When the Moon Hatched

WHEN THE MOON HATCHED

THE MOONFALL SERIES

I

SARAH A. PARKER

HARPER Voyager

Harper*Voyager*
An imprint of HarperCollins*Publishers* Ltd
1 London Bridge Street
London SE1 9GF

www.harpercollins.co.uk

HarperCollins*Publishers*
Macken House,
39/40 Mayor Street Upper,
Dublin 1
D01 C9W8
Ireland

Originally published as *When the Moon Hatched* in the United Kingdom in 2024
by Sarah A. Parker

First published by HarperCollins*Publishers* Ltd 2024
This paperback edition 2025
1

Map by Virginia Allyn
Internal header illustrations by Alice Cao Illustration
All other internal illustrations by Sarah A. Parker
Editing by The Editor and the Quill
and Helayna Trask at Polished Perfection
Author photo by Christine Parker

A catalogue record for this book is available from the British Library.

ISBN: 978-0-00-871026-2 (PB)

Typeset in Goudy Oldstyle Std by Palimpsest Book Production Ltd, Falkirk, Stirlingshire

Printed and Bound in the UK using 100% Renewable Electricity
at CPI Group (UK) Ltd

ABOUT THE BOOK

A glossary and pronunciation guide can be found at the end of this book.

TRIGGER WARNINGS

This book contains explicit content and dark elements that may be triggering for some.

Blood and gore
Death and violence
Sexually explicit
Torture
Implied threat of sexual assault/sexual predator
Explicit language
Cruelty toward a creature/abuse
Abduction of an adult (implied off page and post-recounting)
Death in childbirth (implied, off page)
Abduction/trafficking of minors (implied, off page)
Miscarriage (implied for a secondary character, off page)

THE BURN
GONDRAGH
AGATOTT
DHOMM
LOFF
MEDEON
RIVER LAIN
RIVER AHCT
KOVEN
RAMBEK
OVADHAN
THE BOLTANIC PLAINS
DHAM
THE FADE
BOTHAIM
LETHER
DRELEAD
ORIG
GORE
GUDRIT
PATH OF DAES
VOLERY
BHOGGITH
THE ERGOR PLAINS
PITS OF KHINDARD
OVLAEVE
ARITHIA
MIEL-ET-MUIEM
AMARIEL POINTS
LIMIS
YARITH
OCEREA
AKTAEN
THE SHADE
NETHERYN
NORTH

For those who feel small and quiet.

Spread those wings and roar.

The world began with five.

First was Caelis, God of Aether, invisible to the naked eye. The empty space nobody thought about. Where matter formed, he was simply shoved aside.

His baritone song was so full of substance, yet lacked it entirely. A lonely echo that haunted the empty space between near and distant suns – inaudible in its depth, no matter how loud he sang.

Desperate to be noticed, it was *he* who offered an empty canvas for the others to fill.

Bulder, God of Ground, sculpted the sphere with one belted bellow, building a sturdy globe that did not spin. A world half bathed in sunlight, sprinkled with a rich ripple of rust-colored sand, the other half eternally dunked in shadow so thick it seeped into the stone and cast it black.

With more blunt and droning words, Bulder sculpted the terrain, creating dips, dollops, and cracks in the world. Forging a wall that cut through The Fade – where sunlight and shadow refused to meet – the sky a forever splash of pink, purple, and gold.

The Goddess of Water came next.

Rayne fell upon the ground in a billion yearning teardrops of unrequited love, puddling in Bulder's dips, filling his gorges with her gushing affections. Upon the shaded side, she descended in a patter of heavy flakes, dusting the sharp mountain ranges in a frosty hug.

Her love was a screaming torrent. The deep, gut-wrenching wail of an avalanche. The near-silent cry of sprinkling rain.

Her mournful song was so unlike that of her sister Clode – Goddess of Air – who hinged on the precipice of immeasurable madness. Her voice was a ribbon of silk, soft to touch, unless it turned to the side and slit you with its edge.

Her whispered words swept past branches laden with leaves, tilling them into a flirty dance. Her violent *shrieks* ripped around sharp corners at a voracious speed simply because she liked the sound. Unable to stand Rayne's somber still, Clode's gusty howls often churned the Loff into a heaving mass that dumped upon the shore like a drum.

Ignos was a glutton for Clode. The God of Fire feasted on her. Consumed her.

Loved her so much he could not *breathe* without her.

His searing song was one of ferocious hunger and impassioned greed, but Clode could not be tamed by his rabid affections, even as he blazed jungles and gave her smoke to dance within. Even as he melted bits of Bulder's stone until they were molten rivers of red, desperate to woo Clode with volcanic blasts that shook the sky.

Bound to his mournful solitude, Caelis watched this all, jealous of the other Creators for their ability to be seen, touched, or heard, but thankful to be part of something.

Anything.

And he watched in quiet wonder as, upon this lush and fertile canvas he'd gifted his emptiness, life *bloomed*. A various cacophony of folk who littered the land and snow and sand – some with hearing sharper than the tips of their ears, making them privy to the four other elemental songs. A number of whom learned their languages. Spoke them.

Found *power* in them.

Others fell upon a silver book some say Caelis wrote in his desperation to be heard. Who found a different form of power in those runes nobody could read or pronounce, discovering that the strange markings could be *wielded*. Could mend bones, charm blood, glamor objects . . .

Many beings filled all corners of the world, but none the Creators were more proud of than the great winged beasts that lorded over the sky.

The *dragons*.

Upon the seemingly uninhabitable crown of The Burn, where the sun's harsh rays bubbled skin into fleshy welts, the Sabersythes *thrived* – big, bulky beasts with black and bronze and ruddy scales. With ferocious aptitudes that could not be matched.

They made Gondragh their spawning ground.

Some folk were brave enough to venture close. To raid a nest and snatch an egg.

Brave . . . or *stupid*.

Less volatile than their distant kin, the Moltenmaws found their home in The Fade. In Bhoggith – a foggy scrap of marshland that gobbled almost everything in muddy, sulfuric burps.

Their honed beaks were sharp enough to *slash*, their claws just as severe. Veiled with feathers as colorful as the ever-vibrant sky in their part of the world, no two Moltenmaws bore the same glorious palette.

To steal a Moltenmaw's egg, one also needed to be brave or stupid . . . but perhaps a little less.

Netheryn, however, was almost impossible to raid – the chosen spawning ground of the ethereal and cunning Moonplumes.

Being farthest from the sun, Netheryn was the darkest crown of The Shade, bearing a cold so deep it could turn the blood of most common folk slow and sludgy. But not the Moonplumes, with their luminous, leathery skin so chill to the touch. With their long silky tails and eyes a crush of glitter and ink.

Tucked amongst snow and ice and a hungry quiet that swallowed sounds then spat them out like a warning roar, the Moonplumes *flourished*, growing in number, strength, and brilliance.

Only those as unhinged as Clode or bearing enough power to protect themselves would attempt to steal a Moonplume egg . . .

Most failed, consumed by the fearsome, thrashing beasts or the hostile land.

Some succeeded – a celebrated few who used the dragons to wage wars for sprouting kingdoms.

But as castles grew taller than mountains, and as kings and queens decorated their crowns with bigger, sparklier jewels, so too did folk learn how to shed dragon blood.

For many Moonplumes, Moltenmaws, and Sabersythes . . . their eternal lives were slashed.

The Creators did not expect their beloved beasts to sail skyward upon their end. For many of them to plant themselves just beyond gravity's grip, curl into balls and calcify, littering the sky with tombstones.

With *moons*.

They certainly did not expect those moons to fall not long after they found their lofty perch. For them to collide with the world in a clash of splintering doom that threatened to devastate everything that had come to be.

It took seven moonfalls before Clode, Rayne, Ignos, and Bulder realized Caelis was to blame. That his empty space which yearned to be filled was strong enough to displace a dragon from its resting place and rip it from the sky.

It took them yet another moonfall to devise a plan to save the world they loved so much.

Wielding empty promises and faithless vows, they lured Caelis into their trap and captured him.

Subdued him.

They sang their whipping, burning, breaking songs, mincing Caelis's essence into pieces small enough to trap in a cage of ebony crystal no larger than a pip, henceforth known as the Aether Stone. Threads of his silver cloak tore free as he thrashed and fought, but the other Creators did not bother to round up the scraps, leaving them to tether to both poles of the world. A luminous aurora that spun around the globe, giving folk something to track their daes and slumbertime.

Caelis himself was set within a sterling diadem embellished with a collection of runes that bore malicious strength. Enough to keep him trapped within the stone for eternity, so long as the runes had something to feed on.

A *guardian*.

A mighty fae warrior known for his strength and wisdom was bestowed a gift from the Creators themselves: power immense enough that he was able to host the Aether Stone upon his brow and keep Caelis contained. A gift that passed down his familial line like skipping stones.

Many aurora cycles passed, and more moons littered the sky . . .

Stayed there.

Peace eventually reigned, despite a slew of tragedies and ill-timed deaths that swallowed the Aether Stone's catastrophic origin, its very meaning for existence becoming a scrambled myth passed around campfires or sung to babes to hush their fussing cries.

Until one aurora rise, for the first time in more than five *million* phases . . .

Another moon fell.

Raeve

CHAPTER 1

5,000,165 *phases* After Stone

I curl my shoulders forward, crumbling my posture into something that appears trodden.

Scared.

Rounding a corner, I step onto the stairwell's bottom landing, chased by a parchment lark that flutters so close I'm surprised it doesn't nudge at me to pluck it from the air.

As I twirl the thin iron ring on my middle finger, my gaze climbs the heavily armored guard blocking the gloomy tunnel ahead – arms crossed, his shaved head almost brushing the curved ceiling, a flock of parchment larks nuzzling the door at his back. He's twice my size, boasting a scowl that appears to have permanently dented his face.

His disapproving leer comes to rest on the nick sliced into my left ear, up near the tapered tip. Like somebody with a tiny mouth bit a chunk from the outer shell.

My *clip*.

'No token, no entry,' he grinds out, immediately dismissing me as a lesser. A *null*. Someone who doesn't hear any of the four elemental songs.

I reach into my pocket, retrieving the stone token embossed on both sides with the prestigious club's insignia – a maw of stalactites biting in from all angles. Forging the slightest tremble, I hand it over, feeling the male's probing perusal cut me up and down as he flips the token, his blue armor clanking with the motion.

I'm curious to know why he lets the larks flock the door rather than allow them straight in, but *Raeve* is the outspoken one, and I'm not Raeve right now.

'I'm Kemori Daphidone,' I say, tone soft and submissive. 'Traveling bard.'

'From where?'

'Orig.'

A wall settlement I've never been to, not that it'll stop me from rattling on about it if he asks for specifics.

Preparation is my armor. Don it or die.

He inspects the token, handing it back with a gruff 'No veils.'

I glance up at him from beneath a blaze of feather-tipped lashes. 'Part of my act. I'm part of the scheduled entertainment.' I retrieve a roll of parchment from my pocket and nudge it toward him. 'I was warned about the no veil rule, which is why I've only covered the bottom half of my face.'

Scowling, he unravels the scroll, his beady leer raking over my letter of hire so painfully slow I start to get a crick in my neck, impatience gnawing at me.

Finally, his eyes widen with recognition. 'Oh, you're the stand-in!'

I offer a shy, demure nod when all I really want to do is bang his head against the wall.

Hard.

He rerolls my scroll and hands it back, stepping aside to open the door. 'Third level. Mind the waif. It's always extra hungry this late in the aurora cycle.'

My shiver is far from fake.

I move into the Hungry Hollow's warm, smoky embrace, attacked by a rush of dense musk and the undertow of sulfur, the door banging shut behind me and the flock of dispersing parchment larks. Through a dark tunnel, I emerge at the pinched mouth of a vast, lofty cavern the shape of a stony lung.

A swoop of steps leads me onto one of the many paths that web through a cluster of luminous springs, steam rising from their turquoise depths. Folk are draped against their steps, heads tipped while they languish in the lapping warmth. A pretty paradise for those who wield enough power or political sway to keep themselves on the cushioned side of The Crown.

I huff out a bitter laugh.

Here, it's easy to pretend our colorful kingdom isn't nesting on a bed of bones.

A freestanding staircase leads to the second floor supported by mossy pillars. I head for it, weaving along the labyrinth of paths when a waft of steam congeals into a pale, lanky creature with eyes like ebony jewels.

'Shit,' I mutter, pausing.

Head swiveling unnaturally, the waif looks right at me, sniffs the air, then releases a gluttonous gasp. 'Well, well, well . . . isn't your soul a plump, *juicy* thing?'

Ahh.

'How kind of you to say. I'll just be on my wa—'

'There are screaming spirits desperate to speak with you. How about a small suckle of your soul?' the creature asks, and I swear it sounds like it's salivating. 'Then you can hear *everything* they have to say.'

No fucking thank you.

'I'll pass.'

Heartily.

Seeming to ignore my objection, it flits forward, gathering wafts of steam it uses to stretch in my direction, vaporous fingers reaching.

I spin on my heel and hurry down another path, the hairs on the back of my neck standing on end. Looking over my shoulder, I spot the creature, now hunched over a male lazing against a spring's edge, sucking something shadowed from between his parted lips.

A shiver nettles my skin.

I quietly thank the Creators that waifs are rare, haunting only drapes of mist where they nibble souls in exchange for messages from obliging dead.

Can't think of anything worse. I'm certain the spirits so *desperate* to speak with me have nothing nice to say.

Not that I can blame them.

Thankfully, the creepy soul-nibblers are easily distracted.

I dash up a staircase, rising well above the reaching fingers of steam. The sounds of laughter and clinking glasses come to me as I emerge onto the second level scattered with Skripi tables.

Folk are gathered about, puffing smoke sticks, drinking sparkly spirits, game shards fanned close to their chests. Dice scatter, piles of dragon bloodstone shoved from hand to hand.

I cast my furtive gaze over their attire, some garbed in colorful, gem-encrusted gowns. Others wear finely tailored coats, feathered shapes barbered into shorn hairstyles, elemental beads hanging from their lobes. A boastful token of their ability to hear the different elemental songs:

Red for Ignos.

Blue for Rayne.

Brown for Bulder.

Clear for Clode.

Beads aside, you can usually pick a high-ranking Fade elemental from the other side of a room: those who boast more than ten colors on a single outfit, as if it'll make them mighty like the vibrant dragons that lord this kingdom's skies.

The great *Moltenmaws*.

Funny, since they'd be the first to bleed the beasts if the bloodstone mine ever ran dry.

I'm halfway up a thin staircase chipped into the back wall when somebody tall, broad, and cloaked charges down from above.

I pause, unable to see much of his face bar his strong jaw brushed in a dark, well-shaped beard, his cloak's hood casting everything else in shadow.

He doesn't slow. Just keeps stalking down the stairs despite the fact that I'm dressed in a bold, bright-red gown impossible to miss.

I almost grit my teeth, remembering the metal cap coating my back molar *just* in time to avoid an impromptu activation of my secret weapon.

He barely fits on the staircase *himself*, meaning moving past each other is going to be a tight shuffle.

Lovely.

Typical elemental bullshit, only thinking about themselves.

Sighing, I curl my shoulders further forward and step to the side, reminding myself that I'm Kemori Daphidone, traveling bard from Orig. I'm trodden. Scared. And I'm absolutely not here to *accidentally* trip this male and watch him tumble down the stairs.

Absolutely not.

Back pressed to the wall, I keep my eyes down and wait for him to squeeze past, his heavy steps growing closer. So close I'm struck with a smoky musk pinched with the smell of freshly split stone, softened with notes of something buttery.

My breath catches, then shudders free, as if unwilling to part with the dense, luscious scent that might just be one of the best smells I've ever inhaled . . .

He steps to the side, edging past.

Pauses.

I'm caught in his shadow like a flame in the dark, my heart pumping hard and fast. Nudging up my throat with each lengthy second that ticks by.

Why isn't he moving?

I sidestep farther up the stairs, edging free of his atmosphere. 'Excuse me.'

Places to be, hands to sever.

A dense, grated sound crumbles out of him, like it wrestled loose.

The air shifts.

I shift with it.

Whipping around, I snatch his wrist with the speed of a lightning strike. Tension clogs the air, my gaze dropping to his large, heavily scarred hand – outstretched, paused midmotion, as if he were just about to grab my veil and rip it free.

The asshole.

Though I can't see his eyes, I feel his penetrating stare with such probing intensity my lungs pack full of stones, the trail of his attention traversing to the rounded nick in my ear.

Back to my eyes again.

Sharp words gather on my tongue like thorns that I'm so, *so* tempted to spit at him. Then I remember that folk who stand up to high-ranking elementals end up as dragon chow.

I swallow the words instead. Something that never feels good, no matter how often I do it.

Loosening my grip, I dip my head and shuffle back a few steps, only stopping once I'm high enough that I'm looking down on the male. Far enough away that I'm less tempted to punch him in the throat for thinking he could *unveil* me.

'Apologies,' I bite out, trying to sound submissive. Failing miserably. 'The veil is part of my act.'

Silence ensues, thick like a tacky syrup.

Move, Raeve.

Easing free of his reach, I spin, hurrying up the staircase.

I don't look back, flashing my scroll and token at the second wave of stone-faced guards, one of whom breaks away to escort me toward the stage. I'm led into the shadowy den, engulfed in the scent of peat smoke and mead, struck by the dramatic shift in atmosphere.

Stone fangs jut down from the ceiling, cutting the space into arched segments brushed in rusty firelight spilling from blazing sconces. Dimly lit booths line the outer walls, bracketed with heavy curtains offering privacy for those who seek it. Null servers glide through the space, carrying trays topped with mugs of mead and other foggy beverages, dishing them out to jovial elementals gathered around stone tables pocked about the place.

Tucked in the guard's shadow, I cut a shrewd glance over the eclectic patrons, frustration chewing at my nerves when I don't see the face I'm looking for.

Please be in one of the booths.

The guard leads me toward a central dais crowned by numerous stalagmites that resemble the bars of a cage, and I almost laugh – only because I couldn't imagine anything more morbidly appropriate.

A thin, fine-boned female sits on a stool within, holding a white fiddle etched in luminous runes that probably encourage its sound to carry. She wears a simple full-bustled gown similar to mine, but blue, and much looser around the discreet swell of her babe-laden abdomen.

Eyes closed, she carves a melancholy tune while flakes of white light fall from the arched ceiling like a spill of snow. They settle on her gush of pale hair, extinguishing.

Thanking the guard, I step up and perch on the stool beside the musician, her song reaching a lilting crescendo while I search for an amplifying stick.

'Their Runi's working on it,' she whispers, lowering her fiddle, looking at me through piercing green eyes framed with blue feather-tipped lashes. 'It was cutting in and out last cycle.'

Ah.

'Shouldn't be long. I'm Levvi, by the way.'

'Kemori Daphidone, traveling bard from Orig.'

She flashes me a friendly smile that melts a little when her stare snags on something behind me.

My heart leaps into my throat as a red-haired male strides past, weaving between the crowd, dressed in an immaculate sanguine coat – the color a perfect match to his red elemental bead on boastful display.

Relief prickles through me, eager anticipation making my hands clench and unclench.

Tarik Relaken.

He takes us in, a hungry leer that slithers over my corset-clad bust before he continues toward a booth, three other males lounging within. Leaving the curtain open, he pours into animated conversation, sliding the occasional glance my way. Half-lidded looks that paint me out to be a well-presented piece of meat he'd *love* to gnaw on.

I see you, asshole.

I catch sight of the cloaked male I encountered on the stairs, now moving through the dusky space—

My heart plummets.

He navigates past other patrons, my mind tangling into a messy knot while he makes for an empty booth at the back of the room . . .

He was in such a hurry earlier when he almost barreled over me on his way down the stairs. Now he's back. *Why?*

Business? Curiosity? Or did he catch the wrong impression from me on the stairs?

Creators, is *that* why he's come back in? Because he likes slumming it with nulls and he's hoping for an easy lay?

His head turns in my direction, gaze sweeping across the upper half of my face like a warm, soft-bristled brush, stiffening the air between us.

I swallow a groan.

I fought hard to have this operation approved. It means *everything* to me. If that asshole ruins our carefully laid plans, we may not get another chance for who knows how long. Assuming another attempt is even *approved*.

'You new, honey? I haven't seen you here before.'

Forcing my regard to soften, I look at Levvi, her null clip evident in the ear poking free of her luscious mane. 'Just standing in.'

'I see.' She passes a glance around the room, lips barely moving as she whispers, 'That male with red hair who just walked by? His name is Lord Tarik Relaken. Stay well away. Many performers draw his attention, then disappear.'

I widen my eyes in feigned shock. 'Really?'

She nods.

'The color of your dress, your demure disposition, and long black hair . . .' She sweeps her gaze down my body, up again. 'You're just his type.'

I don't tell her that's the point.

The hope.

At least it *was* until I acquired a cloaked observer now watching me from the back of the room, arms crossed, perched against the table of an otherwise empty booth.

'There's a reason this place hemorrhages null recruits, and it's not the shit wages,' she bites out, flashing me a sour smile.

I don't bother asking why she stays, the swell of her belly evidence enough. There are few options for a null to make a living in Gore besides slogging it out in the mines. No place for a pregnant female. Folk do what they can to get by, even if that means walking the fine line between a safe existence and a dangerous one.

'I appreciate the warning,' I whisper, thinking of the mysterious tip-off Sereme apparently received early in the dae when our current plans were already in motion. Wondering if it was from Levvi – too afraid to muddy her hands by getting involved with *Fíur du Ath* and our sympathizing, albeit *bloody*, dealings.

Understandably.

There's no easier way to piss off our tyrant king than to liaise with his enemies.

A Runi steps close, a white robe hanging off his slight body, dark hair pulled back in a low bun. He looks down his nose at me, and my gaze drops to the only button pinching his floaty garb in place. The symbol of an etching stick upon the round of wood, signifying his ability to etch basic runes.

From the way he's leering at me, I expected two or three. Perhaps some specialty gift like bloodlacing, or something else spectacular. At the very least, I thought his etching button would be more than elementary – made from silver, or gold.

Wish I could say that.

I accept the amplifying stick with a demure dip of my head instead, wrapping my sweaty palms around the hollow length of metal littered with dots and swirls that emit their own radiance.

I slice another glance at Tarik Relaken, my teeth gritted as I look back at the cloaked observer I certainly didn't account for, unease slithering through me.

'You okay?'

No.

A parchment lark flutters close, tips its nose, tucks its folded wings, and plummets into my lap. 'Never sung before such a large crowd,' I murmur, pocketing the message for later.

'I get it,' Levvi says, offering me a reassuring smile. 'They're mostly too engrossed in themselves to notice us.' She lifts her fiddle, resting the base against the scoop of her neck. 'Do you know "Ballad of the Fallen Moon"?'

All the warmth drops from my face, a strand of memory wafting through the back of my mind. Stripped of emotion. Beauty.

Pain.

The ghost of something I can scarcely grasp, its corpse anchored in my icy nether. The place inside me that's vast like the Ergor Plains I once walked alone, blotches of somebody else's blood frosted to the rags that clung to my skeletal body.

'Yes,' I rasp. 'I know that song very well.'

Levvi drags her bow across stretched strings of Moonplume tail hair that shine in the gloom, carving out the first note – so long and deep it's almost tangible. She plays the next few with such passion it's like she wrote the tune herself.

Like the fable's pretty words were tilled from the ashes of her *own* caged past.

I lift the amplifier to my veiled lips and draw my lungs full, shifting a little so the hidden dagger in my bodice doesn't nudge my rib. I close my eyes and plunge into the melody in the same way I once plunged into life – but with the words I've since learnt how to speak. Armored by the horrors I've encountered since.

Flaming horrors.

Mind-*mincing* horrors.

The crowd dissolves into oblivion as I sing of an inky Sabersythe flying into a black velvet sky, balling up, and dying in the dark where she'll never be seen again. Of a lustrous Moonplume that tucks beside the sooty beast, illuminating her shape.

Giving her *light*.

I sing of the Moonplume's gradual dim. Of how little by little, rise by rise, her luster feeds into the Sabersythe and turns the creature's scales white, the tune dipping into deeper, more destructive notes as I sing of the Moonplume's slipping grip on the sky.

Of her fall.

Of the Sabersythe unfurling from her perch amongst the stars, full of gifted life and light, soaring to the world below and hunting for her friend. Of her scratching through inky shards of rock scattered across the snow, trying to piece her back together again.

Failing.

Lids fluttering open, I become vaguely aware that every pair of eyes in the room is turned to us, watching. Wide with greed or wet with emotions that slip down painted cheeks.

But it's the cloaked male that steals my attention, the top half of his face still hidden within the shadow cast by his hood. Despite it, his stare reaches through the space and embraces me in an iron-clad grip I can't shake.

As the words continue to pour from my lips, I become bluntly aware that there's a danger about this male who eclipses everyone else in the room in both size and presence. Who stands with the confident ease of someone untouchable.

A sobering realization strikes like a blow to the side of my head, my gaze drifting to Tarik – perched in his booth, watching me with such condemning hunger I know I'm not leaving this place without him tailing me. The perfect outcome.

Except . . .

I look back to my cloaked observer, into the hooded shadows obscuring his identity.

I came here to lure one monster, and ended up snagging two.

Raeve

CHAPTER 2

Nothing like seven hours of straight singing without breaks to make you feel like you've swallowed a metal scouring brush, then hacked it straight back up again.

Tugging the chain on the privy, I clear my throat, trying to shift the strain from my vocals. I close the lavatory door behind me and move to one of the basins, lathering my hands in suds as I stare at my reflection in the mirror. Powder-blue eyes stare back at me, the bottom half of my face obscured by my thick red veil. In stark contrast to my snowy skin, it half clothes my long inky locks in a dramatic sweep.

'You sing like a Creator.'

I look at the female beside me, drying her hands while she studies her own reflection, chin high as she swings her head from side to side, inspecting her perfectly made-up face.

'Thank you.' *I think.*

Could be an insult. Who's to know with these folk.

She looks at my clipped ear. 'Seems wasted on a null,' she muses, like I'm not even here.

Definitely an insult.

'I'd have Ignos eating out of the palm of my hand if my voice had that kind of range.'

I bite my tongue so hard it bleeds, gaze flicking to the red bead dangling from her ear before I dip my head in servitude. 'Yes. A true waste for someone the Creators did not deem worthy of their songs.'

She hums, looking at her reflection again while she fixes a

tendril of hair into place, seemingly validated by my nod to her ordained superiority. The moment the door swings shut behind her, I roll my eyes, drying my hands.

One of these aurora cycles, I'm going to be forced to bite my tongue so hard I sever the tip. I'm sure of it. The fact that it's still attached is a fucking miracle.

Stepping free of the washroom, I see a male leaning against the corridor wall ahead, blocking the only exit besides the lavatory window in the room behind me.

I pause on the threshold, holding the door ajar, my heart slapped still by this . . . *unexpected* development.

I thought it'd take longer to lure him in. At the very least, I thought I'd be able to pee in peace before we play.

Tarik Relaken stares into the glass he's clutching, swirling an amber liquid, smoke sloshing free. Tangles of red hair hang before his eyes, orange flames barbered into the shorn sides, framing the elemental bead hanging from his lobe like a drip of blood.

'You have a *sensational* voice,' he rumbles, stare still drowning in the depths of his drink. 'And the color of your gown . . .' He tilts his head to the side, flames reflecting in his dark-brown eyes that singe me from afar. '*Exceptional.*'

I ease the door shut behind me, sealing myself in the corridor with the male, mind churning. I've got his attention, now to lure him *away* from this establishment.

I dip my head in thanks, then move to walk past, pausing when he pushes off the wall and turns to face me.

Further blocking the exit.

'Stay,' he mumbles, tipping his glass to his lips. He swallows, purring a smarmy '*Drink* with me.'

My gut knots.

His mouth might be saying *drink*, but his eyes say ugly things that pick you apart, piece by piece, until there's nothing left for the scavengers.

You really are a piece of trash.

'With a voice like that,' he tacks on, stare sliding down my body like an oily brush, making my skin crawl, 'I'm sure your mouth's a fucking *delight*.'

A ball of icy rage gathers within my chest, pulsing with its own violent heartbeat, salivating to end this here.

Now.

It'd be silly not to. He's asking for it so beautifully.

I glance at the closed exit. At the dead bolt *right there* – only three leaping steps away. If I can just get past him and slide it into place, I'll ensure nobody can interrupt this impromptu gathering until the deed is done.

'Apologies, sir, but it's a long walk home. I must be getting on my way if I'm to rest before the rise.'

I move, banking for the sliver of space on his right—

His hand slams against the wall so hard the sconce flame flutters, and my feet still. 'I *insist*,' he grinds out, eyes hardening to dark flints that make something inside me pause.

Listen.

I weigh the value of locking that door. Risky, yes. But to be fair, I wore the veil for this very reason – on the off chance I'd be forced to escape through a back window with a severed appendage in my pocket. So nobody would pull me aside at a later date after passing me on a stairway, recognizing my face, pinning me as the prime suspect for stashing Tarik Relaken – handless and pulseless – into a privy booth.

Screw it.

My attention homes, body poised. The tips of my fingers tingle with anticipation as I reach for the dagger within the hidden compartment tailored into my bodice—

The door behind Tarik swings open, and I curse beneath my breath. We both look over his shoulder at the large, cloaked male who watched me sing all slumber from the back of the room while exuding the stoicism of a stone statue.

The hall suddenly feels like a vein swelling with too much hot, pumping blood. Like an incinerating storm just crammed between the close-pressed walls and sponged all the oxygen, leaving little for me to breathe.

Frustration and anger buck and battle inside me. My hand falls from my bodice, tucking into the gathers of my skirt where I can white-knuckle the fabric without it being obvious.

What an unfortunate time to decide he needs to take a piss, though *less* unfortunate for him. Had he been a few moments later, he would've walked in on something he certainly wouldn't have walked away from.

Clearing his throat, Tarik lifts his *very* lucky hand from the wall and shifts sideways, giving me space to ease past. Honestly, he should use it to shake this male's hand because he absolutely just saved his life.

For now.

'Milady,' Tarik bites out, forging a gaudy smile. 'Have a Creators-*blessed* slumber.'

I battle the urge to let my eyebrows bump all the way into my hairline. Seems I'm not the only one who can sense the combustive energy rolling off this mysterious male.

Wish he'd take that energy *elsewhere*.

'Thanks,' I mutter, my stabby hand twitching as I move past Tarik and make for the exit, cutting a glance at the hooded male holding the door wide. But his attention isn't on me.

It's firmly on Tarik.

Odd.

Sighing, I weave through the thinning crowd, passing folk fucking in darkened corners or stretched across tabletops. Others lumped in low seaters, comatose with drinks still tucked in their loosening hands. Some are still with it enough to see me walk by. To chant for me to sing.

Sing.

Sing.

Little do they know, that's *exactly* what I intend to do.

With a chest full of barely restrained violence flexing for release, I make a straight shot for the exit, certain Tarik will be snapping at my heels with unquenched desires of his own. I've probably only got a few moments to spare while the hooded male relieves himself in the lavatory. Only a few moments to get Tarik out of here without the time-consuming tagalong I didn't account for.

My already tight schedule is suffocating.

'Kemori, wait!'

It takes me two steps to register that it's *my* name being called.

Shit.

I pause, stemming a below-breath curse before I cut a glance over my shoulder.

Levvi's packing her instrument in the case she's flopped open across our stools, hair tucked behind her ear as she looks at me, the black smudges beneath her eyes a testament to just how long we sat and performed without breaks or refreshments.

'Here.' She waves a small pouch through the air. 'Our commission.'

Ah.

She steps down off the dais and closes the distance between us. 'I think the resident Runi docked some,' she says with a roll of her eyes, extending the pouch toward me. 'But there should be enough for a few hearty meals.'

Gaze bouncing between her clipped ear, the blossoming round of her belly, and what's left of the dwindling crowd, I reach forward, wrapping my hand around hers, forcing her grip to tighten on the pouch. 'Keep it. And thank you for playing with me. It was a treasure.'

A line forms between her brows.

I spin, three steps closer to the stairway when her voice chases me. 'Let me walk you home!'

My heart plops into my belly.

'My bound will be waiting out front to escort me,' she continues. 'He's a kind, hardworking male who's never hurt a soul. He can escort you, too.'

I glance over my shoulder, noting the deep-rooted concern in her pretty green eyes. 'Thank you, but I'm fine. My home is so close I'll be sleeping by the time you finish clamping the buckles shut on your case.'

Lie.

My home is all the way down the other end of the Ditch. At this rate, I'll be lucky to reach it by aurora rise, since I don't intend to walk in that direction once I finally make it outside.

I'm two steps closer to the exit before her hand wraps around my arm, snagging me despite my fractious nerves galloping ahead at full speed.

Levvi shoves before me.

Face blanched, she peeks around our dim surroundings, leaning close. 'I saw the way Tarik was watching you, Kemori. I fear for your safety. This time of slumber isn't kind to the likes of us. *Please*, let us walk you home . . .'

The determined edge to her voice dilutes my thickening frustration.

She's growing on me.

I hate when folk grow on me.

Scanning our surroundings, I reach into the left pocket of my gown, shred the safety-seam with my fingernail, then dig into the hidden compartment, pulling out a small glass orb – transparent but for the incarnated depiction of a mythical Elding Bird hatching from a bulb of flame caught in the orb's depths.

'You don't need to worry about me,' I whisper, taking her hand in mine.

Frowning, she drops her gaze, and I loosen my hold just enough for her to glimpse the treasure pressed between our palms, her eyes widening as realization seems to dawn.

'O-oh,' she says, the word a shaken thing, falling out in crumbled bits. Like something inside her just fell apart. 'T-Tarik?'

I nod, pocketing the orb I'd hate for her to get caught with.

She fills her lungs but fails to forge the breath into words, releasing a shuddered exhale, stare caught on her hands now clasping the swell of her belly. A vision that does something strange to my heart. Makes me feel like it's going to burst – and not in a nice way.

I need to get out of here.

'Take care,' I whisper, about to spin again when she grabs my arm. Eyes glazed with unshed emotion, she offers me a fold of parchment.

'What's that?'

'My . . . ah, my details. In case you want to perform together again,' she whisper-rasps, working her lips into a smile that looks more sad than happy. Like perhaps she knows I won't contact her.

That we'll never see each other again.

I take it anyway, dipping my head in thanks, seeing Tarik emerge from the lavatory and catch my eye.

Got you.

I pivot toward the stairs and hurry from the Hungry Hollow.

In another life, I might've befriended Levvi. But—

So many buts.

I think back to *someone else* I once knew. *Someone else* with an easy smile and warm regard. A female who's now a vaporous memory that doesn't bang against my ribs or heart. Not after I tied all those heavy, painful parts to a rock now anchored to the bottom of my icy internal lake.

Companionship is something I work hard to avoid. And *mostly* succeed. The harder you care, the more fragile everything seems.

Easier to just . . .

Not.

Raeve

CHAPTER 3

Snow spews – fat flakes that catch on my feathered lashes and dust the pave anew. Crunching beneath my boots as I walk the dreary Ditch almost entirely bare of life at this late hour.

Both halves of the immense stone wall tower on either side of me, running parallel from east to west as far as the eye can see. Like two lofty bookcases, the path between them large enough for numerous carts to roll down, side by side.

The wall wraps around the world's plump belly like a belt, only split down the middle in densely populated segments like right here in Gore. Deep enough that folk seem to feel a sense of safety within the lengthy trench – away from the immediate threat of predators.

False as it is.

There are just as many down here in the sheltered Ditch, if not more. They're just well camouflaged.

A silver sowmoth splits from a swarm of them churning overhead, fluttering so close its fluffy wings dust me in a spray of luminous powder.

I smile.

I like this time of slumber, when it feels like it's just me, the sowmoths, and the candy-colored clouds. Even though it's not.

Even though I've got a monster on my heels.

Although Tarik times his footsteps to match mine perfectly, planting his feet almost soft enough to meld with the patter of snow, I sense his presence like a looming shadow threatening to gobble me up.

I should be scared. Nervous. Maybe a little sad for what I'm about to do.

Survival's funny. Some wear it like a whisper, others like a scream. Mine's a scorched skeleton of flame-forged rage that keeps me upright. Keeps me moving *forward.*

There's not much that's wet and squishy left in my chest. It's all hard and hostile, impervious to things like *caring* for the likes of Tarik Relaken. In fact, even if he were a pile of shit on the pavement, I'd still go out of my way to stomp on him.

Perhaps that makes me a monster, too.

I don't dissect the thought, shoving it out of the way as I move up a stairway on the inside of the wall's southern half, zigzagging up the levels, past doors shut up for the slumber. I keep going until the wall is just that – *wall.* No more dwellings bored into the sides.

Folk don't like to live so close to the clouds, the air this far up feeling . . . borrowed. Like it doesn't belong to us.

Like it belongs to the *dragons*.

A shiver scuttles up my spine, and I turn south down a lengthy wind tunnel that yawns to the view beyond the wall, packed full of clouds so close I could almost reach out and scoop handfuls of their heavy underbellies.

When I'm only a few long steps away from the deadly plummet to the ground below, I dig into my pocket and ease off my iron ring, exposing myself to a riot of song that threatens to mince my brain into a fine sludge.

Fucking . . . *mayhem.*

The tendons in my neck stretch, the veins in my temples pulsing with too much rushing blood and song.

I tune my mind to the highest frequency – like tightening a sound snare – then cap the opening with a sieve, isolating Clode's manic melody blaring at the top of her billowy lungs. The Goddess of Air works up a howling eddy that makes my veil flutter about, a lopsided grin stretched across my face.

She wants to play.

So do I.

The hairs on the back of my neck lift, Tarik's footsteps drawing closer . . .

Closer.

Come on, you slimy fuck. Make your mo—

His hand latches onto the back of my neck, and he shoves me against the wall face-first, using his weight to pin me in place.

My skin crawls at the heft of him. The disabling might of a male determined to take whatever he wants.

I feign a whimper. A small jostle of desperation.

'Shh, shh, shh,' he rasps against my ear, making my blood curdle. 'Be a good little null.'

Rage explodes beneath my ribs as I consider how many *others* he's done this to. How many have been swallowed by his gluttonous greed like they're nothing more than a snack.

No more.

I lift my boot and bite down on the metal cap crowning my back molar. With a *click*, an iron pin spears free from my heel. '*Glei te ah no veirie*,' I whisper-sing, the words a strangled ache in my mouth, spat free. Coaxing Clode to siphon *almost* every wisp of air from Tarik's lungs.

She giggles.

Tarik sucks a strangled gasp through the compacting organs, and I stomp the nullifying pin through the top of his boot. Biting down on the cap a second time, I shoot the pin so deep between Tarik's fine bones and tendons that the only way to be rid of it is to hack through his own ankle and sever the appendage.

Precautions.

I doubt Clode would loosen her hold on his lungs, but damned if I'm letting him set Ignos on me with a few blazing words. The God of Fire loves to *feast*, and I'd rather be skinned alive than have him gnaw on me.

Again.

Tarik's grip loosens, and he stumbles back, limping, boots scuffing against the snow while I brush my hands down my gown and straighten myself. 'Tarik fucking Relaken,' I mutter, easing the runed dragonscale blade from the secret pocket of my bodice, this one sharp enough to cut through bone like butter.

I turn, head cocked to the side, looking right into his wide, bloodshot eyes – anticipation prickling in the tips of my fingers. 'Are you having a Creators-blessed slumber?'

His eyes bulge, then narrow on the blade I'm twirling. He loses his footing, crumbling against the far wall, mouth agape while he claws at his throat.

Guess that's a no.

His chest convulses, barely a thread of breath whistling down his windpipe, doing little to inflate his suctioned lungs. *Just* enough to keep him present until he's heard my well-prepared speech.

Once, I watched somebody drop a line beneath an icy lake and reel a long, slithering eahl to the surface. It squirmed in the snow, iridescent scales glinting as its mouth gaped and gaped until it became chillingly still.

This game always reminds me of that, except I felt sorry for the eahl.

I feel nothing for Tarik bar the ferocious desire to slit his throat before he ruins any more lives. But not yet.

First, he needs to *suffer*.

I move forward, gaze flicking between his hands, trying to decide on a preference. Tricky – they're both so similar.

'One of the other Elding Blades might have eased you into death the gentle way,' I muse, deciding on the right. I grip it and yank, slicing my blade through his wrist so fast I'm certain he doesn't realize what's happened until I'm waving the severed appendage at him. 'Probably would've done this *after* you were dead.'

Unfortunately for Tarik, I have a special well of rage I reserve specifically for folk like him.

He gawks at me, clawing at his neck as if his hand is still attached, blood spewing from the gory stub – his mouth so wide I can see his tonsils.

'Perhaps I should explain,' I say, pulling a wax bag from my pocket. I stuff my new hand inside and tug the drawstring tight. 'You see, I was roaming the Undercity and stumbled upon your little business.'

Little is an understatement. His sprawling establishment is like a city of its own, fit with an amphitheater-sized battle pit, sleep-suites for those who never want to miss a duel, and cells of caged children. *Nulls* he's snatched off the wall or purchased from desperate parents who lack the wealth to keep them fed, certain they're buying their younglings a fighting chance at life.

A chance to battle their way to supremacy.

None of them looked malnourished, but there's more than one way to starve a soul.

'I tried to free your captives, some of whom – I might add – were in dire need of a healer to mend their small, broken bodies.'

I wave the laden bag at him, shrugging. 'Imagine my disappointment when I discovered I required your *handprint* to open their cells.'

I can tell by the panicked look in his eyes that he's not imagining hard enough. That he's too caught up thinking about himself.

I lump the bag on the ground atop a pile of snow that's blown in as he fumbles, jabs his remaining hand into his pocket, and yanks out a blade. I seize it from his paltry grip, clicking my tongue before I stab it through his thigh.

'Not that I knew who you were at that point,' I murmur, watching him quiver and convulse.

Relishing it.

His face turns redder than his garb, the veins in his temples and neck bulging as I slice his bloodred tunic open, bare his chest, then snag his other hand that won't stop grabbing at me. I hoist it high, flatten it against the wall, and use my blade to pin it in place so I can focus on my task.

His entire body spasms again, wetness leaching down his trousers.

'Funniest thing. The next dae, your bound found a way to reach out to us. You know who we are, of course. The Fíur du Ath.'

From the Ashes.

His features crumble.

I lift my skirt and pull another blade from the inside of my boot. 'She's lovely, your bound. Striking. I'd barter the entire contents of my coffers that you purchased her too – hoping the brown bead she wears would guarantee you powerful offspring.'

More strangled jerks, his heaving chest slicked red from the blood pulsating free of his severed stub. It doesn't elude me that he's now painted in the color he loves so much.

The color he *boasts*.

Head tilted to the side, I study my crimson canvas, dragging the tip of my blade across the expanse of his chest. I plant a little pressure down the length and begin to carve my crude code into his flesh.

'She said you do terrible things to her. To *others*,' I say while I slice.

Slice.

Slice.

'To anybody you can get your grubby mitts on.'

R.

Rapist.

The letter weeps more of his favored color as he squirms, his mouth wide in a silent scream.

Beautiful, blessed silence. I could kiss Clode at times like this.

'She also mentioned that although you don't make your null son fight in your prestigious Undercity battle pit, you often call upon Ignos to paint him in flames for being such a great *disappointment* to your bloodline.'

The words are forced past gritted teeth, that immense, icy presence within me shifting.

Rumbling.

I carve a C. Then an A.

Child abuser.

I'm tempted to give him the entire alphabet, but time is of the essence. Instead, I finish him off with three more letters:

A-S-S.

Self-explanatory.

The wind becomes a cutting torrent, whistling around corners, lifting my veil.

Baring me.

I don't bother trying to cover up, wondering if he still likes my voice.

The color of my dress.

If he regrets following me, trying to assault me against the wall.

His chest jerks to the manic tune of Clode's twirling giggles, practically hanging from his hand nailed to the wall while treasured breath squeaks through his throat.

'Ignos started speaking to your daughter, did you know?'

His face contorts, baring deeper folds of agony as his boots gouge the blood-steeped snow.

'She's been escorted out of the city this slumber, along with the rest of your family, but not before your bound told us everything we need to extinguish your fucked-up operations and set those younglings free.'

Take them somewhere safe and secure where they can learn to be children again.

I repeat Clode's suffocating tune, and she flicks around me at a voracious speed, churning my hair into an inky mess while Tarik's face turns blue.

Then purple.

'How does it feel to be nulled, Tarik?'

His now-bleeding eyes take in the lobe of my ear. The one supposed to be pierced with a transparent bead to signify my ability to hear Clode's ever-changing, riotous song. Way I see it, it would only serve to single me out as a threat to The Fade's militant society.

Fuck their system.

'How does it feel to suffer at the hands of someone "beneath" you?'

Still smacking his throat with his mangled arm, his mouth shapes a single word:

Mercy.

An eviscerating rage torches my spine, licking around my ribs, feasting on my cold black heart.

I wonder how many times the younglings who fought in his pit of death pleaded for that very thing. How many times his *son* said the word, looking up at the male who was supposed to nurture him.

Protect him.

I wonder how many times hope perished in his small chest before he begged his mah to seek us out. To break free of Tarik's invisible shackles.

Too many.

'Your family sends their regards,' I sneer, then slash my blade through his throat.

Raeve

CHAPTER 4

Tarik's blood splashes across the snow, plumes of it spurting from the gory gash.

I reach into my pocket and slip on my ring.

The racket banging against my eardrums snips off, leaving only the organic sounds of Clode squealing past corners without her manic laughter or slicing song.

I crack my neck from side to side, rolling my shoulders – ever thankful for iron's nulling properties. I can tune her out on my own if I concentrate, but it takes effort, and my guard drops while I sleep. Clode's great and all, but not when you're jostled awake by a midslumber squeal. And she's painfully loud. *Plug-fingers-in-my-ears* loud, though I wouldn't dare.

Don't want to get on her bad side.

It's said the louder one hears the elemental songs, the greater the connection, the more power one can derive from learning their language and speaking their words. A blessing and a curse when it comes to the wild Air Goddess, since her squeals can be sharp enough to slit skin. Nothing worse than feeling like your brain's being filleted into fluffy segments.

I tuck my veil back into place, hiding the bottom half of my face as I move to the wind tunnel's entrance and peek out, looking left and right along the thin path etched into the wall like a groove. Making sure my cloaked observer hasn't shown up to play *catch the iron blade between your ribs*.

Not seeing him or anyone else, I step farther forward, glancing down toward the Ditch far below. Eddies of snow tangle with clusters of luminous sowmoths, but I see no other movement, nor can I see anybody on the stair path beneath me. Nor the one below that.

I look across the massive cleft to the wall's parallel half, seeing nobody on the north side, nor on the nearby skybridges that stretch between both.

An appreciated surprise.

I step away from the edge and turn, my footsteps echoing as I walk back to Tarik's corpse still hanging from his hand pinned to the wall, his head flopped to the side. I extract my blade from the stone, and his body heaps into a steaming puddle of red.

Looking at my gown, I click my tongue at the spurts of blood deepening the shade in places. I'd hoped for a clean job this time. Every time.

Never happens.

I unbutton the overlay on my skirt, rip the top layer from my bodice, and pull the tarnished fabric free, revealing the perfect replica beneath – balling the spoiled layer into a parcel I toss down the rubbish chute that's tunneled into the wall. One of many chutes scattered around the city, which delve past ground level, past a few levels of the Undercity, and spew out into the lair of a full-grown velvet trogg that feasts on Gore's trash.

I tip my head to the side, gauging the distance between Tarik and the chute, deciding it's probably a *little* high for me to heft him into it. Better just to shove him out the hole in the wall for the many Shade-born predators to pick at.

Releasing a sigh, I look at his limp body, picturing a world *without* those who like to gobble up shiny things then shit them out broken. 'Imagine,' I mutter, crouching to wipe my blades on his pants before I tuck them away.

Just . . . *imagine*.

I shake my head, grip Tarik around the ankles, and heave his weight with all the strength of my burning thighs, thankful we got almost all the way to the end before he pounced. As I drag him toward the drop, the wind sweeps through the tunnel so hard I'm certain it gives him a shove, and I smile.

Clode's such a crazy, spiteful bitch.

I love her.

I maneuver Tarik until he's so close to the edge his arm is dangling, then wipe my hands on his tunic, crouch behind him, and put all my weight into pushing him over, catching myself on the stone as he slips from my grasp. Leaning forward, I watch him plummet toward the wall's rocky, sawtooth base far below . . .

He impales upon a slice of stone that cuts all the way through his abdomen, and I find myself wishing I'd kept him alive so he could experience it.

Damn.

Missed opportunity.

Standing, I use the edge of my boot to scrape the bloody smear of snow into a pile and kick it off the side.

Pocketing Tarik's hand, I saunter down the wind tunnel, pausing just before the entrance, my stare catching on a bit of parchment stuck to the wall.

I step closer, eyes narrowing on the script.

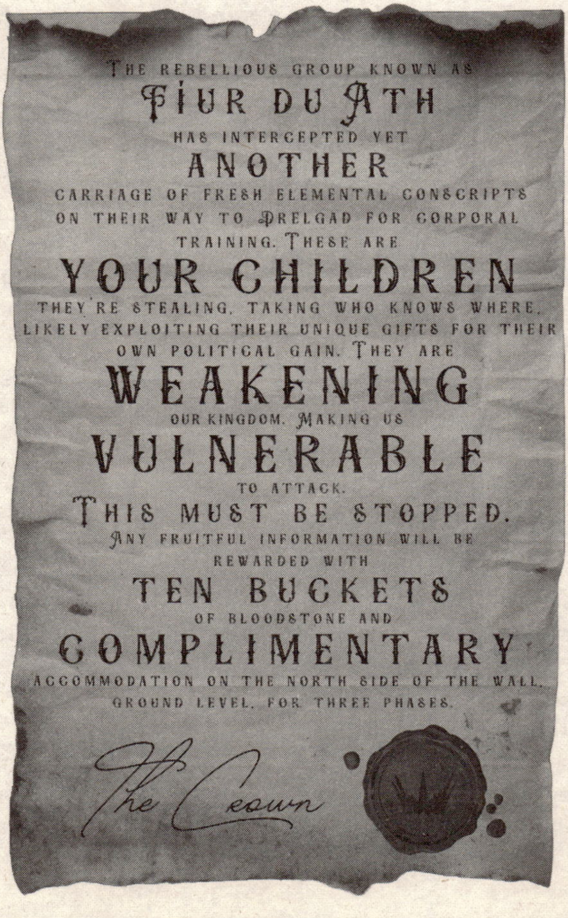

Stealing children?

Exploiting their gifts for our own political gain?

'What a load of spangle shit.'

And The Crown's no longer *threatening* those who engage with us, but rather dangling a bountiful lure impossible to turn down. Especially for those who are homeless, working in the mines, getting by on a few pouches of blood-stone per phase.

This changes things . . .

Snarling, I rip the bullshit parchment free and scrunch it into a ball, just stalking around the corner when I slam into something hard. A firm hand wraps around my wrist, steadying me. The same wrist that's attached to the hand currently clawed around the balled-up bit of parchment offering a hefty reward for, well . . .

Me.

I look up in time for a blow of wind to push back the hood of the mysterious male from the Hungry Hollow.

My heart plummets, breath loosens. For the first time since Fallon taught me speech, I'm lost for words.

He's harshly chiseled, raw . . . fiercely beautiful. My lungs pull full of his scent, so deep and drugging, like smelted stone topped with a ladle of cream.

I hold the breath hostage, taking him in, admiring his black hair that falls just past his shoulders. It's half pulled back off his face that's partially shadowed by a few loose strands failing to soften his regard, his piercing eyes the rich molten color of fired wood.

His brows are thick, the lower half of his face shaded by a dark beard that adds a rugged texture to his already robust appearance. Like he belongs in one of the renowned warrior clans that took root amongst the Boltanic Plains millions of phases ago, wielding an ax and a bloodlusting roar.

His gaze rips from mine, bouncing around our surroundings, searching every shadowed dip. I notice the tapered tip of his right ear is punched through with a small black cuff that encases part of the shell, but no beads.

He's showcasing as a null – minus the clip – but I know better than to assume he doesn't hear any of the elemental songs. Especially given the immense energy rolling off him, shoving against me. Making me feel as if he's so much *bigger* than the space he's currently inhabiting. Which is a lot, being a head and a half taller than me, his broad chest and shoulders reminding me of a Sabersythe. The bold, muscular sort of build often found in those with strong roots to The Burn – the hot, ever-sunny northern kingdom.

His condemning stare lands on me again, and it's like a swift kick to the ribs. Winding.

Chest-deflating.

He's looking at me like I just shoved a dead elemental off the wall. Or maybe I'm imagining things. I'm certain there was nobody else around . . .

The line between his brows deepens. 'Are you okay?'

His dense voice skims my heart like flint scoured across stone, leaving a residue of sparks that crackle through my icy bloodstream in the strangest way.

Am I . . . *okay*?

I mirror his frown. 'Are you mad?'

'Possibly,' he rumbles, voice like a spill of warm, rolling rocks.

A flake of snow lands atop my forehead, and my breath hitches as he lifts his spare hand, bringing it toward my face. Like perhaps he's going to sweep the flake away. I catch myself falling into the motion before I realize he's reaching for my *veil*.

The air between us turns stiff and sterile. Even Clode stops her whipping stir.

'I wouldn't,' I purr, pressing a small iron dagger to his crotch – the dagger always notched just up my sleeve for times such as this.

His brow bumps up. 'Quick hands.'

'It's iron.'

'I can *smell* that,' he growls, his voice thick with the rich, exotic accent of northerners. 'Name. Now. And not the fake one you gave to whoever hired you at the Hungry Hollow.'

Thorough.

Interesting.

I lean more pressure into my little iron blade that suddenly feels vastly inadequate against everything it's pressed against, though I'm not one to stand down from a challenge. 'No. But I'll serve you your own cock if you don't let go of my wrist.'

My words are sultry smooth, passed to him like a ballad I'm certain he's going to appreciate less than the songs I sang all slumber . . . until the corner of his mouth flicks up the slightest amount.

Surprising me.

He makes a gruff sound, drops my wrist, then steps back, forging a small cleft of space between us that feels like a canyon I'm standing on the edge of – the arches of my feet tingling as a strange flutter takes flight inside my belly.

Confusion scrambles my thoughts.

'Thank you,' I announce, straightening my shoulders. Keeping my blade pointed at his crotch, I crunch the parchment into a tighter ball, then stuff it into my pocket.

Maybe I won't have to kill him. He didn't see me kill Tarik, hasn't seen my face nor the notice I tore off the wall. He certainly hasn't tried to take liberties with me.

Perhaps he's not the monster I thought he was while he watched me sing all slumber with an obsessive sort of severity?

Not to mention the time it would take to drag him to the same edge I shoved Tarik over if I were forced to slit his throat where we stand. That's even if I *could* drag him. I'd probably have to hack him into smaller bits – a messy task that sponges time. Something I'm swiftly running out of, Tarik's hand a heavy weight in my pocket.

'If you'll excuse—'

'There's a dead male fae speared through the gut down there,' he says, brow arched, jerking his chin toward the wind tunnel's gaping exit to the unmerciful plummet below – his voice a rough monotone that cleaves an even deeper split between my options.

'I just came from there, and I saw no male.' I keep my dagger steady, muscles poised. 'All I saw was a monster.'

I hold his gaze, perched upon the sharp edge of indecision. Waiting for his response to stretch between us before I decide which way I'll fall. Whether I categorize this male in the same box as Tarik or a different one.

A *safer* one.

His eyes bore into me like he's excavating bits of my soul as he says, 'On that, I heartily agree.'

I frown, open my mouth, close it.

Safe box it is.

'Don't follow me,' I bite out, then pull my dagger from his crotch and stalk off down the nearby staircase without looking back.

Raeve

CHAPTER 5

I dump Tarik's hand down a scarcely used, predesignated rubbish chute, waiting with my head pushed through the hole until I hear a whistle from another member of Fíur du Ath deep in the Undercity. Confirmation the package was caught. That the others will now work to free the younglings.

Being an Elding Blade, I kill. Nothing more. I certainly don't rescue – that task left to others not so comfortable getting bloody. But part of me almost . . . *yearns* to this time.

This mission has been so personal to me. A large-scale passion project I fought hard to have approved. One that tunneled the Ath's resources away from our regular missions that focus on implicating The Crown.

I turn, lean against the wall, close my eyes, and smile, a pleasant warmth spreading through my chest as I imagine the light igniting in those younglings' eyes when they realize they're free. *Truly* free – in a way I doubt I'll ever fully understand.

Make yourself indispensable and folk dig their claws in. Doesn't matter if they're good or bad or somewhere in the middle. If there's anything I've learned from this life, it's that.

Still . . .

I hope those younglings like it at The Flourish. I've never been to the underground safe haven ruled by the Elding, and though I've heard it's somewhere in the south, I don't think I'll ever know for certain.

See it with my own two eyes.

That would be considered retirement, and I doubt the leader of the Fíur du Ath has any interest in relinquishing my usefulness, instead plying me with placating missions I'll happily accept. Especially ones that end like this, filling me with this warm feeling of momentary contentment. Like I've just scrubbed one of the many stains from this big, beautiful world I so desperately want to love.

Besides, I'm not so sure retirement would suit me. Not the sort that would undoubtedly come with a one-way trip to The Flourish. I think my fingers would get itchy.

There's too much trash to take out.

I step out onto one of the perilous skybridges that stretches between both halves of the wall – the silent city so far beneath me. At thirty-three levels up, this one is the highest, never used by others and crusted in layers of snow that crunch beneath my boots.

Reaching the middle, I lie on my back – as close to the clouds as I can get – letting the cold sink through my gown. Into my flesh and bones.

Deeper.

My eyelids flutter shut.

Fat flakes of snow patter upon my face and the lax scoops of my hands, and I focus on each icy point of contact, loosening the muscles beneath, releasing some of the tension I'd collected throughout the slumber.

Picturing myself as a dragon, wings outstretched, I tip and churn through the puffy pink clouds, so far above the world that all I hear is my heartbeat and the heavy thump of my imaginary wings. All I *feel* is the flexing strength of my body. Untethered.

Free.

An icy calm settles within me like a nesting beast, and I wiggle my toes, my fingers, slowly bringing myself back to reality.

Opening my eyes, I look through a gap in the clouds to the moon of a perished Moltenmaw resting above the city. Perhaps the biggest one I've seen – bound in a tight ball, head tucked beneath its wing, its stony plumage brushed in shades of purple, pink, and blue.

I stare at it, recalling the time Ruse mentioned the sad story about how that dragon got there, not that I probed for details. In fact, I think I turned around and walked straight from her store without looking back.

Sadness is like stones that stack inside you, making it harder to move. Ignorance is my self-preservation tonic, and I'll swear by it until I die.

Sometimes, however, when I'm lying on what feels like the top of the world with a sleeping city beneath me, I wonder if that moon is ever tempted to fall. To crush Gore in a strike of spite for whatever caused it to soar up there and perch atop The Fade's decorated capital like a lingering threat.

Maybe I'm wrong. Maybe every last wisp of a dragon's cognizance dissolves the moment they solidify, and they don't *decide* to fall at all. Maybe something else rips them from the sky.

And maybe that dragon didn't consider much of anything when it decided to curl up there. Maybe it wasn't fueled by thoughts of revenge, as I like to believe it was.

Maybe it was just a convenient spot to die.

Gaze still cast on the moon, I wiggle my hand into my pocket, retrieving the parchment lark I received at the Hungry Hollow and lifting it above my face, unfolding its wings, beak, and body until I'm left with a crimped square scrawled in Essi's handwriting.

I hope you got your hand, since I know you won't read this until after you're done. Which is anxiety-inducing, just so we're clear. What if I desperately need a stick of porthonium to prevent the world from crumbling and you're too busy carving words into somebody's chest to unfold my lark still stuffed in your pocket? Think of the world, Raeve. And the hyperfixation I'm currently nursing.

Anyway, here's a very important list I'm sending because I know how you feel about me going to the Undercity alone. Patience is my biggest and most impressive virtue.

I snort-laugh.

Essi has the patience of a waif hungry for a soul to sink its teeth into, and not a pinch more. But good for her thinking otherwise. Enthusiasm suits her.

- *A hand-sized lump of iron (so I can make more pins for your boot)*
- *Three shaves of Sabersythe tusk (ideally from a mature beast well past their tenth shed)*
- *A 0.0112 etching stick reinforced enough to scour diamond (just hand this list to Ruse because this probably makes no sense)*

'Wise beyond your lifespan,' I say, gaze skimming farther down her list.

- *A jar of fluffy sowmoth powder. Or if there's none in stock, can you catch me one? Please? I'll collect the powder myself, then set it free. Promise.*

I cringe, remembering the last time I leapt around the Ditch, armed with a glass jar and a holey lid.

A full-body shudder almost rattles me to the core.

I'll never forget the way the sowmoth squeaked. I didn't even know they *could* squeak.

'Catch your own damn sowmoth,' I mutter, knowing damn well I'll catch her a bloody sowmoth if the bloody store has no jars of bloody powder.

My eyes narrow on the last request half concealed by a blotch of Tarik Relaken's blood.

- *And lastly, please go to the Undercity and*

– S P L A T –

It's very, very, very important.

Course it is.

I sigh, trying to scratch off the blood despite knowing full well it's not going to work.

According to Essi, there are *many* important things to be found in the filthy, rotten Undercity. Which makes sense for somebody whose world once revolved around the deep, craggy cleft in the ground beneath the wall.

My mind tunnels back to the moment I found her dashing from the miners' muck hall with a stolen lump of stale bread in her filthy hands, undernourished, dressed in rags, hair shorn because she'd learned that males get heckled less than the females down there.

She'd told me she was born in an abandoned shaft, and that her parents set off for a shift in the mines and failed to return – long ago. That she'd never seen the sky. Didn't know what the aurora was, or that we wake and sleep in rhythm with its rise and fall.

I was still covered in the blood of a supervisor I'd caught doing terrible things to a miner when I took Essi to meet the sky, then promised to keep her safe. Harder than it sounds when everything she needs seems to come from the fucking Undercity. Contrary to her boast, she's rarely patient enough to send me a supply list.

Frowning at the flattened lark, I try to scratch the blood off again – unsuccessfully – then pocket it and set my sight on the moon, hands clasped over my waist.

Even if I *did* know what's scrawled beneath the splat of blood, I'm supposed to be keeping my distance until I get word the younglings from Tarik's cells are out of Gore. I can, however, fetch Essi everything else if I stay out past the rise. Best I don't head straight home anyway, considering I chose not to eliminate the nice-smelling, mysterious loose end who may or may not believe I killed Tarik Relaken.

Creators.

Why did I do that?

I usually cut first, don't think later. I much prefer myself that way. Now I have to spend a small eternity checking over my shoulder, making sure the decision doesn't swing around and bite me in the ass.

Diary Entry

Elluin Nevǽn

Age: 9 phases
5,000,030 phases After Stone

Mahmi and Pahpi say I'm too young to have a dragon, and it doesn't matter that the Moonplumes in the palace hutch let me sleep with them. They say wild Moonplumes will drop from the sky the moment I step onto their spawning grounds, snatch me up, shake me until I'm limp, then feed me to their young.

I think that's a plop of spangle poop. And I don't think it's very fair that I should have to wait until I'm eighteen to find out for myself how big that plop of poop really is.

Pahpi said I can put my argument forth once I hear the elemental songs and I've learned to speak them properly, but I think that's a plop of spangle poop, too. Haedeon waited a long time and they never sang to him. And I've been listening really hard, every cycle, singing to the snow and the air and the ground and the flames. Nobody's singing back but Mahmi and Pahpi at slumbertime.

Not that I mind. I don't want to wear that silly stone, anyway. Mahmi always looks so tired, like her head's heavy. Pahpi's crown looks heavy too, but not in the same way. The stones on his are so pretty and shiny and make him look proud and important. The stone on Mahmi's is so black it looks like somebody could fall straight through it.

Sometimes, I catch Mahmi trying really hard to pull her diadem off while she screams and cries and folds herself up real small. It makes my heart hurt.

I don't think that stone is very good for Mahmi.

Last slumber, I found her outside, crying in the dark while the falling snow stuck to her hair. Her sad sounds made me cry, too.

I sang a song I'd hoped would make her feel better, but she just cried harder.

She wiped my cheeks and told me she'd be okay. That she lost something important, but that my cuddles made her feel much better.

Pahpi found us then. He picked her up and took her inside, then tucked me into my pallet, kissed me on the nose, and told me it would make sense when I'm older . . .

I don't think I want to understand.

Raeve

CHAPTER 7

The bloated clouds crawl north in time for the aurora to peek above the eastern horizon – ten luminous silver ribbons wiggling into view, moving to their own hypnotic beat. The world comes alive with the distant screech of Moltenmaws, their scratchy yawns threatening to split the sky.

I push up from the skybridge, groaning, my legs a little stiff from disposing of Tarik's body and lying in the snow. Yawning, I make for the north side, trekking down thirty-three levels of steep stairways until I step onto the ground level and into the already churning crowd.

The Ditch bustles with folk completing their early chores: clearing snow gathered before doors, chopping kindling, and fetching bottles of colk milk left beneath the eaves of those who can afford the run. Merchants roll by on colk-driven carts laden with tinctures, runed gadgets, and crates of exotic food, setting up shop for the dae.

A plethora of parchment larks flutter about, darting between folk and landing on outstretched hands, though some have no direction at all. Ghost larks – perhaps meant for somebody lost – that now spend their existence dancing with the fluffy sowmoths I'm feeling far too tired to chase.

'*Please* have jars of dust,' I murmur, jostling through the crowd.

Pausing by a store that's yet to open, I pretend to window-shop while I check I'm not being followed, using the opportunity to ensure my veil still thoroughly conceals the lower half of my face.

That there's no bloody stains anywhere on my gown that's cinched at my waist, the gathered bustle emphasizing my round hips.

The tight bodice makes my already full breasts almost spill from the neckline, and though that played the part last slumber, I look entirely overdressed amongst the freshly woken folk churning about the Ditch at my back. Not ideal.

I grab the tail of my veil, rearranging it so it's draped across my bust, hiding all my perky, pale flesh.

Much better.

I weave through the crowd until I reach a north side shop tucked beneath a wind chute. Pink, powdery sunlight shoots through with a blow of fresh air, rustling the plants that dangle from the store's eave, its name crafted on a stone plaque set amongst the stained glass window fashioned to look like a montage of Moltenmaw plumage.

I yank the door open, taking a step into the long, lofty store lined with rows of ceiling-high shelves packed to the brim with everything a Runi could possibly require: stacks of flat parchment squares with pre-drawn activation lines, small tincture jars choked by dangly labels, leather-bound books dyed an array of colors to match their painted edges. There's an abundance of quills, jars of various etching sticks, and lumps of different ores and gemstones.

Halfway through the doorway, I pause, watching a vibrant flock of parchment larks churn about the shelves with feathers attached to their ends, looking like miniature Moltenmaws.

Every time I come, the flock has doubled in size. I'm sure of it.

'Close the door before my pets escape,' Ruse yells from the back of the shop, 'or you'll not be doing business here for the rest of your existence.'

I tug the door shut and weave between the shelves. 'You know I'd catch them for you, Ruse.'

'Don't sweet-talk me, Raeve. I'm eyeball-deep in inventory and a hair's breadth away from losing my ever-loving mind.'

I round the final shelves, coming to a stone counter that dominates the store's back end. Ruse is seated behind it, slouched over a bowl brimming with bugs armored with brown interlacing shells that can wrap around their wriggling bodies and contort them into tiny balls of stone.

One by one, Ruse is tucking them into bottleneck jars stuffed with a sprig of greenery and half an inch of rust-colored dirt, scoring lines on a scroll to the side with each weighty *plop*.

I watch her work, her wild tangle of curls such a bright shade of orange. 'Looks tedious.'

'I want to impale myself with this quill,' she mutters, then corks the bottle she's currently filling and places a lid on the bowl. She clasps her hands together, slaps a wide smile on her face, and beams at me through pretty, sunburst eyes. 'How can I be of service?'

I pass her Essi's list.

The white tuft of an otherwise lanky tail rises from behind the counter, waving back and forth, making me smile.

'Hi, Uno.'

The tuft wiggles faster before brushing Ruse's jaw affectionately, an adoring softness spreading across Ruse's face as she reaches beneath the counter, no doubt to rub Uno behind the ears.

I wonder how big she's gotten. Miskunns are so scarce and greedily coveted I rarely glimpse more than the expressive tail of the creature who dotes on Ruse like a mother. Which is a shame. She's such a sweet thing.

Ruse hums, gaze still skimming the script. 'Can't help with whatever's supposed to be beneath the splat of blood,' she murmurs, lifting her hand to scratch at it. 'Messy job?'

'Unfortunately.' I shrug. 'He was a squirter.'

'Ah.'

'Do you have any of the other things in stock?'

'You're in luck,' she says, winking. 'I have it all.'

I breathe a sigh of relief, thankful I don't have to repeat the jar debacle.

Ruse grabs a cloth bag and moves around the counter, humming while she shifts between the shelves. Returning, she lumps the laden bag before me and sits again, sliding a large leather-bound ledger into sight. She lifts the front cover, flicking through until she settles on a page titled:

RAEVE
Dragon Bloodstone: 721 BKTS

My eyes widen.

I had no idea I had so much currency, the swelling digits a running commentary on how many bodies I've shoved off the wall to be picked apart by the predators that dwell beneath.

'I see your numbers have grown since—'

The inky scrawl stating my well of wealth bleeds off the page like watery ink blown off a slippery surface, before new digits appear in their place.

Smaller digits.

I frown.

Guess Sereme decided to charge me for the mission I begged the Elding for support on, and only because there was no possible way I could save all those younglings by myself.

Lovely.

A stark reminder that the hand that gives can just as greedily *take away*.

Ruse clears her throat, sliding her pink spectacles further down her nose, glancing up at me from beneath a fan of orange lashes. 'Busy slumber?'

'Not the sort of *busy* they like, apparently.'

She gives me a rueful smile, then recomposes herself back into the vision of *stoic storekeeper*. 'Well, besides your purchases from the list, would you like to spend any more of your *six hundred and ten* buckets of dragon bloodstone?'

I chuff.

'Actually . . .' I look at my gown, brushing my hands over the thick ruddy panels. 'I had to toss a layer of this to the trogg. Am I able to replace it?'

'Won't be a problem.' Her gaze flits over my ensemble, then

back to her book as she lifts a curly blue quill, dips it in a pot of ink, and scratches something on my page. 'Anything else?'

My mind tunnels back to the moments following Tarik's disposal. To the quiet allure I experienced toward a heavily accented male I probably should've slaughtered. But I didn't. Because he smelled good.

'Got any sawtooth blades?'

She pauses, looking at me from beneath an arched brow. 'Planning to hack somebody up?'

Hope not.

I shrug.

Humming again, she spins in her chair and pushes to a stand, snatching at the stone wall behind her. What's *actually* a runed drape ripples as she rips it wide, revealing the full, gloomy expanse of the store that goes so deep it's hard to see the end, the real walls lined with vaults of bloodstone, weapons, armor, and various infantry.

She unlocks one of the many grated repositories, retrieving a small saw she carries my way, tugging the curtain shut before she passes me the weapon.

I weigh it in my hand, tossing it to the other. 'Good shape, but a little less weight in the handle would be better.'

She nods, scratching something else on my page. 'Hiding place?'

'Thigh.'

'Sheath?'

'Colk leather. Preferably dyed fadestone brown, the buckles made of anything other than an iron compound.'

We say the last two words in unison, and the faintest smile tips her mouth as she bobs her head, still scratching. 'I'll have one forged to your size requirements and send a parchment lark when it's ready to be inspected. Perhaps by the next aurora rise if you're wanting a rush job and willing to pay extra?'

'Sounds good.'

I'd like it soon. Just in case *said cloaked male* decides to prove me wrong about the box I placed him in.

'Any withdrawals this dae?'

'No, but I'll return once I've rested to draw down and do another bloodstone scatter. Folk are starving to death in the Undercity, and nobody's doing anything about it.'

'As you wish.'

Ruse jots something on a notepad while I recall my first round of *wages*. Bloody payment for a bloody deed. That's all I could see it as.

Nothing's changed.

I only keep what I need to survive, to do my job, and to support Essi. My periodic donations to the poor, sick, and hungry are my quiet *fuck you* to those who think they can placate me by plying me with payments and approving my passion missions.

It makes me feel like I'm winning, even though I'm not.

'I'll ensure we have enough for the withdrawal,' Ruse says, curly quill wriggling as she scratches away. 'If the King put as much effort into feeding the poor as you do, The Fade would be a much better place to live.'

Like that's ever going to happen.

I doubt he's gone hungry before. Not really. If he knew the weight of a hollow ache, perhaps he wouldn't be so incompetent – though maybe not. You can reshape a turd an infinite number of times, but it's still a turd.

It still stinks.

Ruse closes the ledger. 'I'll be in contact about the gown. Given your . . . *special* requirements, it might take a while for the merchant who imported the material from The Burn to source more of the same color.'

'No rush,' I say, gathering my bag full of Essi's things. 'Any other material makes me cook up. I'd rather have it made with the right stuff.'

She tilts her head in acknowledgment, and I turn to leave.

'Not so fast, Raeve.'

Pausing, I look over my shoulder, brows pulling together as Ruse waves a recently unfolded parchment lark at me.

'Apologies. I know you're tired, but Sereme wants to meet with you.'

All that tension I'd worked so hard to extinguish while lying on the skybridge comes crashing back, making it feel like my heartstrings are being strung out across a rack.

'Tell her I'll be back once I've slept.'

If she can't be bothered coming down the stairs to request my presence herself, she's in no mood I want to deal with. Certainly not while hungry, sleep-deprived, and boasting a dwindling well of patience.

I'm three steps closer to the exit when Ruse's voice chases me like the flick of a whip snapping around my ankles. 'It was an order, Raeve. Not a request.'

Shackle *tugged*.

I sigh, cast my stare to the ceiling, and count to ten before I nod, then make for the bare-faced door in the corner of the store and yank it open. 'How you can stand to exist in the same vicinity as that manipulative serpent is well beyond me,' I mutter loud enough for Ruse to hear.

Maybe Sereme, too.

Ruse's laughter chases me all the way up the stairway and into the serpent's den.

Raeve

CHAPTER 8

'*I heard* that,' Sereme snips out, her voice a whetted blade.

I unwind my veil, stepping into her long office, casting my gaze about the tidy space that boasts an extravagant amount of purple.

Rugs, cushioned seaters, walls, bookshelves . . .

Can't escape it. I think I'd actually *like* the color had I not been treated like a scratching post almost every time I've stepped foot in this room.

'What?' I ask, finding Sereme by the large purple glass window that looks out upon the Ditch below. 'I'm genuinely baffled. Ruse deserves a raise for putting up with your shit on a constant basis.'

Sereme spins, impaling me with her cool silver stare, her angular face perfectly painted – as always. Never a hair out of place or a blemish to be seen, white Runi bead hanging from her lobe. She's donning a thick purple coat that melds with her body, snowy tufts of fur spilling between each seam that match the color of her coiffed hair.

My eyes narrow on the chain around her neck, threaded with a silver vial that's etched in luminous runes, every cell in my body screaming for me to lunge forward and rip it free.

Tip its contents down a drain.

Instead, I move toward the huge desk that dominates the space, everything on it perfectly squared. Setting my bag on the floor, I drop into the boxy chair reserved for visitors and kick my legs up over the armrest. 'I bite my tongue everywhere else; I refuse to bite it here. Feel free to cut me loose if it bothers you so,' I say, batting my lashes. 'Promise I won't complain. Quite the opposite. I might even do the odd side assassination for the cause in between hunting folk I *choose* to hunt.'

Murderers.

Child abusers.

Incompetent kings.

The muscle in Sereme's jaw pops, her eyes hardening like molten ore dropped in a bed of snow. 'You'd struggle without the Ath's unlimited support were you forced to live like the masses, Raeve. Don't forget how well we pad your pockets. There would be no more dragon bloodstone to scatter throughout the Undercity and give you that false sense of importance you can't seem to live without.'

I see neither of us are in the mood to play nice.

Sliding a blade from my bodice, I thump my boots on her desk, nudging a few of her perfectly lined up quills. 'Don't act like you care about my well-being. You don't,' I say, flipping the weapon between my fingers. 'You're just the bitch who clamped a shackle around my wrist and called it mercy.'

The vein in Sereme's temple swells so much I quietly hope it'll burst. 'It's surprising you speak to me with such disrespect, given said *shackle*.'

'Yeah, yeah,' I mutter, using the blade to dig some of Tarik's dried blood from beneath my nails. 'To what do I owe the honor of being summoned into your den, Sereme?'

She glares at me, watching me flick curls of hardened blood upon her plush purple rug. It's always interesting to see how far I can push her before she sweeps me from her space like a long-legged bug she can't eradicate fast enough, hoping she'll eventually decide my presence is more hassle than it's worth.

She paces toward me, lowering into the plump purple throne on her side of what I consider our makeshift barricade, folding her hands together atop the desk. 'I wanted to make sure you received my parchment lark.'

'Is the mission complete?' I ask, brow arched.

'No confirmation yet. I mean the one I sent last cycle, just before the aurora fell.'

Fresh orders.

Lovely.

My interest dissolves, stare cast on my nails again, digging out more filth. 'Must've gotten lost. Perhaps it'll circle back 'round once I've slept, as they often do. So considerate. You should take notes.'

I sense her simmering frustration like a welling storm cloud that clots up the air with a static charge.

Still, I flick.

Flick.

Flick.

'Funny how you're the only one who has trouble receiving my larks.'

'One of the world's great phenomena.'

'Doubtful.' A brief pause, then, 'Rekk's Moonplume is in the city hutch.'

My heart drops, gaze whipping up, plunging into Sereme's stony stare. 'Who's he hunting?'

'Us.'

My responding curse is as sharp as the blade in my hand.

'He's been hired by The Crown, and he's here to put a pin in our rebellion. To stop us from draining the kingdom of its fresh-faced conscripts.'

Well, he needs to die.

I swing my boots off the table and sheathe my blade. 'I'll take care of him,' I say, an eager hitch to my voice. Every time I've seen the bounty hunter, the metal spurs on the back of his boots have been caked in blood. Don't need a grand imagination to work out who the blood belongs to. Likely the poor Moonplume he apparently charmed after slaughtering its former rider, if the rumors are true.

I'll take a vast amount of pleasure in his assassination.

I rise from my seat—

'No,' Sereme bites out, and I frown.

'What do you mean, *no*?'

'*Sit*, Raeve.'

I sigh, then do as she ordered, loathing the spark of satisfaction in her eye.

'Why don't you want me to kill him?' I ask past clenched teeth. 'That's what I do. I take out the trash nobody else wants to muddy their hands with, sweeping the path clear of any filth that might prevent the Ath from completing its missions. Rekk is in the *path*, Sereme. He's endangering other members – *most* of whom I respect.'

She gives me a bland look that doesn't so much as pinch, though perhaps it would if she'd ever done anything to gain my respect.

'Let. Me. At him.'

'No.'

That fucking word again.

'Why not?'

'Because he's well-watched bait.'

'Then I'm perfect for the job.'

'*No*,' she chides for the third time. 'Your instructions are to lie low until he's gone. That means no random slaughterings when you find someone doing something they shouldn't, or hear someone crying out for help. No jobs. Nothing until I say otherwise. You will only leave your home to purchase produce or to come to me if I call on you.'

I frown, thoughts churning hard and fast, whisking into a snowstorm caught beneath my ribs. There's not a single hit Rekk Zharos has failed to bring down, so he's not leaving this city without blood on the tip of his barbed whip.

'If we don't eliminate him, he'll take one of us down, and it won't be pretty.'

'I'm aware,' she says through tight lips, a stern finality to her tone that strikes my nerves with that Sereme-serpent bite.

Meaning . . .

She's going to toss somebody considered *less useful* at him. A sacrifice to the ravenous Crown.

Something inside me splinters, bowing beneath an immense weight pressing against my ribs, my upper lip curling. 'You feed the monster and more will slip from the shadows. Once the smell of blood taints the air, they *don't . . . stop . . . coming*.'

Sereme sighs, reaching across the desk to straighten her quill collection. 'Are you going to tell me how to do my job again, Raeve?'

It's getting old for me, too.

'Every time we intercept a transport carriage full of young elemental conscripts, it's a bandage on a much bigger problem. So long as the King continues to rule, there will be more carriages. More bounty hunters. More death and suffering.'

Still, her eyes are cast on her quills, like she values the task more than she values everything the Fíur du Ath is *supposed* to stand for.

I snarl, slashing my hand across the table, littering the floor with feathers. 'What about the sick? The starving? The nulls?'

Slowly, she pulls her hand back, scouring me with a wide-eyed stare. 'We spent all slumber saving fifty-seven nulls. At *your* bidding—'

'An operation I funded myself,' I snip, brow raised. 'Or perhaps you thought I wouldn't notice, since I don't often check my reserves?'

'Of course I docked your reserves,' she sneers. 'Running such a large-scale operation is costly in ways you'll never understand. We risked our entire cause to keep you happy. Hindered political progress. Someone had to pay.'

To keep *me* happy.

Right.

'You know what that tells me?' I say with a humorless laugh. 'That the Ath doesn't value the nulls as much as it values the elementals. I don't go down to the Undercity just to *scatter bloodstone*, Sereme. I go down there to see if anybody needs help, because nobody else seems to give a fuck.'

She snatches the vial dangling between her breasts.

Shit.

I brace myself as she scrapes the tip of her tailored nail down the groove of my rune—

My entire body jolts, the same scratching sensation scoring one of my ribs like a filleting blade.

'Why can't you just be *happy*?' she snips while my breaths come short and sharp, eyes narrowed on the poisonous female. 'You have the Elding's favor. He does more for you than he's *ever* done for anyone else. Isn't that enough?'

I bind my side with a trembling hand, struggling to wrap my mind around the jealous taint to her tone. Not only have I never met the Elding, but being his favorite is swiftly tumbling to the bottom of my priority list.

She lifts her nail, brows hiked up her forehead, finger poised to mess me up all over again.

Creators, I loathe this female.

'Hard to be happy when the King's mincing young elemental minds until they're brainless killing monsters. When thousands of *less valued* folk are rotting in the Undercity, failing to scratch out an existence in the mines – slaves to the kingdom's well-oiled cogs.' Wiping beads of sweat from my brow, I reach into my pocket, unscrunch the notice I ripped off the wall, and slap it on the desk, though Sereme merely glances at it. 'If we don't usurp the King, I'm convinced things are going to get much, much worse.'

'Not now,' she says in a firm, even tone. 'Not until the Elding deems it so.'

Same story, different dae.

'Screw the Elding.'

Another sadistic scrape of her nail, this one scouring down the knobbles of my spine. Another series of hissed breaths, and I chew on the urge to lurch across the table and pop her eyeballs from their sockets – fuck the repercussions.

But I hold my composure, the pain still slicing down my bowing vertebrae like skipping stones as I speak through gritted teeth. 'Slitting King Cadok Vaegor's throat will not only keep me from being a pain in your ass, it'll protect the cause.'

She releases the vial.

I swallow my breath of relief, refusing to give her the satisfaction, instead jabbing an unsteady finger at the notice that's fully armed to do irreparable damage. 'Nobody will suspect it, given the heat surrounding our name.'

'Simply killing him without a thorough, well-constructed plan would leave the Queen in charge.'

'Perfect.' I throw my hands in the air, wondering why it was presented as a negative when it's *exactly* what this kingdom needs. 'This is her ancestral land. She *should* be in charge.'

'The Tri-Council would never allow it. Queen Dothea can only speak with Clode.'

A sour taste coats my tongue. 'Don't they have a tribead son?'

'Prince Turun hasn't been seen for many phases. Some say he went mad, and rather than make the problem public, the King was all too happy to hide him away.'

'Bet he's still more competent than King Cadok Vaegor. Perhaps he'll pop his head back up once his pah's remains fertilize the ground?'

Sereme looks at me like she's more than ready to grab the broom and sweep me toward the door. 'Again, Raeve, you assume you have some say in the matter. You don't. You have one job, and that's to follow my orders. When I say stab, you say how deep.

When I say leave Rekk Zharos alone, you leave Rekk Zharos well the *fuck* alone.'

It's weird hearing her swear. Perhaps I'd pump my fist and call it a victory if anger wasn't churning in my gut like a snowball that grows with each bouldered roll.

'How do you live with yourself? Honestly?'

She grips her vial again, and my entire body flinches.

Satisfaction ignites her eyes, a smirk curling her lips that boils my blood. 'These aren't easy decisions to make, but I must consider the cause first and foremost. Your strong affinity with Clode, your skill with a blade, and that savage side I glimpsed before you collapsed in the Undercity the first time we met makes you an essential tool we can't do without.'

An icy rumble builds in my chest.

I curse the dae she fell upon me, seeing that side of me I barely understand myself. Not that I remember that part of our meeting – tucked beyond a veil of ice I was all too happy to ball up and wither beneath.

I do remember the screams that somehow found their way down to me. I also remember being pitted with a certainty that whatever I was doing was not okay, but that the part of me in control lived by a different set of rules.

That in their eyes, it was *tame*.

Sereme later told me I'd looked out at her through black, glittery eyes, face splashed in blood, canines bared, and that she knew I was broken beyond repair, in desperate need of an avenue to channel my rage.

I see it differently now.

I think she saw me, surrounded by the mulched bodies of freshly slain folk who'd come to hunt me down, and decided broken things make the *sharpest* weapons . . . so long as you fetter them to yourself so they don't fly away.

'You coped just fine without me before you snatched me from the gutter.'

'I gave you the option,' she volleys, quick as a blink.

A deep belly laugh wrestles up my throat, spilling out in a mirthless tune. 'And what an option it was,' I muse. 'Die or drip my blood into your runed vial and be a forever slave to your whim, able to be yanked to heel at any given opportunity. Except it wasn't voiced that way, was it? You offered me revenge. Painted such a pretty picture I was *salivating* to give you my blood, falling into your web like a plump bug, immediately put to work.'

So many empty promises.

'Ironically, had you simply asked me to join the cause, I may have agreed, given the drowning amount of injustice I soon discovered in this kingdom. But you just *had* to slap a collar around my neck.'

She sighs, long and deep – the breezy confidence of someone who lives in a bubble of safety I can't penetrate. 'Always so dramatic, Raeve. Truly, I've never met someone with so much battle in their blood.' Her elegant hand grips the vial hanging between her breasts. 'Perhaps you wouldn't be so bitter were you not constantly testing me, forcing me to take advantage of the blood bind.'

Yeah, okay. It's my fault.

'Can't you see you're *made* for this?'

'Sure,' I deadpan. 'Nothing quite like the constant threat of a casual torture session to make you feel right at home.'

'It's nothing personal. Everybody puts their blood in the vial—'

'Except *you*.'

'—benefiting from its many advantages. Remember how quickly I was able to heal you?' she continues seamlessly. 'You would've died without it. Besides, you're the only one I'm forced to punish.'

'And what do *you* do for the cause?' I ask, brow raised. 'Besides sucking the Elding's metaphorical cock.'

Her cheeks flush, painted lips falling open. Not that any words come out.

My brows bump up.

Not so metaphorical, it seems.

'You chose to live,' she seethes. 'Sure, it's no longer on your terms, but at least you're breathing. I'd think you'd be more humble toward the one who saved your life.'

I click my tongue, trying to imagine a world where someone would deign to help another without expecting something in return.

Failing.

Thousands of times I've been pieced back together. Only once was it for my own benefit – but Fallon's dead, her light extinguished, all that goodness gone from the world.

Sereme may think she saved my life, but all she did was cage me again, carving Fallon's death into an even deeper tragedy.

I'd rather be back in our cell, looking up at the moons Fallon sketched on our ceiling with blunt bits of coal. Would rather be listening to her vivid explanations for the colorful clouds draped across The Fade, her words so descriptive my mouth would water – like I could taste the colors, feeling their textures puff against my tongue.

She made freedom sound so exquisite with her big, beautiful vocabulary. Made it sound so *magical*.

I couldn't wait to taste clouds with her. To lie on our backs, side by side, and look upon the *real* moons.

Together.

But she's dead, and I'm here, shackled to this purple-scaled serpent. Doing none of the *living* I promised Fallon I'd do before I lost her. Before I woke to find her cold.

Unmoving.

The barbed memory is an icy spike hammered into my hardened heart, all the way to the soft core, pitting me with a twinge of raw, familiar pain—

No.

I sink into my inner self, landing upon the crumbled obsidian shore of my immense frozen lake, struck by the eerie silence that always makes my skin pebble. I pinch a fist-sized stone I use to bind the offending memory around, then creep out onto the smooth, frosty expanse that soothes the bare soles of my feet.

Kneeling, I carve a hole in the thick ice, cold water oozing up the moment it cracks free. I tip the lid, plop the heavy thought down the gap, and rush away, the hairs on the back of my neck lifting as I blink back to my external reality.

My next breath is a blow of icy air, Sereme's earlier words still echoing through my mind:

You chose to live.

Sure, it's no longer on your terms . . .

At least you're still breathing.

I look at the female watching me down the line of her nose like she'd *love* for me to drop to my knees and kiss her purple shoes.

'My life has never been on my terms.' I stand, wrap my veil around my face, then gather her quills off the ground and lump them on the desk, rearranging them in order of size. Just the way she likes. 'And I refuse to accept *this* as living.'

I grab my bag and turn, moving toward the door.
'I didn't say you could *leave*, Raeve.'
'Drag your nail down my rune again.' I shrug. 'See if I care.'
I slam the door on my way out.

Diary Entry

Elluin Nevàn

Age: 9 phases
5,000,030 phases After Stone

Haedeon leaves early next cycle to try and steal his own Moonplume egg. He has to sleigh there and spend many slumbers in snow huts on the way, even though it's dangerous beyond Arithia's walls.

Seems a bit silly to me, since Pahpi's Moonplume could carry him there so fast. But Haedeon keeps saying that's how it's always been done. That he wants to prove himself.

I don't think Mahmi and Pahpi want him to prove anything, because I overheard them beg him not to go. Not that it worked.

This aurora fall, Haedeon smiled big and made lots of jokes while I was helping him fold his clothes and tuck them in his bag, but I can tell he's scared. I can tell because he gave me three butterberry chews from the jar he keeps beside his pallet.

Normally, he never gives me more than one at a time because he says they'll give me a bellyache, which is a lie. I ate all three and my belly feels fine.

Pahpi said it's really hard to get a Moonplume egg. That you have to go to Netheryn – the place where it's too cold for almost everything else to grow or breathe – and climb really high ice towers without being seen. That you have to steal the egg from a mahmi Moonplume's nest, then get back down the tower fast and quiet.

My brother's big and he makes lots of noise all the time. He doesn't know how to breathe soft or make his boots not crunch in the snow. Even his voice is rough and coarse like grain.

He doesn't hear any of the elemental songs.

Maybe those butterberry chews do give you a bellyache after all, because I don't feel so good anymore . . .

I don't think my brother's coming home from Netheryn.

Raeve

CHAPTER 10

Slamming the door shut on The Curly Quill, I charge west through the rowdy Ditch now packed full of merchant carts, folk flocking to claim the cheapest bushels of vegetables they can barter. I'd planned to stop for a cindercream pastry from one of my favorite merchants on the way home, but after having all of Sereme's purple-toned trash stuffed down my throat, I've lost the urge.

A chorus of panicked gasps has me pausing, gaze whipping around, following a sea of upturned stares.

My pulse scatters at the sight of an adult Moltenmaw gliding almost close enough to rip a ballista off the wall with its massive talons. A gust of wind slams down with the might of its magnificent wings – almost unveiling me.

Chest expanding, it lengthens its neck, cranks its maw, and paints the sky in a plume of flame that pours enough heat into the Ditch to turn the snow slushy.

Folk scream, dashing for cover beneath skybridges that are, in all honesty, completely fucking useless. If that beast decided to turn its head and torch us, I doubt a single one of us could do anything to stop it.

Dragonflame doesn't abide by the rules of nature. Ignos's language can't deter it from blistering skin. Melting flesh and bone.

Destroying cities.

Only a *Daga-Mórrk* can wield dragonflame – one so bonded with their dragon they can harness its strength and fire. Though the connection is more myth than reality.

The beast glides toward the coliseum that's clamped between both lengths of wall like a ghastly, blood-splattered crown.

'Creators,' I mutter, watching the Moltenmaw circle lazily above the massive structure.

The feeding bell gongs loud enough that I feel the sound in my marrow, and a haunting hush falls upon the crowd, the air igniting with the frantic thump of beating wings. A thunder of Moltenmaws swarm from every direction, clotting the sky with a riot of ravenous motion, charging for the free meal – their sharp maws pointed toward the coliseum like a volley of arrows.

They converge, snapping at each other, talons slashing, vibrant feathers spraying as they battle for whoever's currently tied to the stake within the structure.

An ear-splitting scream followed by a bloodcurdling howl of anguish echoes into the otherwise silent Ditch with eerie precision, almost like someone willed Clode to carry the sound down just to fuck with us. To remind us of the chilling consequences for those who madden The Crown.

My hands shake with my welling rage, fingers tangling through the folds of my gown, fisting the thick material.

I'd be up there right now, screaming for blood in the spectator seats if the one being fed to the beasts were a monster like Tarik Relaken. But it won't be.

They never are.

They're others like me, caught masquerading as nulls. They're folk who speak out against the King, or parents of gifted children who try to keep their young from being forced through the painful screening process required of every offspring. From being shaved. Pierced. Ripped from their homes in exchange for The Crown's prescription bucket of bloodstone – gratitude for their great contribution to The Fade's swelling militia.

A paltry bandage for a wounded heart.

The searing scream is snipped to the tune of splitting wood, and my guts plummet so fast I'm struck with the urge to vomit.

A victorious Moltenmaw shoves from the coliseum, churns its feathered wings, and heaves into the sky. Blood leaks from its honed mouth as the beautiful, monstrous creature glides west, a sea of heads turning to watch it sail along the wall.

All the oxygen wicks from my lungs.

In that direction, the wall eventually dips, half swallowed by the Moltenmaw spawning grounds – Bhoggith. Whenever they fly west with fresh meat, there's only one place the victim is going to end up.

Spat out in a nest, fed to the dragon's young.

Live prey.

I shiver from the base of my neck all the way to the tips of my toes, my gaze coasting across the silent crowd, most staring skyward through wide eyes, their mouths pinched shut as if under lock and key.

Apparently, the Kingdom of The Fade used to be a Creators-blessed place to live, where children's giggles echoed through the Ditch. Where the wispy watercolor sky inspired an era of music and arts.

Then our current king was sworn in, caring only for his military might.

I'd like to have seen Gore back then, when the kingdom was in its prime. Would like to have experienced the reality that was colorful to the core – not just on the outside.

I think that's the *living* Fallon was referring to. Not this.

This can't be it.

I swallow the rage boiling up my throat, certain there's enough anger inside me to incinerate this city in a single blow of breath. Even so, I force myself to continue forward, ignoring the feral urge to stalk to the city hutch, hire a carter, and fly west to Drelgad. To where King Cadok currently resides, overseeing his militia.

Only a fool would believe I could get close enough to kill him without a fierce amount of backup, the tri-beaded male constantly guarded by dual-beaded elementals and his vicious dragon. Making my anger useless – at least until the Elding decides to stop clipping leaves off this malignant tree and start hacking at its roots.

I take a zigzag path up the Ditch's lofty interior, scaling thirty-one stories, scanning my surroundings as I cross a crumbling skybridge and step onto the side of the wall that looks out upon The Shade. I skulk down a rough-hewn wind tunnel that reminds me of a choking throat, the ground etched in bands of runes that trigger all sorts of terrible responses for anyone other than myself or Essi.

The immediate urge to shit themselves. The sudden loss of vision – like they fell headfirst into The Shade's inky sky. And my personal favorite, the unnerving belief that a Moltenmaw just stuffed its beak down this very tunnel and is trying to pluck them out like a bug in a hole.

I pause by what looks very much like a rubbish chute for the velvet trogg and unlace my bodice, revealing a fade-stone-brown skinsuit that's snug against my form and much easier to climb in. Bundling my veil, boots, bodice, and supply bag within the folds of my skirt, I post the package, watching it shoot diagonally down, then disappear from sight.

Most prefer to make their homes on the other side of the wall, where sunlight shafts through colorful windows and fills rooms with warmth. Where folk can line their sills with potted vegetables that thrive in its constant flow.

Not me.

I like the cold, and I can't keep a plant alive to save myself. Though none of that holds a candle to the reason *why* I chose the brisk, quiet side with the dusky vista.

Wind toys with my hair as I stop at the end of the tunnel with my toes hanging over the edge, looking out upon the snow-covered plains that stretch toward the south. The clouds have almost entirely cleared, allowing me an uninhibited view of the bruised horizon pocked with moons cast amongst a bed of distant stars.

Closer are the vibrant balls of perished Moltenmaws, as if someone took the colorful clouds of The Fade, shredded them, then packed them into compact orbs and tossed them skyward. You can see the outline of their massive, majestic wings bound around them like feathered fans. The lanky plumes of their tails that sometimes fail to tuck in before the dying dragon solidifies, looking like flicks of paint.

Much farther in the distance are rounds of pearl, iridescent, and gray spilling shards of Moonplume light. Radiant bruises smudged against the otherwise dark horizon.

There's something poetic about looking up and seeing that which has passed. A soft launch into grief for those who linger below. If I could ball myself up like a Moonplume and nestle amongst the stars when I know my time has come, I would. Not that I think many would seek me out, but I'd die knowing I left something *bright* behind in this beautiful world sketched in so many shades of ugly.

I also like the idea of being able to fall from the sky and squash somebody if they piss me off. I'd aim myself at the Fade King and obliterate him in a heartbeat for doing such a shit job of keeping his kingdom together.

Petty, but justified.

I seek out the small silver moon of an adolescent Moonplume that's drawn my eye since I first looked upon the tombstone-laden sky, pulling my lungs full of crisp air, a true, untarnished smile stretching across my face . . .

Many call that particular moon *Hae's Perch*.

It's certainly not the largest, nor is it the brightest, nor the most magnificent to look upon. But for whatever reason, I can't imagine not being able to open my eyes each aurora rise, look out past the ever-vibrant clouds in this part of the world, and see that little wonky moon with the malformed wing.

Essi once asked me if I wanted to know its story. I smiled and shook my head. Heartbreak has a tone that echoes through the ages, and her voice was *laden* with it.

I don't want to look at my favorite moon and think of things that hurt. I want to look at that small Moonplume and imagine it had a beautiful life full of happy things that make your heart heavy with love.

Perhaps that makes me a coward, but I have to pinch my smiles from somewhere. And that moon . . . It never fails to give me exactly that.

A smile.

Raeve

CHAPTER 11

I drop from the wind tunnel's mouth, using the abundance of cracks and divots to latch myself to the side of the wall and scale downward, threatened by a fringe of rock shards that hug the base of the wall below. The hungry promise of a swift and brutal death that hasn't yet been able to chomp down on me. Or Essi.

Thankfully.

Gripping a jutting piece of stone, I transfer my other hand to the space beside it, then drop before what *appears* to be more flat wall – a perfect, runed illusion. I swing through what's *actually* a large, ever-open window, into a snuggle of slightly warmer air lush with the smell of something rich . . . buttery . . . freshly baked . . .

I land in a crouch, my appetite returning with a salivating vengeance. 'Yum, is that—'

'Buttermin loaf,' Essi says, slouched over a seeing scope at our small feasting table laden with tools, tinctures, and metal pots, scratching at whatever's beneath the scope with one of her etching sticks. 'I could smell the blood on your boots the moment they shot down the chute.'

Reaching the table, I pinch a finger of loaf from her plate and stuff it in my mouth, groaning through my first bit of sustenance since I set out last aurora fall – the dense pillow of savory goodness drenched in melted butter, slathered in a sweet layer of bogsberry preserve.

I smile.

I love bogsberry preserve. Essi doesn't. Meaning she left this piece *specifically* for me, knowing I'd be ravenous the moment I swung in the window. Not that she'd admit to it.

Not that I'd want her to.

She pretends not to worry about me; I pretend not to worry about her. We coexist in parallel with zero expectations – bar the odd supply list and the fancy things she makes for me – and it works blissfully.

Perfectly.

I wouldn't change a thing.

'Things got messy,' I say through my mouthful, moving into our rough-hewn kitchenette. I lift a cloth on the freshly baked loaf and slice off a fat chunk, topping it with a scrape of butter and a dollop of preserve. Cranking open the icebox, I root around for a bulb of bright-green fruit, slicing it into segments I pile on my plate. 'Want some goro?'

'They're not ripe.'

I spin with the plate balanced in my hand. 'Sure they are.'

'The butt end goes yellow when they're ripe.' She peers up from her task, red brows almost bumping off her pretty freckle-dusted face. 'That one will blow your tongue off.'

I stuff a pale shard in my mouth, and my face screws up as I choke on the zesty tang. 'They're not ripe,' I sputter, spitting it into the trash bowl.

Essi chuckles under her breath, then tucks her head back down, peering through her looking glass and getting back to . . . whatever she's doing.

I slide my fruit to the side and focus on the loaf while watching her work, my gaze shifting from the graceful, deft movements of her fingers to her delicate features. Tawny eyes. Nose slightly upturned at the end. A null clip is cut from the tip of her left ear that's a little longer than mine and with more of a backward tilt, giving her this hypnotic, ethereal visage.

Coils of hair hang well past her hips like a thick ruddy cape that matches the metallic specks in her eyes – such a unique shade of red I've never seen before – the only splash of color that brightens her appearance. Ever.

I take another deep bite of loaf, thinking back to the dae she moved in. I told her she could do whatever she wanted to the previously sparse decor. Naturally, our shared living space is now the same color as her entire wardrobe.

Black.

The rough kitchen counters. The jagged ceiling. The fibrous rug that covers the uneven floor. Even our plump, heavily cushioned seater by the window, big enough to fit three despite the fact that we never have visitors. By choice.

My gaze lifts to the window specially runed by Essi to ward off intruders, remembering the slumber I woke to her standing over me in the midst of one of her episodes. Black smudged beneath her haunted stare as she waved a blade about, screaming at me to fill a cup with my blood. Now. That it was a matter of life or death.

The end result: an entrance that all but murders intruders. Stroke of genius.

'This is delicious, Essi. Thank you,' I say, taking another bite.

'Of course. Glad you like it.'

Understatement. She knows her buttermin loaf is my favorite. No idea what she puts in it, but damn, it's good.

'What're you working on?'

'A diamond cap for your tooth,' she says, etching away. 'I've been trying to find an ore dense enough to withstand these fiddly runes. Freak accident, but I discovered diamond works. Oh!' Hand poised, she flashes me a wide-eyed glance that's so full of life it renders me breathless – no doubt high on whatever thought just threaded through her spectacular mind. 'Did you get my lark?'

'Mm-hmm.' I tuck my hair behind my ears and make for the oddly shaped stone basin that caught all the bits I pushed through the chute earlier. 'I got blood on it but did my best.' I set the plate aside to rummage through my belongings. 'What does the diamond crown do?'

'Emits an invisible, impenetrable barrier around your head and chest without cutting you in half.'

Hand stilling, I look over my shoulder at her. 'Without cutting me in half? You mean . . . my body?'

She nods so fast her hair's a sanguine churn. 'Took me a bit to figure that out. Promise it's good now, though.'

Right.

'Glad you're thorough,' I say, gripping the bag.

'Always. It's almost done. A few fine runes with that new etching stick and it'll be ready to activate. Figured it's a good time to attach it since Rekk Zharos is hunting you.'

'See you've been reading my messages again.'

She shrugs, adjusting the scope of her looking glass. 'It flew through the window after you left. Bumped against the sill until its nose was squished. I put it out of its misery by unfolding it.'

'And reading it.'

'My eyes slipped.'

They have a habit of doing that.

I shake my head, sliding the bag across the table for her to rummage through. Flip side of using so much blood in the active runes etched around the window, the parchment larks sometimes think the window is, well . . . *us*. Ergo, the source of Sereme's eternal frustration whenever she can't get ahold of me.

Essi pulls her head from the bag, her face a tad paler. 'No spangle poo?'

I blink at her. 'I'm sorry, what?'

'From Yeskorn, the Undercity librarian. He's got a pet spangle. Is it in your pocket? Please tell me it's in your pocket.'

'There's no *shit* in my pocket, Essi. Why do you need spangle poo?' She opens her mouth to speak, but I swiftly cut her off. 'Remember my brain's not as big as yours. If you start talking about biophysics, I'll perish.'

She opens her mouth again, closes it, seems to think for a bit, then starts to talk. 'The stone they eat is rich with a special ore that's otherwise hard to find because it forms in minuscule drops that never grow larger than a pinhead. It doesn't break down in their digestive tracts, so it's the most effective way to gather it. It's a creamy color, and it melts at a much lower temperature than most other ores, making it the perfect adhesive for binding runed caps to your teeth.'

'You're joking.'

Her brows crush together. 'For the first time in my life?'

All the warmth drains from my face, my hand whipping out to steady myself against the table. '*That's* what you used to bind the other activation cap to my tooth?'

She nods.

'*Spangle shit?*'

'I rinsed the actual feces off, then sterilized the ore. But yes. It had been . . . shat.'

Creators.

I shove my tongue to the right side of my mouth, feeling around *said* cap. 'Let's file that under *Things Raeve Doesn't Need To Know*,' I mutter, making for the cabinet where I pull out a mug.

Ever.

'Noted. I, ahh . . .' I glance back to see her shuffling in her seat, scratching at the back of her head. 'Given Rekk's renowned accolades, I was hoping to get it attached . . .'

'There's no rush.' With this new, rather revolting information, the least amount of rush *ever*.

'What if he targets you?'

I lift the jug of filtered water from our icebox, filling my mug. 'I've been instructed to lie low, and we both know Rekk can't get me here. The only way we'll clash is if I *accidentally* run into him on my way to pick up my handsaw and *accidentally* slit his throat, *accidentally* going against Sereme's direct orders and *accidentally* saving the life of one of my comrades.'

The only upside to being indispensable? I'm almost certain Sereme won't fatally maim me for the transgression. Just rough me up until she feels like she's got control again.

The usual shit.

Essi's chair grinds against the floor as I gulp my belly full of water, draining the mug before I place it in the basin and grab a band off the counter, using it to pull my heavy hair back into a high updo.

The silence grows prickly and needles me from behind.

I turn.

Essi's no longer facing her project. She's facing *me*, hands on her knees, eyes wide and brimming with worry. A look that impales me through the chest so hard I feel it poke out the other side.

'Stop,' I growl. 'Don't look at me like that.'

Why is she looking at me like that?

Her eyes gloss over with a sheen of sadness that's so much worse. 'Raeve, I can't lose you—'

'We don't do this, Essi. We work just fine the way we are. Don't break something that's not broken.'

Her brows pinch together as she opens her mouth, but nothing comes out. Like the words are too big to wrestle free.

Good. They *should* stay in. I don't want her to tell me she's worried. That she cares. I don't want to say those same words *back* to her.

The folk I care about die.

'The point is moot, anyway.' I spin, rinsing my mug and plate in the basin, eyes firmly cast on the task. 'I can't go to the Undercity until I receive a lark signaling the all clear.' I dry both bits of crockery, put them away, then move to the trough and gather my things. 'I'm exhausted. I'll get these stupid feathers off my lashes, catch some rest, then collect your spangle shit once I receive a lark from Sereme. Deal?'

She doesn't answer.

When the stretch of silence grows too loud, I spin, looking into her big, tear-filled eyes.

Shit.

'*Deal*, Essi?'

Lips pinched into a thin line, she nods – the slow beat of a reluctant agreement.

I make for the trapdoor that leads to my suite and lift the hatch, stilling halfway down the steps when Essi's words impale me like a blade thrown between my ribs, wedging deep. 'I don't like Sereme any more than you do, but for once, I think you should listen to her. Please, Raeve. I ne—' She sighs, pausing before she throws another verbal dagger, this one knocking the breath right out of me. 'You're the only family I have.'

I squeeze my lips so tight together I'm surprised they don't fuse.

Essi's broken. Actually, this entire *cycle's* broken. I need to close the cover on it and flip a new one – a *normal* one – where folk stop voicing their concerns for my well-being and calling me family. I don't get nice things like that without a price tag too heavy for me to pay.

'Please don't go to the Undercity without me. You know I hate it when you go down there alone.' I step out of her line of sight, swinging the trapdoor back into place with a heavy *clunk*.

My suite is sparse compared to the rest of our living space, the only decoration aside from a single piece of wall art being the moons I've drawn upon my otherwise unpainted ceiling with bits of coal. Essi's never asked why, though by the way this dae is going, it wouldn't surprise me if she charged down here and dumped the question at my feet like a steaming pile of spangle shit.

'Dammit,' I mutter, lumping my stuff on the ground. I release a heavy sigh, casting my low-lidded stare on my twill pallet stretched across the ground by the large window that dominates my southern wall.

No stuffy blankets or pillows. Just a comfortable space to curl up and pass out. Something I want to do right now, but if I don't pick these feathers off, I'll wake up looking like a scraggly Moltenmaw midmolt, missing sprigs of my lashes.

Been there. Done that.

'Don't be lazy, Raeve. Deal with your shit.'

I scoop my things off the floor again and move through to my dressing space tucked behind the back wall, hanging my gown, pulling my daggers free from all the hidden compartments like plucking a bird of its plumage. I shelve them all except the one I keep strapped to my thigh, checking my skinsuit for blood. Finding none, I decide it's fine to sleep in and hone the dregs of my energy into scrubbing my boots, removing the damn feathers and taking care of my business, battling through a yawn as I step back into my sleepsuite.

I pause before a flat piece of stone hanging on the wall, carved to look like a nesting Moonplume. Easing it aside, I reach into the hole behind, retrieve a small wooden box that I carry to my pallet, placing it beside the window.

The pane of glass is stretched from floor to ceiling, offering a view of The Fade's gradual smudge into the distant Shade, framed by frosty runes that make the window look like stone from the other side. Another one of Essi's clever adaptations.

Seeking that wonky moon in the distance, I see the rising aurora tangled around it like the frayed threads of a silver gown unraveled by the handsy wind.

A soft smile fills my cheeks despite this weight settling in my chest, like something's sitting on me. Something that feels a bit like . . . *regret.*

My smile falls.

Essi called me family and I walked away. After everything she's been through, *I walked away.*

What the fuck is wrong with me?

How can I look at that moon with so much love in my heart – love that ricochets off my ribs every time I look at Essi?

Stupid question. I know exactly what's wrong with me.

Loving that moon feels safe. Moonfalls are so rare it'll likely always be there, accepting my quiet adoration.

Loving Essi . . . it makes me feel like I'm handling something fragile that'll break apart in my hands if I tighten my grip even the slightest bit.

Sighing, I lift the lid on my small box.

Nee bats her plain parchment wings and rises from the hollow, fluttering around me in a churn of giddy motion, nuzzling my face, shoulder, neck. She tries to wiggle into my ear, making it impossible not to smile.

'Careful not to hurt yourself,' I murmur, gently nudging her away from my face and easing her toward the rest of the room so she can stretch her little wings. She does a few lofty loops, then tucks her head and *plummets* – too fast.

Too far away.

She collides with the floor beak-first, and I flinch.

Fuck.

I scramble up and dash to her, swooping her into my palm. 'Nee, I *really* wish you'd stop doing this . . .'

She jerks, flipping onto her back, baring the three beautifully scrawled letters visible on her abdomen, the rest of her message tucked within the darts of her streamlined body.

nee

I cut her an incredulous glare, unimpressed by the *not-so-subtle* nudge for me to unfold her. 'You know, of all the tricks you use to get me to read you, this is my least favorite,' I mutter, waiting for her to move again. To dart back into the air and burn off all the energy she's built up while I've been out.

Nothing.

'I'm serious.' I jiggle my hand. 'You look dead. Stop it.'

Still, she doesn't move.

I blow on her. Again.

Again.

My heart crimps. '*Nee*—'

She waggles her parchment tail, and all the breath shoves from my lungs as prickly relief packs me full.

I shake my head, rubbing my sternum. 'This is called *rewarding bad behavior*,' I grouse, gently unfolding her crushed beak, head, tail, wings, then body, baring her message that's more than five phases old:

Three small words I'm certain were never meant for me – not that it's stopped me reading them again and again.

I devour the delicate sweep of each tailored letter, brushing the pad of my thumb across them like a Nee belly scratch as I recall the moment she came to me.

She must've gotten lost on her journey to whoever she was intended for, instead nuzzling into the crook of my neck like she was seeking comfort from a storm. I'd opened her, read her message, and realized how important she was – come from somebody who was not okay, though they perhaps didn't know how to say it aloud.

I'd folded her up and blown her back to the sky, asking Clode to carry her high into the currents so she could recalibrate and head in the right direction.

Find the one she was intended for.

The next rise, I'd woken to her resting in my palm, a tear in her wing and a very squished nose, like she'd battled against Clode's currents . . . and *won*.

Hard to part with her after that.

I sweep my thumb over those three words again, then gently fold her back up, flattening her beak crimp and checking that her rip hasn't gotten any bigger. She bursts from my hand in a flutter of motion and bats about the room like she's burning off a furnace full of energy.

'If you're not more careful, I'll pack the room with down feathers,' I warn, and she flips through the air, swooping toward me in a wobbly glide, dipping into the crook of my neck where she nuzzles in. I settle my hand atop her and rock until she stops wiggling, my thoughts drifting back to Essi. To the jarring way she looked at me through those big eyes glazed with . . . *too much*.

Sighing, I make for my pallet, then cast my stare to the sky outside.

Fallon once told me that as a youngling, she used to lie on her back and wish upon the moons – wishes that would sometimes come true.

Magic, she called it.

I've never believed in things that make no sense to me – aside from Essi's magnificence. But perhaps I should start wishing on the moon I love so much. Ask it to find a way to replace my heart with a soft and squishy one so I never have to see Essi's eyes flood with sadness again.

Creators, I'm an asshole.

I curl up on my side, snuggling Nee, looking at Hae's Perch while humming the gentle tune that always clears my mind no matter how loud the world seems.

Diary Entry

Elluin Neván

Age: 9 phases
5,000,030 phases After Stone

Haedeon found me in his sleigh just before the aurora set.

I thought he'd be happy to see me. Instead, he said he was going to take me straight home to Arithia in a big growly voice I've never heard him use before. But when the aurora rose, he boiled me tea, packed our things, and then we kept going in the same direction.

I think he forgave me a little bit because he gave me a butterberry chew this slumber after we ate some felt-ringed fungus soup. Haedeon didn't finish his bowl or eat his chew, but he did spend time shaping a dragonscale blade.

He told me we'll be there in three aurora cycles. That we'll spend one slumber in the hatching hut on the outskirts of Netheryn before he leaves at aurora rise right when the mahmi Moonplumes go off to hunt. That I'm not to leave the hatching hut until he returns or three slumbers have passed without him.

Seems a bit silly to me since I didn't hide in his sleigh to sit in a hut and eat butterberry chews . . .

I came to get my own Moonplume egg.

Kaan

CHAPTER 13

Seated in the back of a gloomy booth, I keep my hood up despite the velvet curtains pulled shut so nobody can see in. My only companion is a heavy mug of mead I bring to my mouth, drawing a frothy glug of the thick, bitter-tasting liquid. Hissing through my teeth, I bang it back on the table, scowling.

The mead in this city tastes like it's been distilled in a muddy barrel, but I prefer it over the murky water that's twice as dirty and leaves grit in your teeth.

The quenching warmth takes only the sharpest edge off this feeling in my chest – like I've been rattled so hard my bones split and stabbed me through.

I know it wasn't her. That it's impossible. That I'm going mad – and have been for phases.

Still.

Those eyes.

That scent.

That voice—

Growling, I lift the mug to my lips again.

The curtain parts.

A hooded female with a proud but delicate stature steps into the confines of my booth, chased by a parchment lark that nudges her shoulder, urging her to snatch it up.

She does, sighing.

Forging myself into a vision of false composure, I draw another muddy sip, swallowing as she settles in the seat opposite me, face hidden within the cowl of her cloak.

'Surprised to see my brother let you out of his sight again,' I rumble, setting the mug back on the table, '*Princess*.'

Kyzari pushes back her hood, brows raised as she regards me through haunting azure eyes. Her white hair hangs well past her waist, bound in a braid almost thicker than my wrist, her complexion so pale I can see the web of veins beneath the skin of her hands.

My gaze lifts to the diadem clinging to her forehead, the black Aether Stone sitting central amongst the curls of silver metal she's been crowned with since the dae she took her first breath.

It's been a while since I saw her last. Since Veya and I went to Mah's special place and found her there. Realized she'd been there for a while – holed up.

Hiding.

Not the first time she'd run away. Obviously not the last.

She reaches toward the sconce protruding from the wall like a gnarled claw and dangles the still-fluttering, unread parchment lark over the flame. Fire gobbles it up, her fingers pinching the thing until it's almost gone before she drops it to the stone table and watches it turn to ash.

I frown.

'I'm devoted to the Creators now,' she announces, brushing off her hands, reaching over the lark's corpse to steal my mug. 'I took the Oath of Chastity—'

'You're my niece. The last thing I want to talk about is your *chastity*—'

'—I can do whatever I want now that Pah's no longer afraid of losing me.'

'Lie,' I growl, low enough my voice won't carry beyond the curtain to where a lone fiddle player is carving a tune in the common area beyond. 'Your Moonplume isn't in the imperial hutch I purposely inspected before meeting you here, and we both know you wouldn't trust her with some loose-lipped city wrangler.'

She rolls her eyes, finally thieving a sip of my mead, face scrunching as her eyes narrow on the offending drink.

'You came via a carter,' I declare, and she thumps the mug back on the table. 'You smuggled yourself out of Arithia after your unveiling ceremony while the skies were busy, figuring it would take your pah longer to notice.'

'How very astute of you. Your drink tastes like mud.'

'It's an acquired taste you'll have to get used to if you intend to spend the rest of your long existence as a fugitive, carving out a life for yourself in a broken kingdom that's no place for a sheltered princess with no wits about the world.'

She arches a brow. 'Who shat in your stew?'

'Who taught you to speak like that?'

The smallest smile pulls at her lips. 'Guess I'm not as sheltered as you think.'

I grunt.

Doubtful.

Silence reigns long enough that she clears her throat, her gaze dropping to the drink still clutched in her hand. 'I, ahh . . . appreciate you agreeing to meet with me. You saved me from a very long trip across the Boltanic Plains.'

She was on her way to Dhomm, then.

'I wasn't aware I had a choice,' I say, crossing my arms, head tipped as I regard her in the firelight. 'Your lark was firmly worded. I'm not used to being ordered around. Not sure I'd take it from anyone else.'

Her cheeks redden, and she nips a guilty glance at me from beneath pale brows. 'Sorry. My tutor taught me to lead with a firm hand. His methods were questionable, but I guess some of his teachings had merit.'

Firm hand?

I raise a brow. Wait.

'Don't look at me like that.'

Still, I fucking *wait.*

She sighs, drops her gaze to the drink, then blurts, 'It was nothing. Just silly things like punishing me with a riding whip across my knuckles whenever I forgot to link my letters.'

My blood turns to magma.

'He whipped you? For forgetting to link your letters?' I ask, my steady voice betraying none of the violence roiling through my veins.

'Asshole, I know. But Pah says only folk with weak hearts complain, so instead, I wrote my tutor hate sonnets I'd send fluttering into the fire,' she says, boasting a victorious smirk. Like she thinks that rights his wrongs. 'Now every time I write something with my *perfectly linked script*, I want to punch him in the throat. Not that I know how to punch, but I'd like to do it anyway.'

'I'd like to cut off his head.'

Her wide eyes snap to mine. She opens her mouth, closes it, shakes her head, dropping her gaze to the drink again.

She probably thinks I'm joking.

I'm not.

I'd like to cut off her pah's head, too. Though I don't say that.

'Was that why you used to run away?'

'No.' She snatches my drink and gulps deep enough my brows pull together, then lowers the mug, cringing. 'Why are *you* in The Fade, anyway?'

'Hunting for something. Queen owes me a favor. Cadok's in Drelgad.' I shrug. 'Timing was opportune.'

'And if he finds out?'

'He won't. Not unless you tell on me.'

'Might consider it. I'm pretty offended by the taste of this drink you let me sip without prior warning.'

I lift a brow. The corner of my mouth tugs up the slightest amount – only because she, too, is smiling. There one instant, gone the next.

My own falls. 'You need help with something.'

She settles the drink on the table much softer this time, still nursing the mug while she looks into its half-drained depths and worries her bottom lip.

I sigh.

Leaning forward, I plant my forearms on the table. 'What is it, Princess?'

She swallows, and I can hear the violent thump of her heart rallying in the way hearts do when folk are preparing for battle.

Her voice is a rasped whisper when she finally says, 'I . . . can *hear* him.'

'Who?'

Another swallow, and she looks up at me with glazed eyes, lifting a pale hand to her diadem.

To the *Aether Stone*.

My blood turns to ice.

I push back against the seat, staring, head full of thoughts I can't tame enough to push free of my mouth.

A tear shreds down her cheek, and I see her.

Truly see her.

The dark dents beneath her eyes. Her frail, almost skeletal

hand, and the way her cheekbones jut out much more than they once did. Her fingernails – chewed so close to the nub she's made them bleed in places.

She's wasting away . . .

Something fierce and feral rears up inside me.

I lean forward, forcing words past my gritted teeth. 'How long?'

She blinks, releasing another tear she's quick to dash away as she drops her stare to the tabletop. 'I'm not certain. My nursemaids said I screamed nonstop the first few cycles after I was born, which they considered strange because the diadem was expected to weaken me. They suspected I could already hear the Creators and that I screamed to drown out their prattle, so they clipped an iron necklace on me. Said I immediately calmed.'

I swallow thickly.

I'd heard she was a restless youngling, but I put it down to the echo of trauma from her start in this world – a world I've grown to hate.

'But as I grew older, the silence *itched* at me in ways I can't describe, and I couldn't shake this feeling that I was missing something. When I was just shy of eighteen, I took the necklace off, and all I heard was . . . was *wailing*,' she rasps.

My throat dries.

'His fear, his *sadness* . . . It flowed through me like a stream. I felt like I was being ripped apart, piece by piece.' Her gaze flicks up to meet mine, and I think a spear through the heart might hurt less.

There's so much *pain* in those big blue eyes . . .

'I put the necklace back on,' she says, wiping her cheeks with her sleeve. 'Left it on for many, many phases. Because I was a coward.'

'You're not a coward, Kyzari. Don't ever speak about yourself like that.'

She cuts me a faux smile, then draws another drink of mead, almost draining the mug before she speaks again.

'I found courage eventually. Removed the necklace for the first time in over eighty phases. I listened to his sounds. Truly listened. I realized it wasn't just screams and wails, but *words*,' she says, voice cracking as her wide eyes plead with me. 'I began threading those words together, shaping his language in my mind, learning . . . too much.'

My gaze nips at the curtain, and I plant my arms on the table again.

There's more, I know there is. She's dancing around the fiery pip like she's afraid to handle it.

'Keep going.'

There's a moment of pause before she lifts her chin, and for the first time since she sat down at my table, I see her as someone with something to guard.

Something to *lose*.

'I'm telling you this not because I want your pity. Pity doesn't help me any more than it helped *him* during those many phases I sat in silence.'

'Then why?'

'Because I want help to set him *free*.'

It's like she reached across the table, swung her hand back and slapped me in the face.

'Impossible,' I growl. 'It'll kill you. The diadem can only be removed from a pulseless host.'

'I don't intend to *die*, Uncle. There has to be another way. I just have to work it out.'

I've never wanted to shake someone so much in my life, my hands bunching into fists so tight my knuckles pop.

'And why do you want to do that?' I grind out. 'The Aether Stone has been passed down for generations. Your mah wore it. Her mah before that. On and fucking on—'

'His name is Caelis,' she announces, her voice stained with a fierce imperial lilt. She pins me with a stare that cuts through flesh and bone. 'And because I've fallen in love with him.'

A rumble boils deep inside my gut, scalding up my throat with such intense heat I swear my flesh peels off.

I know too well how malignant the roots of love can be. I've suffered from the same ailment for over an eon, and I'll continue *suffering* until the dae I die.

Kyzari's suffering, too – I can see it in her eyes. It's taken her, and it won't let go.

If my brother hadn't kept her so sheltered from the world, perhaps she wouldn't have fallen in love with a fucking *stone*. Perhaps she wouldn't be trying to rid herself of a diadem that could very well take her life the moment it's ripped free.

'There is no reality where this ends well,' I snarl through gritted teeth, and something shatters in her eyes.

'You can't know that . . .'

'I know he's in that thing for a reason. That your family line was blessed with the power to contain him for a *reason*.'

She rips her gaze from mine, stare plummeting to the table so fast she probably thinks I missed the stain of guilt clouding her eyes.

'What do you know?'

'Nothing,' she bites out, cheeks flushing.

My eyes narrow. 'What. Do. You. Know?'

She shoves to a stand. 'This was a mistake. Forget I said anything.' My eyes flare as she flips up her hood and makes for the curtain. Looking at me over her shoulder, she says, 'I will leave you with your empty mug.'

She goes – her parting words like drips of poison fed to me on a tarnished spoon – leaving the curtain wide open. Allowing me a perfect, unveiled view of the dais. Of the musician perched on the stool beneath an illusion of luminous snowflakes, the vacant seat beside her haunting me to the marrow.

I look at my *empty* mug, pulling my lungs full.

Holding the breath.

Kyzari's right, but my mug's not the only thing that's empty.

My chest feels pretty fucking hollow, too.

Raeve

CHAPTER 14

Something bumps against my cheek, ripping me from the fiery clutches of a dream that was melting flesh from my bones in slow, sizzling sweeps. My eyes pop open, a scream sitting in the back of my throat like a welling beast threatening to split the world in two.

I sit up, hissing through clenched teeth, trying to refocus my gaze on the *here*.

The *now*.

Nee flutters around me, frantically nuzzling my chest while I scrub my sweat-dappled skin, trying to scour the terror from my flesh.

Unsuccessfully.

I rush to my washroom, fill the stone basin with icy water, and splash my face in laden scoops that do little to douse the burn. 'A dream,' I murmur, repeating the motion again.

Again.

Nee continues to dance around me as I dunk a cloth in the water and use it to dab the back of my neck. I dunk it again, pressing my face into the sodden material.

Just a fucking dream.

I lift my head, looking in the small mirror hanging on the wall. My eyes are bloodshot, ice blue standing out in stark contrast against the red scribbles, my cheeks flushed from the rabid heat that chased me to the surface.

Growling, I screw up the cloth and toss it at the wall, scooping my palms full of water again, splashing my face and dragging the wetness back through my hair. I set my hands on the edge of the basin and close my eyes, humming my calming tune while I focus on my fingertips, then my hands, my arms – moving all the way through my body. Slowly loosening each muscle, convincing myself there's nothing here that wants to hurt me.

To *battle* me.

Nee nuzzles much too close to my sodden hair, and a warning growl boils up my throat. 'Don't, Nee. You know how I feel about water getting near you.'

With a burst of fluttering motion, she rises above my head instead, circling a safe distance away.

I'm not certain she has waterproof runes, and I'm in no rush to find out the hard way that she was constructed before they were invented.

I press my face into the towel and pour a heavy sigh through the fluffy fabric, untacking the sticky remnants of my terror, a full-body shiver racking through me.

That one felt so real. Too real.

I jump a few times to shake it off, then move back into my sleepsuite, chased by a flutter of parchment wings. My eyes widen at the outside view, the sky clear enough that I can see the aurora already beginning to thread below the western horizon.

Falling. Wow.

I slept the entire dae away . . .

My stomach growls, clamping down on its aching hollow.

I'll check on Essi, make us some food if she hasn't already eaten, then try to get back to sleep. Otherwise, I'll be out of sorts for cycles.

I make for the stone stairway as a thump sounds from above, like something heavy just fell upon the floor upstairs.

Frowning, I pause, scooping Nee against my chest to stall the sound of her beating wings. 'Shh,' I whisper, looking at the ceiling as I listen.

Silence prevails.

Perhaps I imagined it?

Slowly, I tiptoe toward the stairs, pulling the small blade from the sheath at my thigh. I edge close to the trapdoor, pressing my ear to the wood.

A soft whimper stills my heart.

Essi.

I release Nee, nudging her in the direction of my pallet. 'Stay here,' I order, shoving the trapdoor open and bursting through, dropping it back down so Nee doesn't escape.

Essi is coiled on the long seater with her back to me, hiding beneath her woolen blanket that conceals all but her tumble of hair spilling onto the floor. Not unusual since she sometimes can't be bothered going up the stairs to her sleepsuite and nods off on the seater.

My next inhale is laden with a metallic reek, and my heart lurches, stare slicing around the room, landing on a red hand-shaped smudge on the windowsill. The size of *Essi's* hand.

Essi's hurt.

She always tries to hide when she's hurt.

I dash toward her, rip the blanket off, and grab her by the shoulder, tugging her gently onto her back despite her coiled reluctance. My gaze is immediately drawn to her hands clutched atop her abdomen, both of them shaking, slathered in . . . in . . .

Blood.

My gut churns as I take in her pallid complexion. The sheen of sweat dappling her brow despite her chattering teeth. I drop to my knees, pulling her hands back and lifting her shirt, revealing a stab wound leaking a constant ribbon of blood.

Every cell in my body stills, my lungs seizing – like jagged shards of ice just slit through them.

I'm suddenly sure I'm in a different place. A different time. Or perhaps I'm caught in one of my slumber-terrors?

Yes. That must be it. Essi's not lying on the seater, covered in blood. She doesn't have a hole in her abdomen, right where there are important organs that take time and finesse and a specialized mender to fix.

No.

She's sitting at the table, working on a diamond cap she's been obsessing over, eating buttermin loaf that makes our house smell like a home.

This isn't real.

Not real.

Not—

'I don't want to end up in the snow, Raeve.'

Our stares clash, her wide eyes wild with a fear that claws through my chest, threatening to cleave me apart.

Snow? What's she talking about?

'Please don't drop me down to the cold or put me in the ground,' she begs through trembling lips, her eyes so wide the tips of her lashes meet her brows, the red flecks in her irises lit like blown embers. 'Feed me to the fire where I'll never be cold again.'

'Stop talking like you're going anywhere,' I growl, stuffing the blanket on her wound to stem the flow. 'You're staying right here with me, safe in our home.'

Just as soon as I get her fixed up.

'You're going to be okay,' I murmur, looking to the kitchen cupboard where my mending kit is stored. I need to grab something to pack the wound full and bind it in place so she doesn't bleed out while I carry her down to the Ditch.

Sereme can fleshthread. She'll help if I fall to her feet and beg. She'll probably drip Essi's blood into the vial, using the excuse that she *needs* the bind to mend her, but I'll find a way to deal with the bitch once Essi's safe.

Fuck the repercussions.

'Put pressure on this.' I shift her icy hand and press it upon the blanket. 'I'm going to grab some supplies so I can get you to Sereme—'

'I'm cold, Raeve.'

Her fractured voice cuts a messy hole in the silence, carving into my chest, deflating my lungs.

I meet her watery stare that's barely holding focus.

Fear erupts behind my ribs with such violent force that cracks weave through my stony heart, exposing the fleshy core – so raw and vulnerable, withering like a juicy fruit tossed to a hungry flame.

'I can't feel your h—' Her words cut off, breath coming in short, sharp gasps as she works to catch her rhythm again, panic exploding in her eyes. 'I can't feel your hand on me. I can't feel it, *Raeve*—'

'You're always cold, Essi.' I swallow the lump in my throat, battling to keep my voice steady. I know the signs. I've seen death too many times not to know the fucking signs. 'We live on the cold side. This is normal.'

It's normal.

It's normal.

It's—

Her face scrunches, and my chest feels like it mimics the motion, making me want to ball up around the ache.

'Hold me?' she asks, a wobbly plea that begs me to fall with her into the hungry maw of resignation. Her entire body jerks, hands clawing at her middle, an angry spill of red seeping through the blanket and squelching between her fingers. 'Please?'

I climb onto the seater and curl around her, my hand flattened across her chest, the other tangling with the one on her abdomen. She releases a shuddered breath, and I crush our bodies together, holding her so tight I picture my strength binding her like a bandage. Picture her sitting at the table, etching a normal trinket into something exceptional, her mind full of magnificent thoughts and an ample amount of blood in her veins. Whole.

Happy.

But she's not.

She's broken in my arms, draining away . . .

'Who did this, Essi?'

She flinches, like my cold, monotone words slit her through.

'I didn't see. I rounded a corner and w-walked straight into him. It was . . . d-dark.'

The Undercity. She went to the *Undercity*.

The realization crushes my windpipe. Makes my hands shake – though I try to still them. Try to force myself to remain calm and composed.

For her.

I'm not going to lie here and chastise her for something I specifically asked her not to do – knowing how dangerous it is down there. I'm not going to break her down further when she's already falling apart.

I'm going to hug her.

Love her.

Avenge her.

'He was h-hooded.'

'Okay,' I whisper, brushing her hair back off her face. 'That helps, Essi. Did you see the color of his hood? Was it red?'

'N-no.'

Probably not from here.

'What did he smell like?'

'Leather,' she rasps. 'S-smoke sticks. When he walked away, his b-boots made clattering sounds.'

Clattering sou—

'Tell me s-something that'll make me f-feel warm, Raeve. P-please.'

'I love you.' The admission spills without pause. A heavy truth tilled from the raw, exposed ache in my chest. I realize the words were there all this time, tucked beneath my calloused bits, hiding in a place I thought they were safe.

Nothing's ever safe.

'Why didn't you go to a Fleshthread, Essi? Why didn't you—'

'Because I knew you'd always w-wonder if I didn't make it out. That you'd think I left you, like they left me.'

They . . .

Her family.

My heart rips straight down the middle.

'You're here,' I whisper against her ear. 'I've got you. We've got *each other*.'

I bind her deeper into my embrace, holding her tight while she drains away. Blood leaches across the seater beneath us, a wetness I can't escape seeping through my clothing, sticking to my skin.

A wetness that should be pumping through her veins, fueling her life. But it's not.

It's not.

I nuzzle her hair, filling my lungs with her warm scent, past and present melding together as I recall another embrace. Another love.

Another loss.

I hum my calming song while she trembles against me, her heart pumping beneath my hand, each beat slower than the last.

Quieter.

Weaker.

'You're the family I never had,' I whisper, and her lungs empty with a shuddered exhale . . .

She doesn't fill them again.

I'm not sure how long I hold her, bound around her body that's no longer moving.

No longer warm.

Long enough that a parchment lark flutters into the room, then bumps against the sill, over and over. Perhaps Sereme's – informing me that last slumber's mission is complete, the children free of the city.

Long enough that I discern the hard segments of my heart aren't going to shift back together and protect the soft core that feels too much. That I'll have to nurse the hurt until it's calloused over, a realization that makes me not want to rise again.

Long enough that I take my time inspecting each moment since I woke, stripping the emotion back like shelling nuts, leaving the smooth pit inside – safe to handle. I bundle all the clutter into piles on the shore of my immense frozen lake that's more silent than it's ever been, then ferry them across the surface.

Silver light spears up from beneath while I carve an icy grave to drop the parcels down. A curious luminosity that hunts every step, chasing me back and forth between the shore and the hole – something that would usually frighten me. But I'm numb.

Hollow.

I've lost Essi, and I've lost the will to care about anything but the thing that keeps me upright. Keeps me moving forward.

Vengeance.

Dropping the final package beneath the frosty expanse, I rise back into myself, raising my hand to brush Essi's hair back from her too-pale face. 'You sleep.' Eyes squeezed shut, I kiss her temple, letting the moment linger. 'I'm going to find whoever did this to you,' I pledge against her cold skin. 'I'm going to find them, Essi.'

And I'm going to make them hurt.

I tug my arm from beneath her stiff body, my bottom lip trembling as I untangle our legs and step off the seater. I swathe the blanket around her shoulders to keep her nice and warm, then make for the stairs on unsteady legs, bracing myself against the wall so I can heft the trapdoor up.

Nee swarms free in a wobbly waggle, bumping against my cheek, neck, and chest while I go about the motions of moving down the stairs, eyes cast blankly ahead. Not bothering to remove my blood-stained skinsuit, I strap a sheath to my other thigh, tucking the many pockets full of small dragonscale daggers while Nee continues to bump against me in a frenzied flutter. She nosedives toward the ground, but I pinch her from the air, gently setting her on a shelf.

Not that she stays there long.

Motions becoming sharp and precise, I thread my arms through my leather bandolier laden with iron blades, stuffing my feet in black boots and lacing them to the knee. I bind a veil around my neck, then move up the stairs, chased by the sound of parchment wings.

I pause by the table while Nee bumps . . .

Bumps . . .

Bumps . . .

She nuzzles into my neck like she thinks she's safe. She's not.

Nobody I care about ever is.

I swallow the thickening lump in my throat and snatch a quill, dip it in a pot of ink, then swoop Nee into my hand and unpleat her face, tail, wings, and body, flattening her upon the table where I read her message – one final time.

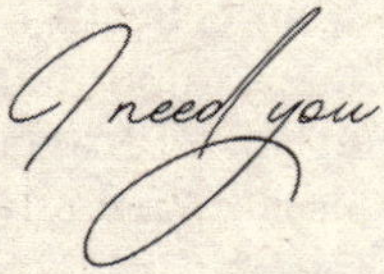

'No you don't,' I rasp, scratching the words upon the parchment in my less than perfect handwriting, butchering beautiful Nee into something far less tender.

Less vulnerable.

The backs of my eyes burn as I fold her up again, tarnishing her with a smudge of Essi's blood as I work her back into shape.

My fingers linger over the final fold. One I haven't pressed before.

The activation line that will return Nee to her sender.

My gaze lifts to Essi – still and silent on the seater.

Dead.

My fingers pinch of their own accord, crimping the fold into place.

Nee wiggles to life, her flapping motions smooth and mechanical. Void of everything that makes her *her*.

That ache in my chest intensifies as she glides toward the window in a steady flutter without another neck nudge or giddy swirl, and I know she's gone. That her soul has slipped free, and that whatever 'magic' tethered her to me . . . it's not there anymore.

Just like Essi's not here anymore.

Just like Fallon—

I cut off the thought, clear my throat, and force myself to watch Nee pass through the window and disappear from sight, into the merciless sky – stuffing down the temptation to rip off my ring. To beg Clode to bring her back to me with a push of wind.

No.

I move to the kitchen and pack the trough with rags that trail over the edge, making a path to the rug. Then I pull a bottle of sterilizing spirits from the cupboard of mending supplies, crack the lid, and douse the rags. The rug.

The blanket keeping Essi warm.

I douse the corner of another small cloth, tuck it in my sheath with a stick of flint, then move toward the window, pausing by the seater where I drop to a kneel.

Brushing my hand through Essi's hair, I take in the sharp slopes of her ethereal face . . . Too beautiful for this world.

Too pure.

'I love you,' I whisper, mapping her freckles. Storing the vision of her somewhere safe where I can treasure it forever. 'I'm going to take away the cold, okay?'

The silence that follows is a cruel taunt that rips at the contents of my chest. Like a Moltenmaw is caught within me, slashing.

Feasting.

With a final kiss on her temple, I force myself to turn. To climb out the window and up the bloodstained wall, sullying my hands with more of *her*. I pull myself into the wind tunnel, stare stabbed at the drop chute as I push to my feet.

Feed me to the fire where I'll never be cold again.

My face crumbles, then knots into a savage twist despite the reluctant shudder tilled from my ashen past.

The thought of burning Essi's body . . . it makes me want to bunch up and scream. The idea of casting her in flames goes against the grain of everything that shaped me into who I am this dae, but I will not cower from this fire she asked me for.

I will not fail her again.

I pull the cloth and flint from my sheath and force myself forward a single wobbly step. Hand trembling.

Soul squirming.

Teeth gritted, I scour the flint across the stone wall, catching the spark on the cloth. It bursts into flames so fast they nip at my skin, and panic wraps its hands around my throat, squeezing so hard I can barely breathe. But I maintain my trembling hold on the cloth, forcing three strangled words past my chattering teeth.

'I'm sorry, Essi.'

I'm sorry I couldn't keep you safe. That I never said I love you before you were dying in my arms.

I'm sorry I wasn't the family you deserved.

I flick the flaming cloth down the chute, followed by the flint, staggering back from the blow of heat that blasts my face, choking on the pour of smoke.

There's the sound of glass shattering, and I squeeze my eyes shut, picturing her jars of tinctures popping – one by one.

The heat intensifies, and I picture the rug burning, the smell of fried flesh coming to me too soon.

Too fucking soon.

A strangled sob squeezes up my throat as I stagger back from the heat. The *smell* – clapping my hand upon my mouth.

Something clatters against my boot.

I open my eyes, looking to the ground splotched red. To the bloody blade resting by my foot and the leather satchel beside it.

Black.

Essi's.

My heart lurches, like something just tossed it against my ribs so hard I'm surprised they didn't fracture.

Tentatively, I bend down and flick the mouth of the bag aside to peer in, seeing a book and a frosted jar. A book she must've gotten from the library.

From the *Undercity*.

I don't bother opening the jar, knowing exactly what's within. The final ingredient she required to bind the diamond cap to my tooth . . .

The cap she'd made to *protect me*.

My lungs constrict.

I reach for the dagger Essi must've pulled from her abdomen. The dagger that did this to her.

That took her from me.

I'm about to sheathe it next to my own when something catches my eye – a slithering motion on the flat face of the blade.

Every cell in my body stills as Essi's blood congeals into a collection of ruddy letters:

A summons. For me.

From Rekk Zharos.

The blade slips from my hand. Clatters to the ground.

He's narrowed his eyes on me. Discovered where I live. Taken down Essi to lure me out.

Somehow.

Which means it's *my* fault she snuck out to the Undercity. My fault she got stabbed, then returned to our home rather than finding a Fleshthread to heal her. My fault she bled out on the couch until she stopped moving.

My fault she's *burning*—

Dead.

A guttural groan ruptures from deep within, bruising my insides as it wrestles free. As the realization crouches upon my chest, slashes me open, then stuffs its maw in and *chews* – masticating my lungs. My heart.

My *soul*.

My face crumbles, shoulders, spine.

Knees.

I heap upon the ground, deflating just as fast as my rupturing resolve, crushed by a mountain of suffocating guilt. Certain I'm being slit through the chest in long, jagged severs – again.

Again.

I flinch with each agonizing slash, my gaze dropping to the blood-soaked hands I used to lead Essi from the dark bowels of the Undercity – so determined I could give her a better life.

I promised I'd keep her safe. Instead, I gave her a grave.

And I—

I—

I can't do this. I can't fucking do this anymore.

Something within me shifts, and a booming collision jars me from the inside out, my bones locking from the impact. A thunderous *crack* ricochets from deep beneath my ribs before a sharp explosion pierces through me, shattering my insides into a thousand icy shards.

My body temperature plummets so fast I hear my heart slow, like it's wrestling slushy blood through my veins one sluggish beat at a time.

I inhale a shudder of air that feels too warm. Like pulling lava into my frosted lungs.

It's coming.

A tear shreds down my cheek as I lose sensation in my fingers and toes.

My arms and legs.

Part of me wants to fight it. To be strong for Essi, despite the fact that I've never felt weaker in my life. To tear the fucking world to shreds until I find Rekk Zharos and string him up. Slit him a thousand times. Wait for him to heal.

Do it all over again.

But there's a bigger part of me that's still lying on that seater inside, tucked around my young, miraculous, beautiful friend who just lost her life because I loved her. A *bigger* part of me that's burning right alongside her. And that part . . .

It's tired.

Lonely.

Lost.

Sad.

More broken than I'll ever admit.

That part of me just wants to stop and never start again.

The icy anger inside me *roars*, its essence expanding with such ferocity my organs feel like they're being shoved aside. I lose sensation in my chest, and my face twists as I slip from my sight, falling backward into a frigid numb that swaddles me so tight I can't move. Can't see.

Can't feel.

A beautiful, blissful numb. So pure – like a cold, silken bandage for my soul. So soft I can almost forget I won't get the glory of killing Rekk Zharos and avenging Essi's death, but as I sink, curled into this frigid comfort, I grow calm.

Resolved.

He deserves to be ripped limb from limb. To have his vertebrae crumbled, brain mulched. To have his insides pulverized by the strange, savage entity that exists within me.

He deserves—

The Other

CHAPTER 15

The Other prowls through the Undercity – a dark, lofty excavation fixed with a web of bridges that reach across the hollow, only a scatter of torches to sketch out the shape of things.

Not that she needs light.

Her inky, glitter-kissed eyes glint in the dark as she hunts, clutching the blade used to bleed the young one until she bled no more.

Breathed no more.

Was no more.

Bringing the hilt to her nose, she sniffs – long and deep – catching another hint of this murderous male's smoky, leathery scent.

He would beg for mercy before the end – of that, she was certain. Not that it would earn him any.

Eyes wild like her bloody thoughts, The Other creeps down an uneven path, scouring the cavern's vast expanse while numerous stares slice across her too-fragile skin. Those of Shade-born predators who've snuck in through collapsed mine shafts. Who *also* have exceptional vision, hibernating in dark corners, eating their prey in peace and languishing in nests of bones.

The Other does not pay them heed. She holds no ill blood over those who kill to survive, to feed, or to protect their young.

But those who kill to hurt the one she loves? The one she *nests within?*

They deserve to be torn apart piece by piece. Skin peeled free like strips of bark. Feasted on while their warm heart still pumps—

However.

The Other stills, gaze dropping to the scrap of material tangled around the thin, vulnerable neck of her precious, pliant host, wondering if she should use it to cover her face. Raeve is always so careful to camouflage when she's spilling blood, strange as it is. Blood should be worn with honor. A boast of fresh meat and full bellies.

Of predators gone.

But The Other respects her host despite her small hands and tiny teeth that are near hopeless for chewing things with any true substance. She decides to adhere to the odd tradition, frowning as she gathers the material and tucks it around her mouth and nose.

There.

She charges down a jagged stairway, deeper into the dark. Pausing midway over a bridge, she peers at another stretch of stone that cuts across the eerie chasm directly beneath, head cocked to the side . . .

Perhaps the armored soldiers flattened against the walls of twin alcoves on either ends of the bridge below believe they are hidden.

Not from her.

She was born in the darkness. To her, their bodies are *luminous* – as if lit by the torches they must've extinguished when they laid their little trap.

The Other feeds on the squishy sounds their hearts make, digesting their near-silent whispers:

'Think I'll get in trouble if I piss over the edge?'

'I wouldn't do it. Not unless you wanna risk gettin' your balls fried.'

The Other scowls at their crude language, wondering if possible mates of their own fae species find that sort of thing attractive. She most certainly does not.

'It's been a while. I think nobody's comin'.' A brief pause, then, *'Perhaps the Ath bitch was the one he already stabbed? Was his informant certain she had black hair?'*

'Long, black, and straight, skin like snow. Heard it with my own ears. She'll come, I can feel it in my bones.'

The Other drops into a low crouch and leans forward, claiming a clearer view.

'What if she doesn't bring reinforcements and this was all a waste

of time for a single rebel? We shoulda just found a way to storm her dwelling, then I wouldn't be standin' here ready to piss myself.'

'Nobody in their right mind would come down here alone. But if she does, at least she'll be easy to dispose of. I'd like to be home before the rise. I'm fuckin' starved.'

The Other decides these fae deserve the grisly end that's coming for them, though she regrets not having more time to draw it out.

Make them *weep*.

She scours every one of the soldiers while pulling deep whiffs of the hot, humid air, seeking the one who stamped his scent on the blade, frowning.

This *Rekk* is smarter than the ones waiting in such obvious places. No matter. He, too, will be lured out by blood.

She cracks a smile.

Lots of it.

Silently skulking farther along the bridge, The Other tucks the dagger away, pausing atop the group of heavily armored males at the northern end. She rips the iron ring off her finger, opening herself to the Creators. To songs she's studied from below the crust of her icy lake whenever they howl, squeal, or shriek down from above.

She does not cower from the clamor against her eardrums. She wears pain like a safety net – *one* with the terrible tunes penetrating her small, too-delicate ears and violent mind.

She leaps.

Falls.

Lands in a crouch before a group of unassuming males – hands clawed, a savage sort of glee spread across her face.

She sings Clode's strangling tune before the beaded soldiers get a chance to speak a single word.

It's not a gentle song. The Other does not leave room for mercy. There are no sips of breath for gasped begging. Instead, she minces their lungs in an instant, reveling in their horrified agony.

Blood erupts from the soldiers' mouths, their bulging eyes leaking ruddy tears as they claw at their throats, some falling where they stand. Others try to escape, staggering into walls or off the bridge, dead long before they hit the ground.

The Other rips twin daggers free of her bandolier, spinning. Flicking them through the air. The blades slice toward the far side of the bridge, into the eyes of two soldiers just beyond the reach of her strangling tune before they have a chance to wield their own words.

They crumble where they stand.

Another soldier trips on the corpses, tumbling over the edge. The sound of his body breaking against a lower bridge thumps through the chaos.

A ruthless smile spreads across The Other's face – no longer reminiscent of her fiercely beautiful host. Now sharp and savage.

Monstrous.

More blades whizz through the air, The Other's deadly sky-borne blows finding home in flesh and bone, slotting into the frail slits between sturdy plates of armor.

Thud.

Thud.

Thud.

Soldiers fall in a clatter of metal and meat while The Other sings the air into nothingness, stripping the oxygen and nulling the soldiers' ability to sing. Making the atmosphere inhospitable for the flames her opponents need to see what she's doing. Where her blades are being aimed.

They thought the darkness was their ally, but it was their ruin. As it so often is for many who underestimate the shroud of a sunless sky.

A storm of unforeseen reserve troops spill from the southern tunnel, screaming.

Charging.

One orders the bridge to split before The Other can pulverize his lungs, and cracks weave through the stone.

The bridge *jerks*.

She falters, hissing through bared teeth, catching her footing with a fist firmly planted on the rock. '*Glei te ah no veirie nahh*,' she screams, whipping up her head. '*Glei te ah no veirie!*'

Clode churns into a squealing dance of snipped breaths and collapsing airways, barging into soldiers' chests in gusty shoves, tossing them off the crumbling bridge with a spray of stone.

Many try to retreat, though only a few make it back into the tunnel.

The Other laughs, pushing to a stand, hunting the clutch of deserters, her swift steps gaining ground until she's close enough to sink iron daggers into the back of their necks with a flick of her wrist. She leaps, pouring upon another like a seething wave, ripping his head back and slashing his throat.

Blood sprays, coating her hands and face.

She charges the remaining two, salivating for the taste of their blood on her lips. She draws closer.

Closer.

The tunnel opens, and she passes into a small circular cavern lit by so many flaming sconces she's forced to squint, her sooty eyes not attuned to the harsh glare.

The hairs on the back of her neck lift—

A loud clanking has her whipping around to see a door of metal bars now blocking the exit. Locking her in.

She hisses, spinning in a churn of black hair, blood, and spitting rage, appraising the many soldiers lining the cavern's wall – arm to arm, red helmets hiding their faces and swords braced at their hips.

A trap.

A *fight ring.*

Some of them sing spitting, hissing tunes, flames whipping from elemental containment wealds and lit sconces.

Spearing straight for her.

With a lashing sneer, The Other sings Clode's suffocating tune. '*Glei te ah no veirie. Ata nei del te nahh. Mele, Clode. Mele!*'

The ribboning flames sputter into oblivion, as with most of the lit sconces dotted around the walls, filling the cavern with a blissful gloom.

Many soldiers drop to their knees, clawing at their throats.

The Other descends on one of the two who beat her here, slashing a blade through the gap in his armor. His intestines bulge from the gory hack, and she's on the next in an instant, wrapping her limbs around his head and lashing it to the side. His neck snaps with a satisfying *crack*, and he falls to the ground in a floppy heap at her feet.

Surveying her remaining opponents, she releases a deep, bellowing word that gouges a path up her throat. Like she just heaved a sharp stone from the pit of her gut.

'*Vobanth!*'

The cavern shakes with Bulder's answer – a jagged cleft prying the ground apart, yawning like the crooked maw of some great beast.

Soldiers scream, hands whipping out to steady themselves

against the rough-hewn wall, some falling into the grinding abyss, crushed by the shifting stone to the tune of breaking bones and popping skulls.

Blood and brain matter spray from the rumbling sever as it *chews*.

The soldiers stagger, looking between each other, the stench of urine wafting through the air as they appear to realize they've trapped themselves inside a cage with a monster. A fierce, *powerful* monster who should have two beads hanging from her lobe rather than the null clip in the tip of her tapered ear.

If they were aware she only knew how to correctly pronounce a few of Bulder's words, perhaps they wouldn't be so scared. Even so, The Other preens at the fear in their eyes, a sharp smile splitting her blood-splattered face into something charmed from the depths of a gory terror.

Such paltry opponents.

She will crush them all, then bathe in their blood before she ruptures free of this cage and hunts this *Rekk*, smothered in the grume of his fallen brethren.

There's a sharp pinch in her right shoulder, and the clamorous tunes penetrating her small, fragile eardrums hush.

Gone.

The Other frowns.

The wet groans of dying fae would be music to her ears if she weren't familiar with this particular form of silence.

She slaps her hand on the back of her shoulder, fingering the stinging puncture, frowning when the tips come away with the smell of her precious host's blood – eyes widening as she realizes she's been shot.

With *iron*.

She spins toward the barred entryway, gaze narrowing on the fae behind it armed with a slingshot that rests against the bars.

Pointed at her.

Tossing a black hood off his head, the male shucks his cloak to reveal black leather pants and a loose white shirt that's partially undone at the neck.

The Other takes in his long pale hair and cerulean eyes. The stick of rolled parchment pinched between his lips leaking smoke that wafts around his face.

The red and brown beads hanging from his lobe.

Most of all, she notes the lax confidence in the way he holds himself – hip resting against the edge of the tunnel like he's enjoying the scenery.

Nostrils flared, The Other tips her head and draws deep, catching a hint of his leathery, smoke-ridden scent. The same dense smell on the dagger still tucked in her sheath.

The veins in her temple and throat bulge, jaw trembling with her welling rage.

Rekk Zharos.

'You're the one who killed our Essi,' she growls, her voice a graveled discord of strained vocals and feral disposition.

'The little redhead?' Rekk drawls, pulling the weapon from the bars and dumping it on the ground. Snagging the smoking stick between his lips, he draws a deep breath, his next words a thick pour of white. 'She screeched like a strangled bird when I slid that blade into her gut.'

The Other sneers, charging toward the bars.

'*Stisssteni tec aagh vaghth – fiyah*,' Rekk spits past curled lips, as if the words burned a trail up his throat before they singed free.

Flames stream from the remaining torches, ribbons of it now churning around The Other in billowing swirls that nip too close to her vulnerable skin, capturing her in a fist of fire impossible to escape. Not without a Fleshthread nearby to mend the burns she would endure.

Hands crunching into fists, she studies Rekk's every move: the fluttered pulse in his neck; the way his lean body shifts as he unlocks the bars and swaggers into the cavern, sharp features lit by the churning flames; the bloody spurs on the backs of his boots rattling every time he steps.

His eyes glint with sadistic satisfaction while he takes The Other in, then the bloody mess she made of his comrades.

He clicks his tongue, pale brows inching up his forehead. 'Impressive.'

The Other snarls, leaning dangerously close to the roaring inferno while sweat gathers on her brow and down the line of her spine. Teeth bared, she froths for his blood. For the feel of his flesh shredding between her teeth, dismal as they are.

Rekk presses the smoke stick between his lips, draws a languid puff, then flicks the butt away and pulls a coiled whip from where it's tethered to a hook at his hip. With a twitch of his wrist, the black tendril snaps through the blaze, binding The Other in a rigid embrace that secures her arms to her sides, legs clamped together. As if cocooned by some silk-threading creature preparing her for feasting.

She falls to her knees, hissing sharp breaths while Rekk charms his flames toward the torches lining the walls. Releasing her from the fiery swirl, though bringing her no closer to the freedom she lost.

She lost.

Rekk snatches the bloody veil, exposing her. His eyes widen as she snarls through clenched teeth, jerking against her binds.

She.

Lost.

'Not at all what I was expecting,' Rekk murmurs, frowning. His hand comes forward, knuckles grazing her cheek. 'Seems a shame to feed such a pretty, powerful thing to the dragons . . .'

With a snap of her teeth, she snags his finger and bites.

Hard.

Rekk roars, trying to yank his hand free. The remaining soldiers bellow, charging toward their growling prisoner while she gnaws through the knobbly knuckle with the fervor of a famished beast.

It pops free, the severed tip dropping into her mouth.

Rekk stumbles back and lifts his trembling hand to his face, blood streaking down his arm. Onto the ground.

Drip.

Drip.

She spits the tip, boasting a smile that's all teeth and blood.

Rekk blinks, stark eyes focusing on the gory stub before he tips his head and roars with laughter, abusing the sound until it's bruised and weary.

The Other's smile falls.

Rekk locks eyes with her again, crunches his bloody, disfigured hand into a ball, pulls his arm back, and swings his fist at her face.

A blinding explosion of pain before darkness consumes her.

Diary Entry

Elluin Neván

Age: 9 phases
5,000,030 phases After Stone

It's freezing on the outskirts of Netheryn, but for a Moonplume egg to incubate, it must stay right here in the cold until it starts to rock. Then I must pack clumps of ice around it and wait for the hatchling to free itself from the shell.

I must do all this on my own because Haedeon can't. Because I found him sleeping at the bottom of a crevice, cuddling his stolen Moonplume egg, unable to move his legs.

I shook him awake. Told him I'd get Mahmi and Pahpi. He said I'd die if I took the sleigh home myself. That his egg would die, too.

That really worried me.

The sleigh can't make it up this far, so I built a snow hut to keep Haedeon safe and warm while he sleeps himself better. Then I made three trips to the hatching hut on my own and moved all our things.

I shook Haedeon awake again and told him I'll try really, really hard to drag him out into the cold when his Moonplume starts to hatch so he can bond with it. He touched my face, told me he loves me and that he's glad I snuck onto his sleigh, then fell back into a really deep sleep.

He's doing lots of sleeping. I'm starting to worry he won't wake. That his chest will suddenly stop moving.

The thought makes my own chest hurt. Makes me want to cry.

I won't. I refuse. I have to be strong for Haedeon because he can't be strong for himself.

But if he doesn't wake, I've decided I'm not going home. I can't get him on a sleigh, and I won't leave him here in the cold and the dark on his own. He hates being alone, and he really hates the dark.

I miss Mahmi and Pahpi.

Raeve

CHAPTER 17

I'm immersed in an icy sleep that's soft like a wispy tail bound around my body, drifting within the tide of nothingness.

Beautiful, hypnotic nothingness.

Until something *snaps* close to my ear, ripping me to the surface and dumping me into the aching scream of reality.

Hot, hurting, *heavy* reality.

My ankles are shackled, and all my weight hangs from my wrists that are tied together, stretched skyward, my shoulders threatening to pop from their sockets. The right one's pinned with a piercing hurt that makes me certain I've been stabbed or poked with something still lodged in the bone.

The pain is a drip in the barrel of aches tormenting every muscle in my body, like I've been wrung at all angles then shaken out like a washcloth. Even my jaw and gums ache like I've been gnawing on something dense and chewy while my consciousness was huddled somewhere far away from the Essi-sized ache in my heart.

Running my tongue across my teeth, I feel a stringy piece of . . . *something* wedged in the hairline gap between my sharp canine and the tooth right next to it.

Shivering, I decide I'd rather not know what that is.

I'm only able to pry one of my lids upward, the other a swell of pain, my eyeball throbbing.

I groan, taking in my smudged surroundings through bloody ropes of hair. My leather sheaths and bandolier are lumped on the floor in a pile not too far away, most of my weapons missing.

Fuck.

My attention lifts to the plain stone walls garnished with a few lit sconces. There's a wooden door directly ahead, from which a trail of ruddy gore leads right here . . . to where I'm hanging . . .

My gaze drops to my skinsuit – previously tan, now drenched red.

Blood red.

My heart plummets.

Whatever happened during my otherwise peaceful blackout landed me trussed up in this unfamiliar room, covered in blood, with a stringy piece of something stuck between my teeth and a likely fractured eye socket.

This is not looking good.

I peer internally, dropping toward my lake, jolting at the sight – the usually smooth, frosted expanse now a litter of ice shards and upturned bergs spearing skyward.

What a mess.

I hightail it out of there, casting my gaze back on the small, muggy room's dewy walls—

The back of my neck prickles. Like somebody behind me just stepped up close.

The rhythmic thud of heavy, clattering steps shatters the eerie silence, and I recall Essi's words:

When he walked away, his boots made clattering sounds . . .

My blood chills.

The noise circles me like one of The Shade's notorious hushlings circling their prey – the deadly dance of a predator near the top of the food chain. A predator who has earned the right to play with their food before they crouch down to feast.

I see his boots first, heels bridled by metal spurs that are caked in enough flesh and blood I'm snarling even before I lift my gaze to the male's face.

Cold, calculating eyes – twin cerulean orbs – lock on me.

Rekk Zharos.

He smiles. 'There she is.'

I jerk against my restraints so hard the flesh around my wrists splits, flushing with a burn that pales in comparison to the swollen ache in my chest.

'You killed Essi.'

My voice comes out fractured and cracked, bringing with it the taste of blood.

'We've gone over this,' he drawls with a roll of his eyes, moving more into my line of sight – a pillar of lean muscle and smooth, feline movements, the length of his iron-tipped whip trailing him like a tail. 'If you want to catch a feral mutt, you must lure it with the right bait. One must be resourceful in my line of work. Much as you probably like to think you're special, it really is nothing personal.'

I'll tell him the same as I'm carving into his chest after I free myself from these *fucking* restraints. Though it'll be a lie he'll glean when I pop a fresh bubble of laughter with every slice. Because it *is* personal.

Very.

I jerk against the ropes tied around my wrists again.

Again.

'At least it *wasn't* personal until you bit off my finger,' he mutters, lifting his right hand and waving the bandaged nub at me.

I still, my tongue coming up to poke at the stringy thing threaded between my teeth . . .

That makes sense. So, too, does my aching jaw.

I quietly hope I didn't swallow the tip, remembering past instances when I've blanked out, then come to with a bellyache and a weird gamey taste in my mouth.

Best not to think about these things too hard.

Rekk pauses before me to retrieve a leather pouch from his pocket, unrolling it, pinching out a smoke stick and tucking it between his lips. 'So,' he says, the word muffled as he pulls a silver weald from another pocket and flicks back the lid, exposing the small, angry bulb of flame hidden within, now dancing from the crown of the instrument. He uses it to singe the tip of his stick, swathing his face in a puff of smoke. 'You're a dual-bead.'

Breath flees my lungs so fast my expression almost twists into a cringe.

Dammit.

Seems my inner psychopath is paying attention, collecting powerful words it's used like rocks to weigh me to the bottom of this lake of doom.

It's an effort not to sigh.

'Am I really?' I force a bemused frown that makes my eye feel like it's about to pop. 'I thought they were just strange voices in my head. Weird.'

He lifts both brows. 'I find that hard to believe.'

'Maybe you should use your imagination?'

He sucks a sizzling draw, then blows his breath in my face, packing my lungs full of the thick, potent waft.

'Go easy on those things,' I say, barking out a cough. 'I don't want them mincing your lungs before I have the chance to do it myself.'

Head tipping to the side, his stare narrows. 'Your eyes are different. They were black earlier. Now they're blue.'

'You *do* have an imagination. Clever boy.'

He grunts, still watching me as he draws another puff, pinching the stick with his injured hand, the next words released with a blow of smoke. 'Kemori Daphidone, traveling bard from Orig . . . What's your *real* name?'

'Die a slow, traumatic death and perhaps I'll consider whispering it against your ear right before your heart gives out.'

'You're a handful.' His gaze drops to my bust, lifts again, lips curving into a slimy smile. '*More* than a handful, actually.'

'*Much* more than you can handle, you pathetic piece of shit.'

He chuffs out a laugh and draws another drag. 'I'm a greedy male—'

'If I have to listen to your drivel, at least tell me something I don't already know.'

'—and you see, with this particular job, I get paid *per head*. So, my foul-mouthed bitch, I'm offering you the chance to avoid retribution for the soldiers you took from me. And for this,' he says, gesturing to his wounded hand.

My attention drifts to his whip, back to his eyes. 'You think I'm scared of your little toy, Rekk?'

'You should be.' He boasts a lopsided grin that's all sharp canines and the promise of pain. 'The iron tip *bites*.'

'I've seen bigger. But hey, if whipping a female makes you feel like a strong boy, then don't let me stomp your dreams. Don't worry, I can handle it. I've got enough balls for the both of us.'

This time when he laughs, it lacks any real substance.

He flicks his hand.

The whip slithers through the air at lightning speed, and breath bursts from my lungs as a lash of pain snaps at my hip, shredding through my skinsuit and slitting skin.

I squeeze my lips shut, chewing the urge to fill the space with a scream, body trembling. My flesh ignites with anticipation – preparing for the next strike that'll undoubtedly land.

'Your lips are tight now,' he says, drawing another puff of his stick. 'But if they weren't so loose while you were speaking to the musician at the Hungry Hollow, you wouldn't be in this predicament and your friend wouldn't be dead.'

My heart skips a beat – another – his words settling amongst my insides like the tips of flesh-shredding arrowheads . . .

Levvi.

He's talking about *Levvi.*

Which means—

'In turn, she handed you a runed note I used to track down your living quarters.'

The room spins, my whirring mind unraveling so fast all the threads that usually hold me together get knotted and bunched until they're a tangled nest of knots.

My details. In case you want to perform together again . . .

Her lips had molded into a sad smile the moment she'd said those words, like they tasted bad.

Creators . . .

I didn't *have* to show her the orb – I would've gotten away without it. But I was in a rush. Distracted. So fucking desperate to complete the mission I'd fought for.

I'd been blind. Stupid.

Selfish.

And now Essi's dead.

I groan, the fresh information a savage slice to the raw, exposed ache in my chest that hasn't yet had a chance to scab over.

'Imagine my disappointment when I activated the tracking rune and realized the note didn't lead me to The Flourish,' Rekk says, pointing the smoke stick at me and tapping off the ash. 'Meaning you're just a grunt. The one they use to do the dirty work. You see, what I *need* is somebody with close-knit ties to the Elding or, at the very least, knows the location of The Flourish. Can you help me out with that?'

Sereme.

I dip my chin, looking at him from beneath my brows, thoughts tumbling over a bristled terrain.

Much as I hate the bitch, I could never hand her over to this sadistic prick. Not only would it endanger Ruse, but if this monster got hold of the vial that hangs around her neck, so many others I respect would fall victim to The Crown.

Not an option.

Ever.

'Oh, don't look at me like that.' He puffs his stick to a nub, then drops it, crushing it beneath the heel of his boot. 'We both know that once I hand you over to The Crown, the Guild of Nobles will make you an example, which will not end well for you – my pretty, feral mutt. However, in *this* room,' he says, caressing the handle of his whip, 'you have a unique opportunity to avoid that fate, should you decide to, I don't know . . .' he tips his head from side to side, '*loosen* those lips again. Do you see where I'm going with this?'

'Yes,' I bite out from between clenched teeth. 'And I *heartily* decline.'

Frowning, he crouches so I'm peering down my nose at him, garnishing me with a look of confusion. 'I don't think you understand. I'm giving you a chance to *live*, you daft cunt.'

'You're mistaken. I know the sick, twisted game you're playing. I simply refuse to partake. So you can flick your little toy at me and shred my skin, but the only thing I'll spill is *blood*.'

My words echo through the space, bouncing off the walls.

I draw my mouth full of saliva and *spit*.

It slaps upon his eye, and I get the glory of watching his upper lip wobble, a frown shadowing his face.

He reaches up to wipe away the bloody slur. 'So be it,' he sneers, shoving up.

In four short steps, he's behind me, gripping hold of my skinsuit.

Something cool and sharp slides down my spine.

There's the sound of splitting fabric as the garment is torn like a sheet of wrapping parchment, my pebbling flesh bared. A blade clatters across the ground – the only warning I get before the first lash rips into my skin like a ribbon of flame.

My body jerks, but I gnaw my scream into submission, refusing to cut it loose.

To give him the satisfaction of hearing me howl.

Another whistling slash severs the air, flaying my flesh from shoulder to bowing spine.

A tremble begins in the pit of my gut and spreads through my organs, my bones, across my ravaged skin as he *lashes*.

Lashes.

Lashes.

Red sprays, my body splitting over and over, until I can feel strips of me hanging loose, flopping around with every flinch from the relentless storm of blows.

But no matter how hard he whips, the snap of sting is nothing compared to the agony I endured as Essi slipped away. As she released her final breath and the warmth leached from her limbs.

As I looked at her one final time, wishing she'd grow wings and flutter into the sky so she could ball up and take her place amongst the moons where I'd be able to see her always. So I wouldn't have to say goodbye.

Not really.

So I absorb the blows. Snarl through clenched teeth as my bladder loosens.

Beg that *thing* inside me not to surge again.

This is my penance for failing Essi – in so many ways. For believing I could love somebody from a distance. Believing they wouldn't suffer the same fate as everyone who sinks past the calloused scabs on my heart.

I wear the strikes of pain like armor slashed upon my body, the smell of my blood filling the room until I'm certain I'm drowning in it.

Until the darkness clouding my vision finally wins the war.

Diary Entry

Elluin Neván

Age: 9 phases

5,000,030 phases After Stone

The biggest Moonplume I've ever seen keeps swooping through the sky, screeching. I think it's a female because the wispy tip of her tail is extra long and sleek like Mahmi's Moonplume, Náthae.

I think she's searching for this egg. Mourning it.

Hunting us.

I think that because she's silver like this egg, and I've never seen another Moonplume that's such a metallic shade of gray.

We could hide in the hatching hut, but we can't hide here. Not properly. I'm worried she'll find us soon, then kill us for raiding her nest.

I keep begging the egg to rock so I can pack all the ice around it that I've chipped off a nearby pillar over the cycles. Once the hatchling breaks free, I can take it inside the snow hut where it'll be safe with Haedeon until I work out what we're going to do next. How we're going to get back to Arithia.

It seems impossible right now.

Haedeon's not getting any better, and it's not just the Moonplume that seems to be hunting us. I can hear a pack of doomquills somewhere nearby, like they can smell death in the air. They make the most horrible rattling sounds that jingle the silence and scare my heart, though I'm not scared for myself.

I'm scared for this beautiful egg sitting in the snow in front of our makeshift hatching hut. It's like a little silver sun, throwing so much light. I use the light to write while I sit here, holding Haedeon's dragonscale dagger in my other hand.

I've never held one before. Never wanted to. But if the doomquills get brave enough to attack, I'll have to protect the egg. And Haedeon.

But I don't like the thought of killing things. I don't want to kill anything.

I really hope they don't get too close.

Raeve

CHAPTER 19

The feel of something splatting against my temple stirs me from a sleep riddled with fire and gulps of poisonous fear, a scream threatening to punch up my throat—

My eyes pop open, teeth clamping down as I hiss breaths and wait for the fiery terror to stop wriggling. The smoky tendrils retreat, revealing my murky surroundings, my vision sharpening on the here.

The now.

My spine locks, blood chilling.

I'm lumped in the corner of a . . .

Cell.

I'm alone in a cell.

Bars slice up and down three sides of my small box of space, a wall of damp stone at my back, the low ceiling collecting moisture on its jagged face. A single drop-lantern lords over each cell across from me and either side as far as I can see, the air a vile, potent mix of blood, vomit, excrement, and rotten flesh.

Bile threatens to charge up my throat, the enormity of everything that's come to pass since I woke in my sleepsuite to Nee's panicked nudges now dumping upon me like an avalanche. A sudden tremble jars me to the bone – a fierce, untamable shake not borne of the cold.

Nor fear.

Nor pain.

The terrible shake of a rattled soul.

My teeth clank together, even my organs quake, and with this terrible full-body shudder comes the agonizing reminder of what Rekk did to my back—

I groan, remembering the way the whip snapped against my skin – over and over – adding to the relentless shudder that

just

won't

stop.

Looking past the oversized brown tunic shrouding the top half of my body, I see iron cuffs bound around my ankles with an interlocking chain. My wrists bear the same, the chain draped between them connected to the one between my feet with a stumpy length of metal. No doubt meant to stop me from doing anything but sit here and rot in my own filth.

The dull ache in my shoulder tells me that what I assume is an iron pin is still deeply embedded in my body. Probably festering.

Shit.

My hand comes up to pluck the stringy piece of what I also assume is Rekk's finger tendon from between my chattering teeth. I flick it away, the motion making my entire back blaze, a serrated howl threatening to rip up my throat.

Instead, I begin humming my calming song, hoping it'll soothe me from the inside out—

'Th-th-thought you were dead,' a high-pitched voice squeaks at me from the cell to the right of mine, and my tremble abates so suddenly I almost believe I imagined it.

I tilt my chin as best I can, half my vision slit as I look at the creature peering at me through the gloom with beady black eyes, furry gray claws wrapped around the bars separating us.

A woetoe. Male, by the look of his long whiskers that are wiggly at the ends, unlike the females of their kind, with theirs straight like blades.

'Surprise,' I rasp.

His glossy black nose twitches, and my gaze drops to the yellow pronged teeth jutting from his maw, the incisors long and slightly curved, pinched together at the tip. His face is mostly shaded in wispy gray fur, a churn of wiry black hair curling around his paddled ears. 'Your eye looks s-s-sore.'

I make a noncommittal sound.

Truth be told, it's the least of my concerns.

'Name's Wrook. What th-th-they got you for?' he asks, releasing the bar to scratch behind his rounded ear, his gaze scraping across the dried blood on my fisted hands.

'Doing bad things to bad folk.'

I think.

The gore that was on my skinsuit suggested as much.

'I heard them s-s-say you're going to t-t-trial with the Guild of Nobles?'

I hack out a laugh that burns my hoarse throat. 'Of course.'

Not everyone gets an audience with the Guild. Only the ones they're deliberating between a public draw and quartering or tying up in the coliseum.

Guess I made the cut. No surprise there.

Based on my interactions with Rekk, there's no way the Guild isn't going to utilize this unique opportunity to lure more Ath to the surface. I guarantee that's the only reason they've deemed me worthy of a trial. To drag it out. Give them time to formulate a plan.

Problem is, it might just work.

'What brought you to this fine establishment?' I ask, trying to distract myself from my slitting thoughts.

'S-s-stealing,' Wrook says, rolling back, twisting his body into a knot. His clawed foot extends up, scratching the seemingly relentless itch behind his ear.

'Isn't that why your lot is so valued? Why lock you up?'

'To punish my master.' Untangling himself, he scurries to the far corner of his cell and begins scratching at the stone in a flurry of motion, tilling up shards that scatter across the ground.

My brows rise.

He's ambitious. Good for him. Though I'm not sure why he's digging *down*. The only thing beneath us is the velvet trogg's den. He'd be trading one death for another, though perhaps he'd prefer to die surrounded by Gore's trash and not the bars of a cell.

Maybe I should dig, too.

A sob comes from across the hall, and I peer into the shadowed corner of the opposite cell, seeing the vague outline of a female bound in a quivering ball, her white garb shredded in places, blistered feet bare of shoes.

'What about her?'

Wrook pauses, whiskers twitching as he looks over his shoulder at the female. 'Refused to t-truthtune for Th-The Crown,' he squeaks out.

My chest packs full of sharp stones that wedge against my ribs . . .

I think of the tents erected about the city, soldiers stationed around the perimeter and herding lines of trembling children through the flap, one at a time, to where a Truthtune is always sitting. Ready to sift through their heads to decipher whether or not they can hear any of the four elemental songs.

There's always a carriage to the side, waiting to swallow the freshly beaded conscripts and trundle them off to Drelgad for training. Always a churn of weeping parents buckling beneath the knowledge that they may never see their gifted children again.

Always a pour of *other* younglings – freshly labeled nulls leaving the tent with a bleeding ear, nursing the clipped flesh.

I release a sigh.

The sound of boots thumping down the hallway has Wrook bunching up a frayed brown blanket and dashing it over the hole. He scurries toward the front of his cell, and I frown, noticing every other inmate except the Truthtune doing the same thing.

The reason becomes clear when rolling cart wheels squeal through the silence, the smell of gruel wafting to me. The same shit they serve up in the muck halls in the mines.

The ache in my chest pangs so abruptly my breath snags, the familiar smell pinching at that raw, fleshy cleft in my heart . . .

When Essi first came to me, plain gruel was one of the only things her sensitive belly could handle – being so used to the bland food she was able to steal in the Undercity.

A black-haired guard with sharp eyes and a tailored beard stops before my cell, crouches, and shoves a board beneath the barred door. I frown, lifting my head off the ground enough to see the piece of parchment stretched across it, pinned down at the corners.

He tosses a sharpened piece of coal through the bars, and I don't dare move fast enough to pluck it from the air before it has a chance to hit me in the face.

Asshole.

'If you want me to draw you a doodle, you'll be happy to know your face is the perfect muse,' I say, flashing him a toothy grin that makes my eye socket ache.

'Sign for food,' he grunts out. 'Thumb print, too. Should you make it out of here alive, you'll have to pay for every meal consumed.'

I snort-laugh.

Drawing a steadying breath, I edge up, teeth gritted, hissing through the searing pain – the flayed flesh on my back shifting at a hundred different angles. An ooze of warm wetness seeps from my wounds as I ease forward, my gaze dragging over the small metal plaque nailed to the floor before my cell, stating its number.

Maneuvering my shackled hands so I can grab the piece of coal, I scratch the tapered tip upon the parchment:

Prisoner Seventy-Three

I rub some coal onto my thumb, then press it against the parchment before sliding the board back under the door.

The guard cuts me a condemning stare.

'What?' I feign. 'Have I got something on my face?'

He extends his hand. 'Coal, Prisoner Seventy-Three. Now.'

'Fine,' I gripe, tossing it through the bars. 'I'll rot from boredom before my trial even begins, and it'll be all your fault.'

He grunts, picks up the coal, and stalks back the way he came just as the slop cart reaches my cell. A much less decorated servant to The Crown ladles a scoop of slimy gray goo into a wooden bowl he slides beneath the door. It skitters to a stop beside me, and the male slams a metal mug of water between the bars before pushing his cart farther down the hall, passing a bowl and mug to Wrook next.

I frown at the goo, back at the server. 'How am I supposed to eat it?'

He looks at me over his shoulder and growls, 'Stuff your face in it for all I care.'

So many assholes, so few fingers to count them all.

My gaze roves to the cell on my left where a male is using his hands to scoop the slop into his mouth. His skeletal frame is all bladed bones, fine hair covering his pale skin, bits of him draped with a shred of gray cloth.

His sallow stare drifts to me, gruel dripping from the bristles of his wiry beard as he heaps another mound in his mouth.

A shiver climbs my spine.

I look at Wrook, who's stuffing the end of his long face into the bowl, chowing it straight from the source. 'Here,' I say, using my foot to nudge my serve beneath the bars separating us, pushing it into his cell.

His beady gaze swivels to me, widening. 'You s-s-sure?'

'Certain,' I say, gaze flicking to his hidden hole in the back corner. 'You need the energy more than I do.'

Love a good hope charge, futile as it is.

Arm extending, the clawed tips of Wrook's paw curl around the lip of my bowl, dragging it close. 'Th-thanks,' he says, clumps of muck littering his furred face.

'No problem.'

I edge back into the corner in slow, agonized shuffles, then lower myself to the ground, closing my eyes. Listening to the sloppy sounds, I pick at the skin down the side of my nails.

My mind festers, thoughts churning at a ferocious speed, remembering another cell.

Another time.

A cell I was born into in my own strange way, bonded with its walls and the smell and the female I shared it with.

I had something to fight for then. Somebody I loved and cherished. All I've got now is a wounded heart and this ravenous hunger for revenge that's as futile as Wrook's hole in the ground.

I'm trapped in a cell, shackled with iron, a pin in my shoulder, scheduled for a trial with the Guild. The only way I'm getting out of this is . . .

Death.

Diary Entry

Elluin Neván

Age: 9 phases

5,000,030 phases After Stone

Pahpi says claiming a mature Moonplume at such a young age makes me remarkable, but I don't feel very remarkable.

Haedeon will never walk again because the bones fused back together, but not in the right way. Pahpi says nobody has the skills to rebreak, then fix such delicate damage so deep without cutting him open and risking more harm.

His Moonplume may never fly because her wing is gammy. Because our makeshift hatching camp got sniffed out by a pack of doomquills just as Haedeon's egg began to rock, and I had to hide it in the warmth with him before it had a chance to fully hatch.

Yes, I fought off the doomquills, but I would've lost if the massive Moonplume that had been circling hadn't shown up and blazed the rest of them. Yes, I then climbed on her back and held on really tight for really long until she listened to my soft song, but I just did what I had to do to get my brother home. Because the Creators wouldn't sing to me no matter how much I begged them to help.

Now they won't shut up.

Raeve

CHAPTER 21

Wrook scratches at the corner of his cell while I hum, sitting in the corner, tapping my foot against the ground to the tune in my head. I trace the dips and spines of the ceiling, hunting the bulbous balls of moisture hanging off the more prominent peaks, trying to guess which one will drip next. A game I've played on and off since I was dumped here.

Not sure how long ago that was. Feels like a while.

Perhaps those who tossed me in here think that by leaving me to rot in this shithole, I'll madden into a pulp. Become pliable enough that when they finally present me to the Guild of Nobles, I'll mold to their stringent will.

Unfortunately for them, I'm well practiced in the art of existing in a confined space, and there are *many* ways to bide time in a cell if you have a rich imagination.

Heavy footsteps thump down the corridor, and I dim my sound, a small smile swelling my cheeks as Wrook stuffs his blanket over his rebellious hole, tucks into a ball before it, and pretends to sleep.

My gaze clings to a water droplet I'm *certain* is the next to fall – disappointment backhanding me when instead one lands atop the peak of my nose, making my face twitch.

I frown, eyes narrowing on the wobbly globule . . .

Drip, you stubborn bastard!

A different one splats on my knee, and a sigh gusts past my dry, split lips.

I'm terrible at this game. Not once have I gotten it right. So help me, I *will* crack the code by the time I'm marched to my doom.

A figure storms past my cell in a flutter of thick white material, and a voice in the back of my mind questions why a *Runi* would bother with a trip into Gore's septic bowels cluttered with half-digested 'traitors' to The Crown. Whoever it is stops before Wrook's cell, crouching. 'I heard you stole the wrong ring from the wrong fae,' the male rumbles in a deep, gravelly voice that skates across my pebbling skin.

A voice I *recognize.*

My heart flops against my ribs, gaze drifting to the broad, cloaked visitor as Wrook feigns a stretch.

The hooded male from the Hungry Hollow, now dressed like a *Runi.*

I tuck farther into the shadowed corner . . .

I was so strong and composed outside the wind tunnel with my iron blade pressed to his member. Now I'm in bits in a cell, chasing drips of mildew, smelling like my own filth and ruin. I'm like a dragon midmolt, and the last thing I want is that assessing stare poking me in my tender spots that are yet to fully calcify.

'Costly mistake,' Wrook forges past a faux yawn.

The male grunts. 'I've been looking for you all over, you know.'

Wrook's ears flick forward, nose twitching. He licks his paws, using them to swipe the hairs back on his face as he rocks up into a crouch. 'Why?'

'Because someone I'm acquainted with saw you scurrying for the nearest sewer with a *moonshard* in your mitts.'

My heart skips a beat.

Why in this Creators-forsaken world is he hunting *moonshards*?

Wrook kicks back his foot to scratch behind his ear. 'I don't know what you're t-t-talking about.'

'I can get you out. Digging won't work. This place is runed against anyone digging farther than a foot. And I have a Sabersythe tusk I'm willing to trade for the shard.'

My brows lift.

According to Ruse, Sabersythes drop their tusks every shed, but they're remarkably hard to find.

I think back to the first time I purchased a sliver for Essi. Ruse said they don't dislodge until the beast is well into its spurt of growth, often swallowed by Gondragh's volcanoes since that's where Sabersythes flock to complete their shed, burrowed away from anything that might harm their delicate state. I also quickly found out they're worth ten times their weight in dragon bloodstone, serving as a bonding agent most Runi's use for their etchings.

Wrook's nose twitches, his scratching foot coming slowly down to rest against the floor. 'How big is the t-t-tusk?'

'The size of my leg.'

My gaze drops to *said* leg, eyes widening.

'Deal,' Wrook spits, his response swifter than the snap of Rekk's whip.

I smile, pride warming my chest.

Good for him. Love a happy ending.

'I'll purchase your sentence and have you out by the rise,' the male says, just stalking by my cell when he stops, drawing a deep sniff of the air, his head turning in my direction slower than a setting aurora.

My breath flees.

His gaze rakes across my shadowed form, like he's trying to sweep past the curtains of filth and shadow to my unveiled face.

I tuck my chin to my chest, loose tendrils of hair falling forward to curtain me.

Leave.

Leave.

Leave—

'It's *you*,' he rumbles, and my heart drops, the hairs on the back of my neck lifting. 'Come forth into the light.'

'Who died and made *you* king?' I rasp past my ruined throat.

'My pah,' he deadpans, and a laugh bubbles out of me, tapering off before the excess motion has a chance to rip my wounds and make them weep again.

'Funny.'

Silence reigns.

He steps closer to the bars, arms crossed over his broad chest, the uncomfortable absence of sound dragging on for so long it pecks at me.

'Were you . . . waiting for something?' I ask, frowning.

'Yes. For you to shift into the light so I can see your face.'

I snort-laugh.

Righteous asshole.

'No, thank you. You'll have to step through those iron bars and drag me into the light yourself.'

There's a moment of pause before he grips the lock hanging from my door, knuckles blanching. The metal creaks and groans, and he rips his arm down—

I suck a sharp breath as the lock comes away.

Broken.

He lifts his hand and makes a show of loosening his fingers, letting the useless lump of metal fall to the ground with a clatter that echoes off the walls to the tune of my rallying heart.

Fuck.

'I'm not usually one to take things from a female that aren't given freely,' he rumbles, swinging the latch off the hook. 'However, your voice reminds me of somebody I used to know, and I've spent five sleepless slumbers convinced I'm going mad.'

He boots the door open, the sound of squealing hinges carving across my nerves, reminding me of times I was dragged from another cell – feet first, fingernails gouging the stone while I snarled through gritted teeth.

He takes the first step in, and I pull my feet back toward my bum, gritting my teeth against a bludgeoning howl as I push my weight against my shredded back and leverage myself to a wobbly stand. 'Hate to break it to you like this,' I hiss, 'but I'd never seen you before that slumber on the south side of the wall.'

'For your sake,' he growls, stalking forward, packing the space full of his massive presence, 'I hope you're wrong.'

'And if I'm not?'

He steps into my shadow, almost close enough for me to reach out and touch him, my next breath laced with a drugging punch of his rich, molten scent.

He flips back his hood, revealing that beautiful, hard face.

My lungs snag at the sight of him.

Lips pinched in a line, he steals another step forward.

'And if I'm *not?*'

'*Vaghth*,' he whispers, the scalding word a flame against my conscience.

My spine stiffens, every nerve in my body tingling in all the wrong ways.

The lantern overhead rattles – like something inside is trying to escape. One of its tiny panes pops, a shred of flame fluttering down into his cupped hand and cradled before my face like a mold of clay.

His thick black brows collide, his face blanching as my teeth clamp together, heart seizing.

Eye bulging.

I look at that flame like the spitting, scalding enemy it is, waiting for him to drag it across my flesh and paint a puckered trail.

A choked sound slips out of him, like his lungs forgot how to work.

He lifts a trembling hand as if to cup my cheek, leaving an inch of space separating us – the heat radiating off his palm akin to a ray of sunshine.

'H—' His stare blazes back and forth across my face, tracing the slopes of me with devastating precision. 'H-*how*?'

Something about the way he rasps the word cuts me down the middle, like he's stuffing those big, strong arms into my frosty depths, churning my lake into a storm of slush.

I open my mouth to speak, but all that comes out is a blow of frosty air.

Tension stiffens in the space between us.

The hand so close to cradling my face pulls back, crunching into a ball. He punches the wall behind my head with such force a hairline crack forms in the stone, weaving across my ceiling.

A litter of mildew rains upon us.

'*How?*' he bellows, and I growl, upper lip peeling back from canines aching to snap forward and sink into his flesh.

'I don't know what you're talking about,' I snarl, wanting him out.

Gone.

Wanting the flame in his hand extinguished before it tills up any more of the hurt I've worked so hard to rid myself of.

'She speaks the truth,' comes a wobbly voice from the opposite cell. From the dark-haired Truthtune who only stopped crying eighty-nine ceiling drops earlier.

I thought she was asleep.

The male frowns, rips his cinder stare off me, and stabs it over his shoulder in her direction. 'You a Truthtune?'

'I am. The female is confused by your interest. She is also petrified of—'

'That's enough,' I snip, my words ricocheting off the walls.

The male turns his attention back on me, his all-consuming stare etched in so many shades of disbelief.

He crushes the flame in his large, calloused hand, though I have only a brief moment of reprieve before he pulls a metal weald from his pocket and flicks back the lid, revealing a bloodred bulb of Sabersythe flame.

My throat constricts, a strangled sound squeezing through the tightening space. A sound I want to crush from existence the moment it leaves my lips.

He raises his other hand, the rough tips of his fingers sweeping a tendril of hair from my forehead, leaving a wake of tingling flesh.

'*Get your hand off me*,' I seethe as he tucks the fall of inky locks behind my ear.

His chest boils with a sound that makes me picture the ground shaking, the tip of his finger tracing the jagged scar on my forehead. A scar that can be seen by dragonflame – the only substance in existence that can ignite a trail of long-ago runes and unearth their glowing ghosts.

'Your head,' he rasps. 'You've been mended.'

Mended . . .

Such a funny word, signifying the end of something. But every hurt has an echo if you look deep enough.

A wound is never *fully* gone.

'Don't remember getting that one.'

Not a lie.

His gaze dips. 'Your eye. What happened?'

'Tripped on a stone.'

His head banks to the side. 'Did it reach up and punch you in the face?'

I offer him a faux smile. 'Strangest thing.'

A beat of silence before he continues, so smooth and soft it chills me to the bone. 'Who are you protecting, Moonbeam?'

My frail, suffocating vengeance, flailing as it is.

Perhaps my skewed vision is making me see things, but he has a look about him. Like if I tell him who *really* punched me in the face, the kill will no longer be mine, and I'm holding on to that promise of hope until I'm masticated by a dragon's maw or sliced from throat to navel.

'That's not my name. And I don't need you to fight my battles any more than I need your presence in this cell.'

He steals a single step back, snapping the lid shut on his weald, sealing the flame back into the runed metal vial. 'Prove it.'

I frown. 'Excuse me?'

'Turn around, lift your tunic, and show me your back. If a stone can cause such damage to your face, I'm *very* interested to see just what it's done to pack this cell with the smell of so much blood.'

My heart plops into my gut. 'I . . . *No*.'

'Always so stubborn,' he bites out, cradling the words like he fucking knows me.

He reaches forward—

Somebody sprints down the hall, cloaked in another white Runi robe akin to the one this male wears – an obvious ruse, given his weald and affinity with Ignos. Unless he's multitalented, I guess.

The approaching Runi slows by my cell, peering into the shadowed depths. 'Sire?' he whisper-hisses, the word pinching me. His eyes are wide with panic, stare bouncing between us both. 'Guards are coming. Lots of them.'

My brows pull together, gaze cutting back to the male standing before me – unmoving.

Unblinking.

Sire.

Fucking *Sire*.

Realization washes over me like a dunk of icy water, whipping all the warmth from my body. 'You're a . . . *king*.'

'As I said.' There's a brief pause as he flicks up his hood, casting his face back in a shroud of shadow, though his eyes still glimmer like a crush of embers caught in the orbs. 'Is that a problem, Moonbeam?'

A swell of fiery rage packs my chest and mouth so full it's impossible to speak. To tell him yes, that's a *problem*.

The Shade, The Fade, and The Burn are each ruled by a different Vaegor brother, each cut from the same vile cloth.

I've seen King Fade from a distance – Cadok Vaegor. This male is not him. Meaning he either rules The Shade or The Burn.

The Shade is said to be even more rotten than this kingdom, if rumors are anything to go by, the cold, shadowed expanse governed by King Tyroth Vaegor. A cruel king with a heart said to fester from the loss of his queen.

The Burn . . . well.

Few who venture deep into the sunny part of the world return to tell the tale, though it's said King Kaan is savage and bloodlusting. That Rygun – his ancient Sabersythe – was too big to fit in any of the city hutches the last time he came to Gore. That he lets the beast hunt freely across his kingdom, firing cities with his blazing breath and feasting on his folk whom he cares little about.

I'm not sure which option is worse. Who I'd least prefer to be sharing this cell with right now, breathing the same filthy air.

One thing's for sure – I wouldn't bow to *any* of them, even if a sword was notched at my neck.

A stampede of booted steps echoes down the corridor while I hold his stare, the racket coming to a halt before my cell. In my peripheral, I note the shadowed silhouettes of heavily armored guards.

'Runi,' one of them bellows, 'what are you doing in cell seventy-three?'

The King doesn't break my stare as he says, 'I'm the resident healer. I was instructed to inspect this prisoner's wounds.'

I give him an incredulous look.

'Impossible. Everyone is under strict instruction not to enter that cell. She is our most dangerous captive.'

I would be flattered, but there's no room for it beside the bubbling well of undiluted rage piling up my throat like a dragon about to wield its first flame.

'I must order you to exit her cell. She's expected at trial before the Guild of Nobles. We're to escort her straight there.'

Music to my ears. I don't want to spend another second in this monster's presence.

'Yes, *resident healer*,' I say, serving him a sour smile, 'kindly step out of my chambers. I have no need of your assistance – now or ever.'

The air between us becomes impossibly tight, and he grunts, stepping back.

The guards flood my cell in a spill of bloodred armor and the smell of polished leather. A male grips me by my wounded shoulder and jostles me forward, a wince hissing past my clenched teeth.

'She's been *pinned*,' the King proclaims, his voice a veiled death threat I want to scrunch up and stuff back down his throat.

I don't want him whipping out his imperial cock for me. Certainly not when he doesn't bother to whip it out for his own folk.

He eyes the guard like he wants to rip out the male's trachea. 'Why?'

'Because she speaks with Clode and Bulder.' I'm held in place while another guard unlocks the metal pole connecting my chains. 'The very reason this cell was off limits.'

'How do you know?' the King queries as I'm attached to an iron leash I consider using to strangle them all – until I see the red elemental bead hanging from the lobe of one of the guards.

Perhaps not.

'She took out an entire unit in the Undercity. Collapsed the lungs of seven soldiers before she even began tossing her blades. She slaughtered another twelve in ways that would make your insides wither, forged a cleft in the ground that took another six, then bit off the finger of a prestigious bounty hunter employed by The Crown.'

Well.

Good for me. I'd pat myself on the back if my skin wasn't flayed.

'Wanna tussle?' I ask the King, flashing him a complimentary grin he can take to my grave, wondering why he doesn't look anywhere near as outraged by my large body count as I expected him to be. 'If I win, you purchase my sentence, and I go back to killing vile males with small cocks and enough ego to justify their sick behavior. And you get to go back to . . . well, hunting *moonshards*.'

I feel the guard's beady-eyed stare bouncing between myself and the Incognito King, the latter stepping so close to me that barely an inch of space separates us.

The world around us fades into oblivion as he looks upon me with such a fierce intensity I almost forget how to breathe. 'Not much point anymore, since I've found the most important piece.'

The air between us grows so tight I'm certain one small tap will make it shatter.

The next breath I pull crushes my breasts against his solid, muscular chest. 'Well, off you go,' I rasp. 'Collect your *prize*.'

'Hard,' he rumbles. 'It's in a problematic position. Difficult to reach.'

I snort.

Please.

'I'm sure you have the resources to work it out,' I mutter, lifting my chin, flicking a look at the soldier behind him. 'Let's get this over with.'

'So eager?' the King asks, and I release a mirthless laugh.

'Yeah, sure. I'm just *itching* to get drawn and quartered or served to the Moltenmaws on a stick.'

Said nobody ever.

I'm led from the cell, down the hall, taking shuffled steps past caged folk clinging to their bars.

Watching me go by.

But the only stare I can feel is *his* – drawing a criss-crossed trail over my back, my tunic no doubt stained in blotches of blood both fresh and old.

I swear the ground shakes.

I'm shoved down another hall free from his line of sight, marched toward a trial that'll pound the gavel on my fate.

No point hoping for a good outcome. There is none. A thought that's almost . . . *freeing*. That lifts a weight from my shoulders and makes my steps feel lighter.

A smile splits my face as I'm nudged up a curl of stairs by one of the boisterous guards . . .

Might as well have some fun before I die.

Raeve

CHAPTER 22

Eight guards escort me through a lofty hall, multicolored windows spilling a kaleidoscope of light that slathers the side of my face in too much warmth. I'm slow, every step a shuffled victory, my damp tunic clinging to the torn, tacky flesh on my back.

Each forward motion feels heavier than the last, as if gravity is crushing me beneath the press of its thumb, slowly applying more pressure.

More.

Black spots begin to blot my vision as my leash is tugged by the guard ahead, luring me to turn a corner. We come to the base of a shadowed staircase, and I swallow a bludgeoning groan.

If I'd known this walk would be so tiresome, I might've eaten my last serving of gruel rather than sliding it down the line like I've done with most of the others.

'Keep walking,' the guard behind me growls, shoving me between the shoulder blades.

A raze of crippling pain threatens to buckle my knees, and my body jolts, air sucking through my clamped teeth. A surge of warm wetness seeps down my spine.

Cracking my neck from side to side, I tackle the staircase one wobbly step at a time until we're spat out onto a circular iron stage at the base of a domed amphitheater. I'm led forward a few jingling steps, the metal smooth and cold beneath my feet as my leash is connected to an iron loop poking up from the ground.

Above me is a low banister that bands the entire circumference, hosting a ring of males, each flaunting more than one elemental bead.

The Nobles, plus the beady-eyed Chancellor.

They're garbed in vibrant robes that blend with the ceiling – a mural of Moltenmaws midflight, boasting multicolored plumage and long, feathered tails adorned with a fluffy tuft on the end that veils their poisonous spike.

I look down at myself smothered in blood and filth and who knows what else. Drawing a deep whiff of my shift, my face scrunches.

I cut a glance at the leering Nobles. 'Apologies,' I say, my voice echoing through the vast space. 'Forgot to bathe for our very important date.'

Silence.

'*Never mind, Prisoner Seventy-Three,*' I mutter in a forged baritone. '*We know you've had a lot on your plate.*'

My guards thread back down the stairway, and my gaze rises to the second mezzanine that loops around the room. It's much higher than the one the Nobles sit at, its banister waist high on most folk standing behind it, looking down from their purchased perch. The ones who get a kick out of watching the Nobles unravel lives. Can't imagine why. But to be fair, I intend to put on a show this dae, so they'll get their bloodstone's worth.

I scan the faces, fearful I might find someone I know – someone who might do something stupid – winning myself a kick to the chest when I see the *Incognito King* staring down at me from his lofty place amongst the commoners.

Fuck.

Even though he's hooded, his face half cast in shadow, I still feel his stare shred across me, leaving a prickly trail.

Not sure what I did to deserve his foul attention, but I wish I could take it back.

I rip my gaze away, looking to the empty stone throne set amongst the Nobles' seats, wondering when King Fade is going to join the party.

Perhaps he's making a late entrance?

The Chancellor slams his gavel three times, my heart thumping in unison. He sets down the tool and breaks the seal on a scroll, unraveling it – signifying the start of my trial.

My heart drops.

I come to the grim realization that our boastful king must still be in Drelgad, disappointment lumping upon me . . .

Damn. There goes all my fun.

I was *so* looking forward to telling him he'd be better off shoveling colk shit than governing The Fade.

Silence roars as the Chancellor leers down at me over his hooked nose, brown and clear beads hanging from his lobe, his ruddy beard whittled into twin braided tails. 'Fade law states that those who hear the Creators' songs are obliged to wear elemental beads,' he says, his voice a conjuring drawl that echoes through the space seemingly runed to amplify sound. 'It is first noted that you wear none and that you are showcasing as a null.'

The scribe three paces away from me – sitting behind a desk beside a white-robed Runi – scratches at a scroll with a bloodred quill, the sound carrying so well it almost feels like the words are being etched into my flesh.

'I thought I *was* a null,' I announce, shrugging. Flesh-ripping pain flares across my back that makes my insides shudder, my next words spoken past gritted teeth. 'Imagine my surprise when Clode whispered pretty words in my ear and helped me pulverize the lungs of all those soldiers.'

A sea of murmurs float down from above.

The Chancellor's eyes narrow. 'From what I understand, you spoke Clode's language fluently enough to suggest you've been hearing such words for a while.'

I offer a wide smile. 'Beginner's luck.'

'Lie.'

I flick a sideways glare at the broad, blond-haired Runi, my gaze dropping, scouring the two gold buttons adorning the central seam of his robe. An etching stick and a small musical note.

Truthtune.

He garnishes me with a stony stare, and I frown.

'Rude.'

'And Bulder?' the Chancellor asks. 'What of him?'

I cock my head to the side. 'Haven't you ever wished the ground would split and chew on your enemies? Guess my dream came true. Lucky me.'

'Not a lie.'

'See?'

The Chancellor condemns me with a seething scowl, like he's picturing *me* being chewed by a hole in the ground as we speak.

Clearing his throat, he begins reading from the scroll. 'You, self-appointed as *Prisoner Seventy-Three*' – he peers down at me, eyes narrowed, and my smile widens in unison with his deepening frown – 'are hereby charged for the murder of twenty-three soldiers of The Crown—'

'Twenty-five,' I correct, and the room bursts with murmurs again as the Chancellor raises a brow.

'Excuse me?'

If he's going to read out my charge, he might as well get it right.

'Personally, I lost count. But the guard who led me here said I killed twenty-five.' The Chancellor opens his mouth to speak again, but I cut him off with a swift, 'Also, I'd like it added to the record that I bit off the tip of Rekk Zharos's finger. I only recently managed to flick out what was left of it from between my tee—'

'That's enough.'

'Pity.'

He flays me with a stare, and even the scribe pauses his incessant scratching. 'Do you find this . . . *amusing*?'

'You misread me.' I let all the humor fall off my face, my response a bite of bloody flesh spat at him with a sawtooth snarl. 'I find it fucking *tragic*.'

This time, there are no murmurs. Just a gluttonous silence that grates my bones.

'Truth.'

Yes, it is.

'Bring in the evidence,' the Chancellor bellows.

I marinate in the seething echo of his outburst while a male comes up the shaft of stairs at my back, toting two sacks he dumps on the ground before me, then loosens the drawstrings. He begins pulling out flaps of preserved flesh, flopping them on the ground in a semicircle around me, each bearing letters carved with my own hand.

Unmistakably.

I'm certain nobody else has handwriting like mine. *Certainly* nobody old enough to be out there slitting throats and dumping bodies off the wall. I hope.

'These were taken from confirmed victims of Fíur du Ath,' the

Chancellor states. 'Each of them important, upstanding members of our society, their loss crippling blows to The Crown.'

I practically preen, chest puffed, about to thank him for the compliment when he waves a familiar board at my face, adorned with three words etched in coal.

Prisoner Seventy-Three

'And this was your . . . *handwriting* when you signed for your rations,' he says, a bemused look in his cruel eyes. 'If you could even call it that. I'm certain my youngling could do a better job, and he's barely out of the crib.'

Some of the Nobles spill a roll of laughter that deflates my chest and makes me feel entirely too small. Makes my cheeks burn.

I learned to write with a piece of coal on the ground of a cell, and no matter how hard I try, I can't stop my words from looking like I'm still scratching them upon the stone. Every letter is a sooty ghost tilled from my past, but I refuse to let them beat me.

I click my tongue, glancing from skin slab to skin slab as the guard continues to slap them upon the floor. 'Well done. You possess a brain cell.' I glance up again, holding the Chancellor's beady glare. 'I would cheer, but I'm certain you'll do enough of that this slumber while you're staring at your floor-length mirror, fisting your microcock.'

Gasps rain upon me as the Chancellor's face reddens, the veins in his temples pushing to the surface. He opens his mouth, and I can see by his narrowed eyes that he's thinking about using a phrase. One I've used more times than I can count, exhibited by the flaps of flesh decorating the floor at my feet.

His lips thin, and he clears his throat.

Lifts his chin.

'You do not deny that you took the lives of these individuals?'

I look up, straight into the shadowed eyes of the Incognito King who just won't stop watching me, wishing he'd kindly fuck off.

A one-shoulder shrug as I meet the Chancellor's stare again, threads of pain lancing across my flesh like fiery veins. 'Seems a bit pointless given the evidence, wouldn't you say?'

'I do not appreciate your attitude,' he scolds, the other Nobles murmuring between each other while they leer down on me, passing me looks of disgust.

Disbelief.

Rage.

'Well, apologies for hurting your feelings.'

He opens his mouth, but I cut in.

Again.

'I, however, do not appreciate being forced to take out the population's *filth* because this kingdom is run by an imbecile who believes that having a cock, three beads dangling from his ear, a cruel dragon, and a powerful army means he doesn't have to iron out the kinks in his rumpling society.'

The upper mezzanine erupts in a riot of sound, the Nobles looking between each other, some of them throwing their hands in the air as they heave words toward the Chancellor. Like it's somehow *his* fault I possess a brain that thinks, a mouth that speaks, but lack the self-preservation to avoid using both while standing in their presence.

Good. Hope I'm making enough of a spectacle that the Nobles will be satisfied with my capture. That Rekk will be given something *else* to chase, and the Ath will flip from the fire – even if it's only for a little bit.

If I'm going out, it might as well be in style. It's not like I've got anything to lose.

Not anymore.

The Chancellor hammers his gavel against the table three times over, silencing the racket. 'You would disrespect our king so publicly?' he bellows, cheeks red like his ruddy cloak.

I cock a brow. 'Is that a rhetorical question, or did you want me to answer?'

The Nobles murmur between each other while I rock back and forth on the balls of my feet, desperate to be done with this. I have a bowl of slop calling my name.

Again, I peek up at the mezzanine.

He's still watching, arms crossed over his broad chest.

I sigh, pick at some of the filth beneath my nails, flick it away. 'I'm incredibly bored with this conversation. Can we get to the point where you condemn me to execution for taking out the trash? That's the part I'm most excited about.'

'You want to die?' the Chancellor asks, not bothering to mask his shock.

'No,' I murmur, picking another curl of filth free. 'I'm just so sick of looking at your ugly face that death is starting to sound rather cushy.'

His upper lip peels back from his canines, and I'm certain the vein in his temple is going to burst. I throw him a wink, though considering my other eye is still half congealed, it probably looks more like a blink.

I tried.

'What's your plea?' he grinds out.

'Guilty. Of all charges.'

'She does not lie,' the Truthtune states.

'Wouldn't dare.' I glance over my shoulder at the scribe, meeting his wide-eyed stare. 'You can probably tack on a few more charges, too. I'm sure I'll fill the quota if you look hard enough. I'm practically a one-folk show.'

Another swell of murmurs.

I'm surprised they still have things to talk about.

'All those in favor of Prisoner Seventy-Three being drawn and quartered next aurora rise?'

I ignore the frantic thump of my heart as over half the Nobles raise their hands, including half the crowd packed into the mezzanine.

I lift my hand, too.

Most would probably prefer the coliseum, but I'd much rather be sliced open while my heart's still beating than be served to a thunder of fire-breathing dragons, thank you very much.

'All in favor of feeding her to the Moltenmaws?'

Another flock of hands rise, and the scribe counts them quietly. 'It's a draw,' he calls out, gaze cast on the mezzanine, appearing to recount.

I frown.

Surely not.

I count too – looking up in time to watch a familiar hooded 'Runi' raise his hand, like he's lifting a gavel of his own.

Casting a vote.

'Oh, no matter,' the scribe bellows. '*Dragons it is* – by one vote!'

My blood chills, my rapidly beating heart making my head spin, certain I'm going to pass out. Not that it stops me from slaying the Incognito King with a glare I hope he feels all the way to his bones.

I should be able to die how I *want* to die, dammit!

The King dips his head, and I picture myself lobbing it off his shoulders and watching it thump upon the floor, but then the Chancellor slams his gavel against the table again.

I flinch, gaze plummeting in unison with my guts.

'It's settled. Prisoner Seventy-Three, you will be led to the coliseum come next aurora rise, and the bell will toll in your name. May the Creators have mercy on your tarnished soul.'

Raeve

CHAPTER 23

I'm escorted back down the long, twisting tunnels of Gore's notorious prison, past cells that smell as rotten as I do. Past folk who cling to their bars with blanched hands, looking at me through wide eyes – faces gaunt, lips cracked and sapped of color.

We pass a boy with his cheek pressed against the bars, his eyes so glazed and sightless I almost wonder if he's—

He blinks, pupils tightening, gaze shifting to me.

The strings of my stony heart tug, because I recognize those yellow irises. That flock of matted golden curls.

On a foggy aurora rise not too long ago, I found him wandering the Ditch, blood spilling from his nose that looked as crooked as it does now, bruises in places that told me someone much stronger had taken their anger out on him.

I'd given him an Elding orb. Asked if he wanted my help in any way. He'd pushed the orb back into my palm and told me he wanted to do it himself—

I look away, a shiver scurrying up my spine where it explodes across my shoulders, down my shredded back.

I'm nudged into my cell, stumbling to a stop. One of the guards unclips me from the leash, reattaches my mobility-restricting pole, and kicks me.

Hard.

Panic erupts beneath my ribs as I pitch toward the back wall, certain I'm about to rip half my face clean off, my feet clamped so close together it's impossible to kick my foot forward and catch myself. Instead, I tip my body to the side and tuck into a ball –

My shoulder collides with the wall, the top half of my back grating down the rough-hewn rock in an explosion of teeth-gnashing agony, violent aftershocks coursing through me – my flesh lit with the whipping pain of a thousand lashes.

A deep, searing scream wrangles up my throat, seeming to echo off the walls, the tapered end of it chased by a chilling silence.

Hissing through the aftermath, I tap my hand against the floor to the beat of my calming song while letting my eyes slit open. Narrow on the offending guard.

He picks my broken lock off the ground, then leers at me like it's *my* fault a king with a fist of iron crumbled it free. He secures my door with a new padlock he plucks off the latch of an empty cell, and leaves with the rest of my armored entourage – their heavy footsteps fading into oblivion.

He's lucky I'm chained and secured in a cell; otherwise, I'd have his heart in my squeezing fist for making me scream.

'Guessing it didn't go well?' Wrook asks from somewhere so close I can feel his whiskers twitching against my arm.

'As expected,' I mutter past gritted teeth.

He reaches through, settling his claw on my arm, and I thank the Creators he's getting out. The world needs more folk like him.

I place my hand atop his for a brief moment before letting it drop.

He does the same.

There's the sound of the slop cart rolling down the tunnel. Of bowls sliding across the floor, followed by the sloshy tune of ravenous consumption.

A bowl skitters into my cell, and I look at it, feeling none of the hunger I was experiencing earlier – the hollow ache replaced with gut-churning dread.

I use my foot to nudge it left since Wrook is apparently getting out soon.

The bony male pauses his frantic gorging, slop dribbling from his beard as he looks at me. 'No,' he rumbles, sliding the bowl back into my cell. 'You will starve.'

I look straight into his sunken eyes. 'I'm to be offered to the dragons next aurora rise. It's wasted on me.'

Everyone seems to pause their feeding frenzy, silence feasting on the echo of my words.

'I am sorry,' the male murmurs.

So am I.

Sorry I won't get the chance to avenge Essi's death, and that I'm leaving this beautiful, broken world.

I love living, painful as it's been at times. I love the colors of our kingdom and the way our clouds are ever changing.

Ever shifting.

I love the way the dragons soar through the tombstone-riddled sky, entirely untethered. Love the feel of fallen snow peppering my skin, and the way a frosty, south-born breeze nips at my nose, numbing the tip of it like an icy kiss.

The backs of my eyes burn as I think of that little wonky moon I'll probably never see again . . .

I love that most of all.

I offer the male a soft smile, pushing the bowl beneath the bars again.

This time, he takes it.

Diary Entry

Elluin Neván

Age: 18 phases
5,000,039 phases After Stone

Ostern Vaegor – King of The Burn – came to visit Mah and Pah and, well . . .

Me.

Since I'm now eighteen, I'm apparently mature enough to be marketed off to the highest bidder, like livestock set for slaughter. At least that's what King Ostern thought. That Pah would agree to an arranged bind between me and one of his sons who has cruel eyes and an even crueler smile, simply because The Shade has a swelling need for agricultural produce we're struggling to service.

Too bad for Ostern, I told Pah I'd rather eat nothing but my Moonplume's shit for the rest of my existence than pair with Tyroth Vaegor – and meant it.

Pah said I have a foul mouth. That if I grew up in the Boltanic Plains like he did, I'd have been made to shovel faunycaw dung for an entire phase for that single comment alone. Or be whipped for my insolence.

I told him I'd happily take a whipping over Tyroth Vaegor.

Pah said that's exactly why he left that place, and that he wouldn't sell me for all the grain in the world. Then he kissed me on the forehead, called me remarkable, and told me to spend some time with Slátra and Allume so kings could talk politics without a foul-mouthed princess listening in.

I love Pah, but I wish he'd stop calling me remarkable. If I could squish that word like a bug and pop it from existence, I would.

I asked Haedeon if he'd like to come with me to the hutch, but he just stared at the wall like he always does. I accepted long ago that he never came home from Netheryn – not really. I swore I wouldn't leave him there, but I did.

He doesn't laugh anymore.

He doesn't eat butterberry chews.

He doesn't speak. Which means he also doesn't argue when I push him into the hutch so he can watch me work on Allume's wing that's growing stronger with each passing phase. Honestly, I think she'll be sturdy enough to take her first flight soon.

Since he was a little boy, all Haedeon wanted was to ride on the back of his own Moonplume . . .

Perhaps if I can give him that, he'll smile again.

Raeve

CHAPTER 25

My foot taps against the floor while I hum soft and slow, 'Ballad of the Fallen Moon' whipping through the otherwise eerily silent cells – most of the other prisoners fast asleep, hidden in some pocket of nonreality where I hope they're happier. More comfortable.

Healthy and free.

Given the fact that the Incognito King watched from the shadow of his hood as I sang the same song in the Hungry Hollow, seeing him stride down the prison tunnel in a flutter of Runi white is . . .

Fitting.

He stops before my cell, arms folded over his barrel chest.

'Go away,' I rasp, letting my eyes sweep shut.

'You don't even know why I'm here.'

'Don't want to.'

Zero.

Percent.

Interested.

My lock jiggles, and I open my eyes to see him delving a key into it, clonking it open.

I sigh.

'Wonder how your *brother* feels about you thieving his keys and breaking his prisoners free?'

'I'm not breaking you out, so don't get your hopes up.'

I snort-laugh. 'Charming.'

He kicks the door open, stepping into my foul-smelling chamber.

'And my brother has eyes in only one direction,' he mumbles, crouching before me, encasing me in the robust medley of his warm scent. A lush comfort in this harsh place, which I ignore the pleasure of, choosing to breathe through my mouth.

'Well, feel free to tell him I'm sorry I didn't get a chance to kill him before I died. I was really looking forward to it.'

'I have no doubt,' he says, producing another key from his pocket that he uses to unbolt the bar connecting my two chains, placing it on the ground beside me. He fails to unshackle my wrists or ankles, meaning he's got . . . *plans* for me.

Plans I want nothing to do with.

He stands, towering above me, blocking the light spilling from my lantern. 'Up.'

'Die in a ditch. Or better yet, a *coliseum* – getting feasted on by a flock of Moltenmaws. I'll meet you there.'

Asshole.

I sponge a little satisfaction from his rumbling sigh.

Even if I wanted to stand, I'm not sure I could. I may have put on a show at the trial, but my entire body feels like a frayed seam.

It hurts to breathe. To blink. It hurts to tap my tapping foot. There's something surging through my veins that's making me nauseous and cold.

I usually like the cold, but this is different. This cold feels *wrong* – wedging into my marrow like it's masticating me from the inside out to make space for itself.

'Now is not the time to be stubborn, Moonbeam.'

'Wrong. There's only *one* thing males see in a shackled female,' I seethe, my words laced with enough venom to stop a heart. 'If you want that, you can take it right here so my cellmates can see what a monster you are.'

A low rumble boils in his chest, making my skin pebble. 'I'm not that sort of monster, Prisoner Seventy-Three. I would not take *pleasure* from you were it not given freely. Now, stand on your own or suffer the embarrassment of being picked up and carried.'

His words wedge between my ribs and stab me where it hurts: my withering pride, the remnants of which I'm determined to take to my impending grave, tied to the stake he sentenced me to die upon.

'Your choice,' he growls. 'Make it.'

'I did make a choice. You *took* it from me.'

'Because it was the wrong one.' He reaches out as if to grip me around the shoulders—

A snarl rips up my throat, and I snap my teeth at his fingers. 'I'm *doing* it.'

'Then do it.'

'Not until you turn around.'

Another rumbling sigh before he spins, giving me the privacy I need to suffer through what's going to be a monumental task I'm not sure I have the capabilities to achieve. Right now, the ground is my friend. Unless I'm standing – then it's my enemy.

At least with his back turned, he won't see me crumble.

'Any progress?'

'Mentally strangling you as we speak,' I mutter, setting my hands on the ground to my left. I pinch my trembling lips together and shove all my weight into my palms, rolling into a wobbly crouch.

The pin in my shoulder grinds against bone, bolts of pain shooting through my arm . . .

Shit.

I squeeze my eyes shut, snap them open, and shove up, rocking to my feet. Warmth dribbles down my back as I sway. As my surroundings split, converge . . . split, converge . . .

'You're not going to fall, are you?'

I lift my chin, steady my spine. Stare at the back of his head while lit with a blaze of retribution. 'Course not. I've never been more sturdy in my life.'

'Good,' he says, then stalks from the cell with a dash of his white robe, condemning me to follow with a curt 'This way.'

I'm led through a tangle of corridors to a quiet tunnel with a single door at the end, nerves popping beneath my skin as the Incognito King pulls the door open and gestures for me to pass.

To enter ahead of him.

'You first,' I rasp with a steadying hand against the wall, not believing a word he said about not being *that sort of monster*.

He's a Vaegor. A tyrant. Tyrants lie to themselves as much as they lie to others.

I know what happens in this prison. I've heard enough stories to wither my guts for eternity. If he's going to have his way with me, I refuse to walk into that room blind. I'd rather force him to look me in the eye as he ruins another part of me. Make him feel every fracture.

Every bruise.

He stands still for a long, hard moment, then flops back his hood and moves into the room, not stopping until he reaches the other side. He turns and leans against the wall, crosses his arms, and waits like a stone statue carved by the Creators themselves. Strong jaw, chiseled cheekbones, muscular neck. Every angle hacked with such precision he's almost painful to look at.

Frowning, I shuffle forward, easing into the room lit by a jar of captured moonlight set on one of the many shelves lining all four walls.

Impressive. Those are pretty hard to come by.

I note the tall mender's pallet and padded chair beside it, my gaze whipping to the female standing in the corner, her hair a crop of brown curls that match her eyes and skin but contrast with the floor-length Runi robe she's garbed in.

She gives me a soft smile that does nothing to stop my heart from plummeting.

I don't bother taking in the buttons pinning together the front seam of her robe – the ones that symbolize her strengths. I already know what I'll see.

She can *fleshthread*.

'This better be a threesome,' I grind out.

'I'm not one to share,' the King says, his voice low and steady. 'But if that's what you really want, it can be arranged once your back is healed.'

He obviously thinks he's hilarious, but I'm not laughing, my pulse a violent churn I can't seem to slow.

The Runi takes a step toward me, her face still warmed by a comforting smile. 'Greetings, Prisoner Seventy-Three. I'm Bhea. Why don't you let me help you remove your tunic so I can take a look at your ba—'

'There's no point healing me,' I growl, cutting a glare at the King. 'It would be a wasteful misuse of this female's skill and energy.'

'Bhea has been well compensated for her service and is more than happy to help.'

'Does she know I'm destined for the *coliseum*?' His lips tug into a tight line, so I stab my stare at Bhea instead. 'Do you?'

'I do,' she whispers.

'Then why bother?'

'Because you're in pain,' the King announces, like that's an answer at all.

'Pain that'll *stop* once I'm fed to the dragons!'

'Please.' Bhea steals another step forward. 'We don't have much time if I'm to do my best work.'

My foot slides back.

She stills, and though the King doesn't shift from his spot against the wall, something locks into place in the void between us. As though physical strings knot around my ribs, stretch across the room, and tether to his, making it impossible for me to draw a single breath without him noticing.

My skin nettles, and I become primitively aware that he's waiting for me to run.

That he will *chase*.

He tips his head, as if in silent appraisal of my tumultuous inner monologue, which just pisses me off. I'm bluntly aware that in my current state I'd make it two steps before he'd be upon me, dragging me back to this very position, waiting for me to concede.

Dammit.

'You will leave your weald at the door.'

'I have three, Moonbeam.'

'The one with the dragonflame, *Sire*.'

A line forms between his brows, gone the next moment as he reaches into his pocket and pulls out his weald, tossing it through the air – a perfect throw that plummets into my outstretched hand.

I lob it down the hall, hearing it clatter across the stone.

This is such bullshit.

I move farther into the room, scanning the worktable that's littered with jars of tinctures, vials, bowls, etching sticks, and containers packed full of medicinal tools. Too many things that remind me of Essi.

The sooner this is done, the sooner I can leave.

With my heart lodged in the back of my throat, I move toward the chair, unpicking the buttons of my loose tunic. 'I was kidding about the threesome,' I snip, releasing the final two while murdering the King with a glare. 'There is no reality where I'd willingly fuck you.'

He doesn't break my stare as he says, almost too soft for me to hear, 'Turn around, Moonbeam. Take a seat in the chair so Bhea can get started.'

I grind my teeth so hard I'm surprised they don't crumble, fingers clenched around the seams of my shirt. There is no point in *either* of them seeing my shredded skin.

None.

I'm so much stronger than these slashes on my back, the story they tell a rippling echo I don't want to be heard by anyone. An echo I'd rather take to my grave than sit here all slumber while they digest it – keeping it alive in some form or another.

Behind me, I sense Bhea stepping into my atmosphere, her hands coming up to help me ease the tunic partway down, exposing my shoulders.

She gasps, pausing.

Moving around the side of me, her glossy-eyed gaze trails across the bared window of flesh from my neck to navel, tears puddling her lower lids.

Confused, I look at her robe, pinched in place by more gold or diamond buttons than I've ever seen on a single seam, my blood chilling at the sight of the one closest to her nape. A tiny dragon blowing a mushroom of flames.

This Runi doesn't need dragonfire to ignite the trail of past runes, because she's blessed with Dragonsight. She can see them with her *own* eyes.

Meaning she's seeing . . .

Everything.

'What is it?' The King's voice hacks through the room like the swing of a sword, and my heart skips a beat.

Another.

Bhea meets my stare, and I shake my head the slightest amount.

Please don't.

Please don't make me go back to that place—

'Nothing, Sire,' she whispers, blinking, dashing a tear from her cheek.

Relief floods through me like a gulp of icy water.

'The damage is more extensive than I was expecting. I will need to retrieve more supplies from the storage closet down the hall.'

With the King's nod, Bhea eases from the room, closing the door behind herself – leaving the space less full, yet somehow *brimming.*

I clear my throat, fingers fisting my tunic, the silence between us tangible. A clay-like substance that could be molded into one of two things: a war horn or a waving white flag.

'This,' I rasp, jerking my chin at the table of tinctures, 'you bringing a Runi in to help me, it changes *nothing.*'

'I'd be surprised if it did.' He pushes off the wall, moving toward me. 'But for now, spend this time sharpening your blades. At least until Bhea has completed her task.'

'That's a big ask.'

He reaches me, warm, calloused fingertips skimming across my knuckles, his gaze a quiet request.

Sighing, I loosen my grip, allowing that white flag to rise between us. A fragile, fluttering thing I intend to shred the moment I leave this room.

'Would you like me to cover you with a cloth before I take this off?'

My breath hitches.

All three Vaegor brothers originated from The Burn, where nudity is considered a comfort for some – far less sexualized than it is this far south – so I'm not too proud to appreciate his consideration of my culture.

For asking.

I open my mouth, close it. Finally, I shake my head.

'Tell me if you change your mind.'

With my nod, and not once breaking eye contact, he eases my tunic down my shoulders until it's bunched around my wrists, the chill air nipping at my bareness while I study his lashes – so long and thick.

A pretty distraction.

He reaches around to gently tuck the drape of material around my hips so it's not agitating my ragged flesh.

'You know this is pointless, right?'

'Not to me,' he rumbles, then takes my hands in his big, sturdy ones – his a tan complexion like the stone walls, mine the color of snow.

He leads me toward the chair, steadying me so I can lift my leg over it and settle on it backward before he lowers with me, giving me the dignity of not looking upon my damage. A mercy I appreciate in this small window of ceasefire.

I rest my chest against the heavily cushioned backrest, hands in my lap as he folds into a kneel.

A soft knock sounds on the door.

'Enter,' he murmurs while I hold his severe stare, like looking into the crumbled remnants of a fire that's lost its flame.

The door swings open. Closes. I hear Bhea's soft, shuffling steps, then sounds of her readying for the procedure.

The King barely blinks as she cleans some of the blood from my back with damp sweeps of a cloth, squeezing the ruddy excess into a bucket on the ground. He barely blinks as she paints my back in a bonding agent – the familiar sting sinking through layers of filleted flesh before she sketches out her paths with the flick of a delicate paintbrush.

'I'm still intent on killing you, if given the chance,' I warn past clenched teeth.

'Don't forget to cut off my head,' he murmurs. 'Or I'll haunt you for eternity.'

'I don't believe in that.'

Not one bit. I've cut off very few heads in comparison to my rather large body count, and I'm yet to see a single spirit claw at me from the shadows.

He lifts a brow. 'Then what do you believe in?' he asks, his voice guttural.

'Revenge.'

All the warmth sputters from his eyes, like part of him just slipped away. 'Revenge is the loneliest deity of them all, Moonbeam. Take it from someone who knows.'

I open my mouth to speak again, but Bhea cuts in. 'If I'm to do this properly, it will take a while. And it will hurt. The cuts are deep. She will have to relive the pain while I mend the damage.'

I realize she's not warning me, her eyes able to see what most others cannot.

She's warning *him*.

'She can do it,' he rumbles, gaze challenging me to do just that.

With my nod, Bhea begins etching her runes, reversing the lifespan of my wounds one vile slash at a time. The King holds my stare as I'm stitched shut in over a hundred ways, though it doesn't feel like that. It feels like I'm being ripped *wider* – my insides bared.

Examined.

Perhaps because I'm used to doing this without an audience besides the Runi fixing me new. Without somebody else timing their breaths to my own, as though reminding me to breathe.

Without somebody else tightening their grip on my hands every time I flinch, wiping the sweat from my brow, rubbing tracks across my blanched knuckles as if to calm my rioting heart.

It's a humble moment of peace despite the pain lancing through me. A quiet moment destined to *scream*.

It doesn't matter how much of my skin is smoothed or how deep he kneels at my feet. I'm still an assassin marked for execution come aurora rise, and he's still a tyrant king.

Diary Entry

Elluin Nevån

Age: 18 phases
5,000,039 phases After Stone

I was working on Allume's wing stretches this dae, singing her a soft, calming song while extending the fine bones as far as they could go – which is now almost a full extension. She was getting restless, swinging her head around and nudging my side, looking at me with those massive glittery eyes. Like she was trying to say something. She even threw a little flame toward the entrance, which is very unlike her.

I now realize she was challenging it.

Suddenly, she began tilling her wings so fast her gammy one clipped me in the head and threw me back toward Haedeon's chair. I skidded across the ground and landed amongst a pile of ice boulders Mah's Moonplume Náthae had recently brought in because we think she might be broody.

I hit my head. Hard.

When I opened my eyes again, Allume was gone, but I could see her through the entrance – fluttering across the sky, light shafting off her brilliant silver hide. Could see her long silken tail dusting the dim with each wonky waggle of her wings. Could see the plumes of aqua flames she kept throwing skyward, accompanied by squealing shrieks. Like a victory cry to the moons.

To her ancestors.

I scrambled up to check on Haedeon . . .

He was smiling.

He looked me right in the eye and said 'thank you' in a voice so rough I think the words might've hurt coming out, and I've never felt happiness so fierce.

For the first time since I climbed in Haedeon's sleigh all those phases ago, I felt remarkable.

Raeve

CHAPTER 27

'Okay, that's the last,' Bhea says, smoothing an oil over my back – her hands soft and tender, rubbing all the tension from my now-healed flesh.

Battling the urge to groan with relief, I open my eyes, looking straight into a pair of intense cinder orbs, a line dug between the King's thick brows.

'You okay?' he asks, tightening his hold on my clammy hands.

'I'm great,' I slur, tugging them from his grip.

Never better. So glad he tortured me back to health during my last living moments. What a way to go out. Fitting, but a bit shit.

I lean back so I can lift my hands up over the chair's headrest without snagging my chain and take the towel slung over his shoulder. The one he's been using to dab at my forehead whenever sweat beaded down into my lashes.

'I'll get my fine-tipped prongs for the pin,' Bhea says while I stuff my face in the towel, scrubbing the tension from around my eyes, hearing the sound of her footsteps before she begins rummaging through something.

Her words finally sink past the fog currently clouding my head.

Prongs?

What do they need fine-tipped prongs fo—

Oh.

I pull the towel from my face, catching the King's stare again. 'You're removing the pin?'

Makes sense. Wouldn't want any hatchlings choking to death on it if I'm carted west and spat out in a Moltenmaw's tinder nest.

'You wear iron cuffs,' he murmurs, his gaze dragging over every angle of my face – like he's mapping out the shape of it – landing on my eyes again. 'The pin is unnecessary.'

'Well, yeah. But *I'm* unnecessary, remember? Skin slabs . . . Rekk Zharos's finger . . . I don't think you appreciate quite how close you came to being hacked into bits, then tossed off the wall. But hey, thanks for mending me before I die, even though it makes no sense.'

The corner of his mouth kicks up. 'Hacked into bits, you say?'

Obviously.

'You're the biggest male I've ever seen.' I shrug, biting down on a wince because that pin *absolutely* hurts. It's blatant now that my skin's no longer slashed to ribbons. 'There's no way I could've dragged you to the edge after I slit your throat.'

'But you didn't . . .'

I frown, wishing he wouldn't stuff my indiscretions in my face like that.

He smelled good.

I fucked up.

Let's not dwell on it.

'The prongs aren't here,' Bhea says, and that small smile instantly falls off the King's face as he pushes to a stand.

'I have some in my saddlepack, but it'll take me a while to get there and back,' he announces, striding toward the window covered by a round of aged, half-rotten wood. 'How are we on ti—'

'Give me a blade.' I wave my hand in the air, jingling my chains. 'I'll cut it out.'

The King abruptly stops, and both he and Bhea glare at me like I just asked them to pretty please bare their throats so I can slice them open.

I roll my eyes.

'I won't stab you. White flag, remember? I won't give it back, either, so don't give me one you're particularly attached to.'

The only thing worse than losing a good blade is losing *all* your good blades, dammit.

The tips of my fingers tingle with the urge to gouge them through Rekk Zharos's throat and rip out his trachea with my bare hands. Now that I'm mended, the injustice is extra crippling. I'm more than well enough to hunt him if it weren't for these fucking chains.

'I can put a salve on it,' Bhea suggests, turning her attention to the King – like I'm not even here.

'That's a terrible idea,' I gripe, reinserting myself back into the conversation. 'I have a *pin* in my shoulder.'

Now that we're all talking about it, I'm growing more and more pissed that I'm going to die with this thing in me, and I think it's only fair that I snatch my comforts wherever I can find them, thank you very much.

I lean back from the chair, spinning so I can see the King properly. 'You have a blade, no doubt. Hand it to me,' I say, flopping my hand out for him to fill. 'Any blade. I'm not picky. Let me root around for a bit. You can close your eyes if you're squeamish.'

He clears his throat, not for one moment dropping his gaze to my naked breasts now on full display while he turns and grabs the wooden window covering. Sliding it sideways, he peers out, muttering a curse beneath his breath. 'Does the salve have rindleroot in it?'

To numb pain?

Interesting.

He wants to ease my suffering as I'm hailed into death. And there I was ordering a handsaw to make disassembling him easier.

'It does,' Bhea responds, digging her hand into a large leather bag she has stretched open on the worktable. She pulls a jar free like it's some sort of trophy, and I frown at the lumpy green paste inside. 'And fermented eahl eggs.'

To disinfect. But most importantly – to make you smell like you've been shat on.

No, thank you.

'You know what?' I say, trying to wrangle my shirt back on. 'Fuck it, I'm good. Doesn't even hurt. Let the hatchlings choke.'

'Do it.' The King slides the window cover back into place, snipping off the extra spill of light. 'We don't have time to cut out the pin,' he says, nailing me with a stare that shoots straight through me and out the other side. 'The aurora's about to rise.'

My heart plummets so fast I almost vomit.

Damn . . .

Guess it's almost time to die.

I side-eye Wrook's empty cell as I rock from side to side, dragging my itchy back against the stone – an itch that threads bone-deep in places, making me want to rip apart all Bhea's hard work just to satiate the uncomfortable sensation.

Guess the Incognito King made good on his promise while I was away. I hope Wrook's satisfied with his Sabersythe tusk and that he wasn't instead fed to whatever beast it previously belonged to.

I'm not stupid enough to believe this scratchy gift I've been given comes without caveats, too. Few folk help others in this world without expecting something in return.

There's a reason I was coaxed to that room. I'm just yet to work out what it is.

Easing my tunic down, I reach back to finger the goo Bhea stuffed in the hole punched through my shoulder blade, frowning at the acrid stench.

Now I get to die smelling like fermented eahl eggs barely softened by a herbal twang.

Lovely.

At least it seemed to finally quench the King's strange, almost compulsive desire to take my pain away.

I frown.

Perhaps it has to do with the one I remind him of? Perhaps healing me assuaged him somehow? Made him feel better about himself?

That must be it.

I breathe a sigh of relief, thankful I worked out the riddle. I did not want to take that question to my gnawing end.

A drop of mildew lands on my nose, dashing my relief. A splatting reminder that I'm in a cell. Waiting for death.

That these are my final moments.

Fuck.

Scanning my surroundings, I take in the resting forms of my cellmates, envying their deep, languid breaths . . .

Sleep would be nice right now. I could exist *elsewhere* for a little bit.

Anywhere but here.

But I can't summon the urge to snuff myself into oblivion. I'm too wound up inside, like there's a lightning storm caught in my chest, zapping me every time I even think about closing my eyes.

For all I know, the guards might be charging down this very moment, ready to drag me to my fiery doom.

My insides knot.

I bat the thoughts away, but just like Nee used to, they keep bumping against me. Nuzzling me.

Loved that.

Hate this.

I pull my chest full of air and slowly blow it out, picking at the skin down the side of my nail.

Don't think.

Don't think.

Don't think.

I close my eyes, tapping my foot to the quiet, calming tune lilting in the back of my mind, timing the beat to the splats of moisture falling from the ceiling.

Splat.

Splat.

Splat-splat.

The hairs on my arms lift—

My eyes pop open.

Through the bars, a waggle of distorted air draws my gaze – no taller than knee height. My eyes narrow as it peels away to reveal a crouching creature with a wild tangle of fur the color of snow, matching her brows and lashes though contrasting with the smooth, pale pink skin on her face, neck, legs, and arms.

Uno lets her cloak fall to the ground in a rumple of inky fabric sketched with luminous runes, flashing me a mischievous smile that's all sharp teeth.

The organ in my chest squeezes so hard I fear it might crack down the middle.

'What are you doing here?' I whisper-hiss through clenched teeth, leaning forward, nipping a glance down the tunnel, my pulse powering so fast my head feels light and airy.

Her large, fluffy ears twitch as they strain for sound. 'Sereme spoke to Master. Commanded I get you out.'

Icy rage rumbles in the pit of my belly.

Of course Sereme ordered this. Which means she intends to replace me with another. To feed The Crown with *another*. What's worse, she put *Uno* in danger to retrieve me . . .

Ruse must be out of her mind with worry.

Uno pulls a pick from one of the many colorful patchwork pockets stitched into her woolen garb, stretches her body into a long line, grabs my lock, and slides the thin metal pin into the opening—

'*Stop.*'

Her delicate hands still, pink eyes flicking to me, slit pupils narrowing. A line forms between her brows, the white, tufted tip of her long tail flitting back and forth.

'Get out of here, Uno. Please. You can't risk being caught.'

Her lips peel back from pin-sharp teeth, buttony features contorting into something honed and horrific. 'You are not Master.' The words slit my skin, leaving a stinging trail. 'You do not command me.'

Stubborn miskunn.

I sigh, glancing down the tunnel again, then back into her fierce eyes. 'They know I'm a threat. If I live, they will double down their hunt.' I pause before landing my kidney shot. 'They will find *Ruse*.'

Uno snaps her teeth together and snarls, lips thinning. Her tail spears forward, brushing against my cheek.

Her eyes flash iridescent.

She goes statue still, her already pale complexion lightening so much her skin turns translucent in places where it's most thin – her temples, the insides of her frail wrists, the lanky bend of her knobbly legs.

Silence stretches as she languishes in one of her rare foretellings, and I swallow, watching the prismatic flecks in her eyes churn. The pink bits congeal, rising to the surface, glimmering red in the warm light.

Her tail whips from my face so fast it's like I'm made of fire, a shuddered breath sucking through her pin-tooth maw. She blinks, pulls her pick from the lock, and folds back down into a crouch, droplets of hope I didn't even realize I possessed splatting against my ribs.

'You know I'm right . . .'

She tucks the pick into the little pink pocket on her woolen garb. 'Master will die if you do not go to that coliseum. Sereme too. I have seen it now.'

My chest deflates, and I nod.

That's settled, then.

'I'm not surprised,' I whisper, forcing a smile. 'I pissed off the Guild of Nobles. Thoroughly. I imagine they'll turn this city upside down to find me if I don't make it to my execution.'

'They will,' she says with stoic certainty. 'I will relay my seeings to Master. She can pass them to her master. Who can pass them to her master.'

My smile softens. 'You do that, Uno.'

She reaches into her orange pocket, revealing a piece of coal. 'Come,' she says, raising it for me to see.

I frown.

With another glance down the tunnel, I lift my metal pole so my chains won't drag along the ground, and shuffle forward. Uno gestures for me to rest my head between two bars, the metal brisk upon the sides of my face.

Her bottom lip wobbles as she drags the piece of coal across my forehead.

I immediately know the shape she's drawing, so thoroughly familiar with the moon I seek out in the sky whenever I'm looking toward The Shade.

'This is . . . *right*,' she whispers, and I swallow the odd thickening in my throat.

'I know.'

She tilts back, knobbed knees up around her cheeks, studying me while I study her . . .

It's on the tip of my tongue to ask whether or not I get munched right from the stake or carted off to Bhoggith and fed to a clutch of hatchlings, despite knowing her visions are sporadic. That the outcomes can shift and sway. But I decide it's better to drown myself in ignorance right until the bitter end.

I close my eyes, not wanting to say a goodbye that'll taste like ash, hearing the near-silent pad of her scuffled steps fade into oblivion. Only when I'm certain she's gone do I open my eyes again, looking into the empty space before me.

I clear my throat, shuffling back to the wall, rubbing my itchy back against the abrasive surface.

'Why a ball?' comes a rasped voice to my left.

I look sideways at the male I thought was asleep bunched beneath his filthy blanket, instead watching me through the bars. 'It's a moon.'

He frowns. 'Then why a moon?'

I cast my gaze forward again, tap-tap-tapping my foot to the soothing tune in my head. 'Because they fall.'

Even when we don't want them to.

Raeve

CHAPTER 28

I'm escorted through the cramped and crowded Ditch, flanked by The Crown's beaded soldiers, the sky weeping flakes of snow that dust the ground – an icy cushion for my barefooted shuffle past tight-lipped city folk.

It's not normal to be marched to the coliseum with a parade of guards and rows of silent witnesses, but with an abundance of posters slapped on the walls alerting of my capture and execution time, I understand.

They watch me shuffle through the thin cleft in the crowd, both sides lined by more Fade soldiers, like fence posts guarding a flock of stock. Swords at their hips, narrowed eyes scanning, perhaps waiting to see if any Fíur du Ath will step forward and show themselves.

Try to help me.

I'm confident they won't interfere. Not after Uno's foretelling.

So I keep my chin high as I pass faces I recognize, fae folk and even a few creatures I've come to trust over the phases. Other members of the Ath who played small but poignant roles in my life before I fell upon this sword I've spent my known life sharpening.

To me, their faces glow like *moons*.

Just like the ones in the sky, I hope they don't fall, sad that I won't be around to see this kingdom restored to its former glory. Sereme will do it, I know she will.

Eventually.

Much as I hate her, the bitch doesn't know how to fail. A seed of hope I'll take to my death.

Stony-faced servants of The Crown cradle bowls of what I can only imagine is some sort of animal blood, splattering me with throws of it. Drenching me in its metallic reek as a thunder of Moltenmaws shadow the sky, the booming beat of their powerful wings *thumping . . . thumping . . .*

Much like my rallying heart.

A speck of snow settles on the tip of my nose, and I look up, smiling, certain everybody else thinks I'm suffering from the brisk weather. But I wonder if our Water Goddess knows otherwise. If Rayne's waving me off with frosty tears that actually bring me a sense of comfort – chilling the fire in my veins and the anger in my heart. There's no point to it anyway. Not anymore.

It's over.

Done.

I'll go to my doom shackled by only two regrets: that I never got to flay Rekk Zharos from cock to throat, and that I failed to experience *life* in the way Fallon explained it before she passed. This beautiful, bolstering freedom that was always just out of reach.

Both regrets feel like splinters in my heart as I'm escorted toward a stairway chipped into the north side of the wall, zigzagging up the levels until I'm almost close enough to the clouds to catch them in my mouth.

To taste them.

Nearing the top of the wall, I begin rolling onto my tiptoes every few steps, craning my neck, determined to steal a peek of the moon I love so much . . . *one last time*.

Just a little higher, and I might be able to—

I scan the low, snow-spewing clouds that blanket the sky in all directions, obscuring the moons.

Every moon.

My heart drops, something sharp pricking the backs of my eyes.

I'm shoved into a tunnel lined with flaming sconces, and I snarl, the cloudy view blocked by stone and flame. The beat of stomping boots echoes off the walls, and I'm certain those boots are stomping my chest with the weight of my disappointment, fracturing my ribs. Crushing my lungs.

Brush it off.

Stuff it away.

I lift my chin as we turn down another tunnel before I'm led up a swirling staircase that spits me out upon the central stage of the coliseum – so vast it makes me feel like a speck of dirt at the bottom of a basin.

Tiny.

Insignificant.

The thick stone awning shelters a single layer of seating that crowns the building, protecting the vibrant elementals who've come to watch me die, willing to risk their lives to witness the grisly spectacle.

They laugh, gasp, and murmur, pointing in my direction as I'm backed against a wooden stake, my feet lost within crusted layers of snow.

I give them a shackled wave, flashing them a smile. 'Thanks for coming to send me off!' I yell, followed by a murmured '*assholes*.'

The guards jostle my hands to my sides, binding coils of fibrous rope around me until I'm secured so tight it's hard to pull a full breath. They thread back down the stairs while my lungs wrestle against the constricting bind.

A burst of panic explodes behind my ribs.

I'm trapped. Powerless.

So fucking alone.

The realization stabs me in the heart, fear seeping through my veins in a rush of boiling blood. My breaths come short, sharp, and fast, that terrible tremble that shook me in the cell resurging with a vengeance.

Perhaps noticing my sudden discomfort, some of the elementals laugh, cackles pelting me like thrown rocks.

Cheeks blazing, I refuse to look at them again. Instead, I throw my stare skyward, eyes widening on the vibrant beasts circling above, cutting through the clouds, whisking the pretty colors into a churning iris focused on . . .

Me.

Flakes of snow pepper my hair and face as I try to halt my chattering teeth and slow my shallow, frantic breaths.

This is a slumber-terror I'm going to wake from. As with every slumber-terror, you don't wake until it breaks you enough you jolt free.

That's it . . .

I just have to break. Then I'll be free.

A swirl of action within the imperial box snags my attention, and I see a female move through a crew of parting soldiers, her pale complexion such a stark contrast to the red crown that garnishes a river of ruddy hair.

The Queen . . .

I didn't think she attended these. Guess I'm high profile enough to earn the privilege.

The feeding bell tolls, and my next breath is a punch to the back of my throat, each gong ratcheting through my bones as her Imperial Highness reaches the balustrade. Her gaze falls upon me, and she stills, eyes widening with a flash of . . . something.

Shock?

Disbelief?

Recognition?

I fail to pin it down. Lacking the heartbeats to care, I let my attention drift to the swarm of beasts flocking the sky . . .

Creators.

A massive Moltenmaw lands on the stone awning, yellow and orange plumage making it look like an angry flame come to devour me. I jolt as it tips its long tapered beak and squalls to the sky, scattering some of the smaller beasts that had begun to descend before weaving its head into the bowl.

So close.

Its slit pupils expand, and it snaps its solid beak at the air right before my face. Like a practice bite.

I hold the dragon's scarlet stare—

A blow of air gusts against me.

The Moltenmaw swings its head to the left, trilling at a second beast almost the same monstrous size now clinging to the awning across the other side of the building. It cranks its beak and releases its own chaotic screech, spraying a haze of spittle and smoke.

I turn my head, trying to shield myself from the blast, my stare delving straight into the imperial box.

The Queen is clutching the balustrade with white-knuckled hands, screaming at the soldiers behind her – soldiers that look from her to me, their faces parchment pale.

Her wide, manic eyes lock with mine, and there's something in those mossy eyes that disturbs my internal lake. Tears flow down her cheeks, and she begins shaping words I can't hear . . . though I can *see*.

Can *recognize*.

She's singing to Clode, begging her to gust.

To spin.

The air around me becomes a cyclonic churn of snow and ice almost impossible to glimpse through. The stake I'm tethered to wobbles like it's about to untether from the stage, my hair threatening to pull from its roots, stringy ends reaching for the toiling vortex.

The two Moltenmaws screech and shove from the roof, wings beating against the stir of air that rips vibrant feathers from their underbellies, scattering them into the swirl that herds the creatures back toward the clouds.

Through the ferocious whisk of snow slicing past my face, I lock eyes with the Queen again – her chest racking with sobs, a warm smile filling her cheeks.

Understanding drops into my belly like a heavy meal after a long stint of starvation, and I frown . . .

She's trying to scare the dragons off.

She's . . .

She's *saving* me—

A deep, guttural pulse shakes the air, thumping from every angle.

Thud-ump.

Thud-ump.

Thud-ump.

All the light leaches from the coliseum, eclipsed by a terrible darkness that almost swallows me whole.

Screams erupt from the crowd now scrambling from their seats, running for the exits – some tripping over each other in their panicked haste. The Queen breaks my stare and looks up past the building's crown, eyes bulging. Confusion punches through me, and I do the same.

My heart stops, breath fleeing as the largest Sabersythe I've ever seen drops toward the coliseum with a till of its billowy wings. It extends its mammoth claws and grips hold of the curved awning, settling its weight on the structure that no longer looks strong and sturdy. Not compared to *this* beast – the color of an old puddle of blood, appearing black in the places where scraps of filtered light don't touch its plate-sized scales.

The entire world seems to tremble, cracks weaving through the stone, bits of it breaking away and plummeting around me, crushing some of the Nobles who failed to get away fast enough.

Violent howls of panic and pain rattle the atmosphere.

The dragon extends its wings to an impossible width, splayed membranes drumming from the force of the Queen's cyclonic song, its clawed tips reaching so far I picture them able to bind around the coliseum more than once.

'Shit,' I mutter, wondering why a beast so large would bother with such a tiny speck of nourishment—

Unless . . .

It wants me for its young.

My stomach drops.

Not only am I going to die, but I'm going to do it slowly, and in the *hottest* place in the world.

Gondragh . . . the Sabersythe spawning grounds.

The King was right, I *am* haunted. All the angry spirits of folk I failed to behead lured this beast to my execution and are now having the final laugh.

Good for them.

Shit for me.

All the breath *whooshes* from my lungs as the dragon shoves its head down into the bowl with a boisterous swoop, its boxy face barbed in horns and tusks that curl and slash it into something monstrous. It blows a searing breath upon me, peering at me through inky globes crammed within a nest of embers.

Something blasts up from the depths of my shattering internal lake like a net that swallows my solid heart. Claws gore into the stony flesh, injecting me with a song that wrestles up my throat and sits on my tongue like a ball of icy flame, prying my jaw wide.

It spills in rhythm with my galloping heartbeat, my serrated voice cutting through the din. A language not of the common tongue, but something . . . *different*.

Something I don't understand. And should probably question.

The dragon blinks, head tipping to the side while the foreign tune clumps against my teeth like fractals of frost and snow . . .

I frown.

Is the beast doing more than just *listening* to my words?

Is it . . . *digesting* them?

Instead of me?

Small drops of hope burgeon in my chest, at least until the Sabersythe cranks its cavernous maw and *roars* – a billowing blaze spiked with the stench of fried flesh. My heart lurches as I stare at that bulb of ruddy flame welling at the base of its ribbed throat, waiting for that incinerating blast to surge.

To *burn*.

The beast strikes.

Sharp teeth close around me, casting me in a pitch of darkness that's hot and wet. Splitting, crunching sounds attack me from all around before the stake I'm bound against dislodges from the stage and lurches sideways, taking me with it. Leaving my plunging stomach behind.

Fear finally masticates me into oblivion.

Diary Entry

Elluin Neván

Age: 18 phases
5,000,039 phases After Stone

I slept in the hutch last slumber, cradled by the silken tuft of Slátra's curled tail, dreaming of happy things. High on the aftermath of seeing Haedeon take his first flight upon Allume's back, smile beaming, both of them hollering victory screams to the sky. High on the ride we'd taken together, drenched in moonlight, soaring between jagged mountain peaks, snow gusting in our wake from the giddy swish of our Moonplumes' silky tails – Haedeon more alive than he's ever been.

I slept in the hutch last slumber, dreaming of happy things while my family slept on pallets they'd never rise from. While some sort of ingested poison threaded through their bodies and strangled them to death.

Mah.

Pah.

Haedeon.

I know their final moments were painful. I can see it in their bulging eyes. In the unnatural twist of their mouths that won't smile or sing or whisper my name no matter how hard I hug them or scream at them to try.

This huge hurt . . . It fills every bit of my chest and makes it hard to breathe. Makes me so heavy I don't think I'll ever be able to move again. Nor do I think I want to.

How can someone you love so much be here one moment, gone the next?

Just . . . gone?

Allume, Náthae, and Akkeri keep swooping past the window,

screeching, blowing their flames. Every time they cry out, more scores slit across my heart.

They must know something's wrong.

I don't have it in me to show them what they've lost. Not yet. I'm still hoping I'll open my eyes to find it's all been one big, horrible dream.

Mah and Pah's aides say I need to let them go. That we need to commit their bodies back to the elements. To the Creators who failed to be there for them when they needed them most.

That feels too final.

I don't want this to be our final hug. The final time I look into their eyes and tell them I love them.

I don't want this part of them to disappear, too.

They say I need to wear Mah's diadem now that it's finally loosened from her head, but only after it suckled every last drop of life from her body and made her unrecognizable. Now the Creators won't stop screaming, spitting hissed words I've never heard before. Words I don't know, nor do I have the desire to learn. Not right now.

I think they also want me to don the diadem.

Mah once told me she's never felt closer to death than the moment she settled it on her brow, so perhaps I will finally put it on . . . if only to be exactly that.

Closer.

Raeve

CHAPTER 30

My new cage reeks of fiery death and sulfur – a spongy, billowing blackness that rumbles all around me, noises echoing. Gurgling, grinding sounds, and the drumming beat of . . .

Wings.

Thud-ump.

Thud-ump.

Thud-ump.

I groan, my face cushioned by a pool of gooey wetness that keeps trying to drown me, slopping over my head and slugging through my hair with every dramatic bank and rise and heart-plunging dip.

A serrated blade of fear slices through my chest.

The Sabersythe hasn't cranked its jaw and nudged me between the wall of sabers my knee is rubbing against. Which means I was, unfortunately, correct. There's only one place I'm destined for, if I don't drown to death in its saliva before we make it there . . .

This beast is lugging me all the way to Gondragh to feed me to its spawn.

Fuck.

I have no idea how long we've been airborne. No idea how fast this beast can fly with its mammoth wingspan. For fifteen buckets of bloodstone, you can purchase a risky one-way passage to Gondragh from Gore's public hutch for those stupid enough to attempt to steal a Sabersythe egg, but it's advertised to take seven aurora cycles – if you make it there at all.

There's no way I have the neck strength to last *seven aurora cycles*.

I release a gurgling breath, finding small comfort in the knowledge that I'll probably die before I'm spat out amongst a nest of molten rock beside a clutch of small hungry versions of this thing.

A shiver rakes up my spine as I imagine them scrapping over my remains while they spit primitive flames that lack the punch to end my life cordially. I'm definitely either haunted, cursed, or a bit of both.

Suddenly and without warning, the beast *plummets*.

My guts splat against my spine, the force of the fall dislodging the wooden stake from the beast's maw and hurtling me backward. I come to a jolting halt at the back of its throat, eyes bulging as I peer down the ribbed cavern to the swollen pip of flame roiling at its base, painting me in a heat so fierce I'm surprised my flesh isn't melting off my bones.

Past and present mince together, mulching my insides . . .

Another tiny jolt backward and that fire will swallow me.

It'll finally *get me*.

My heart races hard and fast, and I close my eyes, squeeze them tight. Tap my foot against the stake while singing a spritely song, picturing myself somewhere cold and dark while a patter of snow dusts my upturned face:

There once was a jolly wee drifter
who harbored a thieving knack.
She gathered her gear upon her back
in a pack bearing dragon tack.
She took to the molten bog in search
of a fiery egg, it's said.
She leapt from mound to mound –
what could be found?

BE FOUND!

Into a tinder nest she stole,
finding an egg that was whole. We're told.
But the egg was already bumping . . . bumping . . .
Then she heard a thumping . . . thumping . . .
Flames began dumping . . . dumping . . .
Our jolly wee drifter now jumping . . . jumping . . .

There once was a jolly wee drifter
who dove into the molten bog to escape
the fiery logs of a hatching molten smog,
Then emerged as a velvet trogg!

I'm suddenly ripped from the back of the beast's gaping throat and flung forward, the log relodging itself against the curving wall of incisors with such force I feel my brain bounce against the inside of my skull.

There's no more rhythmic *thud-ump* of beating wings . . .

Did we . . . land?

Gut-clenching anticipation makes the underside of my tongue tingle.

Creators, this is it. I'm about to be spat out in a nest and eaten.

I don't want to be eaten.

A rumbling sound boils all around me, and the dragon loosens its maw, strings of saliva stretching between the piercing peaks of its catastrophic teeth – each far bigger than me. Brightness shafts between the widening gap, the fierce glare cutting into my aching eyes.

I'm still squinting when the beast jostles its head, then threads its tongue beneath the log and flicks me free like a piece of plaque.

My heart lodges into my throat as I soar through the sky, blocking the scream threatening to erupt.

Thankfully.

I refuse to die with a wail on my lips. I will growl, curse, and snarl at these small, thorny, fire-breathing fuckers until they tear out my windpipe.

Gravity lugs me down, and I face-plant into something warm . . . grainy . . . impossible to breathe through. Softer than I imagined a Sabersythe nest would be. Not as flesh-meltingly hot as I expected either, though I'm sure its spawn will pick up the slack.

The stake jerks backward, lobbing the other direction and thumping down again so I'm lying on *it* and not the other way around – like a perfectly presented meal on a stick.

These hatchlings must be huge. And strong. And they must like playing with their food.

Lovely.

My stomach knots, and a retching spill of Sabersythe saliva

gushes up my throat. I tip my head and cough, hack, heave, guts cramping as my body rejects . . . *everything*.

Between each burping, groaning retch, I pry my aching eyes open a little more, taking in the male standing over me with his arms crossed and a scowl on his beautifully tailored face. A male I've become painfully familiar with, now watching me vomit all over the minuscule grains of stone I garner must be sand.

I've heard about it. First impressions count, and unfortunately for this *sand* that's now scratching my eyeballs and plastered all over my face and hair, we're off to a bad start.

I am, however, alive and currently not burning to death or being gnawed on. A realization that turns my retching heaves into laughter that shakes my entire chest, sounding like one of Clode's manic episodes.

'I'm so glad it's you,' I dredge out between bouts of bellyaching chortles. 'Now I finally get the pleasure of killing you.'

'I just saved your life,' the Incognito King drones, brows raised, black cloak billowing in the scorch of wind that throws more fucking sand in my eyes. 'Perhaps a thank you is better fitting than a dagger dragged across my throat?'

'If you'd almost drowned in Sabersythe drool, you'd disagree,' I proclaim, squinting up at his broody face with the confidence of somebody not shackled in iron and tied to a stick. 'How about we switch seats? See how you feel after you've been marinating in its mouth for a bit. I'm certain you'll want to slit my throat, too.'

The King banks his head to the side, his voice a rumbled drawl as he says, 'You'd rather I have broken you from your cell? Scurried you out of Gore and left an unsatisfied Guild of Nobles still frothing for the blood of your rebellious clan? Perhaps you hit your head in Rygun's mouth, because any sense you harbor is being spat out like minced meat.'

Rygun . . .

Guess this is the Burn King – Kaan Vaegor. Fitting, and just my luck to be snatched by the feared, mysterious King and not the one who's apparently still mourning his dead queen. Sounds like that one has a heart. From what I hear, all *this* one has is a very hungry dragon and an affinity with Bulder strong enough to crush a city with a single word.

Lovely. Think I'll beg Rygun to pick me up again and cart me straight to Gondragh. Spit me out in a nest. I'd rather try my shitty luck with a bunch of famished hatchlings.

'I *did* hit my head, thank you very much. I also choked on your dragon's saliva, was almost *swallowed*, and currently reek of dead things that'll probably never wash off. Now, untie me so we can get this over with.'

'You're not afraid of Rygun?'

I look past his hulking form to the beast at his back, perched on his haunches, inky eyes narrowed on me as he blows whiffs of steam from flared nostrils – ignoring the spike of fear that tries to nuzzle into my callus-encrusted heart.

I've often thought folk look like their pets. This is no exception.

Both beast and male are built from slabs of brawn, casting shadows across the rust-colored sand. Their ember eyes penetrate my soul with cutthroat stares that snatch something inside my chest and grip it tight, leaving me with the knowledge that *wiggling* will be to my detriment. That the grip will only tighten until my eyes pop from their sockets and blood bursts from my mouth.

They're both frightening, basking in their prime. Both devastating to look at . . . in entirely different ways.

I clear my throat, tossing a slop of saliva-laden hair off my face with a flick of my head, eyes narrowing on the King looking down at me with an expression as dry as our parched surroundings. 'No beast is tame enough to cradle a squirming meal in their maw if it's not meant for their young, and your beast looks like he *eats*,' I say, nipping another glance at Rygun, wondering how many living things contributed to his hulking size. 'He would've crunched on me if he didn't like me a little bit. Ropes. Now.'

Kaan continues to watch me, unmoving, not breaking a sweat despite the fierce sunshine beating upon the side of his face, cutting across his strong, striking features that threaten to unpick me from my murderous thoughts.

Again.

'Quick, I'm getting burnt.'

'If you kill me, you'll be stuck in the Boltanic Plains without a ride, without access to water, and with that skin, you'll wither like a Moonplume caught in the sun and be dead before aurora rise,' he grinds out, stating the obvious. I can already feel my skin chapping. 'And that's *if* Rygun lets you live after he sees me bleeding out in the sand. He may like you now, but I can assure you, his loyalty lies with me.'

I scowl at the creature, who blows more puffs of smoke from his flared nostrils, a mighty rumble broiling in his chest that makes me picture being caught between his sabers and crunched into a mulch of bone shards and frothy blood.

'Plus, you have no weapons, a festering pin in your shoulder, and if I'm not mistaken, you haven't eaten in almost two rises. How about we wave that white flag again and you suppress the urge to kill me until after you've feasted, bathed, and you're no longer suffering from an infection that's beginning to weave through your blood-stream, hmm?'

He's so full of dragon shit.

'The only *infection* I'm suffering stems directly from your self-indignant presence.'

'*Wrong.*' His upper lip peels back from canines long and honed, making muscles tighten low in my belly.

Strangely.

He crouches, eclipsing the sun as he pulls the collar of my tunic with such force a button pops free.

'*What are you—*'

He stuffs his finger down the hole in my shoulder, the stab of pain like a fiery poker straight through muscle, sinew, bone—

I scream, a grated burst I immediately regret.

Nobody makes me scream. Certainly not *him*.

His finger retreats with a squelch, and I snarl through bared teeth, heaving short, sharp breaths that do nothing to satiate the rage swelling in my chest like a roil of dragonflame.

He sniffs his bloody finger, the next words powering out of him with such savagery they're almost tangible against my pebbling skin. 'I can *smell* it.'

Wet warmth bubbles from the freshly plundered wound while I study all the bits of him I'd like to slash and dash. 'I . . . *really* want to . . . kill you.'

'Perfectly aware,' he mumbles, flicking my blood off his hand. 'But now is not the time.'

I look at the beast at his back – extending his wings, basking in the sun – then cast my gaze farther abroad, our surroundings a stretch of rippled sand, bits of it being picked up and tossed around in copper eddies. The air above it ripples too, distorting the powder-blue horizon littered with dusky moons almost close enough to reach up and cradle in my palms. Silver ribbons of aurora tangle with the rotund tombstones, a pretty embellishment for the otherwise scorched terrain.

There are no hills. No trees. No stones or rocks or boulders.

No signs of life.

There's certainly no *water* . . .

Just me, a king, and a dragon that's half the size of a mountain.

Great.

'A white flag is a white flag,' he says, and I cut my gaze back to him as he rests his elbows on his bent knees and tilts his head to the side. 'May I free you from your shackles and trust that you won't disregard the rules of our . . . engagement?'

'Probably not.'

'At least you're honest,' he mutters, heaving a low, resounding sigh.

He reaches down the side of his boot and retrieves a bronze blade that's shaped like a petal.

Fuck.

Shoulda lied.

I jerk against my ropes, hissing through clenched teeth as he brings it to my breast, slips it beneath the cord, and . . .

Cuts.

That segment of rope unravels, allowing me to pull my first deep breath since I was bound to the Creators-forsaken stake.

My eyes must express my level of shock, because a glint of humor sparks in his ember orbs. 'Did you think I was going to stab you, Prisoner Seventy-Three?'

'Of course. You saw how many skin slabs they slapped on the ground at my trial, and I'd be lying if I said that was all of them. You're obviously all heft and no brain.'

He chuffs, severing another rope. Another.

Another.

I roll off the stake, promptly face-planting in the sand again.

He heaves me to a wobbly stand and brushes me off, then leans close, sniffing. 'You're right, you *do* smell bad.'

'Screw you,' I mutter, and he cocks a brow.

'You wanted to kill me a moment ago. I can't keep up.'

I snort-laugh. 'Don't worry. Few can.'

'Is that a challenge?' he asks, stuffing his blade back down his boot.

'No. But I *will* issue one to let me go.'

'Heartily decline.'

Of course.

I hope he doesn't mind when I *heartily* slit his throat.

He unpins his cloak, pulling it from his shoulders, giving me an up close view of the powerful way his broad, muscular body moves. My cheeks burn as he swathes me in the airy material, secures the pin beneath my chin, then flicks me on the nose. 'Adorable.'

'I'm going to cut out your tongue with that blade in your boot.'

He whips the hood up over my head, shrouding me in shade. 'I'd prefer you use your *teeth*, but beggars can't be choosers.'

I frown, realization dawning slower than an aurora rise. An indignant scoff escapes me, though it quickly snips off when he crouches, grips my left ankle in one hand, clutches the chain in the other, and *yanks*, shoulders bulging. A link pops free and catapults through the air.

Well.

He repeats the process with my other ankle, severing the length of chain he flings to the side.

'You're good at that.' I wave my hands at him, the metal tether draped between them jingling with the erratic motion. 'This next.'

He gives me a dry look and plucks a bit of rope off the ground. Merging my hands together, he slides my shackles farther up my arms, then binds my wrists, knotting it off.

'That's . . . not what I meant.'

He pries the remaining chain free from my manacles, popping more links like they're made of clay. 'I'm aware.'

Damn.

'Underachiever. I see. No judgment here.'

Releasing a hearty rumble, he begins to stand, then throws his weight forward, wrapping his large arms around me. He flops me onto his back and lifts me like a sack of grain.

'*What are you doing?*' I scream, hanging over his shoulder as he lumbers toward . . . *his dragon.*

My heart leaps so far up my throat I almost choke on it.

'Kaan, *no*. I did *not* agree to this!'

His body stiffens, steps slowing, a low, grating sound coming from him. 'Say it again . . .'

'*What?*'

'My *name*, Moonbeam. Say it again.'

If it'll get me out of this saddle ride, I'll scream it to the sky until my voice box ruptures.

'*Kaan. Kaan. Kaan. Kaan. Kaan!* Now put me down. Quick.'

He fills his lungs, his entire chest inflating – like he just took his first breath since he began a deep dive. 'You didn't say please,' he finally says, then kicks forward again.

Wha—

'Please!'

'Too late.'

I'm going to shatter his bones and use them for toothpicks.

He reaches the side of the heaving beast, to where lengths of knotted rope dangle from its saddle, garnished with an array of foot loops – one of which he threads his boot into.

'Put me back in his mouth!'

He heaves us up the ropes one jerking motion at a time, and I watch in wide-eyed horror as the ground drifts farther and farther away, giving up my wriggling struggle when I come to the gut-tumbling realization that I cannot squirm or slaughter my way out of this.

Reaching the drape of patched-together hides that saddles the mammoth beast, Kaan battles the final few loops, then tosses his leg over the saddle and thumps me into his lap.

Straddling him, I look up into his eyes, mouth dropping open, battered breathless by his immense presence. He looks down upon me, his rough exhale pouring over my upturned face – the air between us becoming charged with a static that makes my skin pebble.

Creators.

Drenched in the smell of leather and the heady blend of his intoxicating scent, this tightening feeling low in my belly yearns for something every other part of me is utterly opposed to, and I consider whether it's prudent to ask this male if he'd like to fuck before I slit his throat . . .

Probably shouldn't.

'You have until the count of ten to decide which way you want to sit, at which stage I'll kick Rygun into the sky and you'll be stuck that way,' Kaan grinds out past gritted teeth, my heart plummeting a little more with each condemning word.

I open my mouth, about to spit something sharp when he says, 'One . . . Two . . .'

Shit.

I wiggle, heaving my right leg up, getting a foothold atop his thigh.

'Three . . . Four . . .'

I try wrestling to a stand but lose my balance and flop back down again, face-planting against his chest as he rumbles a deep '*Five*.'

'*Count slower*,' I growl, flattening my hands upon his abdomen, introducing myself to a stack of muscles that feel more like rocks . . .

My mouth dries.

'Six,' he says, his voice gravel against my pebbling skin. 'Seven.'

Definitely need to move.

I kick my foot up again and shove to a wobbly stand.

'Eight . . .'

I turn so I'm facing forward, heart pounding hard and fast as I glance around us, my feet tingling with the sudden realization of how high up we are.

That this is our *starting* point.

'*Nine* . . .'

Creators, slay this male.

I let my feet slide either side of the saddle, landing perfectly between his legs so hard I garner a deep grunt from him that brings me a burst of satisfaction.

'Ten,' I chirp, and he clears his throat, reaching between us to readjust himself – no doubt throbbing with the wrong kind of ache.

I smile.

'Feel free to drop me off at the nearest village. I can find my way from there,' I say, deciding it's a good time to strike now that the male's cock is bruised. Figure I have two ways to relieve myself of his presence: kill him or make myself disposable.

'Like it or not,' he grinds out, gripping my waist and lifting me, settling me into a more comfortable position – so flush against him my cheeks burn for reasons other than the stifling heat. 'You're coming with me to Dhomm.'

My heart pitches.

Dhomm . . .

So few go to The Burn's capital and return.

So fucking few.

Probably because they all end up inside the beast I'm currently seated atop. Either that or the city has jaws and claws and teeth much sharper than that of the one I just marginally escaped.

I open my mouth, about to spit a barbed rebuttal, when Kaan reaches past me and grips the tug-ropes. '*Guthunda*, Rygun. *Guthunda*!'

The beast heaves beneath us, blowing a steaming breath as he pushes up from his crouched position, making me feel as if the entire world is swaying side to side.

'Hold the leather strap,' Kaan rumbles near my ear, sending tingles down the side of my neck and making my breath hitch.

Snarling, I grip the damn strap. 'You know what I hate?'

'Being told what to do?' he answers, quick as a blink.

'Exactly.'

'Well,' he says, giving the strip of leather a yank, like he's testing my grip on the thing. Something I find deeply offensive, seeing as I don't do anything by halves. 'It's a relief to know you possess a drip of self-preservation.'

'I'd rather possess that *blade* down the inside of your boot,' I grouse as the beast folds his wings flush against his body.

I sense the flow of energy building in Rygun's bunched haunches before he leaps into the sky with a booming slash of his wings, gravity thrusting me into Kaan's chest so hard all the breath bursts from my lungs.

We propel *up* . . .

Up . . .

Any words I had are swallowed into the depths of my tumbling guts, my grip tightening on the strap. My head tucks back into the crook of Kaan's throat, his heart a fierce sledge against my spine, powering in unison with the thump of Rygun's wings.

We whisk through a wispy tuft of cloud, then level out, the entire world seeming to regain its balance.

I pull my first breath since we shoved off the sand, blown out with a shaken exhale.

I miss the dragon's mouth. It was wet, it reeked, and there was a high chance of being swallowed, but at least I wasn't clinging to life by a single strap of leather, pressed close to a male who smells too good to flay.

'You okay?' Kaan asks close to my ear, and every cell in my body prickles with awareness.

I dare a peek over Rygun's side, expecting to be severed with fear as I take in the world below, the barren plains stretching far and wide in all directions like a ripple of rusty water. Instead, something *tangible* swells within my chest. Something that makes me want to spread my arms, tip my head, and release a deep belly laugh that's raw and real and so fucking wholesome it makes me want to . . .

Cry.

'*Answer me*, Moonbeam.'

There's an edge to his voice that whips me from my reverie. Reminds me that I'm a prisoner of yet another vicious Vaegor – dancing from one shackle to the next.

The world shreds past beneath us while I mull over Kaan's question . . .

Am I okay?

'Yes,' I whisper, cradling the strange, giddy feeling with a gentleness I didn't realize I possessed, worried it'll break if I squeeze too hard. 'I'm okay.'

Diary Entry

Elluin Neván

Age: 18 phases
5,000,039 phases After Stone

The Creators are so quiet now, their voices vacant echoes barely loud enough to grasp.

I'm not sure why.

Perhaps the Aether Stone is taking so much of me there's little left to listen with.

That's how it feels. Like my soul's being suckled through the diadem's web of tendrils now magnetized to my skull.

I hate it.

How Mah survived this for over a hundred phases, I'll never know, but perhaps I do understand why it took her so long to bring Haedeon into this world.

Then me.

Perhaps I understand why she was crying in the snow so many phases ago, when my world was small and my heart felt full and whole.

I barely have the energy to breathe, let alone eat. Last cycle, I certainly didn't have the energy to help with the preparations for the committal. To stand on my own two feet while Náthae and Akkeri blew plumes of aqua flame on Mah's and Pah's pyres – committing their bodies back to the elements. Instead, I sat in Haedeon's chair and watched them burn, my heart so raw from cycles of clutching them close that I almost wheeled myself into the fire, too.

Then came Haedeon's turn.

Rather than blow flames onto his body, Allume scooped him up, tilled her wings, then tipped her head to the sky and lifted off the ground with my brother clutched against her. She soared unsteadily toward the deep dark where her ancestors rest, then curled into a ball, tucked Haedeon beneath her gammy wing, and solidified before my eyes – giving herself to death rather than live an eternal life without the one we both loved so much.

Or perhaps she just knew how much he hated being alone.

Everyone else went inside to feast in honor of my lost ones while I lay in the snow and sang to Haedeon's moon, tracing the outline of that small, misshapen wing. Until Slátra came, settled beside me, and curled her tail into a fluffy nest I fell asleep within.

I haven't woken from this terror yet.

I'm losing hope that I ever will.

Mah and Pah's aides say I have very few options. That the folk of Arithia won't accept a queen so weakened by the Aether Stone unless I'm bound with someone who can wield more than two elemental songs. And even so, I'm not yet old enough to rule.

There's to be a meeting in Bothaim where my fate will be decided by the Tri-Council. Of course, I can't attend and speak for myself because princesses are to remain mute and veiled in public until their binding ceremony – something Mah and Pah never enforced . . . But they're not here anymore.

It's just me, and I'm certain the sky is falling.

Raeve

CHAPTER 32

The wisps of cloud burn off as we coast closer to the sun, Rygun's head stretched toward it like a hunter stalking his prey. I decide that's not far from the truth, considering the Sabersythe spawning grounds sit directly beneath the gigantic ball of fire.

I tug the hood of Kaan's cloak down, tucking deep into its shady hollow to avoid the sun's harsh rays. Entombed in his molten musk, I find a smooth, grounding sort of comfort that . . . does things to me. Makes me picture sweaty, snarling warriors scorched beneath this overbearing blaze, a blood-heating smell that muddies my mind and makes me want to slap myself.

Hard.

He may have saved me from the coliseum and had my back mended, but he's still a tyrant. Based on the way he stuffed his finger in my wound and made me scream, I'd say he has the same brutal streak as his kin. Probably worse, knowing my luck.

He wants me for something, I just have to work out *what*.

Bottom line: I can't let him take me to Dhomm. Something low in my gut tells me it'll swallow me whole.

The Fíur du Ath believe I'm dead. The Fade King and his Guild of Nobles believe I'm dead – presumably. I just have to find a way to escape Kaan so I'm free to hunt Rekk Zharos, then slice and dice him for murdering Essi and whipping my back to shreds.

Vengeance crackles through my veins, making the tips of my

fingers itch. A shiver rakes up my spine, and I use the sharp of my thumbnail to scratch at the skin on the side of another—

Rygun coasts to the left, tipping me into Kaan's arm, usurping me from my spot between his legs. I clear my throat, shuffling back into place, his powerful body a mountain stacked around me. Like I'm a fall of snow tucked between his crevices.

'There's a sun-veil in the hood,' he rumbles, his accent so thick it's like it was ripped from the Creators' mouths, not tumbled by the tides of time like so many of those who live in Gore.

So unlike mine – forged in dark places where words were spat, hissed, and shrieked. Where the only softness belonged to the tight embrace of somebody who no longer exists.

'If you roll it down, you'll be able to look around while we fly and better anticipate Rygun's motions.'

The cut of his tone implies everything he's not saying. That I won't almost plummet to death every time Rygun banks or hits a current of air that forces him to dodge, dip, or sway.

Tentatively, I loosen my hold on the strap and reach up, frowning as I blindly pinch and pull at the hood's hem, finding buttons I'm able to wedge free and release a roll of fabric that falls before my face.

Huh.

I lift my chin and dare a glance around, the material a fine sheen that casts me in a mask of shade and even allows me to look almost directly at the sun without fear of going blind.

I take in the vast expanse of our surroundings through widening eyes.

The rippling stretch of sand has given way to sun-scorched dirt torn through with a ribbon of bright-blue silk that I suspect is a large body of—

'There's the River Ahgt,' Kaan announces as I marvel at its wide, interloping weaves. The way it sparkles in the light.

It threads as far as the eye can see, stretching for the sun, back toward the darkening sky in the south – something I confirm by peeking beneath Kaan's arm. Tall, lanky trees cling to the rusty, sun-crusted banks, the tips of their numerous branches boasting blades of orange foliage that look sharp enough to slice. I even spot the odd golden worm-like creature slithering through the dirt, leaving a wiggly trail.

I look to the right, a few tendrils of the aurora still glinting over the horizon, though mostly it's now out of sight.

Guess we'll find somewhere to stop for slumber soon.

I'm just looking at the river again, fawning at the way the water appears to flow so freely between the chapped plains, when I notice Kaan put a little pressure on the left tug-rope.

Rygun's right wing begins to rise.

Anticipating the canting motion, I grip the strap and lean into the sway, finding the movement almost . . . *natural*, this time managing to keep my seat between Kaan's powerful thighs.

The sun now beats upon the right side of our bodies, warming my cloak as we're carried toward a lofty band of auburn mountains stretched far and wide, north to south, emerging from the distant haze of dust torn up by the wind.

'Where are we going?'

'There,' Kaan says, pointing toward a distinct dip in the mammoth range, which expands a little more with each *thud-ump* of Rygun's wings.

Scorched earth gives way to lush, russet jungle, the likes of which I've only seen in paintings on shop walls in Gore, the heavily vegetated mountains before us so large and vast they make Rygun feel like a pinprick in comparison.

The only ranges I've ever seen have been sheer and sharp, but these are the opposite. Like somebody ladled scoops of stone, then dumped them on each other in big mounded heaps, clouds beginning to gather around their heads like puffs of gray hair.

Rygun banks, aiming for a crevice, its soaring, jagged edges severed by the rushing river far below.

'Hold on,' Kaan growls, gathering both tug-ropes in one hand, threading the other arm around my waist. My spine stiffens as he tips his body forward, forcing me to do the same – wedging me between himself and the hard-packed saddle, pitching my pulse into a bellowing roar.

'Why are you not steering?'

'Because he knows where to go,' Kaan says upon the left side of my hood.

Huh?

A tightening of his dense body is the only warning I get before we pitch sideways, the motion so rapid my innards corkscrew the opposite direction. They finally manage to catch up, though just as they do, Rygun tips the other way. Back again, and again, and again, skimming past sheer, rust-colored cliffs the river appears to have worn its path between, like it's reaching for something deep. Perhaps the other side.

Perhaps if it gets there, the world will split in two.

Another tip, Kaan's inhale crushing his body so close to mine that I feel him *everywhere*. The way he flexes as he prepares for the next maneuver. The way his arm tightens around my waist, muscles bulging, clinging to me like I'm going to somehow slip free and plunge to my doom.

Rygun battles the gorge with such precision I realize he's done this many times – tucking his wings when the pathway becomes narrow, dropping momentarily before throwing them out again.

We come to a dead end, water pouring down the rounded mountainscape above in wide, gushing steps, gathering in a large basin at its foot. The teal pool glimmers like a gemstone beneath diagonal beams of sun, the northern side cast in a deep pocket of eternal shade.

Rygun swoops almost low enough to drag his tail through the water, scooping skyward – Kaan's tensing body and my firm grip on the strap the only things stopping me from ripping off the saddle, skimming down the length of the beast and plummeting into the pool.

A smattering of water pelts my cloak as we shoot up, then level so fast a yelp slips up my throat. Rygun thrashes his wings, lowering us gently . . . *then all at once*. We thud upon the ground so hard my canine pierces my bottom lip.

The taste of copper fills my mouth.

Kaan pulls back, ripping me with him. He flips the hood, tilting my head until I'm staring straight up at the underside of his scruff-covered chin.

He clicks his tongue, the rough pad of his thumb dragging across my bottom lip with such tenderness every muscle in my body poises for a few rigid moments before my brain has a chance to recalibrate.

Tyrant King.

My *captor.*

Shoved his finger in my wound.

Snarling, I bat his hand away and push to a wobbly stand, the insides of my thighs so chafed and achy I immediately buckle.

He catches me, making a deep rumbling sound as he flips me over with effortless ease and lumps me on his back, drawing a dense *oomph* from my tormented abdomen now folded over his stone-hard shoulder.

Being treated like a sack of grain is getting very old, very quickly.

'Your hips are sharp,' he grumbles, and I bash my fists against his back, knowing there's next to no point.

Doing it anyway.

'I'll show you something *sharp*.'

'Every word that comes out of your mouth is sharp, Moonbeam.' He one-handedly unbuckles one of his saddlebags and tosses it over his other shoulder. 'I'm half dead already, bleeding out at your feet. Can't you see?'

I scoff.

Please.

Kicking up his leg, he eases down Rygun's ropes, my hood flopping so far over my head I can't see anything but Kaan's brown tunic stretched over his tensing back muscles. He leaps the last few feet to the ground, then he's stalking away from the sound of Rygun's deep, resonating breaths, his booted footsteps softened by something I'm unable to see because of this *Creators-damn cloak*.

He moves down some steps, dumps the bag, and flips me off his shoulder. My feet land on the ground, though I have barely a moment to gather myself before the cloak is unpinned from around my throat and whipped away.

'What are you—'

He grips me around the waist, lifts me, and tosses me through the air.

For two tight moments, I picture myself plummeting down a crevice and straight into the den of a velvet trogg, about to be bound in slimy tendrils of excretion pulled from the gaping wounds in its palms. For *two tight moments*, until I dunk into a body of cool, crisp water.

I scramble, kicking and thrashing, certain I'm about to be consumed by some waterborne creature that no doubt likes the taste of fae flesh, until I stretch my legs down and plant them on a . . . pebbled ground.

Oh.

Shoving up, I push my head above the water and gasp for breath, just in time to see a bar of soap spearing at my head. I dodge it, then scramble to scoop it out of the water and throw it back the way it came – the bar thudding against Kaan's chest, leaving a soapy smear on his tunic.

'You smell bad. Soap *fixes* that,' he says, picking it up and tossing it back at me.

Splashing me in the face.

I snatch it, pelting it at his crotch. 'You need it more than I do!'

'I've got my own fucking soap,' he growls, catching it just before it can make obliterating contact with his cock.

Oh.

Failing to muster any more words to wield, I poke my tongue out at him instead. He returns the gesture, and the corner of my mouth threatens to lift.

The King just stuck his tongue out at me.

Muttering beneath his breath, he tosses the soap again and spins, kicks off his boots, then uses one arm to reach down and pull his tunic up over his head.

My heart skips a beat, mouth popping open.

The scars on his arms extend across every visible inch of his broad, muscular back, covered in so many small sable dots of ink that it appears almost entirely blacked out. And upon the dusky expanse . . . a constellation of white stars and beautiful bouldered *moons*. Almost two dozen of them – both near and far. Most the size of an eye, though a few are the size of my fist.

But they're not just any moons.

My breath hitches as I take in the small wonky one I love so much, sketched so exquisitely I can make out its misshapen wing.

Something inside me stills as the backs of my eyes prickle, certain I'm staring out my window back at home, looking upon the glorious sight.

One I never thought I'd see again.

I almost reach out and touch it. Almost trace the dips and peaks of its visible wing, the delicate swoop of its long neck, and the silken tendrils that hang off its jowls and around the back of its head.

I'm so caught up in the trance that it takes me too long to notice the *other* moons upon the darkened expanse – ones I also recognize. Ones that crowd my favorite little moon in real life, like Kaan sat beneath that patch of sky while somebody mimicked the view with an inked etching stick.

Almost perfectly.

There's one moon that's out of place. The biggest – a silver moon I've never seen before, perched just beneath his right shoulder blade beside my little wonky one.

I frown.

That one doesn't exist. Not anymore.

That's the one that *fell.*

'Not to shock you into strangling me with your hair,' he says dryly, injecting the *perfectly viable* thought into my head, 'but as you so dutifully pointed out, I need to bathe.' He tips his head. 'Feel free to evacuate the west side of the plunge pool so I can use the waterfall to rinse myself to your standards.'

'You'll be at it a while,' I say, scooping up my soap and edging to the right, nipping another glance at the little moon on his back. 'Hope you have refreshments in those saddlebags. You're gonna need them.'

'You really do say the sweetest things, Moonbeam.'

'Thanks. I try my hardest.'

'Hate to see you *not* trying,' he drones, yanking at what I realize are his pant fastenings when they're pushed past his muscular ass, revealing his dusky undergarments. 'I don't think my poor heart could handle it. Now, unless you want an eyeful, I suggest turning your attention elsewhere.'

'I'm not giving you my back,' I growl, my words chased by his airy sigh.

'Suit yourself. But if I wanted to hurt you in any way, I had plenty of chances in the cell I *rescued* you from.'

He spins.

My eyes widen, the organ in my chest thumping to a halt.

He's stacked together like boulders, his abdominals so defined they hardly look real. And though all that's impressive, it's far from the reason my lungs have suddenly stopped working.

More pale scars mar almost every inch of skin on the front of him, too – both big and small.

Long and short.

Some are fine-cut lines that are perfectly predictable, like they've come from the slash of a blade. Some are thick and messy, healed in such an angry manner that I can almost *feel* whatever it was that sawed through his flesh. There's distinct stab wounds and other marks that look like something toothy lunged for a bite and carved off curls of flesh.

My gaze narrows on the round, flat, black and silver carving that hangs from a braided strap of leather bound around his neck, absorbing the intricate design – a Sabersythe and a Moonplume locked in an embrace.

I frown, smothering the strange urge to ask if I can take a closer look.

He kicks off his pants, grabs a small satchel from his saddlebag, then begins striding toward the west side of the pool. My gaze drops to his undergarments, material that does *nothing* to hide the outline of his manhood hanging thick and heavy between muscular thighs lashed in the welted remnants of old—

My breath hitches.

I whirl around, my cheeks attacked with a flush of heat.

Burns.

He has *burns.*

I hear him dump something on the shore, the water disturbed by a wave of ripples. I cast a glance over my shoulder to where Kaan is now wading toward a trickling waterfall that feeds into this small plunge pool, cushioned from all angles by fluffy foliage the color of copper.

The squiggly lines of melted flesh look as though a fiery serpent lashed around his thigh. More than once.

The lump in my chest feels heavier than usual.

I wonder how he got them? They look almost . . . strained. Like they happened when he was small, and the scar tissue stretched as he grew—

I shake my head, jerking away from the thought.

Tyrant King.

Dangerous.

Has a very hungry dragon.

Again, I peruse his many *other* scars while he lathers himself with his own bar of soap, frothing the thick black hair under his arms . . .

He's a warrior, and the biggest male I've ever seen in every way, shape and form. He's probably looked death in the eye more times than I have.

Damn.

Getting away might be harder than I originally anticipated. I'm not opposed to challenges, but I prefer them when I'm not already on the back foot – bound and with an iron pin lodged in my fucking shoulder.

He works the bubbles through his beard and hair, stepping under the fall of water to rinse off while I fail to manhandle the bar of soap beneath my heavy tunic so I can wash myself. Hard with my hands tied together in such an awkward position.

'Bet you're wishing you lied about your murderous intentions when I offered to free your hands earlier,' Kaan drones.

'You have no idea,' I mutter, *also* wishing I had a spare change of clothes so I could rip this tunic off my body. Finally be done with this scratchy cell garb.

The soap slips from my hands *just* as I was about to wedge it up beneath the fabric, and I groan, settling instead for scrubbing my face and hair, working the bind from my thick, matted locks for the first time in . . . a while.

So focused on the task of trying to untangle my sodden tendrils, it takes me too long to register the *off* sensation tickling my skin, making it pebble.

I frown. 'This water tingles.'

'Dunk lower,' Kaan says, tipping back, allowing the waterfall to wash over his head again before easing free. With a dash of both hands, he pushes his shoulder-length hair back off his face, next running them through his beard. 'It has healing properties.'

Well, that's handy.

He stalks through the pool, making for the shore, beads of water peppered across his beautiful body. I do as he said, needing my strength if I'm going to make a swift escape when the opportunity strikes, dunking low enough that the ripples he makes fold over my shoulders.

He reaches for the small satchel he left on the bank, loosening the leather drawstring. Cradling the pouch, he digs through the contents until he reveals a pair of prongs, yanking my heart into my throat.

Fuck – I forgot about them.

I dunk so low the water's lapping at my chin as I scurry backward, keeping my narrowed eyes firmly locked on his – that flinty stare now puncturing me like a couple of arrow-heads. 'If you stick those in me, I'm going to knee you in the cock.'

'That's an improvement on being slaughtered,' he says, charging through the water.

'You'll certainly *wish* you were dead,' I warn through clenched teeth, though all my confidence dissolves the moment my back collides with the stone wall that cups this side of the pool.

Shit.

'There is only one thing that could take me back to that dark place,' he mutters, such a hard punch of honesty in his words that my heart stills, some innate part to me pausing.

Listening.

Wondering.

'And I will *never* let that happen again,' he finishes, drawing closer, eyeing me like I'm getting in the way of that very prerogative. Of this strange promise he seems to have made to himself.

'What's that got to do with the pin in my shoulder?'

'*Everything*,' he growls, snatching me by the collar and yanking me into his atmosphere. In the same motion, I thrust my bound hands down, fist his undergarments, and hold him exactly where I need – my knee poised to spear forward and charge straight into his cock. Considering the size of my target, I'm more than confident in my chances to land a crippling blow.

We both freeze, energy prickling between us that has every cell in my body standing on edge.

His gaze softens, and he releases an exhale that's tangible against my skin. 'It's been a long ride. I'm not untying your wrists because I'm in no mood to suture myself together this slumber, and you can't pick that pin from your own shoulder. It's wedged too deep in the bone.'

I open my mouth to speak, but he cuts me off.

'Your lips are already a shade paler than they usually are, your heart pumping at a faster rate. By this time next rise, you'll have a fever, you'll feel lethargic, heavy. By the following rise, you'll be dead.'

I frown.

I can't smell the infection he boasts carnal knowledge of. And unfortunately for both of us, trust is not a word I readily wield.

'So what's it to be? The easy way or the hard? I'd prefer not to brace you against the wall if I can avoid it, but I certainly will if you give me no other choice.'

Holding his fiery gaze, I cling on with clenched fists and stony pride.

It's not that I don't want the pin out. I do. I'd just prefer to do it myself. The moment you let your captors weave their weapons between the cracks in your armor, you're already slit, guts spilling.

Heart weakening.

Dying.

'You can't be strong if you're dead,' he murmurs, quiet enough that even Clode would struggle to catch it.

I sigh, his firm logic a blow to my spine.

I hate the sensation of my vertebrae crumbling as I loosen my hold on his undergarments and turn, resting my cheek against the mossy stone, watching the burbling waterfall pour down the jutting clefts. 'How do you know about the pool's healing properties?' I ask, trying to distract from the fact that I just yielded to this male and accepted his help.

Again.

It chafes.

I'm sure he's collecting these favors owed, preparing to shove them down my throat at his convenience. Like when he needs somebody suffocated from the inside out or disembodied. Or something else I haven't yet considered.

The possibilities are endless.

Kaan clears his throat, easing my collar off my wounded shoulder. 'I spent most of my adolescence and a number of my later phases as a warrior of the Johkull Clan. They have always nested close to these mountains and recently claimed the crater formed by the fallen Sabersythe moon, Orvah.'

I frown, his scars suddenly making a lot more sense . . .

'I used to sneak here during the slumber, soak until I no longer bled, then ride back before the aurora rose.'

'You're the King,' I murmur as he threads his prongs into my wound, making all the nerves beneath my tongue tingle. My next words are wrangled past clenched teeth. '*Why did . . . you spend most of . . . your adolescence in . . . a warrior clan?*'

'Because my pah sent me there when I was nine after it was discovered I could only hear Ignos and Bulder,' he mutters, pincers digging through my flesh while a warm leak of blood dribbles down my shoulder, leaching into the water. 'Said that if I survived their harsh and grueling training methods, I might earn his respect.'

My heart squeezes painfully.

Creators . . .

If that male were still alive, I'd slit him from chin to navel, then braid his fucking entrails while he was still conscious.

'What . . . h-haaappened to . . . him?'

'I cut off his head, then fed him to Rygun.'

The words land like a kick to the ribs, almost winding me.

Deserved, but—

'Wh-why?'

'Because I was mourning someone I loved very much. I discovered my pah had done something unforgivable, and I took her revenge because I thought she no longer could. Now I have regrets.'

'What was . . . h-her name?'

'Elluin,' he murmurs, and *pulls* – yanking the pin free. I open my mouth in a silent scream, certain he just siphoned half my skeleton through the tiny hole.

Fucking. Ouch.

I spin, gaze dropping to the bloody thing pinched between us, Kaan studying the length, perhaps checking to make sure it didn't snap on its way out – that name echoing in my mind with the blaring throbs of pain still rioting through me.

Elluin . . .

I swish some water into my wound while he dunks the pin, running his finger up and down the length.

My gaze narrows on his amulet, absorbing the intricate design – the two dragons embracing in such an intimate way that I wonder if it's a symbol of their lost love.

A wave of . . . *something* sloshes through me.

Sadness?

Envy?

No, of course not.

'What happened to her?'

His eyes flick to mine. 'She died,' he mutters with such finality the words feel like a shiv to the gut.

He storms from the water, pulls on fresh clothes from his pack, and tucks the others away. He stuffs his feet into his boots, grabs his cloak, then charges up the stone stairway toward Rygun – leaving me to marinate in a blossom of blood and unease.

Raeve

CHAPTER 33

Drenched, tingling all over, and with a now-itchy shoulder wound, I follow the path Kaan took back up the red-stone stairway, frowning at the tufts of copper grass that have sprouted in the cracks. Pausing to run my hand over the soft blades.

Seeing foliage this color is . . . strange. In The Fade, anything that manages to sprout from beneath the snow is a vibrant shade of green. And though I like it, I like this better.

Looks sturdy. Harder to kill.

Maybe if I lived here, I'd actually be able to keep some form of vegetation alive.

Something smooth and round catches my eye, my gaze sliding to a dark, ruddy Sabersythe scale half the size of my hand, resting amongst the grass. Probably Rygun's, perhaps flicked from a leg during one of his previous sheds.

It's here. On this step. And I'm entirely unsupervised.

Maybe I'm not so cursed after all?

I grab it, cutting a glance at the top of the stairs while using my fingers to wedge the scale down between my wrists, hiding it from view, my heart thumping so loud I'm half convinced every pair of ears in the jungle can hear it.

I pull a steadying breath, victory bursting through my veins with such potency I almost do a dance.

Nothing to see here.

A rumbling sound has my gaze whipping skyward to the dense clouds gathering overhead.

My brows pull together.

I've heard it rains here where the air is well above freezing, these mountainous areas a lush spawning ground for drenching storms. All I know is the slice of sleet and the soft, gentle fall of snow . . .

The pale clouds bulge and swell, and I shiver despite the sticky heat, an electric current caught in the air I can't seem to shake.

I crest the rise just in time to watch Rygun leap over the edge of the massive grassy plateau, his barbed tail the last thing to disappear – the entire mountain seeming to shift with his displacement.

There's a clamorous roar, the *thud-ump* of his wings, and then he's scooping skyward.

Kaan stalks toward the edge with something round and wiggly caught in his fist, scowling as he watches the beast carve off through the gorge and disappear from sight.

'Where's he going?' I ask, moving closer, weighing my chances of reaching the male in time to shove him off the cliff.

'Like you,' Kaan mutters, waving the shiny black bug at me, 'Rygun is allergic to help.'

I frown, eyeing the creature, its spindly legs waggling, clawlike pincers protruding from what I suppose is its face nipping at the air. 'What's that?'

'A tick I found nudged up under Rygun's armpit where his scales are still hardening from his last shed.' He flicks the thing at his feet, crushing it with the heel of his boot. It *pops*, purple innards splatting across the grass. 'If left unattended, they release a toxin that can turn a dragon rabid.' He cuts me a hard look shaded by thick lashes and the darkening sky. 'There is no cure for an animal intent on torching cities and slaying everything in its path except a swift and merciful death.'

My blood chills.

Torching cities . . .

Slaying everything . . .

Swift and merciful death . . .

None of it stacks up for a king who apparently *condones* that from his beast. At least according to rumors.

Confusion wrestles through me, my gaze dropping to the purple splat on the ground.

'Come.' Kaan hefts a saddlebag over his shoulder, wrapping his arms around another and heading toward a path etched through the dense foliage ahead. 'If you want food, that is,' he tosses back at me. 'Can't escape until you've eaten. You'll pass out and wake up right back where you started.'

He's got a point.

Sighing, I follow his lead, the ropes around my wrists now swollen with moisture. 'I think you accidentally tied this too tight,' I say, looking left to right. Trying to trace the chirping sounds that keep scratching through the air – like somebody's dragging sticks up and down many ribbed, hollow logs.

'I assure you,' he says, kicking a fallen branch off the track like it personally offends him, 'that was no accident.'

'If my hands fall off, so will my iron cuffs, and then I'll call upon Clode to suffocate you in your sleep.'

'Such pretty promises,' he muses, his tone so dry it could wick all the moisture from my body.

The path opens to another plateau, though this one supports a small stone dwelling that looks like it grew straight from the ground. It's got two levels, bearing oddly shaped windows not round or square but somewhere in the middle. The dwelling is crooked one way at the bottom, the other way on the second floor, the roof peaked. The walls are knobbled in places and dipped in others, like little thumbs pressed them into place.

I pause, transfixed by it, a smile catching the corner of my mouth.

It's like a youngling drew the building on a piece of parchment, then peeled it off and whispered life into its walls, giving it the strength and substance to stand.

This south wall boasts a makeshift trellis of crisscrossed branches clothed in a vine heavy with fat purple molliefruit, their scent zesting the warm air. Beneath it are rows of raised garden beds, each bearing a flush of frilly vegetables, some of which appear to have gone to seed . . .

My gaze lifts, sweeping over the structure, unable to shake the feeling that this place isn't attended as much as it once was despite the warm sensation that fills my chest just looking at it.

I wonder what song it sings, picturing it a deep, rumbling, happy one. More content than a regular slab of stone. I wonder if Clode twirls past its rounded edges, sipping from bits of its serenity.

Most of all, I wonder why just looking at it makes the backs of my eyes sting – blisters of emotion I pop faster than Kaan popped that tick.

He moves between the garden beds, drops his laden bags on the ground, then grips a lush tuft of vegetation around the neck. He rips a canit root from the heaving dirt, its squiggly length dusted in rust-colored soil that falls back to the ground as he shakes it off, then thumps it against my chest.

Frowning, I curl my arms around the vegetable, cradling it while he repeats the process, over and over, adding to the growing pile until I can hardly see over the top of it.

'Are you cooking Rygun vegetable soup?' I mutter, wondering how I'm expected to see where I'm walking with my arms packed so full.

'I'm making enough so we don't have to stop at any villages before we reach Dhomm,' he tells me, dumping something that's particularly hard to balance upon the pile and almost undoing me. 'I'd prefer not to be seen with you if I can avoid it.'

Fuck you too, Kaan Vaegor.

'I'm not particularly fond of being seen with *you* either. Not unless I'm toting a pike with your head on the end.'

He lumps another vegetable on the pile without shaking it off, dusting me in soil that peppers my hair and clings to my damp skin.

Maybe he's getting sick of me . . .

Good.

I'll keep agitating him until he drops his guard, then make a move. I quite like my chances of surviving in these mountains, given the abundance of water and fertile vegetation. In fact, I'll probably *thrive* – gather my strength as I move south. I think these mountains finally kneel somewhere near Bhoggith. Perhaps if I charm a full-grown Moltenmaw, I can easily hunt Rekk Zharos. My options are endless now that I'm free.

Well . . .

My thoughts drift to my rope-bound wrists. To the nulling iron cuffs still locked around my arms and ankles.

Almost free.

First, I have to get away from this male and his dragon and these filthy *Creators-damn* vegetables. And this cozy little house with its pretty, idyllic view and a warmth that tells me it's held so much more happiness than I'll ever understand.

'I think we have enough,' Kaan rumbles, placing a flush of herbs atop the pile before I hear him gather his saddlebags, the sound of his heavy boot steps making my ears twitch. 'Follow me.'

Ahh . . .

'How?'

'Tether yourself to the alluring tone of my voice,' he drawls, and I roll my eyes, tentatively following the sound of his steps instead – sliding my bare feet through the fluffy grass at a slow and steady pace in the effort not to trip.

I crash right into the back of him and dust myself in another layer of dirt, suppressing a cough so I don't drop anything. I wait for him to place his bags on the ground, then unlock the door, hearing the squeal of metal hinges before he shifts out of my way.

I'm about to step into the dwelling when he says, 'Wait. I'll unpack you first. Don't want you dragging more dirt across the rug than necessary.'

'Ever heard of a bucket? You just threw me in a pool and tossed a bar of soap at my head. Now I'm more filthy than I was before.'

'No,' he grinds out, relieving me of my pile one bulbous, overgrown root vegetable at a time. 'Before, you smelled like spew, rage, and dead things. Now you smell like soil. This smell calms me.'

'You don't seem particularly calm.'

He removes the final vegetable, transferring it into a large wooden bowl with all the rest of the produce. 'I'm calm.' He cuts me a dark look. 'You've just been lucky enough to avoid witnessing my other temperaments.'

Yet.

The unsaid word slams between us like a gavel.

I hold his pointed stare, clumps of dirt rolling down my cheek and falling from my jawline. I, too, have many temperaments I'd like to test against his *not calm.*

Grunting, he severs our stare-off and strides through the room.

I attempt to brush myself down, flicking more dirt onto the grass while I take in the dwelling's cozy, eclectic interior, rich with a soft assortment of organic furnishings – mostly in Burn tones.

Burnt orange, warm umber, black, bronze . . .

A large kitchen takes up half the floor, bearing three long benches that run the walls in the shape of a giant U. There's a butcher block that breaks the space in two, the right half of the room garnished with two low seaters and a small table – all without any gaps beneath. Like they were grown from the ground, embellished with plump cushions and tufted throws.

A crooked staircase on the right leads to what must be the second level. My gaze cuts to the windows – tawny glass that's distorting to look through. Quirky and organic like the rest of this tiny home.

What really catches my eye are the stone carvings lining the windowsills. Sabersythes in all shapes and sizes, though no bigger than my fist. No two are the same, some bearing more tusks than others, more or less spears adorning the tips of their tails. Almost as if they have little lives and personalities of their own.

'What is this place?' I ask, stuck on the threshold.

'It was Mah's retreat,' Kaan says from his spot before the basin, rinsing a vegetable beneath the gushing tap. He places it in a different bowl, then grabs another, drenching it.

Was . . .

I didn't know his mah had passed. Have never researched The Burn's reigning history beyond the fact that the three Vaegor brothers each rule one of the three kingdoms.

Now I wish I had.

I glance around, failing to shift the heaviness now sitting on my chest, crushing my ability to breathe properly. 'Is there somewhere else I can spend the slumber?'

He pauses what he's doing, turning his head the slightest amount as he says, 'Somewhere else?'

Feels wrong to step into a female's warm, homely dwelling when I've fantasized about killing her son.

'This feels like a family space,' I murmur, taking in the artwork littering the walls. The crooked alcoves and shelves packed full of bits and pieces that can only be precious memorabilia. 'I'm not family.'

Kaan's coarse growl fills the space so abruptly I jolt, stare whipping back to him as he says, 'Get in the dwelling, Prisoner Seventy-Three. Or you'll miss out on this meal.'

His shoulders appear taut and stiff, and there's a tension in the air that makes it hard to inhale. Part of me wants to tell him to choke on the order he just gave me and die a painful death, but then my stomach rumbles loud enough to wake a sleeping dragon.

He raises a brow.

I roll my eyes. Chew my bottom lip. Try to wriggle this situation into a spot that fits comfortably beneath my ribs.

I don't know a lot about northern traditions, but I once read that it's considered rude not to offer something in exchange for shelter. Maybe that's the answer. And maybe I shouldn't shed Kaan's blood while staying here.

That would feel wrong, I think.

'I have nothing to gift in exchange for the time spent under your mah's roof.'

There's a moment of utter stillness before Kaan turns his head a little more – just enough for our eyes to meet. 'Your name will do.'

My name . . .

I open my mouth, shutting it as I reconsider, then shake my head and blurt, 'Raeve.'

All the color drains from his face.

He pulls a breath – slow. Like he's consuming a meal he's been looking forward to for longer than I care to admit. 'Just Raeve?'

Another name sizzles through my soul like a burning scream.

Fire Lark.

Fire Lark.

Fire Lark.

'Just Raeve,' I say, stuffing the other down. Far away.

Gone.

He nods slowly, the ball in his throat rolling. 'Well, thank you for the offering,' he says, followed by a soft, 'Raeve. Please, enter my mah's dwelling.'

He handles my name with such care and precision a shiver rakes up and down my spine – a sensation I try to ignore, stepping over the threshold and into the space that feels much like a warm hug. Perhaps the reason it chafes. Haven't had one of those since—

Clearing my throat, I lift my chin and move toward the butcher block, sitting atop one of the three knobbly stools that each appear to be carved from a single stump of wood, placing my bound hands on the counter.

Kaan resumes his rinsing, time ticking by. He finishes cleaning the vegetables, dices them with a blade I duly note the location of, then piles them into a large pot with water, herbs, and salt. He sets it on the stove and clunks a lid on it.

He opens the small grated door of the stove's plump metal belly, then pulls a weald from his pocket and flicks the hood. I cast my attention elsewhere as he whispers a sizzling word that coaxes a bulb of flame through the opening, kindling the prepacked pile of sticks into a roaring flame.

Closing the metal grate, he turns, his warm gaze roaming the side of my face while I stare out one of the windows to the world beyond. The room darkens by the moment – more and more clouds crowding the sky, sponging most of the light bar the flickers of orange spilling through the grill.

He snaps the lid back on his weald. 'You don't like fire.'

'I don't like males with cocks bigger than their brains.' I slay him with a stare I hope cuts the head off his observation. 'Unfortunately, that eliminates half the population.'

Silence bleeds between us, a victim of my slashing ire.

Arms crossed, he watches me. Unblinking.

Unyielding.

I watch him with the same intensity, sharpening more barbs to sling should he decide to have another pick at the subject. One that is, in fact, none of his fucking business.

He clicks his tongue, then moves around the butcher block.

Perfectly still, I watch from my periphery as he lumbers to the door and retrieves his saddlebags, dumping them on the long, cushioned seater. He brings the smaller one to the bench and flips the satchel open. Rooting through it, he pulls out a scroll of leather he unrolls, bearing a tidy collection of tools. He lifts a small hammer from one section, a tapered nail from another, and jerks his chin at my hands.

Frowning, I ease them toward him, remembering too late that I have a scale tucked between my bound wrists.

My heart leaps so high up my throat I almost choke.

Shit.

I silently beg him not to notice while he settles my hands on a folded piece of cloth, sets the nail against the pin of my right cuff, then taps it.

My brow lifts as the pin slides out, allowing him to loosen the iron cuff and wriggle it free, though he shows no inclination toward the one on my left wrist.

'What about my other one?' I ask, nudging my still-bound hands at him.

He bats them away. 'Oddly enough, I'm in no mood to have my lungs minced.'

'Well, what about my ropes?' I shove my hands at his chest again. 'I had a perfect opportunity to shove you off the cliff earlier, but I didn't.' Only because I got distracted by the tick story, but he doesn't need to know those finer, rather embarrassing details. I'm not usually so bad at . . . slaughtering. 'That should earn my hands some freedom, surely. Small sign of good will?' I say, winking at him.

'Foot,' he drudges out, and I scowl.

'What in the Creators do you think I am? Some sort of filthy animal who goes around putting her muddy feet on cute, oddly shaped butcher blocks?'

He frowns. 'You think it's oddly shaped?'

I shrug. 'Lil bit.'

'Huh,' he says, scanning it, a deep line still etched between his thick brows.

'That only adds to the cuteness, in my humble opinion. Wish I had one just like it.'

Guess I could, except I can't shape stone well to save myself. The flipside of blocking Bulder out so much I can only wield a few roughly-hewn words, and none of them very well.

That, and I don't have a home anymore to put one in.

Ouch.

Kaan clears his throat and slaps his hand on the top. 'Foot, Raeve. Before the soup burns.'

Bossy *and* a bad listener . . .

Definitely needs to die.

'I'm not putting my filthy foot on your mah's butcher block, King Kaan Vaegor. End of story.'

His head cocks to the side. 'And *I'm* not kneeling before you for fear of being kicked in the head hard enough to knock me out cold so you can steal a blade from the drawer, slit my throat, and escape.'

Valid concern, honestly.

'Foot. Unless you want to keep your pretty anklets on?' he goads, and I kick the damn thing up on the stool beside me instead, tarnishing the surface with a smear of dirt.

He glares at me.

I flash him a smile.

'You're very stubborn,' he says, moving around to crouch by the stool.

'So nice of you to say. I sharpen that weapon daily.'

'I can tell,' he mutters, tapping the cuff free of one chafed ankle, then the other. When he's done, he tucks the tools in the pouch and rolls it up, stuffing it in his satchel, a waft of cold air blowing back at me from within the packed hollow.

Frowning, I catch a glimpse of something silver and shimmery inside. Something that stills my heart, my next words cut with a serrated blade. 'What else is in there?'

'None of your business.'

'Your precious moonshard?'

He strikes me with a stare that chills me to the bone, then flips the satchel's flap. Giving me his back, he strides toward the stove, lifts the lid on the pot, and stirs the soup.

I blow a wisp of dried hair from my face, gaze shifting from the satchel to Kaan, back again. Scratching at the skin beside my nail, I tap my foot against the ground, drawing a breath so big I'm certain it'll shift this heaviness from my chest.

It doesn't.

Moonshards come in all different hues, depending on which fallen beast they split from. Most are dug up by those who work in the mines – from long-ago moonfalls from long-forgotten times.

There's only been three documented moonfalls since folk began scribing our history onto scrolls, and each occurred somewhat recently.

An adolescent Sabersythe barely three phases old that fell within the Boltanic Plains. A Moltenmaw large enough to destroy a chunk of the wall, littering the sky with a cloud of dust and sand that could be seen all the way from Gore. And a *Moonplume* . . . the first to fall in more than a million phases. Perhaps longer.

That beast was not small, and it did not fall lightly.

It did not plummet without aftershocks of carnage.

Silver as the aurora ribbons, that beast shone with the light of a thousand moons before gravity lost its grip on the thing. Before it fell, bursting into a litter of shards that blasted a crater within The Shade so large a city could dwell within its dimpled depth.

Or so I'm told.

I've seen shards of it before, in a place where I was remade more times than I could count – those glorious shards one of the only forms of luster that didn't cause me some sort of pain.

I don't know why Kaan's collecting bits of the fallen Moonplume that ripped from the sky more than twenty phases ago, but my gut tells me that's a secret best kept stuffed in his leather satchel.

For that reason alone, I let silence have its crown.

Raeve

CHAPTER 34

Standing over the other side of the butcher block, Kaan splits his focus between stirring the soup and crafting one of Rygun's scales into a blade, chipping off bite-sized crescents with a round-mouthed tool.

It must be handy to have a ready supply of Sabersythe scales, given most dragonscale blades maintain their slitting edge forever. They're also lighter than any metal and hardier when shaped correctly – the very reason I have so many despite their steep price tag in The Fade.

Had.

Fucking *had.*

Rekk probably has most of them now, the fuck. Can't wait to stuff one so far down his throat he chokes on it.

Kaan inspects his makeshift blade from all angles, loose hair hanging around his face. His black tunic is rolled to the elbows exposing slash marks up and down his corded forearms, half the buttons popped, offering peeks of dense chest muscles that tense with each strong clamp of his tool. Another thumbnail-sized crescent of scale chips off and flicks into the large clay bowl he's working over.

I avert my gaze toward the pot of bubbling soup, steam escaping from around the rim of the waggling lid . . .

Killing him is looking harder by the hour.

I thought it strange that he had no beaded soldiers with him. No powerful entourage. At least not for the part of his journey he's sharing with me. Though I'm beginning to wonder if he simply doesn't require the protection. Perhaps so confident in his own abilities that any extra bodies are unwanted baggage he can't be bothered to cart around.

My stare drifts to his satchel . . .

Or perhaps he just wanted to travel incognito because he doesn't want folk to know he's hunting *moonshards*.

Either way, he knows how to shape a damn fine blade.

I flick another glance at it, jealousy rippling through me as he places the pretty weapon in the bowl with the excess shards and sets it all on a back bench, far from my reach.

Clever tyrant king.

He moves toward the stove and lifts the lid on our meal, releasing an eruption of steam he bats away, stirring the fragrant concoction with a wooden spoon before scooping some of the broth to blow on it. He sets the edge against his lips, sipping—

My stomach gurgles, and I cough in an effort to smother the sound, though not before Kaan raises a brow and flicks me a look I ignore.

Wish I wasn't so hungry. Feels wrong accepting a meal from somebody I eventually intend to kill. And behead. Just to be safe.

He ladles two clay bowls full of the soup, hearty curls of steam wafting off the top of each lumpy pour. My gut makes another one of those gurgling sounds, my cheeks burning as he settles a copper spoon in the bowl and slides the meal in my direction. He places another on my right, lowers himself onto the stool beside me, and begins spooning the meal into his mouth.

My gaze bounces between his profile . . . my bowl . . . my spoon . . . my rope-bound wrists . . .

Right.

I maneuver the spoon's handle into my incompetent grip, discovering that if I tip my arms to the right, I can actually scoop the soup at an angle that *should* be accessible to my mouth.

Should.

I lift a small serving from the bowl, leaning forward—

My fingers fumble, sloshing it everywhere.

Teeth gritted, I try again, this time bringing it halfway to my wide-open mouth, tongue lolling, before the utensil wobbles from my grip, splatting my arms and chest with soup.

My spoon clatters to the ground, along with the remaining drabs of my patience.

I make to move off the stool, but Kaan grips my shoulder, as if to keep me in place. 'I'll get—'

I whip my head around and sink my teeth into his forearm so fast I barely register it happening until it's done. Until the taste of his blood is in my mouth and he has me on my feet, backed against a wall with his thigh shoved between mine. With my hands pinned above my head and his hand clutched around my jaw.

Our bodies are flush, breaths sawing through our bared teeth.

Our noses and foreheads collide as the remaining light is wicked from the room, the only source now spilling from the stove's kindled belly – making Kaan look like an angry shadow poured over me, his eyes crackling embers glinting in the gloom.

'You want to play rough, Moonbeam? We can play rough. But only after you eat.'

'Is that a command, *Sire?*'

I swear the ruddy specks in his eyes flare, his body a strong, resonant force pressed against me. Too hot.

Not hot enough.

'There's a difference between being *cared for* and being commanded. Know it.'

I chuff a humorless laugh, notching my chin forward. 'You give me a bowl of soup and expect me to eat it with bound hands? Your perception of *caring* is warped.'

Can't believe I'm thinking this, but I miss my shackles. Or more to the point, the chain draped between them. At least I could do things, like stretch. And scratch. My wrists are bound so close together that wiping my ass is going to be an experience when I finally make it to the privy.

'Try being open to accepting *aid*, Raeve. You'd be amazed at how the grain no longer chafes. A simple request for my help doesn't make you weak. It makes you *real*.'

I open my mouth to tell him I don't want the help of a tyrant Vaegor King, when my stomach gurgles again, casting its unwanted vote.

Something loud and rancorous unleashes upon the roof, a thundering assault unlike anything I've ever heard.

My heart leaps into my throat, gaze ripping from Kaan's and darting around the room, searching for cracks in the walls since the building is obviously crumbling.

Did a moon fall?

Shouldn't we be running? Hiding under the table?

Why the fuck is he so calm?

'It's just a heavy rainstorm,' he rumbles, his voice a tender stroke to my hackled heart.

My body loosens.

Oh.

'It's very . . . loud,' I say, still hunting the walls for cracks. 'Are you certain it's not a moonfall?'

'Positive. You are safe.'

I meet his cinder stare. 'Debatable.'

'You are *safe*.'

'Because you need me for something – they always do. What is it? Might as well get it out in the open now, don't you think? Expectations really *pinch* when they stab you in the back.'

He frowns. 'All I want from you is for you to eat your fucking soup. And maybe for us to get through this slumber without any more bloodshed – a concept I'm aware you struggle with.'

My eyes narrow, seeking the fissures in his stare, finding only stone-hard conviction. 'You're a good liar, I'll give you that.'

A growl boils in his chest, and he releases my wrists, stepping back. For some strange reason, it feels almost like ripping a seam open, my breath shuddering free.

He turns on his heel, picks up my spoon, rinses it under the tap, then sets it back in my bowl. Settling on his stool, he continues to eat in stoic silence, such a contrast to the battering of rain on the roof.

The air grows tighter by the second.

My gaze nips to the bite wound on his arm, blood dripping onto the ground. Still slicked across my lips.

I cringe.

I bled him in his mah's home. *Dammit.* And dropped soup everywhere.

Turns out, I'm a shit houseguest.

Another grumbling belly gurgle, and I think of my beautiful, fallen Essi. She often baked for us. Loved experimenting with all the different foods I'd bring home from the markets.

I always thanked her, appreciating her efforts.

I'm almost certain I didn't thank Kaan when he slid me the meal. Just began wrangling my spoon after watching him prepare it from my somewhat-relaxed perch on the stool.

Wow.

I'm a really, really shit houseguest.

No matter how much I dislike the male and everything he stands for, I should at least show my gratitude for the fragrant meal he cooked for us both. And persevere with trying to get some into my mouth.

With a deep sigh, I push off the wall and settle back on my stool, still wearing his blood on my face as I say, 'Sorry for being disrespectful. And thank you for this meal. I appreciate the effort you put into it.'

He pauses, spoon midscoop. 'It's my pleasure, Raeve.'

I nod, toss my hair over my shoulder with a swish of my head, flick him a shy glance, then lean forward, pucker my lips, and shove my face in the bowl – sucking a long slurp of broth.

A moan slips out.

This.

Is.

Delicious.

Not too rich or salty. Subtle notes of whatever herbs he threw in here. There's even the hint of something citrus. Don't know what, but I like it.

I'm just swallowing my second glorious mouthful when Kaan erupts, his deep, gravelly laugh loud enough to battle the clamorous sky.

My cheeks heat, and I almost snap at him again, but then his laughter weaves a thick ribbon beneath my ribs that flutters up my throat and bursts from my mouth so fast it also spurts from my nose with a spray of soup that coats the butcher block.

My nostrils burn like I just snorted flames, but the laughter keeps coming, my entire body shaking from the force of it.

I've never laughed like this before. Not truly. I didn't know it could feel this . . .

Good.

Why does it feel so good?

Tears streak my cheeks, soup drips from my nose and chin, my guts ache as my sound continues to spill . . .

And spill . . .

It takes me a while to realize the male next to me has gone quiet.

My laughter tapers, face muscles loosening. I unscrunch my eyes, looking sidelong at Kaan.

My heart stills.

He's watching me with a haunting intensity that threatens to peel off one of the many calluses crusting my heart. A look that presses against my chest. My soul.

The sort of look that buckles spines, heartstrings, and knees in the same swift strike.

The air between us hollows, hungry for something I certainly don't have the substance to fill, and I realize I might've been wrong about him. That he doesn't want me for my affinity with Clode or Bulder or the ease with which I slay. That he wants something much, much worse . . .

Me.

Just me.

'Don't do that,' I bite out.

'Do what?'

'Pretend we're cozy. We're not. I don't know you, you don't know me. I'm plotting your death as we speak.'

A tick in his jaw pulses, something flashing in his eyes that chills me to the bone. 'Of course.'

I clear my throat, break from his gaze, and sink my stare into my soup. Another beat of chest-cracking silence before he reaches for a cloth on the bench and uses it to wipe my face.

I don't stop him.

I don't stop him from grabbing my spoon and feeding me like a youngling. I don't stop him from ladling another serving he also feeds me before offering me a mug of water freshly poured from the tap.

I don't stop him from wiping the soup from my shirt once we're done. From leading me up the crooked staircase, through a skewed wooden door that's high on one side, short on the other, and into a cozy sleep space with a single lopsided window and a large pallet topped with enough cushions and covers to drown in.

A sleep space that smells like *him*.

'The only exit is down the stairs and out the back door. That's if you can creep past me quietly enough, since I'll be sleeping on the seater. If you succeed, I'll enjoy hunting you down, so be my fucking guest.'

'Privy?'

'Through there.' He points to another much smaller, more oddly shaped door as a burst of lightning ignites his beautiful, barbaric face in frightening undertones.

I lift my bound hands. 'How am I supposed to—'

'I'm sure you'll work it out,' he mutters, then closes the door so hard I jump.

Raeve

CHAPTER 35

I nudge at the scale pressed between my bound wrists until it flops onto my lap, then pinch it between my knees and get to work. Gaze homed on the door, I rub my rope across the tapered edge, severing the twirls of twine in fraying increments.

It cuts through much faster than I was anticipating, my hand slipping as the rope gives way—

The scale slices into my arm, and I suck a sharp breath, clamping my jaw against the slit of pain.

Shit – fuck – dragon balls!

Dammit, Raeve . . .

I use my teeth to unravel my binds before pressing a hand on the cut, blood leaching through the gaps between my fingers and dribbling onto the pallet.

I sigh.

Guess I broke the *no more bloodshed this slumber* rule.

Definitely time to kick myself out.

I rush into the washroom and crank the copper faucet barely visible in the dull light, dragging my arm beneath the gushing flow and doing what I can to clean off the blood. Tearing a strip from my shirt, I bind the wound, using my teeth to tie off the knot before smiling at my handiwork – victory popping beneath my ribs in giddy bursts.

I might've wounded myself, but I'm free.

Free!

Fuck yes. Now I just have to get away.

I use the privy, lavishing in the freedom of being able to wipe my ass comfortably. Tucking my hair behind my ears, I move back into the sleep space, nipping another glance at the still-closed door.

Drawn to the drawers at the end of the pallet, I pry the first open and rummage for something more comfortable than the scratchy garments I thought I'd die in, finding a black shirt that's butter-soft. I pull out some equally soft pants that are short enough they likely cut off at Kaan's knees.

They'll probably still swallow me.

Shrugging, I tug them on anyway, discovering they have a drawstring that allows me to cinch them at my waist.

I keep my hair tucked beneath the oversized shirt now hanging off my shoulder as I creep back onto the pallet. Pulling the blankets up around myself despite the humid heat, I stash the scale and severed binds beneath the covers while I watch the door.

Giving Kaan time to fall asleep, I wait – entombed in the smell of cream and molten stone.

The storm howls, dumping rain upon the roof, pelting against the little window. The space dark and gloomy as I bide my time, picking at the skin down the side of my nails, picturing all the gory things I'm going to do to the male who killed Essi and slashed my back to shreds.

I'm coming for you, Rekk Zharos . . .

You fuck.

But first, I have to escape a king.

I edge the door open, my breaths soft and steady.

Mind calm – sunken into that quiet place I go when I have a job to do.

With the scale clutched in my right hand, I make for the stairs, timing my movements to the ferocious beat of the storm lashing against the dwelling, dragging my left hand down the wall to steady myself. I descend toward the ground floor, movements soft and slow, four steps from the bottom when a bolt of lightning ignites the room.

Ignites *him*.

My cheeks heat, thunder rumbling as I consume the vision of Kaan Vaegor stretched across the long seater.

Naked.

More lightning, and I see the fluffy throw draped across his groin, covering *that* part of his body but leaving his scars and his fierce, formidable stature on bold display.

Creators.

He's so big his legs hang off the end, feet flat on the ground, legs partially spread.

Another thump of thunder, and I swallow thickly, gaze dragging up to where he has a pillow beneath his head that's tipped to the side, both arms tucked beneath it . . .

I shake my head, admiring.

I had a lot of time to think while I was sitting in his sleep space, bound in his scent, biding moments until I was certain he'd be asleep. Realized he's shown me kindness when I've shown him none. Certainly done nothing to deserve *his*.

And the way he looked at me while I laughed . . .

I release a slow, silent breath, taking in the relaxed slant of his face. Peaceful.

Serene.

My fingers itch, but not with the need to kill. Not the feeling I get when I think about the male I'm about to hunt.

They itch with the need to *touch*. To trace the sturdy lines of his eyebrows, then his nose – ever so slightly crooked. As though somebody punched him one time and he didn't bother to set it completely straight.

The urge to tangle with his thick beard and tug at the strands, then drag across the broad expanse of his shoulders, smoothing across his bouldered chest. To trace the dips between his abdominals, down the slick black trail of hair that leads beneath that blanket—

My cheeks flush with another spread of heat.

Of all the things I've seen in my life, he's one of the most magnificent. I can admit that to myself now that we're parting.

Another reason why I need to go.

Perhaps he's a good male. A good, honorable king. I don't have the heart to peel back the layers and find out. I'm broken in ways he'll never understand, condemned to a lonely existence I've found peace with.

So no, I don't want to kill him. Not anymore.

I simply want to be free of him.

I spear my gaze at the door and ease off the final few steps, tiptoeing past the seater. My hand is just settling around the doorknob when my mind tills up the haunting echo of his previous words. Ones I'd barely absorbed when he'd said them, because I was so caught up on other things.

The only exit is down the stairs and out the back door. That's if you can creep past me quietly enough, since I'll be sleeping on the seater. If you succeed, I'll enjoy hunting you down, so be my fucking guest.

A shiver rakes through me as I digest the conviction in his tone, crippled by the distinct impression that not even a *moonfall* would prevent him from finding me . . .

Gaze cast over my shoulder, my heart misses a beat.

Another.

Shit. I *have* to kill him. If I don't, I'll never be rid of him. He'll haunt me. *Truly* haunt me – just as he promised.

This weird feeling gouges at my throat. Like a claw reaching up through layers of flesh, muscle, and sinew, fisting my trachea, tightening its grip.

Choking me.

I realize with a start that it's *hesitation.*

Again.

I don't know what to do with this. I've never dealt with it before this male came along. I kill. That's what I do. Somebody needs taking out, I fucking do it.

This decision should be easy. He's in the way. Get him out of the way.

Why is it not easy?

I squeeze my eyes shut, pitching myself back to the moment I discovered he's one of the three Vaegor kings. To the rage I felt, bolstered by the knowledge of all the terrible things he's rumored to have done.

Monstrous things. Heinous things that are unforgivable.

The world will be a better place with one less tyrannical Vaegor brother.

Yes. That's it.

That's the hook.

I snap my mouth around the thought's sharp point as I slip

inside myself, stripping back the sprouting emotions I feel for Kaan until I'm left with a bare skeleton I leave lying on my internal shore – bundling all my budding curiosity and tentative appreciation and tying it to a stone. With stout determination, I creep across my lake, shards of silver light spearing up from beneath the ice like something bright and bold is soaring through the water.

Following me.

I shiver, plonk the stone down a carved hole and into the dark expanse, then brush off my hands.

There.

Good riddance.

The huge, luminous presence darts forward in a whip of motion, appearing to chase the stone like a predator hunting its prey, its glow fading into the depths with a billowing swish that sends icy water gushing up the hole and sloshing around my feet.

Breath caught in my lungs, I blink back to the now, heart pounding hard and fast . . .

It's never chased something I've discarded before. At least not that I've noticed.

A shiver scurries up my spine, and I shake my head, centering myself, ignoring whatever just happened.

Do the job.

Get out.

Hunt Rekk Zharos.

Cradling a stark indifference toward my sleeping target, I creep closer to the seater, Rygun's scale clutched in my steady hand. In one swift motion, I straddle the King, scoring the sharp weapon to his throat—

Kaan's eyes pop open, glowing like pots of crackling embers as my internal lake *erupts* – the complex bundle of discarded emotions spat back at me, splatting against my heart where it sinks between the gaps, leaching toward my fleshy core.

I gasp, speared through by the fire in Kaan's eyes. By the pierce of *feeling* that just infected me like a disease – ten times more potent than it was when I threw it away.

A whimper wrangles free as I repress the urge to delve my hand between my ribs, goring a hole in my chest cavity. To scratch the thumping organ like it's an insect bite, or maybe wedge my fingers deep and scoop out this . . . *sensation.*

Heavy. Swollen.

Alive.

His nostrils flare, gaze flicking to my injured arm, back to my eyes while breaths saw in and out of me. While I poke at my crippled resolve, trying to work out why my desire to kill him just melted into a puddle of desperation to be closer.

Not just *closer* . . .

As close as we can be.

This strangest need to kiss him surges through my veins. For us to clash against each other until we fuse in intangible ways. To taste him and feel him move inside me . . .

A luscious, hungry shudder crawls up my spine.

Another flash of lightning ignites the fierceness in his stare, and his chest deflates, like all the breath just shoved from his lungs.

Slower than a rising aurora, he pulls his arms from beneath the pillow, one strong hand settling on my hip. Gripping hard. The other settles around the side of my face, cupping it in a way that feels so jarringly familiar. So *right* it makes me want to crack my aching heart into shards because it's obviously confused.

'I see you, Raeve . . .'

My breath hitches, the scale still indenting Kaan's throat. 'I don't . . . I don't know what—'

'*You*,' he growls, tightening his hand around the side of my face with a tender jerk, eyes lit with a soul-crushing blaze. 'I fucking *see* you.'

His voice is a jagged wound – raw and grisly. Painful in a way that makes that sensation in my chest ache with a deeper, more destructive throb I'm so *desperate* to dislodge. Or at the very least, distract myself from.

It's too real. Too piercing.

And this . . .

Why does this feel so right?

The room ignites again, illuminating him in devastating detail. Strong, proud body slashed in too many scars to count, hair mussed, lips a perfect pillowy shape I imagine pressed against mine, moving with mine, *claiming* mine—

Fuck.

'What do you need, Moonbeam?'

To scratch this primal itch in the hopes it'll assuage the emotional blade now lodged in my chest.

With fumbled motions, I reach for my waistband, untethering the bind and loosening the cinched material before grabbing his hand that's sitting on my hip and urging it down the front of me.

A rumbling sound spawns in his chest, vibrating up my spread legs where it meets my tender core now pulsing with a hungry beat. A sensation I intend to fall into – headfirst with a blindfold on.

'You want me to touch you?'

The words are a flint scored down my spine.

Lower.

My muscles loosen, making my flesh heat as I nod – the motion fast and desperate. 'Yes,' I plead, grinding my hips, trying to rock myself against his fingers that aren't quite where I want them. '*Please.*'

He growls, his thick manhood swelling beneath my ass, growing impossibly hard. Another grind of my hips ignites every nerve in that sensitive spot between my legs, and I groan, this deep, heady sound that's like a wanton fracture in the room.

Kaan pushes his hand closer toward my aching center, making my flesh pebble, my nipples pinching into hard, sensitive peaks from the coarse feel of his skin against my needy softness.

I throb with anticipation, knowing he's close.

So close.

Another hitch of my breath as his finger sweeps across my wet flesh, the tender tease zapping me with a ravenous bolt of pleasure.

'Cut me if you want me to stop,' he rasps, his thumb sliding across my cheekbone. 'I'll *gladly* bleed beneath you, so don't be shy.'

'*Touch me*,' I groan, my voice shrill with a neediness I don't recognize.

Not in myself.

His fingers skim my stretched expanse, feathering around my flushed, swollen slit.

My mind muddies – *empties* – another deep, heady groan pouring up my throat.

He makes a gravelly sound as he traces a path around me, slow, steady circles that wind me up and unravel me in the same luscious motion. His other hand drops from my face and weaves beneath my stolen shirt, palming my aching breast, tweaking my nipple, sending zings of electric pleasure through all my fine ligaments.

Fuck.

I let my head tip back, bottom lip tucked between my teeth.

Surrender to his ministrations.

'*More*,' I groan, and he pinches the sensitive peak. I gasp, my attention tuned to my breasts, then struck with a bolt of shock when he sinks two fingers into me.

I moan to the slashing sky as he pumps them deep, then stills.

Holds them there.

Another flick of my nipple, another zing of pleasure that pours into my throbbing core. 'Take what you want, Moonbeam.'

The words till something inside me, my mind drifting somewhere bright and breezy.

A dream, maybe.

Somewhere that smells like salt, spices, and sweet, succulent flowers. A place where the only thing that matters is . . . *this*.

Us.

I snap from the luminous tendril of thought woven up from beneath my icy lake.

Desperate to scrub that beautiful, impossible feeling of *rightness* from my chest, I chase the pulse of rapture between my spread thighs. A heady, primal distraction that I can make sense of.

'I need you,' I groan, tossing the scale aside, hearing it clatter across the ground. 'Now.'

'You fucking *have* me.'

'No, I need *you*,' I growl, trying to tip us sideways.

Seeming to catch on, he makes this throaty sound, and in one swift, powerful motion, he flips us, making my breath catch.

He shoves my pants down and tosses them aside, my legs now splayed beneath him. Flushed core bared, aching and ready to take his thick, hard length now resting against the inside of my naked thigh.

I'm just about to reach down and grab him – to guide him toward my throbbing entrance – when I catch him looking at me with the intensity of a chapped wasteland desperate for even a drop of rain. The sort of look that *consumes*. That clutches heartstrings and braids them together for eternity . . . forever bonded.

Can't he see that my heartstrings are stubby and frayed?

He grips my leg with one of his calloused hands, right up by my knee. Widening me. The other comes up and cups the side of my face with captivating tenderness, his thumb dragging back and forth across my parted lips.

My pulse slows . . .

Stills.

He's so beautiful, poured over me like molten lava. So, so fucking beautiful that it's tempting to let him fall into the illusion I think he's woven over me.

Over *us*.

To take him into my body and give him a little bit of what he's so obviously seeking in my eyes.

'Are you sure you want this, Moonbeam?'

The deep, gravelly words are coarse and sharp . . . yet somehow not. Somehow, they're the softest words I've ever heard.

Cut me if you want me to stop . . .

Take what you want . . .

Are you sure you want this, Moonbeam?

Creators.

He's definitely not the monster I thought he was.

'Certain,' I rasp, tilting my hips to offer him better access. 'I want you *in* me, Kaan Vaegor.'

He groans, lids lowering as he looks at me with another tender crush of intensity that overrides that ache between my legs. Makes the one in my chest flare with renewed vigor, and I'm suddenly sure a hand just plunged down my throat, punched through the side of my esophagus, and gripped my stony heart.

He fists himself, lining up with me as I say, 'But first you have to stop looking at me like it means something.'

He flinches, as if struck with the metal tip of a barbed whip. 'You want a *meaningless* release?'

I nod, jerking my hips.

'Right.' Another flash of lightning, and I see his eyes have shuttered black. 'Well . . . you won't find that here, Prisoner Seventy-Three.'

His voice is monotone.

Detached.

Severed from . . . whatever *this* is.

He eases back onto his knees, dropping my leg, leaving me open and exposed – his thick manhood standing strong and proud and ready, webbed in veins, a pearly bead of precum leaking from the tip.

He pushes his hair back from his face, lips pinched into a tight line while confusion wrestles beneath my ribs.

Is he . . . *joking*?

He's ready, wanting. I'm here, asking for it. Why not just get it out of our systems so we can move on?

I blink, gaze lifting to his eyes, mine wide. 'What are you—'

'Get up and go back to your sleep space. Get some rest. We have a long, nonstop ride when the storm clears.'

There's such a chill in his tone that for a moment, I don't breathe. Don't move.

I open my mouth—

'*Get. The. Fuck. Up.*'

His words rumble through the room with such violence I'm certain I'm going to be crushed beneath them if I don't move.

Fast.

I scramble off the seater and snatch my discarded pants, clutching them close to my chest as I edge back toward the stairs, maintaining our eye contact while my cheeks flame with a shame I don't understand.

Don't *want* to understand.

With a shake of my head, I spin and sprint up the staircase to the drum of the thunderous storm.

Raeve

CHAPTER 36

I slam the door behind myself and lean against it, lungs heaving, heart galloping. Still flushed and *wanting* between my trembling legs.

What the flying fuck was that?

I toss my hair back off my face, groaning at the smell of *him* now staining my fingertips. Like he seeped through my pores and melded with me, creating an aroma that's so carnally *us*.

And it smells good. So damn good that part of me wants to dash back down those stairs right now and apologize. Let him fuck me like it means something. Let him beneath my skin.

The *stupid* part.

A flash of lightning ignites the room, and my stare narrows on the illuminated window being lashed at by the storm, head tipping to the side as a roll of thunder rattles the pane . . .

I'm small enough to fit through that.

Just.

Actually . . . this side of the dwelling supports a trellis perfectly convenient for me to use as a ladder!

Thank you, little crooked home.

I smile and shove off the door, crossing the room as I step into my short pants and cinch them at the waist, tucking my shirt in so there's less of me to catch a snag. I may not be able to bring myself to kill Kaan Vaegor, but I still need to get away.

Far, far away, before any more damage is done.

I climb onto the raised pallet, then onto the side table. Reaching the window, I glance over my shoulder at the door before I pry open the latch and push the pane wide. The storm is drumming the roof like a thousand flat hands – a booming diversion for what little sound manages to squeeze from the window's hinges.

Threading my arm through the hole, I grip the trellis and haul myself out into the deluge, feet tingling with a flush of paranoia. I don't have time to dwell on the strange sensation of heavy raindrops pelting my skin as I wiggle free of the sleep space.

Get out – get out – get out—

I grip the knobbly trellis, trying to avoid the lush, fruit-laden foliage as I clamber down, drenched by the time I drop onto the sodden soil that squelches between my toes. A small zap of victory pulses through my veins, and I sprint for the jungle path, my heart pounding in rhythm with the angry storm.

I'm out. I'm free.

Now to put some distance between us.

My mind flashes to a different time, a different place. When I was escaping somewhere vile during a storm of a different variety, darting through eddies of snow that stuck to my hair and threatened to crust my lashes shut.

Hard to ignore the stark difference. Then, I was running from a place of pain, starvation, and suffering. Now, I'm running from a place of pleasure, wholesome meals, and deep belly laughs.

Don't think about it. This is right.

This is right.

All that good stuff is not for you.

I repeat it to myself with every splashing step through puddles and over fallen logs, the jungle's dense foliage seeming to swallow me as I trace the path we took to get here while the storm shrieks and shudders. Slowing, I emerge before the clearing Rygun landed upon earlier, relieved to see the beast hasn't returned.

Sheets of rain fall around me, and I cast my gaze right, taking in the steep cliff that fringes the plateau.

If I run that way, there are only so many places I can go. And with a warrior king intent on hunting me – likely familiar with these mountains – I'll be caught in no time.

But if I climb *down* . . .

I can follow the river all the way to the wall. I'll have a constant supply of drinking water, a delightful view of the River Ahgt, shade coverage from the shoreline trees.

What more could I want?

I dash to the left, taking a moment to stare down the cliff and map my chosen pathway.

'Creators,' I mutter.

The cliff is a vertical drop that levels onto another plateau, cradling a churning basin fed into from the now-heaving waterfall. The pool spills over the edge, down another cliff, where it feeds into a second basin far below – the one I saw when we first flew in. Though it looks nothing like it did then.

Now it's a swollen catchment gushing into the gorge with hazardous force.

I wince.

This is not ideal, but it's this or the cliff behind me and a probable dead end.

The rainfall tapers a little, a single shaft of light splitting through the bulbous clouds above . . .

I shrug, taking it as a sign.

Turning, I push my iron cuff farther up my arm so it won't get in the way, cutting a glance toward the jungle walkway before I fold into a crouch. I ease my feet over the edge, find a foothold in the stone, and drop – swallowing the heart-plummeting sensation that always ensues the moment I'm hanging off the edge of something treacherous.

The stone is slippery but sturdy enough that I'm able to climb in semiconfident increments, making my movements swift and methodical.

Nearing the bottom of the cliff, I leap the final few feet, landing upon the grassy plateau. I run toward the edge of the pool to see angry water lapping at the sides, though it's still a few feet off from challenging the bank's generous easements.

Should be fine.

For a moment, I watch the heaving waterfall shoveling over the edge with such roaring might it's hard not to marvel . . .

Rayne's an exquisite Creator. Such a dominant force.

I turn, just easing over the cliff's edge when a flutter of movement snatches my gaze. A flock of tawny birds ripping from the jungle, squawking as they shoot skyward.

My heart leaps into my throat.

Birds don't fly during storms, everybody knows that. They hunker down. Hide.

Did something spook them?

A deep seed of knowing sinks into my chest, riddling me with blazing roots of adrenaline.

He's coming.

Shit.

I begin to clamber down the cliff, not bothering to check my hand placements. Tearing up my fingers and feet with the frenzy of my frazzled descent.

If Kaan finds me, there's no way I'm getting free again. He won't take his Creators-damn eyes off me.

A terrible creaking sound fissures the air, and I look up in time to see an explosion of water – a gushing torrent of froth and stones and torn-out trees pouring toward me so fast I barely have time to pull a breath before I'm struck, ripped from the wall.

Something hard collides with my head—

Darkness.

Diary Entry

Elluin Neván

Age: 18 phases
5,000,039 phases After Stone

They came for me while I was sleeping, curled beneath the furs in Mah and Pah's pallet like I did when I was sick. Where they'd sing me songs that always made me feel better.

They came for me – an entourage of beaded guards from The Burn, The Fade, and the neutral city of Bothaim, residence of the Tri-Council.

They must've known I'd put up a fight despite my weakened state, because they shot me with an iron pin before I'd even opened my eyes.

Cowardly fucks.

They allowed me to gather a single bag of belongings before I was veiled, shackled in iron, and escorted from the sleepsuite. Mah and Pah's aides must've fought, because they were also bound, on their knees, being guarded along the corridors as I was led outside to where a thunder of Moltenmaws were perched along Arithia's walls. Upon the rooftops of Arithia's buildings and gusting through the sky, blowing their orange flames and making the city folk scream.

I'm told they didn't come to conquer my kingdom. That they're simply helping to ward it until I'm able to bind with the male who's been chosen for me by the Tri-Council.

Tyroth fucking Vaegor.

One of King Ostern's three sons. The one with cruel eyes. The male Pah promised he wouldn't trade me to for all the grain in the world.

I screamed at them. Told them I'd rather rot. Earned a smack to the side of the head by one of The Burn's barbed guards.

Everything went black for a bit.

I came to on the back of the biggest Moltenmaw I'd ever seen, Slátra trailing us all the way to the Imperial Fortress near The Fade's capital where we're to spend this slumber – screeching without pause.

Now I can't drift off. Can't do a thing but stare out the window, nurse this chest full of grief, and watch Slátra flick through the colorful clouds, throwing icy flames while my escort Moltenmaws keep trying to herd her back toward the shadows of The Shade.

Once the aurora rises, we're set to soar across the Boltanic Plains, straight on to Dhomm – The Burn's illusive capital. Where I'm to spend the next three phases biding time until I come of coronation age, after which Tyroth and I are to be bound. Until then, it would be 'uncouth' for me to be living under the same ceiling as the male now charged with running my kingdom.

My. Kingdom.

Earlier, while I was slumped here watching Slátra tear three Moltenmaws from the sky and fry the feathers of many more, The Fade's young queen came to visit me in my guest chamber. Offered to remove the iron pin from my thigh.

We spoke in hushed tones as she worked, and she apologized for the actions of her male – King Cadok Vaegor – who offered his aid to the Tri-Council and sent their thunder of mercenary Moltenmaws to secure me.

I got the feeling she regrets that she let the male 'slither into her sleep space,' conceiving a youngling who forced them into a binding that tied The Burn and The Fade together in a secure knot.

I took my veil off and let her see my face, gaunt as it is.

She wrapped me in a warm, sturdy embrace, reminding me that there's still some good in the world.

Together, we watched Slátra wage a lonely war until the Queen was done mending my wound and retired to her chambers. Still, I rest on the windowsill runed against my escape and pray to Clode despite the chilling silence brought on by these cuffs of iron.

I beg her to tell Slátra to fight her battle this slumber but, once the aurora rises, to turn around. To return to Arithia, curl up in the hutch, and wait for me.

Moonplumes don't survive in the sun, and I can't lose her. My heart can't take another hit.

I'd rather die than watch her turn to stone.

Raeve

CHAPTER 38

Cold water splashes my face, sloshing me to consciousness. An unrelenting thump in my temple makes me wonder if I've cracked my skull.

Rushing water drags at my legs while I cling to something round, my arms draped over the curve of it, cheek pressed against its gnarled surface. Probably a tree.

I must've had enough wherewithal at some stage to grip hold of something buoyant and save myself from certain drowning. That's nice.

I pry my eyes open to a smear of orange water and blue sky above that's threaded with a middae aurora. Sheer, rusty cliffs press in on either side of the river I'm currently bobbing along at a rapid pace. A gorge, but it doesn't look like the one we flew through to get to the dwelling. Meaning I've drifted farther, though based on the rich color of the cliffs, not quite far enough to be clear of The Burn.

Damn.

Guess I'll pass out for a bit longer. Sleep off this rampant thump in my head. Hopefully wake up closer to the wall.

I let my heavy lids fall shut—

'*Gafto'in nahh teil aygh' atinvah*!' The coarse words echo through the gorge, nudging me. '*Agní de, agní*.'

That's no language I've ever heard.

Should probably inspect.

I lift my head, turn it, then settle my left cheek on the trunk and pry my eyes open. A large shape is running along the thin shore, trying to keep pace with me. A male, I think. Pretty sure he can't reach me from there – which is good. I'm too tired for stops.

'Hi.'

Bye.

I close my eyes again.

My log comes to an abrupt halt, jostling me so hard I almost roll off. I groan, opening my eyes to see I've snagged on a collection of debris, my trunk still banging and bumping into place amongst a pile of uptorn trees.

The blurred figure draws closer, yelling more words I don't understand. But I don't think he's yelling at me, his head facing another direction, though he continues to point my way.

Cold dread slips through my veins, something innate telling me I need to get up.

Now.

I lift one weighty arm off the log, then the other, and immediately plunge beneath the water, wrestled by its churning might – realizing my mistake when I lack the energy to kick or flounder to the surface.

My lungs rebel, battling for breath, sucking a wad of water that feels so heavy and *wrong*—

There's a splash, bubbles exploding.

Hands gripping me.

I'm lugged skyward, hauled toward the bank and torn from the water, up over the shore's sharp lip before I'm dumped on the ground so hard any moisture I sucked down is quickly expelled in a retching heave.

Muddy water splatters, not discriminating between my sodden hair and the dirt I'm aiming for, air rasping into my heaving lungs between chest-cracking coughs.

My gut and chest continue to convulse in staggered synchrony as I nip squinted glances at my company between the violent upheavals.

The male is huge and muscular with yellow sunburst eyes, garbed in leather pants that hang off his trim hips. He's littered with pale scars, bearing long red hair adorned with coils of copper thread. The leather strap braced across his chest is laden with an array of finely crafted weapons – dragonscale blades and bronze ones in the shape of lanky petals, akin to the one Kaan had. There's also a hook-type tool similar to the one I saw being used to pull that eahl up from beneath the ice south of the wall.

What have I gotten myself into now?

The male lowers, his massive scarred hand coming down to point at my iron cuff. '*Guil dee nahh?*' he asks, and I shake my head, figuring he must be asking about the evidence of my past imprisonment.

'Just ornamental,' I burp out, chased by another splatter of spew. 'Isn't it' – *reeetchhh* – 'pretty?'

Definitely wouldn't want him to think that I'm an escaped prisoner who barely avoided getting ripped apart by a thunder of Moltenmaws. I might end up back there again.

The male turns, yelling more unfamiliar words to another in the distance, the latter standing on the shore's severe lip, hacking storm debris from a damaged fishing net.

I'm so busy heaving half my guts on the ground that it takes me too long to notice the markings on the back of the male closest to me. A dotted tattoo of some kind of bird, wings stretched around his ribs as though hugging him from behind.

I frown – *retch* – continue frowning.

It reminds me of the dots that make up . . . Kaan's . . . tattoo . . .

Realization flays me through the chest, another surge of water gushing up my throat, splashing on the ground.

Warriors of the Boltanic Plains.

This might be where Kaan spent his adolescence.

My nausea instantly abates, and I curse, using the back of my arm to wipe my trembling lips.

More yelling in that language I don't recognize, the other male now running toward us. The one closest grabs my arm and helps me to my knees.

There are many clans scattered across this chapped and grainy wasteland no others have the tenacity to carve out a living on, and I seem to have drifted right into the clutches of two such folk, their way of life even *more* mysterious than those who reside near The Burn's capital.

But I do know one thing.

These clans produce warriors with unmatched abilities . . .

Think I'll give this place a miss.

The male before me drops to one knee, his ruddy beard

concealing half his tan, freckle-dusted face, his sharp stare cutting across my features. He reaches forward and lifts a coil of my sodden hair. '*Achten de. Kholu perhaas?*' he says, pointing at the long, vomit-drenched tendril coiled in his palm, looking back at the other male who's now drawing close – the latter shrugging. '*Sheith comá Rivuur Ahgt . . . en?*'

I gather my hair and push his hand away.

His brow bunches, and he grabs me by the shoulders, helping me to my feet. The moment I plant them on the ground, I lurch from his grip, backstepping, lifting a hand to cradle my throbbing temple.

'*Acht etin aio?*' the male asks, gesturing to me.

'I don't understand.'

He touches his hand to his temple – to the same spot where mine's throbbing – his next words presented so slowly it's obvious he's trying to help me comprehend. '*Surva etin agavien?*'

Is he asking how I hit my head?

'I fell off a cliff.'

His frown deepens, and he murmurs something to the male beside him – more of those words I don't understand.

I can tell by the glances nipping my way and by their general body language that they're discussing how to get me from here to *somewhere else*. I don't want to find out where that is, nor do I want to find out what they want to do with me there. I've got a headache. The last thing I feel like doing is breaking necks.

Unless it's Rekk's, of course.

'Well, it's been grand, but I've got a tree to catch,' I say, jerking my thumb toward the rushing river that looks nothing like it did the previous cycle, now so orange and full of debris, no doubt torn up from the abated storm. Unfortunately, it's nowhere near as tranquil and inviting, not that it'll stop me from leaping into it the moment another log bobs by.

The males pass each other stares of uncertainty, speaking in those foreign words again before they advance as one – almost stepping through my puddle of half-digested soup.

The determined hardness in their eyes stiffens my spine.

Shit.

Looks like I'm not waiting for another log after all.

I spin, about to leap into the gushing river when a blur of motion catches my eye, drawing my attention to the cliff on the opposite side.

A piece of rock displaces, plummeting before thumping against the riverbank below. I wouldn't think it strange were it not for the claw marks also scoring down the cliff, like something invisible is *climbing* it.

I frown.

How hard did I hit my head?

'*Jakah tu . . .*'

I glance back to see both males staring wide-eyed across the river, their complexions turning so pale their freckles stand out in stark difference.

Maybe I'm *not* seeing things . . .

There's a shrill yowling sound, and I whip my head around, seeing a huge metallic smudge now perched on the opposite bank, contrasting the stone's warm tones.

'What's going on?' I murmur, ready to leap into the river and never learn the answer to this particular riddle.

The shape sharpens, becoming a fluffy silver beast that looks like it could swallow me in two mouthfuls, twin metallic sabers protruding from either side of its upper jaw – so long they reach well past its chin.

Big pale eyes stare at me, unblinking, slit through with a line of slate that contracts and tightens.

Contracts and tightens.

Like it's imagining what I'd taste like lanced through by its munching maw.

'*Fait Hatdah*!' one of the males behind me yells, pointing past. As if I can't already see the enormous creature perched over the other side of the river, certainly large enough to stomach all three of us.

'I really hope that thing can't—'

It *leaps*.

My heart drops.

For a moment, all I see is this massive creature flying through the air, claws outstretched, like it's reaching for me – lips peeled back from its bared teeth. Until one of the males grabs my arm and yanks me backward.

I fall into a pile of limbs, a heavy thud telling me the creature has landed on our side of the shore.

Fuck.

I scramble to get up again.

Get *away*.

Finally making it to my feet, I whip around, finding the animal between us and the river. It oscillates between an argent haze of barely-there shape and a strong, sturdy feline with a tufted tail and flowing mane that tangles with the wind. Like the tendrils are dancing with Clode.

My heart leaps into my throat as it lowers onto its thick, powerful haunches, the piercing tips of its sabers almost scoring across the ground.

It looks me right in the eye, lifts its upper lip, and *snarls*.

I sigh.

I survived a thunder of Moltenmaws and nearly choked to death on Sabersythe saliva only to be eaten by *this* thing?

'*Fait Hatdah gah te nahh*,' one of the males beside me says, the tone of his voice laced with a twinge of wonder. '*Fait Hatdah. Fait Hatdah . . . comá feir* Kholu.'

Fait Hatdah? What the fu—

My eyes widen, heart skipping a beat.

Fate Herder . . .

It's the fucking *Fate Herder*.

The creature is more legend than reality, so rarely spotted in the flesh. Those who *have* seen it are often considered crazy or delusional, boasting stories about the beast nudging them to make a different decision from the one they'd intended.

Physically nudging them. Like a bossy handler.

The creature's slit pupils swell, its large flat tongue coming out to lick across its muzzle, as though in confirmation of the revelation.

My shoulders loosen, some of the tension leaving my body.

Surely this thing doesn't go around eating folk . . .

Surely.

Flicking a glance behind me, I wonder which of the two males the creature's here to herd, my heart stilling when I find them both on their knees – looking at me with reverence. Certainly not like I just heaved my guts all over myself in front of them.

Weird.

'I'll just . . . move out of your way,' I say, holding the Herder's jarring glare as I step to the right.

It prowls sideways, keeping itself firmly positioned between myself and the river, a low growl boiling in its fluffy chest.

I frown, passing a glance over my shoulder at the others, certain they must have *also* moved – my heart plopping into my stomach when I see them still in the same place, looking at me with raised brows.

You've got to be kidding me.

No.

Not happening.

Narrowing my eyes on the creature, I shift my weight like I'm about to leap to the left, then throw myself right and sprint along the bank as fast as my legs can take me, curving toward the river—

A snarl cuts through the air a split moment before something big and dense charges into my side, knocking me off my feet. I careen along the ground, certain flesh is grating off my shoulder as I grind to a halt in the dirt.

Groaning, I lift onto my grazed elbows so I can look right into the slit eyes of the creature now doing slow, prowling arcs between me and the fucking river. 'No!'

It growls, the sound like a sawtooth slice.

Maybe it does go around eating folk.

'I want to go *that* way!' I say, pointing in the direction the water is flowing.

The Fate Herder begins tightening its arcs in loping strides, crushing the space between us, its message blatant.

Get the fuck up.

'This is a heap of spangle shit,' I mutter, pushing to a stand.

It continues to move in sweeping arcs, pushing closer with each prowled step.

I walk backward, keeping my eyes mostly on the animal, though passing the odd glance over my shoulder. It doesn't take me long to realize where it's herding me.

Toward the *warriors*.

I stop, widen my stance, and narrow my eyes on the beast. 'I am *not* going with them,' I say, pointing at the males.

It *roars* – baring a maw full of honed teeth, its breath buffeting me with such force I have to squint. The sound bounces off the canyon's sheer walls like an echoing volley.

Maybe I am going with them after all.

Groaning, I tip my face to the sky and close my eyes, dragging my fingers through my wet, tangled hair.

All I want to do is slit Rekk Zharos's throat. Is that too much to ask?

'Fuck!'

My curse bounces off the walls, hitting me over and over.

Pretty sure going to war with this thing wouldn't end well. And I can't hunt Rekk if I'm dead.

Dropping into icy resignation, I spin and charge toward the warriors, cutting a few sharp glances at the creature now prowling close enough to my heels that it could snap at them if it wanted to.

Reaching the two males, I stop, throwing my hands up in a show of displeasure. 'Let's get this over with, whatever *this* is. Try anything questionable and I'll gut you both with my nails.'

Frowning, they stare at me for a long while, pass some words between themselves, then dip their heads at me, almost like a sign of . . . *respect*. They do the same to the creature at my back, then gesture toward a path that clefts through the sheer, rust-colored cliff on this side of the river.

'*Comá, Kholu.*' They gesture me forward. '*Comá.*'

No idea about the other word, but *comá* must mean *come*.

Truly, honestly, the last thing I want to do.

I cut my majestic, mythical beast another scathing look. 'Unless Rekk Zharos is up that path, nice and cornered for me to slaughter, I'm going to be pissed. Just so you know.'

The Fate Herder licks its chops, steps closer, and nudges me forward with its big fluffy head.

Muttering beneath my breath, I trail the warriors, pausing at the base of a stone staircase cut into the cliff, casting a forlorn look at the river.

One step closer, sideswipe to the head.

The Fate Herder growls, and I growl back, baring my teeth at the beast. 'Stop being so bossy,' I gripe, charging up the stairs, chased by the sound of its great paws padding on the stone behind me. 'You won.'

Raeve

CHAPTER 39

The pathway is like a crack formed in the world's crust, weaving off in all directions, seeming to go on.

And on.

'This is quite the tour,' I mutter as we cut left up another vein of stairs. Or perhaps I'm just impatient, being herded by a massive feline close enough that I can feel its hot breath puffing against the back of my neck.

We take another turn, the air thickening with the rich smell of roasting meat. We move between a tall, lofty entrance framed by . . .

Bones.

Two colossal bones so large they can only belong to *one* thing. A dragon that died before it had a chance to soar into the sky, curl up, and turn to stone, instead rotting where it fell.

My eyes widen as we step past the macabre entrance into a massive chest cavity four times the size as I imagine Rygun's to be. As though the mammoth beast fell many phases ago, its corpse swallowed by the elements.

It's been mostly hollowed bar a few swooping pinnacles reaching for the clefts in the ceiling – holes bored between some of the thick arching ribs, allowing sunlight to pour down.

The ground is pocked with domed tents made of smooth animal hides all stitched together, reminding me of Rygun's saddle blanket, the tents like tumbled boulders, painted to look like the scorched terrain in this part of the world. Likely camouflaging this place from anyone soaring above who might otherwise look down the holes in the ceiling.

Clever.

Stone arches frame the entry of each dwelling, all so beautifully carved, boasting creatures of every caste. But predominantly *dragons* – their realness embossed upon the stone in such immaculate detail.

A shriek snaps my gaze to the arched walls of the chest cavity littered with faunycaws. Winged beasts less than half the size of an average Moltenmaw, looking like knobbled bulges of leathery stone. Perfectly disguised were it not for the way their heads swivel on stumpy necks, big, gloomy eyes blinking.

One of them loosens from the wall and flits between the pinnacles, screaming, saddle ropes fluttering in its wake. My mind clutches the vision like a newborn babe seeking comfort. Seeking an anchor in this place I have no knowledge of.

My key to acclimatizing: don't get bogged down by the overwhelming details.

Pick something.

Hone my focus.

Don't drown.

I'm led down a path that wiggles between the tightly packed tents, clusters of silk-swathed females and bare-chested males milling about the space, forging weapons from bits of wood, bronze, or plates of dragonscale bigger than I've ever seen. Others are weaving troves of golden silk thread into draped lengths of material or gathering around smoking fire pits saddled with metal spits, each laden with haunches of roasting meat that season the air with that rich, gamey smell.

Though many of them have red hair and bronze, heavily freckled skin, there are also folk with white hair. Black hair. Brown hair. With skin of all shades. Like folk from all corners of this world have fallen through those holes in the ceiling and found a home in this place.

I notice many of the cavity's inhabitants boast tattoos similar to Kaan's but depicting various creatures, some more of an outline rather than a full, shaded rendering.

'*Kholu haf comá*!' one of the warriors who led me here bellows, the words seeming to echo through the hushing cavern.

Everyone stills, wide eyes taking me in, then the creature

following me like a majestic silver shadow I certainly didn't ask for. But here we fucking are.

Some of the females cry out, eyes watering as they repeat the words:

'Kholu haf comá!'

'Kholu haf comá!'

'Kholu haf comá!'

Everyone drops their tools, some folk pushing from tents and immediately falling to their knees, kissing the ground. Like they're thanking Bulder for . . . *something.*

Aside from my two escorts, myself, and my prowling Herder, not a single male, female, or youngling remains upright.

A surge of nausea spears up my throat, making the underside of my tongue tingle. I'm not sure if I've upset them or made them really, really happy, but either option is concerning.

If they revere me, *expectations.*

If they fear me, *death.*

That's the general formula the world seems to be brewed with, and both those things are heavy time wasters. I've got a male to hunt down and strangle with his own intestines. I don't *have* time to waste.

I pick at the skin on the sides of my nail, cutting another condemning glance at the beast herding me forward. 'You're in trouble.'

It cranks its jaw and yawns, stretching its mouth so wide I could almost crawl down its throat.

Nice to see somebody's relaxed.

I'm led over a small hump, then down what I can only imagine was once this ancient beast's throat, its knobbled vertebrae protruding from the ground just enough that a bony tunnel is exposed – a hole I imagine once housed the dragon's spinal cord. The way is lit by glowing runes etched into the sides, casting the tunnel in a warm hue.

It must've taken great affinity with Bulder to find these remains, to excavate them so precisely without disturbing their position.

I'm still marveling as we come to twin flaps of hide hanging from above. My escorts pull them open, stepping aside to give me enough space to pass.

I frown, pausing. 'Not sure I want to go in th—'

The Fate Herder headbutts me between the shoulder blades,

shoving me through the gap and into the humid embrace of the dragon's massive skull.

I cut a glance over my shoulder and scowl at the bossy creature before I take in my curved surroundings etched in more of those luminous runes, the ground lined with leathers painted with an array of colorful dots, streaks, and jagged lines.

On the left is a low table that runs the length of the space. Slabs of wood are piled high with hunks of meat being carved up by a white-haired male wielding a huge bronze blade.

He pauses the moment he casts his gaze on me, eyes widening, shifting to the beast at my back. He immediately falls to his knees, kissing the ground.

It occurs to me that it's probably what I was supposed to do when I first saw the Fate Herder.

Kiss the ground.

Instead, I tried to run from it, yelled at it, snarled at it, and essentially told it to fuck off. It'll probably give me a shit fate, and honestly, it's warranted. I've certainly got enough blood on my hands to justify it.

I notice a small cluster of golden-silk-clad females perched around baskets heaped with the lanky, blade-like foliage I saw from the sky. They're folding them around bits of dried meat, though their hands pause as they look at me, then at my prowling shadow.

Their eyes go impossibly round.

They, too, kiss the ground before they rise, nipping glances at the entrance while they gather their things and dash out of the way. Frowning, I look over my shoulder, past my fluffy non-friend, eyes bulging.

A swell of folk are pouring in between the flaps of hide, splitting both ways, packing the space full on either side of the twin bloodstone thrones at the far end of the space. Not sure how I didn't notice them earlier, given that they're huge, dominant, and so intricately carved I think they might've taken many aurora cycles to construct.

A female occupies the throne on the right, a babe suckling her breast. Her pale hair pools around her like gushing water, her skin so fair I'm certain a single blade of sun would cause her to sizzle like a Moonplume caught in The Burn.

Her bright-green eyes widen at the sight of me, then soften

with something akin to relief before she looks to the broad male on her right, placing her hand on his arm. Squeezing gently.

His features are hard and harsh, short beard tailored to his strong jawline, his eyes like mini suns staring out at me from beneath russet brows crunched together in a disbelieving frown. Unlike the other bare-chested males, his broad, freckle-dusted shoulders are draped in strings laden with copper rods, and he wears a bony crown that claws down through his long hair, his ear pierced with a black cuff.

I frown.

It's the same as the one *Kaan* wears . . .

He passes a wide-eyed glance to the female on his left, placing his hand on hers. They dip their heads our way in combined homage, though I suspect that's more aimed toward the creature that herded me here, considering its mythical status. Certainly not *me*.

Can't be me.

I'm wearing a shackle, for shit's sake. And there's vomit in my hair.

My cheeks heat as I bring the offending tendrils close to my nose and sniff, my face scrunching up at the sour reek.

Damn. I thought it was more diluted than that.

'This is what happens when you don't let me jump in the river,' I grind out to my unwanted Herder. 'I'm presented to important folk smelling like bile.'

Its only response is to leap ahead and do a prowling loop around me, forcing me to stop.

'Message received,' I mutter, and it lumps itself beside me, sitting on its haunches. It lifts a paw, licks it, and swipes at its face with a smooth sort of contentment I certainly don't appreciate – surrounded by strangers, standing in a dragon's skull in the middle of fucking nowhere.

The space packs so full there's scarcely any hot, humid air to breathe, and the male on the throne lifts his head. His gaze shifts between me and the creature at my side.

Boasting a warm smile, he shakes his head. Like he's wrestling with some kind of disbelief. '*Kholu* . . .'

'Yes,' I say, cutting a glance around all the silent, wide-eyed onlookers. 'Folk keep saying that.'

Again, he looks at the female beside him. They press their

heads together, both relishing in some form of relief I can see clear in their expressions.

The male cups the head of their babe and plants a kiss on its brow—

I pull my attention from the intimate moment that's strangely painful to watch, looking skyward, noticing the vast domed ceiling is strung with toothy skulls. Enough for me to come to the swift realization that these folk have no qualms in killing.

We'll get on fine so long as they don't try to kill *me*.

The maybe-King stands – slow. Everyone in the room bar the white-haired female pounds their fists against their chests before dropping into a bow so low their mouths meet the floor again.

I should probably do the same. Don't want to piss anyone off, given the fact that I'm incredibly outnumbered and still bound in a shackle of iron.

I clear my throat, drop to my knees, then dip my head, holding the stance for a long moment.

The male steps down from his throne, looking between me, the Fate Herder, and the two males who plucked me from the river – both now standing off to the side. '*Hagh toth?*' he asks, pausing.

The male with the bird tattoo responds. '*Rivuur Ahgt at nei del ayh.*'

'*Rivuur Ahgt . . . uh surt?*'

'*Ahn . . .*'

A stretch of silence before the crowned male speaks again. '*Teni asg del anah te nei. Tookah Téth ain de lei . . . Sól aygh tah* Kholu!'

My mind drifts, clawed fingers scrambling to cling to the now. The present.

It all begins to remind me of a different place, a different time. When I was just as confused about what the hell was going on, my vocabulary failing to stretch further than a few huffing grunts I'd use to try and explain my needs.

I recite my calming song internally as the maybe-King moves back to his throne, a tall female stepping free of the parting crowd. She's clothed in lashings of copper body paint and a black-beaded cloak that clatters as she strides toward us in long, hip-swaying steps. Her feet are bare, russet hair so long it smothers half her cloak.

My gaze lifts to her eyes, and all the breath flees my lungs.

They're white.

Unseeing.

She looks my way, and I feel the *opposite* of unseen – shafted through with the sense that she sees far too much.

'*Kholu*,' she whispers, smiling before raising both hands skyward. '*Kholu haf comá. Haf de neil da nu . . .* Tookah te!'

The skull erupts with victorious yells and the pounding of fist to flesh, thumping hard like my rallying heart before the crowd becomes a bustle of motion – an energy about the space that prickles with anticipation.

'What in the Creators have you gotten me into?' I grind out to the beast at my side, who simply curls into a great mounded ball of fur, tucks its face beneath its tail, and appears to fall asleep – oscillating between its solid form and smudging at the sides.

Hmm.

Maybe if I ignore it for a bit, it'll smudge out of existence entirely. Then I can leave.

Two hulking males push free of the bellowing crowd, the larger of the pair so massive his hand could thread around my throat and crush it with a single squeeze, his hair the color of clay and reaching down between his shoulder blades. When he turns to bow at the folk occupying the thrones, I see his back is *littered* with dots, the image of a serpent coiled around his muscular frame more whole than blotted in places. The smaller male has brown hair and tawny, freckle-dusted skin, bearing a faunycaw with its wings reaching up, draped over the warrior's shoulders.

Both turn to me, dipping into an even deeper bow.

I frown, my attention drifting to the female sitting on the throne, seeking answers in her eyes. All I find is a soft, comforting smile that makes me want to growl.

I don't want comfort. I want cold hard truths so I can work out what this *Fate Herder* has gotten me into and how I can remove myself from the situation the moment the creature drops its guard.

Clopping sounds come to me from behind, and I look over my shoulder, seeing a big leathery six-legged creature being led down the path between the crowd. It has no ears and three sets of beady black eyes that are clustered on either side of its long face, its jaw rocking as it chews something tucked between its molars.

My frown deepens. I think it's a colk, but the ones I've seen have a thick, fluffy pelt. The creatures look so strange . . . *naked.*

It makes a snorting sound, settling between myself and the two males watching me with intrigue.

The milky-eyed female steps between me and the peaceful, masticating beast. With one swift motion, she rips a curved bronze blade from a sheath I hadn't noticed strapped to her leg and slits the animal's throat faster than I can track.

My lungs seize, heart hammers.

The poor animal lets out a shrill honk, its spilling blood caught in a bowl while my head goes light and airy. The beast is gently lowered to the ground, settling into a kneeling position that mimics my own. But still.

Dead.

I waver.

I've killed folk in the same manner. But seeing this poor, innocent creature loosen its final, gurgling breath jostles something inside me. Makes me feel sick to the stomach.

Fuck this.

I'm out.

I push to my feet and spin, stalking for the exit when the Fate Herder leaps in front of me, snarling. The crowd gasps, murmuring while I bare my teeth and growl back.

It drops its head lower, prowls closer, urging me back toward my starting point.

'I'm growing less and less fond of you,' I grind out, then shake my head and turn, storming back, toiling rage whipping at my ribs like ribbons of icy water.

This verbal barrier is growing deeper by the second. If I don't find out what's going on soon, I'm going to lose my fucking mind.

The male and female on the thrones frown at me, passing each other wary glances as I pick at the skin down the sides of my nail, watching the two warriors get painted in colk blood like it's something to be proud of.

I try not to look at the dead animal. Hard when it's *right there*, still bleeding out in a bowl.

A group of females converge around me like a fence, breaking off my view of the poor colk. Rows of them, until I'm hidden behind a circular wall of shapely, silk-garbed folk, most of whom have their backs turned.

Every cell in my body stiffens, my eyes darting left and right.

It takes me noticing the nervous glances being passed between the few folk still facing my way for me to realize I'm snarling.

One dons a soft smile and steps forward. '*Eh tah Saiza. Téth en. Aygh ne.*'

'I don't understand. Any of this.'

She lifts her hands. 'My name is Saiza. It is okay. No hurt.'

Saiza's peaceful words do little to soothe my hackles, though I do wrangle my upper lip down over my teeth, thankful somebody can speak my language.

This is good. I can work with this.

'Please tell me what's happening.'

'We have need to cleanse your body,' she says, and my brows fly up.

'Because I got vomit in my hair? I assure you, there's a very easy solution to that. Just lead me back to the river and toss me in.'

A small smile picks up one corner of her mouth, her sunburst eyes warming, reminding me of Ruse. 'Because you are *Kholu*,' she whispers, pointing to some colorful marks painted on the leather beneath my feet, crouching to touch a black slash. 'Your hair is like the eyes of the faunycaw – in your common tongue,' she says, then points to an azure squiggle. 'You came to us on the eternal ribbon of blue – the *River Ahgt*.'

Debatable. It looked pretty muddy to me.

She traces a dark-red line that coils around these markings like a rope binding a bouquet, spearing off to the right, cradling an impression of three moons.

A Sabersythe.

A Moltenmaw.

A Moonplume.

Another line surrounds the entire image, silver like my unwanted companion coiled at my side, Saiza's finger tracing it. 'It was foretold that the Fate Herder would bring you to us. That your offspring will tether the moons to the sky,' she says with a hitch of awe. '*Forever.*'

My heart thuds to a stop, gaze rising to meet hers. 'Well, that's a load of spangle shit,' I snap, jerking my chin at the paintings. 'I am no Kholu, and I will *never* carry offspring.'

The words are a weapon hacking through the space between us, their honed edge whetted on my stony heart.

Never.

The Fate Herder cracks an eye open, watching me.

'*Never*,' I repeat, infusing every ounce of condemnation into my tone as I meet its slit stare.

It blows a deep, rumbling breath that puffs against my face, and something settles within my chest. Like it just reached through me and stroked my frazzled heartstrings.

Might just be me, but I get the potent sense that it doesn't want me here for . . . *that*.

'I know not of this spangle you speak of,' Saiza says, 'but the Sól is never wrong. She drew this foretelling many cycles ago, and she herself has called you Kholu. The Fate Herder escorted you here, so the Tookah Trial will proceed, as it was ordained by the Creators themselves and approved by our Oah and Oah-ee. King and Queen in your tongue.'

Another trial?

I groan.

Wonder how many more of these I have to stand through before I finally get to kill Rekk Zharos?

I glare at the problematic Fate Herder still watching me with lazy intrigue, its tail flicking back and forth. 'This is your fault.'

A vibrato *dong* rattles the air, its echo tapering before striking again, making my skin pebble. Another female steps into my circle of relative privacy, carrying a bowl of soapy water.

'May I remove your clothes and prepare you for the trial?' Saiza asks, and I sigh, reaching for the hem of my oversized shirt.

'Sure,' I mutter. 'Let's get this over with.'

The sooner I'm *cleansed*, the sooner I can be done with this trial, the sooner I can leave.

Hopefully.

A length of silk is passed around my protective ring of females, draped like a curtain before Saiza helps me out of my stolen clothes, then rinses my hair and sponges me down – painting lathered sweeps over my body to the daunting beat of the gong.

'You have beautiful shape,' she boasts, patting my skin down with an absorbent bit of cloth. 'Such lovely curves.'

'Thanks,' I mutter, mind elsewhere.

Another.

Fucking.

Trial.

What are they even trialing me *for*? It's not like I murdered any of them.

I don't think.

Perhaps they want to question me on my procreation intentions, given they think I'm going to magically produce some world-saving offspring?

Better not. I take a tonic every phase that renders my womb inhospitable and have *no* intention of missing a dose.

Streaks of blood are slicked across my skin by two other females before a long strip of bloodred silk is draped around my waist and knotted. Another shred is wrapped around my breasts, a string laden with copper rods pushed over my head and settled atop my bust.

The gong sounds again – swiftly followed by a rapid foray of beats.

The curtain drops, my band of privacy dissolves, and I see the two painted warriors watching me with honed regard. I'm about to ask Saiza if they're the ones who are trialing me, but then the Fate Herder gets right in my face and nudges me to a stand, smearing some of the freshly painted blood.

The crowd begins to disperse, funneling through the exit, my fluffy non-friend herding me in the same direction while uncertainty churns in my chest, making it feel tight.

Constricted.

Pick something.

Hone my focus.

Don't fucking drown.

I hum my calming tune, stare narrowing on the flow of folk before me as I count my steps, imagining each one brings me a little bit closer to that mystical fucking word that's always *just* out of reach . . .

Freedom.

Raeve

CHAPTER 40

I'm herded through a warren of tunnels to the beat of the pounding gong, the thick, stagnant air becoming easier to inhale only moments before we spill into a big, dusty crater. My eyes bulge at the impossible height and width – large enough to cram four coliseums in here and still have room to move.

It's as though something collided with the ground with such velocity the stone was displaced.

Frowning, I recall Kaan's earlier words . . .

I spent most of my adolescence and a number of my later phases as a warrior of the Johkull Clan. They have always nested close to these mountains and recently claimed the crater formed by the fallen Sabersythe moon, Orvah.

Guess that's what this is. Orvah's crater. The small moon that fell a little over eight phases ago.

Folk pour into the space behind me and my prowling Herder like gushing water, and my mind churns as I take in the chapped surroundings.

There are tents dotted about the circumference, each sturdy structure consisting of four wooden poles plowed into the ground and a flap of patched leather stretched between them – forming a roof. They cast rectangular shadows occupied by woven rugs and many clay urns etched with glowing runes.

Between the tents are a number of wooden racks stacked with weapons, most of which I've never seen before: batons with a length of chain attached to the end, topped with spiked balls that look like they could shatter a skull; giant hooked swords; and small flat blades with pearly teeth mounted around the edge. *So* many weapons it makes Ruse's armory look juvenile.

The crater's blanketed with a stretch of sand, though when I look at the grains sifting through my toes as I'm escorted around the perimeter, I notice gray shards amongst the rusty majority.

Iron. To nullify those who can hear the elemental songs, no doubt.

I frown, then cast my stare at the powdery sky threaded with the aurora's wispy silver tendrils, a scatter of inky Sabersythe moons perched in the distance. The crater's lip bears a crisscross of fraying rope heavy with skulls – most sun-bleached. One with shreds of decomposing meat and tufts of hair still hanging off the bone, a small tawny-colored bird perched on it.

Pecking at it.

My heart skips a beat.

Unlike the skulls in the tent we just came from, these ones are not from fallen animals. They have rounded heads and tapered canines, the fresher one retaining the rotten remnants of a tapered ear.

They're *fae*.

Creators . . . This is a *battle* ring.

Is that what my trial is? Am I expected to fight?

The tips of my fingers tingle, unease slithering through me like a serpent.

The gong continues to sound as I'm guided further around the crater's circumference, past tent after tent, the folk before us threading into a large dome-shaped one similar to those I saw in the chest cavity of the fallen dragon. Though *this* one's much bigger than them, and with many entrances, each framed by more of those intricately crafted archways.

Saiza stops before one opening, pulling a woven flower from one of the few baskets dotted around the tent, offering it to me. 'Would you like to honor Orvah?'

My heart leaps so high up my throat the next words are choked. 'The fallen Sabersythe?'

Saiza nods, smiling softly. 'He did not break apart upon impact. It took many warriors to roll him to the crater's side. We now pay him great respect in the hopes that no other moon will fall on our place of living.'

Pulse pounding hard and fast, I accept the flower, cutting a glance back at my oscillating Herder who cranks its muzzle and yawns again, skulking toward one of the doorways and curling into a sleepy ball.

Guess that's permission.

Swallowing, I push my hand between the tent's flaps, steady my breath, then step inside, drawing on the hot, humid air trapped beneath the pelts.

My heart stops.

Nestled amongst the sand before me is the most spectacular mottled moon. Like the Sabersythe was rolled through puddles of black and bronze ink that sunk into his small, overlapping scales.

The backs of my eyes prickle as I take him in, his slight stature and lack of spikes a tribute to his adolescence. The dragon's left wing is swooped around his body, his sparsely tusked head dug only partially beneath it, still exposed enough that I can see almost an entire half of his face, his lid closed. Looking like he just slipped into a quiet, peaceful sleep he'll never wake from.

One of my frayed heartstrings pangs at the thought, because this dragon . . . he's so *small*. A little under twice my height. Just big enough to support a rider, as evident by the damaged remnants of a saddle secured to his scaled back.

It feels like a hand claps around my neck and squeezes tight.

Tighter.

Although some dragons *choose* to soar into the sky when they feel their time has come to an end – to ball up and solidify – many don't make that decision on their own.

Many are devastating victims of wars waged by *us*.

Then there are the ones that don't make it into the sky at all. That die in the dirt or the snow or the sand and rot where they lie, their blood fossilizing. Later mined by *us*.

Used by *us*.

I reach out a hand, pausing just before my fingers are able to brush across the stony scales as a mourning presence deep inside urges me to turn around. To stop looking.

No, not an urge.

A gentle probing *request*.

A *plea*.

Clearing my throat, I drop to a kneel and settle my woven flower on the ground at the dragon's base like others are doing, adding to the growing piles of offerings – old and new. Then I listen to that plea. Respect its desperate, mournful request.

I turn around, and I don't look back.

I'm led upon a raised dais beneath a patch of shade – relief for my already chapped skin.

I look at my feline non-friend who coils up beside me, releasing a satiated rumble. It tucks its face beneath its long, bushy tail and appears to go to sleep.

I'm obviously not expected to fight. Otherwise, it would've herded me right into the ring.

Surely.

Folk finish paying their respects to Orvah, then pack into the slabs of shadow. The two blood-soaked males kneel before me, the larger one lifting a necklace up over his head. He bows, hand outstretched, and my eyes narrow on the black pendant engraved with a serpent. The same image as the one dotted on his back.

The pendant hangs from his clenched fist, swaying in the dusty wind, reminding me of the one Kaan wears – though less intricate.

Less *alluring*.

Saiza leans close to my ear. 'You must accept Hock's málmr now.'

'Why?'

'It is an important part of the trial,' she says, and I frown, reaching out. He drops it into my open palm, the coil of string coarse against my skin.

The dark-haired male extends his, too – a tawny diadem bearing an embossed faunycaw. Not as polished or finely crafted as the other piece.

'Now accept Zaran's and set both málmr on the rug before you.'

I do as she said, my frown deepening as both males bang their fists against their chest three times, then stand, dispersing toward separate weapon racks.

'So . . . we're going to watch them fight?' I query, and Saiza nods. 'Of course.'

'What does this have to do with my trial?'

'This *is* your trial,' she says, and my brows bump up.

'I just have to sit here and watch them knock each other around?'

She nods.

I frown, very little of the unease loosening from my chest.

Zaran chooses a partially curved sword that reminds me of the serpent on his opponent's back, while Hock picks a bludgeoning stick with metal spikes sprouting from its bulbous head. A weapon which seems to suit the monstrous male.

My gaze stabs right beneath another large tent where the Oah and Oah-ee sit upon bloodstone thrones, the latter being fanned with a massive flat leaf while she continues to feed her squirming babe. The Sól is there, too – sitting on a smaller throne to the Oah's right.

Their combined attention is firmly cast on the males who make for the ring's flattened epicenter.

Wind churns my hair into a lash of black tendrils but fails to whip the heat from the air. To ruffle the tension stretched across the crater as Hock and Zaran begin to circle each other in wide skulking strides, their eyes locked, upper lips peeled back from bared teeth. It feels like they're stalking those same churning steps inside my gut while the gong continues to bang to a chest-thumping beat that rattles through my ribs.

Zaran dips low, growling as he charges Hock, curved blade slashing for his guts so fast mine plummet.

This is no practice match. They're fighting to *kill*.

Fuck.

Zaran is booted back. He lumps onto his ass, barely rolling out of the way in time for Hock to pound his club into the ground instead of directly upon his opponent's chest with a mighty, muscle-rippling heave, a burst of sand spraying skyward.

I flinch, watching the males slash, hack, dodge, and sway, tearing deep gashes in each other's leather pants and skin, splashing the sand red.

Unease wraps its bind around my chest again – pulling it tighter. Tighter.

Something's not right.

'I'm confused. What does this have to do with me?'

Raising a single brow, Saiza flicks me an amused look. 'Everything, Kholu. They're fighting *for* you.'

My heart drops so fast my next words choke out. 'They're fighting to the death to *entertain* me? Are you serious?'

She frowns. 'No, not to entertain.'

'Then wh—'

'This is a *Tookah* Trial,' she says, attempting to smooth some of my unruly hair behind my tapered ear. She gestures with her other hand toward the males now grappling in the sand, fists throwing. More blood sprays with the ferocity of their violent swings. 'They are fighting for the great honor of being bound to you. The honor of building a life and producing offspring with Kholu is the greatest one could wish for. To pin the moons to the sky for good will ensure the future for offspring of the entire Johkull Clan, and their offspring, and *theirs*. To secure such peace is a great privilege.'

Her speech flays me, little by little, slicing skin, sinew, and bone in swift, icy blows . . .

No.

No, no, no, no—

Hock uses Zaran's own blade to hack through his opponent's neck in short, slitting increments, cracking his neck halfway through. The rest of it tears free from his motionless body now splayed across the sand, and all the breath bursts from my lungs. Like Clode just siphoned it free.

Crouched upon the lifeless corpse like a feasting beast, Hock fists Zaran's blood-matted hair and lifts the head like a trophy, roaring triumphantly as he shakes it, blood slipping from the gory wound.

The crowd roars, folk bashing their chests with fisted blows, the gong sounding in rhythm to my thrashing heartbeat.

Hock sets his eyes on me, and all the heat escapes my body, violent unease exploding in my chest.

No, no, no—

'Hock is your victor,' Saiza murmurs against my ear, and my thoughts churn like a tangled length of barbed threads. 'You are lucky. Aside from his roskr and the Oah, he is our strongest fighter. There will now be great celebration, after which he will escort you to his tent and show you the pelts of his kills, upon which you will hopefully make many strong sons and daughters in the cycles to come once your bond grows sturdy.'

Sons and daughters . . .

A heaviness settles on my chest and belly, making me feel crushed, yet somehow so incredibly . . . *empty*.

Failing to pull breath into my lungs, I slit a glance at the Herder, now almost smudged entirely from view. So close to turning invisible that I'm certain I could shove my hand straight through it.

I'm not surprised it's hiding. It should be fucking *ashamed* of itself.

I'm just about to tell it as much when Hock lumbers forward, kicking up blows of sand with his charging steps. He thumps Zaran's head on the ground before my dais.

I gasp, gaze dropping to the male's lax face. To the fleshy mess of tissue, tendons, and bone.

The blood puddling upon the sand.

I'm still looking at it, trying to work out how the fuck I got here – scarcely garbed, painted in blood, and staring at a severed head – when Hock kneels before me. He plucks his sooty málmr from the rug and reaches for me, trying to thread the loop over my head. Like a shackle for my neck.

Rage explodes beneath my ribs.

'*No*,' I snarl, jerking back.

Hock's eyes flare with a mix of confusion and scarcely veiled wrath.

He growls, grips me by the shoulder, and jostles me closer to the tune of rumbling murmurs—

I fling my head forward, feeling his nose crack from the force, whipping back to see blood spurting from his flared nostrils.

The world around us stills.

I shove to my feet, scurrying backward while he stalks into my patch of shade, growling through the stream of blood pouring from his face. 'I will fight for myself!'

A hush falls upon most of the crowd, buffeted only by a few gasps. Perhaps from those who understand the common tongue.

Hock pauses, gaze darting to Saiza who translates my frantic request, his brow becoming a bunched mantel above his stormy sunburst eyes.

He looks to the Oah. '*Géish den nahh cat-uein?*'

His words are a brutal clash of sounds, tension thickening.

The Oah seems to deliberate, his wide-eyed Oah-ee paler than she was before. She looks at me, her babe now bunched and squealing at her breast.

Her lips move, soft words pulled straight to my ears on a gentle twirl of wind. '*What are you doing?*'

She can speak my language, then.

She can also speak with Clode.

Interesting.

'I do not choose this,' I seethe, the ruddy silk bound around my waist ruffling in the wind, my entire body taut with the urge to *move*.

To *fight*.

My gaze drops to my Fate Herder, now watching me through slit eyes that are far more solid-looking than the rest of its body.

Though it's still coiled, I sense its welling unease in the air between us. Like it's waiting to see what foot I'll step out of line next. But if this is my fate – if this is what it was leading me to – I don't accept it.

Not one single bit.

Over the last few aurora cycles, I've cradled my Essi while she slipped away, said goodbye to Nee, been shot with an iron pin, and received so many lashes I passed out from the pain. I've been fed to a thunder of dragons, nearly swallowed, been turned down by the only male who's ever made my heart skip a beat, was swept off a cliff, and I am at my wit's end.

I am not *accepting* this male's málmr, no matter how exceptional his battle skills are. I'd rather slam the small disk so far into his skull it cleaves through bone and punches into his squishy brain than bear this male's children.

I have no idea who he is, and I don't want to. I don't *want* to grow a child – first and fucking foremost. If I have to go to war with the Fate Herder to avoid this, I will. Beautiful, mythical beast or not.

A dribble of Hock's blood slithers down the line of my nose, my upper lip peeling back. 'I will fight for *myself*.'

My words hiss across the crater.

The Oah-ee swallows, leaning toward her male, whispering something against his ear. He looks at me, gaze shifting to Hock, to my sleepy Herder, then back to me. He says something to his Oah-ee, and she releases a shuddered breath, gaze dropping to her babe nuzzled amongst folds of gold silk.

Silence beats by.

She sweeps a hand over the youngling's brow, then clears her throat, though her words still come out choked as she looks me in the eye and says, 'So long as the Fate Herder does not prevent you from entering the ring, we will not oppose your decision.'

Raeve

CHAPTER 41

Saiza paints me in more parchment-thin streaks of blood while I stand statue still. While I watch Hock stalk back and forth across the sandy battlefield, his gaze firmly cast on me as he sucks and shoves deep breaths through bared teeth like a ferocious, meat-eating animal chomping at the bit to launch forward and chow down on his prey.

I sigh, nudging my shackle into a more comfortable position on my arm.

The escape plan was simple: climb down the cliff and follow the river to the wall, sticking to the shade as best I could. Charm a Moltenmaw. Hunt Rekk Zharos and torture him to death. Now I have to behead this male only two steps from the starting line.

I cut another glare at my near-invisible Herder, currently little more than a rumbling metallic smudge, cursing the moment it leapt into my life.

Saiza swirls another streak of blood across my midriff. 'You don't like the male who won for you?'

Won for me . . .

That's not what this was.

'I do not choose this male,' I rebuke, and she frowns, confusion swirling in her pretty sunburst eyes.

She drags the brush down my nose, over my lips, chin, and neck. 'He has hunted many wild gruuc – great, tusked beasts almost impossible to bring down. His tent is large, wrapped and lined with many of their pelts. Proof of his famed strength. You are

Kholu. Your offspring will tether moons to the sky and bring great peace. Do you not want a strong sire?'

I bristle.

How much clearer do I need to be?

There is no reality where I lift this silk and let that male into my body. No reality where I step a single fucking foot in his impressive tent. No reality where I bare my throat to him – the tilt of deep, primal respect.

I'd rather him slit it from ear to ear.

'I don't want this male, this title, this *anything*,' I growl, cutting another sharp stare at the smudge of metallic air particles beside me, hoping the Fate Herder is paying real good attention. 'My body is mine, and I will do with it as I please. *Nothing* more.'

Saiza's face blanches, and she drops her eyes, dipping her head in submission. 'I understand, Kholu. We cradle different values. I apologize for overstepping.'

'It's okay.'

I just want to be done.

Gone.

Saiza passes me a small smile, then paints more swirls down the length of my arm while I continue to observe Hock's movements – studying the way his body shifts. The way he eases his weight from foot to foot. The damage already inflicted on his hulking form.

'Do you know how to fight?' Saiza asks, and I bob my head. 'Like a *warrior* fights?'

My gaze flicks to her, brows bumping together.

She pauses. 'Nobody fights like those from the Johkull Clan. We are the strongest in the Boltanic Plains. This is why we earned this land where no moon will fall again,' she says, gesturing to the crater surrounding us. 'All Hock must do is get you to submit, and the trial is over. You must *kill* him to be the victor. To earn the right to slay wild gruuc and to build your own tent. Then you must cut off his head.'

I don't bother telling her I have no interest in killing wild gruuc and building a tent. Once I kill Hock, I'll retrace the path back to the river, then follow it until it freezes and eventually meets the wall. If the Fate Herder tries to stop me . . . well.

Hopefully it doesn't come to that. I love animals, and I loathe the thought of killing them.

'I've taken the heads of males before,' I murmur past tight lips. *Though obviously not nearly enough, considering how cursed I absolutely, without a doubt, one hundred percent am.* 'This will be no different.'

A stretch of tension-riddled silence ensues while Saiza continues preparing me for the looming battle, my copper necklace lifted and set to the side. My hair is brushed, then threaded into a braid that falls almost to my hips, tied off with a stretch of string while the gong continues to sound.

Once I'm fully prepared, I cut a glance at my Fate Herder transitioning into view again, opening its eyes to look at me.

Those slit pupils swell as I hold its fierce, intense stare. 'Don't try to stop me.'

All I get is a tail flick, as if to say, '*Off you go. Get back in the ring where you belong. Do your job.*'

I bristle, the entire congregation seeming to hold its breath as I lift my chin and charge from the shadow, refusing to pay the beast any more heed. Not a single drop of it.

It's not going to stop me. I know it's not. I should've known this is where it wanted me all along: back in a battle ring, shedding blood.

Perhaps Fate – whoever *Fate* is – needs Hock and Zaran taken out for some reason, so the Herder deviated me here to do the deed. Whatever it's for, it's hard to shake the sense that I'm being *used* again.

I should be used to it by now.

I move toward a weapon rack, lifting a few off the hooks that I quickly discover are too top heavy or too thick in the handle for my fingers to securely wrap around. I pick up a small iron ax with a bound leather pommel that feels comfortable in my grip, tossing it from hand to hand before using it to shear off the excess material of my shirt so it doesn't get in my way.

Tossing the blood-tinged scrap of silk to the wind, I move into the ring, beginning a slow, steady circle around the outer perimeter while maintaining Hock's eye contact. He's swapped his spiked club for one that's smooth, no doubt reluctant to disfigure me in his efforts to earn the 'right' to bind with me.

Such spangle shit.

I crack my neck from side to side, steadying my breaths until they're deep and slow.

Calm.

Waiting for *him* to make the first move.

Hock shakes his head, muttering beneath his breath before his face distorts with a bellowing roar. He lunges, kicking up sand as he powers across the arena like a charging beast.

I wait until he's so close I can feel the vibrations of his hammering steps. Can see the orange flints in his bold-yellow eyes.

I flick to the side, bending my upper body away from his swinging mace to the collective gasp from the crowd. I spin, whipping around with a slash of my ax.

Blood sprays, my weapon slitting through skin and flesh, nicking bone, severing the side of his abdomen. Not deep enough to kill, I realize – scurrying back, gaze firmly locked on my roaring opponent while fisting a handful of sand.

Hock slaps his hand against the wound, inspecting the slick of blood now coating his palm, a flash of undiluted shock kindling his eyes, followed by a flare of rage violent enough to sizzle skin.

I've seen males look at me like that, right before I've pierced their hearts.

The look of *wounded pride*.

I don't give him time to digest the emotion, charging, dodging left and right. Drawing his attention to my feet, hoping he boggles over the direction of my next move rather than what my hands are doing.

With a flick of my wrist, I toss my scoop of sand into the air as Clode lashes the wind into a gust, spraying it into his eyes – helping me of her own accord.

Hock roars.

I smile.

Love you too, Clode!

Miss you!

While Hock bats at his eyes, I dive upon his back, wrapping my arm around his throat, just about to slash my ax across his jugular when he grips my arm and hauls his body forward.

I feel my blade make contact as I'm whipping through the air, bracing myself for impact so that when I collide with the ground, I'm immediately rolling out of the way. Marginally avoiding a blind swing of his mace that bashes the ground at my back.

I leap to my feet, seeing him scurry back, padding at the too-shallow slit in his throat.

Damn.

He leers at me through bloodshot eyes, seething, bellowing boisterous words while he reaches into the pocket of his pants. Probably trying to check that his balls still exist.

Not wanting to give him too much time to recalibrate, I charge again, dodging left and right, a few long leaps away when he pulls his hand free.

I see the thin aureate tendril dangling from his fingers too late, already throwing my body in that direction – ax swinging as he thrusts his hand forward. As a small, hissing serpent is tossed through the air between us, maw bared.

Fangs stretched.

My weapon slits through Hock's thigh just as the serpent strikes my chest with a bite of sting.

I roll, tumbling across the ground, throwing myself onto my feet again and backstepping. Watching the small serpent wiggle off through the sand – practically blending with the grains.

What.

The.

Fuck.

I cup the throbbing hurt on the upper swell of my left breast, not taking my eyes off the asshole now smirking at me from a handful of long leaps away. Like he's already won despite the fact that he's baring three fresh slash marks that are leaking blood all over the sand.

'Who goes around carrying *those* in their pocket—'

A sudden flash of dizziness makes me wobble, and I throw my hand out to balance myself to the tune of the crowd's gasps and murmurs.

Creators . . . That serpent spiked me with its venom.

Hock chuffs, then charges.

I charge too, because there's no way I'm standing stationary while this fuck comes at me again.

Hand fisted around my ax, I consider which two ribs I'm going to slice between, dodging to the left, another tip of dizziness making the ground rock with such violence I stumble a step.

His weapon collides with my shoulder, and a burst of pain explodes across my collarbone, down into my elbow.

Scurrying back, I cradle my arm close to my body, gaping at the stalking male, sawing breath into my parched lungs . . .

What was that?

My dodge was *perfect* . . . until it wasn't.

Another wobble, and a bulb of fear explodes behind my ribs, realization dawning like aurora ribbons rising in my belly, tangling around my spine, wriggling up my throat.

The venom is moving through my system fast.

Too fast.

The entire world seems to tilt sideways, my steps floundering with it, forcing me to plant my hand on the sand to catch myself. A flash of satisfaction ignites Hock's features, his lips curling into a victorious smirk.

'You dishonorable *fuck*,' I snarl, charging – dodging side to side, finally dipping low and sliding along the ground. I whip my ax out and slash it through his calf muscle in the same instance his weapon *whooshes* past the side of my face.

He roars, catapulting forward in stomping stumbles, taking himself far enough away from me that he's able to check the laceration in his pants, the fresh wound pouring blood down the back of his leg.

His eyes bulge with disbelief.

'Couldn't swallow the fact that you were going to lose to a female half your size, huh?' I push to my feet, still sneering. 'I will fucking *ruin* you, then boot your severed head all the way to The Fade.' I growl, charging again—

The world jerks, taking me with it. My hand flies out to catch myself, only for it to plummet straight through what I thought was the ground.

Heart lurching, I stagger into an awkward, sideways crouch, catching myself on the *actual* ground – my heart pumping hard.

Fuck.

I meet Hock's slashing gaze as he tests his weight on his injured leg . . .

This is not good.

I need to finish this – *fast.*

I shove up, prowling in a wide arc Hock mimics in limping strides. With my stare firmly cast on my snarling opponent, I pick at the leather bind wrapped around the pommel of my ax, unraveling the taut, sturdy length of material.

Come on, asshole. Make a move.

He charges.

So do I – converging toward him at a rapid pace.

A few long lunges away, I whip my hand back and toss my ax. It slices through the air with the speed of a lightning strike, propelling straight for his chest—

He moves faster than the flying weapon, dodging it with a dramatic dip of his immense body. The ax whirs past him, and I leap, latching onto him. Clambering up his compromised form and kicking my foot against the gouge in the back of his leg.

Hock tips his head and *roars*, dropping to his knees with such heft the ground trembles, the crowd gasping as I bind the leather ribbon around his thick neck and tighten.

Tighten.

Choking sounds rupture from his no-doubt gaping mouth, fuel to spur me on. Hock may look like a mountain and move like he slid from the womb swinging, but his neck is still delicate.

He still needs to *breathe*.

I pour all my strength into keeping the bind taut, the muscles in my arms and chest ripped with a tearing burn from the immense effort. Hock claws at his throat, failing to get his fingers beneath the leather, instead jerking his entire body forward.

Using his heft to his advantage.

Anticipating the maneuver, I latch my legs around his waist, becoming a willing passenger to the shift. We collide with the ground, our left shoulders boring into the hot sand.

He lurches, spine arching, trying to shuck me off his body. I tighten my legs and fists, moving with his frantic motions, clinging to him like a life-sucking parasite.

The strips of leather cut into my palms, my lips pull back from my teeth, my brain pumping so full of blood that my head goes light and airy. The world rocks around us, like we're on a raft in a lake of undulating sand, and I just *know* that this is my only shot.

That if I don't get him now, I'm fucked.

'*Die, you corrupt fuck!*' I growl, pouring the last of my strength into another wrench of my arms, further tightening the bind.

He reaches back, swatting around my head, clawing at my braid. He yanks it, but I can tell by the lack of force that he's fading.

Warm anticipation bubbles in my chest.

My scalp burns from his desperate tugs that grow weaker . . .

Weaker . . .

All the tension loosens from his body, and his head flops to the side with the drop of his arm. Relief flurries through me like a snowstorm, pouring up my throat as a whimpered exhale.

I did it.

He's out.

Now to cut off his head.

Battling for breath, I look through the haze of heat waves, straight into the sun's harsh glare, locating my weapon that looks both close and incredibly far away.

I release the bind, shoving at Hock's big, limp body with my wounded hands, trying to wiggle my leg out from where it's crushed beneath him. Finally inching free, I clamber to a wobbly stand – the entire world tipping, swaying. The ax as one, then splitting . . .

Splitting again.

I focus on one and charge forward, folding over to swipe it up, scooping only grains of sand, the illusion disintegrating like it's made of fog. Groaning, I tumble forward, catching myself in an unsteady crouch, the bite on my breast thumping with a deep, destructive ache that spurs my hunger to hack through his throat. To fist his hair, raise my gory trophy, then walk out of here and *never* look back.

Gaze whipping around, I seek the weapon.

Where is it—

Where is it—

Where is it—

My stare latches onto its honed head glinting in the sun, cushioned in the sand just to my right. Another flurry of relief ices my insides.

I stretch out, reaching.

A shadow burdens my peripheral – the only warning I get before something hard *cracks* against the side of my head.

Pain explodes in my temple as my body soars too fast.

Too slow.

Lights flash across my waning vision, and I collide with the sand so hard my teeth impale my tongue, something warm spilling down the side of my face while I stare at the crater's sheer side.

Unblinking.

Unmoving.

I just . . . lie. Lids heavy, head heavier. Feeling weaker and more brittle than I did when I woke confused in that cell so many aurora cycles ago – way back at the very beginning.

My sluggish mind churns as I try to grapple this new, warped reality into something that makes sense . . .

Was he not dead?

Did I not strangle him for long enough?

Was he playing me the fool?

Get up, Raeve.

Groaning, I roll sideways, then push to my hands and knees.

Wobble.

I lift my head, seeing double the tents. Double the crowd. Double the big, glaring ball of sun.

My arms buckle, and my face collides with the sand.

Hock's weapon whirls through the air, thumping to a halt beside my ax before I'm cast in his broad shadow.

Get. The. Fuck. Up!

Snarling, I finally manage to clamber to my feet and spin.

The ground tips.

Heavier than I've ever felt, I stumble with the world's violent tilt, barely catching myself.

Hock stalks toward me, muscles rippling with each prowling step, his neck slashed with deep, ruddy indents to match his eyes – the whites now stained red from his choking strain. Making him look wild.

Rabid.

'*Gúide*,' he growls, which must mean submit because Saiza's screaming it from the sidelines. '*Gúide, Kholu*.'

'*Fuck you*,' I slur, spitting a wad of blood on the ground, my lids threatening to slam shut. 'And my name's Raeve, you corrupt piece of shit.'

He grunts, lunging. Cracks his fist against my jaw so fast I barely realize I'm falling, watching the strings of skulls sift by in rapid motion, until I collide with the ground. All the breath erupts from my lungs, and I cough, hacking for breath. Trying to scramble to my feet again—

He straddles me, his dense weight packed upon my hips.

I thread my hand up his right thigh and work my fingers past the gaping leather, into the long slice Zaran created earlier with his rounded sword.

Hock roars, snatching my wrist, then the other. He pins them to the ground above my head, the beating gong somehow tilling the air with its harrowing throb, dashing sand into my eyes.

The back of Hock's hand collides with my cheek with such force the entire world rips sideways, my head snapping with the motion, mouth lax and caked with sand.

My body shuts down from the hurt. The pain.

The ability to move.

'*Gúide*.'

I'd rather die than be bound to him against my will. The Fate Herder must surely know that.

That creature brought me here – to this very moment – knowing I'll never submit. Meaning this . . .

This is an *assassination*.

Of *me*.

Definitely should've bowed.

'Gúide!' he repeats – a slashing command that shreds the air.

'Fuck . . . you,' I puff through bloody clumps of sand.

Fuck the Fate Herder.

Fuck *everything*.

A laugh crumbles up my throat as he fists my hair so tight I'm certain he's about to tear big clumps from my scalp. Using it to lift my head again, he scowls down at me. My vision splits, converges.

Splits again.

That gong continues to beat, harder and harder, until the entire arena is a swirl of pulsing wind and sand.

I continue to laugh in Hock's face, even as he raises his other hand—

A shadow eclipses the sun.

A roar cleaves the air.

Hock tips his head to the sky, his hand still set to strike me as a Sabersythe soars into view, dragging its monstrous claw through the crisscross of skull-laden ropes and ripping them skyward.

Skulls rain, pelting the sand like mini moonfalls.

Folk scream, but my pulse screams louder.

I'm certain I'm seeing things as Rygun drops upon the crater's lip with a ground-shuddering *thump*. As Kaan uses Rygun's ropes to propel himself down into the dip, shirtless but for his own málmr hanging around his neck, his beautiful face ripped with the wrath of a million maddened men.

I'm certain I'm seeing things as Kaan's boots thump upon the ground. As he crunches his hands into fists, stalking toward me with footfalls that seem to shake the world while his lips shape words I recognize, the tendons in his neck straining as he wrestles with Bulder's dialect.

I'm certain I'm seeing things as the crater begins to shake, a slash of relief almost severing me in two despite the massive crack weaving across the ground. Despite the way those ember eyes are locked on me – scarcely dressed, sprawled across the sand beneath another male intent on claiming the *right* to bind with me . . .

Probably not a good time to commend him on his hunting skills, but damn – *it's tempting*.

Raeve

CHAPTER 42

Kaan dominates the crater, each long stride hailed by another shake of the ground, his body a tower of rippling brawn dappled with sweat that glistens in the sun, his scars pale against the rusty surrounds.

His hair is pulled back, sooty brows pinched above his savage stare that clings to me. That casts a cord between my ribs, down into the depths of my icy internal lake where it snags something heavy and thrashing that I can't quite glimpse.

I begin to tremble, my teeth clanking together so hard I'm surprised they don't shatter. I blame it on the fact that my skull is probably on the verge of cracking. It's certainly not something deeper. I'm not shaking like an egg threatening to hatch from this overwhelming surge of relief now packing my chest full. Relief that he's here. With me.

That—

It's definitely not that.

Every other clan member aside from Hock smacks their fists to their chests four times, the thumping clamor filling the crater with a drone of respect. Kaan does it once – a vision of ruin and rage.

His gaze shifts to the male still straddling me, his eyes blazing so full of flames I should be scared.

Frightened . . .

I'm not.

'*Dagh ata te roskr nei.* Ueh!' His dense, gravelly voice carries the foreign words with such carnal ferocity I feel each syllable abrade my pebbling skin. He smacks his fist against his chest again, this time splaying his hand, dragging his nails diagonally down his torso. Four distinct scratch marks bloom – risen and angry. '*Gagh de* mi *dat nan ta* . . . aghtáma.'

The words cut like blades, making me wince. I don't have to understand the language to know the King is . . . well . . .

Pissed.

Hock rises – Kaan's match in size. '*Agath aygh te nei dahl Tookah atah. Agath dein* . . . vah! *Lui te hah mat tuin*.' He repeats Kaan's motion, scratching his own skin, then again with his other hand, creating a welted X upon his heaving chest.

Kaan snarls. '*Heil deg* Zaran *dah ta réidi*. Heil deg dah ta réidi!'

Hock spits on the ground, repeats the clawing motion, then *charges*. Kaan mimics – like two great mountains merging toward each other.

Clashing.

I feel the motion like a boulder lobbed at my ribs.

Heads pressed together, clenched hands firmly cast at their sides, they *snarl*. Such violent intimacy in their almost-embrace that I'm certain the energy they're exuding has the power to cleave another crevice in the ground.

Saiza is suddenly at my side with another female, both scooping me up, threading my arms around their necks and dragging me toward the tent.

'Whas being sssaid?' I slur past my clanking teeth, trying to blink away the haze beginning to cloud my vision.

'Hock is claiming the victory over your battle, despite the fact that you did not submit,' Saiza says as I'm carried past the Sól now making her way to Hock and Kaan in long, hip-rolling strides. 'Kaan is declaring you are not free to be claimed by anyone. That you were not raised in our ways and are not accustomed to such traditions. He is demanding the trial be void. As Hock's roskr – his *greater*, in your tongue – he is demanding Hock accept his great victory over Zaran and step out of the battle ring to add a dot to his réidi. Hock, in turn, is challenging the roskr order and wants to battle Kaan. If he wins, he will earn many more dots for his réidi.'

My heart dives, the thought of Kaan battling Hock to the death spawning something spiky and uncomfortable in my chest.

'Kaan isss King of The Burn,' I force out. 'Hock would dare to challenge the crrrown?'

'Your crowns mean little here. We claim part of no kingdom. Only the réidi matters. We only pound chest four times for the roskr-éh. The *greatest*.'

My brows collide, and I look over my shoulder at the snarling males still spitting words at each other. 'If Kaan is ssstrongest, why is he not Oah?'

'He was, until his pah died,' Saiza whispers when we reach the tent. 'He offered uith-roskr – second greatest – the bones of our ancestral Oahs. Oah Knok has been a worthy Oah.'

My gaze sways to Oah Knok as I'm helped onto the dais before I'm spun and settled upon the rug, the hurt on my temple dabbed at with something cold and damp.

I sway, the scene before me splitting, converging.

Splitting again.

Rygun reigns over the arena from his lofty perch on the edge, his mammoth size casting half the crater in shadow. Set amongst that fearsome pronged face, his inky eyes trace Kaan's every move with crushing intensity – not helped by the fact that he multiplies every time the world splits.

I feel the opposite.

There's not one single part of me that wants to watch this fight unfold. Just a slumber ago, I wouldn't have batted a lash at watching Kaan Vaegor have his head sawn off in an arena. Instead, I would've *cheered*.

Now, even the thought makes me want to vomit.

I don't understand it. Don't want to understand it.

Don't want to watch.

'Well,' I rasp, bringing a shaking hand up to feel the hurt on my head, frowning when my fingers come away bloody, 'while they're occupied, howww 'bout I pretend to be dead and yyyou two throw me back in the river?'

'It is not that simple, I'm afraid.'

That's not the right attitude to have.

'The Fate Herder'sss gone,' I slur, looking around my wobbly surroundings, not seeing it anywhere. 'I think it can be that sssimple if we believe hard enough.'

She swipes some of the blood from my chest. 'I do not think it is gone; I think it is just choosing not to be seen.'

I frown, searching the crater, still trying to make sense of this fated mess.

Failing.

Every time I think I've got a grasp on it, the grains of understanding slip through the gaps between my fingers.

If it wanted me dead, that would've been the moment.

So what *does* it want?

'You have a vahli serpent bite,' Saiza says, running the pad of her thumb over the two stinging prickles on the mound of my breast, all the color leaving her face. 'Where did this come from?'

Guess nobody saw Hock flick his pocket python at me. Wonder how many other opponents have fallen victim to his vile, dishonorable methods.

I don't respond, mainly because there's no point.

It's done. The moment I no longer feel like I'm going to crumble if I stand, I'll launch back out there and hack off his head, then mulch his brain with my fist.

Saiza's eyes widen, whipping toward the ring. '*Gas kah ne*, veil dishuva!' she sneers, her words so honed I swear they could slit skin.

She stands and makes for the cluster of urns at my back, clanking around while she mutters beneath her breath. There's the sound of her stirring something before she presents me with a cup of chilled water perhaps pulled from one of the runed urns. Though it looks almost . . .

Lumpy.

'Drink this,' Saiza instructs through gritted teeth, cutting another sharp glance in Hock's direction. 'I mixed the water with an antidote that gives it a strange feel, but it will counteract the venom in your system.'

I dip my head in thanks, my features twisting as I sip down globs of the sour jelly-like concoction, feeling the icy swallows seep through my bloodstream at a rapid pace. Chilling me from the inside out.

Smoothing some of the wobbles from my mind.

The Sól crouches in the sand, pinches some between her fingers, then sprinkles it on her tongue just as I drain the rest of the mug in a single face-scrunching gulp. Tipping her head, the Sól begins chanting, reaching for the sky. She stops, slams her palms on the sand, grips two handfuls, then flicks her fists over so fast most of it sprays free.

'What's she doing?'

'Reading the will of the Creators,' Saiza whispers, taking the empty cup from my hand.

Slowly, almost eerily, the Sól loosens her fingers, milky eyes searching the grains left in her lax grasp. '*Gath attain de ma veil set aygh te*,' she says, her murmured words somehow echoing across the dusty expanse. '*Hailá atith ana te lai . . .*'

A hush falls over the crowd, and Kaan's face pales. He spears me through with a wide-eyed stare that chills me to the bone.

'Did she say something b-bad?'

'The Sól has announced that since blood has already been spilled in your honor, you must not leave this crater unclaimed. That if you do, more moons will fall in this place of ill-spilled blood and the Johkull Clan will lose our place of sanctuary. That many will perish. Her word is final.'

My shudder abruptly stops, like every muscle in my body just pumped full of mortar.

The ball in Kaan's throat rolls, and he breaks from Hock, holding my stare. He stalks toward me, his eyes taking on an empathetic softness as he pulls his málmr off.

My blood turns to ice.

He falls to his knees before me and lowers his head between his shoulders, bowing so deep his back is bared – his cupped hands outstretched, cradling his beautiful málmr . . .

Silence.

Even the wind stills its frantic stir.

My heart lodges so far up my throat it's hard to breathe past.

I look at the piece – at the dark Sabersythe and silver Moonplume tucked in their forever embrace – admiring the exquisite workmanship. The love he's poured into every dip and curve of the carving.

A vision saddles me with such intensity my breath snags:

Kaan's málmr resting between my naked breasts, my body slicked with sweat as I writhe in rippling pleasure, looking past my navel. Down between my split thighs that are gripped by large, powerful hands . . .

Down to where Kaan's ember eyes are blazing for me, his tongue laving at my—

I pop the hallucination like a bubble, gasping for a rush of air that only succeeds in making my head spin. Making it throb with a deeper, more painful hurt. No matter how hard I scrub the specter from my mind, I'm left with this oily residue of possession that slicks my insides.

A single surety stakes my heart like the roots of a mountain range – impossible to shift.

I want to accept that beautiful, dangerous object.

Hold it.

Cradle it close.

If even for a little while.

Fueled by that single blade of knowledge – ignoring its problematic implications I'll battle another dae once we're past this treacherous hurdle – I reach out, fingers wrapping around the málmr and bringing it close to my chest.

Something settles inside me like a key notched into place, though I don't look too close. Don't assess it.

This isn't real.

It's survival.

Kaan remains crouched before me, hands empty, holding the stance for so long the crowd begins to murmur. A few even gasp.

'What's he doing?'

'He is asking for you to place your print upon his réidi,' Saiza rasps, her voice hitched with awe. 'He is saying that he respects you above himself and, most importantly, above his honor.'

My heart stills, eyes widen.

'I—' *I don't know what I've done to deserve that.* 'That doesn't make any sense.'

'He is announcing you as his roskr. His *greater*. Should you accept this honor, his title will be passed to you should he fall this dae.'

Should he fall—

A strange piercing pain lances through my chest like a dagger plunged deep. 'Wh—' My voice cracks, and I look at Saiza, a question in my eyes that I hope she can see, certain that if I try to speak, everything will come out in strangled bits.

What does it mean?

Saiza's eyes soften, and she places her hand upon my cheek, cupping it. 'It means that if Kaan loses, any decision you make will not be challenged. You can leave despite being claimed and receive no dishonor because you will be considered Hock's greater.'

Every cell in my body charges with a current of thick, primal understanding, my next breath shuddered.

He's ensuring I get out . . .

No matter what.

My gaze drops to the male before me, something swelling in the back of my throat that's hard to swallow past, and I realize just how right I was to run.

To leave.

He's much, *much* too easy to care about.

Saiza sweeps some of my own blood off my collarbone and uses it to paint my hand. 'You may choose to print upon him and accept this great honor.'

I crunch my hand into a fist, release, looking at my blood slicked across it, then at the málmr caught in my other palm.

I don't deserve this. Not one bit. But I also don't want to disrespect him by refusing his beautiful gesture that weighs so much more than I'm now certain this magnificent male thinks I'm worth.

Silence reigns, and I battle to stuff those feelings down, wrestling them beneath my ribs while I look at the mural painted across his back. At the wonky moon half the size of my fist – like I could sweep it into my palms and cradle it.

I fall toward it heartfirst, pressing my hand upon the moon I love so much.

Kaan trembles all over, the motion vibrating up my arm and into my heavy heart, making my breath hitch.

He stands – too fast.

Too slow.

Some strange, unfamiliar part of me wants to reach forward and grab him. Scream for him to stay.

Beg him to live.

He keeps his stare to the ground and raises his fist, strikes his chest six times, then spins – stalking toward the weapon rack to the tune of the gasping, murmuring crowd.

Raeve

CHAPTER 43

Tension cuts the air, hundreds of stares scraping across my skin.

Delving beneath it.

I scan the leering crowd, then look to Saiza, her complexion pale, eyes bulging as she watches the King's retreat. 'Why six?'

'I am not certain,' she says. 'Five for Oah. Six is unheard of.'

I swallow, tightening my hand around Kaan's málmr.

He rummages through the weapons stacked upon a nearby rack, clunking things to the side, finally gripping the small knife I noticed earlier – the one with a maw's worth of tapered teeth mounted around the fringe of the flat blade.

He passes it from hand to hand, grunts, then rips his boots off and tosses them aside. '*Hach te nei, Rygun*,' he growls, pointing to his beast, his stern words echoing off the crater's sheer walls. '*Hach te nei, ack* gutchen!'

I lean into Saiza. 'What's he saying?'

'He is ordering Rygun to stand down . . . whatever the battle's outcome.'

The last four words land like boulders upon my chest.

Blazing eyes still pinned on Kaan, the beast fills his chest with a breath he rumbles free, the sound so abrasive it packs the crater with a thick promise of fiery violence I understand perfectly.

Too perfectly.

Kaan bellows another order. '*Hach te nei, Rygun*. Ack!'

Rygun stretches his wings, turns his face to the sky, and releases a searing screech – the sound accompanied by a mushroom of red flames that scorch and lick and flick at the powdery blue.

Folk scream, crouching over their younglings to shelter them from the heat. Others dive upon the ground, as if that could save them if the massive dragon decided to tip his head and pour his flames into the crater.

I also crouch, but for different reasons . . . binding myself into a ball as my skin *illuminates* with the remnants of a million wilted runes. Turning such a stark shade, the light emitting from the old etchings rivals one of the Moonplume moons perched within The Shade's otherwise gloomy depths.

I'm so crouched over myself, trying not to look too close at the residue of runes sketched across my skin – at the layers upon layers of tiny etchings used to stitch me together more times than there are moons in the sky to count – that I forget Saiza's beside me. At least until my eyes open and I catch her bulging perusal.

Her gaze drifts up my body, meeting mine. My heart leaps into my throat, and I open my mouth to speak—

'No wonder you laughed,' she says, then reaches behind me, flicking a blanket over my back and easing it around my shoulders. 'The unbreakable always do.'

I don't correct her. Don't tell her I've broken too many times to count. That I laughed because the pain I've felt in my heart eclipses any damage that could *ever* be inflicted upon my flesh and bones.

Instead, I give her a dozy smile of thanks, tucking deep into the corded fabric as Rygun throws his fiery tantrum toward the sky, like he's trying to sizzle the moons.

Seems he's more than displeased about being told what to do. To be fair, if I could rip off this iron cuff, I'd be taking fate into my own fucking hands.

His flame snips off, and he shoves into the sky, bits of rock raining from where his claws were pierced into the crater's lip. He tills his massive wings, stirring the crater into a billowing gale, forcing us all to shield our faces from the whip of sand.

He circles higher . . . higher . . . until he's far enough away that the clan's folk grow comfortable enough to unbundle themselves.

My mouth dries as Kaan stalks toward the crater's center, to where Hock has resumed his pacing, again wielding the same spiked mace he used to defeat Zaran. A spiked mace I picture swinging through the air with untraceable speed, colliding with the side of Kaan's face.

Shattering his skull.

I flinch, my body reviving its terrible tremble, more blood leaking down my temple. The antivenom is working hard to smooth the wobbly crinkles from my equilibrium, but not fast enough.

Not fast enough.

Even so, I force myself to my feet. Saiza leaps up to help me rise, acting as my post to lean against. The other female dabs at the wound on my head again, slathering it in something thick and potent while the males circle each other in prowling strides that trample through my chest.

Finally, they *charge* – clashing in a bludgeoning bash of fiery rage, again and again, each meaty, growling collision ricocheting through my bones so hard I jolt.

Skin splits.

Blood sprays.

Weapons turn wet and red.

There is no rhythm to their rippling motions that remind me of cracking earth and shattering stones. Of quakes that rattle the world hard enough to knock you off your feet. They're a chaotic dance of bulging muscle and feral regard I don't want to see, don't want to hear, my chest crushing a little more with each new scar slashed across Kaan's beautiful skin.

But despite the crippling sensation, I can't bring myself to look away.

Saiza leans close. 'You should sit, Kholu. Your legs are shaking, and that cut on your head is losing a lot of blood.'

Kaan fails to parry another swinging attack that lacerates the air, hacking shreds of skin from his abdomen.

A strangled scream slips up my throat, and his bloodshot stare latches onto me as something painful grubs through my chest like a flesh-eating worm.

My knees give way.

Saiza lowers me to the rug while Hock rains upon the King in a flourish of deadly strikes. As I cling to Kaan's málmr like the motion alone could hold his body together and protect him from the advancing blows that

don't

stop

coming.

Snarling, Kaan reaches into the swinging mass of lethal force, eating a spiked blow to the chest in order to snatch Hock's arm, and I think another sharp sound wrestles up my throat.

I think it might be his name.

I think I might've ordered him to *live*.

Hissing blood through clenched teeth, Kaan drags his toothy weapon through Hock's inner bicep, severing the bulge of muscle with a splash of red.

The mace drops to the sand.

Hock roars.

Kaan roars louder, stepping around the monstrous male and fisting his hair, ripping his head back far enough to bare Hock's throat in my direction.

My heart stops, the rest of the world smudging into oblivion.

Holding my stare, he lifts his toothy, bloody weapon to the stretch of flesh and *saws*.

A breath shudders into me.

Hock's screams start fierce and frantic before tapering into a gurgled groan as his throat is severed in messy, bone-grinding increments, plumes of blood ribboning down his jerking chest like a ruddy aurora.

His body drops. Head stays.

Something warm slips from my eyes. Drips down my cheeks.

Kaan steps over Hock's motionless mass and stalks toward me, chewing up the space between us. Still fisting Hock's hair as the world begins to split and sway.

Split and sway.

Kaan reaches me, teeth bared, his ravaged chest leaking blood. He lumps Hock's head on the ground before my low dais, and I feel that same weight thump within me, a choked sound wriggling past my trembling lips.

I drop my stare, taking in the rough, weeping sever of flesh around Hock's neck, his wide-open eyes. His mouth caught in a perpetual scream I'm certain I'll never stop hearing. The very reason I snip their breath.

Kaan drops into my line of sight like a crouching dragon, having just proved he's every bit capable of being the monster I thought he was. But right now, I feel only cold, plunging *relief*.

I cast a noose around the delicate, vulnerable feeling. Hang it from one of my ribs where I can look at its rotting corpse whenever I feel my heart doing the fluttering thing it's doing right now. Because that's what happens when I get attached in *any* way at all.

Death.

I look into Kaan's devastating eyes, a darkness toiling within the fiery depths that's so unhinged it brings me a strange sense of calm. Makes me feel a little less alone in this fucked-up world.

I lift his málmr and drag the leather loop over my head, settling the heavy carving between my breasts.

That darkness deepens.

Boldens.

A rumbling sound boils in his chest, planting a seed of ease in me even as my world sways with so much violence my entire body flops with the motion.

He catches me, lifts me.

Tucks me close to his chest.

Then his steps are thumping, *thumping* . . .

Or perhaps that's Rygun's wings.

I become quietly aware of the shadow. The wind. Of the fierce, feral roar that tears at the air, and the fact that we're likely leaving.

I settle my hand on Kaan's chest, finding comfort in the heavy pound of his heart, my eyes prying open just in time to see a silver smudge clawing up the crater's side.

Leaving.

Something else I decide not to assess too closely, certain that line of thought can only lead to more pain.

Suffering.

Loss.

'Moonbeam.'

'Hmm . . .'

'Please don't scare me like that again.'

Scare?

What a nice thing to say.

'You shouldn't spend such lovely words on me, Sire,' I murmur groggily, wishing I didn't find such comfort in his scent. In the feel of his arms wrapped around me.

In *him*.

'You should save them for somebody special.'

His guttural growl is the last thing I hear before darkness consumes me.

Diary Entry

Elluin Nevárn

Age: 18 phases
5,000,039 phases After Stone

Slátra flew across the Boltanic Plains while I was strapped to the saddle of a Moltenmaw, begging for one of the blue beads to summon a cloud of moisture and shelter her from the sun's singeing rays. The rider ignored every word.

Every plea.

Every fucking scream.

She followed me all the way to Dhomm, her silver flesh bubbling and bursting. Flying until her wings had too many holes to maintain her soar.

She plummeted, and I felt what was left of my heart rip from my chest and plummet with her, hopeless and powerless as she crawled across the burning dunes, making keening sounds I'll never be able to unhear. Nor will I be able to unsee the milky sheen of her eyes from staring at the sun while she screeched – over and over again.

I doubt a healer will be able to help her regain her vision, nor do I expect her to trust anyone to get close enough to try.

I certainly wouldn't, nor would I have blamed her if she never let me cuddle her again.

But she did.

The moment she balled up in the safety of a hutch near the Imperial Stronghold, she tucked me so close to her chest that I could feel the fluttering thump of her heart – barely clinging on. For me. Of that, I'm certain.

She didn't want to leave me here alone.

I almost begged her to solidify around me and take our pain away.

King Ostern agreed to let me sleep in the hutch with her, so long as its entrance is heavily guarded.

Don't know why he bothers. We both know I'd never leave this place without Slátra. Since I donned the Aether Stone, I can no longer summon a cloud for long enough to escort her back across the plains. Meaning I'm stuck here in this hot, humid place while my kingdom is run by a vile male I did not choose for myself. A horror that pales in comparison to the pain I feel whenever I look at my beautiful, broken Moonplume . . .

I'll never forgive myself for climbing upon her back all those phases ago. For riding her until she listened to me.

Trusted me.

I'll never forgive myself for taking her from her home. I'd do anything to go back to mine again.

Kaan

CHAPTER 45

I fold forward over Raeve's too-limp body before we plunge, spearing through a clot of cloud. We shred free with a flick of Rygun's wings, the jungle-encrusted mountains rolling by beneath us much slower than I'd like them to.

'Hast atan, gaft aka.'

Faster, my friend.

Rygun's raging adrenaline churns in my chest, making me feel like I'm burning from the inside out.

'Hast atan, Rygun!'

He *roars* – blowing a plume of ruddy flames through a web of low-hanging clouds, dissolving them.

The mountain range comes to a lofty head, and he chases the updraft with a pump of his wings, slingshotting over the rounded peak crowned with the domed lookout housing several Sabersythes and a Moltenmaw. Their riders blow horns in sharp bursts to hail our arrival, and I finally sight the Loff stretched far as my eyes can see.

I consume the vast, unpredictable body of water like the welcomed relief it is, Rygun roaring to the constellation of spiked Sabersythe moons peppered above the glistening turquoise depths. To the Moltenmaw moons, too – though only a few.

Home.

Relief loosens some of the weight stacked inside my chest.

'Almost there,' I murmur close to Raeve's hooded head as Rygun cuts so close to the lookout I'm certain his tail skims the roof. He tucks his wings and plummets down the cliff's sheer face toward

The Burn's sheltered capital packed around the sloping shore. Like Bulder took a blade to the bulbous summit and sliced a cove wide enough to cradle the second-largest city in the world.

Sunshine batters the auburn dwellings rounded like the mountains they spawned from, folk yelling from the veined walkways – waving. Younglings jump up and down, arms stretched as they hoot and roar and pretend to soar across the cobblestones.

Rygun aims for the Imperial Stronghold that oversees it all, protruding from the mountain like a growth pocked with stained glass windows and open archways, clothed in vines heavy with the black ukkah blooms Mah loved so much.

Pah used to have them hacked back, but not me. They have my permission to swallow the city.

The entire *kingdom*.

Rygun lowers us toward a flat landing patch, the balmy air rich with the smell of salt and braised meat. I brace around Raeve as Rygun drops his weight upon the ground, packing so much heft a cleft forms in the stone I'll have to patch up later.

I throw my leg over the saddle, my heart dropping when I see Veya jog through a domed doorway, her long brown hair tossed about by the wind. She's garbed in her ever-present riding leathers I suspect she fucking sleeps in, wearing a broad smile that disappears the moment her stare cuts across the blood I'm wearing . . . the female tucked against my chest . . .

'Shit,' I murmur, working my way down the ropes.

I love her welcomes. Treasure them. But for the first time in my life, I would've happily gone without it just so I can get inside the door without—

'Who's that?'

My salvation. And the very reason you're probably going to gut me with your pocket blade before I even make it into the Stronghold.

I leap down the final few rungs and land upon the stone, scouring Rygun's lathered hide. '*Glatheiun de, Rygun. Hakar, glagh, delai.*'

Thank you, Rygun. Bathe, replenish, rest.

He releases an ear-splitting screech and bounds into the sky, slamming us with a gust of wind that whips at Raeve's thick black braid hanging free from the cloak I draped her in to protect her from the sun.

'Kaan, who's in your *Creators-damn arms?*'

I turn, storming toward the doorway. 'I love you, Veya, but I can't do this here. I need Agni.'

Now.

I'm almost through when Veya screams at me from behind – her voice so shrill I picture a blade whirring toward me. 'Kaan Llúk Vaegor. Tell me who that is, or I *will* fill your pallet with hurky beetles every slumber for the rest of your long, miserable existence, so fucking help me!'

I blow out a sigh and turn.

Cutting me another sharp look, she steps close, gaze dropping. She tugs back the hood, eases Raeve's blood-soaked hair aside—

And gasps.

I look down, my heart dropping at the sight of Raeve's face – her skin so pale it's almost translucent.

My chest stirs full of flames.

Her features are too lax, thick lashes fanned across bruised cheeks, her plump lips barely parted.

Not pursed with rage.

Not peeling back with a lashing sneer.

Not battling a smile, as it did when I poked my tongue at her.

Veya's trembling fingers dance around Raeve's face, like she wants to touch her. Like she's afraid she'll disappear if she does.

A feeling I know too well.

I look to where a patch of dressing covers the deep gash in the side of her head. A gash that follows the same trail as the scar I saw via dragonflame.

More blood has seeped through the dressing since I checked last . . .

Fuck.

Perhaps finally noticing that some of the blood on Raeve's body has been *painted* on, Veya cuts me a glance, then peels the cloak farther back, revealing Raeve's red silk attire. Revealing my málmr draped around her neck, the carving rested upon her blood-slicked chest.

Veya stumbles back a step, her wide, tear-puddled eyes condemning me. '*How*—'

'She's wounded,' I rumble, tucking the cloak back into place to protect her modesty for my impending charge through the halls. 'I stopped by a mender's hut on the way, but they only had the expertise to stabilize her for the journey here.'

Veya swallows, nods once, then dashes a tear off her cheek, not meeting my gaze as she rasps, 'Come, I just passed Agni on her way to the feasting hall.'

I charge through lofty tunnels lit with flaming sconces, Veya keeping pace. We storm past mercenaries who flatten themselves against the walls – right fists thumping against their chests.

'*Hagh, aten dah*,' many of them yell as we pass, packing the air with the clamor of welcome and respect.

We barrel down another lengthy tunnel, the Stronghold almost the size of the city itself – a city *within* itself – tunneling into the mountain range, spilling out in cleverly hidden clefts farther south. Enough space to house the entire cavalry, their families, and the dragons of those who have charmed one.

There was a time when the entire place was maintained for the imperial family alone, but I filled it with enough noise to drown out the plague of silence after I tore Pah's head from his shoulders and took the city haunted by the ghost of *her*. Blood rained, the Loff blushed, and Rygun feasted that dae.

I thought it would make me feel better.

It didn't.

We round a corner, storming into the rowdy clatter and chatter of the feasting hall as Pyrok exits the wide-open doorway with a mug of Molten Mead in his big fist. His blaze of rebellious locks is a fucking mess as usual, hanging around his scar-riddled shoulders, black piercings through his nipples, lip, septum, and lobe.

He looks me up and down, whistles low, and spins, charging back into the hall. 'Meal time's over! Grab your plates and get the fuck out. Yes, you too. No, not you – you stay right where you are, Agni dearest. Your miraculous skills are required.'

Nice of him to be helpful for a change. Guess we look worse than I thought.

I barge through the doorway in time to see him reach over the long stone table, using his arm as a sweep to shove everything down the far end – copper plates, cutlery, and chalices clattering to the ground, splashing mead and meat and flaps of spiced dahpa bread all over the stone.

Folk scatter, exiting the vast hall in a silent riot I barely notice, heading for the half-empty table lit by a single jagged blade of sun slicing through the cleft in the roof. I lay Raeve's listless body on it, directly before a wide-eyed Agni – her white Runi cloak such a contrast to her dark skin, more than twenty gold, silver, or diamond buttons lining the middle seam.

A boast of her vast accolades. Even more than her sister, Bhea.

Agni looks between the still-weeping gashes on my chest and the bloody dressing on Raeve's brow.

'Her first. Please.'

She nods, tucking a lock of brown hair behind her ear before she peels the cloak away and examines Raeve's battered body, clicking her tongue.

I look at Pyrok. 'Can you find Roan? The extra pair of hands could help.'

'Can't,' he says, twirling the piercing through his bottom lip. 'He's not here.'

'Where—'

'Bothaim. Trying to get a look at that book again. He's certain there are more pages that haven't been transcribed and released to the public.'

I sigh.

Pyrok shrugs. 'You ask me, the place has been awfully peaceful without my nagging brother around. And you.'

I glare at him as he chugs his mead.

Agni lifts the dressing to inspect Raeve's gnarly wound, shaking her head. 'The bone is fissured,' she murmurs, poking at the gape of skin in a way that makes me want to vomit. 'I'll have to melt her skull smooth again before I thread her flesh. She's very lucky this didn't kill her.'

I would've split the world if it did.

Then split my fucking self.

She uses the dressing to blot at the wound. 'Someone will need to get me a cloth and a pail of water, and fetch my kit. Pyrok, you look like you need a job. Is this all *her* blood?'

Surprisingly, Pyrok jogs from the room like something's nipping at his heels, though not before casting an assessing stare between me and Veya – the latter standing over the other side of the table, gaze narrowed on me like an arrow notched and aimed.

'No,' I say, holding Veya's stare. 'A lot of it is colk blood, my blood, and the blood of another male.'

'You fucking bastard,' Veya growls, then launches across the table at me – arm swinging. I let her get three good hits to my jaw, gut, and the fucking wounds on my chest before I snatch her wrists and shove her toward Grihm, who'd silently eased off the back wall the moment she started speaking.

With a big pale hand wrapped around her wrists, he bands his other arm across her chest, looking at me through a flop of snow-toned hair that mostly hides his icy eyes, the tic in his square jaw pulsing. The only sign the male ever gives that he's on edge.

Veya snarls, looking up at me with the ferocity of an uncharmed adolescent Sabersythe – eyes blazing, upper lip peeled back from bared canines. Failing to jerk out of Grihm's hold. '*How could you take her to that place?*'

'The *gorge* took her to that place,' I growl, wiping a wad of blood off my lip. 'I got there just in time.'

'She's dressed in the garb of a Tookah Trial, Kaan. A *Tookah Trial.*'

'Well aware, Veya.'

'Who was the male?'

'Hock.'

Shadows cloud her eyes, and she stiffens. 'Good,' she fires, no longer wrestling Grihm – not that he lets her go.

Not that she asks him to.

She lifts her chin. 'How did she kill him?'

Rage crackles through my veins like crumbling embers as I fail to shake the image of Raeve sprawled on the sand, covered in blood, straddled by a male who had every intention of claiming her as his own. As I fail to shake the image of her laughing, like she was mocking her impending death.

You shouldn't spend such lovely words on me, Sire.

Fuck.

I crunch my hands into fists. 'She didn't.'

Veya's eyes narrow on the málmr around Raeve's neck, then widen. 'Creators . . .'

I grunt, another pulse of stone-crushing energy shooting through my veins.

My muscles.

I intercept Pyrok as he re-enters the room. Taking the pail, I use the damp cloth to clean around Raeve's wound, then wipe the blood off her face while Pyrok helps Agni spread her tinctures across the table. When he looks up again, he stills, the jar that was in his hand dropping to the ground.

Shattering.

'Who in the Creators-damn *fuck* is that, and why does she look like Elluin Neván? She's dead,' he says, looking from me to Veya to Grihm, his skin turning just as pale as the latter. 'Am I the only one that thinks I'm going mad right now?'

No.

Agni looks between us like we're *all* mad, dabbing some purple liquid on a piece of cloth and patting it over Raeve's mouth.

'She doesn't know herself as Elluin,' I mutter, slopping my cloth back in the pail and dragging both hands through my hair, pulling it back off my face. 'To her, she's Raeve, and she has no recollection of anything prior to the past twenty-three phases.'

My words echo through the hall, taunting me.

'Well . . . fuck,' Pyrok murmurs. 'You sure they're one and the same? That you didn't just bring some poor stray home because she looks like Elluin?'

'You think I'd do that?' I growl.

He shrugs. 'Seen some crazy shit over the past eon. Not gonna lie.'

I clear my throat.

Granted.

'It's her. Any doubt I might've had was squashed the moment she told the High Chancellor of The Fade he has a microcock – and at her own murder hearing.'

There's a stretch of silence before Pyrok chuckles, snatching some random chalice off the table. 'I'll toast to that.' He drains the vessel, slamming it back on the table. 'Hate that dusty old piece of shit.'

'If she has no recollection,' Veya says with slow, steady precision, 'how do you explain the fact that she calls herself by her *middle name*?'

I shake my head. 'I don't know, Veya.'

'Then how is she here? Alive?'

'I don't know that either.'

A line forms between her brows – the stain of frustration I feel in my marrow. 'Well, what are her first memories of *this* life?'

Another shake of my head.

Veya finally loosens from Grihm's grip, the latter crossing his arms over his broad chest, gaze firmly cast on my sister stalking toward me with war waging in her blood-shot eyes. 'Do you know *anything*?'

Fuck all.

'The only time I tried to pry, she compared my cock to the size of my brain,' I bite out. '*Unfavorably*.'

Some of the anger drains from Veya's eyes, the corner of her mouth twitching as Pyrok chuckles. I slice him a glare, and he drowns the sound in another guzzle of someone else's mead.

He won't be laughing when she cuts those sharp teeth on him.

Agni hands Pyrok the purple-blotched cloth. 'Wave this in front of her nose every few moments. I don't want her rousing mid-etching, and your hands look like they need something better to do than drink everyone else's mead.'

'Agni, you know perfectly well how good I am at multi-tasking,' Pyrok says, flashing her a grin.

Agni's cheeks flush, and she shakes her head, muttering beneath her breath.

'Where did you find her?' Veya asks, seemingly immune to the shit coming out of Pyrok's mouth.

'I stumbled upon her at the Hungry Hollow, but her face was half-hidden. I thought I was going mad.'

Still do.

'I later found her rotting in a cell.' I scrub my beard as Agni paints a bonding agent over the snowy flesh I've kissed more times than I can count. 'A Truthtune confirmed she had no prior recollection of me before our chance encounter. None.'

'So she doesn't know about—'

'No,' I say, cutting Veya off.

She opens her mouth, closes it, shaking her head. 'And you're *certain* you watched Slátra—'

'On her life,' I growl, my words bouncing off the walls like one of Rygun's rumbling exhales.

Saw it. Lived with the bruising memory for the past one hundred twenty-three phases – while sleeping and awake.

I'll never outlive the vision nor the jagged cleft of pain that broke through my chest at the sight. Even with her here, on this table, *breathing* . . .

I'll wake up from this utopia eventually. I'm sure of it. I'll jerk up off my pallet and realize it was all one vicious, beautiful dream.

Veya moves around the table and tucks Raeve's hair back from her pointed ear – the one that's clipped into. 'She bears the southern mark of a null.' She frowns, inspecting both lobes. 'No beads. Not even a hole for them to hang off. Do the Creators still speak with her?'

'Clode and Bulder,' I say, crossing my arms over my ravaged chest. 'Though I'm not sure about the other two.'

Straightening, she mimics my stance – twice as fierce but half the size. 'Her veins flow with *Neván blood*, Kaan. And she wears no song-silencing Aether Stone. If Tyroth finds out she's here, he'll be blowing flames upon our doorstep before we've had a chance to properly prepare. He'd be stupid not to, and we both know he's far from stupid.'

'I'm well aware of the risks.'

She cocks her head to the side. 'Well . . . what are you going to do?'

'I don't know. But if you want to talk about war strategy, now is not the time.'

I'm tired.

Angry.

Bleeding.

Hungry.

I have a million things to attend to and only *one* I'm interested in.

My gaze flicks to Raeve, Agni beside her mixing tinctures, preparing for the procedure—

'Are you afraid she'll see him and . . . *remember* him?' Veya asks, her narrowed stare like iron arrows shot straight through my chest. 'Leave you again? That the note was *true*?'

I don't let her see how much the words sting. How I feel them punch through one side, shred muscle, sinew, and bone, then burst out the other.

Yes.

Yes.

Fucking *yes*.

But I lost the right to be greedy with her.

I watch Agni work, Pyrok juggling between his menderaid duties and guzzling pilfered mead. 'She's a dream come true, but she's not just *my* dream,' I say, packing the space full of truth-laden stones. 'Not anymore.'

Even the air seems to still, and an eerie quiet blankets the room, gnawing at me from all angles.

I look at my bloody hands, stretch them out, inspect both sides before I crunch them into balls. 'She's so much more than a power play. So much more than the love of my existence. There's someone out there who needs her more than *any* of us do, and it's not our fucking brother,' I growl, looking straight into Veya's glazed eyes.

She blinks, and a tear slides down her cheek.

'I will slowly, gently ease her into her truth – painful as it is. Then she can choose her own path. Make her own choices.'

Come what may.

Veya drops her stare to the floor as another tear drips down her cheek.

I look away.

She never cries, so when she does, it feels like the world is cracking. Like I've failed to protect her.

Again.

My hands loosen, fist again, trembling with a crushing amount of untethered energy.

Agni uses a metal tool to cleave Raeve's wound wider, giving her direct access to the fissure in her skull so she can first mend the bone—

I look away from that, too – wanting to crush the image from my memory. But its claws are already in.

Digging deep.

'I'll be back,' I mutter, then jerk my chin at Grihm and make for the door, expecting Veya's final hit well before it lands.

'Nobody can suffer what she's been through and not be pitted with a well of dragonflame – whether she remembers her past or not. Tread carefully, Kaan, or she'll incinerate herself and turn to ash in your fucking hands.'

I growl, charging down the hall, chased by the heavy thump of Grihm's boots.

I know.

Kaan

CHAPTER 46

I stalk down tunnel after tunnel, the air chilled by glowing runes etched onto the curves of russet stone, flaming sconces shrieking at me as I charge past.

Those who can't hear Ignos probably think flames are happy to be alive no matter their size.

Wrong.

A candlestick flame will stretch and squirm in the presence of anyone who wanders by, screaming for more sustenance to burn. Desperate to *grow*.

Ignos doesn't like being small and unimpressive. He craves rugs to singe. Forests to obliterate. Fields of dry grass to rip across.

I call a small flame to my hand, and it writhes in my palm with hissing excitement as I pass mercenaries shoving against walls, fists thumping against bare or garbed chests.

'Hagh, aten dah.'

'Hagh, aten dah.'

'Hagh, aten dah.'

Their respectful bellows drone into oblivion, paling in comparison to the rage rumbling through my bones, heating my blood, licking against my organs with fiery malice.

I haven't slept in cycles. Not since before I woke to Raeve straddling me, one of Rygun's scales poised at my throat, her eyes flared with the promise of a death I'd rather have at her hand than anyone else's.

Before they softened.

Before I caught a glimpse of . . . *something*. A tender emotion that split my chest. Made me think her memories are in there.

Somewhere.

Fucking *somewhere*.

The aurora rose and fell three times while Rygun beat across the plains to get us here as fast as he could, and still, I don't crave sleep – a rabid amount of energy thumping through my veins, pumping my muscles full. Making me picture blood on my hands, fingers shredding flesh, bones snapping beneath my tight grip.

Grihm's heavy steps echo mine as I crack my knuckles, turning down the wide stairwell that spills into a dusky training ring.

I whisper my flame into segments that flit through the air, latching onto the flammable heads of many wall torches. Engulfing them in hissing shrieks – casting the wide, round, rough-hewn cavern in a rage of amber light.

I didn't craft this space with gentle precision. The ceiling isn't high or paved in grandeur. I didn't bother willing the walls into a fine polish.

This space is exactly what is required, nothing more. A crater-sized arena to throw fists and split skin. To break bones and fray feral tendencies before they grow their own blood-letting pulse.

Stepping down into the sand peppered with grains of iron, the voices in my head extinguish like a blown flame. I make for the arena's epicenter, the doors thumping shut, followed by the sound of Grihm removing his boots.

I stretch my arm across my chest, then the other. The fine scabs that had begun to form on some of my wounds reopen with the motion, warm blood slicking down my torso and dripping onto the sand.

'I'm not in the mood to hold back,' I rumble, spinning.

Grihm's jacket is on the ground by his boots, head dipped as he loosens the strings on his black tunic before pulling it over his head, exposing his back, his pale flesh a puckered mess. Like it melted, got stirred up, then abruptly solidified.

He begins to turn, and I look away.

'Neither am I,' he grates out, and it's a battle to keep my face stony. To contain my shock at the sound of his voice – its coarse texture a tribute to how little he uses it.

He stalks toward me, looking at me from behind the flop of

snowy strands half concealing his face, broad shoulders flexing as he fists his hands at his sides.

'Good,' I growl, then *charge*.

We collide in a clash of white-knuckled blows that break more than they build, our blood spraying the sand as we exert the menace from our systems in the only way either of us understands.

Fists to flesh.

Snarl to bloodlusting snarl.

Rage to fucking rage.

Veya

CHAPTER 47

Agni closes the wooden shutters, blocking out most of the light while I drape Elluin atop the large pallet in one of the many guest suites, placing her lax hands upon her chest. Pausing, I take in the ravaged skin down the sides of her nails, my brows pinching together.

Interesting . . .

Either a bad habit or she's lusting over the thought of having someone's blood on her hands.

Wonder which it is?

I pull the silk sheet up to her chin, sweeping a tendril of freshly brushed hair from her now-healed brow. Not even a trace of a scar she would've forever worn like a fucked-up version of the diadem she once bore.

'You did well,' I tell Agni, who dips her head in thanks, pausing by the end of the bed. Gaze caught on Elluin, she chews her bottom lip, fingers knotting – like she's deliberating. 'Something the matter?'

'Yes.' She looks at me, slowly filling her lungs. 'There's something I didn't want to bring up in front of the males. Mostly because they seemed . . . on edge. Didn't want to add fuel to the flames, so to speak.'

So she's telling the one who threw herself across the table and punched the King three times before she was manhandled into submission?

Nice.

I mold myself into a vision of poised composure and say, 'Go ahead.'

Her cheeks flush. 'The patient's, ahh . . . As you know, the gift of Dragonsight runs thick in my family line. So once the blood was cleansed from her skin, I could see the layered stain of many runes. Many, *many* runes.'

I frown, looking at Elluin. 'Recent?'

'It's hard to tell.' Agni makes her way around the pallet, peeling back the sheets. 'But she has *one* wound that doesn't appear to have been mended by runes. It glows a shade of silver I've never seen before. Right . . . here,' she says, placing her hand directly over Elluin's heart.

My blood chills.

'A killing wound,' she continues. 'Not one folk survive, since healing a stab to the heart takes more time than the patient usually has.'

All the heat drains from my face.

Creators . . .

I swallow the thickening lump in my throat, rubbing my hands down my cheeks, threading my fingers through my hair. 'Don't tell the King. Not until we know why . . . or how.'

Agni's face blanches, stare flicking to the door at my back, to me again. She drops into a swift curtsy, clears her throat, then turns her attention back on Elluin.

Frowning, I look toward the door, moving out into the hallway just in time to see a shirtless Pyrok disappear around the corner at the far end.

I sigh.

Charging forward, I spill into the sitting room and cut my gaze across the cluster of colk leather seaters curled around a low stone table that's seen more games of Skripi than there are stars in the southern sky.

Pyrok's sprawled across a large seater, his long, disheveled hair the same blazing hue as the flame dancing between his fingers. 'Don't tell the King, huh?' he says, condemning me from beneath raised brows.

'Don't look at me like that,' I mutter, stalking toward the opposite seater and dumping myself on it. 'He's so fucking *happy* to have her back he's not asking nearly enough questions. Besides, you don't slaughter your enemies with a blunt blade. You sharpen it until it's so honed you're certain it'll do the job.'

Pyrok flicks the flame from one hand to the other like a ball, its illumination casting his face in fierce, angular shadows. 'What do you know?'

That Elluin was stabbed to death – contrary to the story we were all spoon-fed like younglings desperate for a scrap of sustenance.

'Let me rephrase,' Pyrok says with a roll of his emerald eyes. 'Is whatever you *do* know going to lead us to war with our fledgling army?'

I shrug.

He curses, squashing the flame in his fist, fingers still steaming as he runs them through his hair. 'For someone who's never officially *been* to war, you're incredibly hungry for it.'

'What have we been preparing for all these phases if not to swipe the filth from the board and undo all of Pah's hard, bloody work?' Tucking one leg beneath myself, I pivot, unlacing my leather vest from where it's threaded down my front and sides. I loosen it, pull it over my head, then lift my loose brown tunic, exposing the ancient firelash marks I know make a damn good mess of the pretty skin on my back. 'You know I didn't keep *these* because I like the look of them,' I say, tossing him a backward glance, though he keeps his eyes on my scars – stare bouncing from one deep, mangled slash to the next. 'I kept them so that every time I look in the mirror, I'm reminded of why Tyroth and Cadok need to *rot*.'

Nothing quite like winning your own Tookah Trial, then being scored to shreds by your own blood for soiling the family name.

Yes, I'm war hungry. I've earned that right. Seventy-eight times, to be exact.

Pyrok clears his throat, dropping his gaze as I spin, wiggling my tunic back into place – not bothering with my vest.

'I didn't get to rip off Pah's head,' I mutter, reaching for the mug of brandy and tipping myself a glass. 'I'll rip off theirs.'

'Well, let me know if you want me to fry their cocks.'

'Maybe. See how I feel at the time.' I jerk my chin at the stack of Skripi cards and the eight-sided dice tucked in a tall clay mug beside it. 'Deal us.'

'I hate when you're bossy,' he groans, sitting up and reaching for the deck, swiping away some of the thickening tension.

'If I don't boss you around, nobody will. As it is, you're about as useful as a pretty mead-stained floor rug.'

'*Pretty*, you say? Fuck me,' he boasts, chest puffed, elbows on his spread knees as he leans forward and shuffles. 'I'm flattered.'

'Course you are.'

He winks, dealing the hard parchment shards. I snatch each one that slides onto the table before me, features smooth as silk despite my *delectable* hand.

This game loves me.

'I don't want to play for gold. I've got enough gold.' I fan my deal, reordering them from best to worst – left to right. 'I want to play for favors.'

Pyrok snort-laughs. 'Take it you've got the Moonplume?'

'Don't know what you're talking about,' I purr, batting my lashes at him.

He cuts me a dry look, then lays the rest of the deck around the board that never leaves the table. That's absorbed more spilled Molten Mead than Pyrok – and that's saying something.

'My roll,' I say, reaching for the cup containing the dice. 'Since your face annoys me.'

'You said I was pretty.'

'Yeah.' I toss the dice across the table, rolling a six, picking the eighteenth shard from the far left corner. Choosing to add the spangle to my deck, I set my sowmoth face down on the empty spot. 'Pretty *annoying*.'

Pyrok chuckles, shaking his head. He throws the dice, picking up a shard he ponders, the smile smoothing from his face. 'Grihm seen your scars?'

'Course not. Why?'

He slides the shard into his fan, placing another in its spot on the grid. 'Just wondering. Don't tell the King what?'

'Not telling, and if you try to pry the information from poor, vulnerable Agni with your charm stick, I'll murder you in your sleep.'

'The fucked-up thing is, I actually believe you,' he mutters, and I cut him a sharp smile – gone the next second.

I roll the dice again, picking up the hushling, face stony as I say, 'Elluin used to keep a diary, you know. I once caught her tucking it into a hole in the wall. In the suite she's sleeping in right now, actually.'

'What's that got to do with anything?' Pyrok asks, pouring himself a glass while I deliberate what to trade out.

'Never felt important before.' I shrug, placing the huggin face down on the empty space on the grid. 'Does now.'

'Okay, well . . . where is it?' He scoops the dice into the cup and rolls a seven, though he's swift to discount the card he picks and leaves it face down on the grid.

'Think she took it back with her to Arithia,' I mumble, rolling a two, this time picking up the Moltenmaw.

Luck, it seems, is licking my ass.

'Over a hundred phases ago,' he says with a thick tone of sarcasm I certainly don't appreciate. 'It's probably dust.'

'It's cold there.' I watch him over my fan of shards, holding his stare as I set the flotti face down on the empty spot. 'Perfect atmosphere for preservation.'

He looks at me like I'm daft, which we both know is far from true. 'Think you can visit Tyroth and not cut off his head, forcing your only decent brother into a war that starts off on the back foot?' He slams a shard on the table, and I frown at the thieving woetoe leering at me from the painted side.

Cute. He thinks he's got tricks.

'I'm not *that* irresponsible.' I ease my hand forward so he can blindly steal whatever shard he wants, smirking when he plucks the fog slug from the far right. 'And you're incredibly shit at this game.'

He scowls down at the shard, growling as he threads it into his fanned hand. 'I hate playing with you. I've watched you play over your shoulder before. You usually stack your good shards from the right to the left.'

'*Exactly* why I stacked them left to right,' I tell him, draining my glass before thumping it on the table. 'Skripi.'

'*Already*?'

'Want me to say it louder?'

'No,' he mutters, slamming down the Sabersythe I trump with my Moonplume, all the colors leaching from his shard – like the Sabersythe just perished. 'Fucking knew it.'

I set my colk down, but he trumps it with a velvet trogg, also winning the following stomp when his miskunn trumps my enthu.

Perhaps high on the smell of impending victory, he slams down the doomquill I'm quick to trump with my hushling before I slap my Moltenmaw on the final slot, knowing there's nothing left in the deck for him to beat me with.

'You lose.' I fill my glass and kick back in the seater, taking a deep draw, the brandy casting a fiery trail down my throat – my next breath hissed through clenched teeth. 'I reserve my right to a favor. To be used at a later date.'

'I'm never playing with you on my own again.' He flops back on the seater, using his bent arm as a pillow. 'It's not so bad when you beat me and Grihm at the same time.' He spits a word beneath his breath that peels a whip of flame from one of the sconces. It flits into his hand where he twirls it between his fingers like a slithering snake.

I look to the ceiling, the pretty bronze, black, and red tiles making up the face of Pah's snarling Sabersythe, Grohn. Constantly staring down at us. Constantly judging my indiscretions – or so Pah used to say when he discovered I was fucking one of the hutchkeepers after I'd given myself to the Creators to escape any future Tookah Trials.

He called it unbecoming. Disgraceful.

Embarrassing.

He *also* said Mah would be devastated to know she died giving birth to such a filthy whore.

I called it sweet, pleasurable revenge and decided Mah would've smiled at me, given me a pat on the head, and told me I could fuck whoever I felt inclined to fuck. Or nobody at all, if that's what I wanted. Hard to know for sure since I never met her, but she made me, and I like to think I inherited all my fabulous traits from her.

Certainly not the asshole who sired me.

'Guess I'm going to The Shade,' I mutter, drawing another deep sip of my drink, the spicy liquid heating my belly. 'Yay for me. Wanna come?'

'Shit no.'

'I could make you,' I drawl, lifting my glass above my head, closing one eye to look at Grohn through the fractals – the menacing fucker. 'Call on the favor I just won.'

'You're not that cruel.'

He's right. I'm not.

Unfortunately.

Sighing, I turn the glass, further fragmenting Grohn's horrific face, remembering the way Pah used to cue him to chase folk across the plains if they displeased him in any way.

I shiver.

'You're not gonna wait until Elluin wakes? Reintroduce yourself?'

'Haven't decided.'

What I *mean* to say is that I don't trust myself not to rip at her the same way I ripped at Kaan, despite the unrecognition and confusion I'll undoubtedly receive.

What she did was, in many ways, completely unforgivable.

Perhaps the diary will shed some light on the black hole she punched through my heart when she left without a word to me and a single pathetic note to the male she supposedly loved.

Diary Entry

Elluin Neván

Age: 18 phases
5,000,039 phases After Stone

I was singing to Slátra while I dozed amongst her fluffy tail when the gates were suddenly lifted by the guards standing watch over the hutch. Through the door, the biggest Sabersythe I've ever seen entered, sponging the light.

A male climbed down off the beast's back.

Tall.

Broad.

Beautiful.

Creators, he was beautiful.

There was something about the way he moved that made me picture a mountain crumbling.

He looked right at me through eyes like crackling embers, and I think my heart stopped.

His feet stopped, too.

That moment seemed to go on and on, and I almost begged Slátra to lift her wing and cut it off. Give me something to hide behind so I could catch my breath. She didn't, though she did lift her head and growl in the direction of the massive dragon looking at us like we were in its sleep space.

To be fair, that's probably correct, but this hutch is the only one Slátra was able to access in her injured state.

I didn't bother to put my veil on. The male had already seen my face and the Aether Stone latched upon my brow like the disease it is.

He coaxed his beast back from the burrow, though he returned a while later without his dragon.

This time, Slátra didn't growl.

He stole steps toward us, asking what happened to Slátra's eyes – his voice so rough and thick and accented that I almost couldn't understand his words, wondering how often he spoke. By the looks of all the scars on his arms, I've decided he spends most of his time screaming, not speaking.

He inquired about the last time I ate. If I was living down here.

I didn't respond to any of his questions. Not because it's forbidden for me to speak with strangers, but because I simply didn't have it in me.

I'm tired.

Tired of losing things I love. Tired of trying to rip this stupid diadem off my brow so I can wield the power I need to get Slátra home and take my throne from the asshole who thinks he owns me. Tired of being spoken down to by males who believe they know what's good for me and my kingdom I miss so much, now being run by a cruel, selfish, greedy male I wouldn't trust with my worst enemy.

I'm just . . . tired.

Raeve

CHAPTER 49

A scalding word burns hot on my tongue,
sputters against my lips, hopelessness stomping
me like a world lumped on my chest.
There's an ache in my heart that's leaking . . .
Leaking . . .
I think I'm leaking with it,
reaching for something I can't grasp.
Fingers outstretched.
Desperate to tangle with—
Something important.
Something . . .

Mine.

But I drain . . .
Drain . . .
Gently drain away . . .
Yanked away too fast.
Too slow.
Cold
Empty—

Jerking up, I battle for breath, clawing at my chest, ribs, and belly. Trying to untangle from the tacky tendrils of a slumber-terror that felt too real.

Too painful.

I slap my face, open my eyes, taking in the humid room, shards of light peeking through shuttered curtains I think I might've seen before. Somewhere. Perhaps in a dream. But I'm not dreaming anymore. I just woke.

I just woke—

Where the fuck am I?

I thread my fingers through my hair and push it back off my face, trying to piece together the bloody segments of my mulched memories.

The Fate Herder . . .

The kneeling, motionless colk leaking blood from its slit throat . . .

Two unfamiliar males slashing each other's flesh, trying to claim the rights to my body.

Hock's fist colliding with my face . . .

Kaan decapitating Hock . . .

Kaan—

Gasping, I reach for the málmr hanging heavy from my neck and cradle it in my palm, admiring the two embracing dragons . . .

Creators. That happened.

That.

Actually.

Happened.

'Shit,' I mutter, cutting my gaze around the room again, the walls all made from russet stone, the ceiling a mosaicked clash of black, bronze, and dark red. The space is sparsely furnished, most things grown from the wall or floor – the massive pallet, the twin side tables, the dresser protruding from the far wall packed with woven baskets used as drawers.

Light. Simple. Organic.

I glance down, seeing my attire has been changed, brushing my fingers across the black silk shift buying me all the modesty I could hope for in this oppressive heat. A good sign that accepting Kaan's málmr is *not* going to lead me to a life on my back, staring up at stitched-together hides while I grow some mystical offspring meant to save the world from impending moonfalls.

This is good.

I can work with this.

I let the málmr thump against my chest, shove the sheet off, and push to a wobbly stand, my stare landing on a gold and copper framed body-length mirror mounted to the wall. I frown at the image of myself staring back.

The black sleep shift spills off my curves, the neckline draped across my full bust, the hem falling to midthigh and baring my long pale legs. The sheath is a perfect match to the tone of my loose hair that's cloaking me like a sheet of silk, falling all the way to my hips in long, ruffled tendrils.

Somebody washed me, dressed me, and brushed my hair. Not sure what I did to deserve such service.

I step closer, hands lifting to my face, noticing my cheeks are flushed pink from the heat, my lips a deeper tone of red – my body so unattuned to this oppressive temperature that all my capillaries appear to be working overtime.

Tipping my head to the side, I ease my thick, heavy locks away from the dull throb in my temple, fingers skating over the unblemished flesh.

My frown deepens.

Not a single scar paying tribute to the mace that cracked me open.

Huh.

Kaan must've organized a Runi to thread me back together. That's nice. Fine treatment for a prisoner still bound in an iron shackle. Not that I'm complaining. Pretty sure one more smack to the skull would've been the end of me.

I turn away, am about to move to the shutters so I can see *where* in this Creators-forsaken world I've ended up, when a vision flashes, striking me like another blow to the head, making me feel like the world's tipping.

Plummeting.

I grip the burnished mirror, easing it to the side, revealing a hollow cavity in the stone behind. I thread my arm into the hole, pulling out a leather-bound book I tug close to my chest—

The memory disintegrates, like crumbling dirt sifting through the gaps between my fingers, refusing to clump back together again no matter how hard I try to fist them into shape.

My heart lodges so far up my throat it's hard to breathe past.

What the fuck was that?

Swallowing, my gaze drifts back to the mirror, an unsteady hand extending toward the frame and gripping tight. I slide it right, and my heart dislodges from my throat, then *whumps* into my gut when I see a rough-hewn cavity. Empty. Big enough to fit a book and not much else.

My blood turns to a thick, icy sludge . . .

The door behind me snicks shut, and I whip around, letting go of the mirror. The heavy thing *scuffs* back into place as I take in the female leaning against the door, one leather boot kicked back. She uses a small dragonscale blade to slice crisp milk-colored shards off a round black fruit, biting into them, zesting the air with tart sweetness.

The female's skin is sun-kissed, her long hair full of body and a warm shade of brown, threaded with natural highlights that complement her ember eyes. It's braided on one side, decorated with brown beads.

Freckles dust her nose and cheeks, a roguish elegance to her shapely stature that's hard to look away from. She's fiercely beautiful, exuding an aura of confidence that's palpable in this small, stuffy room.

'Who are you?'

'Kaan's asshole sister you don't want to get on the wrong side of,' she says, lashes lifting as she gives me a once-over, then goes back to slicing her fruit, crunching through its watery flesh.

My stomach rumbles, clenching around its hollowness, eyes narrowing on the blade. Becoming primally aware that this prickly female has a weapon.

And I absolutely *do not.*

'You don't like me,' I muse, edging right to rest my hip against the side table. She doesn't shift her gaze from the fruit as I grip the unlit sconce – tall, gold, and heavy enough to knock somebody unconscious with minimal effort. Precautions. 'You don't even know me.'

'Debatable.'

I arch a brow. 'Meaning?'

Her lashes flick up, that sharp stare scraping across my face, down to the málmr resting between my breasts, bowing the silky material into the generous dip. '*That* means something, you know.

You don't just accept one, then toss it in your jewelry box to wear with your favorite outfit.'

Joke's on her because I have no outfits.

Her gaze meets mine again, and she bites into another segment of fruit, chewing it while I chew on the way she's looking at me – seeping enough hostility to make me feel utterly unwelcome. Perhaps if she saw the way Kaan sawed off Hock's head while the male was still well and truly conscious, she wouldn't be so concerned about me hurting his precious heart.

'Where is he?'

She swallows her mouthful, slicing another segment free. 'Probably getting threaded back together. He got pretty messed up trying to save you from a life on your back, tits out with a belly full of some brute's babe.'

My other brow lifts.

'Let me guess,' she continues, piercing the tip of her blade through the milky shard as she pops her hip against the door, looking me up and down, flourishing the weapon about like a pointer stick. 'He took you to a quaint hut in the hills, cooked you a meal, then looked at you like he loves you more than life itself. So you ran away, fell down the waterfall, and ended up being stripped in a skull full of half-naked warriors?'

All the blood drains from my face. 'How do you kno—'

'Because I'm magnificent. I'm also loyal, but *intolerable* when you get on my bad side.' She brings the blade to her mouth and snatches the piece of fruit with her teeth, chewing through it. 'I'm yet to decide where you fall.'

Unfortunately for her, I don't draw self-gratification from the acceptance of others. Not to mention I'm so fucking hungry I could eat a large mound of those strange juicy orbs of fruit, and hearing her crunch through its crispy, tart-smelling flesh is stirring a feral amount of jealousy I'm struggling to tame. I've never tasted one of those before, but the tingling nerves beneath my tongue are *ready*.

'You'd be amazed at how little that bothers me,' I mutter, tortured through another crunchy bite that almost has me leaping across the room and knocking the female out just to steal what's left of it. 'If you're done pissing circles, feel free to show me the exit so I can exercise my newfound liberty of no longer being chained, bound, or pinned.'

I *shoo* her with my hand, but she just stares at me, head cocked to the side as she chews her fruit.

'Kaan was brought up constantly being told he's not good enough. He'll never admit it, but in his mind, he doesn't deserve the honor of *that* being around your neck,' she says, waving her blade in the direction of Kaan's málmr.

I don't think she gets it – desperate times and all that.

He's probably looking forward to getting it back.

Wearing a sharp smile, she says, 'Break him again and I'll break you.' She shoves off the door and swings it wide, fluidly stalking down the hall while her last words sink their teeth into my brain and *gnaw*.

'What do you mean *again*?' I snarl, stalking to the doorway, still white-knuckling the candlestick.

She keeps walking, just turning the corner at the end of the hall when a word bludgeons up my throat unchecked – my mouth shaping the sound as if from muscle memory alone.

'Veya!'

She stops, head turning – slow.

Precise.

Her wide-eyed stare collides with mine like salt to a raw, vulnerable wound that's not on my body but *within*. On a portion of the shore lining my icy internal lake that's not as high as it was before. That's dropped a foot, leaving a ring of ebony stones achingly bare.

Maybe I'm seeing things? Maybe it was always like this?

'What did you just call me?'

Frowning, I rub my head, wondering who I'm confusing her with. Somebody, surely. Do I know a Veya? I must.

'Nothing. I don't know. Go away, you're hurting my head.'

My body must've gone into starvation mode, restricting blood flow to all my important bits.

Damn, I need food. And water.

She storms back down the hall, her eyes blazing embers. Tossing the core of her fruit on the ground, she bashes her hand against her chest as she bellows, 'I'm Veya. *Me*. Do you remember me?'

My eyes almost roll out of my head.

Not this again.

'No. My brain just belched in the right direction. I've never seen you before in my life,' I mutter and slam the door in her face, clonking the lock into place. 'Let's chat again when you've learned how to share.'

There's the sound of her boot colliding with the wood before she belts at the top of her lungs: 'I'm going to work this out. You hear me? *I'm going to work this out.*'

She's nuts.

'You do that,' I mutter. 'Careful not to strain your brain.'

The only response is the sound of her footsteps stomping down the hall.

Away.

I sigh, toss the candlestick on the pallet, and move toward the wooden shutters, sliding them aside and half blinding myself in the process. I lift my other hand as a shield from the fierce ray of light and heat, eyes widening when they finally adjust to the stark glare.

'Wow,' I whisper, gripping the rustic wooden handle on the door before me, shoving it wide. I step out onto the small stone balcony that overlooks a civilization crammed upon a vast bay that stretches into the powdery horizon, its borders smudged by rippling heatwaves. A shame since something about the western point piques my interest. Makes me want to peel back the layers of distortion and see what's hidden beneath.

I look directly toward the city below.

From up here – partway up the swooping cliff – the buildings look like a tumble of rust-colored boulders, some paved in mosaic swirls, others capped with round windows that glint in the sun. The pale-blue sky is heavy with dusky Sabersythe moons, as well as a few colorful Moltenmaw moons reflecting in the silky turquoise water that stretches into oblivion, the blazing sun perched directly ahead, lathering me in heat.

I draw my lungs full, shaking my head . . .

Looks like I made it to Dhomm.

Raeve

CHAPTER 50

I rummage through the woven baskets to discover a pair of black knee-high boots with thick soles and laces down the front. Tugging them on, I find they fit and immediately fall in love with them.

Perfect for tucking blades down and stomping toes.

I pull out a bundle of sheer black fabric from a different basket, unraveling it, discovering it's actually a hooded robe.

'Huh,' I say, tugging it on, checking myself in the mirror – turning left and right.

This.

Is.

Adorable.

I can still see my silky sheath beneath, giving a layered effect that also doubles as my own portable slab of shade that doesn't restrict the airflow to my body.

I admire the floor-length hem and the bell sleeves that almost fall to the tips of my outstretched fingers. A convenient length to *mostly* hide my cuff so I don't look like an escaped convict while I'm traipsing through the city, hunting for a Curly Quill.

In the same drawer, I find some pants that look too small, but I yank the black belt free and bind it around my waist, discovering it fits if I thread it all the way to the final hole.

I flick up the hood, look at my reflection again, and smile.

Perfect.

Grabbing the candlestick, I charge from the room, down the hall that spills into a domed sitting room. I frown up at the ceiling

– a mosaic Sabersythe that looks like it's about to blow flames all over me.

A shiver skitters all the way to my toes.

Kaan needs to fire the decorator before somebody dies of a heart attack.

I cut my glance around, a third of the wall a stretch of glass doors with tawny windowpanes, looking out on a paved courtyard buttoned with a fire pit. Massive urns spill plush vines that appear to clothe the building, heavy with inky flowers the size of my head, their faces tipped to the sun.

The room itself has a cozy feel despite its horrific ceiling art, more urns gushing vines that smother the internal walls, drenched in sunshine pouring through the many windows – those inky blooms flavoring the air with a spicy sweetness.

Around a stone table no taller than my knee – and sitting atop a curl of plush leather seaters – are two large males. One with his body facing me, his expression hidden by a flock of pale locks half covering his eyes. The other watching me over his shoulder, brow arched, his face and shoulders covered in freckles. A blaze of hair making him look like he just woke from a middae nap.

Both of them wield a fan of Skripi shards, with more face down on the table also adorned with a glass of amber . . . *something* and a dish of crispy-looking nibbles.

'Love that game,' I say, striding toward the table, pausing to pinch a snack from the dish. I drag it through a swirl of pale dip and sweep it onto my tongue, scrunching my face at the creamy concoction threaded with notes of something that tastes a lot like dirt. 'Not my favorite. What is it?'

'Trufflin cream,' the red-haired, heavily pierced male croaks. 'We import it from a nearby village. The fungus that goes into it is hard to grow, so it costs its weight in gold.'

I swipe the rest onto my tongue, confirming it is – in fact – terrible.

'Definitely not my favorite.' I toss the crisp into my mouth and chew, brows bumping up. 'You've redeemed yourself. *These* are delicious.'

Rich.

Salty.

Fatty.

They even *pop* against my tongue with each bursting bite.

I crunch through another. 'What are they?'

'Fried colk fat.'

Huh.

Not my snack of choice since I just watched one bleed into a bowl, but beggars can't be choosers.

I scoop the entire dish against my chest and wrap my shackled arm around it – the one still gripping hold of my stolen candlestick. I pluck out another crisp of fat, crunching through it. 'You don't mind, do you?' I ask, pointing at the bowl.

'Not enough to stop you,' the shirtless male says, his raised brow inching up his head until it's almost lost amongst his rebellious locks. 'Do you want a bag for the candlestick?'

I smile. 'How thoughtful! Yes, I'd love one.'

He shares a look with the quiet male and stands, wanders over to a drink bar, grabs a thin cotton bag, and empties a bunch of dimpled orange fruit on the bench. He lumbers back toward me, opening it. I drop the candlestick inside, and he threads the handles over my arm.

'Thank you.' I look between them both. 'You don't need me to kill anyone in exchange for it, do you?'

Silence prevails for so long I almost repeat the question.

'Ahh, no. We'll pass,' the red-haired male says.

'Nice.'

And strange. That's usually how it works.

'Let me know if you change your mind. I'm trying to get out of conscription work, but your king saved my life a couple of times, so I'm happy to offer a one-time-only favor.' I hoist the bag farther up my shoulder. 'Where's the front door?'

The male on the seater continues to stare at me like I'm some strange creature he's never seen before, his complexion so wan I wonder if he's coming down with something. Poor guy. Probably best I leave before I catch it too, else I'll never make it back to the wall to flay Rekk Zharos from cock to throat.

The redhead points behind me. 'That way. Eighteenth door on your right is the fastest route to the city center.'

I turn, seeing a hallway I hadn't noticed earlier – lined with windows, beams of light shooting through.

'So helpful.' I pinch another crisp from the bowl cradled against my chest and spin, tossing both males a wave with the same hand. 'Nice chatting with you!'

Have a great life.

Silence chases me as I saunter down the hall, gorging on fried fat and the glory of being free.

Supposedly.

I didn't wake in a cell, strung up, or in a dragon's mouth. Nobody's called me a filthy null or made my stabby hand twitch too much. I didn't get tackled to the floor the moment I stepped free of my suite, painted in the blood of a sacrificial beast, or tied to a stick and offered to the Sabersythes. Nobody called me *Kholu* or ordered me to stay and breed some *world-saving offspring*, nor am I being herded by a mythical silver feline.

I'm cautiously optimistic that my short stay in Dhomm is going to be far less traumatic than I was previously anticipating.

Two large, stony-faced guards grip the handles of the double doors and pry them open.

'Creators,' I mutter, squinting against the overwhelming flood of sunlight. I pluck the last crisp from my dish, crunching through it as I step out into the sticky, sweet-smelling heat, drawing my lungs full.

Blowing out a sigh.

Freedom tastes like fried colk fat and too-hot air, but I've never been more thankful. The only thing that could blunt my whetted optimism is a large, scarred, ember-eyed king who sawed off somebody's head for me.

My heart squirms, like it's trying to burrow between my ribs. A feeling I want to crush in my clenching fist.

The quicker I get out of here, the better.

The doors snip shut behind me, and I spin, a different set of guards bracketing the doorway on this outside wall catching my attention. I take in their dragonscale armor, the way both males wear their dark hair loose around their shoulders, each armed with a bronze sword in one hand and a wooden spear in the other.

Sucking the last of the salty seasoning off my fingers, I step close to the male on the right somehow not squinting or sweating despite the violent sunlight pouring upon his face. 'Would you mind holding this for me?' I ask, nudging my empty dish toward him.

A line forms between his brows, and he glances at the pendant hanging against my sternum, brows bumping up. He dips his head for a few long beats – like a bow – then looks up at the clay dish. Clearing his throat, he extends his sword, which I take, thanking him as I place the dish upon his now-empty hand.

Stepping back, I swing the weapon around, getting a feel for its balance. I frown, yet to find a sword I've immediately fallen in love with.

'Too heavy for my hand.' I jerk my chin at the dagger strapped around his thigh. 'But I'll happily swap you for that. And the sheath.'

After a moment of pause, the guards share a look before the male sets the crockery on the ground, along with his spear. He unbuckles his sheath, and I first weigh the dagger's feel before surrendering my stolen sword.

'Nice doing business with you,' I say, winking.

He clears his throat, stepping back into position with my dish on the ground between his feet. I notice a few beads of sweat now gathered on his brow.

'Quick question.' I set my candlestick bag on the ground and part my robe, easing up the hem of my shift so I can thread the leather strap around my hip and thigh. 'You don't happen to feed folk to the dragons here, do you? In, say . . . I don't know, a giant blood-soaked coliseum with a stake in the middle that's *really* uncomfortable to be tied to?'

I cut a glance at both males who are casting each other wary looks. They shake their heads in unison, and my brows bump up.

Interesting.

'What about your young elementals? What happens to them?'

'They attend Drohk Academy,' the guard on the left announces in his thick northern accent, dipping his head.

'And the nulls?'

'They're given the option to discover if they have an affinity for the runes. If not, they may choose to study something else or gain an apprenticeship.'

Apprenti—*Huh?*

'Right,' I say, head cocked to the side as I blindly thread another buckle.

The doors shove open.

The big shirtless male with fiery hair stands in the hallway beyond, arms crossed, brow raised. 'Harassing the guards?'

'Rather presumptuous of you.'

'Your reputation precedes you.' He pokes his head out the door and looks left and right, as though checking we're all still in one piece.

Mainly them.

His emerald stare shifts between the dish on the ground, the guard's reddening cheeks, and my freshly donned weapon. 'I see you've managed to scam your way into being equipped. Quick work.'

I drop my hem. 'Hidden talent. What's yours?'

'Sweet fuck all.' He dashes his hand at the stairs that swoop toward the bouldered city below. 'Let's go.'

My heart drops, frown returning.

Am I not as free as I thought I was?

'What did I do to deserve an escort?'

He flicks me an up and down look, both brows raised. 'You look like a tourist unaccustomed to the heat. If you're going to hock off a solid gold candlestick, you might as well get a good deal. A merchant sees you with me, chances are they won't short you.'

Actually, that's thoughtful. Though I wonder if he'd be so supportive if he knew I intended on swapping said candlestick for an armory's worth of Sabersythe scale blades?

'Thank y—'

'Unless they caught me tangled up with their daughters,' he tacks on, shrugging. 'Or their sons. Then they'll probably refuse to do business with you altogether.'

Creators.

'Weren't you in the middle of a game you should probably finish?'

'Yes. And I was getting my ass kicked. Grihm's lethal when he's in a shit mood, and my pride's already bruised. Besides, somebody stole our snacks and the fucking brandy ran out.'

Right.

Guess I'm stuck with him.

'In that case,' I say, bending down to snatch my bag off the ground, 'shall we?'

He stuffs his hands in the pockets of his tight brown leather pants and leads the way, his long steps smooth and light despite his hulking size. The sun beats upon us like a distant blow of dragonflame, so I tuck my hood farther forward, casting my face in shadow, immediately easing the discomfort.

'I'm Pyrok.'

'Raeve. Though I suspect you already knew that.'

'Correct.' He extends his left hand across his body toward me, pointer and middle finger outstretched, the others curled in. I frown at it, looking up into his eyes, then back at his hand again before I mimic the motion, our fingers meeting.

He flashes me a half smile that's so nonchalant it's infectious. 'There you go.'

I stab my stare down the stairs as we ease amongst the bouldered buildings clothed in more of the big inky blooms Essi would've loved.

That organ in my chest pangs, and I rub at the ache.

'So, Raeve, what sort of store were you hoping to dump that candlestick at?'

'A Curly Quill. If you have one.'

He casts me a sidelong look. 'We do.'

My eyes widen. 'It's called that? The Curly Quill?'

'*Parchment, pawn, and all your Runi supplies*,' he chimes, and relief bubbles through me, popping against my ribs.

Lightening my steps.

I knew they were elsewhere; I just wasn't certain there would be one this far north. This is my lucky dae.

'You need a quill?'

'I do.'

Lots of *quills* with sharp, pointy ends honed enough to slit through all of Rekk's important bits.

Slowly.

Painfully.

'Then I need a sweet drink and a good view,' I tell him, moving the handles of my bag so they're resting on my shoulder, repressing the urge to scratch at the skin on the side of my nails that's starting to get a little raw.

'Drink sounds like a premium part of the plan. What sort of view are you after?'

'Best you can find.'

It's a big city. Figure if I have a view broad enough, I'll eventually work out where the carter hutch is without forcing any tongues to wag. Then I'll know where I need to go once I've liquidated this heavy golden asset and am packed with a lethal amount of weapons, toting a satchel full of those crispy black fruits Veya was eating.

In front of me.

Shard by crispy, watery shard.

The muscles beneath my tongue tingle . . .

If I leave this place without some, I'll never forgive myself.

Raeve

CHAPTER 51

The aurora sits low, edging toward the west as we move between rounded buildings the color of burnt clay. Urns sprout from the ground, gushing plants and trees and vines that climb all over the rich, organic city, buskers perched within sloped corners blowing tunes from copper flutes.

We jostle through a bustle of folk clothed in garments that drape, pinch, and twist around their bodies like cleverly worn veils, and I can't help but wonder if *everyone* in Dhomm has the same garment in brown, black, or rust and just wears it differently – a pin here, a clip there, a copper belt looped around the waist.

Seems likely.

Parchment larks flutter in the space above our heads, diving into the outstretched hands of smiling, laughing folk. Nobody appears starved, homeless, or has a clip in their ear. Not that I can see, anyway.

'Folk appear to enjoy existing here,' I muse, watching two younglings dash after each other, their lilting giggles hitting the most beautiful notes. Two folk I suppose are their parents watch on from beneath a crooked tree, licking at dollops of something creamy-looking that's cradled within coiled black cones. 'It's nice.'

And I couldn't have been more wrong about this place.

Pyrok cuts me a sideways glance. 'I hear you lived in Gore until you were—'

'Offered to the dragons?'

'Yes. That.' He pulls a flat gold token from his pocket and

flicks it through the air, snatching it. 'Have you traveled elsewhere?'

There's an easy lightness in the way he hands me the question, but it still feels like catching an ember.

I consider the cold journey north toward the wall after I finally escaped from . . . *there*. Consider the horrors I encountered.

Fought.

The loneliness that bit so deep it gouged bone.

'Just here,' I say, batting the memories aside. 'Though I was mostly unconscious or inside Rygun's mouth. I wouldn't exactly call it sightseeing – unless you count the ball of flame in the back of his throat that kept threatening to incinerate me.'

A perfect reminder that this city may glow with a happy radiance, but its beautiful king still toted me around like a toothpick. *Perfect* reason not to fall too far in love with the place. And it's hot here – I hate the heat. And Rekk needs to be skinned alive, cured, then used as a fucking floor rug.

'You seem to be taking me on a tour,' I mutter, pointing at a tree that's woven its way around a building like a gnarled crown, boasting big coppery blooms that look like flapping wings. 'I'm certain we passed that earlier, when the aurora was sitting *much* higher in the sky.'

'Relax,' Pyrok drawls, pausing by a market cart. 'Unless you've got somewhere you need to be?'

Not here. Not in this inviting, wholesome city where folk are too easy to be around. Too easy to *want* to be around.

Too easy to grow attached to.

'There's always somewhere to be. What are you buying?'

'Molten Mead.' He swaps his token for a terracotta mug ladled with a red-toned drink. He looks at me over his shoulder, brow popped. 'Want one?'

'Maybe later.'

More small gold tokens glint in the sun as the merchant drops them in Pyrok's hand. His change, I assume.

Pyrok threads in beside me, whistling to the sway of his steps, leading me on what I suppose will be another lap of our tour.

'Gold is your currency here?'

'Sure is.' He draws a deep sip from his mug, releasing a satisfied hiss. 'This kingdom doesn't support the mining of fossilized dragon blood,' he says, a hardness to his tone that wasn't there before. 'Mining it promotes *spilling* it.'

My brows pinch together. 'Is it *used* here? For its medicinal purposes?'

He shrugs. 'What finds its way into the city wasn't mined by folk under this kingdom's protection.'

Interesting.

I move around a busker plucking a pretty tune from a large emberwood string instrument that draws my eye.

My ear.

That makes me want to stop, sit, and *listen*.

'So The Burn has untapped reserves of bloodstone?' I ask, looking left, only to find Pyrok nowhere.

Just . . . *gone*. Like the ground ate him up.

I whip around, catching sight of his blaze of hair down a side alley, standing at least a head taller than everyone else. He waves a hand for me to follow without bothering to turn, and I roll my eyes, pushing through the throng to catch up.

'Thanks for the warning,' I mutter.

'You got one. Not my fault you weren't paying attention.' He pauses, leaning against a wall clothed in more of those russet vines bearing the bold black flowers, one hand still in his pocket while he sips his mead with the other. 'Through there,' he says with a jerk of his chin. 'Tell Vruhn I say hi.'

I spin, turning my attention to the wooden door of the domed building opposite him, an aged sign hanging from the awning.

I smile and grab the handle, pausing to glance over my shoulder. 'Need anything?'

'Not unless Vruhn's decided to stock brandy alongside his collection of bug wings,' he says, then takes a deep drag of his drink.

Shaking my head, I shove into the rounded store, drawing the smell of leather and dust. I glance around the curved wall of shelves stacked with books, tinctures, etching sticks, and bits of volcanic rock. Sabersythe tusks hang from the ceiling, suspended from lengths of copper chain, each bearing price tags that mean nothing to me since I'm not used to dealing in gold.

Fingers crossed this heavy lump of a thing I've been lugging around the city is worthy enough to fetch the supplies I need, hopefully with some coins left over so I can hire a carter back to the wall.

I move through a labyrinth of shelves until I reach the back of the store pinned with a mosaic of small, medium, and large bug wings, making me frown.

Wonder where the armory is . . .

My gaze lands on a male with wiry white hair that sticks out in all directions – presumably Vruhn. He's sitting behind a cluttered stone counter mixing tinctures, white and blue beads threaded through his rebellious locks.

A line forms between his brows, and his hand stills, gaze lifting. His airy eyes cast my feet in stone and pitch my pulse.

They're milky like the Sól's – such a contrast to his dark skin – and they're staring straight *through* me.

My heart flops into my gut as something flashes to the forefront of my memory, like a piece of flesh thrown on a bed of flaming coals:

A big pair of ivory eyes stare blankly in my direction, a blow of icy breath battering my face as a cold, luminous, leathery nose nudges my chest. My chest that's so full of love. So full of . . .

Hurt.

So much hurt—

'Welcome to The Curly Quill,' a serrated voice says, snapping me back to the here.

The now.

Shoving the unsettling image toward my icy lake, I clear my throat, looking at the male, struggling to hold his milky stare. 'Hi. I'm—'

'Here to hock off a candlestick you stole from the Imperial Stronghold. I'm quite aware, Raeve.'

I frown, narrowing my gaze on the male's white robe, searching the many buttons down the front of his seam, seeing one that boasts a branded knot of threads.

'You're a Mindweft,' I murmur, my voice hitched in awe. 'I thought your lot were hunted and forced to work for the imperial families?'

'Painfully aware,' Vruhn says, his voice like a scratchy string. He tips his head sideways, metal mixing stick held between his thumb and finger. 'You, my dear, have a very interesting mind.'

His words stuff me full of mortar, making my body feel heavy. *Laden*.

'There's a hidden . . . *depth* packed with more hurts and secrets than I can count,' he says with a swift shake of his head. 'How do you manage it?'

I force my lungs full. Convince them to work.

'I ignore it,' I rasp. 'Mostly.'

'Ahh.'

He sets the stick on a piece of folded cloth, wiry brows pinching together. 'You've come for a flush of dragonscale blades, six iron ones, a bandolier, a handful of iron pins – regular size – and you'd like to be fitted with appropriate garb you can carry with you in a small, manageable bag to The Fade where you intend to hunt the bounty hunter Rekk Zharos.'

Well. This is handy.

'Correct.' I dip my head in respect of his abilities.

'Quite a list.'

'Yes, well. I had a house fire. Lost—'

Too much.

The vision of Essi too still on the seater strikes me like a shiv between the ribs, and it's an effort not to flinch.

'I can see that,' Vruhn tells me, his voice thick with emotion. 'I'm sorry, Raeve. For Essi. Regret is the heaviest burden to bear.'

I turn my stare to the mosaic ceiling.

The shelves.

My hands.

'I'm also sorry for your little Nee. I know how hard it was to activate the return fold.'

'Your mental fishing rod is very good at catching things,' I say with a forced laugh, pushing the shackle farther up my wrist to give my skin some room to breathe.

'It is. I'm sorry. It's more a compulsion than a gift, I'm afraid.' A brief pause, then, 'You *also* want one of my metal mixing sticks to punch that iron cuff from your wrist . . .'

I look up, brow lifting. His own is hitched in a quizzical arch.

'An idea you got when you walked in here. You're going to pluck a stone from the shore and use it to tap the linchpin free.' He flashes me a mischievous smile that's immediately infectious.

'Think it'll work?'

'I do, though I have something more appropriate that won't bend beneath the pressure. You also want a few things off the shelves to maintain the vision that you came in here for regular supplies. I can help with that, too.'

'Thank you,' I say, followed by another dip of my head. 'Pyrok says hi. He's right outside.'

'Tell him he needs to lay off the mead. *Oh* . . .' His eyes widen, then squint again, like he's peering through the folds of my brain. 'I see why you brought the candlestick rather than make use of your reserves . . .'

Yes.

That.

'The Fíur du Ath believes I'm dead. My page should state as such. I'd like to keep it that way. At least—'

'For the time being.'

'I'm sure you can understand why.'

'Indeed,' he muses, nodding slowly. 'This *Sereme* is quite a nasty piece of work. I see she's kept you on a very tight . . . leash . . .'

Choker collar more like it. But sure.

All the warmth falls from his face, his eyes glazing with a sheen of tears. 'You're missing something, but you don't know what . . .'

A bolt of chill shoots through my veins, boring all the way to my marrow.

'I—'

'Oh . . . my dear.' His face scrunches, hand clutching his chest as a tear slides down his cheek. 'Something so . . . *special*,' he sobs, his words a convulsing ache in my belly.

A swift stab to the left side of my chest.

'The answer is within you. In the place where you hide everything. I could help you drain the—'

'That's enough,' I snap, thumping the candlestick on the counter.

His eyes widen, breath shuddering. For a long moment, he just . . . *stares* – all the color leaching from his face, more tears gathering in his eyes that fall freely down his cheeks. Drips of a truth I don't want to look at. Don't want to see.

Not when I can already imagine the sad sounds his tears are making just by looking at them.

'I said *enough*.'

Please . . .

He blinks, crushing his brow together, not bothering to wipe the trails of sadness from his cheeks. 'Of course. I'll do my best to stop. I just—' He shakes his head, then stands, moving out from behind the counter. 'I'll collect your decoy purchases so you can be on your way.'

My knees almost buckle the moment he's out of sight, my hand coming up to rest on my hammering heart as he shuffles about his store, pulling things from the shelves.

I don't watch. Don't pay attention. Just stare at the back wall and pretend I'm somewhere else where my mind's not being picked at.

It was nice when he began plucking through my thoughts, leaving my words redundant. Like a convenient tickle.

Now it *stabs*.

He returns with a black leather-bound book with a pearly Moonplume embossed on the cover, a pot of ink, and a bundle of coal sticks. He also has a small metal sharpening tool that looks capable of withstanding the force of the stone I very much intend to use to punch the linchpin free of my shackle.

He piles some gold coins into a pouch I suspect is my 'change,' packs it all into a brown leather tote with a flap that buckles into place, then slides it across the counter. 'Your measurements are in the ledger?'

'I believe so.'

'Then I'll send a lark once your purchases are prepared and ready to be collected.'

'Thank you.' I take the bag, the leather supple beneath my grip.

Such a beautiful, high-quality knapsack. It seems wasted on m—

'It's not,' he says, garnishing me with a soft smile. 'Rain is coming. I don't want your diary to soil. It's such a beautiful one, and I want you to be able to enjoy it.'

Frowning, I look to the ceiling. To where a round window is spilling a bold beam of sunlight that ignites eddies of dust. 'It looks perfectly fine to me.'

'You'd be able to hear it coming if it weren't for the iron cuff. And if you bothered to listen.'

His words pinch all my tender spots, my blood chilling as I realize how deep he's dug. 'It's easier not to,' I bite out.

'You listen to Clode.'

I grind my teeth so hard I fear they might shatter, feeling like a skeleton picked of all its meat – just bones left to bleach in the sun. 'Clode's playful, wild and vicious. Strong and feisty. She doesn't wallow or sulk or feel *sorry* for herself.'

'Rayne is—'

'*Tears*. She's bloodshed. Rayne's the frost that sticks to the skin of the dead who are tossed over the wall for the beasts of The Shade to feast upon. Rayne's the snow that coats the shaded half of this *fucked-up* world. Rayne's—'

'Power, my dear.'

My next word sputters on my tongue.

'Rayne is *power*,' he continues. 'Half a world coated in powdered *power* no one is strong enough to wield. Though *you* could, if you did not tuck sadness into that icy lake within you, along with—'

'Thank you, kind sir. For accepting my candlestick as currency.'

There's a stretch of silence before he dips his head so low it could almost be a bow. 'It's been my greatest honor, Raeve.'

With the leather satchel clutched close to my chest, I spin, making for the door, feeling like a sour bogsberry was just squeezed all over my brain and rubbed between the folds. Massaged real fucking deep.

This dae may have started off on a high, but it's swiftly losing its luster.

Diary Entry

Elluin Nevān

Age: 18 phases
5,000,039 phases After Stone

A female came to me this dae with the same ember eyes as the male who visited last slumber. Just as remarkable to look at, with thick, curly hair and freckles on her nose and cheeks. She cradled a bowl of food she was brave enough to set down beside Slátra's coiled tail.

I took one look at it and fell back to sleep, only to be woken some time later by the beautiful, heavily scarred male scooping me into his arms.

I thrashed and screamed, but Slátra did nothing. Nothing! Not even a growl.

The male tucked me against his chest, his arms so strong I realized that fighting was useless. And tiring. I had so little energy left and not much left to fight for anyway.

He carried me up the tunnel of stairs and into the Imperial Stronghold. He dumped me in a tub full of warm, bubbly water, fully clothed, then stormed from the room, leaving me alone with the female I suppose is his kin.

She undressed me, and I lacked the care to stop her, but I did try to hide myself as she bared my breasts. She pushed my hands away and scrubbed me down, telling me that where she was brought up, bodies are not seen as something to be shy about, no matter their shape or size. That flesh is not treated as some great secret, and breasts are worshiped for the way they nourish the younglings of their clan.

She introduced herself as Veya Vaegor and apologized for her brother's behavior, talking to me as if I was conversing back.

I wondered which brother she was speaking of. I don't believe I could ever accept an apology for what Tyroth Vaegor has so willingly taken from me.

My *kingdom.*
My *independence.*

She spoke of many things and asked many questions while I stared at the wall and wondered if this is how Haedeon felt all those phases he was mute. Like there was so little point in it all. But then she stopped scrubbing my body, tucked my hair back off my face, told me she teaches combat at Drohk Academy, and asked if I'd like some lessons.

The words lit something in me, and I felt more alive than I have in a very long while, like an aurora had just risen in my chest.

I told her yes – I want some fucking combat lessons.

Her smile was blinding.

Raeve

CHAPTER 53

Pyrok watches on from the booth seat opposite me – reclined, hands clasped behind his head, an ever-present smirk on his face I certainly don't appreciate.

I leave the thin metal sharpening tool standing atop the linchpin embedded in my cuff, willing it to *stay*.

'This is it,' I murmur, attention honed as I move . . . my hand . . . slowly . . . away . . .

'You think?'

'Gut feeling.' I grasp the rock I stole from the Loff's bouldered shore and lift it above the rod, count to three, then slam it down—

The rod skitters across the stone like a fucking arrow.

Sighing, I thump the rock on the table, scrambling for the tool to the tune of Pyrok's deep belly laugh.

The asshole.

'Glad somebody's finding this amusing.' I reset the scene, trying to get the cuff perfectly level so the pin will stand on end.

Still laughing, Pyrok wipes a tear from the corner of his eye. 'Thirty-seven.'

'Shut up.'

Feeling the hairs on the back of my neck lift, I slash a stare around the space to see if anyone else is taking enjoyment from my erupting well of frustration.

The cozy, domed building consists of three levels, the outer rim segmented into plush leather booths – one of which we're currently occupying – with a delightful view across the Loff I wish I could fully appreciate.

Cuff free.

A circular bar dominates the center of the room, surrounded by stools mostly occupied with chatting patrons snacking on meat skewers, sipping from tall glasses of foggy liquid, or guzzling mugs of Molten Mead. Upon my surveillance, I catch two folk looking my way, perusing my cuff, passing whispered words to each other.

Waving with my shackled hand, I flash them an exaggerated grin that drops straight off my face the moment I set my attention back on the task at hand.

Essi would've had this off in a heartbeat.

'Vruhn hit a nerve?' Pyrok asks, and I flick my lashes up to glare at him. He shrugs. 'Your mood plummeted. Significantly.'

Such a nice way to say I'm being a bitch.

'Several,' I mutter, turning my attention back to leveling my cuff. Think I'll pay a busker to collect my package when it's ready so I don't have to face the Mindweft again. Lately, folk are taking far too much interest in my life – past, present, and future.

I'm sick of it.

Kholu this. *Offspring* that. *Let me peer into your mind and help excavate your past grievances—*

No fucking thank you.

'I hear you and Veya got off on the wrong foot,' Pyrok muses, then nabs a honey-glazed nut from one of the three terracotta bowls of snacks he ordered with our first round of mead, tossing it in the air. Catching it with his mouth.

'I hadn't eaten in a while,' I say, setting the rod atop the pin, trying to release my hold without it toppling. 'She ate fruit in front of me.'

'Ahh.'

I pull my pinching hand away, slow . . .

Steady . . .

'I think you'd like her if you got to know her.'

'I'll have to take your word for it,' I respond, not bothering to mention that I don't intend to stay here long enough to find out. Nice city, happy folk. I admit I was wrong. But I've still got a hankering to punch my fist through Rekk Zharos's chest and rip out his heart, the urge itching at my bones like a swarm of frost flies.

I pick up the stone, raise the thing, then slam it down. The rod scatters across the table to the rhythm of my sharp-tongued curses while Pyrok chuckles himself into an impending grave.

'A little help?' I growl, waving my cuffed hand at him while reaching for the rod.

With a shake of his head, he picks up his drink and drains it to the dregs. 'That thing is on there for a reason, I'm sure,' he says, wiping his lips with the back of his sun-brushed arm.

'Might have something to do with the fact that I bit off the tip of Rekk Zharos's finger,' I mutter, frowning when the sky releases a heady rumble that seems to shake the air.

I glance out the open window to my right, scouring the picturesque Loff ruffled by the wind. Since this establishment sits amongst the bouldered shore on the eastern hook of Dhomm, we have a perfect view of the swooping city. Of the western point that keeps drawing my eye – appearing desolate of civilization, completely clothed in rust-colored jungle. 'What's there?'

Silence.

I look at Pyrok, who's now staring at me like I sprouted an extra head.

'What?'

'Nothing,' he says, releasing a full-body shiver likely attributed to the finger story.

I get it. I felt the same at first, but I've since bonded with the thought.

'It's walled off.' He jerks his thumb toward the point. 'A hushling lives there.'

I frown. 'Really?'

'Wanna go investigate?'

I cast another glance toward the point.

Sort of.

'I want this cuff off more,' I grind out, and Pyrok pushes to a stand.

'Another drink for the long battle ahead?'

'Absolutely.' I drain my glass – the mead a rich conglomeration of smoked chezberries, hobs, and burning wood. Not too sweet or bitter. Undoubtedly the most delicious drink I've ever tasted. 'I'll pay you back with the change I got for trading the stolen candlestick,' I say, sliding the empty glass into his hand.

'You sure you don't want a glass of water? It doesn't taste like dirt here, and your cheeks are pretty flush—'

'Mead,' I murmur, turning my attention back to the cuff, lining up the rod. I doubt my purchased items will be ready before tomorrow's rise, meaning I'll probably be escorted back to the Imperial Stronghold for the oncoming slumber. 'Please.'

The only way I'm sleeping beneath the same ceiling as his *Imperial Highness* without saying or doing something stupid is if I'm so utterly smashed I'm too comatose to lift my body off the pallet. I'm not usually one to drown my sorrows, but I see no point fighting the tide that obviously wants to dunk me beneath a pall of mindless oblivion.

I'm just steadying the rod again when movement outside catches my eye, my seat allowing me the perfect view of the domed lookout perched atop the mountain far above. Of the many massive hutch holes burrowed into the swooping cliff.

Twice now I've seen the same adolescent Sabersythe leaping from a rocky plateau cut within the bulging Stronghold – the beast's only adornment a leather saddle blanket, perhaps getting it used to the feel of something draped upon its back.

Though interesting to watch it swoop through the sky in a giddy dance, frolicking about like it's burning with a belly full of energy it doesn't know what to do with, it's not what I've been looking for. Sabersythes aren't typically used for carter crossings since they can't travel much farther south than The Fade for risk of freezing to death. They can't stand the snow any more than a Moonplume can stand the sun – and I don't want to go toward the sun.

I want to go *away* from it.

Thankfully, most major cities have a reserve of charmed, generally *placid* Moltenmaws trained enough to cart paying passengers to their chosen destination, escorted by the one who charmed the beast. And that Moltenmaw right there – now bursting into view from behind the mountain range, skimming through the sky as the wind ruffles its pink and red plumage, a double saddle cushioned between its feathered wings . . .

That's my ticket out of here.

The massive beast lowers onto a plateau, throwing its head around to gnaw at an itch beneath its wing as Pyrok pulls the booth's curtains closed, then settles into the seat opposite me.

'Tell me,' I murmur, pointing out the window with my rod, 'is that the carter hutch?'

'Thinking of going somewhere, Moonbeam?'

My head whips around, heart plopping into my guts at the sight of Kaan reclined in the booth – hair pulled back, loose bits hanging around his fiercely beautiful face. He's dressed in a black leather tunic that fits his frame like a second skin, stitched together with thick thread, the lines accentuating the broad scope of his powerful chest. What little sleeves the garment has are cut off across his wide shoulders, his scarred arms crossed as he watches me from beneath an arched brow.

I suck a breath into suddenly parched lungs, filling them with his molten scent that makes my heart rally.

'Hmm?' he coaxes, and I realize I've been sitting here staring at him, cheeks aflame, dry mouth empty of words, marinating in the stiff waves of tension undulating between us.

'I . . .'

Creators, it's like he stole my tongue.

Where did Pyrok scurry off to? A big, tipsy buffer between myself and this male would be really nice right now.

'I've got all slumber,' Kaan rumbles, and I swear his deep, raspy voice was designed by the Creators themselves to disable me. To tamper with my insides, rearrange me into a mindless idiot. 'The rest of my life, actually.'

Fuck.

'I've seen some of your city,' I manage to blurt – not at all what I intended to say, but *that* thread of conversation was going in dangerous directions.

His other brow bumps up. 'And?'

'Not what I expected.'

The corner of his mouth curls into a half smile that makes me want to squirm in my seat, picturing his face between my thighs, right here on this table for everyone to hear me scream.

'Are you giving me a compliment, Prisoner Seventy-Three?'

'Don't let it go to your head.'

'I most certainly will,' he says, and I roll my eyes, reaching for the fresh mug of mead Pyrok must've told him I'd asked for before feeding me to this proverbial Sabersythe – the untrustworthy asshole. I'm just wrapping my fingers around the mug when Kaan's hand whips out.

Grips mine.

Flattens it against the table.

In another swift motion, he has the sharpening tool poised against the linchpin, the rock in his other hand, and begins tapping it with shrill, tender hits that sweep a hush over the establishment.

My brows rise, and I picture everyone looking toward our closed-curtain booth as the pin slides free.

Kaan sets the tools down while I pull back my arm, cleave the iron free, then toss it through the window, watching it splash into the Loff. I close my eyes and rub my wrist, tightening that mental sound snare on all the other clamorous clatter I have no interest in listening to right now.

Probably ever.

A smile graces my lips while I relish in the melody of Clode's fluttering giggle . . .

Welcome back, you crazy bitch.

'Awful trusting of you.'

'I trust my folk, and I'm eighty percent certain you won't kill me now that I've saved your life twice.'

I open my eyes, smile gone as I look into his intense ember orbs. 'Depends.'

'On?'

I grip hold of my mead and drag it close to my chest. 'Your kingdom may be lush and full of smiling, happy folk, but I doubt you've experienced life under your brother's reign. Are you complicit in the way he snatches children from their mahs at the tender age of nine?' I ask, cocking my head to the side.

All the color seeps from his eyes, leaving cold, sooty coals.

'A whisper of power and they're immediately snatched from screaming parents and replaced with a bucket of bloodstone. Conscribed. Carted off to Drelgad where they learn how to speak murdering words, practicing on small, fluffy creatures. Ripping out that delicate part of a youngling's heart that can *never* be replaced – turning them into true, tortured monsters.'

'Raeve—'

'Did you know,' I say, gesturing to the hole I sliced into the shell of my own ear, 'that younglings confirmed as a null are held down and clipped? That this becomes a marker for vulturous folk who target them, coaxing them into Undercity battle pits with vacant promises of enough bloodstone to feed their families. Discounted folk otherwise forced to live in the Undercity. Where the air is too thick. Where there is no sun, and every slumber is a gamble on whether or not *this* is the time that you get woken – immobilized by a hushling squatting on your chest, gently slurping your brain through your nostrils.'

The wind begins to gust, tilling into a violent swirl that snaps at the curtain, Clode echoing my rage with a roiling song of sharp words and high-pitched squeals.

'Or worse,' I rasp with a clash of thunder, 'that some skeevy, more powerful *fuck* might take liberties in the dark where innocence goes to die – all because your dear brother cares only about his plump, powerful army and how many charmed Moltenmaws he has in his military hutch.'

I lift my mead and drain half the mug in three deep gulps, wiping my mouth with the back of my arm. 'If you are complicit with *that*,' I say as the wind churns my hair into whipping tendrils of black, much of the light sponging away, 'then yes, I will find the courage to kill you despite your smiling city, this strange chemistry between us, and the fact that you've saved my life twice.'

Our stares hold while the air continues to wrestle with our atmosphere, the silence thicker than water. So much so that I think the establishment may have abruptly emptied.

'This strange chemistry, you say?' he asks, the intensity of his gaze sizzling a hole in my soul that makes it hard to breathe.

I shrug.

He reaches across the table, fingers brushing against mine as he grabs hold of the mug. I let my own hand loosen, and he brings the vessel to his lips, drawing from the opposite side while he studies me over the rim.

The ball in his throat rolls.

Again.

Again.

He sets the drink down with a heavy thump. 'It has taken many phases to secure The Burn and build an armada *almost* strong enough to rival my kin, who'd already dug their talons deep within the stone and obsidian thrones by the time I found incentive to take the bronze. A war with Cadok or Tyroth will be catastrophic, but it's only a matter of time. My brothers deserve the same mercy my pah received, and it *will* be served,' he says, voice thick with a daunting tone that casts a chill across my skin. 'But it will be costly.'

Silence reigns while I chew on his words.

'You don't mean gold . . .'

'I mean *innocents*,' he growls, and my blood turns to ice.

'Hire an assassin. Eliminate them without flair rather than a violent overthrow. I volunteer. Heartily. I'll even do it for free.'

Then dance on their fucking corpses.

The tic in Kaan's jaw pulses, a line forming between his brows. 'There is no honor in this in our culture. A battle is either waged with brute force or between two Oahs upon a nullifying battlefield – though my brothers would never agree to that. Not since Rygun and I became Daga-Mórrk.'

My eyes widen, brows rise as my heart skips a beat.

Another.

That explains the weald.

The strength.

The—

'You're—'

'Most importantly,' he interrupts, 'they hold a strong, steady alliance forged in the womb that is unshakable. Dangerous. *Deadly*.'

I hear the silent message threaded between the rumbled statement. To attempt to take on the weight of either kingdom would mean war with *both*.

'A battle would puncture our world and scatter the skies with many more moons,' he says, dropping his voice to a haunting grind, his next words a sizzled swipe at my nerves. 'It would pour flames across flesh. Drown many. Suffocate more. As you pointed out, a great number of those conscripted in The Shade's and The Fade's armadas are still younglings who should be running around barefoot, laughing and enjoying life. Less fluent than seasoned warriors, *they* would be the first to die—'

'*Stop*.'

The word belts out of me so fast it scrapes the back of my throat, a strangled breath pouring into my lungs.

I break from his gaze. Gather the embers of his scorching declarations and cart them into my frosty expanse, shoving them down a hole in the ice where I don't have to look at them.

Attention stabbed at the table, I keep shoving . . .

Shoving.

He leans forward, elbows resting against the stone, finger sliding beneath my chin and tilting my head, forcing me to meet his softening stare. 'War is messy, Moonbeam. Even when it's raised for the right reasons, no one truly wins until eons have passed, memories have faded, and all the hurt and loss starts to blur—'

'I understand,' I grind out. 'You can stop.'

My eyes scream the word my mouth doesn't shape.

Please.

The moment stretches while he searches my eyes with an intensity that threatens to dig beneath my skin and skim across my hardened heart.

'I'm not going to kill you, if that's what you're waiting for.'

The corner of his mouth kicks up again, and it's like staring into the eye of a storm. So hauntingly beautiful you almost forget you're in danger.

Almost.

'I'm honored. Let me know if you change your mind.'

Doubtful. I've actually decided his death might be one of the greatest losses this world could suffer. Not that I'm going to tell him that, of course. This . . . *whatever* between us will grow into a ravenous beast unless I starve it to death – I'm certain.

'Hungry, Raeve?' There's a tender hopefulness in his warm gaze that grates. 'Would you like to share a meal with me?'

Clearing my throat, I pull away from his touch. 'No. I don't think I should,' I murmur, reaching for his málmr, feeling the air stiffen as I lift it over my head. 'Thank you for lending me this. I very much appreciate what you did for me in the crater.'

I don't go into more detail. Certainly don't speak of the Fate Herder or the Sól's odd foretellings, not wanting to open that messy topic up for inspection as I untangle the loop of leather from my hair, the world a rumbling roar outside. I dangle the precious pendant between us, looking up into hard eyes that still the beat of my heart.

He makes no move to take the málmr. He doesn't even look at it.

'It was not lent, Raeve.'

The words land slow and hard, lacking the softness of his previous sentence, casting my skin in little bumps.

I shove my hand closer to his chest. 'This means things I can't give you.'

He watches me with the honed regard of someone inching toward a wild dragon, head tilting. 'What do you think I want?'

I break from his stare and look through the window, seeing a tumor of gray clouds rolling toward the bay, light scribbling across the surface to the tune of crackling thunder.

A warm heart.

Offspring to carry on his heritage.

At the very least, someone who gets along with his swaggering sister.

I swallow, refusing to meet his gaze as I settle the málmr on the table and stand, shouldering my satchel. I edge from the booth and push free of the fluttering curtains.

Around him . . . sometimes words just feel inadequate.

Raeve

CHAPTER 54

Wind snatches my hair and tosses it about, Clode's song a mix of tittering mania and high-pitched screams. Like she's working herself up to slit the atmosphere straight through its bulging, electrical gut.

I feel somewhat similar.

I charge down the esplanade in a flutter of black fabric, not bothering with my hood, the sun blocked by a boil of gray clouds burgeoning toward me like some rumbling beast – the horizon lost to a hazy smear that appears to be falling from the storm cloud's underbelly.

So unlike the earlier bustle, the esplanade is empty and still. So at odds with the rowdy thump of my boots.

My thoughts toil with the churning wind, that phantom heaviness sitting on my chest like a mountain, each breath a labored pull.

Sighing, I recall the way Kaan's eyes lost all their warmth when I offered him back his málmr . . .

He was hurting. I know he was.

I could see it.

Perhaps I should've explained. Told him the last fae who saved my life did it to her detriment. That folk who care about me enough to put themselves in harm's way tend to end up dead. He dodged that blow in the crater battling Hock. I'm not stupid enough to believe he could dodge another.

Life doesn't pat me on the head and praise me for making connections. It thunks arrows through hearts. Stabs bellies. It makes damn fucking sure I know loneliness is the only acquaintance I'll ever have, waiting until the roots of connection bore deeper than I'd like to admit before it rips out flesh and bone. Sheds blood. Stops hearts.

Hardens mine with another calloused layer of disconnect.

But to explain, I would've been forced to fish heavy, painful memories from that ice-covered lake inside myself, and I'm not doing that. Going within is eerie enough as it is. I've dumped all sorts of shit down there, adding to whatever else is already hiding beneath the surface.

Who knows what I'd pull up.

Probably my elusive Other, and I'm really not in the mood to wake with more tendons between my teeth, strung up to endure another whipping, completely oblivious to whatever trail of carnage was left in my wake.

Nope.

Not happening.

That's what led me here in the first place.

If Kaan wants me to keep his málmr, he might as well slip his head through a noose and tighten it himself, then hang his weight upon the loop until he chokes. And though that would've been a balm to my burning rage just a few short slumbers ago, the thought now plows its fist through my chest and rips, rips, *rips* at all my important bits.

I need to get out of here.

Casting my stare toward the plateau where I saw the Moltenmaw land, I slow, frowning. The assassin tack I ordered would've been handy, but fuck it. Looks like I'm going bare.

I've got a dagger. And Clode. Once I reach The Fade, I'll work out the rest.

I charge down a side alley that appears to weave in the right direction, pausing when a drop of rain weeps right past my ear and splats against my shoulder.

My heart stills.

Grappling with my internal sound snare, I make sure it's the right tautness. That I've got the right sieve tucked over the opening – the one that allows Clode to slip through but prevents Rayne's frosty, snow-falling sobs from penetrating my brain.

Keeps her *out*.

I cast my stare upward, and another wailing bead plunges toward me. I flinch as it collides with my cheek in an agonized splat, my hand lifting to sweep its weeping corpse from my skin . . .

What's happening?

I study the wetness smeared across my fingers like the anomaly it is, the raindrop's forlorn whimper cleaving a crack through my chest. Like she broke apart on impact, achingly aware she'll never be whole again.

Not as she was.

More heavy droplets wail as they plunge, singing foreign words I don't understand, splashing upon the pavement by my feet. Howling from the shock of their savage deconstruction, like they're begging the stone to absorb them.

To pull them back together.

I edge away from each sad little blotch wetting my heart in all the wrong ways . . .

This—

This is not good.

Eyes wide, I search the sky, chasing the cloud's mournful tears as they sing their fatal song. Like each tiny raindrop is innately aware they're caught in a descent that can only end one way. That they will *never* be more whole than they are right now, plummeting to their doom.

My hand flies to my chest to rest upon my thumping heart, the heartbreaking melody growing in strength as the rain falls harder.

Faster.

Pins prick the backs of my eyes, the same weeping upheaval threatening to mimic within me.

Again, I check my mental sound snare. Find no flaws.

None.

Meaning the song of rainfall must be a different frequency than I'm used to blocking . . .

Lovely.

This dae can go right ahead and eat a jar of spangle shit.

With a wary glance at the smudged wall of rain charging toward me, I realize I have no time to fiddle around and try to work out how to block myself from the encroaching clamor, cursing myself for throwing the fucking cuff in the Loff.

Idiot.

I tighten my mental sound snare until it's squeezed entirely shut, gulping air as that sheet of water whips forward and crushes the space between us.

Drenching me.

My snare wobbles like pinched lips desperate to part. To draw breath and *scream*. I barely get a chance to brace before it erupts – Rayne's devastating song spewing through me like iron-tipped lashes to my unguarded eardrums.

My unguarded *heart*.

A sob dredges up my throat – an ugly splat of unwelcome sound.

I stumble back a step, another, scrambling to tighten the snare and shut myself off. But it's like contracting a muscle that's never been used. Not against this blaring force. And Rayne—

She's *everywhere*.

Screaming past me, drenching my hair, dribbling down my skin. She's splashing up at me from the puddles forming around my feet – a sloshing melody that grips my frayed heartstrings in clenched fists and *rips*.

Rips.

Rips.

Like plucking feathers from my heart.

Like poking fingers through the holes.

Like packing salt in the now-gaping wounds.

My face twists, the pain in my chest pulling me into a bunched knot. 'S-stop . . .'

Hands clapped over my ears, I stagger toward a stubby awning and spin, forehead pressed against the stone as something inside me splits open like the gates of a gushing dam.

And I cry.

Like I've never cried before.

Warm tears leak down my cheeks that only add to the gut-wrenching clamor flaying me with small, precise slits.

And it doesn't

stop

cutting.

No matter how hard I crush my palms against my ears, I can't escape the shrieking wails that echo within me. That shatter my composure with the force of a fallen moon, scattering the bits so far and wide I can't see them.

Can't feel them.

'Stop,' I sob.

Beg.

Scream.

'STOP-STOP-STOP-STOP-STOP-ST—'

A hard warmth presses against me from behind, shielding me from the rain. Pulling my hands from my ears and wrapping them around my chest, encasing me in a snug, sturdy embrace.

I know it's Kaan even before he speaks, my posture folding into his. Seeking a silent refuge in his comforting presence and the strong bind of his powerful arms.

More ugly, messy sobs wrestle up my throat unchecked.

Unguarded.

Raw.

'I once knew a female who'd cry when it rained, though she thought I never noticed,' he murmurs against my ear, his dense words battling the torrent of mournful cries like a boom of thunder. 'Her name was—'

'Elluin.'

His arms tighten, my body a pool melding with the stony slabs of his resilient form. 'The cuff was a kindness, Moonbeam. There is little need to weaponize yourself here, but it storms. Often. *Violently.*'

Hindsight.

My least favorite way to learn.

Clode squeals a slashing melody, like she's pissed at the rain for *existing* – something I can commiserate with her over. Her air-tossing tantrum dredges a torrent of rain into a horizontal sheet, lashing the side of my face.

Rayne weeps with newfound ferocity, like she just crushed her body into a ball, wrapped her arms around her legs, tipped her scrunching face to the sky, and *unleashed.*

My knees wobble, threatening to buckle from the weight of her deep, mournful yowls. 'Give me something else to focus on. *Please.*'

The words have barely left my lips when Kaan presses his against my ear, a dense hum rumbling from his chest and cutting through the din as he tucks me impossibly close.

A song I'm *achingly* familiar with.

I don't dissect it – not right now – allowing myself to fall into his calming baritone, letting the melody seep through my pores like grains of stone that gather in all my dips and hollows, weighing me down in a comforting crush. Sanding the jagged sadness in my chest into something rounded and smooth.

My shuddered inhales begin to lose their shake . . .

Still, he hums . . . threading me together one familiar note at a time until I can draw enough steady breaths to sing along with the tune. Words I've only ever heard murmured through the hollow of my mind – distant echoes I've never been able to grasp the dusky origin of.

Words that have given me solace in times I've felt alone or uncertain. Brought me peace when my soul screamed the opposite. Words I think might've belonged to somebody special . . . once.

In another life.

Another time.

The storm stops just as abruptly as it began, Kaan planting the final note against the arch of my neck like a phantom kiss – the tender press of his lips infusing me with a burst of knee-buckling familiarity. Like I've been here before. Caught in his grasp. Crushed close to his chest.

Kissed.

Like I've been lulled by his comforting presence in a dream I can barely remember the shape of.

Only the sturdy bind of his arms keeps me from crumbling into a heap on the puddled ground, my lungs now powering for a different reason . . .

'You know my song,' I whisper.

Silence ensues – so thick and heavy my heart rate spikes.

'How, Kaan?'

I regret the question the moment it falls from my lips, a bulb of dread swelling in the back of my throat. Threatening to choke me.

What if he says something too big and painful for me to discard? What if his words resonate with another unsettling strike of familiarity? Drains more of my icy lake? Exposes more stones?

What then?

'There's something I need to show you,' he murmurs against my neck, then grabs my hand, plants a warm kiss upon my blanched knuckles, and *tugs*.

For some strange, uncertain reason . . . I don't argue. Don't dig my heels into the ground.

I follow.

Raeve

CHAPTER 55

Deep within the heart of the Imperial Stronghold, Kaan unlocks a chain threaded between two mammoth black wooden doors carved to look like a pair of warring Sabersythes going head-to-head, the handles twin tusks curling from their pronged faces. I cut a glance down the empty, dim-lit tunnel behind me as I wait for him to unwind the chain, tugging the left door open.

With a sweep of his hand, he gestures for me to step inside. The dark room. Ahead of him.

I don't think so.

'You first.'

He sighs, charging into the gloom with a barrage of heavy footsteps.

I follow, sketching out the shape of the space, slivers of sun coming through from what I suppose are curtains over on the far side. Kaan moves toward them.

'*Veil de nalui*,' I whisper, whipping Clode into a giggling churn. She twirls across the room, tangles with the curtains, and rips them wide, dousing the room full of light.

Kaan stops before the glass doors, hand outstretched. He clears his throat. 'Thanks.'

'Pleasure,' I say, taking in what I suppose is his personal suite based on the dominance of his warm scent. I'm certain he dabs something on his skin each aurora rise that makes him smell so inconveniently moreish.

This sitting room is packed with curved bookshelves, plush

leather chaises, and a black rug stretched across the floor. Beside a deep, upholstered chair that's worn to the padding in places sits a large string instrument resting on a stand, the frayed strings in desperate need of replacing. On the other side of the same chair is a small round table with a bottle of spirits, an empty glass, and a corked jar that holds something misty.

Swirling.

He snatches it, tucking it inside a drawer within the table.

I arch a brow. 'Don't want me to see your jar of mist?'

'Not particularly,' he murmurs, hanging his málmr on the instrument.

I look away, seeing various weapons haphazardly dumped on shelves and a pair of boots kicked off by the door. My stare glides to a map of the world that stretches across a large curve of wall, the yellowed parchment littered with tiny black crosses – most of which are south of Gore.

Thousands of them.

'Keep your secrets,' I say, gaze bouncing from cross to cross. To the map's left, a blade's been stabbed into the stone, and from the constellation of indents surrounding it, I garner it's not the first time it's wound up there.

'Believe me,' Kaan mutters, gathering some bits of clothing he'd left lumped on the seater. 'I'm under no false assumption that you're even the slightest bit interested in my secrets.'

'Realistic expectations are healthy.'

He grunts, carrying the clothes through a wide doorway to the right, disappearing into the darkness within while I do another visual sweep of the space, noticing a fine sheen of dust on his shelves. Actually, pretty much upon *everything* except his instrument, the seaters, that bottle of spirits, and the dagger stabbed in the wall.

Huh.

'Guessing you don't . . . entertain much?'

Or even let somebody in to clean.

'The bolted door puts most folk off,' he says from somewhere within the adjacent room. 'Suits me just fine.'

Right.

Likes his privacy.

Got it.

I look to the lofty domed ceiling adorned with overlapping

dragonscales I suspect are Rygun's based on their burnt-blood tone. A huge chandelier hangs from the peak, pieced together with more Sabersythe tusks than I've ever seen in one place, all of varying shapes and sizes.

'Wouldn't want to be standing here if the mountain shook,' I murmur, gaze shifting to my right as Kaan emerges from the shadowed doorway with two towels – tossing one at me.

'Thanks,' I say, using it to sponge some of the water clinging to every inch of me like the remnants of a slumber-terror, drying off my garments while he does the same. I drape my towel across the back of a seater, along with my satchel.

'This way,' he rumbles, tossing his towel next to mine, then moves toward the twin doors ahead. They look out onto what appears to be an overgrown private garden doused in so much shade I'm surprised anything grows out there at all.

He unlocks the doors and steps through, and I follow into the humid midst, down an unkept path that often requires me to duck – insects creaking, water beading off the faces of round velvety leaves the color of clay.

A ruffle of wind offers me a glimpse through the dense foliage to the sandy view beyond, and I realize this garden looks south toward The Fade.

Away from the sun.

'It's just down here,' Kaan says, moving toward a fall of coppery vines that clothe segments of the steep, uneven wall surrounding this garden. He parts the natural drape, cleaving an opening through to a hidden tunnel beyond, then ducks and shoves in ahead of me.

I frown. 'I'm not following you down there.'

He pauses, looking at me over his shoulder. 'Why not?'

'Because that's how folk *die*, Kaan. I know because that's how I—'

His brow bumps up.

I pause, reconsider divulging my trade secrets with a king I only decided to semi-trust two seconds ago, then figure it's best he knows I'm a bloodstain on his pretty paradise.

'*Assassinate*. This right here' – I gesture to the tunnel he's leading me down – 'is a prime location for you to slit my throat, then carve some letters on my chest.'

Wonder what he'd give me. Probably:

RETURNS PRECIOUS GIFTS

He turns to fully face me, eyes beseeching as he says, 'Listen, Raeve.'

'I am. Obviously.'

'No,' he growls, placing his hand on the smooth, rounded wall. '*Listen*.'

I open my mouth, close it when his meaning sinks in. 'But he's so—'

'What?'

Stable.

Sturdy.

The absolute opposite of me.

Crossing my arms, I shake my head and sigh, loosening my internal sound snare almost wide enough to let *him* in . . .

Bulder.

I hold Kaan's stifling gaze a moment, then loosen the snare that little bit more, slapping a wide-holed sieve atop the opening and bracing myself for Bulder's grinding vibrato that . . . doesn't come.

Because he's not singing – not at all.

He's *humming*.

A deep, droning roll . . . almost like a baritone *coo*.

My brow buckles, my own hand coming out to flatten on the burnished stone. 'It's—'

'This is a place of nurture, Raeve. Of love and worship. If I wanted to harm you, I certainly wouldn't do it within this cavern,' he says, holding my stare with chest-crushing intensity.

'Can't you just tell me what's down there?'

His eyes soften. 'I can't. This is something you need to see for yourself.'

Creators.

'Fine,' I snip. 'But just so you know, I coaxed your guard into swapping an empty crockery dish for his dagger that's currently strapped to my upper thigh, and I'm not afraid to use it.'

He blinks, shaking his head as I step into the tunnel, letting the fall of foliage sweep shut behind me – engulfing us in shadow.

The tight stairwell is littered with small glowing bugs that remind me of Moonplume moons, offering a meager amount of light for our journey down the endless coil of stairs I wish I'd counted from the beginning. I'm certain we're over a thousand steps down by now, my skin no longer warm but delightfully cold – my exhales like puffs of smoke.

Kaan fills the stairwell so entirely the top of his head nearly brushes the light-smattered ceiling, his shoulders almost too big for him to be moving down faced forward. Every now and again, I try to peep past him and see if there's an end in sight, but it's useless.

He's a giant stairwell plug.

I collect the damp length of my hair to squeeze the gathered moisture from the ends, frowning when I realize the water has begun to stiffen.

To *frost*.

'Much farther?' I ask, brushing the fractals off my hands, wondering if he's walking me all the way through to the other side of the world. If we're going to emerge near Netheryn – the Moonplume nesting grounds.

'Not far.' Kaan looks at me over his shoulder, his eyes glinting in the dark as he assesses me. 'Are you okay with the cold? You can have my tunic if you—'

'I'm fine.'

Something flashes in his eyes, like perhaps he assumes the thought of wearing his tunic makes me uncomfortable.

It doesn't. At least not in the way he probably thinks.

I don't tell him the deeper we've drilled, the less tentative I've been about this decision to follow him down a twirling tunnel into a dark abyss. I certainly don't tell him the growing cold feels a lot like . . .

Home.

The reason I keep trying to peep past him isn't because I'm worried he might be taking me down here to murder me. Not anymore.

No . . .

Some innate part of me is *drawn* to whatever's at the bottom of this never-ending stairwell.

The frosty nether nips at my skin, turning the tip of my nose so blissfully numb, the chilled air beginning to lap at me like an undulation of icy waves that tug in their withdrawal – urging me deeper.

Deeper.

Each step folds me further into that tiding tug until the darkness gives way to a silver light that kisses the walls and steps. That turns Kaan into a gloomy silhouette against the radiant luminosity trying to squeeze past him from whatever's on the other side.

'We're here,' he murmurs, his voice a shockwave through the hungry silence that lifts the hairs on the back of my neck.

He steps to the side, dousing me in *light*.

So much light.

My heart stops, an icy cleft of awe fracturing my chest as I take in the circular cavern, the swooping walls embossed in magnificent, detailed carvings of *Moonplumes*.

The same magnificent creature in hundreds of different stances – long neck; big, wistful eyes; spindly tendrils that trail from its jowls and whisk with its crafted movement. Elegant tri-membrane wings fit for speed and unmatched agility, wispy tail with silken threads that sweeps and coils and flicks with a gush of personality.

The carvings meld together much the same way as the dragons on Kaan's málmr, though the extravagant mural pales in comparison to the massive silver moon the cavern cradles like an egg – the ground dipped in the middle like cupped palms, no doubt keeping it from rolling around.

A choked sound slips up my throat, and for a moment I don't move.

Don't breathe.

Don't blink.

Something within me settles, nuzzling into a comforting curl that makes the backs of my eyes sting for the second time this dae – so overwhelmed by the moon's rounded beauty that I feel like the world is tipping.

My shuddered exhale is so thick and milky it's hard to see through, a loud smudge upon the gobbling silence.

I stagger forward, hand outstretched, the tips of my fingers aching with the need to touch. To trace the divots and mounds of the fallen Moonplume forever tucked in a sleeping curl, head half nudged beneath the fan of a frayed membrane. The dragon's silky tail is woven up beneath its winged embrace, spilling out in tufts about its neck and head like a once soft pillow.

Drawing close to the fallen beast, I feel smaller than I ever have. A hatchling in comparison to its vast size.

Bulder continues to hum, the heavy baritone an audible cradle of droning comfort so complex it's impossible to grasp. Like looking up at the stars and trying to work out what's in the dark gaps between those distant prickles of light.

He's a nest, I realize. Can almost picture him crouched, hands cupped before his chest, curled under this beautiful moon while he looks down upon it.

Treasures it.

Nurtures it.

My throat thickens so much it's painful to swallow . . .

I reach forward, brushing my hand across the Moonplume's once-leathery hide now fossilized. So hard and cold it's like caressing a frosted mound of ice.

'Your moon,' I rasp, a small smile picking up the corner of my mouth as a tear slips down my cheek that I'm swift to bat away.

'Her name was Slátra,' Kaan says, a rawness to his voice that I've never heard before. 'I'm yet to find her final shards. You can't see on this side, but there's a small crevice around the back of her I still need to fill.'

A chill climbs my spine, and I trace a hairline fissure with the tip of my finger, looking up to see so many more webbed across the metallic beast – proving she smashed into thousands of shards upon impact. Shards that have been painstakingly pieced together in this rounded tomb.

'You did this?' I ask, my voice wobbly.

'I did, yes.'

I shake my head, realization gushing down my throat like a drowning shove of water.

My rage – my rabid thirst for revenge – was *blinding*. I thought Kaan was a tyrant. A heartless monster. But he has such a big, warm heart I'm surprised it fits in his chest.

'Why?'

'Because it hurts knowing she's not whole,' he rasps, casting another sweep of sting across the backs of my eyes.

I step around the dragon, pausing at the spot where Slátra's head is nuzzled deep into the tuft of her tail.

My heart stills, breath catches. A bludgeoning *bang* inside my chest almost makes me lose my balance.

Ignoring the sounds of splitting ice ratcheting through me, I ease up onto my tiptoes, peering over the cleft of her wing to the small hollow it's shielding. Not sharp and jagged like bits are still missing, but a smoothed ingress close to the tip of the beast's wide nose, as though Slátra gave her final breath cradling . . . *something* bundled within the silken tendrils of her once soft tail. Shielded by her cupped claw.

My brow furrows, stare pouring into that snug hollow, almost *feeling* its clefts and bulges nudged against my body.

Cradling *me*.

Almost feeling the cold expanse between her slit nostrils pressed against my brow, the solidified tuft of her tail cushioning my . . . *chest—*

I stumble back a step . . . another . . . sucking breath into lungs that seem to have forgotten how to work.

No—

'You're familiar with it,' Kaan says, his baritone wrestling the silence like a rockslide.

Battering me.

'I—'

My thoughts tunnel to a memory I discarded long ago, its corpse laid out on the shore of my internal lake, stripped of all the frilly emotion I plucked from it, leaving only the bony skeleton of something that might've hurt one time.

Felt heavy in some way.

I allow myself to assess the remains from an angle of relative disconnect:

A strange trundling sound had roused me from my eternal sleep. I'd blinked my eyes open for the first time, taking in the world I'd been born into through the iron bars of what I now know is called a cage.

My brutal waking was fraught with confusion while I tried to work out how I fit inside my body. How it worked and moved. Why everything was blurry.

Warm.

Yet I trembled – violently. I thought it was the heat, but now I know that's not the case.

My soul was shuddering from the inside out.

I'd reached forward, finding something heavy and cold clamped around my wrist, an item I now know to be a shackle. I'd clung to the bars in the effort to steady myself in this strange existence where I had hands that moved, lungs that breathed, and eyes that could see – my stare narrowing on the source of the sound that had drawn me into existence.

A cart being wheeled down the length of a dusky burrow, past my place of waking.

In its deep hollow sat jagged shards of silver brightness that gave off a lapping chill I wanted to splash upon my face.

The shards were so beautiful against the dim of my surroundings that I was immediately certain my place of waking was not good, but bad. Because no matter how hard I grunted and screamed, trying to beg the creature that was pushing the cart to please bring it closer so I could have a proper look at the pretty, pretty shards I desperately wanted to touch, he did not so much as look at me.

The shards disappeared, and I realized mere moments into my existence what it meant to be trapped.

'Answer me, Raeve.'

Again, I feel trapped. Forced to look at something I'm certain has the potential to shred me from the inside out if I look any deeper.

Any harder.

Because those shards I saw when I first opened my eyes to the world . . . I now understand they were scavenged at the same time as me. *That's* why the cart was lugging them past my cell. They'd just been snatched from the snow, dragged inside a mountain of stone and ice that held a belly full of fire.

'Are. You. Familiar with it?'

I leave the stripped memory where it belongs.

Within.

'I have no idea what you're talking about,' I snip, whirling around, storming toward the exit.

Kaan banks, cutting me off, his leather tunic dusted in a fine layer of frost.

My gaze snaps up to meet his fiery glare that's so at odds with the icy fractals dusting his hair and beard, making it glimmer in the luminous light. '*Move*.'

'See, I think you're lying.' He pushes forward a step, emitting the immense energy of a mountain-size beast in his prime. An energy impossible to ignore. 'I think you know this moon better than *anyone* else.'

There's a rumbling within me, from somewhere deep beneath my lake. A hum of acknowledgment I neglect, focusing instead on the anger swelling within my chest like a ball of dragonflame.

My foot slides back, upper lip lifting from my canines.

'I think this beast cradled you for a hundred phases, breathing life back into your broken body until you both fell from the sky. I think you broke from Slátra's tombstone like a hatching dragon—'

'You're fucking *mad*,' I hiss as my back collides with the moon.

'Am I?' He arches over me like a rocky overhang, leveling me with a look that sucks all the oxygen from my lungs. 'Because I knew a female who died. Tragically. Whose lifeless body was sailed into the sky by the adoring beast at your back with my torn-out heart in her fucking fist,' he rasps, lifting his hand into a claw that he shakes in my face. 'Her name was Elluin, and she laughed with the wind, cried with the rain. She angered with fire and bellowed with the ground. Her heart thumped in synchrony with—'

'*Enough.*'

He growls, and there's a clicking sound. He says a word I don't hear over my roaring pulse as a flame dances to life in his hand.

My body stills, paralyzed by the sizzling sight. A deeper, almost *sentient* silence hollows the cavern surrounding us. A silence that seems to spawn from . . . within.

Me.

Like I'm sponging the sound. Absorbing it.

Kaan brings that flame so close to my face I'm certain he's about to smear it across my skin, and I become innately conscious of the fact that something inside me is *watching*.

Listening.

'You look me in the eye, Moonbeam – right in the *soul* – and tell me you don't hear this fire's hissing shrieks. Look me in the eye, sharpen those words, and don't fucking blink as you plunge them through my heart.'

I struggle to gather the breath to tell him exactly that. That his flame does not shriek or hiss or spit. It is but a flame, and it does *one* thing.

It burns.

'Crush your flame, Sire. Or I'll crush you,' I seethe with cutthroat certainty – violently aware that my Other is on the brink of bursting free. I may be utterly against hurting this male, but I cannot speak for . . . *it*. 'That's a promise.'

A line forms between his frosty brows.

He whips his hand away, crushing it into a fist of smoke, flooding my system with a cold deluge of relief. 'Who hurt you?'

'I do not *hurt*, King Burn. I harden. And no – your *pet flame* did not sing to me. Not even a little bit. Otherwise I would've sung it up the hall and ordered it to suicide itself in a puddle.'

His frown deepens, his hand coming up as if to cup my cheek. Like he wants to touch me but is worried I might slice it off. 'Don't lie to me, Moonbeam. Lie to the world, but please don't lie to me.'

'Stop talking to me like you know me. You don't. Even if I did fall with your precious moon, I owe you nothing. Elluin is *dead*.'

'*Stop*.'

His word commands. His eyes plead.

Both ricochet off my armor like arrows I snatch, lodging them between his ribs. 'Saving my life, dragging me away to your big, bright kingdom where everybody fucking loves you is not going to reincarnate her. I'm not yours, and I *never* will be.'

He steps back, leaving me arched over Slátra's solidified wing. Allowing me space to draw my first full breath since our atmospheres clashed.

I ignore the unveiled pain in his eyes as I charge toward the stairs without a single glance over my shoulder, every step skyward pulling me farther from the comfortable nest of chill.

I ignore the tugging sensation that tries to lure me to turn around. To climb over that folded wing, tuck within the hollow, and fall asleep in Slátra's stony embrace.

Most of all, I ignore the sense that every step skyward is another step further from my truth.

Instead, I strip the moment of all the soft wisps of attachment and curiosity, bind them into a parcel, then tie them to a stone, finding my internal lake already crushed near the shore. A convenient hole cracked through the ice, making it easy for me to discard the package.

I don't believe in much, but I do believe that the unknown needs to be handled with caution – much like a dragon. Leave them alone, and they rarely decide to attack. You can exist in harmony for eternity, so long as nobody makes any sudden movements.

Try to climb on their backs or steal their eggs? Well.

Chances are you're dead.

I happen to like living in my blank oblivion. It's lonely, but lonely folk have nothing to lose.

That suits me perfectly.

Raeve

CHAPTER 56

I explode free of the stairwell and burst into the ruffling breeze. Shoving past a low canopy of big round leaves, I storm for the door to Kaan's suite.

'I *knew* I shouldn't have followed him down there,' I mutter to my stupid self. When has following somebody into a dark tunnel to the words of 'it's just down here' *ever* been a good idea?

'Idiot,' I bite out, hammering the word into my brain like a nail that obviously wedged loose, landing me in a cavern with a deceased Moonplume he thinks was mine. The same Moonplume he has drawn on his back – a realization that threatens to cleft me straight through the heart, leaving me with *another* package to discard in my icy nether.

Snarling, I slap myself. Hard.

Idiot, idiot, idiot.

I charge through the sitting room and snatch my knapsack, flipping the flap as I move toward a bookshelf, pilfering a few dragonscale blades and a number of iron ones because – despite my lapse in brain function – I'm incredibly resourceful.

I'm almost at the door when Kaan shoves before me, cutting me off. Like Rygun himself just pushed before the exit with a belly full of flames and fire in his eyes.

'Stand aside,' I growl, scouring his savagely beautiful features cast in a stony frown.

He grabs my hand, pressing a small leather satchel into my palm – heavy with the promise of what I suspect is a significant amount of gold.

'Bloodstone,' he says. 'You'll need it once you cross the border.'

'Oh . . .'

Thoughtful.

He takes my face in both hands, snatching my breath. Pulling me so close our noses press together, his shuddered exhale a too-welcomed fever upon my flesh. 'Chase death, Elluin Raeve.'

A gasp cuts down my throat like a blade – whetted edges goring deep.

Elluin Raeve . . .

'Spend your life alone, forever wondering why you scream in your sleep. Calling for that very Moonplume I've spent the past twenty-three phases piecing back together, hoping it would bring your spirit peace. All because you *loved* that beast so fucking much,' he utters, shaking my head, 'I knew it would break you to know she was scattered all over the world after scavengers raided her impact zone.'

'I—'

My words catch on the tip of my tongue as he takes my hand and brings it close to his heart, the pad of his thumb running back and forth across the torn skin down the side of my nail.

His gaze implores, voice plagued with a sadness too heavy to bear as he says, 'Chase death, Moonbeam. And I pray your blood-lust brings you the same sense of peace I feel just knowing you exist.'

He plants a kiss on my temple, so swift and light I barely register it until he's gone. Until he's storming into the adjacent room where he disappears into the shadows – the ghost of his kiss still a brand upon my pebbling skin.

For a moment, I consider chasing him. Asking if Raeve was Elluin's last name on the off chance I ever want to unveil a past that'll undoubtedly burn just like the rest of it.

I reach up. Touch my temple.

Whip my hand away.

No.

Snarling, I tighten my fingers around the sack of bloodstone and storm through the open door, hoping the hutch doesn't shut for the slumber. That there's a Moltenmaw already saddled, ready for a swift escape from this beautiful, haunting place riddled with too many sinkholes to bear.

It's not until I'm tromping across the Loff's rocky shore toward the western tip of the cove I've been drawn to since I arrived – the city hutch well and truly at my back – that I realize I have no intention of leaving yet . . .

Another foreign compulsion that'll no doubt bite me in the ass.

Diary Entry

Elluin Neván

Age: 18 phases
5,000,039 phases After Stone

It's been a while since my last entry. My attention's been . . . elsewhere. Tangled in a web of confusion. That's the only way I can describe this feeling in my chest.

After my first fighting lesson with Veya beneath the harsh rays of Dhomm (which, by the way, is nowhere near as easy as I thought it was going to be), I moved through the halls of the Imperial Stronghold – body aching, smelling like the sun-deterrent poultice she always cakes me in before I step outside. I came to the grated door that leads to Slátra's hutch. Only it was closed.

Locked.

Sitting beside the door was the male I now know to be Kaan Vaegor – the eldest son of the King, only recently back from the Boltanic Plains to watch over Dhomm while his pah helps Tyroth secure his foothold in Arithia.

It was the first time I'd seen him since he threw me in the tub then stormed off to let Veya scrub me down.

He was sitting on the ground with a beautiful string instrument resting over his lap, carved from what appeared to be a hunk of emberwood. Such a deep, ruddy tone – like aged blood. He was plucking out a simple tune from the three thick strings, his fingers moving so delicately I felt like they were plucking the chords of my broken heart.

He didn't look at me, but the instructions were clear based on the key beside him. Based on the massive bowl of red stew and the lump of bread sitting atop a meal tray on the ground across the hall.

I leapt for the key, but he snatched my arm, his grip so strong I was immediately aware of how easily he could snap bones.

He told me to eat first.

One – who does that?

Two – I'm a mood eater, just like Mah was. And this thing on my head makes me feel nauseous ninety percent of the time. Doesn't make for much of an appetite.

I didn't bother telling Kaan Vaegor that. He had this look in his eye like it wouldn't have mattered if I did. The rules wouldn't change. And technically, while his pah's gone, I'm living beneath Kaan's roof.

Kaan's rules.

Such bullshit.

Furious, yet desperate to get back to Slátra, I did as he asked – slurping down the stew so fast I only realized the meal was too rich and spicy when it was far too late, a small sun burning in my gurgling gut. I made it to the privy just in time for my stomach to turn inside out. Or at least that's how it felt.

When I came back, the door was unlocked.

Kaan was gone.

The following slumber, he was there again, but this time there was a much smaller serving of a much milder stew that almost reminded me of home – with notes of jumplin bulb and frostfruit. There was also a glass of colk milk which cleansed my mouth and belly from the mild amount of spice.

Every slumber since has been the same strange routine. Me sitting in his vast atmosphere while I fill my belly with meals I can feel flooding me with strength.

We don't talk. He simply plays while I eat and earn the key that unlocks Slátra's hutch. Then I leave, his plucked chords chasing me down the tunnel where I huddle within the curve of Slátra's tail, lulled to sleep by the baritone tune . . .

I don't understand what he's doing. Why he's doing it.

I don't understand why I'm starting to look forward to it.

Veya

CHAPTER 58

Sunshine punches the side of my face as I climb the jagged stairwell scored into the mountainside, my laden leather satchel banging against my leg every time I take a step. The aurora's yet to rise, the city silent, the air still thick from the downpour.

Objectively, I should wait a few cycles before I set out for Arithia in search of Elluin's diary. Take time to prepare for the lengthy journey. But I have the patience of a Sabersythe and twice the energy – making for a sleepless slumber fraught with spiky thoughts and feet so itchy I finally gave up and packed a bag.

The path cuts left, then flattens into a wide stone shelf dedicated to some of the larger burrows. Like cells of a búsinbee hive, the hutch has been integrated into the mountainside, bearing two hundred twenty-seven holes in all different shapes and sizes.

Some Sabersythes like to tuck deep within the mountain, others shallow. Some prefer a wide space, others tight and cozy so they can blow the burrow full of flame, then curl up pressed against near-molten walls like they're still tucked in an egg.

Like Rygun, the adorable monster.

I smile at the thought, sweeping my hair back behind my ear, but then a *different* thought slaps that smile straight off my face. 'Shit,' I mutter. '*Tick prongs*.'

Did I pack them? I can't remember. Kaan may be fine with ripping them off with his bare hands, but that never works for me. The head always dislodges and then I have to get my fingers in there and fish it out.

I lump my pack on the ground and crouch over it, shifting through things I don't remember stuffing in here – no idea why I'd need *two* forks.

My hyperactive, sleep-deprived brain had its reasons, I'm sure.

I continue rifling through, trying not to look to my right. To the burrow that's been abandoned since I was five phases old.

Threading my entire arm into my satchel and feeling around the bottom, my thoughts churn into a black smog as I cast my stare up at the large thorny moon perched directly above the Stronghold. A little lower than many of the other moons in the sky.

Jógo.

Mah's beloved dragon that she nursed back to health after finding him kicked from a nest as a hatchling.

After she passed, I'm told Jógo refused to leave the big round burrow to my right – an abnormality for a Sabersythe, since they like to switch dens more often than a huttlecrab switches shells. The very reason we provide so many burrows. An effort to keep our charmed beasts content enough not to mourn their hatching grounds.

Jógo's uninterest in emerging was the first sign something was wrong. That he'd fallen into a *different* form of mourning.

The only time I ever saw the light hit his beautiful bronze scales was when I sat on this very plateau waiting for Kaan to finish tending a tear in Rygun's wing. Jógo emerged, hobbling. Barely able to keep his head off the ground.

He'd looked me in the eye, huffed a hot breath upon my face, and I'd never been so scared. Then he made a sharp mewling sound, squinted up at the sky, tilled his droopy wings, and *flew*.

Five phases old, and I watched him ball up and die in the sky. Something else for Pah to blame on me. Being so young, I actually believed it *was* my fault, until I grew old enough to understand the beast was mourning Mah. Then I knew for *certain* it was.

I shove the prickly thought aside, clearing my throat.

Finally finding the prongs, I shake them victoriously, then tuck them into a pocket that's easy to access, tossing my bag over my shoulder again. I'm just walking past Rygun's burrow – the mouth of it gouged from the way he scraped against it while preparing for his last shed – when I see Kaan bent over a saddlebag he's currently repacking.

I pause, looking into the burrow's rumbling depths where Rygun is likely sleeping with one eye open, well aware Kaan is about to force him from his tight, heated nook.

'Where are *you* going?' I ask, watching Kaan tuck one of his packs full of dried flaps of dahpa bread. Enough that I realize he has every intention of being away for more than a few slumbers.

He cuts a glance at me over his shoulder, brow creased. 'Ticks are out with a vengeance,' he mutters, reaching into his pocket and pulling out a rumpled parchment lark. 'A charmed beast turned rabid and torched half a village.'

Frowning, I set down my pack and advance, taking the lark from his outstretched hand. I smooth it against my thigh, skimming the messy script. '*Blóm*? Chief Thron's beast?'

Kaan grunts.

Creators . . .

'He blazed an entire herd of colk with no intention of eating. If the beast is left, there are many other villages nearby that he'll decimate before the poison corrodes his heart. I'm getting a head start. Grihm's gathering his gear, then meeting me on the way if he can catch up. The keepers are helping to saddle one of the carters for him now. Lane's beast, I think.'

'Nevut?'

'Correct. She's the fastest Sabersythe in the hutch that hasn't yet been turned out for The Great Flurrt, and haste is of the essence.'

My gaze drifts to the three metal spears resting on the ground in a bundled heap, bound with a leather holster that'll attach to Rygun's saddle. I nod, not that he sees it, his attention cast back on his pack, movements stiff and precise as he stuffs it full.

Poor Kaan. There's nothing worse than hunting a rabid dragon. It's hard to convince yourself that you've put a beast out of its misery when it falls to the ground rather than soars into the sky, curling up beside its ancestors.

For his sake – and for the sake of his massive, tender heart – I hope someone else has grounded the beast before he makes it there. Help folk rebuild their stone homes and you're a hero. Slaughter a Sabersythe and you're a fucking murderer, no matter how many pats on the back you get.

No matter how many folk you save.

Clearing my throat, I fold the lark in half and pass it back.

'I saw you lead . . . *her* toward your suite. Please tell me you didn't take her to your shrine.'

Kaan pauses, then continues rearranging his pack as if I didn't speak at all. He pulls the drawstring taut, knuckles blanched with tension as he knots the strips of leather.

Guess that's a yes.

I pinch the bridge of my nose, eyes squeezed shut. 'You said *slowly ease* . . .'

'I did.'

'This is not that.'

'It's not.'

I sigh, opening my eyes. 'I assume by your general demeanor that she didn't throw herself into your arms before the corpse of her dead dragon and thank you for the missing piece of her mind puzzle?'

'No, Veya. She didn't.'

'Shocker,' I say on a faux laugh, threading my hands through my hair, contemplating the possibility that his mind's just as lost as the beast he's flying off to slay. 'So, what, you gave her enough gold to buy her safe passage across the Boltanic Plains so she can chase her welling bloodlust? Where there's a big chance she'll eventually be recognized by either of the twins, both of which have access to a certain *tool*. Perfect leverage to fold her into submission once they blow the lid off *that* jar. Lovely.'

Kaan stands, crosses his arms, and frowns down at me – his black and red riding leathers sculpting him into a larger, fiercer, more formidable form of our pah. Something I'm certain he despises every time he looks in the mirror.

'They get hold of her, we're dead, Kaan. How long do you think it'll be before they're swarming our borders, ready to paint this city red and carve into our rich, untapped reserve of bloodstone? We're living on borrowed time, and you *fucking* know it.'

'You done?'

I plant my hands on my hips, tossing my stare skyward.

Why is he calm? The kingdom he's worked so hard to capture, protect, and grow is probably going to be ripped to shreds, all because he dropped the Elluin boulder on Raeve before we had a chance to assess the situation from *all* angles.

It's a disaster.

'Yes. I'm done,' I mutter, realizing I need to track back down to the carter hutch. Tell the Moltenmaw riders they need to make themselves scarce – at least until I have a chance to make it to Arithia and back with her diary in hand.

Hopefully.

There's no way she's getting across the plains on her own. She'd sizzle like Slátra did.

'All going to plan, I should be back before The Great Flurrt to help raise the platforms.'

My gaze snaps to him so fast my head spins. 'The miskunn predicted that'll be in thirty aurora cycles . . .'

'Correct.'

'You're leaving for *thirty aurora cycles*?'

'It's a big kingdom, Veya. I can't just fluff around here when there's shit to do. I've been south for a while, and the kingdom doesn't run itself.'

'Sounds like a convenient excuse to run away.'

He tips his head to the side, eyes narrowing. 'You told me to tread carefully or she'll incinerate herself. This is me treading carefully.' His stare softens a little. 'She doesn't want me around. I'm simply abiding.'

'You tossed her a sack of *gold*, Kaan. She's probably halfway out the door. It's only a matter of time before she's wielded *against* us.'

'Dragon bloodstone,' he corrects, and I groan. 'And she's not halfway out the door. She walked straight past the carter hutch and headed for the western point.'

My heart stops, all the blood rushing from my face. Sharp prickles of emotion pierce the backs of my eyes.

'She's still in there,' I whisper past the swelling pip in my throat.

Elluin.

Kaan nods – just once. 'Somewhere.'

I swat a tear from my cheek.

He looks away, puts his fingers to his lips, and whistles loud.

Rygun releases a rumbling exhale that rattles my bones, followed by the scraping, creaking sounds of his immense body nudging free from his tight sleep space. The beast emerges from the darkness in world-trembling increments, cinder eyes glinting in the gloom, plumes of steam billowing from his flared nostrils – the curved tusks protruding from his boxy face a fearsome tribute to his size and age.

Kaan shoulders his pack and the trio of spears, stalking toward the emerging beast when he stills, looking back at me, then *past* me to my pack on the ground. 'Where are you going, Veya?'

Crap.

'Well, you see . . .' I edge backward, swipe the bag off the ground, and swing it over my shoulder. 'As I'm sure you recall, she used to write in a diary.'

'*No.*'

'Pfft. You know I feed off that word,' I boast. 'Besides, I'm not just doing it for *you*. I need to know things she can't tell me. It's messing with my head now that she's . . . *alive* again.'

'Then I'll go.'

I snort-laugh. 'While Cadok may be aloof enough to let you roam his kingdom unguarded, Tyroth is not. And he hates you. Fiercely. I can make myself unseen. You can't.'

He levels me with a stare to match that of his beast barely protruding from the shadows at his back. A single look that makes me feel more valued than Pah *ever* did – even though he knows I'm more than capable of taking care of myself.

Sometime, I'll thank him for that.

'You got rid of that bangle. You told me so.'

'I lied,' I say with stony precision.

I didn't lie. It's gone. Meaning I have to get it *back*. Not that I'm going to tell him that. He'll blow a fucking artery if he knows where I tossed it.

His eyes narrow.

'Oh, and I intend to be gone awhile. Taste some *delicacies* on the way,' I say, waggling my brows.

He immediately breaks my eye contact, shuddering. 'I don't want to know about that, thank you very fucking much.'

No, but I need him to shuck this conversation like an itchy cloak. My insinuation that I'm going to prowl for a few good lays is a certain way to repulse him enough he'll—

'*Fine*,' he growls, probably knowing I'd do it without his blessing but that it'd hurt me more than it'd hurt him.

Love him for that.

I flash him a smile. 'Dear brother, are you worried about me?'

'Since the dae Pah shoved you in my arms – squirming, bloody, and screaming.'

Since he realized he was all I had.

He doesn't need to say it. I can see it in his eyes. Our one good parent died bringing me into this world.

Hard for me to mourn someone I never knew, but I hate that I took her from him. That Kaan was forced to raise me because Pah didn't care whether I lived or died.

The prick.

'I wish he had another neck to sever.'

'I wish he had *three*,' Kaan snarls, stalking deeper into the darkness, followed by the grunting sounds of his ascent onto Rygun's saddle.

I frown after him, wondering what he means by—

'*Oh* . . .'

Shit.

Kaan can't contain a secret for long before it gnaws through his gut. Eventually, he'll have to tell Elluin what Pah somehow accomplished that terrible slumber over an eon ago when her life came crumbling down.

When she woke to find her entire family poisoned to death.

For someone already misted by the beginnings of blood-lust, that's the sort of news that can paint your vision red. Plant you with an appetite that can only be quelled by revenge.

I've seen bloodlusting folk who've failed to satiate their savage desires, rabid like a tick-bit Sabersythe, the only cure their own swift and merciful death.

And with Pah already dead, slain by *Kaan's* hand . . .

Rygun begins to edge forward like a mountain shifting from its perch, and I press myself flush against the wall – pack in hand.

'Be careful,' I yell at Kaan, despite not being able to see him from all the way down here, trying to become one with the stone.

'Always,' he bellows before Rygun hefts off the plateau's edge, his tail the last part of him to slither from the burrow as he plummets from sight.

Raeve

CHAPTER 59

The booming *thud-ump* of dragon flight has me spinning to see Rygun soaring toward the east, Kaan saddled between his massive wings, a cluster of spears notched by his boot.

My heart bangs against my ribs like a gallop of hooves.

Snarling, I flip up my hood and whip my head back around, large stones shifting beneath my heavy-booted stomps to the Loff's lapping tune.

Chase death, Elluin Raeve—

I slap myself.

Hard.

It's all some strange, fucked-up coincidence. Or perhaps someone messed with my head while I was knocked out. Fiddled with the threads of my brain. Tied knots where they shouldn't exist. Patched me up incorrectly.

That must be it.

That has to be it.

I come to a red-stone wall that stretches from within the jungle, across the shore, and disappears into the Loff's ruffled depths, many luminous warding runes carved into its stumpy height as well as a bunch of painted words:

DANGER

TURN BACK NOW!

KEEP OUT OR DIE A HORRIBLE DEATH

BEWARE! A HUSHLING LIVES HERE

Shrugging, I leap it and continue on, whistling my calming tune to distract myself from replaying Kaan's caustic words in my head.

If there's a hushling living somewhere over this side of the fence, I'll be gobsmacked. Being one of the few folk who've likely gotten within swiping distance of one and lived to tell the tale, I know full well no warding runes can hold them off. They'd step right over those things with their pale, lanky legs to get to the brains on the other side.

It would've ravaged the city long ago, meaning this heavily jungled, uninhabited point of the bay is being protected for some *other* reason I'm determined to discover.

Not sure why. It's an itch I need to scratch before I finally ditch this place and hunt Rekk to the other end of the world. Preferably as far from *here* as I can get.

I'm nearing the peak's sharp, rocky tip when a tree catches my eye, its roots gouged deep into the rocky over-hang that fringes the shore. Its gnarled branches stretch in all directions, riddled with knots – *one* that makes me pause, oddly smoother than the rest, as though it's been touched many times.

With a lilting giggle, Clode swishes past my ear and toys with the tree's long coppery leaves, making them look like dancing blades.

I frown.

Drawing closer, I reach out to touch the knot that drew my attention, fingers skating over a small handle-type nub that sticks out from the center. I pinch it, give it a wiggle, and the thing pops free, revealing a small hollow behind.

Huh.

Casting a glance over my shoulder toward the sleeping city, I search the skies, the esplanade, deciding I'm little more than a speck. No need for me to be sneaky like I've got something to hide, rooting around in tree trunks that don't belong to me.

I stuff my entire arm inside the hollow, flopping my hand around the smooth internal cavity, fingers grazing something hard that rattles around. Frown deepening, I grab the cold lump and pull it free—

My heart *whumps* fierce and fast as I cradle the small stone carving. A three-dimensional depiction of Kaan's málmr – a Moonplume and a Sabersythe bound together like two halves of a circular whole.

My skin prickles despite the muggy heat.

Another glance in the direction Kaan disappeared before I plug the knot back into place. My hand tightens around the carving, and I grab the branch, using it to haul myself up the overhang, then move into the jungle's dense, overgrown guts.

I push past low-hanging vines and round velvety leaves, insects buzzing about my face, certain I'm hearing a playful giggle through the trees.

The echo of a thundering chase.

The sounds are there but . . . *not*. Snuffed out, leaving nothing but the smoke from a once-frolicking flame.

I frown, the underbrush crunching beneath my boots while I trace the sense of a path that certainly doesn't exist in reality but is somehow vibrantly clear in my mind. A different color to the rest of my thoughts – luminous and with its own pulsing beat that spikes me full of warm anticipation.

Swatting beads of sweat from my brow, I emerge amongst a clearing at the base of a cliff, the sheer stone draped in a leafy, vining plant. I stare up at it, unable to shake the feeling that there's something here.

Something . . . *important*.

Remembering the way Kaan parted the fall of foliage in his private garden, I tuck the carving into my satchel and step forward, pushing at the vines, growing restless when all I find behind is stone . . . Stone . . . *More damn stone*.

Perhaps I'm going mad?

Creators, it certainly feels like it.

I'm palping a stone wall when I could be on the back of a Moltenmaw, soaring toward The Fade, drunk on thoughts of how I'm going to make Rekk break before he dies.

I sidestep farther along the wall, cursing beneath my breath, shoving, *shoving* – heart lodging into my throat when I plunge all the way through the wall and into a hollow beyond. I wrestle the foliage, sucking sharp breaths as I free myself from the tangle that's much too reminiscent of a hushling's web for my liking.

'Imagine that,' I mutter dryly, a small laugh bubbling up.

Imagine. That.

I shake my head and look right, moving deeper into the tunnel that's tall and wide enough for a grown male to fit through – *just*.

Clode giggles past me on an eddy of wind, tilling dried leaves that dance about my boots with each slow step forward.

I make for the coil of stairs illuminated by dull natural light falling down from above, curious anticipation fluttering through my belly like a cluster of tiny sowmoths. It's five whole turns before I reach an open archway on the right that gives me the option to veer off. I take it, those fluttery things multiplying as I step into a small cavern lit by an overhead skyhole, the cozy space riddled with blooming copper vines reaching across the walls.

The ceiling.

Hundreds of those bold, inky flowers that dominate the city spice the air with a zesty sweetness, the sight of them warming my chest and making me smile.

'Pretty.'

I move toward an organic, grown-from-the-stone cooking bench that reminds me of the butcher block in that little crooked dwelling in the mountain range, dragging my hand across the rough-hewn surface heavy with a layer of dust. The metal door on the stone range creaks when I open it to peer inside the ashen hollow, rusted from lack of care, my brow buckling as I run my fingers over twin terracotta mugs hanging from hooks on the wall above.

It's tempting to lift one off and tuck it in my bag. They look lovely to drink from. It's hard to find the perfect mug. When you do, they always break.

I pause beside a table that sprouts from the wall below a massive vine-clothed window, glowing runes etched into the frame, shredded curtains hanging limp at its sides. Two seats are tucked beneath the table, the leather padding on one pecked at by some animal, most of the feather stuffing pulled free and probably used in a nest somewhere.

I'm not sure why that makes my throat ache. A feeling I try to ignore as I move past twin leather seaters, stepping close to a large wall shelf and finding a pot of ink, an old quill, and a stack of flat, ready-to-fold parchment larks with pre-etched activation lines. I slide a thin leather-bound book from a pile next to the ink, blow off the dust, and crack it open, discovering the pages are blank.

Strange.

Crouching, I find the shelf below boasts a collection of small stone creatures – mostly dragons. All carved in the same style as the one currently tucked in my satchel. Pulling it out, I shake my head, setting the carving amongst the rest, right beside one of a sharp-tipped palace.

This is a couple's home, packed with relics of their love.

I should go.

Moving toward the exit, I intend to ease back down the stairs when Clode nips past my ear on a whip of wind that swirls *up*.

'*Geil. Geil asha.*'

My heart stills.

Come. Come see.

It's not often she speaks to me so directly. She's too wild and aloof to maintain any semblance of a honed, sturdy presence.

I rest my hand on the dagger at my thigh and edge up the stairs. '*Halagh te aten de wetana, atan blatme de.*'

If I die this dae, I'm blaming you.

Strokes of luck aside, Clode's perception of danger is just as skewed as her perception of my ability to dodge it, my thoughts tumbling back to the time she lured me into the Undercity, bringing me face-to-face with a rogue doomquill buck about to gut a young huggin I guess Clode took a liking to. Not surprising, since those things are damn adorable.

Not yet versed in the art of willing Clode to implode lungs, I'd only survived due to some swift maneuvering down an abandoned rubbish chute where I'd perched for half a dae with the balled-up huggin bound in my lap.

Utterly unfazed.

My muscles trembled with the effort not to plummet into the velvet trogg's den while the huggin nibbled its nails, whiskers twitching, looking at me through googly, iridescent eyes that never seemed to blink – until the doomquill finally stopped clawing at the chute and clattered off.

I'll never unsee the way it gnashed its prickly maw at the entrance, pink tongue wagging as it screeched for blood.

With a full-body shudder, I open myself to Bulder's song, deciding he's likely more reliable in situations like these – though all I hear is a low, droning hum that pours me full of a warm, heavy sense of peace.

Contentment.

Similar to the sound he made in Slátra's tomb.

Frowning, I wind around another curl of stairs, spilling into a cozy chamber that's fed with a beam of sunlight shooting down from the skyhole above – casting the lush space in devastating detail.

I pause, heart in my throat, hand slipping from the hilt of my blade.

The space reminds me of the cavern that held Kaan's pieced-together moon, bearing the same embossed walls boasting a passionate clash of Moonplumes and Sabersythes.

But it doesn't house a moon.

It houses a massive circular pallet pressed against the wall, softened by a spread of white sheets so fine it's no wonder they've disintegrated in places, the pallet picked apart in others like gaping wounds spewing feathers that eddy with Clode's giggling tune. A sound that echoes with another giggle that seems to rise from beneath the depths of my icy lake . . .

A vision strikes like a blow to my brain. My heart. My *soul*—

Me, crawling across this pallet – naked.

Laughing.

Flipping onto my back, looking up at a male at the end pulling his shirt up over his head while I part my legs and touch myself – desperate and wanting.

Needing.

At the sight of his sweat-dappled body, I release a throaty groan, close my eyes. Sink my fingers inside myself in an effort to sate the hunger that never quells.

Not when it comes to him.

The pallet dips with his weight, his hefty presence dropping close – electrifying my skin, making my heart pump in hard, rapid beats.

A kiss is planted on the stretched slope of my neck. A nip below my ear that sends shivers scuttling through my body and almost unravels me upon my fingers.

His lips are at my lobe, coarse words poured into me:

'What do you want, Elluin?'

'You.' I turn my head, open my eyes. Get lost in Kaan's ember gaze as a smile fills my cheeks. 'Forever.'

The vision loosens its hold on me, and my knees buckle. I fall to the ground amongst a litter of feathers, gasping for breath that won't come, hands gnarled into claws that drag at my chest. As I realize with soul-crushing finality the reason I've been drawn to this point since the moment I opened the shutters.

This place isn't the relic of somebody *else's* love . . .

It's *ours*.

Diary Entry

Elluin Neván

Age: 18 phases

5,000,039 phases After Stone

This slumber, Kaan played a song I recognized. The same song Mah and Pah used to sing to me when I was sick.

I sang along until my words got choked by the first tears I've been able to cry since I brought Haedeon back from Netheryn. They didn't spill like a soft snowfall, but like a storm lashing the windowpanes.

I cried for Mah and Pah. For Haedeon and Allume.

I cried for Slátra.

I cried for things that were taken from me, and for the voice I'm not allowed to use.

I didn't realize Kaan had stopped playing until he scooped me up, tucked me against his chest, and held me so tight I could barely breathe, his strong body absorbing every one of my sobs.

It reminded me of the way Pah picked up Mah when she was crying in the snow. The way he carried her back inside where it was light and warm . . .

For some reason, that just made me cry harder.

Kaan

CHAPTER 61

The heavy smoke haze makes the sun look like a pink smudge, a quiet reminder that this village was a battlefield earlier this dae.

Now it's a graveyard.

We step around the blistered corpse of a fallen colk yet to be dragged into the pit, and I clear my throat.

Chief Thron keeps my pace as we walk past bouldered homes, some reforged in the past few hours, though shattered glass still litters the ground at their base. Others are black from where dragonflame fired the stone, the glass from their windows now puddled on the ground.

Solidified.

Uprooted trees lie across the path like dead bodies, their foliage withered or singed, roots still clinging to slabs of ground that lifted with their upheaval. Folk cut into the trunks with long bronze saws, hacking them into pieces small enough to be used as firewood or other supplies.

'We have lost much,' Thron says, a somber hitch to his deep voice. 'But we'd have lost much more had you not arrived when you did.'

Had I not slaughtered his dragon.

I grunt, stepping over a scatter of crushed ginku fruit, the bright-yellow flesh browning beneath the sun's harsh rays. Souring, just like this feeling in my gut.

We move into the open, past fields of tawny crops that have been gouged, many plants uprooted from the skirmish that took place before I was able to lure Blóm into the sky again. Toward the rolling hills that sit as a backdrop for the village of Rambek, like great crouching beasts.

I could've done it here, but I wanted to give him somewhere private to curl up since it was clear he wasn't going to make it into the sky.

As it was, he didn't manage to curl up at all. Didn't solidify.

Just died, and will eventually rot where he lies.

I clear my throat, trying to scrub the image from my mind, gaze sliding to the clay silo – once tall and strong, now shattered. A phase's worth of grain spilled across the scorched ground, dampened by the downpour that came just after the beast was slain. As though Rayne herself was crying over the loss of the majestic Sabersythe Rygun slung to the base of a gully, releasing his own tortured shriek that rivaled the howling wind.

The ground had rattled just as much as my fucking bones.

I pull my lungs full, the air thick with the stench of death, smoke, and despair. 'I will have barrels of grain shipped to the nearby port,' I offer, watching some of the village folk move about the fields, snapping nearly ripe heads off the top of cormah fronds and gathering them in carts. Salvaging what they can. 'As well as some slow-perishing produce to tide your folk over until you can replenish your crops.'

Thron turns to face me, his hand flat on his broad sable chest as he dips his head. 'Thank you, Sire.'

'Of course.'

He lifts his head, stark-brown eyes heavy with the weight of loss. 'And on a more personal note, I'd like to thank you for felling Blóm.' He brings his hand up to the lower half of his face and smooths it down his black beard threaded with a few ruddy beads. 'Had we been able to get a clear shot, I'm not sure I would've been able to order it taken . . .'

'I understand,' I say, placing my hand on his shoulder. 'He has been your companion for many phases.'

Thron clears his throat, glancing toward the vast stretch of colk pastures at my back. 'There's your second-in-command. I'll leave you be, but please join my family for a meal before you leave.'

I offer him a clipped nod, watching him move toward the shattered silo.

'Fuck,' I mutter, my gaze lifting to the hills, certain I'll never look at them the same again. They used to be so picturesque, now they look like fucking tombstones.

Shaking my head, I turn, seeing Grihm standing by the stone fence that appears to be entirely repaired – spoken back into shape. When we'd arrived, the herd had scattered, many of them felled and now bloated in the streets, caught by the blow of dragonflame that poured all over the village.

The surviving members of the herd now graze on patches of shrub, long tongues wrapping around the stiff twigs and pulling them into their mouths. Young ones wobble about or punch their heads up at laden udders, stubby tails wagging as they drink.

I move down the ashen path and lean against the fence beside Grihm, planting my forearms on the stone. Silence prevails while we watch the herd graze on what little vegetation wasn't razed by the flames, their large padded feet picking up a mixture of damp ash and mud.

'Something on your mind, Grihm?'

He clears his throat, like checking to see if it'll work before he speaks in a voice rusty from misuse. 'I would like to request leave.'

I look sidelong at him, taking in his pale hair streaked in ash, his black leathers smeared in the same orange dirt the soles of his boots are caked in.

'For?'

His eyes remain cast ahead. 'It's rumored the Great Silver Sabersythe has laid a trio of eggs.'

My heart stills, realization sinking through my skin, chilling me to the bone. 'You want to go to Gondragh and raid the nest of the Great Silver Sabersythe?'

A single nod.

For a moment, all I can do is stare at the side of his face, trying to sort my thoughts into a manageable hand.

Failing.

So I go with the fiery facts.

'I stole one of her scales many phases ago. She almost ripped off my arm. For a *scale*.'

He turns his head, and I see fragments of his pale-blue eyes through the flop of his hair.

Silence.

I shake my head, laughing low, bringing my hand up to scrub my beard. 'Fuck, Grihm.'

'I don't wish to replace Inkah, but being bound to her grave has taken a toll.'

It's an effort not to gape at him.

I've never heard the male thread so many emotionally bound words together in one sentence, and I'm all but certain I'm the only one he speaks to. He doesn't even say *Skripi* when he's ready to show hands. Just taps the fucking table with two fingers like he's ordering a mead.

He's never told me what happened to Inkah, and I'll never ask. I know enough about his past to know it's riddled with veins of pain that will forever throb.

'Did you inform the others about this decision?'

He shakes his head.

Course not.

He and Veya are cast from the same stone. I'm almost certain they'll quietly dance around each other for eternity.

'And if you die there, will you have any regrets?'

'Perhaps.' He shrugs. 'But I'd be dead.'

Right.

I sigh, scrubbing my face again. I was baffled by the size of his saddlebags. Makes a whole lot more sense now. Going to Gondragh, you need to be prepared.

Meaning he's been planning this for a while.

A heaviness settles on my chest, and I hang my head, then nod and push off the wall. 'I'll take you there and drop you near the hatching hut,' I say, feeling his gaze on me as I stalk toward the village. 'Least I can do since it's probably the last time I'll see your sorry ass again.'

Veya

CHAPTER 62

The wind howls, nipping the tip of my nose numb.

Eight aurora cycles in and out of the air, sleeping beneath Zekhi's wing or nudged next to sunburnt boulders – doing what we could to avoid civilization. It was pleasant until the sun lost its strength and The Fade swallowed us whole with its snow and endless buffeting wind.

I'm homesick already.

I'm sure Zekhi feels the same, nudged in an unfamiliar hutch he blew into a molten dribble before he tucked himself inside. Trying to keep warm until I return.

Another pushy gust, and the massive colk pulling Noeve's cart trembles all the way to his thick fluffy hind, though he keeps his plodding pace along the frail Path of Daes, snorting milky plumes of air that tangle with his curly horns.

I lean my head over the side, looking down the sheer drop to our left, finding the below still hidden by a swirl of mist that creates a false sense of security.

Very false.

I've traveled this part of the wall on mistless cycles. We're so high the plummet looks endless. Like falling into a pale, moonless sky.

Another howl of wind crams a flurry of snow into my hood, and the entire cart jolts right toward the equally brutal fall on the other side of the Path. My heart jolts with it, my hand whipping out to white-knuckle the side of the cart. Not sure why, we're all fucked if this thing goes off. The cart, too.

I clear my throat, busying myself by brushing away some of the snow that's gathered in my lap. 'That was a bad one.'

Beside me, Noeve chuckles – the maniacal sound of an old crone who's done this so many times she clearly believes she's invincible. I sure hope so.

I intend to die doing something brilliant and heroic. Not free-falling to my doom.

'You're out of practice,' Noeve says, her voice a husky rasp from all the smoke she's inhaled over the phases. 'A blow like that never used to ruffle your feathers.'

I look sidelong at the fae – a short, stumpy female who must be over a thousand phases old to have earned the dollop of gray hair she keeps coiled atop her head. Not that I've ever inquired about her age.

Seems rude.

'How are you not cold?' I ask, eyeing her simple gray tunic and pants, only embellished with a fluffy patchwork belt that knots around her waist and dangles to the floor, made from the hides of her favorite beasts from times past.

Or so she told me once.

She quirks a quizzical brow my way, the reins draped within the loose grasp of her bare hands.

'I've never seen you in a cloak,' I continue. 'No matter the weather. How you haven't frozen to death yet is well beyond me.'

She clicks her tongue. 'Have to be tough to live east of the Path of Daes, my dear. Especially in times like these. You know as well as I do that it's a hotspot for renegades and folk a few eggs short of a clutch. The cold is a *cushion* compared to some of the shit I've seen.'

I don't doubt it, and I don't particularly like going there myself. But flying into Gore's hutch would publicly announce my arrival to my not-so-darling brother. Making use of one of the old, abandoned hutches in the east has always been my safest bet since I'd rather risk falling off this very sheer cliff than tempt a run-in with Cadok.

At least until I finally get the chance to meet him in a battle ring and cut off his head.

There's a jingling sound from somewhere ahead, tolling through the din. Noeve pulls her own handheld bell from a compartment by her feet, rattling it, informing whoever's waiting to move onto the frail Path that it's currently occupied. That they need to wait until we pass before they move onto it themselves.

I tuck deeper into my fur-lined cloak. 'Here I was thinking the Path would be quiet at this time.'

'Often times, others have the same thought,' Noeve says. 'You can clamber into the back if you're worried about being seen.'

I twist around and lift the flap of leather that saddles the deep wooden tray, frowning at the flock of goggin birds pecking at a scatter of seed, clucking away. One of them tilts its plump feathery ass, then paints the thick drape in a splash of white.

Gross.

'Think I'll take my chances,' I mutter, dropping the leather, Noeve's chortling laugh making it impossible to keep a straight face. 'You're terrible.'

'You missed me.'

'I did,' I admit as a squeal of wind whips past us so fast it makes the cart wobble again. The colk tosses his head and snorts at the sky rather than buck us over the edge.

That's the difference between Noeve's Path-traversing colks and almost anyone else's: they're *truly* charmed. Less chance of death. Well worth as much bloodstone as I can pack into her very deep pockets.

No wonder she turns them into belts.

'It's been a while since you've graced my cart, my dear. I started to think you'd gone off me.'

'Never. I just decided I don't like the wall anymore, or most of its inhabitants – present company excluded,' I say, giving her a soft shoulder-nudge. 'Feeding folk to dragons because they piss you off rubs me the wrong way.'

'I couldn't agree more,' she murmurs, and a heavy silence elbows between us.

I have no doubt she's considering times past, when this colorful kingdom was at its prime. Until Cadok marked his scent all over it and turned it into a military nest.

'Heard you were sneaking folk out of the city for the Queen?' I ask, reaching into my pocket for one of my few remaining sticks of dried meat, chewing on the lanky end.

'Not since she tried to stall an execution.'

My eyes widen. 'Really?'

Noeve nods. 'I believe it got back to *His Imperial Shit Stain.*

Apologies,' she's swift to tack on, flicking me a quick glance. 'I know he's your blood.'

'Not gonna stop me from decapitating him,' I mutter.

Noeve chuckles, taking a while to recompose herself before she speaks again. 'Anyway, I haven't heard from her since. Guess it doesn't look good for your significant other to publicly oppose a ruling of your Guild. *Especially* when that ruling's against a member of the *Fíur du Ath*,' she says, waggling her brows.

'Interesting . . .'

Very.

'Mm-hmm.'

I rip into the meat, chewing through the leathery chunk, taking the edge off my hunger but making me incredibly parched. Unfortunately, I have only gritty water to look forward to when we reach our destination. And a date with someone who'll probably eat me.

Noeve transfers both reins into one hand and pulls a leather roll from the pocket of her pants, unraveling it. She plucks out a smoke stick and waves it in my direction.

'Thought you gave that up?' I ask, reaching into my pocket for my fire weald. Well, *Kaan's* old fire weald I stole when I was young, imagining I'd need it one dae. Or more to the point – wishing.

Hoping.

Wasted hopes they were.

'Over thirty times since you last sat in that seat. But I've decided I quite enjoy it.'

I smile, flicking the metal lid, using the dancing flame to singe the end of her death stick. She draws on it, blowing a swathe of sweet smoke that gets lost amongst the fog while I polish off my meat strip to the tune of our trundling cart.

'Why are you here, Veya?' Noeve asks between deep drags.

'Left something important in Gore,' I say, removing a glove to pick the meat from between my teeth.

'How long ago?'

I think back to the moment just after the *blank* in my head. The inky smudge that somehow feels both void and unfathomably hefty. 'Over a hundred phases?'

'Ahh,' Noeve muses, taking another deep pull of her stick, blowing a plume of smoke that soils my next breath with the overly sweet residue of whatever herb she's wafting. 'And where did you leave this . . . *thing*?'

'Tossed it down the rubbish chute.'

I thread my hand back in my glove and cross my arms over my chest, settling deeper into the cold wooden seat. Frowning, I try to wiggle my ass into a more comfortable position.

Given how much Noeve charges for crossings, I'm surprised the seats still have no padding. Next time, I'm packing a cushion rather than two useless forks I haven't even looked at since I left Dhomm.

Suddenly registering the void of silence beside me, I glance right, straight into Noeve's wide gray eyes – the smoke stick hanging from her pinched fingers, a curl of ash threatening to blow away on the next whirl of wind.

'What's wrong?'

'There's a *velvet trogg* at the bottom of the rubbish chutes in Gore, Veya.'

'Oh, that.' I reach into my pocket for another piece of meat, inspecting both ends, picking the stumpier one to gnaw on. 'Unfortunate, isn't it?'

'You're not intending to—'

'Confront her? Course I am. How else am I going to get the damn thing back?' I mutter through the leathery mouthful. 'She's obsessed with jewelry, correct?'

'From what I've heard, yes . . .'

'Wonderful,' I say, swallowing. Biting off another big chunk.

Hope she hasn't eaten my bangle, otherwise this'll be for naught. Especially since there's next to no chance of me finding Elluin's diary without this *particular* piece of jewelry I stupidly decided to part with many phases ago, tossing it down the chute like some cursed trinket. Certain it had something to do with the reason I had a blank spot the size of thirty aurora cycles smudged in my mind.

Seemed like a good idea at the time. Now it might cost me my life before I get to do something grand and heroic with it.

'You paid for a return trip,' Noeve says, and I shrug.

'If I die, keep the change.' I wiggle in my seat again, trying to find a more comfortable position while I stuff my mouth full of meat. 'Perhaps use it to invest in some Creators-damn padding.'

Diary Entry

Elluin Nevàn

Age: 18 phases
5,000,039 phases After Stone

It's been seven slumbers since I saw him last. Since I heard him play Mah and Pah's song, dropped my shield like a battle-weary soldier, cried in his arms until I finally drifted off, then woke wrapped in Slátra's tail. Though there's still a fresh meal set by the door each slumber, accompanied by a small stone carving I add to my growing collection of pint-sized pity-dragons I want to toss against the wall, there's no song.

No him.

Every time I walk around the corner and find the hall empty, I'm weighed down by another brick of humiliation I throw into my punches.

My kicks.

Veya says I'm improving. If that's what I get for trying to beat the shit out of this feeling, I'll take it.

Veya

CHAPTER 64

Tucked in one of the quieter wind tunnels, I stuff my head through the hole in the wall and peer down the rubbish chute, face twisting at the sour reek wafting up from the trogg's lair.

I sigh, pull my head back, and unravel a length of rope from where it's bound around my shoulder, attaching the large metal hook to the chute's lip. I toss the rope down the hole, hoping it's long enough to skim the top of whatever rubbish pile I'm about to become uncomfortably familiar with.

'Veya, you know what?' I mutter to myself. 'You're marvelous, but you really screwed yourself with this one.'

In the future, I intend to make much better decisions. Preferably ones that don't land me in one of Gore's rubbish chutes, preparing to have a conversation with a creature that nests somewhere near the top of the food chain.

With another sigh, I give the rope a tug, then climb into the hole feetfirst, slowly lowering myself down the chute's lengthy throat toward a blue glow radiating from below. The warming air thickens with the stench of sour, rotten things, and the underside of my tongue tingles.

If I vomit all over my leathers, the trogg won't take me seriously.

I swallow a wad of bile, tipping my head back while I try to keep it down.

Next time life throws me a magical bangle, I'm just going to put it in my jewelry box.

Wherever it is.

Reaching the opening, I ease down a touch farther, dangling midair above a pile of reeking trash.

'Fuck me,' I mutter, casting my wide-eyed gaze around the large cavern, taking in the ceiling – a splintered mess of stalactites. From their tapered tips hang long, blue, dripping strings that are draped across the ceiling like the threads of a web, igniting Gore's refuse in a bold glow. Mountains of it.

I quirk a brow, noticing how there are separate, very organized piles for things: old chairs, clothing, footwear, plates, glass—

Everything.

She'd work wonders in my sleepsuite.

My attention snags on a shimmery pile in the distance. A stack of glinting goods.

Maybe I won't have to confront the trogg after all. I just have to spend the rest of my life hunting through that pile. Silently. While living off trash to sustain myself.

I sigh.

This entire plan is flawed and I'm going to die a horrible death.

A dense *thump* attacks me from above, and I glance up, struck with the terrible realization that something is currently plummeting down the chute above me. The mostly *abandoned* chute. Mid-slumber.

Probably a dead body.

Groaning, I loosen my grip on the rope and plunge toward the pile of trash. Colliding with the clanking, slushy mound, I roll sideways, tumbling groundward, simultaneously coating myself in an oily fluid I refuse to acknowledge.

I clamber to the ground, plucking fruit peels off my tunic and egg shells from my hair, tiptoeing along the frail pathway threaded between the mounds – pointing myself in the direction of the glinting treasure pile I saw in the distance.

I'm struck with the sound of something *chewing*. Of popping, crunching, slurping sounds that chill me to the bone.

I pause for a moment, listen, then soften my steps, moving closer to the pile of mostly broken chairs and peeking around the edge of it.

My blood chills.

Crouched on a nest of ramshackle garbage is the velvet trogg – bony knees up around her fiercely tapered ears as she brings a piece of chair to her lipless mouth, wraps her maw around it, and bites. More popping, cracking, splintering sounds, her second set of arms preening her oil-slicked hair that falls about her bony body, coiled around her limbs like a nest.

For a moment, all I can do is watch. Morbidly transfixed.

She must be three times the size of me, her blue velvety skin so at odds with the holes in her four palms. Round gapes of flesh that glow with the same fluorescence as the threads draped across the ceiling.

Her numerous black beady eyes narrow on the piece of chair before she stuffs the rest in her mouth, moaning with satiated delight.

Something glints in my peripheral, my gaze latching onto the silver, gem-encrusted bangle sitting atop her head like a tiny crown. My silver, gem-encrusted bangle.

Dammit.

Guess she likes it more than I did. She's certainly *looking after* it more.

Definitely getting eaten.

Sighing, I grab a three-legged chair from the pile and drag it across the rough stone floor that's surprisingly clean, aside from the odd splat of fluorescent goo, stepping into the small patch of empty space before the trogg's nest of hair and trash.

The creature goes eerily still, a shard of pottery poised halfway to her mouth.

I place the chair down and perch upon it as the trogg cocks her head to the side, lowering the shard, her many eyes blinking at me. 'You're a brave little morsel, planting yourself before me like a midslumber snack.'

Internally, I quiver so much I swear my bones rattle.

'You have something that used to be mine,' I say with a loose shrug.

Those beady eyes narrow further. 'What is it?'

'My bangle.' I point to where it's resting atop her head, stringy bits of hair curled around its circumference and binding it in place. 'I want it back.'

She releases a shrill cackle that ends as abruptly as it began, cutting me through with a predatory leer. 'She's a *bossy* little morsel . . .'

Guess that was a little bossy.

'Apologies. I would like it back, *please*.'

'That's a good morsel.' She raises a hand, her knobbly finger reminding me of the stalactites hanging from the ceiling.

Silence stretches as she unweaves the piece of jewelry from her head one limp, oily strand at a time – my heart pumping hard and fast.

Can it really be this easy?

'You know,' she says in her odd, scratchy voice that makes me battle another full-body shudder, 'things have *memories*.'

'Really?'

Pretending to be interested is hard while I'm quietly begging she doesn't flick the circlet of silver into the air, then swallow it down in a single gulp.

She nods, hanging the bangle on the tip of her tapered nail, bringing it to her flat, slit nose, all her lids growing heavy as she draws a deep whiff.

Internally, I wince – beginning to see where this is going. 'Smells good, does it?'

'Clever, clever little morsel.'

I *am* clever. Most of the time. This entire situation puts an unfortunate chink in my armor.

Splaying a hand, she plugs her thumb and pointer finger into one of the gaping holes in her palms. Pinching, she extracts a fluorescent string that emerges with a thick, gluey secretion, making me want to hurl. 'The richer the memory, the more of *this* I make.'

'I see . . .'

She keeps pulling until there's a lengthy coil of the substance bound on the ground before her, throwing light up at the underside of her honed chin.

The last of the thread slurps free of her palm hole, flopping before her. 'Isn't my palace pretty?' she preens, tossing her arms wide.

I lift my gaze to the ceiling, taking the space in with a whole new, gut-twisting appreciation, a wad of stretchy wetness dripping onto my cheek from what I suspect is a recently strung thread.

It's an effort not to loosen my guts all over the floor.

'Very pretty. Wish I could secrete like that.'

Fucking glad I can't.

'This right here,' she says, tapping a nail upon my gem-encrusted bangle. 'I've been saving it for a special occasion.' She brings it to her nose and draws a long, haunting whiff, groaning. 'I can tell it's going to be tasty.'

Unfortunate. I was hoping I wouldn't have to part with what I currently have stuffed in my pocket.

I reach in, pulling out a loop of braided colk leather heavy with a round of black dragonscale carved to represent the pronged face of Pah's vicious Sabersythe. 'What about a trade?'

The trogg's head snaps to the side, like her neck just popped a bone. 'Trade, you say? What's that my little morsel has in her bony hand?'

'It was Mah's málmr,' I say, dangling it before me. 'Gifted from my pah, the late King Ostern Vaegor.'

'And how did you . . . *obtain* it? Did my little morsel steal it?' She draws a whiff of the air. 'Smells stolen . . .'

'It is. I stole it from his sleepsuite when I was seventeen.'

Figured if he noticed, his hate toward me would feel at least a tiny bit justified.

He didn't.

The trogg's head snaps the other way, the motion so unnatural looking, I'm equally as repulsed as I am concerned for her safety. She sniffs again – long and hard – and I decide her lungs are somehow bigger than her willowy body suggests.

'This is richer, little morsel.' She waves the bangle at me, her face carving into the most terrifying smile I've ever seen. '*Just*.'

I grind my teeth together, surprised they don't shatter. 'You can also have the catch chain on the bangle. I don't need that.'

I think.

Her chest shakes with a haunting shriek that slowly tapers off before she garnishes me with a gleeful stare. '*Deal*.'

A warm, prickly wave of relief washes over me.

She plucks the chain free before throwing me the bangle. I catch it, my three-legged chair toppling onto the ground without my weight keeping it vertical.

I toss the málmr at her, and she snags it by the string, dangles it from her wrist, then flicks the tiny chain into her mouth like a grain of sand. Shrill crunching ensues, and I picture teeth cracking. Her eyes widen so much I think they might all pop out of her head and pepper the pile of memory-excrement coiled on the ground by her nest.

She stops midchew, releasing another clamorous laugh. 'Oh . . . you are a *naughty* little morsel, aren't you?'

Ice snaps through my veins.

I clamp the bangle around my wrist. 'Don't remember using it. Just remember what it does.'

'Interesting,' she murmurs, followed by another jarring tip of her head while she chews.

Crunch.

Crunch.

Crunch.

'Does my little morsel want to know its secrets?'

'Pass,' I say, watching her pull a thread from one of her right palms – so much brighter than any other draped across the cavern's ceiling. '*Definite* pass.'

'Such pretty, pretty secrets,' she purrs, her words pinching my nerves.

Think it's time I get the fuck out of here.

Shaking off the tension climbing my spine, I drag my chair back to the pile, passing her a dubious stare. 'You're not going to eat me on my way out, are you?'

Hard to say, but I think she frowns. 'Course not, little morsel. I don't eat those I strike bargains with. Only the ones I don't.'

'And how many have you struck bargains with?'

Still dragging the bright thread from her palm, she rubs her chin with a spare hand, appearing to think long and hard. 'Six,' she announces, lifting Pah's málmr to her nose and drawing another deep sniff. 'Including you.'

'Right.' I glance at the steadily growing pile of slurpy string glowing brighter than a Moonplume egg. 'Lucky me.'

I give her a wave she doesn't appear to notice, too transfixed on her task. Or maybe she does and she just doesn't care?

Probably the latter.

I move around the piles of trash, arm heavy with the bangle I once won from a deeply troubled Mindweft who claimed she knew how to speak the language of Aether. That she'd studied the Book of Voyd in length and knew the secret to our insignificant existence.

She told me the bangle would serve me in two ways. That both would be painful but necessary.

Don't remember the first, so can't speak for that.

Probably won't want to remember the second, either.

Diary Entry

Elluin Neván

Age: 18 phases
5,000,039 phases After Stone

He came back.

He didn't explain why he'd left, nor did I ask, nor admit how much I'd missed him.

Too much.

Like one of my ribs had been snapped free, leaving an ache right over my heart.

He had a fresh scar on his arm – the one he uses to strum. He was also wearing a necklace. A long braided piece of leather attached to a flat, circular pendant. A silver Moonplume and a reddish-black Sabersythe bound together, their jagged and sweeping bits fitting against each other.

From what I understand, only one Sabersythe has silver scales, and she lives in Gondragh. Nobody has been able to get close enough to climb on her back and attempt to tame her – and honestly, I hope they never do.

I ate my meal in silence, watching Kaan play his instrument with that pendant hanging proudly against his chest . . .

Wondering.

I wanted to touch it. Weigh it in my palm. Ask him where it came from. All things that are absolutely none of my business.

If he caught me looking at it, he didn't let on or even lift his stare from his strings – not that he ever does.

Normally.

When he began playing 'Song of the Silent Sun,' I closed my eyes and sang, getting lost in the tune and his sturdy, comforting presence. So when the song finished and I opened my eyes, I certainly didn't expect to see him staring at me.

For a long moment, we sat there watching each other, unspeakable truths thrumming between us, more palpable than the pluck or strum of his chords.

Something I'd never felt before fluttered through my belly and up into my chest. Like I had a fluffy sowmoth caged beneath my ribs, dusting me in its powder and lighting me up from the inside out.

Pulled toward him like I was caught in a current I had no interest in fighting against, I'd risen.

Edged closer.

He was stone still as I pushed aside my veil and leaned close, so desperate to know what his lips felt like. If they were smooth and warm like I'd imagined them to be.

I brushed against him – featherlight.

It was barely a touch, but it ripped a hole in my perception of the world and bared the guts of a whole new version of existence . . .

Bigger.

Brighter.

Happier.

I wanted to stay right there forever, caught on that quiet yet clamorous threshold, my heart pounding so hard and fast I was certain my chest was cracking open.

I knew it was wrong. That I was breaking a thousand rules. But how could something so wrong feel so fucking right?

He cupped my face with such tenderness it was like he was cradling a dragon's egg, and I nuzzled his palm. Found so much comfort in it that I wanted to stay right there.

Forever.

Then he asked me what I wanted, and I told him my truth. One three-letter word that weighed too much, being promised to his kin.

You.

I pulled away with the key in my hand, just unlocking the door when he gripped me from behind, swung me around, ripped off my veil, and kissed me with such ravenous intention I lost myself.

Found myself.

It was the kiss of someone who wanted to give me everything.

Take nothing. Yet I gave him my whole heart anyway. Realized it was rightfully his.

That it had been for some time.

I was about to drag him down to the far corner of the hutch where there's a pile of hay Slátra has no interest in, but then someone came running down the hall, requesting his help on an urgent matter.

They almost caught us kissing. As it was, they blushed at the sight of me unveiled, no doubt noticing the scrap of material clutched in Kaan's fist before they spun and apologized for intruding.

I didn't care.

I don't feel like Haedeon anymore. I feel like Allume – wobbling along, being forged into something strong despite my broken bits.

Perhaps I'll fly, too.

Raeve

CHAPTER 66

I wander down the twirling staircase, yawning as I push past the fall of vines and move through the jungle, following a well-worn path I've forged back into existence over the countless cycles since I came here.

Time works differently in this place. It folds into itself like a parchment lark, hiding scrawled secrets I keep tucking away.

And away.

And away.

The path opens to a small spring puddled beneath a burbling waterfall, and I smile.

Dropping my bag and towel on the stone shore, I strip, taking tentative steps into the cool water with a bar of purple bogsberry soap and a piece of pumice I foraged from the Loff's pebbled shore. I scrub my clothes, myself, then lather my hair and rinse it beneath the fall of water, combing some conditioning oil through the heavy length, leaving it to drip-dry down my back. I wring out my clothes, drape them across a low-hanging vine, then bind a towel around my body and tuck all my things back in the mesh bag I purchased from one of Dhomm's market stalls.

Moving through the jungle, I pause to pick handfuls of black bogsberries from clusters of wild shrubs that grow tucked at the base of trees, collecting them in a sack of threaded fiber. I forage through the underbrush for fallen gongnuts I pile in there, too, as well as a copperdew melon I cradle in my hand as I make my way back to the dwelling.

Humming a merry tune, I climb the staircase and empty my

foraged goods into a large clay bowl, rinsing the berries, cracking the nuts, slicing the melon into juicy segments I arrange on a platter. I settle my spread on the table next to my terracotta mug of water and sit, about to bite down on a piece of melon when my gaze flicks to the shelf.

To the diary I acquired from The Curly Quill.

I stand and move toward it, reaching out to pluck it from its resting place, tracing the Moonplume embossed on the cover. My stare drifts to the old quill I dusted several aurora cycles ago, then to the jar of ink.

Shrugging, I carry all three items to the table and settle them beside my spread, cracking the diary open, brimming with the strangest urge to . . . *write*.

I've never felt inclined to journal before. But this place does weird, unexplainable things to me, and for the most part, I've been going with it. Exploring these odd urges in this quiet place where there are no eyes. No ears.

No *commands*.

In the beginning, I called it an experiment. Now I see it a little differently.

I think I'm learning how to exist without shackles and expectations. Without the hurt and the crippling fear of loss that hacks my head from my heart.

I think I'm learning what it means to *live*.

Fallon would be proud.

Mostly.

I ink my quill, pausing to pop a bogsberry in my mouth, the burst of tart sweetness exploding over my taste buds as I scratch my thoughts on the parchment, the words flowing easier than I expected them to . . .

I've tried to leave.

(*Creators, I've tried.*)

But every time I've packed up my stuff and set out with the intention of catching a Moltenmaw across the plains so I can snap Rekk Zharos's neck, I've instead returned with new towels.

Sheets.

A sewing kit to repair the ruined pallet.

An iron ring so I don't cry with the rain.

With lengths of material and shears to craft new curtains, and then a roll of colk hide I used to patch up the chairs and seaters because apparently I'm crafty now.

Essi would be proud. I'm just . . . baffled. Haunted. Maybe a little crazy.

Maybe a lot *crazy?*

I'm not sure how to handle this strange part of me that seems determined to sing new life into this small forgotten home. The same part that seems unable to dislodge from this sense of belonging I've never felt before.

Not once.

Here, I'm more alone than I've ever been, completely cut off from the rest of the world. Yet somehow the opposite.

It's been hard to turn my back on the me that thrived within these walls, like studying a slow-moving tragedy that slugs along at such a languid pace you never reach the painful part.

I'm living in the in-between. In the bubble of lust and buoyant hopes, drunk on the giddy feeling that flutters through my belly every time I see a flash of something so very . . . him and her.

Elluin and Kaan.

As the cycles flip by, I've come to the slow, uncomfortable realization that Kaan fell in love with a distant, bygone version of me that was probably softer.

Kinder.

A version of me that was brave enough (or perhaps stupid enough) to love.

I know this is dangerous. That I've spent my life trapped and starving, and now I'm a gluttonous escapee gorging on the ancient scraps of a happiness that belonged to somebody else. Because it was somebody else.

It certainly wasn't me.

Call it morbid curiosity, but a pinch of me is desperate to know what pried me from this place, while every other part is certain I never want the answer to that poisonous question. Not even my lust for Rekk Zharos's blood on my hands can pull me from this pocket of happiness right now, yet somehow I left. Somehow, I lost him.

Lost myself.

Lost a dragon who apparently loved me enough to sail me into the sky with her and calcify around me like a tomb-stone built for the both of us.

It's hard to grapple that into a shape that doesn't make me choke. Every angle I inspect, I feel like I'm only seeing the small rounded peak of something too big and heavy to bear.

Intuition tells me I don't have the capacity to swallow all that sadness, which is why I've come to a decision. Now I just have to build up the courage to do it.

To let this go. For good.

But not now . . .

I'm not done imagining yet.

Kaan

CHAPTER 67

I charge down the hall, using the back of my arm to swipe the sweat from my eyes, plowing around a corner to see Pyrok jogging toward me – shirtless, looking like he just rolled off his pallet at the sound of the lookout's horns hailing my arrival.

'You look sober.'

Ish.

'The cycle is young,' he says, falling into step beside me. 'Welcome home.'

'Take it Veya isn't back yet?'

I'd hoped that, when I landed, she'd run out to greet me like she usually does. Feels weird without her dashing out with a thousand questions on her tongue, ready to sling them at me.

Feels . . .

Hollow.

'No. Last lark I received, she was almost at the wall but anticipated a few stops were going to slow her down. I'm guessing she's almost at Arithia by now. Maybe even on her way back.'

I grunt, wanting to know nothing about these *stops* he speaks of.

'Why do you smell like sulfur?'

'Took Grihm to Gondragh,' I mutter as we charge around another corner.

'What?'

'Dropped his sorry ass off at the hatching hut so he can try and steal an egg from the Great Silver Sabersythe.'

A beat of pause as the two sentries standing guard over my office stamp their spears upon the ground at the sight of me, opening the doors.

'He's going to die,' Pyrok mutters. 'And he didn't even wave goodbye. What the fuck is that?'

I don't bother responding.

I've had a long time to work through these same emotions, and I'm now sitting somewhere close enough to acceptance that I no longer want to punch my fist through a wall or kick myself for letting him convince me to leave him there. Telling me he was going to do this by himself or not at all.

I get it. Going to raid a nest or charm an already grown beast is a deeply personal journey for those doing it for the right reasons . . .

Still chafes.

I charge into my office, the large space empty but for a stone desk and twin leather seats – appearing exactly as I'd left it all.

Moving toward the wall of curtains at the back, I rip them wide, scouring the view of the Loff beyond and filling the room with a blaze of light. Illuminating the char marks all over the walls.

The only embellishment this room deserves.

I think back to the shelves that used to line these walls, packed full of memorabilia from Pah's reign. Think back to how good it felt watching it all burn after I stormed the Stronghold still splashed in his blood with his head hanging from my fist.

He put too much effort into this space and not enough into being a decent pah to Veya.

To me.

Now this room resembles a vacant chest cavity, and I wouldn't have it any other way. Anything more would be doing his memory a service he doesn't deserve.

'I saw Grihm carrying runed boots into his sleepsuite,' Pyrok muses as he lumps into the leather seat opposite my own. 'Makes a fuckload more sense now.'

Yes, it does.

I drop my saddlebags on the ground, scrubbing my hands over my face before I turn toward the desk.

'So what now?'

'If he makes it back to the hut, he'll send a lark for one of us to collect him,' I say, lumping heavily into my seat.

Catching a waft of my shirt, I frown, pulling up the collar, drawing a sniff of sweat, sulfur, and ash.

Definitely need a bath. And a meal. And some fucking sleep – preferably on something other than sand or dirt with only the shield of Rygun's wing to keep me from being mauled to death by predators. To be fair, I think he would've happily stayed north forever, basking in the heat and the vast smorgasbord of creatures that tried to skulk past him and snatch me while I slept.

I'm certain he's grown.

'Collect him and his freshly hatched *dragon*,' Pyrok says.

'Let's not get ahead of ourselves.' I reach into my pocket, fishing around for all the parchment larks that've been flocking me over the past thirty slumbers I've been away. 'It's one thing to steal an egg. *Hatching* it is a different story.'

I dump around fifty crushed larks on the table, pinching the bridge of my nose as I glare at them.

'Behind on your paperwork, I see.'

'What do I pay you for again?'

'Certainly not *that*,' he chuffs.

I lift a brow, waiting. Genuinely curious. All I ever see him do is drink mead.

'To sit around and look pretty,' he finally says, flashing me a smile. 'Roan's the helpful sibling, remember? He got the brain, I got the hair. And the cordial nature. And I'm pretty fucking good with my tong—'

'Got it.'

His smile widens, and he crosses his ankle over his knee, playing with his bottom lip piercing. Making no move to help me sort through the notes.

I sigh, reaching across the table for the pile of pre-runed parchment squares and my black quill, flattening one of the larks and skimming the note, wincing when I see the date.

Poor Krove's been waiting over twenty cycles to have his huttlecrab quota signed off for final approval.

I ink my quill and begin scratching out an apology. 'Speaking of which, is Roan back yet?'

'Nope.'

I shake my head.

Might send someone to check on him. Make sure he's alright.

'So . . . are you gonna ask about her?'

My blood chills, that stupid organ in my chest impaling itself on a rib.

'No,' I grind out, dipping my quill in the ink again and continuing to scribe my message.

'She's still here.'

I pause, eyes closing as I release another sigh. Slowly, I set my quill on the desk, lean back in my chair, cross my fucking arms, and give Pyrok my full, undivided attention. Lifting a brow, I wait for him to continue.

'I've seen her at the markets.'

I quirk a brow. 'Oh?'

He nods. 'Buying shit.'

I stare at him, waiting for him to continue. Which he doesn't.

'Well, what kind of *shit*?'

He rolls his eyes, like it's an outrageous question – except it's not. Not to the organ in my chest that's far too soft for its own good.

Pyrok begins ticking things off his fingers. 'Leather, soap, poultice, towels. She did go to The Curly Quill and waited outside while a kid went in to pick up a bag of something for her, but I can't tell you what because I can't see through leather. And I *think* she bought a sack of feathers from the local goggin bird breeder, but it could've been grain.' He shrugs. 'I tried to keep my distance.'

I frown, my gaze dropping to the pile of crushed larks while I pick through his words. It sounds to me like she's settling in, not preparing to leave. Which makes no sense. Unless she's been . . . *remembering* things. Perhaps forming a new attachment to the place.

My chest aches at the thought, and it's an effort not to groan as I scrub my face again – in desperate need of a bath and maybe a wall to bash my head against.

'Are you attending The Great Flurrt celebrations?' Pyrok asks, and I lean forward, getting to work unfolding the rest of the scrunched larks.

'I'll be lifting the platforms, of course.'

'I mean the *actual* festival.'

I quirk a brow, sliding him half the pile. 'Have I ever?'

He still makes no move to help, instead narrowing his eyes on me. 'You really think now's the right time to turn all stubborn prick?'

Perfect time, actually.

'The last Great Flurrt we spent together was the last time I saw her alive.' I flatten another lark and slap it on the pile. 'We spent the slumber together, and the following dae I flew off to help rebuild a village. The next time I saw Elluin, her limp body was being carted into the sky by her mourning dragon,' I growl, slamming another lark on the fucking pile. 'So no, the idea of inviting her to The Great Flurrt celebration doesn't thrill me, nor will I apologize for my reluctance.'

'Maybe this time will be different?'

I chuckle – low and without humor. 'Maybe she'll fillet my heart in a different direction? Undoubtedly. She's quite fond of filleting. Quite good at it, too.'

Pyrok sighs, bashing his fist against the arm of his chair. 'Look, all I know is I heard her ask a merchant if they'd seen the King around. Do with that as you will,' he mutters, then shoves to a stand and stalks toward the door.

I frown. 'Where are you going?'

'To get drunk in Grihm's suite while I raid his dagger collection,' he drawls, moving through the doorway. 'Since he's probably dead already, the asshole.'

The sound of his boot steps tapers off, and I tip my head, staring at the ceiling.

Fucking . . . fuck.

Abandoning the larks, I push up and drift toward my balcony doors, pull them wide, then step out into the sun's harsh glare, overlooking Dhomm and the Loff.

The western point.

I walk all the way to the vine-clothed balustrade, resting my elbows against it, my heart blocking my airway when I see a shape in the distance – right where the water laps at the bouldered shore. Frowning, I stalk into my office and snatch my seeing scope off the desk, then move back onto the balcony and stretch the tool, putting it to my eye and pointing it in the direction of the shape.

My ribs crack at the sight.

Raeve's stepping from stone to stone – feet bare, hair mostly piled atop her head, her cheeks and shoulders a little sun-kissed. She's dressed in the short black sleep shift she was wearing when I took her to visit Slátra, one of the thin shoulder straps falling down her arm.

She doesn't bother to lift it back into place, like she hasn't even noticed, instead bending down and plucking a shell from between the stones. She inspects it from all angles before placing it in a basket hanging off her arm.

I swallow as she straightens, casting her crisp, glacier eyes toward—

My heart stills.

Toward Rygun's hutch . . .

Well, fuck. Guess we're on her mind.

'Ready for another round, Moonbeam?'

She tucks a loose piece of hair behind her ear, a yearning in her eyes that messes with my heartstrings.

I slam the looking glass against my palm, closing it, considering the implications of ripping my own heart out and smashing it against the stone. Giving her a head start.

Though maybe Pyrok's right. Maybe this time *will* be different.

Maybe it'll be worse.

Either way, there's no one else I'd willingly serve my heart on a platter to – over and over and over again – like a hopeless, lovesick stray begging for a treat.

Diary Entry

Elluin Neván

Age: 19 phases
5,000,040 phases After Stone

I attended a Tithe this dae.

Since his pah's absent, Kaan sat on the bronze throne, accepting offerings, giving back to those who had little to offer in the first place.

I watched from the back of the hall as he spoke with each of the folk with such raw grace and fairness it reminded me of the way Mah and Pah used to run their kingdom, feeling a deep pang of homesickness at that thought . . .

Pah didn't respect King Ostern. He said their values didn't align. That Ostern had little care for anyone who couldn't hear the elemental songs.

I watched Kaan offer a young, struggling family a plump sack of gold and decided Pah would've respected King Ostern's eldest son.

Kaan saw me from across the vast space, our eyes locked, and I'm certain the world stilled.

I felt so bare before him, infused with a fiery heat that had nothing to do with the ever-present burn that scalds this place. Certain my body was going to sizzle from the inside out if we did not collide, struggling to see much else through the haze of my unquenched desire.

I moved behind a pole before anyone noticed, desperate to catch my breath that had suddenly fled.

I know the things I desire are forbidden.

I'm all out of reasons to care.

For almost two phases, I've existed in this Stronghold like one of the shadows . . .

I'm done living the life I've been told to live and not the one I want for myself.

Raeve

CHAPTER 69

He's broad, dense, alive beneath me,
his bent knees pushed between my legs, prying me open.
Entirely exposed, I jerk my hips, trying to force
his touch upon that coil of tender nerves. 'Please . . .'
'You don't have to beg for me, Moonbeam.'
His words shake my bones, his fingers sweeping
around my entrance – so featherlight it's but a breath of touch.
My body ignites, my heart a violent hammer of feisty need.
I grip his málmr, holding it close.
'If you want me' – he presses his mouth to my ear,
nipping gently – 'I'm fucking yours.'
Groaning, I slide my hand down the taut muscles
of his strong arm, over his wrist, his knuckles.
His fingers.
I push him into me, tiding with the thrust of pleasure,
thighs loosening.
Widening.
'Forever,' I whimper, working him deeper. 'I want you forever.'
He makes a dense rumbling sound, his other hand gripping
my jaw and turning my head to the side. I catch a glimpse
of fierce ember eyes before he takes my mouth in a kiss
that devastates my ability to breathe or think – prisoner to
his insatiable taste. To the way he commands my lips and tongue.
Devouring me.
My hips roll to match the deep thrust of his fingers
and his all-consuming kiss, my body winding up . . .

Up . . .
He flips us, knees my legs wider, then grips my hips and tugs, lengthening my spine. A firm hand presses between my shoulder blades before he rubs the solid head of his cock against my wet, pulsing entrance.
So open.
So ready—

An air-shredding roar rips through my dreamscape, like snapping a book shut right at the good part.

My eyes pop open, a passion-fueled moan of frustration bludgeoning up my throat – hungry and feral and laced with *need.*

I slap my hand on my face and groan, still crushed beneath the feel of Kaan's body upon mine. Moving with mine.

In mine.

Trembling from the dream's vibrant shockwaves, I push up, beads of sweat gathered between my breasts, my nipples hard and peaked.

I shake my head, threading my hands through my damp hair.

It's getting worse.

Well – better, actually. Substantially better. But a whole lot harder to let go of.

A shadow falls upon the sleep space.

Frowning, I cast my gaze up through the skyhole, seeing a flash of dark ruddy scales. Another screeching roar slices through the din, and my heart rallies as I register what *actually* woke me.

A dragon. Flying almost close enough to whip its tail down and slash this place to shreds.

I leap off the pallet and flatten myself against the floor, waiting for the booming thud of the beast's wings to ebb. When I finally risk a peek at the ceiling, my heart stills.

High in the sky, almost close enough to graze the spiky bronze moon that sits above the city, a pair of Sabersythes spin together, shrieking as they twist and tumble amongst a spill of aurora ribbons. *Too* many.

Is the sky broken? And has war come to Dhomm?

Keeping low to the floor, I reach for my small pile of clothes I've collected over the cycles, pulling my trusty black slip on and shoving it over my hips. I stuff my feet into my boots, then snatch my leather sheath on my way down the stairs. Blindly buckling it to my thigh, I dash out into the jungle to the tune of another screeching roar.

'Shit,' I mutter, flattening myself against the stone, heart thumping hard and fast. I secure the final buckle while searching for any sign of danger, finding nothing amiss. Though there is a faraway song lilting to the distant thud of drums that certainly doesn't sound like I'd expect *war* drums to sound – the beat . . . playful?

What's going on?

Dashing my hair off my face, I dart through the jungle, cutting my surroundings into surveyed segments. Hunting for any irregularities.

More near and distant dragon shrieks rattle the air lusted with a sweet, spicy smell, almost like the world is a flower in full bloom.

I inch free of the dense foliage, down the tide's vertical lip, and onto the Loff's pebbled shore.

My eyes widen, something inside me going so still I feel like every beat of my heart is an earthquake in comparison.

Terracotta rocks grind beneath my boots as I edge toward the lapping water, taking in the sky . . .

Definitely broken.

A scribble of silver aurora threads dance to their own pulsating beat – *thousands* of them. Like the tap that usually lets no more than ten of them dribble free sprung a leak.

A *big* one.

Dragons soar and spiral through the metallic ribbons of light, some on their own, some paired off with other dragons that match their spectacular motions.

Frowning, I cast my gaze across the city in the distance.

Almost every bouldered structure boasts a silver flag – a riot of lengthy ribbons fluttering about, tangling with each other. The esplanade is a vibrant smudge of motion, the smell of Molten Mead and braised meat brought to me on a whip of wind.

There certainly appears to be no *war* happening. Just some sort of celebration the likes of which I've never seen before.

That, and the broken sky.

I pick apart an old conversation I once heard between two merchants a long while ago. They spoke of something called *The Great Flurrt*. Said the miskunns were predicting one would bloom sometime this decade, and that they hoped there would be an influx of fertilized eggs at the spawning grounds afterward.

Perhaps this is that? The dragons in the sky certainly look like they're . . . *flurrting*.

My cheeks heat.

Good for them. At least somebody's fucking in real life and not just in their dreams.

Again, I look at the city, a surge of adrenaline spiking through me, making my heart pump harder. Faster.

Something about those silver ribbons and the drums and the dragons makes me want to run *toward* something for a change. To rip down the bars of my self-restraint and crack open my hungry heart, crumble it into a silt, mash it together with some moisture, then mold it into something soft again.

Exactly why I should not go there.

Over the other side of that heavily runed terracotta fence, reality prowls like a skulking beast ready to hunt.

To kill.

I turn my back on the city, charging toward the jungle, but something in my peripheral makes me pause.

I look at the tree where I found the carving, a black woven basket now hanging on a short, knobbly branch.

My heart stills, breath catches.

Whoever left it there knows I'm here despite the fact that I've been discreet. Most importantly, they know there's no damn *hushling* living over this side of the fence.

The riddle's not exactly hard to untangle.

I move toward the tree, eyeing the basket like the ember it is, knowing one purposeful breath blown upon its surface will lead it to ignite.

To *burn*.

Swallowing the lump of trepidation rising in my throat, I take the basket's weight in my hand and lift it from the branch, settling it on the ground. I rip back the cloth draped over the contents, entirely expecting the motion to rip off a scab in some way or another.

'Creators,' I mutter, studying the delicate, ethereal mask tucked amongst a nest of silver silk. An elaborate craft of argent wire and flat pearly disks that glimmer in the sun's blaze. Ribbons are attached to the sides, perhaps meant to bind it around the back of my head.

I set it aside and lift the puddle of silken fabric, revealing a gown unlike anything I've ever seen – all strips of draped material clamped in places with diamond brooches. Beneath the garment, I find a pair of crystal-encrusted slippers to match, as well as a corked bottle of sun-shielding poultice. The same sort I purchased from a store many slumbers ago when I realized bathing naked in the spring was a recipe for chapped skin and fevered sleep.

The final thing in the basket is an elaborate fold of parchment I side-eye like it's going to leap out and bite me.

Cutting another glance toward the city, I pull out the note and unpleat the folds.

Kaan's málmr tumbles into my lap, and my heart drops into my belly.

For a long moment, I stare at the beautiful pendant before finally taking in the note.

My eyes squeeze shut as I pluck the málmr from my lap and hold it tight, a quiet trepidation thrumming through me.

There's a weight to the note that's threaded between those three small words. A weight in the mask. The gown.

This málmr which speaks of an *us* that existed long ago.

I think he's asking me to *pretend*. To let down my walls and open my heart to him for this special occasion.

I draw my lungs full of sweet, smoky air and cast my stare across the city, a certainty settling within me. An energy ripe to pop.

To deflate.

This is it. The pin that's finally going to burst the bubble of imagination I've lost myself in. *Found* myself in, if I'm honest with myself.

Not that it changes anything.

But what a spectacular way to go out? A goodbye fit for everything we used to be. The quiet acknowledgment I now see that I owe . . . *us*.

Him.

Before I erase it all.

Diary Entry

Elluin Nevàn

Age: 19 phases
5,000,040 phases After Stone

This aurora fall, there was no carving, no meal. Just a half-folded parchment lark and a strange rusted key.

I folded the final activation line, and the lark took flight, soaring down the stairs that led to Slátra's hutch, then taking to the back where it flapped down a shadowed tunnel I hadn't noticed before. I followed it for a long way, the key opening a different door that shot out on the pebbled shore that cradles the glistening turquoise Loff that was ruffled by an approaching storm.

That poor lark . . . It was getting too soggy, struggling to maintain flight, so I cupped it in my hands, cradling the frantic thing like a caged sowmoth.

I tried to discern its desired direction based on the way it nudged against my fingers – weaving a crooked, confusing path through the jungle.

I began to get nervous, wondering if it was an ambush. If someone wanted to slaughter me to steal the Aether Stone, thinking it some priceless treasure and not the soul-sapping curse it is. But then I came to a dwelling carved into the cliff. A home so hidden away from the world that I suspect it would be impossible for anyone else to find.

Kaan was inside, sitting at a stone table he'd set for us, the air flush with the smell of colk and canit root stew.

He told me this place was his gift to me but that he didn't have to come with it. That one word from me and he'd step out into the jungle and never return.

I was upon him before the sentence fully left his lips.

He's fire and brimstone. I'm shattered ice. Our collision is steam and destruction, destined to dissipate, but I'll gladly burn beneath him until the world comes crumbling down.

Raeve

CHAPTER 71

There's a familiar male leaning against the stone wall with his back to me, a blaze of rebellious locks dashed around his shoulders.

'You look like you were dragged backward through a bush,' I say, striding toward Pyrok, the gifted mask upon my face like an elegant shield.

He spins, flashing me a teeth-glinting smile. 'All part of my charm. Females love it. They tug on it like *reins*.'

'This one won't be.'

His eyes widen. 'Fucking hope not. I quite like my head. And my cock. And *living*.'

Clearing my throat, I pretend I don't know *exactly* what he means, taking in the red leather tunic cut to emphasize his broad chest. The top half of his face is hidden behind a mask fashioned from the orange and red down feathers of a Moltenmaw, and he's even replaced his piercings with ruddy ones to match. 'So. Guessing you're my escort?'

'Strictly platonic.'

'If you had *more* platonic relationships, perhaps your hair wouldn't look like a bird's nest.'

He smiles, digging his fingers into a small sack of something lumped in his hand. 'Nice to see the hushling didn't suck out your brain through your nostrils.'

'Shocking, I know.' I pause before the wall and set my slippers on the ground so I can readjust the material draped across my bust, making sure it's keeping me well contained. 'Who finger painted the warnings on the wall?'

'Veya.' My brows bump up, hands stilling. 'Kaan lost it after you passed,' he says with a shrug. 'She knew he'd have regrets if the place fell into complete disarray.'

'Oh,' I murmur, stashing that prickly parcel beneath my icy lake with the speed of a lightning strike. 'So you knew me . . . *before*?'

'Little bit. It was a long fucking time ago—'

'You don't remember much?'

'Quite the opposite,' he counters, winking at me. 'My memory's the sharpest weapon in my sparse armory.'

Right.

'Good for you.'

Mine, as it turns out, is quite shit. Not that I'm complaining.

He tosses a small red thing into the air and catches it with his mouth, crunching through it. 'Wanna know anything?' he asks, a hopeful hitch to his voice that I squish before it can crawl up my leg and pinch me.

'Creators no. I was just curious.' Knowledge is power and all that. When I have Kaan erased from my memories, I'll need to snip all tethers to the *past* me.

To Elluin.

That now includes Pyrok. Probably a good thing, since he's really starting to grow on me.

He clears his throat, tugging the string taut on his treats like he's suddenly lost his appetite. 'Well,' he says, twirling his finger, a heaviness to his tone that wasn't there before, 'let's see.'

I do a spin, my hair woven into a braid that starts at the crown of my head and brushes the bare skin at the small of my back, secured with one of the clamps I removed from the gown. A strip of gathered fabric is draped upon my breasts, others pulled tight across my hips before they fall in a gush of silver tendrils.

I've never worn something so fierce.

Flattering.

Sexy.

My favorite part is the twin triangles of sparkly sheer material tethered to my shoulders that chase me in a flutter of motion. Like wispy wings. Though I left Kaan's málmr in the dwelling.

Felt safer there.

'It was hard to get the back panel clipped in place, but I think I got it right,' I murmur, glancing over my shoulder at it.

'Looks right.' He pockets his treats, gaze sweeping across my gown again. 'Though it appears you've left half your dress behind . . .'

'I did,' I say, collecting my slippers before I kick my leg up over the wall. It's hot, and I've grown accustomed to being naked in the bush – though I don't tell him that.

All that fabric felt unnecessary, so I unclipped a few tendrils here and there. Crisscrossed some. Tied knots in a few places.

Released my inner crafty bitch and let her shine.

Pyrok chuckles, shaking his head. 'Come on,' he says, strolling toward the city. 'We're missing out on all the fun.'

The esplanade is a riot of color and cheer.

We weave between a churn of eloquently dressed folk, masked kids darting around with sticks clutched in their hands – the long silver ribbons attached to the ends being twirled and flicked through the air. They roar like dragons as they chase each other. Catch each other.

Fall in giggling heaps of ribbons, feathers, and makeshift wings.

Everyone is masked, crafted masterpieces fashioned from all different materials. Moltenmaw feathers and the scales of Sabersythes. There are some made from sheets of copper bearing the dents from whatever tool was used to bang them into shape, others from slopes of pearl that trail tendrils about their jowls like the elegant Moonplumes.

We near a cart that appears to be offering free serves of prepoured Molten Mead, Pyrok going out of his way to snag a mug. 'Want one?'

I lift a brow. 'Bit early, isn't it?'

He gives me a look of genuine bafflement before he drains the entire thing in three deep gulps. 'To hydrate?' he asks, drying his mouth with the back of his arm as he settles the now-empty mug on the same tray, grabbing another. 'Don't think so. The sun's fierce this dae. And even if it wasn't, what better way to break my fast?'

I shake my head, hoping he knows somebody strong enough to scrape him off the pave later, morbidly aware of just how hard it is to get a body his size to budge.

Unless it's in pieces.

We come to a path that shoots out from the shore and splits three ways, spearing toward a trio of risen platforms, each capped in a dome of shimmering air. Like bubbles large enough to house a small village were blown from beneath the splashing waves, paused midbirth, then solidified.

The domes look empty, my gaze cutting straight through what *appears* to be simple bulges of distorted air. The noise tells me otherwise, the space around me alive with the deep thump of drums and the drone of stringed instruments coming from ahead. Like the bows are being dragged across my ribs, planting the music inside my chest and making my blood *sing*.

Others siphon down the path ahead, the stone knobbled with disk-shaped shells. It's almost flush with the Loff's lapping surface, the folk traversing it appearing to walk on water as they glide toward the domes, some with crafted wings fluttering in their wake.

Pyrok offers me his arm, and I tuck my hand in the crook of it, my heart a blunt and indomitable hammer against my ribs. We come to the junction where the path splits three ways, sun beating upon my face while we pause.

'The three domes each house a faux representation of the different nesting grounds,' Pyrok says, gesturing from left to right. 'Netheryn, Bhoggith, and Gondragh.'

Each path is saddled with an arch – the one on the left adorned with a twist of silver vines and white, frost-encrusted blooms, tendrils of mist leaking from their pointed petals despite the heat.

Netheryn.

The middle one is clothed in a burst of feather-tipped flowers that match the varying vibrant shades of a Moltenmaw's plumage.

Bhoggith.

My gaze drifts to the one on the right, finding it bound in thorny vines, the rounded black blooms singed at the tips and smelling like scorched wood.

Gondragh.

'Where's the King?' I ask, and Pyrok gestures to the right, looking down at me with what I picture as a raised brow expression. Hard to see much with his mask on.

'That narrows it down,' I say, gaze bumping between the other two before I tug him to the left, stepping beneath the fall of mist that smells fresh and crispy.

If Kaan wants to dance, he can have fun finding me first.

'Interesting choice,' Pyrok muses as we stroll down the path, stuck behind a couple of slow-moving folk garbed in bustles of faux plumage.

'I've never been much further south than the border between The Fade and The Shade.' I shrug. 'I'm curious.'

He clears his throat, the folk before us tugging at the waggle of air, parting it like a curtain before disappearing into the dome with a puff of fog. Our steps slow, and Pyrok grips the invisible barrier like he's handling a tent flap, pulling it back. Another pour of fog seeps out and tangles with our feet, the drumming *thump* pounding against my chest in rhythm with my thrashing heart.

A flock of . . . *something* takes flight within my belly. Something that makes no sense.

Kaan's not here. He's elsewhere.

Why won't my feet move forward?

'You okay? I didn't take you for the *hesitating* sort.'

I search for a sharpened edge I can use to throw something quippy back, finding them all blunt and rounded.

Soft and floppy.

I swallow, still staring at that triangular opening to the swirl of dusky motion beyond.

No, I don't think I am okay.

'I'm fine,' I lie, then straighten my spine, force my feet forward, and shove past the flap – engulfed by a swallow of darkness.

Raeve

CHAPTER 72

Each step forward is another crunch of my slippers through the layer of fluffy snow. Another whisk of the fog churning about my feet.

I've stepped into another world, the sky a stretch of black velvet buttoned with pearly moons, scribbled with ribbons of aurora that cast my eerie surroundings in a flood of silver light. Clusters of hexagonal ice pillars reach for the moons, each large enough to support a nesting Moonplume.

It's like standing within a painted depiction of Netheryn, minus the deadly chill. Minus the threat of being swooped by a broody Moonplume protecting her clutch from thieves who'd risk the climb up one of those sheer, seemingly unscalable pillars in the efforts to snatch an egg.

The air feels hollow but for the thud of the drums and a harp's lilting tune – like someone called for Clode to sit so chillingly still within the confines of this dome. A hollowness that nests in my chest. An invisible weight I can't grasp the shape of.

The *origin* of.

Shaking it off, I step into the swirl of masked folk tiding to the smooth, ethereal melody, as though they're caught in some sort of trance.

I clear my throat, whipping a crystal flute off the tray of a passing server. 'What's this called?' I ask, gesturing to the azure liquid spilling milky mist down the sides.

'Moonplume's Breath,' the server says, his lips tinged blue from the cold, a line forming between his brows as he takes in my scant garb. 'There are fur shawls by the entrance . . .'

'I'm fine.' *Perfectly fine*. 'Thanks!'

I continue on, setting the frosted rim of the glass upon my lips. I take a sip, filling my mouth with sour sweetness – crisp and so cold it's an icy balm to my tongue, throat, and belly.

There's a momentary thinning of the crowd, and my stare delves into the chasm between two lofty pillars.

My heart skips a beat, and I pause, spinning the iron ring on my finger . . .

I'm certain there's something between them I need to see. That if I don't go and investigate immediately, something *bad* will happen.

Not sure what. Feels important.

'Is everything alright?'

Definitely not.

It's on the tip of my tongue to ask if Pyrok knows how I ended up with the Moonplume I supposedly charmed in my previous . . . *existence*. To ask if I raided a nest for an egg, or perhaps inherited someone else's previously claimed beast.

To ask if I've been here before – the *real* here.

'Of course,' I say, flashing him a smile over my shoulder that falls off my face the moment I stab my stare forward again and charge through the crowd.

'Where are we going?' he yells as I weave between bodies draped in heavy layers of leather and fur, between tables and stools, moving toward the tallest cluster of pillars in the epicenter of the celebration.

'Don't know,' I murmur, taking another sip of my drink, holding the puddle of chill in my mouth until I'm verging on a frostbit tongue before I swallow it down.

The crowd thins, giving way to a barricade of guards standing shoulder to shoulder, barring entry to a frail path that appears to thread between two immense icy pillars. Bronze armor molds to their bodies like Sabersythe scales, black masks covering the top half of their faces, dark fur shawls draped around their shoulders.

'What's behind there?' I ask Pyrok when he finally catches up to me, a Moonplume's Breath in one hand, the other cupping a dragon's egg filled with curly fried things capped in a glob of white sauce.

'A game table for the highfliers,' he says. 'You don't go in there unless you have a *lot* of gold to waste and an ego large enough to absorb a few blows.'

Huh.

Not what I was expecting to find. But now that I'm here . . .

I spin and pat down Pyrok's pockets, discovering a bulge in the left one that I dig out to the tune of his disgruntled mutterings.

'You know what you remind me of?' he grinds out as I wave the pouch of gold at the guards who part ways to let us through. 'A woetoe.'

'Met one of those while I was in prison for serial murder,' I say, loud enough a few of the guards turn their heads, looking at me over their shoulders. 'Nice fellow. Kept his face hair smooth and slick despite the squalor they kept us in. What game are we playing?'

'Skripi,' Pyrok mutters, following me along a frail path woven between the lofty pillars that certainly aren't quite cold enough to be *real* ice. Perhaps just stone runed to look like it. 'You play?'

I throw his pouch in the air, snatching it. 'Lil bit.'

'Great,' he gripes. 'Can't wait to lose a sack of gold to a clutch of elitists who use pebbles of the stuff to decorate their garden beds.'

'That's not the right attitude.' I take a few more turns down the zigzagged path, tossing back another deep glug of my Moonplume's Breath. 'Take it King Burn doesn't pay too well?'

'Very well. For sweet fuck all, if I'm to be perfectly honest. Not the point.'

There's an edge to his voice that makes me pause, glancing over my shoulder, seeing a hardness to the line of his mouth that wasn't there before – his own Moonplume's Breath entirely untouched.

Odd. He usually tosses drinks back like they're split moments away from evaporation.

'Care to elaborate?'

'Care to get this over with so I can find a barrel of Molten Mead large enough to drown myself in?' He jerks his chin, urging me on. 'Quick, before my squinn curls get cold.'

Frowning, I continue forward, wondering if Pyrok has a prickly history with some of these *highfliers*.

Another jagged bend, and the path opens to a wide cavern,

like somebody took a spoon to the ice and carved out a dead-end dollop. A hexagon-shaped table sits in the center, six high-backed chairs perched around it, all but one inhabited.

My feet still.

Four males clad in fine black garb and sooty fur cloaks wield a fan of game shards close to their puffed chests, each bearing the same simple half-face masks sculpted from polished gold. A fifth seat is occupied by a creature I'm somewhat familiar with.

An octimar.

The bulbous creature's skin is a mottle of icy shades, allowing it to blend almost entirely with our surroundings, its numerous vine-like appendages coiled around a mound of gold piled before it. No eyes. Just a tumorous head, the skin thin enough to garner a view through to its large, luminous brain that's throbbing a little.

My gaze drops to its mouth – a pouty pucker that looks harmless, though I've seen them stretched. Seen how many teeth those things pack.

Enough to chomp off an arm with a single crunch.

Seems fitting that these highfliers have the company of such a rare and coveted creature, given the fact that octimars can weave promises upon flesh, binding them to blood, body, and soul.

Each of the fae garnishes me with narrow-eyed perusals, one pulling on a pipe, blowing rings of ruddy smoke. His stare spears past me to Pyrok, and his mouth curls into a sly grin. 'Looks like our Little Flame is not so *little* anymore.'

Pyrok's energy stiffens.

The male draws another deep puff, blowing a second ring of smoke into the air. 'Come to play with us, have we?' He gestures to the table adorned with a Skripi spread, crystal cups of amber liquid, and wiggly stacks of gold coins gathered in piles. 'You know how much I *love* it when you have debts to pay . . .'

The other three males chuckle.

I cut another glance over my shoulder, but Pyrok's stare is pinned to the male smoking the pipe, his cheeks ablaze as he white-knuckles his flute of Moonplume's Breath.

The tips of my fingers itch.

'Not him,' I say, whipping my head around and swaying toward the Skripi table with a pep in my step.

All the laughter snips, five pairs of eyes trailing my every move as I settle into the vacant seat, set my glass on the table, loosen the drawstring on Pyrok's sack of gold, and empty its contents.

Gold coins puddle before me.

'Finish your game, then deal me in.'

Silence prevails while I busy my hands, stacking Pyrok's coins into tidy piles somewhat smaller than the mounds packed before each of the leering males.

The one to my right settles his hand on my arm, and I still, looking past his mask to bold brown eyes. 'Sweet thing, although I admire your enthusiasm, your tiny pile is only large enough to buy you in,' he croons, one of the octimar's tentacles slithering out and wrapping around my gold, tugging every coin from me in a clattering commotion. 'Whatever will you bet with?'

I pinch the tip of his finger, peeling it from my arm. 'I'm not sweet, and I'm certainly not a *thing*.' I flick the male's hand back toward his own allotment of personal space, then look to the octimar, palm up. 'Buy me in with a favor owed. To *each* of the other players.'

'*Raeve—*'

Pyrok charges forward, not reaching me before the creature's tentacle scribbles upon my skin, leaving a tickling trail.

'*Fucking* – Fuck!' He pelts his flute at the icy pillar, glass shattering, blue liquid seeping down the sides with a tumble of fog. His squinn is the next to sail through the air, the eggshell smashing, spraying the floor with a litter of fried treats quickly lost beneath the reconverging fog. 'I need to go and find—'

'Wait,' I say, a request in my hard stare for him to stay right here.

For him to watch.

I mouth a silent *please*, and he stills, taking in the males now polishing off their game, the octimar cutting their winnings and gathering shards.

Lips a thin line, Pyrok clears his throat, then leans against the pillar, arms crossed as he offers me a small nod.

'So lovely of you to stay,' the male with the pipe drawls, sliding Pyrok a slimy look that makes my hackles rise. 'I can't wait to show you how real males play with pretty females who have too much confidence and not enough sense.'

I laugh, scanning my opponents from atop the fan of illustrated creatures staring back at me.

The octimar's tentacles spear out, slicing into the stacks of gold before each of my opponents – collating a mighty, toppling sum that makes my brows rise.

Guess my *favors* are a rather worthy pledge.

Good for me.

'Does the *pretty thing* want the first roll?' another male drawls, and it's an effort not to choke that title from his throat, wondering how he'd feel if I gave him a derogatory name that whittled him down to nothing more than a well-cut piece of meat.

'Course not.' Gaze cast on my shards, I reorder my hand. 'Then you'll contribute my win to the advantage, and we can't have that.'

He chuckles, holding my eye contact as he picks up the crystal mug and shakes it, the contents rattling. 'Your confidence is beguiling, however *ill-spent*,' he spits out, then tosses the dice.

Raeve

CHAPTER 73

I slap my Moonplume on the final stomp of shards, flashing the four seething males a smile so wide it makes my cheeks ache. 'Are you all sick of me yet?'

The octimar tangles its tentacles around a mountain of gold that *absolutely* weighs more than I do, sliding it toward me.

A smoking pipe goes sailing across the table, scattering my latest winning play in all its glory. The male who threw it shoves to a stand, snarling as he stalks from the chamber in a flutter of black and gold.

'Keep practicing!' I holler after him, straightening my piles, flashing the three remaining males another smile that does little to sponge their antagonistic leers. 'Another round? I'll accept favors owed if you're not carrying more gold. Or your masks. They look hefty.'

Not to mention how much I'd *delight* in seeing the faces of the pricks I forced into submission with a few lucky hands, earning enough gold to not only pay Pyrok back immediately – *with interest* – but also purchase a small village. Or perhaps the patronage of a charmed Moltenmaw for the rest of eternity. *Certainly* long enough to hunt Rekk Zharos until I get the chance to feed him his own entrails.

'Unless you want time to reinforce your crumbling egos?' I ask, batting my lashes.

The air tightens.

Heats.

The males about the table stand so abruptly their chairs go

skidding across the ice, all three of them turning toward the exit and bowing at the hip, holding the stance for a long, tense moment.

Long enough that I surmise we have a visitor.

Looking left, I see the exit shadowed by the imposing male my body immediately responds to – heart racing, a flock of those fluttery things taking flight within my belly.

Kaan's an image of muscle and poise in brown pants and a leather tunic embellished with bronze Sabersythe scales accentuating his broad shoulders. His bare arms are crossed, his pale scars standing out in stark contrast against his tawny skin.

His mouth cuts a harsh line, a plain bronze mask casting the top half of his face in mystery, the pierce of his cinder stare catching me despite it.

Snagging my breath.

He's crowned in bronze, the metal wreath perhaps once reaching skyward in eight points now melted in places, folded down, like it got caught in a blaze of dragonflame that almost turned it molten. His mask almost melds with it.

Accentuates it.

He moves, his muscular thighs tensing with each powerful shift forward, the thump of his boots pounding in rhythm to my galloping heart. He holds my stare every step of the way, and I picture Rygun clawing through the cavern like a shifting mountain range. All the muscles in my body clench, primed to buffer his vast presence that crushes against me.

Finally breaking our eye contact, Kaan sweeps his stifling attention across the highfliers. '*Out*,' he growls, his voice a violent slash.

The remaining three males scurry toward the exit with empty hands and even emptier pockets, another dip of their heads toward the Burn King.

Ripping my gaze away, I look to where Pyrok was standing, surprised to find him already gone.

Damn.

He must've dipped out during that last round while I was slapping down my Moonplume, Moltenmaw, and Sabersythe to the tune of disgruntled mutterings. Too bad, considering I drew most of my delight from the fact that those assholes had somehow wronged him in the past.

The last male disappears down the frail pathway, leaving only myself, Kaan, and the octimar still seated in the dealer's throne – apparently exempt from the King's ferocious order.

Kaan moves around the table, gripping the back of the seat opposite mine, knuckles so blanched I imagine the piece of furniture seconds from shattering. Everything about him is immense, like a shadow that eclipses every light source, swaying my ability to see anything other than *him*.

My small stint alone with the memories of *us* gulped me into his gravity. Now I'm *falling* – too heavy.

Too fast.

The sort of plummet that ends with a crater large enough to swallow half the world.

'This is not what I meant when I asked you to dance,' he says, stare dropping to my pile of gold.

I draw my lungs full of his drugging scent, flashes of memory carving into my chest like razor blades:

> *Me, planting a constellation of kisses upon the scars on his back and arms, pretending I could mend them with my lips, while he chopped vegetables for our soup.*
>
> *Him, teaching me how to shape clay into bowls, mugs, and plates, his hands and arms smothered in so much of it that eventually made its way onto me.*
>
> *Us, moving together beneath a shaft of silver light, my chest pitted with a noxious seed of fear. Like every touch, every kiss, every whisper of breath on my skin brought us one step closer to an unknown end.*

'I was someone to you,' I whisper. 'Someone important.'

'Correct.'

'Until?'

The word is a stab – the sort of offensive motion that comes before my mind catches up to the shift of my surroundings or truly registers the lurking danger.

'You bound with another male,' Kaan answers equally fast, and my lungs empty in a shuddered exhale as all the warmth escapes my cheeks. As I try and fail to grapple that prickly reality into a shape smooth enough to swallow.

That piece of puzzle feels jagged and abrupt. Ill-fitting. The sort of piece I'll need to hammer into place.

'Would you like to know who?'

'No,' I say, my gaze dropping to chase the octimar's slithering motions, the creature gathering shards. Shuffling them.

Over the past who knows how long, I've become fondly familiar with the *us* that existed within the jungle home.

With *Kaan*.

You don't simply *scratch an itch* with Kaan Vaegor, then throw him away and move onto another. You peel back your skin and open your ribs to the male. You tuck him somewhere deep and safe, fight others off with weapons forged from secrets sharp enough to slice, then perish with those secrets clutched close to your chest.

There is no way I gave him up for anyone else . . . *willingly*. And there's only one answer to that particular riddle.

Elluin had secrets just as barbed as my own.

But secrets earn their title for a reason, often painted in an illusionary veil because they're painful to look in the eye.

Kaan hasn't felt the shape of my emotions while we were together in that place, but I have. And I'm almost certain my lost memories are a blessing in disguise. That Elluin's secrets *hurt*.

I have no desire to uncork that bottle and condemn myself to sipping the poison it undoubtedly holds, if even for a moment.

'After all that,' I say, lifting my stare, 'you still saved my life.'

'Yes.'

'Twice.'

The right side of his mouth kicks up in a half smile that wrestles with my heartstrings. 'Hard to turn down an opportunity to gift you the severed head of a male who made you bleed.'

I open my mouth, close it. My next words are rasped past a dry throat. 'I don't understand how you still look at me like you *want* me.'

Silence prevails, tension thickens, his eyes burning embers when he finally says, 'Raeve, you could flay me down the middle and I'd still fucking love you.'

All the breath shoves from my lungs.

Love . . .

The word is a quiet death that slips away without so much as a whispered goodbye – an abrupt shove into an eternal loneliness I'll never deign myself to claw free of.

'Such a waste of that big, beautiful heart,' I whisper, and his eyes flare.

I sever our eye contact, looking down at the shards the octimar has been collating into shuffled piles. Kaan makes a deep rumbling sound, and I swear the entire world shudders around me.

Creators . . .

I think I missed the meaning of the note, mask, and gown. I don't think he wants to *pretend* at all. I think he asked me to come here hoping to rekindle whatever we had in the past – back when we thrived within those hallowed walls – hoping I'm still the same female beneath the shell.

I'm not. There's nothing there but scorched stone, heartbreak, and a million reasons why I *can't*.

But perhaps . . .

Perhaps this magical send-off that Elluin and Kaan deserve can still be salvaged?

'There are two options.' I signal for the octimar to deal a round.

Kaan's gaze follows the creature's slithering motions before impaling me with another stare that promises everything I want.

Everything I don't.

'Which are?'

'I leave right now with this pile of gold,' I say, eyeing my impressive stack, 'and hire a Moltenmaw from your carter hutch for the foreseeable future.'

'So you can hunt the one who turned your back into mince-meat?'

'Among other things,' I grit out past clenched teeth.

A moment of perfect stillness while he studies me with such precision I'm certain he's hunting for answers in the flecks of my eyes. 'Or?'

'We play.' I gesture to the spread laid out between us – already dealt. 'A wager.'

Kaan looks from me to the octimar, down at the shards, before pulling his chair into place and taking a seat. My brow bumps up as he presents his left palm to the octimar.

I follow suit, but with my right.

Holding my stare, Kaan says, 'If I win, you will answer three questions from me. *Truthfully*.'

I open my mouth, words clogging on my tongue as the tip of the octimar's tendril flicks across my palm in etching trails, the pledge's hot pulse sludging through blood and sloshing against bone.

Bastard.

The octimar finishes his prickly inscription while secrets squirm in my belly like a knot of worms.

I clear my throat, scrunching my tingling hand into a ball. 'And if I win, we pretend we're the ones who existed in that place I suspect you built for us, but only until next aurora rise. At which stage, you'll owe me a single wish.'

Confusion swims in his eyes as the octimar scrawls upon his palm. 'What happens once the aurora rises?'

'Not important.'

'What. Happens?'

I sigh, gather my allotted shards off the table and begin sorting them, stare cast on the vibrant illustrations. 'I will have a Mindweft smudge you from my brain. Get back to reality. The wish is precautionary.'

I need a full stop in my back pocket. Something I can stake in the ground if it comes to it. He may think it's cruel, but I refuse to barter with his well-being. And loving me?

It's a fucking death wish.

I shift my hushling to the far left, move my enthu to the right, silence stretching for so long I glance at Kaan over my fanned deck.

He's watching me, his stare so intense it almost siphons all the breath from my lungs – not that I let on.

'What?' I ask, tipping my head to the side.

'You lost someone . . .'

My heart splats against my ribs.

My mouth opens. Closes. Opens again. When I can't forge my scrambling thoughts into a single word to throw at him, I slam my fan face down on the table and shove to a stand, stalking toward the exit.

Fuck this.

Fuck him.

Fuck everything.

Something long and leathery lashes around my throat – *tightening*. Snagging my ability to breathe or speak.

I try to weave my fingers beneath the noose and pry it loose but fail to get any traction, all the blood in my head threatening to burst my bulging eyes.

My mouth gapes, and I fall to my knees, mist wafting up like reaching claws.

A shadow shifts into my atmosphere, my gaze rolling to Kaan now crouching before me. Arms resting on his bent knees, he banks his head to the side. 'You can't leave, Raeve.' His finger comes up to support the underside of my chin, tipping my head so I'm forced to meet his blazing perusal. 'We're bound to the table until the game is through.'

I look at the octimar now shoved to its full, unimaginable height, the beast's puckered lips pulled back in a gaping yowl that exposes hundreds of sharp teeth. Big and small. Long and stumpy.

Kaan helps me up, then nudges me toward my chair. Only when my hand slaps upon the back of it does the creature let me loose, breath heaving into my starved lungs.

'*Sit*,' Kaan growls from the other side of the table.

I swallow, rubbing my aching throat as I look at him, seeing a fire in his eyes that reminds me of the bulb of dragonflame nesting at the base of Rygun's throat.

Chugging the rest of my Moonplume's Breath in three deep gulps, I slam the flute back on the table, clear my throat, and obey – knowing *exactly* what Kaan is going to ask should he win this round.

What have I done?

Raeve

CHAPTER 74

I toss the dice, rolling a four, deciding to pluck the twentieth shard from the top left corner – keeping my face smooth when my gaze coasts over the smox. A black swirling splotch that can transform into any creature, immediately inheriting its strengths.

Its weaknesses.

A risky shard that can't represent the same creature as any other played in the final lay or else it's immediately void, that play lost. Problem is, by the end, all the best shards are generally played, leaving it useless. A waste of space when you could be holding something genuinely valuable.

I pinch the flotti from my fan and set it back in the empty space.

'You know,' Kaan says, rolling the dice, taking a shard from the square and threading it amongst his hand, filling the gap with one of his previous shards, 'I taught my sister how to play this game.'

'She any good?' I ask, scattering the dice.

'Excellent.'

I purse my lips, pick a shard, look at it. Set it straight back down again. 'Better than you?'

'Hasn't beaten me once,' he mumbles, tossing down.

My eyes almost roll out of my head. 'How conceited of you.'

'Just hopeful, Moonbeam. Ever hopeful.'

I arch a brow in question.

'Unless you were playing Skripi with Slátra while you were

balled up in the sky, I have at least an eon on you.' He shrugs. 'I pray to the Creators that it gives me the advantage I need to win.'

I slay him with a stare while he lifts another shard, swapping something out, his features cast in stone as he spears me through with a simmering gaze.

'Your turn.'

Right.

Clearing my throat, I sweep the dice into my hand and flick it across the table, swapping my sowmoth for the Moltenmaw.

He rolls, but rather than pick a card from the board, he slaps the woetoe on the table, its furry face leering out at me from the upturned shard.

Fuck.

I flash him a smile, further fanning my deck as I extend my arm across the table to give him easy access to whatever card he decides to steal.

Holding my stare, he pinches the Moltenmaw, and I grind my teeth so loud I'm certain he can hear it.

'Apologies,' he says before he's even had a chance to look at the powerful shard in his hand, threading it into his fan while still holding my eye contact.

'Don't want your apology.' I toss the dice, my mood immediately brightening when I pick up the Moonplume. 'I certainly won't be offering one if I beat you.'

He throws the dice again, lifting a shard and swapping it out for another. 'And the Mindweft? Will you apologize for that?'

Clearing my throat, I collect the dice in the cup, giving it a shake.

He lifts his gaze, meeting mine as he says, 'Skripi.'

The dice flies free, bouncing across the board. '*Already*?'

Silence.

Internally, I groan – placing my nilacle he trumps with a colk. He places his Moltenmaw next, forcing me to reveal my Moonplume.

'Ouch,' he says, and a sour smile spreads across my face.

I slam down a swamp hag he trumps with a velvet trogg. Teeth gritted, I play my hushling – my remaining power card seeing as he ended the game so fucking quickly.

A beat passes before he slowly – almost *gently* – sets his doomquill on it, effectively handing me the play.

I look up, catching his stare.

Holding it.

Holding my breath, too.

'If I'm losing you again, I need to know why,' he implores, his gravelly words shaped more like an apology than an admittance.

My brow furrows as he pulls another shard from his fan and settles it on the final spot.

I break his stare, looking down.

My heart plummets so fast I almost vomit.

He sets the rest of his shards face down on the table and leans back in his chair, crossing his arms.

I release a shuddered breath, scouring the heavily tusked face of the roaring Sabersythe, a ball of red flame illuminated at the back of its throat – the only other shard that can possibly trump it already placed in the second stomp.

My *Moonplume*.

'Well played,' I rasp.

He dips his head.

I tap my finger against my shards, dropping my stare to my remaining spread, filling my lungs before I pull the smox free and set it on his Sabersythe.

A moment of pause, then 'What is it?'

'A tick.'

The smox swirls, then congeals into the shape of the tiny bulbous bug . . .

Kaan's eyes darken, a heaviness settling, like gravity just bore down on us.

'Your Sabersythe is feral,' I whisper. 'Now it's dead – slain. Unable to so much as lift its wings and soar into the sky to rest with its ancestors.'

All the color leaches from his shard, like the Sabersythe just perished between us.

Silence.

The promise that was scrawled across my palm squiggles free, releasing me from its clutch.

Kaan draws a deep breath through his nose, exhaling slower than a setting aurora. 'Impressive,' he says, barely moving his mouth.

'Thank you.'

Another stretch of silence burdens the space between us, his eyes dark shadows still set on the final play.

I clear my throat, filling my cheeks with a blow of air I audibly release. 'So . . . is there somewhere for me to store my gold so we can enjoy the festival without lugging it everywhere?'

Kaan blinks, drawing another deep breath. He lifts his head, evading my eye contact. 'I have guards beyond the exit. I'll send them in to bag it up and take it to the hutch so it's ready for your departure.'

I nod, more of those fluttery things swarming through my chest at the thought of what this cycle could hold.

Anything's possible.

We get to live this fantasy out, then I can get back to living my solitary life lifted by the knowledge that he's *safe* from whatever curse seems to follow me around like an invisible scythe, slaying anybody I form attachments to.

'I'll need to pay Pyrok back the gold I borrowed—'

'I'll see it done.'

The words are so clipped they sting.

There's a hardness in his eyes I've never seen before. Cold.

Detached.

'So,' he says, and a chill scuttles up my spine as his upper lip peels back from his canines. 'Would you like me to come around and bend you over the table?' He tips his head to the side. 'Fuck you right here so we can get it over with? Or would you like to draw it out a bit?'

I drop my gaze to the table.

He doesn't get it . . .

If I wanted to fuck, I'd find someone without the laden baggage to scratch the itch with.

A few lusty glances here, the crook of a finger there. I could have some faceless male in a darkened corner in no time, parting the tendrils of my skirt and giving me what I need without the pressure of leaving with our fates intertwined.

This is not about . . . *that.*

All I want from this slumber is to allow myself to *love*. Or at the very least *try*.

For him.

For me.

Though I may not be the one he lost, I could give him the goodbye I don't believe he got but undoubtedly deserves. I could pretend my heart is soft and warm and vulnerable. That I'm worthy of everything this spectacular male embodies, even though a stone in my gut tells me that's not the case. That Kaan Vaegor is too good for me in every way, shape, and form.

But I won't think about that right now.

No . . .

I'll save that thought for when I'm stepping into The Curly Quill. For when I'm preparing to pass Vruhn a sack of gold, then beg him to remove Kaan like a prickly weed when he's actually a *forest.*

Lush.

Strong.

Beautiful.

Too vulnerable to the nip of flames for me to bear.

Maybe he'll follow my lead. Remove *me*.

Perhaps this slumber will give him the freedom to finally say goodbye to the female he used to know. To bury the past. Find happiness with someone *worthy* of his big, warm-hearted love.

Perhaps.

I stand, move around the table, Kaan's stare still speared at my now-empty chair when I finally reach his side and extend my hand.

His gaze dips to it, then lifts to my smile.

My eyes.

'Dance with me?' I whisper.

The ball in his throat rolls as his eyes take on slightly softer lines. As my heart thumps harder, those fluttering things inside my chest multiplying. Nuzzling against my ribs and making my entire body tingle.

'Please?'

A moment of pause before he stands, towering above me, ignoring my outstretched hand. 'Lead the way, Prisoner Seventy-Three.'

I take his hand anyway, then tug him toward the exit.

Kaan

CHAPTER 75

Raeve's hand is so warm and alive snagged around my wrist. Such a contrast to our frosty, jagged surroundings. To this shard of bitter emotion lodged between my ribs, swung with the same hand she now uses to lead me through the pulse of celebration.

Some folk glance at me as we pass, then at the breath-taking female dragging me along, weaving us through the throng in a trail of silver tendrils that gust behind her. She looks at me over her shoulder, eyes like glaciers, her soft smile the gleaming slash of a blade that strikes home, bleeding the vulnerable organ that so eagerly pumps for her.

Only her.

The only beam of light I'll ever need or want in this world, my love for her sitting like a moon in my chest. Only this moon will *never* fall, no matter how hard she tugs on it.

She snags a crystal flute from a passing server, then downs the drink in a single gulp, thumping the empty glass atop a table on our way past.

Stealing glances at the sky, she stills within a somewhat less-crowded area of the dance space framed by clusters of icy columns, only a few other couples dotted about, swaying to the beat. Raeve lifts my arm above her head, and I stand still as she closes her eyes and twirls – smiling. Kicking up the fog and packing my lungs full of stones.

The aurora casts her skin in a silver sheen, her smile so wide her dimples pucker. Dimples I've not seen since she burst into laughter at Mah's special place, reviving me despite the vicious words that followed. Before that, not since the last slumber we spent together, when the aurora was just as flush.

Another slumber we spent *pretending*.

If I'd known that slumber would be our last, I would've spoken the words I'd been edging around for cycles. Begged her to take my hand forever, despite my weaknesses.

My shortcomings.

Begged her to break from the Tri-Council's decision – for *us*. Because I thought that's what she wanted.

Us.

That the Creators had blessed me as the one she chose to love.

A very big part of me still believes it. Refuses to accept that what we had was light and flimsy enough to scrunch up and toss in the bin. And perhaps that makes me weak. Soft of heart. *Incompetent* – just like Pah used to say.

I proved him right too many times before I took his head.

Yet here I am again, standing stationary while Raeve dances around me with my soft heart in her fucking hands, dripping blood all over the floor. Here I am again, looking at her like she crafted the world with a few whispered words, every sweep of her eyes twisting that jagged weapon lodged in my chest. Only this time, I'm not blind or in denial.

This time, I fucking *see*.

She's hurting. Lost someone. Maybe more than one. She thinks she doesn't deserve . . . this.

Us.

That if she opens her heart and lets me in, something bad will happen.

It most certainly will, but what she doesn't see is that her love bolsters me. Strengthens me. When she shines that light my way, *nothing* can hurt me.

Nothing.

'*Dance* with me,' she pleads, grabbing my right hand. She wraps herself around me, giving me a nudge so I untangle from her hold like *she's* the lead.

Feels fitting.

She coaxes me to twist with her to the music's droning tide, and I give her the bare minimum, turning as she drags me about the floor, feeling like I'm standing in the path of an impending moonfall – too transfixed on its plummeting beauty to step to the side.

To save myself.

She spins into my arms this time – so close.

So unbearably far away.

It's tempting to accept this scrap she's offering. To lean in and embrace this 'goodbye to Elluin' Raeve seems to think I want.

'You did request a dance, correct?' she asks, looking up at me from beneath a thick fan of black lashes.

'Correct.'

'Doesn't look like it,' she jests, brows raised. 'You have to actually *move your body*. Shocking, I know.' She tosses herself free in a churn of silver tendrils and whisking fog, boasting much of her body to a loose ring of curious onlookers who've gathered behind my fence of austere guards to watch her dance.

They look at her like the enigma she is – more untouchable than Clode – while she moves as though oblivious to their stares, lost in her swirl of make-believe.

I clear my throat, the song taking on a slower, deeper drone.

She spins toward me, tripping on a tendril.

I dip low and catch her just before she hits the ground, my arm bracing her bare back, our noses almost touching.

Her wide eyes lock with mine as she puffs a breath upon my face . . .

The celebration falls away. The crowd.

The song.

There's nothing but a pair of big azure eyes, our tangling exhales, and the welcome weight of her in my arms.

A fucking *moon* could fall and I wouldn't notice.

Her gaze drifts to my mouth, and my heart becomes a ferocious beast pounding for release. Begging me to crush the barrier between us and kiss her, like throwing myself to a nest of Sabersythes to be torn apart – slowly.

Painfully.

'Was this a bad idea?' she rasps.

'Yes.'

Very.

She squeezes her eyes shut, and I can almost feel her mind ticking before she spears me through with that glacier gaze. 'We'll stop. I'm sorry. I wanted to give you—'

'The perfect goodbye?'

She opens her mouth, closes it, a flash of tender embarrassment staining her beautiful cheeks.

I don't *want* the perfect goodbye. I want to say hello to *Raeve* – whoever that is. Whoever's tucked beneath that hardened exterior, I want to know her.

Be around her.

Love her.

'I'll go,' she whispers. 'I'm sor—'

I move, hearing her sharp intake as I throw her into a spin in tune with the song's crescendo. She stills, eyes twin pools of blazing blue wide enough to swallow me whole.

'Backing out of a battle, Prisoner Seventy-Three?' I ask, forcing a fake smile. 'I didn't take you as a quitter, but perhaps I was wrong?'

She's silent for a beat before another smile breaks across her face – so big and bold her dimples pucker again. She smooths her features, clears her throat, then lifts her chin. 'Perhaps I don't want to dance with you after all.'

'Lies,' I growl, then spin her back into my arms, crushing her body against mine. Perfectly.

Too perfectly.

'You want to dance with me, Raeve.'

You want to love me, too. But you're in the way of yourself.

I don't know what happened to her after Slátra's fall, but I can see the fractures she hides so well. The missing pieces.

The pain.

She's just like Slátra. Just as broken.

What I wouldn't do to help her feel whole again. To piece her back together, much the same as I did her dragon. Weathering the cuts to my flesh. The frostbite. The endless fucking regressions when the entire thing would crumble and I'd have to start all over again.

And again.

And again.

Keeping her tucked close, I move with her, breath stilling when she settles her head on my chest like she means to stay, braiding my heartstrings into a perfect rope she *tugs*.

Forcing myself to relax again, I graze my fingers up and down the silky skin at the small of her back – maneuvered by lures of the past.

She shivers against me in the way she always did, deepening my grave with another shoveled scoop.

It's an effort not to groan. To break away and smash my fist into a wall until my knuckles bleed.

I should've let her walk away rather than pretending I'm okay with this.

But I'm *weak.*

Soft hearted.

I drift my touch up the side of her long, elegant neck, and her entire body trembles, melting against me, our fingers interlacing like a quiet dance of their own.

'Your hands know me,' she whispers.

'Yes,' I murmur against her hair. 'Know you, crave you, worship you.'

Her breath hitches.

I could go on. Tell her our bodies clash like they were made to tangle for eternity. That I could spread her in the mist and make her body sing. Have her unravel in seconds from a few tender touches coupled with a nuzzled nip to her neck, just below her ear.

I'd mulch her enemies with my bare hands to see those dimples. Or at the very least, pave a bloody path for her to slaughter them herself.

I was living an eternal solitude, more than prepared to spend forever feasting on her memory, yet here she is, fully intent on erasing me like a stain. Despite knowing – at least in part – what we had.

What we *were.*

History is repeating itself all over again, and it makes me want to rip the fucking world in two. Crack it open in hopes of finding the answers to the heartbreaking riddle of . . .

Her.

A deeper beat pounds at the air—

Folk scream, and my stare whips up at the same moment a large Sabersythe plummets from the sky, straight toward the dome.

A buck, based on his heavily spiked tail.

He spreads his wings and scoops around, giving us his back, looking toward a second Sabersythe now charging him from above – jaw cranked so wide I can see the churn of fire welling on the back of its tongue.

Fuck.

Folk drop, flattening to the ground. I tuck Raeve behind me as a plume of dragonflame pours across the dome, preparing to catch it should my blood-runes fail.

The ruddy blaze clamors against my shield, volcanic heat boiling my blood until I'm certain my organs are mush—

The beast bites down, gnashing the air, and a cool breath of relief fills my lungs when they churn into a skyward chase – the smaller beast luring the bigger one to court her closer to the moons.

I spin, heart plunging as I scan the now-empty dance floor, screaming folk still ducking beneath tables or clustering at the base of frosty sculptures. Raeve nowhere to be seen.

Like she vanished.

My heart resumes its rampant beat when my stare latches onto the slab of shadow between two ice pillars. The entry to the maze.

Raeve peeks around the corner, her gaze cast on the retreating dragons. Almost like she's . . . *hiding* from them.

Something fierce rises inside me like a boil of liquid flame, setting every cell on edge.

Raeve doesn't hide. Not unless she's got something *to* hide.

I frown, studying the tightness around her eyes, her blanched knuckles a tribute to her crushing grip on the ice, certain I'm peering through a looking glass to something that wasn't meant for me. But I've seen it now.

I've fucking *seen* it.

Her eyes widen, face pales. She inches deeper into the maze before she spins on her heel and sprints out of sight moments before another flare of dragonflame ignites the sky. All but confirming my suspicions.

Something cold and jagged slides through my chest, and I chase – weaving through a tangle of thin paths pressed between pillars of ice that reach for the moons above. Following the intangible path of her butterberry scent.

I take a sharp left that's a dead end, dragging my hand across the frosty wall, inhaling her on the tips of my fingers. Like she ran in here, slapped her hand against the wall when she realized there's no way out, then turned around and sprinted back the other way.

Another blow of dragonflame ignites the sky, threading down the clefts between the paths, warming my skin with its luminous heat – the blaze of light making the ice look like it's burning.

But not just that.

The pale remnants of otherwise invisible runes sketched into the pillars *glow*. Runes that cast the terracotta stone in a glamour of frosty ice.

Runes only visible because of the *dragonflame*.

Frowning, I look up, watching the Sabersythes wrestle above. Again skimming so close their spear-headed tails threaten to slash through the dome as they tussle for dominance.

'Do you have something to hide, Moonbeam?'

Her huffed response comes almost instantly – brought to me on an icy breeze. Like she's standing right beside me. 'What an absurd assumption.'

I don't miss the nervous hitch to her voice. A rasp I've heard only *once* before.

When I flicked the lid on my weald back when I found her in the prison cell, revealing a bulb of Rygun's dragonflame I used to ignite the mended wound on her head.

I squeeze my eyes shut, threading my hands behind my neck and gripping tight. 'Then why did you run?'

A beat of silence.

Another spill of fire.

Another crack in my heart.

'I thought you enjoyed *hunting me down*?'

It's presented as a jest, but I see it for what it really is:

A *distraction*.

'Or was that a lie, Your Majesty?'

No.

Elluin used to hide in the jungle, her playful sounds echoing through the trees.

I used to chase her.

Catch her.

Make *love* to her.

This is different. I'm now *certain* she's hiding something – building her walls sky-high.

It's getting lonely on the other side.

I stalk forward, look left and right, drawing deep breaths of the air laced with her scent – finding it stronger to the left. 'I've hunted your *spirit* for one hundred and twenty-three phases, Raeve. Forgive me if I'm a bit jaded.'

'What do you mean by that?'

'Exactly what I said,' I grit out, charging through troves of mist.

Exactly.

Fucking.

That.

'Show yourself. Now, Raeve. Or I'll crumble these pillars and you'll have nothing to hide behind.' I pause, splaying my hand against one, a clash of robust words sitting in my chest like boulders. 'They may look like ice, but I assure you, they're not. I could turn them to dust in a heartbeat.'

Though my voice is big, it's pitched with a desperate, hopeful plea.

A *beg.*

She's probably picturing me on my knees, and perhaps that should bother me. It doesn't. I'd spend eternity looking *up* at her if she'd only fucking let me.

'Okay,' she whispers – so quiet.

So loud.

My heart hitches from a hook of hope, though I'm *certain* I heard her wrong.

'Okay?'

'Close your eyes first.'

Four small words never felt so heavy.

So *crushing.*

They sit on my chest like mountains as I cast my stare to the sky for a long, agonized moment, looking at the moon almost directly above, watching the Sabersythes blow their flames while they wrestle through the dim. Wishing for a reality where she could be as vulnerable with me as I am with her – her words from the cell a haunting echo in my ears.

Not until you turn around.

It's like watching Slátra fall apart all over again, feeling that crumbling grief inside my chest as the pieces scattered right when she was taking on such sturdy shape.

But my hope is a flame that'll never blow out. Not when it comes to her. She could sink me to the bottom of the Loff, and it'd still burn like a sun.

Leaning back, I tip my head against the ice and squeeze my eyes shut. 'They're closed for you, Raeve . . .'

Small flapping things swarm through my chest while I wait, for better or for worse.

Broken or whole.

Wanting.

Loving.

I feel her presence before I hear her, the hairs on my arms lifting as her lips brush my temple, so featherlight I'm almost certain I imagined it. But then her hands are threading through my beard, tipping my head to the side.

Her lips press against my neck, mining a gravelly sound from deep inside my chest – the kiss so real I know it's not a dream.

'You're here,' I murmur, a tremble rattling through me. Like I just dislodged a ghost from my bones and set it free, scrubbing some of the weight from my chest that was packed tight from phases and phases of dreams that felt so real.

That never were.

'Another,' I beg, the next kiss pressed to the spot just below my ear.

My cheek.

The corner of my mouth.

'Where now?' she asks, her voice tentative. Nervous even.

Like she's standing on unsteady ground.

'My lids.'

She used to kiss them when she thought I was asleep. Of all the things I've missed during the many phases I've lived, I've missed that the most.

I hear her swallow before she leans so close her exhale tickles my lashes, her lips pressing upon my left lid, then my right – like a warm, pillowy gift from the Creators themselves.

My next breath is more unsteady than my knees.

Another blow of flames warms my skin—

She stills, and I hear her heart skip a beat, feeling mine mulch.

Oh, she's hiding . . .

I squeeze my eyes tighter, and she softens against me even before the flame snips off.

'You're remarkably good at keeping your word, Sire.'

'I'll take it to my *grave*, Moonbeam.'

I feel her cheeks swell in a smile, hearing the flame-throwing Sabersythes scream off into the distance, wings beating into an echo.

'Count to ten,' she whispers against my neck. 'Then come find me beneath the moon.'

What?

My hand whips forward to thread around her waist and pull her close, only to tuck around my *own* abdomen.

My stomach dips, eyes snapping open.

I search both ways, but she's gone – not even a swirl of mist to mark her retreat.

'*Moonbeam*!'

The name bangs off the walls like tossed boulders as my head cuts left and right.

'You're not counting,' she chastises from afar, and I sigh, crunching my hands into fists. Releasing them. 'Are you doing it in your mind?'

'*Two*,' I grind out, shaking my head. '*Four* – *Six* – *Eight*—'

'You're a terrible counter.'

'—*Ten*.' I lunge forward, kicking through troves of mist. 'Sing me a song, Raeve. Give me something to chase that's *real*.'

Please.

Nothing while I stalk down path after path, but then her voice comes to me. A melody that weaves across my heart in silky notes that both slice and soothe.

I pause, close my eyes, and absorb – pulling my lungs full, like her tone is a meal my soul just sat down to feast upon.

There she is . . .

I've heard folk speak of Rayne's voice. Of how it's so achingly beautiful it makes you want to weep. Of how Clode makes you question your own sanity.

I imagine Raeve is a blend of both, sewing knots in my chest I treasure despite the agony they cause.

With a single lyrical order, she could will me to the edge of a cliff.

To jump.

I charge through the maze like I'm following a map in my own mind – turning left then right, racing down a jagged path before turning right again. I come to a lofty ice pillar with an opening carved in one side, moving into the hollow and up a curled stairwell, every turn bringing me closer to her haunting melody. The same song she once sang to me while she cried outside Slátra's hutch.

I burst onto the pillar's flattened top that's large enough to support a nesting Moonplume, directly beneath a luminous moon. Almost close enough to the aurora to touch the threads of light.

'Lie with me?'

I look down at Raeve – on her back, her stare pinned to the moon overhead, hair unraveled and cast around her in crimped waves. Her mask has been flung aside, her dress a scatter of ribbons mostly draped across the ice, less so against her pale skin, like she just fell from the sky and landed here.

My heart aches at the sight.

The *thought*.

Clearing my throat, I lift my crown and set it on the stone beside her mask, then do as she asked, placing myself beside her, arms at my sides as I study the moon – its appearance altered by the dome's distorting veil.

Usually black and spiky.

Now silver and smooth.

'I like this moon,' she whispers, followed by a lengthy pause. 'It's the same color and size as the little wonky one I could see from my window back in Gore.'

The same one on my back.

I swallow, the silence between us growing its own mournful pulse. 'Do you want me to tell you why you like it?'

'No.'

Of course not.

Glimpsing movement to my right, I frown as she rolls atop me. With her back to my chest, she reaches down, grabs my arms, and weaves them around her body – now bound in a hug she built for herself.

I forget how to breathe. To blink.

To fucking *think*.

I close my eyes, speaking past the noose threatening to strangle me. 'This hurts, Raeve . . .'

'I don't want that,' she rasps, and her arms tighten their grip on mine, like a clenching comfort that fails to soothe the burn. 'I wanted—'

'I know what you wanted. But I find no joy in pretending to have something we don't.'

'I can't do anything *but* pretend . . .'

'Because you lost someone?'

She stiffens in my arms.

This time, I'm the one to tighten my hold, tempted to squeeze her until our bodies fuse.

After a long pause, she finally whispers, almost too soft for me to hear, 'Yes.'

My heart splits, the knowledge of her devastating past sitting in my chest like a lump of lead. A cruel, burdening weight I loathe to pile atop whatever grief she's already carrying before she slips through my fingers again.

But a necessary cruelty.

She needs to be able to make a justified decision about her future based on the facts of reality. Not this smoke-screen she's living behind.

I thought I'd have more time to pick the right moment. Wait for her to grow curious and seek the answers out since the moon reveal went so fucking poorly.

Now I see the truth.

She senses the weight of her past, or she wouldn't be resorting to such extreme measures. She's poisoning her curiosity, refusing to let it sprout.

Meaning she'd rather be alone for eternity. Alone, and *happily* naïve.

Unfortunately for her, I have a responsibility I refuse to cower from.

'I envy the dragons, Kaan. They worship death so beautifully. We just . . . *lose*. Left with nothing but ghosts and memories that feel like wounds.'

The throaty husk of her voice forces me to keep my eyes closed. Raeve doesn't break when she's being watched. She stuffs it all down, pretends it's not there. And right now . . . she's not pretending.

At all.

'Have you ever wished the dead could come back? Even for a fleeting moment so you could feel them in your arms? Tell them how much they meant to you?'

'Yes.'

For a hundred phases, I looked upon Slátra's moon and wished for her to bring Elluin back to me. Begged the Creators, too.

Just another dimpled smile.

Another touch.

Another kiss upon my lids.

Anything.

She releases a shuddered breath. 'I'm not back – not really. Much as I'd like to be . . . that.'

Her.

Elluin.

Weaving her fingers through mine, she lifts my hand.

I open my eyes. Watch her use our fingers to sketch the shape of the rounded graveyard hanging above us, tracing the slope of the Moonplume's wings.

'This moment is a gift we either waste or treasure, but I'm thankful for it either way. For the time I've spent here. I've finally learned what it means to *live*, and I'll never forget that, Kaan.'

Every cell in my body stills as she pulls my hand down again, coaxes it into a cup, and nuzzles her face against it. Just like she's done so many times before . . .

'Never.'

My composure snaps.

I rip off my mask and tip her, catching the side of her face, dragging my thumb across her lips. Her breath stills – her eyes wide and glazed, cheeks wet with tears.

There's such bold shock in her stare that I feel like I'm seeing the *real* her for the first time since she fell back into the world. Not just Elluin. Not just Raeve.

A beautiful, devastating blend of both.

A pained groan grates up my throat, and I take her mouth in a crushing kiss, tasting tears on her lips as I finally jump off the cliff she sang me to the edge of.

Diary Entry

Elluin Neván

Age: 20 phases
5,000,041 phases After Stone

The stone is happy here, like Kaan asked Bulder's permission before he hollowed out the cliff to make our space. As if Bulder gladly yielded.

I love it. Being here . . . it feels like a small home away from home.

Each slumber, we feast together before Kaan plays for me, and I sing to him of The Shade. Of the wind, water, ground, and flames.

Of my beautiful fallen family.

Then he makes love to me on our large pallet carved by his own hands until we fall asleep in each other's arms.

We're in a bubble. I know we are. The rest of the world doesn't matter here within our special place.

It can't touch us here.

Last slumber, Kaan got on his knees, took his necklace off, and offered it to me. He called it his málmr and told me he went all the way to Gondragh to collect the scale of Ahra – the Great Silver Sabersythe – in order to craft the pale half. He said Ahra had come to him in a dream, and he'd gotten the distinct message that if he couldn't secure a scale from her shed, he was undeserving of the love we shared. That he would not have the strength to face our biggest challenges that have not yet come to pass.

But he got it. He survived.

So I cling to this málmr and the hope it serves, pouring my love into it even when we're not tangled in the sheets of our pallet or within our special place. I cling to it, and I beg the Creators to let us have this love with every beat of my heart. Most of all, I beg for them to keep Kaan safe.

Living.

Breathing.

I've lost so much already. The thought of losing him, too . . .

It's buckling.

Raeve

CHAPTER 77

A crackling sound nudges me from a sleep that slicks to my mind like oil. A sleep so deep and silent my body feels like stone.

I pry my way toward awareness, lulled by the patter of rain upon the glass stoppering the skyhole. Groaning, I nuzzle deeper into the calloused scoop of warmth cupping the side of my face, a dense weight draped over my waist that's comfortable.

Familiar.

Another crackling *boom* clefts the air, a flash of light igniting the backs of my lids. The weight moves, a hand sliding across my ribs, tucking me closer to a solid wall of breathing, pulse-pumping heat . . .

He's still here.

My eyes pop open, breath catching. I take in the domed room I've grown so fond of, the dragons carved all over the rounded walls barely visible in the dull, stormy light.

A rumbled breath blows upon my ear, a shiver crawling from the base of my spine all the way to the tips of my toes as I settle into the conclusion that this is not a dream. Nor is it a chest-squeezing memory.

The immense presence pressed against my curved spine . . . The muscular legs tangled with mine . . . The hot breath upon my flesh . . .

My heart labors.

Real. All real.

I draw my lungs full of air laced with the scent of cream and molten stone. Releasing a slow exhale, I think back through my drink-sodden memories, recalling our pillar-top kiss. A dusky scramble of moonlit dips and twirls. Chestaching laughter. The tangy taste of Moonplume's Breath smacked upon my lips.

I remember the rain hammering down, me gripping Kaan's hand and tugging him along the esplanade. The shore.

Through the jungle and up a twirl of stairs.

I remember him giving me privacy I didn't want as I dressed into my sleep shift. Remember climbing amongst the sheets, then ardently *wishing* for him to crawl in beside me and hug me until I fell asleep like he used to do with Elluin – feeling my well-won Skripi leverage yank from my chest like a flower ripped from its pot. Because drinks and laughter and love obviously turn me into a fucking idiot.

It's an effort not to groan at the realization that I tossed my contingency wish out the window just like I tossed that iron cuff into the Loff after Kaan picked it free.

Hindsight and all that. Though it's hard for me to find a true flare of regret beneath my ribs. Not with the memory of me drifting off while he ran his fingers through my hair – humming my calming tune.

Although . . .

My mind latches onto the vaguest wisp of memory. Of his voice upon my ear as unconsciousness clawed at me. Something about . . . a painful truth I need to know?

Creators.

Don't want that.

Another flash of lightning floods the room full of static energy, raising the hairs on the backs of my arms.

Kaan groans, shifting, and I use the opportunity to churn in his hold until I'm facing him, breath stilling when I see his sleeping face. Instantly regretting it, realizing I should've just crawled out and left without looking back.

His black hair is skewed, bun loose, tendrils strewn across his brow that I want to trail a line of kisses upon.

I lift my hand, dancing my fingers over his shapely lips, pretending to touch them. Pretending to thread my fingers through his beard, then brush his long black lashes.

Sucker for punishment, my gaze travels farther down.

He's shirtless, his body so bold in the flashing light, etching his rounded muscles into a work of art slashed in too many pale scars to count. Harshly chiseled.

Raw.

Beautiful.

I think back to some of the memories I've been struck with since I almost died from that head injury at the crater, frowning . . .

In not one of them was he so covered in scars.

It's hard to imagine him surviving some of the wounds he's obviously endured in the time we've been apart, that stony organ in my chest squeezing at the thought of him curled on a seater with a puncture in his gut – stiff and lifeless.

Pale.

At the thought of waking beside him, holding him close to keep him warm – only to find that he's not. That he's just as cold as our little snow cave, and that his eyes aren't closed at all. They're wide open, and they won't blink, no matter how hard I shake him.

Scream at him.

Beg him.

Just like I begged Fallon.

I can't do that. I can't lose somebody else.

Exactly why I need to get the fuck out of here and leave. Now.

I look at his lashes again, imagining myself leaning forward to kiss them both – soft and slow. Imagining my nose nuzzled into his neck, drawing my lungs full of his scent. Imagining myself pressing my forehead to his, telling him the three words I know Elluin felt in every fiber of her being, planting a final kiss upon his cheek—

Go, Raeve.

My heart throbs with an agonizing ache as I rip my gaze away, shift his arm to the side, and sit up. I drop inside myself and begin shucking the beautiful memory of all the warm, lustrous layers that could make me want to stay and live this past slumber again, and again, and again.

Forever.

Kaan's arm lashes around my middle, snapping me back to the now. With a surge of might, I'm lugged against his chest, bound in his embrace.

'Wh—'

'The aurora's still in bloom,' he murmurs into the dip of my neck, his voice gravel laced with groggy wisps of sleep.

Despite my frown, my body bows to the shape of him, like we were made to fit together.

Move together.

Fall together.

'You don't know that,' I scoff, and another bolt of lightning ignites the room.

'It is,' he says, settling around me like he intends to fall straight back to sleep. 'You can't tell because of all the clouds.'

I sigh.

Sounds like a load of spangle shit to me. A perfect excuse to draw the pleasure out and put off the painful bit. But I've been doing that for the past who the heck knows how long, and all it's done is land me on this big, comfortable pallet with the male, nuzzling his hand. Indulging in a love I'll never be able to keep.

It's cruel.

I'm cruel.

'I have to go, Kaan.'

'Bluntly aware of your intentions, Raeve. But as I said before you fell asleep, we need to have a serious conversation first.'

I go stone still, swearing internally.

I'd hoped he'd forgotten.

He lifts his face from my neck, then tilts my head far enough that I'm looking up at him, crushed beneath the sizzle of his earnest stare. 'We can either do that now or we can keep pretending for a little while. The choice is yours.'

I scowl. 'And if I don't want to have this *talk* you speak of? Ever?'

He shrugs. 'Then you'll have to kill me on your way out of Dhomm. Simple as that. Otherwise, I'll be on your fucking heels for the rest of eternity until you decide you're ready to face your past.'

I physically recoil, like he jabbed me with a shiv and marginally missed a vital organ. 'You're horrible.'

His smile is soft. Gentle, even.

'I'm a horrible male that *loves* you, Raeve. That wants the best for you, even if it's not the best for me.' The smile falls, his eyes darkening as he pauses – like he's grappling with the words on his tongue. 'There are . . . *others* who would be affected by your sudden return. One in particular. You need to know the truth.'

I open my mouth, close it, shafted by the hardness in his stare. The same hardness I saw in his eyes when he leapt down off Rygun's back at the crater in the Boltanic Plains.

Whoever this *other* is, I'm half convinced he'd cut off a head for them. Meaning I'm not getting out of here without this *talk*. Especially since I threw away my leverage for a midslumber snuggle and a lullaby.

Who *am* I? A dose of love from the past has tamed me into something soft, squishy, and . . . *stupid*.

'I don't like this.'

'I know you don't,' he murmurs, reaching up to tuck a tendril of hair behind my clipped ear. 'Growing pains are called *pains* for a reason.'

Don't like that, either. I've had enough *pain*.

A bit sick of it, actually.

'So what's it to be, Moonbeam? Are you in a listening mood?'

Definitely not.

A little more blissful make-believe with the male who's looking at me like I shaped the sky versus a conversation about my prickly past that'll probably break more than it builds?

Not even a competition.

'Tell me,' I muse, falling back into our lustful illusion like falling through a cloud, 'what sort of . . . *things* did we used to do in this room when we'd wake before the aurora rose?'

Kaan softens around me, a husky sound building in his chest as his eyes blaze. 'You haven't dreamt about us in this sleep space?'

Yes.

'No.'

He quirks a brow. 'Really? Because you said otherwise while you were four drinks deep, being thrown about the dance floor to a thumping jig in the Bhoggith dome.'

My cheeks heat.

Course I did.

He threads his fingers through the strap of my sleep-wear, edging it down my shoulder, planting kisses across my collarbone – tangling with my senses.

Loosening my body.

'Tell me, Raeve . . .' Another soft kiss is planted on my neck, his next words rumbled against my ear. 'How did I fuck you in your dreams?'

Raeve

CHAPTER 78

Warmth pools between my legs.

I nibble my bottom lip as my mind tunnels toward the vivid memories I've seen . . .

Lived.

Memories of *us* tumbling between the sheets together, laughing.

Loving.

Memories of him working my body into a precipice of pleasure that can only exist when hearts collide in synchrony with a passion-fueled clash. Something I never thought possible until I dreamt it.

One of the reasons I found it so hard to go, while at the same time making me equally desperate to do just that – leaving me torn two ways. Unable to move at all.

And here we are.

Me, like a charmed dragon struggling to rip from Kaan's atmosphere. And him—

Him.

Fuck.

To think I almost slit this male's throat rattles me to my marrow.

Kaan pulls the strap farther down my arm, freeing my aching breast, his thumb brushing the peak of my hardened nipple. 'Did we play rough or gentle?'

Another kiss on my neck as his fingers slide across the gathered silk of my black sleep shift, feathering over my navel.

'Did I tease you until you were wet, shuddering, and mindless, screaming for me to take you?'

He nips my neck, and I jolt.

Yes, Kaan. I've screamed for you in my dreams. Woken with your name still hot on my lips, pulsing with the memory of your hand . . .

Right where I need it now.

I press my ass against his swelling shaft, putty for his touch skating over my hip, dipping lower.

Lower.

A languid roll, and I lift my right leg, the hem of my shift slipping up my thighs. He gathers it a little farther, leaving me entirely bared.

'Did I take you hard?' he coaxes, grazing his fingers along my seam, parting me, swirling around my throbbing entrance.

Again.

Again.

Two fingers circle that sensitive nub of nerves while he kisses my neck, working me into a knot. 'Was it deep and slow?'

'All of the above,' I rasp, and a dense rumble rattles his chest as he pushes into my slick, fluttering core—

Pleasure ripples through me, making me shudder.

Another unhurried thrust, and I widen my legs, trailing my hand down his arm, just like I did in my dream. Using my *own* fingers to press him deeper into my aching heat – grinding to the same famished rhythm.

He nips the shell of my ear, then kisses it with devastating tenderness.

I rock to a steady beat, keeping his hand between my thighs, coaxing my flesh to flush with a swollen warmth that's hungry.

Wet.

Wanting.

Another kiss to the side of my neck casts a trail of tingles to my breasts. Past my navel.

Down into my core.

All my fine ligaments twinge and tighten, and my body deepens its rolling ride, building my pleasure from the fill of his fingers.

I tip my head in a quiet request for him to kiss my neck again, groaning when he laves at that tender stretch of skin with such voracious confidence. Picturing his tongue doing the same thing *elsewhere*.

Every nerve ending below my belly button begins to tingle, intensifying until I can't speak.

Can't think.

Can't breathe.

Another lavishing kiss to my neck, and every muscle in my body clenches with fierce, greedy violence. My release rips through me like a rockslide, splashing me with wave after wave of explosive pleasure.

He gently withdraws his fingers, and a moan bludgeons up my throat as he rubs my tender coil of nerves while peppering kisses around that spot beneath my ear – winding me up.

Unraveling me.

I continue to pulse, Kaan's low, satisfied growl shuddering through me, and I laugh, shaking my head. So high it feels like I'm dancing through the clouds.

If only I could live in this imaginary existence forever. Things feel *good* here. Wholesome and happy.

Free.

He plants a kiss at the corner of my mouth, sending another *zing* straight between my thighs despite my ebbing release.

My attention homes in on his hardness pressed against my backside, the muscles under my tongue tingling . . .

I roll out of his arms, and his eyes flare as I reach for the clasp of his pants, popping the button.

Yanking them down.

Tossing them aside, I straddle him, greedy gaze sweeping his body. He's a work of art tangled amongst the silken sheets, his manhood resting against his belly, the tip almost meeting with his belly button.

He reaches up, cupping my face, looking at me in the same way he did in that small, lopsided dwelling. Like he'd catch a fallen moon for me. Only this time it doesn't chafe, because we're shaping memories from silt. Something that can be washed away with the next torrential downpour.

I fall into that look like it's my salvation, nuzzling his hand.

Cupping it closer.

He groans, brows bunching. 'You're magnificent.'

My heart skips a beat.

The words . . .

The look in his eyes . . .

The way he's holding my face . . .

I could revel in him for eternity and never stop marveling. More evidence that whatever pulled Elluin away *hurt*.

I lift a brow – a pitiful effort to lighten the mood. 'You're biased, Sire. And perhaps forgetting the fact that I almost hacked you open more than once.'

'No. I'm fucking *obsessed*,' he growls, wrapping his other hand around my face and jerking me forward.

Our lips crush together, and I swallow his guttural sounds as I grind against his solid length, rekindling that ravenous throb. His fingers feather down my spine that curves into his touch, his firm hands gripping my hips, urging me to roll deeper.

Harder.

Breaking our kiss, I pepper more down the column of his throat to the sound of his gravelly moans, savoring each languid press of my lips upon his skin like a sip of life. I plant more upon each of the scars on his chest.

Around the side of his ribs.

I map the constellation of his pain with my mouth – imagining each slow, tender kiss absorbing a little of his violent history – moving down his abdominals, past his navel, taking his thick, hard cock in my hand.

My mouth waters, core pulsing at how hard he is for me.

How ready and wanting.

My lashes flick up.

I hold his volcanic stare and flatten my tongue against the velvety base, then drag it all the way to the tip, traversing a web of bulging veins. His hips buck as my tongue sweeps over the rim, lapping the salty bead of precum dripping from the slit.

He hisses, jerking.

I wrap my lips around the swollen tip and drop low, opening my throat, taking him so deep I can't breathe – my hand still wrapped around the girthy base. Again, his body jerks as I pull back, keeping my lips tight until I pop off the top, flicking another glance up into his eyes.

My pulse scatters at the way he's looking at me. Like a male who's been living on air, on the verge of starvation, and is now seated before a feast for kings and queens.

I smile. Take him into my mouth again. Slide up and down

until he's taut and shuddering, hissing sharp breaths that fill me with liquid satisfaction, his hips rising to meet me. Until he's so thick and firm I'm certain he's about to—

He fists my hair and gently tugs me back until he's free from my mouth, my neck stretched as he watches me with cutthroat intensity.

Something in his stare has changed, braced with an assertion I don't understand.

I frown, and it takes me a moment to register the thick tension in the room. That his energy has gone from warm and playful to hard and serious.

Before I have time to untangle that thought, he loosens his hand and flips me onto my back – now kneeling between my spread legs, lording over me like a savage silhouette.

The air stiffens.

'Why did you stop m—'

Another flash of lightning, and he grips my thighs, widening me so much there's no place for me to hide. 'I've made a decision,' he growls, spreading his hand across my lower belly, the pad of his thumb circling my swollen clit in slow, ruinous circles.

My hips buck, and I thread my fingers through my hair, strums of pleasure thrumming through me as he plays me like an instrument. 'Good for . . . y-you.'

The fact that he can think at all right now is beyond me.

Seriously – *good for him*.

He sinks his fingers into me, curling them, rubbing at some deep, tender patch of nerves that strikes me with a bolt of knee-shaking rapture.

I wail from the startling sensation.

Fuck.

What was that?

He strokes that sensitive spot again, again, *again* – winding me so tight I can hardly breathe. 'You're not erasing me,' he rumbles, thumbing my clit faster.

Faster.

'Not this again,' I moan, but the words don't hold the punch I intend, his fingers working me so expertly my mind has withered into compost. The sort where bad decisions go to sprout.

'I'll cut you a deal,' he spurs with a flash of his canines.

'Fuck your deals.'

'No, Raeve. Fuck *yours*,' he growls, pushing another finger in. Stretching me.

'I spent over a hundred phases crushed beneath the weight of your death, wrecking myself, trying to shed the hurt from my heart. Do you know how much easier it would've been to simply *remove you* from my mind?'

I groan as he pumps me full, my body singing for his ministrations, wet sounds filling the room.

'But I didn't, because I'm not a fucking *coward*.'

I snarl, arching up to snap my teeth at him, flopping back upon the pallet with a pleasure-filled groan as he pushes me full again.

'I don't take you for a coward.'

'Stop t-talking. You're ruining it.'

'*No*.'

Another thrust.

Another.

'You don't get to treat me like a secret this time,' he grinds out, strumming my clit with his thumb.

My pleasure begins to peak, a mighty wave cresting—

'I'm not your secret. I'm your *truth*.'

He pulls his fingers free, dissolving the climax before it has the chance to curl over.

I cry out, my sound turning into a needy whimper as I tug my foot back to shove him in the chest for being a teasing asshole.

He snatches my knee, then the other, pinning my spread legs to the pallet, his eyes shadowed embers glinting in the flashing storm. 'I know you're a feral creature that likes to swipe at everything that moves into your atmosphere, but there are only so many hits I can take before I start swiping back. Once upon a time, I listened to you. Let you push me away. Then you *died*. So no,' he growls, 'I don't accept your deal. But I will offer you a new one that's favorable to *all* parties – not just your own selfish whims.'

'*I'm not selfi*—' He dips his head between my thighs, flattens his tongue against my throbbing entrance, and licks a hot line all the way up me. '*Ohhh*, you're good at that,' I moan, bucking.

He does it again, my fingers tangling with the hair at the back of his head as I rock my hips to his laving beat.

Okay, I am a bit selfish.

I press him closer, his tongue spearing into me. He lifts my hips, cranking my rapture to an entirely new level.

My center begins to clench—

He pulls back.

I cry out, though my frustration sputters as he thrums my clit with his thumb again. 'Reach back and put your hands on the wall,' he commands, such calm authority in his voice that I immediately obey, certain my compliance is going to earn me the orgasm he keeps dangling just out of reach.

He tosses one of my legs up over his shoulder, grips the other, and spreads me wide. He fists his length, then thumps it against my swollen core.

Again.

Again.

I soften with each heavy thud to my tender clit, picturing him inside me. Filling me.

Moving in me.

Creators, this male . . .

'What's the deal, asshole?'

'Yield and I'll fuck you.' He flashes me a sharp smile that's all canines and feral delight, devastating me with more teasing thumps. My hips buck up to meet each one. 'Then I'll tell you.'

'That's a shitty ruuuu – *Creators*,' I grind out as he swirls the thick head of his cock around my entrance, dipping in the slightest amount.

Pulling out.

Swirling again.

Maybe it's not such a shitty rule.

'You made the rules last aurora fall when you fucked me at that play table. You had me agree, knowing full well you planned to *remove* me with a wish up your sleeve to ensure you saw it done.'

I *really* don't appreciate having a mirror shoved in my face while I'm edging toward an orgasm.

'I hate you,' I whimper, lifting my hips to meet the next heavy thump.

'No, you don't, Moonbeam. You love me. You're just too busy feasting on my heart to notice.'

I would flinch from the barbed accusation if I weren't wound so fucking tight.

Another luscious swirl binds me into a mewling knot, his next word snarled. '*Yield*.'

'Fuck you, asshole. I fucking *yield*.'

One hand grasps my thigh, the other threading up around the side of my face and cupping my cheek as he meets my eyes, challenging me – no, *begging me* – to hold his blazing stare.

'Don't blink, Moonbeam.' *Please.*

'I won't,' I rasp, all my welling frustration toward him popping into a honeyed cloud of chest-crushing need. Of yearning to meet him on this bridge of connection that's so frail and uncertain . . . but *exquisite.*

Brimming with a magical, prickly warmth that makes me want to cry.

My mouth falls open as he strikes his hips forward, claiming me in one swift lunge, my body tiding with the motion – crammed so deliciously full.

He stills – hilt deep – our gazes caught in a clash that feels like a fissure in time and space. All I see is molten adoration. A fierce, untamable love so heavy it stomps me breathless.

All I feel is *him.*

He releases a shuddered exhale that reminds me to work my lungs, drawing a gulp of our tangled scents that might be the best smell in the world. His hand tightens around my face, stare deepens. 'Tell me if it's too much.'

I swallow, nod, then lift my pelvis to urge him on.

With a guttural growl, he begins devastating my body with deep, rhythmic rolls of his hips that strike me with luscious bolts of rapture. I whimper, moving to match his ferocious pace, his body surging in muscle-clenching waves.

We clash in a snarling beat until I'm cresting on a combustion that might just ruin me.

His thick length swells, making me feel impossibly full as he moves his hand between us, fingers flattening against my lower belly.

His thumb circles that slick, tender bud. Faster.

Faster.

My core clamps down, a tremble starting in the tips of my curling toes, traveling up my legs, into my sex, and along the line of my spine until I'm certain I'm going to split into a thousand jagged pieces.

I run my hands over his tensing arms, across his shoulders, my right palm pressing upon his heart that's ratcheting to the same gorging rhythm as my own.

'You feel that?' he rumbles, setting his hand on top of mine and holding it over the thumping organ. His eyes take on a lighter shade that almost looks like reverence. 'You found us, Moonbeam.'

I fissure.

Split.

Shatter.

Every fiber in my lower belly goes tight and tingly, lit with a crippling surge of hot, hungry euphoria. My mouth pops open, short, sharp moans rending the air as I clench around him, pulsing with such ferocity my mind melts, lights flashing across my vision.

I lose all sense of space and time – tumbling. Landing somewhere within his gaze where I drown in the most gluttonous way.

Kaan's hand curls back around the side of my face, tightening. He *roars*, then snarls through gritted teeth, throbbing inside me. Pouring me full of liquid warmth and a primal satisfaction that butters my muscles.

My nerves.

Everything loosens, my body lax as he leans forward and nuzzles my head to the side, growling softly. He opens his mouth around my neck and gently bites. A nip that calls to my base instincts. Has me wishing he'd dig his teeth a little deeper.

'What did I just agree to?' I pant, melting beneath him.

His nip turns into a kiss he plants below my ear. That spot I never knew was so sensitive. 'You're not erasing me – no matter how much our impending conversation hurts.'

My breath catches, a chill slithering through my veins.

He plants another kiss on my neck, as if to soothe the scathing wound he just left. Another on my jaw.

The corner of my mouth.

'This is so much bigger than *us*, and you need to soften that heart or you're going to break someone who's not attuned to being stabbed through the chest by your reluctance to build connections.'

My body stills, every cell standing at stark attention.

I've been told off before, but never like this.

This is . . .

This *chafes*. Ringing with a tune of truth that makes my frayed heartstrings coil and squirm.

He grips both sides of my face, another flash of lightning filling the room with white light, his eyes volcanic as he says, 'This truth is going to hurt, and you're going to hate me for it. But there's someone out there who *needs* you, and you're going to change their life even more than you changed mine.'

My heart fractures, the crack weaving so deep it hits the soft, fleshy center.

I picture little Nee fluttering about, dancing the giddy swirls she danced whenever I lifted the lid on her box. Picture her nudging against me, nuzzling my neck, remembering all the times I gave her a belly rub. Unfolded her delicate pleats. Flattened her.

Read her.

Need.

My throat thickens so much I'm forced to swallow.

I always thought that little parchment lark came to me by accident, but maybe she wasn't lost at all. Maybe she was *exactly* where she needed to be . . .

'So, Raeve. You can swipe at me all you want, pretend you don't love me as much as I love you. I can take more scars, despite how much they hurt. But you're not running away.' He plants a kiss on the tip of my nose, the tender motion so at odds with the hard edge of his words. '*That's* what you just agreed to.'

Diary Entry

Elluin Neván

Age: 20 phases
5,000,041 phases After Stone

King Ostern returned on his Sabersythe, trailed by his two youngest sons – Cadok and Tyroth – both here for The Great Flurrt celebration. It's the first I've seen the male I'm to bind with since the slumber I set foot in his pah's kingdom.

Call me untrusting, but I took one of the dragonscale blades Kaan had shown me how to forge and kept it close to my body. Until the moment Tyroth corralled me in a hallway and tried to shove me into a darkened corner. Then I pressed it against his throat.

He laughed. Said his sister had been a bad influence on me. My response was that I felt her influence was quite the opposite. He told me I wasn't allowed to speak yet, so I told him he could eat dragon shit and that I hoped he choked on it.

Wishful thinking.

At feasting, I was made to sit beside him, donned in my veil, awkwardly eating the food that had been served for me like an animal. Hard with a clothed mouth. Even harder when all the food I'd been given was either too rich or spicy for my palate and I wasn't allowed to speak – to ask for other things stacked farther down the table.

Kaan kept his stare firmly locked on Tyroth while I suffered in the silence expected of a princess unless she's either bound or given herself to the Creators. Like Veya.

Speaking of which, Veya was strangely silent – closed off, eyes downcast – as she ate beside her nephew. I didn't understand why until her pah started pecking at her, harping on about all the ways she'd disappointed him.

With each of his scalding words, she shriveled a little more, until he said he regretted the slumber he'd sown her in her mah's womb.

A tear slid down her cheek – the first I'd ever seen her cry.

I snapped.

I ripped off my veil, climbed on the table, and charged to the other end. I slammed my fork through a pile of colk meat that I'd been salivating over since the meal began, then I proceeded to sit back in my chair, stuff my mouth full, and toss King Ostern a fake smile.

The fuck.

He glared at me as I chewed with my mouth wide open before plucking some blanched muji beans off Tyroth's plate, stating that I'm certain he didn't mind sharing with me since he was currently ruling my kingdom.

He glared at me, too, and I could see in his eyes that he was pushing down the urge to backhand me across the face for my bad behavior.

Wish he had. I desperately wanted an excuse to slam my fork through his thigh.

I was just sucking the meat juice off my fingers when King Ostern announced Kaan and Veya would be leaving with Cadok and Tyroth after The Great Flurrt so they could help rebuild a village torn apart by a rabid Sabersythe.

Everyone looked shocked except the King himself.

Kaan joined me in our home later and took me so slow and tenderly, speaking a million words through every touch, every kiss, every desperate clutching embrace. I soaked in his presence until the aurora rose like a burst of silver ribbons woven across the entire sky, and we spent The Great Flurrt tangled beneath the sheets in our quiet bubble of delusion and denial.

In thirty cycles, I turn twenty-one. Preparations have already begun for the binding ceremony in Arithia between myself and Tyroth.

For my coronation.

I think Kaan and I both feel as if ignoring the future will prevent it from coming . . .

If only that were true.

Raeve

CHAPTER 80

I stare at Kaan's immense, beautifully tattooed back as he moves through the kitchen space, rinsing a bowl of berries, slicing a globe of copperdew melon into juicy segments that spritz the air with tangy sweetness.

Every confident, fluid shift of his body reminds me how well he broke me down into a trembling, *begging* mess of corrupted thoughts and short-term decisions.

Chewing the inside of my lip, I strum my fingers on the tabletop, stuck in this strange limbo. Half drunk on lusty satiation while also welling with a ball of static energy that's flicking at my ribs, urging me to leap across the room and wrestle the male currently filling two bowls with a vibrant cacophony of freshly foraged fruit.

He wraps his fist around a gongnut and cracks it, plucking the shell away from the pale insides he then crumbles atop both servings.

I shake my head.

A fully stocked cupboard with a handful of options to break our fast, and the male knows exactly what to serve me. Not that I asked for a meal, or a spring water served in my favorite mug. Or for my soul to be cradled while he was so deep inside me there was no place to hide.

Yet here we are.

Him, half naked, moving with the mirth of someone who just stepped off a battlefield, blood barely blotted from his skin before dashing a cloth over his shoulder and preparing food he personally foraged. And *me*, festering in the aftermath of our emotionally charged coupling, hair askew, mind mulched. Trying to work out how I went from winning the most important game of Skripi I've ever played to sitting at this table, wishless, boggled, and annoyingly aroused.

Head tipping to the side, I watch Kaan's perfect, muscular ass as he moves about the space, shucking a sprig of minty herbs he uses to garnish our bowls. Certain the brown leather pants he's wearing must cut off blood supply to areas that should *always* have a ready supply as far as I'm concerned.

I sigh.

The purpose of last slumber was to role-play something I'm incapable of maintaining long term. I don't look at males wistfully and remember all the luscious things they did to my body, then want to do it again immediately after. I don't do relationships. I certainly don't do *love*.

That word has a single definition: *dangerous, potentially devastating inconvenience*.

Kaan looks at me over his shoulder, brow bumped, strokes of black hair loose from his bun hanging over his eyes. 'Are you ready to have our talk yet?'

I flinch, like he just snapped his hand out and struck me. 'Thanks, but I'd rather skin myself with a blunt blade.'

He gives me a look that suggests he thinks I'm being a bit dramatic, but it trumps a conversation that makes me feel like my ribs are being snapped off one at a time.

'Okay, well, you're obviously feeling things—'

'Regrettably.'

'Do you want to fight or fuck about it?' he asks, his coarse accent cradling the question in such a visceral way that a flush of warmth hits my core.

Squeezing my legs together, I sip my drink to wash down the impulsive desire to beg for the latter, reminding myself that his cock waged the war we now find ourselves maneuvering.

I thump my mug back on the table. 'Haven't decided yet.'

He grunts, spinning, his eyes a rich shade of auburn in the low light struggling to filter through the skyhole. With both bowls cupped in his hands, he lumbers toward me like some great beast wrestled down into the confines of his muscular physique.

'Well, while you think on that,' he says, setting both bowls on the table, 'shall we enjoy a lovely meal together?'

I look at my beautiful, colorful serve . . .

It *does* look delicious. Too bad it comes with the bitter aftertaste of an impending conversation I absolutely, one thousand percent do *not* want to have.

There has to be a way out of this. I can't just live here for the rest of my life lavishing in good sex, freshly foraged cuisine, and crafty side quests. Something's itching at the back of my brain, telling me this perfect paradise will eventually burn – just like everything else. That death will slither up those stairs like a serpent and sink its teeth into somebody else who's lodged themselves within the clefts of my heart.

I flash him a faux smile. 'Sounds delightful.'

Grunting, he pinches a berry from his bowl and tosses it in his mouth, then moves through the room, lifting one of the pre-runed parchment squares from the shelf. He uses my quill and ink to scratch something on it, then folds the square into a wiggly lark he cradles in his cupped hands before releasing it out the window.

'Who was that to?'

'Pyrok.' He settles into the seat opposite me, picks up a shard of copperdew melon, and bites into the crispy flesh. 'There's only one Mindweft in Dhomm – I believe you've already met him? I'm moving him to a safe house.'

My heart stops. 'You're joking.'

'Joking?' His eyes flick up, slaying me. 'Forgive me, Moonbeam, but there's nothing funny about it. You have a history of dipping out a side door the moment my back is turned, then winding up dead in the sky.' He offers me a forced smile that stings as much as I imagine mine did earlier. 'I'm simply taking precautions.'

I make a huffing sound and shove against the backrest, shaking my head. 'I liked you better when you were yielding to *me*.'

He shrugs. 'And I liked you better when you were drunk with a smile on your face, singing to me, telling me you were only running because you couldn't bear the thought of watching me die.'

I wince.

Those drinks should've come with big, bold warning signs.

'The great news is you're free to butter me up for eternity with those dimpled smiles, because it's not your job to keep me safe,' he says, tossing another berry into his mouth. 'Now, eat your fruit.'

He stands, taking his mug to the sink for replenishment while I simmer in my seat.

'I don't want my fruit,' I snip as he drains half his mug in three deep gulps. He lowers it, brow lifting, his regard casting a molten trail down to my lips.

Up again.

'Then what?'

'Revenge.'

'For?'

Bypassing my defenses like a fucking picklock.

I ease the iron ring off my finger, welcoming Clode's mischievous giggle while I move around the table, slide his bowl aside, and plant my ass in its place. I lift both legs, setting one foot atop his chair, stretching the right toward the windowsill.

The ball in Kaan's throat rolls.

I edge the hem of my shift into the crook between my hip and wide-open thighs, his blazing stare dropping to my naked core – plump and hot and wanting.

Wet.

I lick two fingers and part my swollen flesh, baring myself to him as I whisper a stubborn word beneath my breath, Clode's dialect gusting from my mouth like a flick of wind.

Kaan slams his mug down, striding two steps forward before he collides with a hardened wall of air. Chuffing out a low laugh, he crosses his arms and shakes his head, his eyes volcanic. 'This is *war*, Prisoner Seventy-Three.'

'Oh, I certainly hope so.'

I smile, sinking my fingers into my hot, clenching core, looking at him from beneath lusty lids. I moan, soft and sensual, imagining they're *his* fingers now slicked in the residue of my wanton need – stroking me with deft, confident thrusts.

A rumble boils in his chest. 'Does that feel good?'

'Mm-hmm.' I tuck my bottom lip between my teeth, working myself deeper . . .

Deeper . . .

Pulling my fingers out, I paint slick circles around my swollen clit, bowing my spine so I can look down at myself.

Watch myself.

I thrum that tender nub of nerves, releasing short guttural groans. Sweat prickles the back of my neck, my hips rocking – chasing the warm, thrumming pleasure. Clenching nothing.

Wanting *him*.

I peek up, my smile sharpening at the severe outline of his swollen cock that makes me throb with a fiercer ache. At the vein popping in his temple, the tendons in his neck stretched as he watches me with feral precision.

'Why the long face?'

'Any lost opportunity to worship you is a tragedy.'

Well.

Another slick swirl. Another languid dip that stokes me full of clamping pleasure. 'What would you do if I let you pass?'

'Kneel between your legs and stuff my face between your thighs,' he growls instantly, as if the words were already poised behind his pinched lips. 'Eat you until your hips are jerking and you're clenching around my tongue.'

I picture it.

Ache for it.

Another teasing swirl around that tender nub of nerves, my hips tiding toward him with each jerking thrust, my entire body heating.

I quicken the strum, legs widening.

Mind muddying.

'Then what?' I plead, every cell in my body charged, verging on the precipice . . .

'I'd flip you. Slip a pillow beneath your hips so your ass is in the air. Fill you with my fingers while my thumb threatens to push into you from behind.' My shoulder shifts up and down as I work myself to the illusion. 'Once you're so wound up your entire body's shuddering, I'd spread you, *marvel* you, then split you like an egg.'

I snap, chin tucking close to my chest, every muscle in my center pulsing with violent waves of rapture, my harsh moans tackling him from afar. I ride my fingers with deep, desperate thrusts – every muscle tight and tenuous, then turning loose and long as the pleasure begins to ebb.

A laugh bubbles up my throat, and I shake my head, looking at him from beneath a single raised brow, hand threading up to sweep my hair back off my face. 'That was good,' I say, spreading myself so he can see the residue of my release.

His eyes are black, jaw gritted, veins embossed all over his bulging muscles.

He's never looked so big. So severe.

So heartachingly beautiful.

Too bad he's in love with a death wish.

He swallows, eyes on my core. 'You're not done, Moonbeam. You're *ripe*.'

Chuffing, I plant both feet on the ground, the hem of my shift slipping into place around my thighs. I whisper a softening word to Clode, then stand, collect my bowl of fruit, and toss a berry into my mouth.

Sweet nectar bursts across my tongue.

'There are no more white flags with me, My King.' I sway toward him, stepping into his smoldering atmosphere. 'They're all used up.'

I reach him, planting my hand on his chest, his tense muscles twitching beneath my touch as I sully him with my scent.

'Good to know,' he grinds out, every bit a shadow-bathed beast in his prime. 'I'll burn mine, shall I?'

'Please do.' I toss another berry in my mouth and flash him a smile. 'Thanks for the fruit. It's really, *really* good.'

I leave the room without looking back.

Diary Entry

Elluin Nevár

Age: 20 phases
5,000,041 phases After Stone

King Ostern waved his sons and daughter off this aurora rise. We both watched them disappear into the distance before two of his guards snapped iron cuffs around my wrists.

I was shoved into a bland room, forced into a chair. The King crouched before me, looking like he wanted to slaughter me.

He told me my behavior was unbecoming of a future queen. That he'd seen the way Kaan watched me. Acted around me.

That he knew we were 'fucking.'

He told me Kaan is not fit to rule a kingdom because he can only wield two elemental songs. That he is not, and never will be, worthy of a crown.

I spat in his face. Told him I'd choose my own king or I would not bind at all.

That I would give myself to the Creators.

He sucked all the air from my lungs and made me feel like my ribs were caving, then told me that he'd noticed how friendly I am with Veya. That if I didn't bind with Tyroth, he'd rid the world of the little bitch who took his bound. That he'd inform the twins of Kaan's transgressions, and the three of them would hunt him down, then saw off his head. That he wouldn't stand a chance.

I've never felt fear so real.

He said that if I left the next rise to prepare for the binding ceremony, he'd offer Slátra safe passage back to Arithia.

Alternatively, he'd leave her hutch unguarded as I'm dragged across the plains, and I'd be forced to watch her kill herself trying to follow me home.

Then he got real close and looked at me like he could see straight through my skull. Told me he'd been informed that my bleeding is late – something I hadn't considered until that very moment.

Hadn't even realized.

He said this is the only way my youngling will have a chance at life. That if Tyroth believes he sired the small seed apparently growing in my belly, all will be well. Otherwise, there will be nowhere Kaan and I can hide where they won't find us. They'll hunt us down for this filthy dishonor we've bestowed upon our families.

I've decided this is the trade-off for finding such a great love like Mah and Pah's. That mine, too, must end in tragedy, bearing the curse of my family name.

Raeve

CHAPTER 82

More fire smudges across my abdomen – an incinerating trail
that seeps through my flesh, muscle, and bone, filling my
lungs with the acrid smell of burning meat.
I jolt against the cold stone bench, muscles spasming. Shackles biting.
Another scream threatens to burst past my gritted teeth, but I refuse
to release it, shaking my head again and again while he paints . . .
paints . . . paints me in bubbled, blistering welts. 'I know it hurts
. . .' The orange flame tethered to the tip of the Scavenger King's
finger glints off his sooty eyes. 'But pain hardens you, Fire Lark.
It makes you so exhilarating to watch in the pits, and my coffers
love it.' He moves about me in a flutter of frayed fabric,
he outline of his bony crown jutting from his head like
mangled fingers. 'Just remember – you wouldn't be so
marvelous without this. Without me.'
I've heard the same words more times than I know the numbers
to count. But what makes him so special that he gets to make
me hurt, but I don't get to do the same to him?
Fallon's been teaching me many things – big words and big
world things that are hard to grapple – and the more I learn,
the less this makes sense. The more I want to get my hands
around his neck and make it crack.
I think I'd like that. Then Fallon and I could escape.
She could finally show me the moons – the real ones.
Not the ones we draw on our ceiling.
She could also show me the colorful clouds
she's always talking about.

The Scavenger King whispers his flame into a ball he spreads down my leg, searing me all the way to the tips of my toes. My muscles spasm as I chew on a scream, gaze speared through the cleft in the ceiling to where his beast peers down from the shadows – always watching.

Always rumbling.

I picture my pain pouring into that same cleft, disappearing. Draining away before it gets a chance to take root as I hum a tune in my head. A slow, peaceful song that's been with me since the start.

'Sometime soon, I'll wear my bronze crown and you won't ever have to hurt again. I'll be on my rightful throne, and you'll be by my side, enjoying the spoils of your battles.' More fire is smeared down my shin, and I become deadly certain of one thing:

I don't want to sit by his side. Not now.

Not ever.

'Look at me,' he growls, gripping my jaw and turning my head.

I stare into ebony eyes, the scorch of pain making it hard to focus, my gaze sharpening.

Smudging.

Sharpening again.

He'll have to stop soon. I'm about to pass out.

His brows bunch together while he studies me, his hand smelling like smoke and burnt skin. 'Why don't you ever speak? I know that little bitch I shoved in your cell is teaching you. Perhaps I should burn her, too? Give you something to scream about?'

'Touch her and I'll tear you down the middle, then flip you inside out,' I rasp, my words cold and stony.

Raw.

His eyes widen before a low chuckle rattles his chest, growing in strength until his head tips back.

Deep, roaring laughter echoes off the walls.

'There she is,' he says, snapping his stare to me as I realize my mistake, my heart stilling when I catch the cruel glint in his eye.

He summons another ball of flame he spreads down my thigh. A slow, sizzling smear that burns through layers of muscle the Fleshthread will struggle to heal before I'm due back in the pit.

But that's not the reason another scream threatens to bludgeon up my throat – not even close.

'My Fire Lark does have a voice,' he purrs, summoning another flame into his hand. Another promise of pain that pales in comparison to the fear now flaying me. 'I just needed the right motivation.'

Raeve . . .

Raeve . . .

Raeve . . .

'RAEVE.'

My eyes pop open, my chest packed full of a scream I refuse to release.

I hiss air through bared teeth, filling my lungs with breaths that do nothing to unstick me from the scalding slumber-terror still slicked across my skin, the smell of smoke and fried flesh thick in the back of my throat.

My vision sharpens on a pair of hard cinder eyes shadowed by thick black lashes, a dent of concern etched between Kaan's brows that jolts something inside me.

Makes me want to squirm.

I shove at his naked chest, trying to get him to unstraddle me. When he doesn't so much as budge, I shove again – this time releasing all my pent-up energy into one volcanic word. 'Move!'

Finally easing sideways, he gives me room to roll off the pallet and stand, face tipped to the skyhole, fingers threading through my sweat-slicked hair and shoving it off my face.

Just a dream . . .

It was just a dream.

'What's a Fire Lark, Raeve?'

Fuck.

I charge for the doorway, halfway down the stairs when his thickly accented voice attacks me from behind.

'What's a fucking *Fire Lark?*'

'None of your damn business,' I snip, powering toward the exit, needing to submerse myself and scrub this *feeling* from my skin.

Kaan's heavy steps chase me through the jungle as I stalk toward the Loff, wind whipping my hair into lashing tendrils of black. I explode free of the jungle and leap onto the shore, the sky blotted with dark clouds, thick blades of sun striking through.

In another few strides, I'm waist-deep in the water and kicking my feet out from under me, dropping below the surface. I scrub my face, my arms, my legs, and for the first time ever . . . I let loose the firestorm scream that chars a path up my throat in a spill of bubbles racing for the surface—

Firm hands grip my arms and lug me skyward.

I'm spun, jerked into Kaan's roiling atmosphere, his face a sculpted clash of ruin and rage, mouth thin. Waves slosh against my back while he holds me captive. 'Who were you talking to, Raeve?'

'We're not having this conversation,' I grit out past the ribbons of sodden hair plastered to my face, trying to rip free of his firm grip.

He pulls me so close I can scarcely breathe without crushing my breasts against his firm, heaving chest as he looks down upon me, his molten stare burning into me. 'You seem to be under the illusion that I'm going to drop every bone you accidentally toss my way simply because you command it, but that was before I watched your entire body knot like you were being fucking tortured in your dream,' he growls with enough fortitude to dissolve my next breath. 'Now, my beautiful, spectacular, *indignant* Moonbeam, let's try this again. *Who. Were. You. Talking—*'

A pained, ear-splitting screech rattles the atmosphere.

Both our heads whip to the south. Toward fluttered movement emerging from the belly of a low cloud clinging to the mountain's rounded head.

Horns blow – ten short, sharp bursts that pinch the air.

I frown. 'What's that me—'

Two large vibrant Moltenmaws plunge through the cloud, both trailing white flags from the tips of their plumed tails, their riders donning silver armor to match their gray saddles.

My heart chills.

'Shade emissaries?'

Kaan remains still.

Silent.

Another chest-cracking scream cleaves the sky, followed by a deep honking sound that rattles me to the core.

A pearly Moonplume dives through the heavy tuft of cloud, the white flag tethered to its ankle fluttering in the wind – its shredded wings scrambling to catch air and keep the creature from wobbling around.

Volcanic rage boils my blood as the beast churns, its head whipping around. It cranks its maw wide and leaks another screeching whine.

My gaze homes in on its beautiful, lustrous flesh riddled with blistered welts—

Everything inside me goes eerily quiet, my lungs compacting, a wedge of hurt I didn't realize was tucked in my chest splitting wider . . .

Wider.

The beast plummets toward the city hutch, and my stomach drops when I catch sight of the saddle bound around its hide. Of the blond rider pressed flat against the poor dragon's back.

Rekk Zharos . . .

Kaan threads his hand behind my head and forces my face into his wet chest, breaking my view of the tortured Moonplume. Like he wants to protect me from the horrid sight. But it's already branded in my brain like a blistered boil that's bulging . . . bulging . . .

Destined to *pop*.

Another pained screech, and Kaan curses beneath his breath, every cell in my body now blitzed with a slicing rage. My vision tunnels, mind numbs, a vengeful serpent slithering through my chest, weaving around my ribs, charming my stony heart into a slow, steady beat.

The promise of revenge tickles the tips of my fingers . . .

I'm going to peel the skin from his body. Pierce his eyes. Rip out his teeth – one by one. Rip off his nails just as leisurely.

He's.

Fucking.

Dead.

I shove away from Kaan and storm from the water, the world around me smudging into oblivion. I barely feel the underbrush crunching beneath my bare feet. Barely feel the cool stone steps as I charge toward our sleepsuite – the distant drone of *something* bellowing behind me barely banging against my conscience.

All that exists is my dense, pulsing lust for Rekk's blood on my hands. All that *matters* is how, exactly, this is going to pan out. Like sitting down to a ten-course meal, each plate boasting multiple ingredients all beautifully presented.

I grab my sheer sun-protection robe, shoving my arms down the sleeves and threading the belt around my middle. Flipping the pallet, I reveal the cache of weapons I purchased from The Curly Quill. I saddle myself with the bandolier and both sheaths, snatching at the perfect line of blades I'd meticulously stashed – imagining the way each sharp tip is going to bite into Rekk's flesh.

My hands are swift as a lightning strike as I pack my sheaths full, blade after blade, picturing them stabbing through Rekk's jaw.

Into his ear.

Flaying him from chin to navel.

He's a filthy shit stain on this world, and I will exterminate him. Slowly.

Painfully.

I stuff my feet into my boots, lace them tight, tucking blades down the sides before I spin, making for the door. The ground shakes, the only warning I get before a chunk of stone falls before the exit, stalling my escape, the room filling with a blow of wind tunneling in from outside.

Frowning, my gaze climbs skyward, to where a jagged hole in the ceiling spills a thick shaft of sunlight all over my recently refurbished, upturned pallet. Again, I look at the chunk of fallen stone, the beautiful, elaborate images carved into it now cracked through, smaller bits of it scattered across the ground.

My attention stabs to where Kaan is standing by the end of the pallet, arms crossed as he watches me through shadowed eyes.

'You broke my wall.'

'*Our* wall,' he grinds out. 'And I had to get your attention somehow.' His gaze drops down to my chest and thighs, up again. 'What are you doing?'

I look down at myself, appearing almost feathered with the amount of blades I've packed upon my body. Most of which I barely remember wielding. 'Hunting,' I say, lifting my eyes, meeting his sooty stare. 'Anybody who treats an animal that way deserves to be flayed. Without remorse. Now, move the stone.' There's a brief pause before I remember my manners. '*Please*.'

I could try to move it myself, but chances are I'll just create more of a mess. I have no interest in making a fool of myself before the Burn King who can famously build or crush cities with a few well-crafted words.

No thank you.

Too much finger-itching silence slips by before Kaan says, 'He's toting a white flag, Moonbeam.'

'I can fix that.' I whip a blade from my bandolier, flicking it between my fingers. 'I'll use it to mop up his blood when I'm done. It'll be red by the time I'm through.'

Red like Essi's hair.

Red like the color of his beast's fleshy welts.

Red like the blood he lashed from my body.

Kaan watches me with feline precision, like he's assessing a battlefield, trying to work out the best angle of attack. 'There will be war with whomever his patron is if that rider ends up dead on my doorstep.'

My heart rallies into a wild, rib-crunching churn, my upper lip peeling back from my canines. 'Anyone who hires that monster deserves to die, too.'

Just as slowly.

Just as painfully.

'I agree. But this is not the dae for it. He's traveling with two Shade emissaries who've not shown the same cruelty toward their Moltenmaws. Are you going to kill them too?' he asks, tipping his head to the side. 'Because if you don't, word will get back that an emissary was killed on Burn soil – a perfect excuse for my brothers to shred across the Boltanic Plains and batter me with a war they've been *so* looking forward to since I murdered our pah.'

I open my mouth, close it, then crunch my hands into fists so tight the hilt of my iron dagger bites into my palm. 'So what do you want me to do?'

His eyes soften the slightest amount while I imagine mine do the opposite. 'Much as I loathe to say this,' he rumbles, too slow, too assuaging, 'I need you to put your blades down. I will leave now and speak with the riders. Find out what they want.'

I grind my back molars, tasting blood, the ravenous energy churning beneath my skin threatening to split me at the seams. 'You're not going to kill him?'

If he takes this kill from me, I will be so intolerable he'll have to cut me from this world.

'No,' he says, his voice remorseful. 'I'm sor—'

'Promise you won't?'

The faintest line forms between his brows. 'I . . . promise I will not kill the male. You have my word.'

Good.

Nodding, I stuff my dagger back into my sheath, the boiling bloodlust strumming through my veins dropping to a low simmer.

I know where he is.

I can hunt him the moment he leaves.

The soothing knowledge eases the itch at the tips of my fingers, if only a little.

Spinning, I begin unsheathing my daggers, lining them up on the pallet's stone base again. I slip my arms free of my bandolier, then unbuckle my sheaths.

'Can I trust you to stay here, Raeve?'

I look over my shoulder at Kaan – still standing in the same place. Still watching me with cutthroat precision.

'I'm not going to slay him on your soil, Kaan. Now that I understand, I will not put your folk in danger. I promise.'

'That doesn't answer my question.'

It doesn't.

I turn, arms crossed as we lock eyes – stances matching – a thrum of tension pounding between us that's almost palpable enough to shake the ground.

Twice he opens his mouth to speak, then snaps his teeth shut. Finally, he clicks his tongue, snatches his Great Flurrt tunic off the ground, grabs his crown, and releases a dense command that shifts the beautiful, broken piece of stone to the side.

Without another word or glance in my direction, he leaves.

Kaan

CHAPTER 83

Shadowed by six armed guards, I charge through erratic beams of sunlight shafting into the Stronghold's corridor, a stony silence hanging over the lot of us. 'Hutch twenty-seven?'

'Yes, Sire. The other emissaries settled on platform twelve. They've already dismounted and are under beaded guard until you're ready to accept them. But the Moonplume just fell into the first patch of shade she could find rather than listen to the keepers.'

'Yeah, well, I don't blame her,' I mutter as we round a corner, almost bowling over two soldiers who flatten their backs against the wall and pump their fists to their chests.

'Hagh, aten dah.'

'And did anyone get the name of the Moonplume's rider?' I ask.

'Rekk Zharos, Sire.' My gaze whips to Brun on my left, his flinty eyes flicking to me. 'A bounty hunter. He's well known in the southern kingdoms.'

'Oh, I've heard of him.'

Pretty sure Raeve bit the tip of his finger off. Now I wish she'd been able to tear out his throat while she was at it. Based on her reaction to seeing him, I'd say she's feeling somewhat similar. 'Anyone have iron cuffs?'

'Me,' Colet says from my right.

Good.

Another screeching roar belts through the Stronghold, splintering my self-control.

I grind my teeth, quickening my pace, storming up a flight of stairs. The two guards bracketing the doors at the top rip them wide the moment they catch sight of us, exposing the flat stretch of chapped stone large enough for almost any beast to land, the odd coppery bush growing from the cracks.

One of the earliest hutches, somewhat isolated. Distanced from the rest of them.

Rarely used.

I look out upon the massive kidney-shaped landing patch forged in an otherwise sheer drop of cliff, the hutch's mouth drenched in a pour of sunlight on the eastern side. The other half is steeped in shadow currently occupied by Rekk's trembling Moonplume pawing at the stone, coiling away from the sunlight with Rekk still saddled.

I'm not surprised she's distressed. Frightened.

With the storm clouds dissipating rapidly, there's a dense, humid heat this creature's not built to withstand and no hope of the sunshine letting up to allow her a painless crossing to the hutch's shadowed entrance on the other side.

'Creators,' I mutter, taking the creature in. A black mask is fitted to her face, shielding her eyes and protecting her from blinding, not that it helped the rest of her. Her leathery skin is bubbled, blistered all over, blood and puss leeching from her mottling of sun-exposure wounds, smearing across the stone as she binds herself into a tighter ball.

A shape that reminds me too much of Slátra – solidified in the same position deep beneath my sleepsuite.

My heart pounds as I scour her shredded wings that look barely capable of catching air, and I wonder how she made it here at all.

Hutchkeepers inch toward the broken beast, yelling commands for her to pull from the shadow and move into the hutch. Her silky tail sweeps across the ground, threatening to flick them off the cliff, some leaping out of the way just in time to dodge their plummeting fate.

'*Beuid eh vobanth ahn . . . defun dah*,' Rekk bellows to Bulder – a groundbreaking timber that clefts a web of hairline cracks through the stone directly beneath his beast. Attempting to force the poor creature from the small patch of shade.

Rather than scurry from the unsteady ground, the tormented Moonplume tucks into an even tighter ball, almost crushing Rekk against the cliff at her back in her squealing efforts to avoid the sun.

Scowling, Rekk mashes the thorned heels of his boots through gory holes in his saddle blanket. 'Move, you stupid bitch!'

The Moonplume tips her head, releasing another deep, droning lament that shreds my fucking heartstrings.

'Wait here,' I growl at my entourage, stalking forward—

A hefty *thud-ump* pounds the air, an immense, more *predatory* form of rage swelling beneath my ribs, falling amidst the churning pool of my own violent wrath.

Maintaining a healthy distance from the sweeping reach of the Moonplume's tattered tail, I signal for the keepers to clear out, stopping in Rekk's line of vision, arms crossed so I can hide the clenching of my fists.

He meets my gaze, opens his mouth to speak again, the tendons in his neck stretching with the strain required to shape Bulder's language—

'Do it. Put another crack in my ground. I'll enjoy filling it with your grated remains.'

He snaps his teeth together, the corner of his mouth curling. He releases a slow, bloodcurdling laugh that snips off the moment Rygun explodes into sight.

Massive, billowy wings wrap around the air as he hovers before the landing patch, oozing bone-crushing strength, every part of his body a heaving mass of motion but for his heavily thorned head. Plumes of smoke spill from his flared nostrils, blazing eyes narrowed on Rekk – now statue still, his Moonplume so small and delicate compared to my hulking Sabersythe. So broken and bound.

She releases another pained lament, this one softer.

More scratchy.

A deep rumble emits from Rygun's chest, his lips peeling back, flames flickering between the gaps of his bared teeth. His desire to plunge forward and rip Rekk off that saddle folds through our bond, making every muscle in my body feel like it's at war with itself.

'Order your beast to stand down,' Rekk bellows, throwing me a panicked stare I take far too much delight in, tasting smoke on the back of my tongue coupled with the sweet nectar of his fear.

'Unwedge your spokes from that Moonplume's hide, get down from your saddle, and I'll consider it.'

'Imperial cunt,' he mutters beneath his breath, probably thinking I can't hear him. Like a youngling tossing a tantrum for being told what to do.

His words are dust in my boots, but his actions are fucking stones.

Again, my gaze drops to those bloody gouges in his Moonplume's hide . . .

'As his Imperial Highness *commands*,' Rekk says, then throws his leg over and scales the short length of rope, black whip coiled at his hip, his stare caught on my hovering beast as he leaps down and charges toward me. In an impressive surge of strength, the Moonplume spears her head forward, snapping just shy of Rekk's heels.

With a hiss of sharp words, he leaps out of the way, reaching for his whip—

'Lash that dragon and I'll tie you to a stake and whip you to ribbons,' I scold.

His hand pauses around the handle. 'That's two threats and not a single formal greeting. I'm toting a white flag, *Sire*.'

I'm tempted to shove it up his ass, then deliver him to Raeve. But *kingdom*.

Rules.

'Well aware. But we don't condone animal cruelty in this kingdom. You've severed your bond with the beast. That's on you.'

'I'll just have to lash it back into her later,' he seethes beneath his breath, cutting another glance over his shoulder at the bundled creature.

Like he thinks I'll let that happen.

'Order your handlers back out here to move Líri into the hutch so she can drink and feast,' Rekk commands, an imperial lilt to his tone that makes my brows lift. 'I'll also require the services of your Fleshthread to patch up her wings.'

My stare drifts to the luminous beast – bubbled and blistered, head tucked beneath her frayed wing. Looking moments away from solidifying right here on the landing patch.

Rygun continues to leer at Rekk, smoke still pluming from his flared nostrils, an immense, pulsating *plea* pounding from his chest to mine.

One word and he'll lunge forward and snatch the male. Crunch him into a bloody mulch.

My self-restraint has never had such excruciating exercise.

'I'll have refreshments wheeled to her until I can have a blue bead brought up who's strong enough to shift a cloud,' I grit out as he unrolls a leather pouch, revealing a line of smoke sticks. 'I'll also call for the Fleshthread. Unfortunately, she attended celebrations for The Great Flurrt in a neighboring village. It'll take her some time to get here.'

Not true. Bhea's away, but Agni's here. I'll be sending someone to wake her the moment I leave this landing patch, but he doesn't need to know that.

'By the way that Moonplume's curling into herself, I doubt she has time to wait. But we'll do what we can for her. Make her comfortable.'

Rekk sniffs, passing me a glance from beneath pale brows as he plucks a smoke stick from his crammed collection and tucks it between his lips. 'Well, that's fucking useless to me, isn't it?' he murmurs, keeping his lips pinched on the tight-packed roll of parchment.

I don't answer.

'So what am I supposed to do?' he asks, throwing his hands wide, as if it's my fault he's in this predicament.

'When it's time to leave, I can organize you a carter back to The Fade,' I grind out. 'You can try your luck in Bhoggith for a beast more suitable to your . . . *needs*.'

'Fine,' he sneers, cutting a glance over his shoulder at the poor trembling creature – who goes eerily still, lifts a leathery lip, and growls at him. 'She's your burden now. She's a stupid, feral bitch who's more trouble than she's worth. My advice? She'd be better off chunked up and dumped in your feeding troughs.'

'Your advice is worth less to me than a smear of colk shit on my boot,' I say, voice monotone.

Huffing out a laugh, Rekk cocks his head to the side, his long, sharp features severe against the burnt terrain.

Looking at me from beneath an arched brow, he tucks the leather satchel back into his pocket and retrieves a weald, using a bulb of flame to singe the end of his stick. He pulls a deep puff before blowing a plume of smoke that tangles around his face. 'You gonna call off your beast, or will I go down in history as the male who stoked the war between The Shade and The Burn?'

Tyroth is his patron, then . . .

Interesting.

'Hach te nei, Rygun.'

My dragon shakes his head, displeasure rippling through our bond like a flow of lava. He snaps at the air before he *roars* – thrashing his wings with such force a burst of wind barrels into the landing patch, tilling dirt and smoke.

He cuts off in a wide, arcing path, leering at Rekk as he powers through the sky, releases another screeching roar, then tucks his wings and plummets out of sight.

Rekk brings the stick to his lips, draws on it, then blows a plume of smoke in my direction. 'This is cozy.'

My eyes narrow. 'You have some gall bringing a *Moonplume* to my kingdom without a blue bead in tow.'

The tone of my voice says everything my words do not: if his beast wasn't shackled with that tattered white flag, I'd hammer him to a wooden pole on the esplanade. Let the sun bubble and blister his skin until it's falling from his bones. Then I'd cut Raeve loose. Sit myself center stage and watch her have her bloody way with whatever's left of the fuck before carving his head free and tossing it to Rygun as a snack.

He shrugs. 'Líri's not large enough to carry two riders, and with The Great Flurrt looming, most of Gore's flock had been turned out,' he says past a slashing smile, dragging on his smoke stick again.

In other words, he didn't have the patience to wait. To put his beast's well-being before his own selfish whims, expecting *us* to patch up the mess when he arrived.

My muscles bulge and swell, tendons stretching as I battle the will to lunge forward and rip his head from his shoulders – promises and wars be damned.

Another suck of his smoke stick, and I notice his other hand is gloved.

I jerk my chin at it. 'So it's true.'

'What is?'

'A member of the Ath bit off the tip of your finger.'

'She did. I'm yet to find a Runi talented enough to undo the damage.' He pulls off his glove to boast the gory nub, inspecting it from all angles. 'She, too, was a feral bitch.'

My hands fist so tight my knuckles pop.

'I heard your beast was in the vicinity at the time of her

execution. That he shoved a couple of Moltenmaws out of the way to snatch her off the stake.' He looks at me through slit eyes – a look that chills me to the marrow.

My gut sours with the thought that this fuck has even the smallest inkling of what went down in that coliseum.

'He was turned out. Can't fault the beast for liking the taste of fae,' I lie, cutting him a threatening grin.

'Ah.'

'Tell me, Rekk Zharos, why have you soiled my ground with your presence?'

'I'm hunting someone.' Head cocked to the side, he pulls on his stick again. 'The Princess went missing just after her anointing. Her pah sent me to track her down.'

I almost laugh.

Of course he did.

Everybody knows this male has hung off Kyzari like a sticky shadow for many phases, desperate to vie for her affections. Only *Tyroth* would use that to his advantage in the urge to find his precious daughter, who won't stop slipping free of the cage he's kept her in for far too long.

'Well,' I mutter, looking at him down the line of my nose, 'find comfort in the fact that if she were *my* daughter, I'd do anything in my power to keep her well the fuck away from you.'

He makes a chuffing sound, pulling another sizzling draw before he taps a wad of ash away. 'I tire of your words. How about you take a stroll into your chambers and wash whatever whore you're wearing off your cock while I scour the city, hmm?'

I consider the implications of popping a single eyeball. I could probably get around it politically, but Raeve's another story . . .

I think she'd be disappointed in me, and that's the last thing I want.

'Look all you want, you won't find Kyzari here. And you won't scour my city without wearing iron cuffs, escorted by a barrage of beaded chaperones,' I say, gesturing to my guards lined up at the entrance to the Imperial Stronghold, each of them boasting red, clear, or brown beads in their beards or hair. 'I, too, will escort you. I'm sure you understand.'

'Of course,' he grits out, flicking his stub on the ground, the embers hissing like a dying serpent before I crush it beneath my heel. 'And my saddlebags?'

'Will be removed and brought to your temporary quarters where you'll be under full surveillance every second you sully my kingdom with your putrid presence.'

He extends his hands, a sadistic smile curling his lips as Colet approaches with the cuffs and latches them onto his wrists, locking them in place. 'Is this an honor you bestow upon *all* who visit your Stronghold?'

I return his smile, exposing the full length of my canines. 'Only the ones I fucking *loathe*.'

Raeve

CHAPTER 84

I pace sweeping semi-circles around the pallet, clenching my hands into fisted balls, releasing them. Clenching them again. Energy lashes at the underside of my skin like a metal-tipped whip, slicing through my resolve with every powered stride.

I crack my neck from side to side. Scrub my face. Rip my hands through my hair.

White flag.

White flag.

White fucking flag.

Another pained yowl slits across my heart, tangling with a flash.

A vision strikes like a blow to the brain:

Pale, blistered skin. Shredded wings. Milky, unseeing eyes—

A deep groan bludgeons up my throat.

I'm in the jungle before I can even process the stabbing pierce of my thoughts. Leaping over the stone wall before I register the suffocating noose bound around my throat. Charging up the esplanade when I become vitally aware of the heaviness sitting upon my chest, crushing my ribs.

The city is sleeping, leading me to ponder the hour as I charge up a path winding between terracotta homes draped in bronze vines, their inky blooms bobbing in the wind, facing shafts of sun that paint my back.

Rygun shreds through the air above, carving large loops that keep churning back to the faraway ledge I saw the wounded Moonplume plummet toward.

I've never seen him act this way before . . .

The ground becomes more uneven beneath my boots as I weave to a higher altitude, pulling tight breaths of muggy, sweet-smelling air, making for the sheer cliff ahead.

A dead end.

I unlace my boots, tuck them behind a bush pressed close to one of the bouldered homes, then rest my hands on the stone, looking up the vertical expanse. Rygun makes another swooping pass of the isolated landing patch far above, almost like he's *guarding* it.

Frowning, I wedge my fingers into the clefts, find a sturdy foothold, and pull myself up – ascending the cliff face in teeth-gritted increments. The wind tangles with my hair and toys with my trailing robe as I climb, moving with speed and agility.

With poise and purpose.

Another pained lament tapers into oblivion, tangling with another blinding flash:

Me – aboard the back of a vibrant feathered beast gliding through the sky, an oppressive heat pressing down on me as screams rip my throat raw.

A bloody, blistered Moonplume bobbing through the air behind me, tethered to my wake, rays of golden light glinting off her big, glistening eyes that weren't fit to peer at the sun. That lost their sparkle, then faded into a dark gray.

Light gray.

Paler—

The vision slits my chest straight down the middle, takes my heart in its hand and crumbles it through a crushing fist.

I slip, hand whipping up, catching myself on a tree root protruding from the cliff.

Dangling, I fail to scrape the residue of the vision from my mind's eye, that noose around my throat tightening.

Tightening.

All the light seems to wick from my surroundings, the vision's suffocating tendrils lashing my mind like blazing ribbons of searing sunlight.

A massive roaring shadow swoops past me, gusting my face with a slap of air.

I pull a shuddered gasp, my stare finally spearing past my swinging feet, honing in on the bouldered city far below. I blink away the blur, my heart lurching as I properly gauge the potential drop just waiting to yank me into its slaughtering void.

Fuck.

Again, Rygun swoops past, the thorned tip of his vast wing slicing the air so close to me I'm certain it's not an accident.

'Stop fussing!' I scream in his direction, head tipping as I take in my tentative grip on the crumbling root, my next words mumbled. 'I'm fine . . .'

I reach forward with my flailing hand and wedge my fingers into the cliff, find a foothold, and transfer my weight back onto the stone, dumping the painful image on the shore of my icy lake where I can deal with it later.

When I'm not scaling a cliff.

I secure myself to the stone, then loosen my grip on the root and continue my ascent, threading my arm over the ledge when I reach the top. I slap my hand on the landing patch and pull myself up, stare stabbing left toward the hutch's gloomy hollow. Heaving myself onto flat ground, I peer over my shoulder to see Rygun still circling through the sky behind me, watching on from a distance.

Still *fussing* from a distance.

Sighing, I creep toward the hutch, pausing by a black mesh mask big enough to fit a dragon – ripped through, as though a talon tore it free.

I crouch, running my fingers across the sheer fabric not dissimilar to the roll of material Kaan instructed me to veil my face with while on Rygun's back.

A shiver crawls up my spine, something inside me shifting heavily. Paying attention.

I pause.

Turn.

My blood ices at the sight of the coiled Moonplume trembling in the lump of shadow over the other side of the landing patch, emitting a dull light.

A frosty wail of mourning threatens to carve up my throat from somewhere deep beneath my ribs as I scour the dragon's leathery skin riddled with welts, shreds of sizzled flesh hanging off its haunches. The massive holes burnt through the elegant sweep of its shimmery wings.

Through one of those tattered lacerations, a single glistening globe peers at me, snatching my breath and the frayed tips of my stubby heartstrings.

That slit in my chest widens, a lump swelling in my throat that's hard to breathe past as I study the wounded creature – a quarter the size of Slátra's moon. As I take in the hole gouged into its saddle beneath the stirrups. The trail of blood weeping from deep, fleshy wounds.

My knees threaten to give way, my fizzing, spitting rage yielding to ribbons of icy sadness that bind around my brittle ribs and chill me to the core.

Somebody has wheeled a barrow of chunked-up meat close to the dragon, not that it appears to have been touched. Same goes for the copper trough of water that's still filled to the brim, the surface rippling with each rumbled breath the creature releases.

A crackling *boom* rips across the sky, and I draw on the sweet scent of impending rain, a single drip plummeting past my ear. Splatting against the ground.

The sky is crying for you . . .

'I have them too,' I whisper, and the Moonplume blinks.

I swallow the swelling lump in my throat and study those welts, moving forward a step.

Another.

'You can't see mine,' I rasp, stepping over a web of hairline cracks in the ground. 'Not anymore.'

I release my truth like a charred skeleton dredged up from the shore of my icy lake, spat on the stone beside this beautiful, broken creature.

I steal another step toward the trembling beast.

Another.

'The pain . . . it never goes away. No matter how hard you pretend.'

My voice cracks on the last word, memories of my own burning flesh shoving up my nose, muddying my lungs. Making my gut clench, the muscles beneath my tongue tingling with a surge of nausea.

'I used to believe the Creators were punishing me for something.'

I move closer still, more drops of rain splashing upon my shoulders and weeping down my skin, recalling the memory that struck me on the cliff and almost tore me to my death. A jagged blade now wedged in my chest as I dip inside myself, lift the memory from the obsidian shore within, and put it where it's meant to be.

In my chest – where I can feel it always.

Forever.

'I think that might be true,' I sob past the pit in my throat growing bigger with each tentative step toward the beast still staring at me. Like she's taking me in, weighing my words, my actions. She sniffs at the air, perhaps pulling my scent into her lungs.

'I think I failed my Moonplume Slátra many phases ago,' I admit with soul-crushing certainty, like finally chewing a splinter from my hand that was rooted deep, the flesh around it swollen.

Infected.

The admission . . . it feels right.

So *heartbreakingly* right.

Another tear slips down my cheek as the sky continues to weep. As I draw close enough to the trembling beast to settle my hand on an untarnished patch of cold leathery skin—

A *thump* pulses through my spine, like somebody tore the cord of bones from my body, whipped it against the stone, then threaded it back through me.

This brisk, flesh-biting cold . . . It feels like *home*.

The creature blinks, a truth settling in my marrow, deep and yearning.

Vulnerable.

A truth that's both frightening and abrupt.

'I think you and I were supposed to find one another,' I whisper, peering into the Moonplume's glimmering globes as another tear slips down my cheek. As a promise plunges between the calloused ridges of my heart like a thorn – straightening my spine. Reinforcing my bones.

My resolve.

Like an icy sun just crested the horizon in my chest and filled my lungs with the first full breath I've pulled since I woke in this strange, foreign reality of pain.

'No one will *ever* hurt you again.'

Raeve

CHAPTER 85

Barely any light threads through the mouth of the cave, the storm rattling the sky outside, howling against the din. Heavy clouds that blocked the sun long enough for three hutchkeepers to help me coax the Moonplume into the shadowy burrow.

They told me her name is Líri. That she's just shy of adolescence, based on the length of the tendrils dangling from her jowls, but that she's very small for her age. She certainly looks it – curled up in the middle of the lofty cavern. A delicate loop of interlacing runes surrounds us, creating a chilled environment that makes every soft word I sing expel with a puff of milky air.

My hand circles over the wide curve of Líri's nose, her flesh an icy nip against my palm that calms something inside me.

She blows a cold, rumbling breath across my leg, lids threatening to sink shut over her gloomy eyes, and my gaze drifts between her and the Imperial Stronghold's Fleshthread.

'This one will hurt,' Agni says, her words muffled past the thick woven material bound around her head, keeping her warm.

She's crouched beside one of Líri's half-stretched wings, sketching a preliminary path of runes around a gaping hole in the largest panel of membrane – doused in the glow emitting off Líri's hide.

She flicks me a dubious look. 'It's a tender spot, and the tear is—'

'Large.'

She nods. 'There's a lot of flesh to be remade with a single bind of runes, but I really didn't want to have to repeat the process more than once in this spot. So . . . we're going to try.'

I reach behind me for the hard, wiry tuft of ghorsi grass, cracking some of the stems to release the sedative stench and resting it against my thigh – right before Líri's left nostril. Running my hand up between her eyes, I give Agni a tight nod.

She dips the sharp tip of her etching stick in a jar, gaze nipping at Líri before she tucks her head and begins carving the runes.

Líri's lids pry open to slits, her upper lip lifting from a row of piercing sabers as her eyes narrow on Agni. The long muscles in her lanky neck bulge, tendons tightening, as though she's deciding whether or not she wants to whip her head around and *snap*.

Agni pauses, stare set on the snarling creature.

'*Hais te na veil de nel*, Líri.' I crack more fronds of ghorsi grass, slicking my palms in the milky residue and rubbing it across her snout. '*Hais te na veil . . . catkin de nei.*'

Líri's muscles soften, and her upper lip stops wobbling, nostrils flaring. She blows a cold plume of breath on me, and I give the signal to continue.

'You know how to speak in the southern tongue?' Agni asks, resuming her tedious task.

Still rubbing my hand across Líri's snout, I look up. 'Not that I'm aware.'

She peers at me. 'That's what you spoke right now. My mah used to be an emissary. She had to be familiar with the language because some folk south of the wall choose only to speak in the southern tongue. Especially in some of the communities south of Arithia.'

Huh.

I hadn't considered the words that were coming out of my mouth – simply spoke them.

'Did I speak it fluently?'

Agni nods, pausing to dip her etching stick in her tincture again, passing me a gentle smile. 'Like you've been speaking it for a long while. Have you spent much time in The Shade? That you can remember?'

That you can remember.

My thoughts sink down that coiled staircase beneath Kaan's sleepsuite, into a cavern pregnant with a luminous, icy tombstone – the weight of which I can suddenly feel beneath my ribs.

Weighing me down.

I let the silence ruminate between us, cracking more ghorsi grass upon my hands to smooth over Líri's nose. Agni clears her throat and continues etching her runes, her own lids appearing to grow just as heavy as her patient's.

Hardly surprising. She's been working nonstop since she got here almost an entire aurora cycle ago, during which neither of us have slept nor barely even eaten. The entire time, the storm has raged, clapping the sky into luminous shards, rumbling like a caged beast. Like Rayne is overflowing with teeth-gnashing anger – a similar storm churning within the confines of my chest cavity.

But I'm mindful.

Uncharacteristically, painfully *patient*.

A *thud-umping boom* rattles the cave. Rattles the very air we breathe as Agni completes the misshapen loop. She lifts her hands, and we both still as the hole's tattered circumference illuminates – tightening.

New flesh *spawning*.

'Please be enough,' Agni mutters, etching stick poised as the hole shrinks in nail-biting increments. '*Please* . . .'

It seals shut.

Agni's face contorts, like something just stabbed her through the gut.

'Are you oka—'

Her eyes roll into the back of her head, and she slumps sideways, glass shattering with the heavy thump of her head hitting the ground.

Fuck.

I unravel myself and dart around Líri's crimping wing to where Agni is bunched in a shuddering heap. 'Agni? Shit.' I crouch beside her, heaving her up against my chest.

Her lids flutter open. 'I fainted, didn't I?'

'Yes,' I grind out, brushing my hand across the lump on her forehead. 'You need sleep.'

'I need sleep,' she mimics, allowing me to help her all the way to her feet.

'I'll escort you back to the Stronghold.'

'I'm fine,' she assures, passing me a weak smile before she reaches up and touches the lump, wincing. 'This isn't the first time I've come to with an egg on my head.'

I consider telling her about the time I came to with the remnants of Rekk's finger between my teeth to lighten the mood a smidge, but think better of it.

'Are you sure you're okay?'

She nods, her drab gaze dropping to her spread of tools and tinctures, some shattered, others scattered across the ground. She sighs. 'What a Creators-damn mess.'

'I'll sort it. You go rest.' I kneel to collect the strewn vials, corking some, doing what I can to salvage the spilled contents.

'I'm terribly sorry I can't work any faster, Raeve . . .'

'You're easing her discomfort at the cost of your own health and well-being. Don't be sorry. Go. Eat. Replenish. Get some rest. I'll still be here when you return.'

'It's just . . .' Frowning, I look up to see her stare scraping across my arms, my legs – tears welling in her eyes. 'Anyone who's been through the process knows how much it hurts, and I understand her suffering must be . . . *hard* for you to endure.'

Her meaning sinks beneath my skin, whisking my pulse into a rapid churn.

I clear my throat, carting a bundle of corked jars to the table we had set up on the far side of the cavern, my gaze caught on my task of putting them back into place. 'We don't need to talk about—'

'To me, you shine far brighter than Líri . . .'

I sigh, set my hands on the table, and stare at the wall. In all my known life, I hadn't met a single folk blessed with Dragonsight. Now in less than sixty rises, I've met two.

They're supposed to be blessedly *rare*.

'I don't want the King knowing,' I say, turning to look at her.

'Veya said the same when I brought it up with her. Your secret's safe with me. I just—'

'And I have no desire to speak of it. None. I don't need coddling, Agni, though I appreciate the sentiment. All I need is for you to get some rest before you pass out again.'

Her mouth snips shut, cheeks flushing. 'Of course.' With a dip of her head, she moves toward the cavern's mouth, stepping into the misty curtain of rain.

'Creators,' I mutter, shaking my head.

I make for Líri's head, her heavy-lidded gaze following my every motion, blinking with a flutter of wispy, pale lashes.

Such a contrast to her dark, fathomless eyes.

I settle before her, doused in the frosty blow of her soft, rumbling exhale. Rubbing my hand back and forth across her rounded nose, I marvel at the unique texture of her skin – like crumpled leather pressed smooth, veined in a web of fine creases.

Her slit nostrils flare, and she whuffs at me, the tasseled tendrils hanging from her jowls fluffing as my hand threads up between her eyes, rubbing. A trilling sound rattles in the back of her throat, and a smile kicks up the corner of my lips—

'What is it you don't want me finding out, Raeve?'

Though my heart lodges itself on a rib, I keep my features smooth.

Impassive.

Heavy footsteps echo behind me, and every hair on the back of my neck lifts as I realize how close he is, his scent wafting around me like a soothing blanket part of me is desperate to nuzzle into.

Ignoring his question, I reach forward, taking one of Líri's tendrils and running it through my fingers, her trilling sounds softening to a high-pitched purr that saws in longer, more languid drags until her breaths turn deep and even.

Slowly, I edge away. Careful.

Quiet.

She doesn't so much as twitch as I ease to a silent stand, walking free of the rune's frosty embrace, mindful not to disturb the luminous drawings smudged into the stone.

I make for the cave's clamorous entrance, Kaan's thumping footsteps following close behind.

Reaching the fall of water, I pause, arms crossed, peering out at the downpour – unsurprised to see Rygun coiled on the landing patch, though barely fitting on it. A single ember eye peers at the hutch's entrance with lazy intrigue while he rumbles through long, heavy breaths.

'The hutchkeepers confirmed that Líri belonged to Rekk Zharos,' I say, my tone cool and calm. Precise.

It speaks nothing of the well of rage simmering beneath my ribs like a firestorm.

I've spent all of this past aurora cycle listening to that Moonplume howl as she's been forced to relive the sizzling pain of each weeping welt that *asshole* dealt her, and there's only one remedy to this brewing fury.

One.

'They also informed me that he's hunting for The Shade's missing princess. Is that right?'

'It is,' Kaan rumbles from just behind my left ear. There's a lengthy pause, then, 'This male did more than simply . . . *capture* you in Gore.'

Such a dangerous, prickly question, passed to me like a freshly sharpened weapon I'm wary enough to handle gently. With careful precision.

'Correct.'

He steps so close I'm engulfed in the dense aura of his body heat, a shiver crawling up my spine despite his welcome warmth. 'Would you like to enlighten me, Moonbeam?'

My mind tunnels back to a churn of red hair, the smell of blood, soft pale skin that was too cold when I pressed my lips against it and whispered an acrid goodbye—

'He took someone from me,' I rasp.

'Who?'

There's menace in his voice.

Fiery, ferocious menace.

I swallow, battling the urge to release another violent shiver, his electric rage feeding the feral part of me chafing for release. 'Someone I loved.'

A heavy beat of silence, and I can feel the thump of his thoughts like tumbling boulders clanking against each other. 'Was he the one who whipped you?'

The words are blazing coals – too hot to handle. Give them a single breath of life and they'll incinerate.

I leave them there. Don't touch them or feed them. Don't even acknowledge their sizzling existence.

I believed Kaan when he said he wouldn't kill Rekk, understanding the political implications if he were to harm him on Burn soil. I also believe there's a line that borders that well of self-control. A line I can sense, just like I can sense him standing behind me. A firm, hot-blooded male containing a churn of barely tethered rage.

Sometimes, it's best to leave things unsaid.

'How long will he be here, being escorted around the city?'

'Another few cycles, perhaps. He's thorough. I suspect my brother's emissaries are here to scope our military weight more so than to hunt for his missing daughter, so I've got them under arrest in their guest suites.'

A streak of lightning momentarily splits the sky. 'Do you know where he plans to go after he's finished here?'

'I had his saddlebags searched after they were removed from Líri.'

When he says no more, I turn, looking up into broody eyes that see so much.

Too much.

His arms are crossed, the sleeves of his black tunic rolled to the elbows, his hair held back in such a loose bun that tendrils hang around his face. He's the picture of savage regard – a fierce, sturdy presence. With his beast at my back and this massive, impenetrable male at my front, I should feel small.

I don't.

He's only ever made me feel vast. Mighty, even. And perhaps he's right.

There's something *big* brewing within me. Something monstrous. I don't want to be here when it bursts.

'Well?'

Resolve softens his eyes. 'He's heading back to Gore to chase down a lead. Most dragons can't fly for as long or as far as Rygun can, so they'll likely stop at Ovadhan on the way for supplies, then again at Bothaim.'

'The city that straddles the border between The Fade and The Burn?'

'Correct. Neutral territory. Home of the Tri-Council Citadel.'

I nod, my eyes unfocusing, mind ticking. Tracing.

Weaving.

Neutral land.

I snap my attention back to Kaan, opening my mouth—

'I will have everything arranged for your departure once Líri is healed, and will do everything in my power to keep Rekk in Dhomm until the dae after you leave the city.'

A wrestle of words dies on my tongue as a warm sprout of knowledge nestles between my ribs.

He's letting me go rather than clipping my wings and telling me all the valid reasons why I shouldn't do this. Rather than telling me we're yet to have our conversation or demand he come with me to assure I don't remove him from my mind.

Rather than shackle me in any way, shape, or form . . . *he's blowing me back to the wind.*

My chest becomes heavy with the weight of a realization too multifaceted for me to ponder right now – with itchy feet and a whirring mind and bloodlust nipping at the tips of my fingers.

I can understand why Elluin loved this male with her entire heart . . .

He threads his hand around the small of my back, tucking me into his chest, warm lips brushing against my temple. 'Come back to me, Raeve. To *us*.'

Then he's gone.

Diary Entry

Elluin Neván

Age: 20 phases
5,000,041 phases After Stone

We left this dae with a storm cloud big enough to soften Slátra's journey across the plains, a parchment lark fluttering around Kaan's sleep space for when he returns – stating that I'd enjoyed our time together, but that Tyroth's a more gifted sire and everything I need if I'm to breed healthy younglings to maintain my family line. To maintain our ability to protect the Aether Stone.

I've never felt so vile. So rattled by the poisonous lie that I'm certain my heart solidified.

Kaan may never know he's everything to me. That I'd fall just to watch him fly.

He may never know the youngling I carry is his or that I'm pitted with a fear that I won't survive long enough to find a way to make this right.

Pah thought I was remarkable, and once, I believed it.

Now, I can't stand to look at my own filthy face.

Rekk Zharos

CHAPTER 87

Bothaim

I drop onto a barstool, the Velvet Snog alive with the whistle and drum of a small band perched on stools in the corner of Bothaim's infamous inn. A place of comings and goings, of sealed deals and neutral agency.

You never know who you're going to find here. Or what.

Exactly why I like it.

I cut a glance around the space, the irregular ceiling held up with stumpy stone pillars that remind me of rock trolls. Sconces reach from the wall like metal claws, casting the space in a bronze light that offsets the many dark corners folk like to fuck in.

Another reason why I like it.

Nothing better than a hot meal and a good show to get me in the mood for eating pussy and spilling blood.

My two Arithian escorts settle on empty stools to my right, shucking off their silver cloaks and draping them on the bar. To my left, the male whose mount I caught a ride on the back of barely fits on his own stool – his chest a barrel, legs and arms the size of trunks. A brown bead hangs from one of the braids in his black wiry beard.

Terros. Decent guy. Bit quiet, but I like that. Nothing worse than feeling like you've gotta talk to the cunt carting you across the kingdom on the back of his mount like a fucking priss.

Sniffing, I catch a lingering whiff of ashen musk clinging to my cloak. The scent of the dragon I've taken a liking to.

Hard to resist. Terros's large Moltenmaw performed so beautifully during our long journey here from The Burn's capital. Never once tossed his head or complained.

Unlike the feral mutt I left in Dhomm.

Líri couldn't travel long distances. Couldn't travel past Bothaim without a fucking mask or squirming from a bit of sun. Moonplumes are supposed to be swift, cunning, and disastrous to their opponents, but all Líri gave me was bad attitude and twitchy heels. The bitch.

Fucking glad to be rid of her.

I'll be even more glad once I charm Bruus – the strong, sturdy mount. He bears thick ruddy plumage that can ward off both the biting chill of the south and the harsh rays of the north, and he'll be *mine* once I slit Terros's throat.

But first, I'll let the Dhomm male have one final meal. Let him take one of the Velvet Snog's famous whores and fall into a sleep he'll never wake from. If there's anything I learned from Pah's regular whippings, it's that manners are of the utmost fucking importance.

Terros looks sidelong at me, raising a dark brow.

'Hungry?'

He nods.

'Good. It's on me.' I gesture to the barmaid to get her attention. 'Two Molten Meads and two colk steaks, the thick ones still on the bone, and with a side of canit slaw.' I lean closer to Terros, dropping my tone as I ask, 'How do you like yours cooked?'

'Still bleating,' he grunts out.

'Nice.' I pull a smoke stick from my stash before relaying the details to the lusty-eyed barmaid. 'I also want a whore sent to my sleepsuite. Blue eyes.' I reach into my pocket for a small sack of bloodstone, dumping the lot on the bar. 'And I want the entire floor cleared out so I can make the bitch squeal without others listening in.'

'Of course.' She sweeps the sack off the table, pocketing it, then serves our meads and disappears through the back door.

The four of us sit in silence, drinking while I watch a male finger a moaning whore who's draped across the bar with her tits out – jiggling with each rough thrust of his hand.

It's tempting to jerk my hardening cock as I drag on my stick, blowing smoke rings skyward, listening to the hungry moans and conversations tittering around me. Picking for threads on Princess Kyzari's whereabouts.

She knows I love to chase. That I fucking *feed* off it. I've decided that's why she chose to hand herself to the Creators.

Why she chose to *run*.

When I find her, I'll give her exactly what she refuses to admit she wants.

Me.

The barmaid slides meat-laden plates before myself and Terros, boasting hunks of chargrilled colk wafting rich, fragrant steam. I cut into my serving, revealing shreds of fatty pink flesh I couple with some of the creamy slaw, moaning around the gluttonous mouthful.

'Good, right?' I ask, looking at Terros.

He grunts, stuffing his mouth with another laden bite, stare stabbed toward the back wall while he chews.

Moody fucker. Not even a *thank you*. Doesn't he know manners are important?

Maybe I will make him suffer after all. Lash him a little.

I finish my meal, drain my mug, then stub my fifth smoke stick in the tray as I ease off the stool. 'I'm turning in.'

'Were we not going to debrief first?' one of the Arithians asks, frowning at me. Probably pissed I didn't buy him and his comrade a meal, too.

I only buy meals for males I'm about to slaughter, so really, he's the lucky one.

'Debrief?' I ask, playing dumb.

'Yes.' He cuts a beady glance toward Terros, who's still munching through his meal, pretending he's not listening – that he hasn't been asked to report back once he returns to Dhomm. 'Since we're . . . you know, *splitting off*.'

Since they're expected back in Arithia with any information they gleaned about Dhomm's military status. Information they didn't get since they ended up locked in their rooms under beaded guard the entire time.

I shrug. 'Not my fault you failed.'

His face pales.

I've got one job: find the Princess. Something I *will* achieve. Their shortcomings don't belong to me, the useless fucks.

'I've got a warm mouth waiting for me in my sleep space, so unless you want to drop to your knees and choke on me while I tell you everything you want to know, you can practice some fucking patience.' I snatch my cloak and key from the barmaid who comes to clear my plate. 'We'll do it with the rise before we part ways.'

If I can be bothered, that is.

I pull the door open, a smile cutting across my face when I see the shapely piece of ass stoking the large fireplace at the back of the room.

Warm satisfaction spreads through me at the sight of her clothed in scraps of lace visible through the sheer dark-green cloak she's draped in, black hair piled on the top of her head. Her legs are long, hips round, waist tight – a curvy elegance to her that shoots straight to my hardening cock.

'Fuck,' I grind out, kicking the door shut behind me, tossing my cloak and gloves on the ground. I stalk forward, lifting loose tendrils of hair off her elegant neck, wrapping my hand around the back of it and gripping hard.

Perfect fit.

I pinch the edge of her cloak, easing it off her pale shoulder.

'Aren't you a *treat*,' I groan, unbuttoning my leather pants. I reach in and fist my solid cock in slow, tight drags.

Just my type.

She stuffs the metal poker deeper into the flames, making the sizzling logs crumble and hiss. 'You know,' she murmurs in a smooth voice that pumps more blood into my loins, 'I'm not really a fan of fire.'

Weird thing to say to the male who just bought your body for the slumber.

'Why not?'

She makes a soft humming sound. 'Might have something to do with the time I spent in the Pits.'

'Fighting pits?'

'Mm-hmm.'

Ahh, role-play. Not what I ordered, but fuck it. I'll bite.

'Which ones?' I ask, easing her cloak off her other shoulder, feeling it drop to the floor at our feet.

'The Pits of Khindard . . .'

I chuckle against her warm flesh. 'Sweetheart, nobody makes it out of those pits alive. That's half the fun.' I use the tip of my finger to paint a slithering line down her spine. 'Unless you're trying to tell me you're *Fire Lark*.'

This time, my chuckle is met with her own lilting laugh.

'*Glei te ah no veirie*,' she whispers, and all the breath escapes my lungs in the same instance her hand swings back.

Something sharp impales my thigh before she tosses a wooden handle into the fire, dispersing a blast of sparks as a chilling, *nulling* silence settles within me.

What.

The.

Fuck.

I stumble back, cradling my throat, my chest jerking for breath I can't catch. My other hand drops to my thigh, sweeping through the warm, wet liquid leaking from the wound, fingers coming up so I can see the—

Blood.

The bitch stabbed me with an *iron pin*.

I reach for the daggers stuffed in my bandolier, finding both empty, looking up in the same instant she tosses them in the fire, too.

My lungs squeeze so tight I'm certain they're about to collapse as all the blood drains from my face, realization kicking me in the gut.

She's been hunting me. The bitch has been fucking *hunting* me.

I stumble toward the door, clawing at the spot where the handle's supposed to be, but all that's there is a fucking hole I shove my fingers down, whipping them away when they slice against something sharp.

Razors.

The cunt.

My bulging eyes threaten to burst from my sockets as I bash the door with my bloody fist.

The air displaces to my right, and something smashes against my temple, a burst of sharp pain pitching through my skull—

Gone.

The Other

CHAPTER 88

The Other straddles Rekk Zharos while studying him with overt curiosity, wondering where she should start. Which part of him she should burn first.

Difficult decision, given there's so much of him to play with. And an entire slumber to have her fun.

The tips of her fingers tingle with bloodlusting anticipation . . .

She reaches for his left wrist, making sure the bind is as well secured to him as it is to the palletpost, then repeats the process with his other hand and both feet, all the while musing over the silence inside her. Not even a flicker of presence seeping up.

The one she loves did not fall easily into the watery den. She battled and slashed, kicked and screamed, then only went still and quiet once The Other packed her in a tomb of ice.

To *protect* her.

This *Rekk* must suffer a similar fate to the one he bestowed upon his dragon, something her precious Raeve would've struggled with. Much as she acts fierce and impervious to pain, it's mostly because she tosses the hurtful things down to gather like tombstones within The Other's den.

The Other understands loss, death, and pain differently from Raeve, who is but a hatchling in her eyes. But Raeve will grow. Adapt. *Embrace*, and therefore conquer – if she is open to it.

But first . . .

The Other slaps Rekk's cheek, probably a little too hard considering the way his head cracks to the side so fast his neck almost snaps and ruins all the fun.

He groans, opening his eyes – blue like the glaciers in The Shade. A nostalgic color that doesn't fit in his vile face.

No matter. She will scoop them out and rid him of them before the end.

His pupils tighten, his face turning a sickly shade of gray.

A sharp smile stretches across The Other's face.

Rekk thrashes, lifting his hips, trying to buck her off, bellowing, '*Hoar heg*!' over and over again.

She can't be certain, but she wonders if he's trying to say 'You're dead' through the material she stuffed in his mouth.

The Other chuffs.

Strictly speaking, he's not incorrect.

She pushes off and sways toward the fire with animalistic grace, gripping the end of a stoker roasting in the flames, poking at embers that glint off her black, glitter-kissed eyes. She pulls it out, the space alive with Rekk's panicked grunting sounds as he jerks and wrestles against his restraints.

Then he stills, eyes widening on the sharp tip of the metal tool blazing with a hot, radiant beat.

She prowls toward him in long-legged strides. 'You know, I saw what you did to that Moonplume,' she muses, climbing onto the pallet again. 'I heard how she *wailed*.' She brings the poker's fiery tip to his left eye, sizzling the ends of his lashes, lacing the air with the potent musk of burning hair.

His bloodshot eyes water.

The Other clicks her tongue, whipping the weapon away. 'No, you protected her eyes, didn't you? That was nice.'

A small mercy that was not bestowed upon *herself* many cycles ago.

'I'll deal with them in a different way.'

She drops the blazing poker to his naked chest and draws a jagged line.

Rekk screams, his muffled cries of pain turning to whittled whimpers, his tendons taut and risen. He begins to tremble beneath her – the room packing so full of the smell of roasted flesh that The Other realizes how hungry she is. Not that she intends to eat him.

No.

Raeve was quite repulsed when she learned The Other had chewed off this male's finger, leading The Other to spend some time pondering whether or not she should be more considerate with the way she uses her host's pliant, precious body.

Eating this Rekk is probably a step too far. Unfortunate, considering how delicious his fried flesh smells—

No.

Must not.

Shoving down her natural urges, The Other lifts the weapon from the line of sizzled flesh. 'Though you may not have understood Líri's pained sounds, *I did.*'

His eyes bulge, and he looks at The Other like she's utterly mad, his nostrils flared, chest bucking with the violent beat of his panicked breaths.

'Unlucky for you,' she sneers, tipping her head to the side, 'I'm here to show you *exactly* how she felt.'

The acrid smell of his urine fills the room.

She paints another sizzling trail across his chest, down his tensing abdomen. Rekk jerks and jerks – fierce, primal satisfaction shaping The Other's features into a vision of savage glee.

'Then I'm going to use your *own* metal spurs to dig holes all over your body, before slashing what's left of you with that whipping tool you cart around.'

Another groan as she digs the poker deep . . . *deeper* . . . then tosses the thing. It clatters across the stone floor, coming to a halt by the wall.

Rekk chokes and heaves, his wide, wild stare bouncing around the room, like he's searching for something that can help free him of this predicament. Too bad for him, the one she loves was thorough with her preparation. Impressively so.

There is nothing here to save him.

'*Vaghth*,' The Other whispers, and Rekk's gaze whips up to meet hers.

She hears his heart skip a beat. *Feeds* on the pulse of his surprise as a bulb of flame flutters from the open fireplace and settles in the palm of her clawed hand.

She can almost hear the thump of his thoughts, no doubt churning over the fact that she can wield three elemental songs – not just Clode and Bulder as he'd witnessed in the Undercity.

He doesn't know about Rayne. Doesn't know it's actually *four*. Neither does the one she loves, The Other having gone out of her way to absorb Ignos's spitting, scalding tune so it doesn't trigger her strong but delicate host.

Until she's ready.

She tilts her head, the motion smooth and animalistic. 'Do you know how it feels for a Moonplume to scald in the sun's harsh rays, *Rekk Zharos?*'

He shakes his head, whimpering, his stare flicking between the fire in her hand and her rattling leer.

'A bit like this,' she sneers, then paints his face in flames.

Veya

CHAPTER 89

There's a coldness about this place that digs all the way to your marrow.

I blame it on the fact that I'm not used to it. That I was born and raised north of the wall. Toss me amongst endless plains of snow, flurried storms, and breaths that make your lungs feel frostbitten, and I'm suddenly questioning every life decision that led me here, to this moment – walking through the sable halls of Arithia's grand Imperial Palace dressed in the stark-silver garb of a servant.

My long, flowing skirt rustles with every step, a plain blouse buttoned to my nape where it meets a collar of fur that matches the tufted cuffs around my wrists. Not nearly enough layers to battle this bone-biting chill.

The vast size of this palace is boggling, the building cut into the side of a jagged, snow-covered mountain like spears of obsidian shot up from the ground, reaching for the numerous rounded moons nesting in the sky. All of Arithia is cast in a whimsical pearly glow that penetrates through the many windows in this haunting palace. *So* many windows that, with every turn up the obsidian stairway, I'm granted another fragmented view through panes crafted to look like shattered glaciers, made from thousands of shards in every tone of blue, silver, and white.

On and on I go, up the ever-winding stairs that are buffed to a high gleam, skirt shushing in my wake. Unsure why I'm going *up*.

Something in my gut, I guess. *Not* something I want to look in the eye any longer than I have to.

Get in.

Get the diary.

Get the fuck out.

Coming to an ornamental mirror on the wall, I pause, tucking strands of pale hair behind my pointed ears, checking my sharp, pretty features and blue eyes for any cracks in my imitative appearance – jarring as it is to see myself as *not me*.

Truly, very weird.

My silver, appearance-altering bangle hangs heavy around my wrist as I rearrange some strands back into place. A bangle with a hidden spike I used to poke both my finger and that of the female now bound, gagged, and unconscious in a cupboard in the servants' quarters on the ground floor. With a pillow under her head – because I'm nice like that.

Too bad I didn't think to ask the poor thing for directions before I knocked her out. This palace is a labyrinth, each doorway bracketed by stern, silver-armored guards known as Thorns, the hallways haunted by a constant stream of stone-faced maids bustling about the place, keeping its many sharp edges perfectly polished.

A bit like a gleaming trophy Tyroth is obviously *very* proud of. The fuck.

A dark-haired female dressed in the same garb as myself pours down the stairway in a swish of silver, her eyes widening when she sees me. 'Ayda?' She nips a glance over her shoulder, her next words a quiet hiss. 'You're not supposed to be down here.'

Ayda.

Guess that's my name. Good to know.

She slows, frowning. 'Are you okay? What are you doing?'

Hunting for the ancient diary of Elluin Raeve Neván, hoping it hasn't turned to compost in a wall somewhere.

'Well, you see—'

'Have you already been up there?'

That's a baited question I certainly didn't prepare for. Beginning to think I might've pricked the wrong maid . . .

'No?'

Her eyes almost bug out of her head. 'You're expected in the King's chambers *right now*.'

My heart lurches.

Actually, that's exactly where I need to go.

'I lost my way,' I say, offering her an awkward smile. 'I didn't sleep well. In fact' – I rub my temple – 'I'm suddenly all confused about the levels. I think I lost track somewhere down—'

She snatches my arm, tucks it into the crook of hers, and tugs me farther up the stairs, past two Thorns moving against our grain before she leans close, speaking in a hushed tone. 'We're on eleven. You have another twenty-three to climb.'

'Of course.' I let loose a soft laugh similar to the one I heard the *real* Ayda make while I trailed her momentarily in the bowels of the palace, right before I knocked her unconscious. 'Silly me.'

The female pulls a silken dusting stick from the pocket of her apron and wraps my hand around the cold handle. 'You need to at least *look* useful going in there or the other females in the palace will talk, and that will displease him greatly. You know what he's like.'

Yes. I *do* know what he's like.

Sadistic.

Fucking.

Asshole.

I flash her another smile. 'Thank you. I left mine . . . somewhere.'

Muttering something beneath her breath, she peels away, then turns back down the stairs, disappearing from sight.

I keep shoving up the twisting stairway that seems to go on and on, doing my best to count the levels. Easier said than done since some are stouter than others. Some, the stairway is woven through the air of wide-open atriums like a black squiggle – the atmosphere spiced with the sweet, intoxicating smell of illuminated flowers in full bloom, their glowing heads tipped to the windows.

I step onto a level with a lofty ceiling veined in silver threads, a grand double door directly ahead that's bracketed by two sets of Thorns, their shoulder pads flaring to pointed peaks. Silver helmets cover most of their faces, wings splayed from the sides that accentuate the tapered tips of their ears.

Each of them wields a long iron sword, pointed down, both hands wrapped around the hilt. Swords that are almost longer than *me*.

My breath catches at the sight of the door, something inside my brain wiggling like a worm I can't quite manage to pluck free and inspect.

Even if it weren't for the extra guards, I'm somehow certain this is the place.

This is the sleepsuite where Elluin died.

My gaze darts from guard to guard. 'I've got . . . dusting to do,' I say, waving my stick.

None of them even glance my way, though one of them raises a brow.

Right.

Permission to proceed.

Clearing my throat, I move forward when the door swings inward, releasing a familiar ashen scent.

My heart leaps into my throat.

I slide back a step, dipping my head.

Holding.

Paralyzed.

In my direct line of sight, a silver thorn-tipped boot pierces my view as I'm shoved within the crackling atmosphere of Tyroth Vaegor. Heart thrashing.

Thoughts churning.

Certain he's looking at me with scarcely veiled vitriol in his eyes, like I'm a bug he wants to burn. Certain he's about to shape his mangled thoughts into words that'll crush my throat with their monstrous fists. That'll make me feel small and weak and so fucking quiet – my tongue too heavy to speak.

There's a long beat of silence, and I find my trembling hand tightening around the duster, the other reaching for the dagger I have stuffed in the deep pocket of my skirt—

'You're late, Ayda.'

The foreign name snaps at my spine. Reminds me that I'm not Tyroth's sister – not at the moment. I'm not the one that took his mother from him. The one he *hates*, and has since I was far too young to hate him back.

To even understand.

I force my fingers to loosen their hold on the weapon I promised I wouldn't use, pull my hand from my pocket, and fist the fabric of my skirt instead.

'Apologies, Sire.' I dip lower, willing my heart to ease up on the white-knuckled blows to my ribs. 'I overslept. Won't happen again.'

My breath snags as his fingers pinch my chin, forcing me to

look into his cruel, cutthroat eyes. One green, like Mah's apparently were. One pitch black, just like the pit of his septic soul.

His black hair is half pulled up, the rest hanging loose around his shoulders, tumbling all the way to his elbows. His beard is, as always, adorned with a trio of beads.

Clear.

Brown.

Red.

He's bigger than I remember – two heads taller than me and almost as wide as Kaan in the shoulders – his presence one of scarcely veiled chaos that contrasts his impeccable silver garb.

'Well. Nice of you to finally show up,' he says with that cutting sort of serenity that always makes me picture myself bleeding out with a stab wound I didn't realize he'd stuck me with. 'Tell me, Ayda. Do you think that carrying my bastard brings you certain . . . privileges?'

My mind empties so fast I'm certain the ground tips beneath my feet. Like the entire palace just dislodged from the toothy mountainscape and is now swaying side to side, trying to decide which direction it wants to fall.

What do I say to that?

'I have a child. An heir – disobedient as she is,' he grits out, like there's a fireball of frustration welling on his tongue. 'I don't need another, and my tolerance of your condition dissolves the moment you no longer prove useful to me.'

My guts knot, words choking past my swollen throat. 'I . . . Of course, Sire. Apologies. And thank you.'

'For?'

'Your tolerance.'

Definitely picked the wrong maid to prick.

A line forms between his brows, though it smooths when a parchment lark flutters close, quickly returning again when the damn thing dips between us and nudges against *my* chest.

My heart drops so fast it almost falls out my ass.

'This is unusual,' he says in that chilling way he speaks, snatching the thing, keeping his eyes on me as he unfolds it while my pulse pounds in rhythm with my slashing thoughts.

Fuck.

Fuck.

Fuck.

'I—'

He waves it at me, both brows bumping toward his hairline. 'It's blank.'

Internally, I smile. Because it's not blank.

Not at all.

Whenever either of us are beyond the safety of Dhomm, Kaan and I write our notes in invisible ink illuminated only by dragon-flame we both carry a weald of.

Precautions. Never came in handy until now.

'A dud, perhaps.' He's swift to rip the wings off the thing and toss its nonfluttering corpse to the floor – a visceral reminder of my brother's brutality I didn't need.

'I have business to attend to, but I'll be back in a couple of hours. Go inside, get on your knees with a polish cloth, and make yourself *useful* until I return.' He turns and stalks toward the stairs. 'Keep me waiting again and I'll have your head.'

The tips of my fingers tingle with the sudden, violent urge to spray his blood across the perfectly polished floor, my upper lip twitching to pull back from my canines.

My foot kicks forward, hand digging into my pocket as if to grip my blade so I can leap and *slash*—

No.

I tug my hand free and fist it at my side, trying to squeeze the tingles away.

One, I said I wouldn't kill him and start an impromptu war Kaan's not yet fully prepared for.

Two, not like this. Not coming at him from behind, wearing the skin of another. I want to look him in the eye. Make him bleed the way I've bled. Hurt the way I've hurt. I want to spit the words that have been festering in my mouth for far too long, bruising my gums every time I stand paralyzed in his presence.

Anything less will be like a sip of water that turns to lava in my throat.

I tell myself that over and over as I watch Tyroth move down the stairs, relieved I spent a few hours folded over an ice boulder on the city's outskirts, vomiting from this dagger of dread lodged in my gut. If I'd had anything left in there, it would be on the floor at my feet right now. Or splattered against Tyroth's silver boots.

Can't believe I knocked out his pregnant mistress. How horrible, when the poor thing is already living a slumber-terror.

I make a mental note to pad her pockets with enough bloodstone to buy her a better life before I wake her from her forced sleep and go on my way.

Tyroth disappears from sight, and I release a shaken exhale, my body loosening in places I didn't know had tightened. I spin, picking up the deceased lark and tucking it in my pocket, then move into the vast chambers, letting the doors click shut behind me.

Eyes squeezed shut, I rest my head against the ebony wood and pull my lungs so full they ache, trying to shift the tightness from my chest. I pass the duster from one hand to the other, shaking both out, dashing the last of the tingles away.

Get the diary.

Get out.

Wake Ayda up so she can rush up here and avoid getting her head lopped off.

I open my eyes, widening as I take in the stark-black sitting room with panoramic views of the glittering city far below, seeing his sleepsuite through an open door to the left. I move through, pausing at the foot of the huge obsidian four-poster pallet.

My eyes narrow on a large mirror on the far wall . . .

It has to be there.

I make for it, cast a quick glance over my shoulder, then set the duster on the pallet and slide the mirror sideways, expecting to see a hollow—

My heart drops.

Nothing. Just a flat wall.

I appraise the space . . .

There's nothing else on the walls in this sterile room. Meaning she can't possibly have hidden it here. But this is where she spent the last chapter of her life. I know that for a fact – that she was too unwell to even make it into the streets and see her folk. To celebrate the impending birth. Something that meant so much to all Arithians, since conceiving has never come easy to those who don the Aether Stone.

I look to the balcony, realization slapping me so hard my knees almost give way.

Half the room was crumbled when her Moonplume broke through the wall after Elluin passed away, scooping up her lifeless body she then carried into the sky where she curled around her and died.

Perhaps she tore up the diary, too?

'Shit,' I mutter, dropping to the pallet, dragging my hands down my – *Ayda's* – face.

I should've thought of that before I flew all the way here.

A deep wash of failure sweeps over me, the weight of it shoving me back onto the thick, cushiony pallet, tossing my arms out as I stare at the black velvet canopy.

I've been compulsively chasing a truth that doesn't belong to me. That never did. Guess this is what I get.

Sweet fuck all.

Creators, this room feels morbid. And cold. What a shitty place to be stuck – rise after rise – pitted with the knowledge that you'll probably die giving birth. Probably too exhausted to even walk to the balcony and get a clear view of . . . the . . . moons . . .

I lift my head, looking toward the balcony door – panes of glass that frame the sky littered with balled-up gray, pearly and iridescent moons.

My heart skips a beat.

If she were pallet-ridden, she would've hidden it within *reach*. Surely.

Why make things harder on herself?

Frowning, I sit up, imagining my belly is laden with life. Imagining I have a diadem on my brow that's draining me to death, making it almost impossible for me to draw enough energy to breathe, let alone nourish my youngling into existence. Imagining that I'd want to look out at those moons right there. Mostly – the one belonging to . . .

Haedeon.

I edge myself off the side of the mattress, dropping straight down onto my ass on the floor beside it, looking out the balcony door to a perfectly framed view of Hae's Perch. A sad smile lifts the corner of my lips . . .

This feels right.

Devastatingly *right*.

I plunge my left arm under the risen pallet, eyes on that gimpy-winged moon spilling its silver luster upon Arithia as I feel around the back post.

Across the back wall.

My hand pushes into a jagged hollow, a lump forming in my throat as my fingers graze across the face of a leather-bound book.

There you are . . .

I pull it into my lap, tracing my finger over the black and silver depiction of Kaan's málmr. Something she must've painted on the otherwise black front.

The backs of my eyes sting at the sight.

'Oh, Elluin,' I whisper, hand trembling. I nip a glance toward the door before I lift the front cover, flipping through the yellowed flaps of parchment, each so beautifully scrawled upon. Even when she was small, her handwriting was immaculate – all dainty curls and twirls.

Just looking at each entry makes me feel as though I'm tumbling through a veil into another world seen only through *her* eyes.

First the young her. Then the adolescent.

Then the *mature*.

Lacking the time to read the entire thing right here, right now, but *also* lacking a single shred of patience, I flip straight to the end – to the final three entries. Immediately regretting it, realizing I shouldn't have read this here.

I shouldn't have read this at all.

My hand flies up and cups my mouth that I can't seem to shut, my heart growing more laden with each barbed word I swallow. With each soul-crushing, life-changing word that doesn't belong to me.

But I'm already there. I'm already invested.

Intertwined.

Reaching the final entry, I pull a shuddered breath and force myself to continue.

Diary Entry

Elluin Neván

Age: 21 phases

5,000,042 phases After Stone

Every cycle I grow bigger, yet weaker in my bones. Almost too weak to reach into my hiding spot to retrieve my diary and read of happier times that remind me there's still some good in this world.

The city folk celebrate in the streets each dae, as if my youngling is already here. As if the ashes of my loved ones don't still taint the very air we breathe.

If Tyroth suspects the babe isn't his, he hasn't let on – not that we speak at all. Not that I have anything I want to speak to him about.

I've heard from one of his loyal aides – the only folk I'm allowed contact with – that a Bloodlace has arrived on dragonback this rise. If she's here to test my youngling's blood once I give birth, the paternal line won't draw in Tyroth's direction.

It'll draw north – to Kaan.

All I'm allowed to do is wither here, bleeding my life force into this youngling, occasionally drawing enough energy to slide off the pallet and garner myself a clear view of Haedeon's moon. I sing to it, and I swear I can hear it singing back.

Like it's calling me.

I want to curl up with Slátra – to be with her while I labor – but I struggle to move on my own anymore. All but stuck on this pallet where Mah and Pah died. Where I pretended to conceive a youngling that was already seeded inside me. This pallet that used to be filled with love and song but now reeks of death and pain.

A battle is coming, I can feel it in my bones. Like my body is shoring up the courage to charge into a war I don't think I'm going to survive. Even if I do, I feel like there's a scythe hanging over my head, waiting to slice.

Either way, my heart is heavy with a seed of understanding I can't dislodge. That I will climb back upon the pallet once I whisper goodbye to Haedeon's moon, and I won't rise from it again.

Casting my stare up at the sky, I sob through short, sharp breaths that are so far from adequate . . .

She lied for us. For *him.*

Kaan.

She lied for the youngling she carried all the way from their love den in Dhomm to this cold, caustic room where she'd lost so much already, all because she believed the words that spat out of my pah's mouth. And for what?

To die right here.

To not see Kyzari grow.

For Tyroth to raise Kaan's daughter as his own.

I close the diary, a venomous truth settling in my chest like a serpent poised to strike . . .

These pages are going to rip the world to shreds.

The Scavenger King

EPILOGUE

From deep within the inky clutches of a shadow too dense for the average eye to see within, the Scavenger King studies the young female fae coiled in the corner of her cell, rocking back and forth, hands threaded deep into her pale hair. Eyes squeezed shut, she mumbles a chain of incoherent words perhaps hewn from the crevices of her swelling insanity.

She's speaking to someone, of that he's certain. Just as certain as he is that this particular *someone* only exists within the confines of her peculiar mind.

His head tips sideways as he studies her more deeply: red lips, large eyes mantled with a thick fan of lashes, a shapely elegance the likes of only *one* he's encountered before.

His *Fire Lark*.

She holds such uncanny resemblance, but her eyes are softer, her skin a touch darker. And though his Fire Lark came to him without words, this female . . . well.

She has plenty. Entire rambling conversations. They just make no sense.

To him.

Yet, on she mumbles, the dark dents beneath her eyes a tribute to the diadem clinging to her brow, its fine silver tendrils seeming to meld with her skin.

Her face twists, a tear slipping down her sallow cheek . . .

The Scavenger King watches it drip off her chin and seep into her soiled tunic, a crease forming between his brow as he muddles over this other . . . *difference*.

His Fire Lark never cried. Not once. She bit into life like some wild animal, snarling around her messy feast.

She did not leave scraps. She simply *consumed.*

This female, however, exists delicately, with all the decorum of someone raised in a palace with servants to feed her, groom her, teach her.

A loving pah to *speak* for her.

Stepping free of the shadows, Arkyn clears his throat.

The female stops rocking, eyes snapping open – glossy bold-blue orbs staring at him through the gloom. 'You *will* release me,' she bites out, dashing the tear from her cheek.

Arkyn clicks his tongue, glancing around her cell, taking in its plush details: a crumpled blanket, a straw pallet, a tray bearing an empty bowl from one of her regular meals. She even has a wooden bucket so she's not forced to shit where she sleeps. More home comforts than he offers other prisoners.

She is, after all, his niece.

Not that she knows that. Not that *any* of his half-brothers knows he exists, as far as he's aware.

But they will.

'That's *exactly* what I've come to offer,' he says, crouching before the curve of bone bars and easing his hand through, a piece of parchment pinched between two outstretched fingers. 'Release.'

Her eyes widen.

She scurries forward in a clatter of iron chains, snatching the piece of parchment and smoothing it on the ground. She frowns up at him, tucking strips of matted hair behind her pointed ear. 'It's blank.'

'I need you to sign your name,' Arkyn states, threading a runed quill through the bars.

She takes it, scratching out her signature while he studies the pretty skin on her hands, stuffing down the urge to burn it . . . if just a little bit. See if she, too, refuses to scream.

He certainly doesn't acknowledge that it's more complicated than that. That he's *resentful* of her plush life. Of the way her pah dotes on her.

Loves her.

Nor does he acknowledge that he's curious to see how *she* would fare were she cast into the Boltanic Plains and told to run while a roar of fire nips at her heels. Sizzles her flesh.

Would she carve out a life for herself in the barren hollows of an unloved terrain? Would she forge her weakness into a fearsome strength?

Would she *thrive*?

She passes the note and quill back through the bars, a hopeless sheen to her eyes.

No wonder his half-brother protected her so. She's but a pretty ornamental flower, and flowers singe in the face of flames.

He decides she would not thrive at all. She would die as he almost did too many times to count.

He leaves without words or flair, the torn hem of his cloak fluttering in his wake as he moves through the elaborate tangle of cold, dark burrows, only stopping once he comes to his personal suite. He sits at his perfectly polished desk lit by a blazing candelabra stolen from someone long ago and spreads the parchment upon the tabletop.

He studies the bounty of treasures surrounding him – his suite a conglomeration of only the best, most *interesting* bits he's scavenged over the phases.

The Princess had fallen into his lap as a sign from the Creators, he was certain. Too good an offer to pass up, given she immediately demanded he send a lark to the Burn King himself.

Not a single mention of her doting pah.

Handy, seeing he has no interest in The Shade. The only seat he cares about is the bronze throne of The Burn that rightfully belongs to *him*.

This is it. The very moment he's been channeling toward for so long.

Arkyn sits straighter, quill poised as he looks down. For the first time, he examines the flat of parchment, pausing.

Smiling.

She signed, yes . . . but amongst the scrawl, in a tiny, almost indiscernible script she did well to meld with the shape of her name, is a single sentence:

He chuckles, scratching his own note upon the empty space before folding the parchment lark down its activation lines, giving it life, whispering a name upon its fluttering wings.

She has more bite than he'd anticipated.

Perhaps he was wrong about her. Perhaps she *would* survive after all. The same, however, cannot be said about her uncle.

No . . .

He has plans for the great *Kaan Vaegor*, who took Arkyn's revenge for himself, and none of them are pretty.

The parchment lark takes flight, soaring from the Scavenger King's personal suite and out into the halls. It weaves through the underground warren toward the world outside, bypassing a *different* lark on its way past the cells . . .

A small, wobbly one with a tear in its wing and a blood splotch on its tail.

The damaged lark dips between two bars to where Princess Kyzari is bound on the ground in a ball beneath her filthy blanket, the scoop of her hand a landing pad the little lark dives toward – face-first, crushing its nose against her fingers.

Kyzari flinches. Opens her eyes.

The lark flips onto its back, bearing three small, perfectly scripted letters upon the underside of its belly . . .

nee

Family Tree

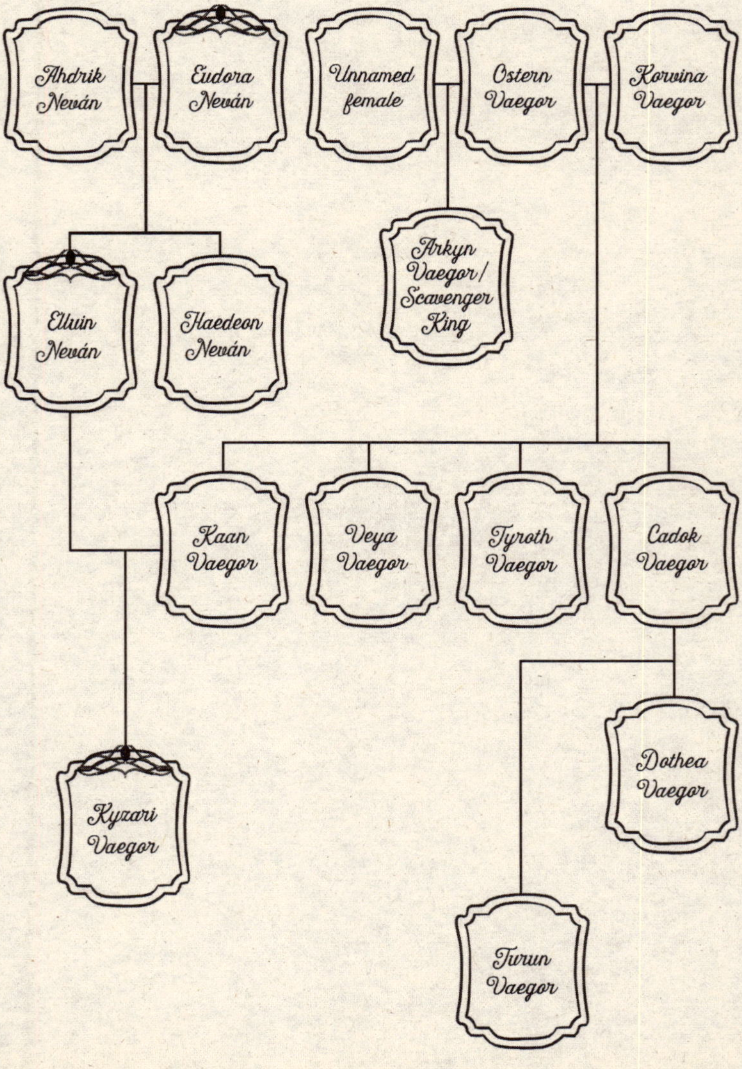
Ahdrik Neván
Eudora Neván
Unnamed female
Ostern Vaegor
Korvina Vaegor
Arkyn Vaegor / Scavenger King
Elluin Neván
Haedeon Neván
Kaan Vaegor
Veya Vaegor
Tyroth Vaegor
Cadok Vaegor
Dothea Vaegor
Kyzari Vaegor
Turun Vaegor

GLOSSARY

AGE & TIME EXPLAINED

• AS/After Stone
The tracking of time/phases – after the Aether Stone was gifted to the Neváns.

• BS/Before Stone
The tracking of time/phases – before the Aether Stone was gifted to the Neváns.

• Aurora Ribbons
A band of silver, luminous ribbons that are tethered to both poles of the world (north and south) and orbits the world on this axis. The aurora ribbons are what folk use to track their sleep/awake time.

• Aurora Cycle
A complete aurora cycle is the amount of time it takes for the aurora ribbons to orbit the entire world once. An aurora cycle is equivalent to our twenty-four hour day.

• Aurora Rise/Rising
The time of the aurora cycle when the aurora is dawning on the eastern horizon.

• Aurora Fall/Falling
The time of the aurora cycle when the aurora is setting on the western horizon.

• Dae
The time of the aurora cycle when the aurora is tracking through the sky overhead. This is the time when the folk of this world are often awake.

• Slumber
The time of the aurora cycle when no aurora ribbons paint the sky. This is the time when the folk of this world sleep.

• Phase
1,000 aurora cycles (akin to a year). The aurora ribbons grow marginally thicker over the course of the phase, then thin out on the thousandth cycle. This ebbing rhythm tracks the phase from start to finish.

• Eon
100 phases / 100,000 aurora cycles.

• Age explained
1 phase of life = 1,000 aurora cycles.
24 phases of life = 24,000 aurora cycles.

TERMS

• Aether Stone
The small, black stone (the size of an adult thumb pad) that is set amongst a silver diadem. This diadem fuses with a host's head and is guarded by the Neván family line. Caelis (God of Aether) is within the stone.

• Arithia
Capital of The Shade.

• Bhoggith
The Moltenmaw nesting grounds. This is in The Fade and is a vast stretch of boggy wasteland. There are stable mounds that the Moltenmaws form their nests atop of, building great circular globes from trees and branches and laying their eggs within. Once their eggs begin to rock, the paternal Moltenmaw blows flame upon the structure – a vital part of the hatching process.

• Binding ceremony
Much the same as a marriage ceremony.

• Bloodlace
Someone who is gifted with a unique power over blood. They can source familial origin, use someone's blood to make them hurt or feel pleasure, etc.

• Bothaim
Neutral city. Residence of the Tri-Council.

• Bound
The equivalent to a spouse. To say we are 'bound' is also to say we are 'married'.

• Clip
A circular notch cut into the peak of a fae's ear, almost as if a tiny creature took a bite from the shell. If someone has a clip, it signifies that they are a null, and that they can't hear any of the

elemental songs. This is not something that is prevalent everywhere – just in specific kingdoms.

• Daga-Mórrk
One so bonded with their dragon that they can harness its strength and fire. This connection is more myth than reality.

• Dhomm
Capital of The Burn.

• Dragon Bloodstone
Mined from the ground in areas where dragon blood has been spilled. It's the main form of currency in The Fade and The Shade. If ground up and consumed, it's packed full of medicinal properties.

• Dragonsight
The ability to see the trace of old runes – something that can only otherwise be seen via the light of a dragon's flame.

• Drelgad
A segment of the wall that is dedicated to The Fade's army, housing its fresh conscripts.

• Elding Blade
An assassin for the Fíur du Ath.

• Elemental Bead
These are worn to show if an individual can hear any of the elemental songs. There are different fashions for different kingdoms. In The Fade, they are worn as earrings. In The Burn or The Shade, they adorn the wearer's hair, beard, or garb.

Red: *Ignos (fire)*
Blue: *Rayne (water)*
Clear: *Clode (air)*
Brown: *Bulder (ground)*

• Fíur du Ath
The rebellious group who are working to counteract the tyranny leeching across the kingdoms (predominantly The Fade). Their reach stretches all over the world.

• Fleshthread
Someone who is trained in the art of using runes to mend flesh, muscle, and organs.

• Gondragh
The Sabersythe nesting grounds. This is directly beneath the sun where it is very hot and uninhabitable for most folk. Very rocky, with lots of volcanoes and rivers of lava. The Sabersythes nest within the nooks and hollows in these volcanoes. Once their eggs begin to rock, they either scoop lava from the volcanoes and spit it into the nests or douse the nests in dragonflame – a vital part of the hatching process.

• Gore
Capital of The Fade.

• Grandmah
'Grandma'

• Grandpah
'Grandpa'

• Hatching Hut
A hut that's generally on the outskirts of the different dragon nesting grounds. This is usually where someone who has stolen an egg will make camp so they can successfully hatch the baby dragons in their natural habitats, ensuring a safe and healthy hatchling.

• Johkull Clan
One of the many warrior clans that reside in the Boltanic Plains. These clans are renowned for producing strong and gifted warriors. Kaan grew up with the Johkull Clan.

• Kholu
The one foretold to bear an offspring who will eventually tether the moons to the sky indefinitely.

• Mah
'Mother'

• Mahmi
'Mommy'

• Málmr
A hand-carved pendant that those in the warrior clans of the Boltanic Plains offer someone they are courting. They are often made from things like dragonscale, bone, copper, or stone.

• Mindweft
Someone who has the unique ability to dig into another's mind. They are extremely rare.

• Netheryn
The Moonplume nesting grounds. This is situated in The Shade, at the southernmost pole of the world. Here, the bitterly cold environment is inhospitable to most folk. The Moonplumes nest on giant hexagon pillars of ice. Once their eggs begin to rock, the paternal Moonplume will either blow its icy flames upon the eggs or pack ice and snow atop them – a vital part of the hatching process.

• Null
Someone who doesn't hear any of the elemental songs. In certain kingdoms, their ears are clipped to show this.

• Pah
'Father'

• Pahpi
'Daddy'

• Parchment Lark
Runed squares of parchment that have activation lines. Once folded (into the shape of a lark) these notes will flutter to the one the

message is intended for. A reliable form of communication in this world.

• Reídi
The dotted tattoo on the back of a warrior from the Boltanic Plains. Each dot represents a victory won, and a heavily tattooed back is a show of great strength and honor.

• Runi
Someone who has learned how to wield the symbols found in the ancient tomb some believe Caelis (God of Aether) wrote in his desperation to be heard. They wear a white bead and/or white cloaks boasting buttons down their center seam that pinch the cloak into place. These buttons are stamped with different symbols that announce the Runi's talents. For different levels of skill, the buttons are made from different materials – wood being the elementary level, diamond being the most advanced.

• Skripi
A luck/strategy game played throughout the world. The shards that are used are similar to playing cards, but boasting pictures of different creatures.

• The Burn
The northern third of the world. It's always sunny here, so it's very hot, and it storms often in certain parts. There are lots of rainforests and vast, sandy plains, as well as vast bodies of water.

• The Ditch
The main thoroughfare in the city of Gore.

• The Fade
This is the middle third of the world – the girthy band of the globe. Here, the clouds are always colorful, as it's forever cast in the light of a 'golden hour'. It's cold here, often snowy, never rainy, though it sometimes sleets. There is a massive stone wall that circles this girthy part of the world like a belt. Most of The Fade's civilization have built homes within it. In heavily populated areas, a trench is dug down into the wall, effectively splitting it in two – creating a sheltered ditch with skybridges stretching between both sides.

• The Great Flurrt
A celebrated phenomenon where the aurora 'duplicates' and ribbons of light spill all over the sky. This does not happen often, but when it does, the dragons will dance together and mate. After a Great Flurrt, there will often be an influx of fertilized eggs.

• The Loff
The vast body of water that halos the Sabersythe nesting grounds like a turquoise iris. It is renowned for being home to ancient beasts and unpredictable weather patterns.

• The Flourish
The underground safe haven ruled by the Elding, nesting in an undisclosed location somewhere in the south.

• The Shade
This is the southern third of the world. No sunshine reaches this area, therefore it's forever cast in darkness – the only light being the aurora ribbons and the light emanating from Moonplume moons. It's very cold here, covered in snow, the coldest part being the southernmost pole known as Nethereyn.

• Tri-Council
This is a council of ancient tri-beaded elementals and very knowledgeable Runis. They hold a certain amount of sway over the kingdoms because of their great power and sometimes intervene in political matters. They reside in Bothaim – neutral territory that does not fall under the rule of any king or queen.

• Truthtune
Someone who has the unique ability to tell when another is lying. They aren't as strong as a Mindweft, but they are more common and prized by The Crown for their ability to tell if someone can hear the elemental songs – mainly younglings who have just begun to hear the songs and are trying to escape conscription.

• Tookah Trial
Two warriors fighting for the privilege to bind with another.

• Undercity

The big, jagged cleft in the ground beneath the wall of The Fade (directly below Gore – The Fade's capital). It's riddled with abandoned dragon bloodstone mineshafts and is a hotspot for homeless folk. Some of these mineshafts collapse, and creatures from either side of the wall sneak in to find shelter, making it a very perilous place to live.

• Unveiling Ceremony

When a princess gives herself to the Creators (rather than binding to a partner) she is unveiled to the public for the first time. Otherwise, this unveiling happens during the binding ceremony.

• Weald

A small, handheld device that's runed to be able to contain different elements in their purest forms. Fire, air, water, ground, and even dragonflame – though these wealds are rare as they require the blood of a Daga-Mórrk to construct.

CREATURES/BEINGS

• Elding Bird
A mythical bird-like creature born from ashes and flames.

• Faunycaw
Winged, leathery beasts with stumpy necks and big gloomy eyes. They are less than half the size of an average Moltenmaw and are able to blend with the rust-toned stone in The Burn. They can cling to cliffs and ceilings and have bat-like wings. They can be ridden.

• Fae
The more common folk in this world. They aren't immortal, but they have exceptionally long lifespans. The fae have pointed ears and sharp canines and are primal by nature.

• Fate Herder
A large silver feline-like creature that is more legend than reality. Those who have seen it are often considered crazy or delusional, boasting stories about the beast nudging them to make a different decision than the one they'd intended.

• Miskunn
A knee-height creature with white hair and complexion, buttony features, and sharp teeth. They have willowy bodies that fold up like a marsupial and long, tufted tails. They can see into the future, though these visions are sporadic and subject to change. These creatures are verbal.

• Moltenmaws
The dragons that live in The Fade. They are covered in feathers, their faces sharp and beaked. Their plumage is a vibrant mix of colors – no two Moltenmaws bearing the same color palette. They can travel anywhere in the world comfortably and are the easiest dragons to charm/steal an egg from.

• Moonplumes

The dragons that live in The Shade. They have leathery, luminous skin that comes in shades of gray, pearl, iridescent, and white. Their eyes are big black and glittery, their faces rounded, necks long, bodies elegant. Their tails are long, like brushes of silken strands. They are cold-loving creatures, and they cannot handle the sun or their skin burns, nor do their eyes adapt to such brightness. They are very cunning and are therefore the hardest dragons to charm or steal an egg from.

• Sabersythes

The dragons that live in The Burn. They are large boxy creatures with scales, spikes, and heavily tusked faces. They come in many different colors, such as rust, bronze, red, brown, black, and gold. They are heat-loving creatures and cannot survive for long in the fierce cold of The Shade. They can be very boisterous and aggressive and are almost as hard to charm or steal an egg from as the Moonplumes are.

• Velvet Trogg

Large lanky creatures that like to hoard and feast on trash. They have four arms, long black hair, and blue velvet skin. They consume memories from the bits of trash they eat and purge them as luminous, sticky tendrils they pull from gaping holes in their hands, using these tendrils to decorate their lairs. These creatures are verbal.

• Waif

Rare, lanky, fog-like creatures that haunt drapes of mist where they nibble souls in exchange for messages from the dead. These creatures are verbal.

• Woetoe

Furry creatures with big, paddled ears, long noses, pronged teeth, and whiskers. They are around two-thirds the size of a regular fae and are prized for being able to steal things from tricky places. They are great hoarders. These creatures are verbal.

CHARACTERS

• Agni
A very gifted Runi who lives and works at The Burn's Imperial Stronghold.

• Ahdrik Neván
Former King of The Shade. Partner to Eudora Neván, and father of Elluin and Haedeon Neván.

• Allume
Haedeon Neván's Moonplume.

• Arkyn
Also known as the Scavenger King.

• Bulder
One of the five Creators – the God of Ground.

• Cadok Vaegor
Current King of the Fade. Partner of Dothea Vaegor, father of Turun Vaegor, son of Ostern and Kovina Vaegor, sibling of Kaan and Veya and twin of Tyroth Vaegor.

• Caelis
One of the five Creators – the God of Aether.

• Clode
One of the five Creators – the Goddess of Air.

• Dothea Vaegor
Current Queen of The Fade. Partner to Cadok Vaegor, and mother of Turun Vaegor.

• Elluin Neván
Former princess of The Shade. Daughter of Ahdrik and Eudora Neván, and the sibling of Haedeon Neván. Descendant of the familial line entrusted with the Aether Stone.

• Essi
Raeve's young friend whom Raeve rescued from the Undercity. Essi lives with Raeve in Gore and is very smart.

• Eudora Neván
Former Queen of The Shade. Partner to Ahdrik Neván, and mother of Haedeon and Elluin Neván. Descendant of the familial line entrusted with the Aether Stone.

• Fallon
Raeve's friend whom she lost a long while ago.

• Grihm
King Kaan's second-in-command.

• Haedeon Neván
Former prince of The Shade. Son of Ahdrik and Eudora Neván, and the sibling of Elluin Neván. Descendant of the familial line entrusted with the Aether Stone.

• Ignos
One of the five Creators – the God of Fire.

• Kaan Vaegor
Current King of The Burn. Eldest son of Ostern and Kovina Vaegor, and sibling of Cadok, Tyroth, and Veya Vaegor.

• Kyzari Vaegor
Princess of The Shade. Grandchild of Ostern and Kovina Vaegor. Descendant of the familial line entrusted with the Aether Stone.

• Ostern Vaegor
The former King of The Burn. Partner of Kovina Vaegor, and father of Kaan, Cadok, Tyroth, and Veya Vaegor.

• Pyrok
A not-very-helpful member of King Kaan's Imperial Court. Sibling of Roan.

• Rayne
One of the five Creators – the Goddess of Water.

• Rekk Zharos
A renowned bounty hunter.

• Roan
An alchemist and a member of King Kaan's Imperial Court. Sibling of Pyrok.

• Ruse
The owner of The Curly Quill in Gore.

• Sereme
A high-ranking member of the Fíur du Ath.

• Slátra
Elluin Neván's Moonplume.

• The Elding
Head of Fíur du Ath.

• Tyroth Vaegor
Current King of The Shade. Son of Ostern and Kovina Vaegor, sibling of Kaan and Veya and twin of Cadok Vaegor.

• Uno
Ruse's pet miskunn.

• Veya Vaegor
Princess of The Burn. Daughter and youngest child of Ostern and Kovina Vaegor, and sibling of Kaan, Cadok, and Tyroth Vaegor.

• Vruhn
Owner of The Curly Quill in Dhomm.

• Wrook
The woetoe Raeve meets in the cells.

PRONUNCIATION GUIDE

Allume
Uh-loo-m

Cadok Vaegor
Kah-dock Vay-gore

Elluin Neván
Ell-ew-in Neh-v-ah-n

Essi
Ess-ee

Fíur du Ath
Fee-er doo Ah-th

Haedeon Neván
Hay-dee-on Neh-v-ah-n

Kaan Vaegor
K-ahn Vay-gore

Kholu
Kh-oh-loo

Kyzari Vaegor
K-eye-zar-ee Vay-gore

Ostern Vaegor
Ohs-tern Vay-gore

Raeve
Ray-vv

Réidi
R-eh-di

Rekk Zharos
R-eck Z-arr-ohs

Rygun
Rye-gun

Sereme
Ser-eam

Slátra
Slah-trah

Tyroth Vaegor
Tie-roth Vay-gore

Veya Vaegor
Vay-ah Vay-gore

The Ballad of Falling Dragons

PROLOGUE

It was unnaturally quiet that dae, the Loff a sheet of tempered glass that offered only the sharpest reflection. Not a breath of wind ruffled the grass or squealed past honed corners. The volcanoes that blistered Gondragh quelled their grumbling ruckus for the first time in many phases. Not a single rock rolled out of place unless specifically ordered to, the action carried out swiftly and without strain. Even the clouds refused to weep, like a crumbled face holding breath before the anguished sob.

It was as though Ignos, Bulder, Clode, and Rayne had pooled their consciousnesses . . . elsewhere. As though they'd been watching.

Listening.

Folk spoke of the strange occurrence, and those who could hear the Creators' songs would later speak of it as a bad omen, given what was soon to unfold that very dae. Given that the large silver Moonplume moon perched in the sky in The Shade was about to unwedge itself from its lofty perch.

First came a scream from the mouth of someone buckled with too much pain and loneliness. Like bursting a seam that had been sewn too tight. Then came the words – tilled from a thirsty heart and without much thought beyond hopes of easing the ache in the female's own chest.

What happened next had the Creators screaming with equal might, their voices hitched with a foreboding lilt.

Then . . .

Slátra pitched from the sky like a luminous egg, plummeting with such velocity fire plumed in her bouldered wake. Those who witnessed the event and lived to tell the tale would later say the ground around them seemed to heave a sigh of acceptance, right before the moon struck with such force the entire world rattled for a beat; like a tremor. Fitting, given the event would later bring about a reckoning that was well overdue.

The Creators watched as the one who hatched from that moon stumbled free of the beautiful, luminous wreckage with eyes a crush of glitter and ink, blood leaking from a bone-deep gash in her head. As she tore toward Arithia with vicious intent . . . before she was captured. Subdued. Tossed in a cell beneath a mountain that housed a male who frothed with his own form of bloodlust.

Watched as she was tortured. Hardened.

Sharpened.

They knew the end began here, amidst this echo of something that took place so many phases ago. That the male this moon-fallen fae once loved roamed the plains bearing a heart full of ache and a mouth full of words that could crumble the world to dust. That he could end things faster and with more ferocity than continued moonfalls.

That fate was working against them to make things right, herding them into a corner too small and suffocating.

They didn't fight, for they knew they were in the wrong. Knew that if they did, they would lose. For the dae they laid their little trap and tore Caelis to shreds, packing him into a cage that crushed him into a screaming mulch, there was but one *thing they hadn't counted on. Something bearing a potent strength that would forever go unmatched.*

Love.

THANK YOU

Since 2020, I've been picking away at this story, visiting it in the evenings while trying to drift off. While driving. Showering. Cooking. But part of me knew I wasn't ready to tell the tale and (hopefully) do it justice.

Looking back now, I think the story was biding time, pulling breath until it could sing loud enough that I wouldn't be able to tune it out. As it was, that happened when I needed it the most. When I, myself, needed to remember how to *breathe*.

I hope you fell in love with this world as I did.
That the story gave you a smile. A tear.

A warm feeling in your chest.

I hope that, for just a moment, you felt as though you were pressed between these pages, coasting through the sky on Rygun's back or looking up at the moons. That you were bound around a silver egg and writing in your diary, or tucking *nee* into the crook of your neck and rocking her to sleep.

Thank you for taking this breath with me.
For allowing me to take you on another adventure.

For trusting me with your heartbeats.

All my love,

Sarah xo

ACKNOWLEDGMENTS

I wouldn't have been able to publish this book without the help of my incredible team and the unending support of my family.

Josh. You took a world of weight off my shoulders by becoming the primary caregiver to our three beautiful children, allowing me to fully immerse myself into this story. I cry every time I see that snippet from Game of Thrones – you know the one where Jon Snow has an army charging towards him? He's beat down, preparing to go to war on his own, and then just before the clash . . . *another* army charges in from behind him and takes the hit.

You're the army, my love.

Thank you for saving me.

Mum – thank you for taking the time to read over this story not once, but *twice*. For talking things through on the phone with me.

For your support and never-ending encouragement.

I love you.

The Editor & The Quill – Chinah – thank you for *everything* you poured into this story. For first alpha reading, then your developmental edits, then line and copy. You go above and beyond with every book I write, and I'm so lucky to have you in my life. For not just your amazing editing skills, but for your precious friendship.

Forever wishing we lived closer.

Polished Perfection – Helayna – thank you for the many hours you spent making this beast of a book sparkle. For hunting down inconsistencies in my plot and for your love and devotion towards the story. I'm *so* thankful that you were able to fit me into your schedule.

Raven, you know I love you to the moon and back.

Thank you for encouraging me to take this leap of faith. For being the voice of reason when I so desperately needed it, and for setting me on the right path again when I got caught in the rewrite spiral of doom.

Thank you for taking the time to beta read this story, and for your love and support of it. Of *me*.

I treasure our friendship.

A.T. Cover Designs – Aubrey, thank you for the stunning paperback/kindle cover. I still can't believe you painted me a MOONPLUME!

Thank you for pouring so much heart and soul into everything you design for me. Words can't begin to describe how thankful I am for all the hours you spend bringing my stories to life visually.

Forever thankful for our friendship.

Lauren – thank you for reading my very raw alpha doc. For your thoughtful critiques, and for not being afraid to speak your mind. Just like with Flame, you helped Moon become the best version of itself. For that, and for our lovely friendship, I will be forever grateful.

Angelique, Talarah, Ivy and Ann – a huge thank you for taking the time out of your busy lives to beta read this story. For your positive reinforcement, constructive criticism, and for bolstering me in SO many ways. Love and adore you all.

Lois and Kim, thank you for reading before I sent this beast to ARC. You both gave me all the confidence to pass this baby off to the rest of the world.

So grateful.

Alice Cao – thank you for the amazing chapter headers. I know I say this all the time, but you really are *so* talented. I'm incredibly proud to have your illustrations all throughout this story, beautifully representing the creatures and characters.

Rachel from The Nerd Fam, thank you so much for all the hard work you have poured into my release campaign. Your attention to detail is exquisite, your enthusiasm infectious, and I can't wait to work with you for many releases to come.

Brit – thank you for your unwavering friendship and support. Love you always.

And to my marvellous readers, thank you for every tag, every message, every review, like, comment, or share. Thank you for taking a chance on my stories and trusting me with your hearts.

Here's to the next!

ABOUT THE AUTHOR

Sarah A. Parker is an internationally bestselling author who grew up on a farm in New Zealand, where she spent her days getting lost amongst the rolling pasture, building forts in the hedge, climbing trees and exploring the forest pathways – making up elaborate stories that never lost their grip on her. She now lives in Australia with her husband, dog, three children and countless plants, and spends her days pouring her stories onto paper rather than throwing them to the wind. Her genre of choice is epic fantasy romance, and she thrives off dreaming up real, complex characters and immersive worlds to get lost amongst.